The Ghastly Gothic Tomes

Vol. 11

The Ghastly Gothic Tomes

Vol. 11

Published by NRM Books.

ISBN: 978-1-965179-14-7

CREDITS
Cover Art by: Nathan Reese Maher

COPYRIGHT

The Ghastly Gothic Tomes are protected under the copyright laws of the United States of America. Any reproductions or unauthorized use of the contents herein including, but not limited to, artwork and text is prohibited without written permission from the author. Novels, poems, plays and short stories published herein are part of the public domain.

Copyright 1st Edition October 14th, 2024, all rights reserved.

Table of Contents

"The Moonstone"
by Wilkie Collins
Published 1868, p. 2-531

"Carmilla"
by Joseph Sheridan Le Fanu
Published 1871, p. 532-619

"In a Glass Darkly"
by Joseph Sheridan Le Fanu
Published 1872, p. 620-734

The Moonstone

By Wilkie Collins

PROLOGUE

THE STORMING OF SERINGAPATAM (1799):

(Extracted from a Family Paper.)

I

I address these lines—written in India—to my relatives in England.

My object is to explain the motive which has induced me to refuse the right hand of friendship to my cousin, John Herncastle. The reserve which I have hitherto maintained in this matter has been misinterpreted by members of my family whose good opinion I cannot consent to forfeit. I request them to suspend their decision until they have read my narrative. And I declare, on my word of honour, that what I am now about to write is, strictly and literally, the truth.

The private difference between my cousin and me took its rise in a great public event in which we were both concerned—the storming of Seringapatam, under General Baird, on the 4th of May, 1799.

In order that the circumstances may be clearly understood, I must revert for a moment to the period before the assault, and to the stories current in our camp of the treasure in jewels and gold stored up in the Palace of Seringapatam.

II

One of the wildest of these stories related to a Yellow Diamond—a famous gem in the native annals of India.

The earliest known traditions describe the stone as having been set in the forehead of the four-handed Indian god who typifies the Moon. Partly from its peculiar colour, partly from a superstition which represented it as feeling the influence of the deity whom it adorned, and growing and lessening in lustre with the waxing and waning of the moon, it first gained the name by which it continues to be known in India to this day — the name of THE MOONSTONE. A similar superstition was once prevalent, as I have heard, in ancient Greece and Rome; not applying, however (as in India), to a diamond devoted to the service of a god, but to a semi-transparent stone of the inferior order of gems, supposed to be affected by the lunar influences — the moon, in this latter case also, giving the name by which the stone is still known to collectors in our own time.

The adventures of the Yellow Diamond begin with the eleventh century of the Christian era.

At that date, the Mohammedan conqueror, Mahmoud of Ghizni, crossed India; seized on the holy city of Somnauth; and stripped of its treasures the famous temple, which had stood for centuries — the shrine of Hindoo pilgrimage, and the wonder of the Eastern world.

Of all the deities worshipped in the temple, the moon-god alone escaped the rapacity of the conquering Mohammedans. Preserved by three Brahmins, the inviolate deity, bearing the Yellow Diamond in its forehead, was removed by night, and was transported to the second of the sacred cities of India — the city of Benares.

Here, in a new shrine — in a hall inlaid with precious stones, under a roof supported by pillars of gold — the moon-god was set up and worshipped. Here, on the night when the shrine was completed, Vishnu the Preserver appeared to the three Brahmins in a dream.

The deity breathed the breath of his divinity on the Diamond in the forehead of the god. And the Brahmins knelt and hid their faces in their robes. The deity commanded that the Moonstone should be watched, from that time forth, by three priests in turn, night and day, to the end of the generations of men. And the Brahmins heard, and bowed before his will. The deity predicted certain disaster to the presumptuous mortal who laid hands on the sacred gem, and to all of his house and name who received it after him. And the Brahmins caused the prophecy to be written over the gates of the shrine in letters of gold.

One age followed another—and still, generation after generation, the successors of the three Brahmins watched their priceless Moonstone, night and day. One age followed another until the first years of the eighteenth Christian century saw the reign of Aurungzebe, Emperor of the Moguls. At his command havoc and rapine were let loose once more among the temples of the worship of Brahmah. The shrine of the four-handed god was polluted by the slaughter of sacred animals; the images of the deities were broken in pieces; and the Moonstone was seized by an officer of rank in the army of Aurungzebe.

Powerless to recover their lost treasure by open force, the three guardian priests followed and watched it in disguise. The generations succeeded each other; the warrior who had committed the sacrilege perished miserably; the Moonstone passed (carrying its curse with it) from one lawless Mohammedan hand to another; and still, through all chances and changes, the successors of the three guardian priests kept their watch, waiting the day when the will of Vishnu the Preserver should restore to them their sacred gem. Time rolled on from the first to the last years of the eighteenth Christian century. The Diamond fell into the possession of Tippoo, Sultan of Seringapatam, who caused it to be placed as an ornament in the handle of a dagger, and who commanded it to be kept among the choicest treasures of his armoury. Even then—in the palace of the Sultan himself—the three guardian priests still kept their watch in secret. There were three officers of Tippoo's household, strangers to the rest, who had won their master's confidence by conforming, or appearing to conform, to the Mussulman faith; and to those three men report pointed as the three priests in disguise.

III

So, as told in our camp, ran the fanciful story of the Moonstone. It made no serious impression on any of us except my cousin—whose love of the marvellous induced him to believe it. On the night before the assault on Seringapatam, he was absurdly angry with me, and with others, for treating the whole thing as a fable. A foolish wrangle followed; and Herncastle's unlucky temper got the better of him. He declared,

The Moonstone

in his boastful way, that we should see the Diamond on his finger, if the English army took Seringapatam. The sally was saluted by a roar of laughter, and there, as we all thought that night, the thing ended.

Let me now take you on to the day of the assault.

My cousin and I were separated at the outset. I never saw him when we forded the river; when we planted the English flag in the first breach; when we crossed the ditch beyond; and, fighting every inch of our way, entered the town. It was only at dusk, when the place was ours, and after General Baird himself had found the dead body of Tippoo under a heap of the slain, that Herncastle and I met.

We were each attached to a party sent out by the general's orders to prevent the plunder and confusion which followed our conquest. The camp-followers committed deplorable excesses; and, worse still, the soldiers found their way, by an unguarded door, into the treasury of the Palace, and loaded themselves with gold and jewels. It was in the court outside the treasury that my cousin and I met, to enforce the laws of discipline on our own soldiers. Herncastle's fiery temper had been, as I could plainly see, exasperated to a kind of frenzy by the terrible slaughter through which we had passed. He was very unfit, in my opinion, to perform the duty that had been entrusted to him.

There was riot and confusion enough in the treasury, but no violence that I saw. The men (if I may use such an expression) disgraced themselves good-humouredly. All sorts of rough jests and catchwords were bandied about among them; and the story of the Diamond turned up again unexpectedly, in the form of a mischievous joke. "Who's got the Moonstone?" was the rallying cry which perpetually caused the plundering, as soon as it was stopped in one place, to break out in another. While I was still vainly trying to establish order, I heard a frightful yelling on the other side of the courtyard, and at once ran towards the cries, in dread of finding some new outbreak of the pillage in that direction.

I got to an open door, and saw the bodies of two Indians (by their dress, as I guessed, officers of the palace) lying across the entrance, dead.

A cry inside hurried me into a room, which appeared to serve as an armoury. A third Indian, mortally wounded, was sinking at the feet of a man whose back was towards me. The man turned at the instant when I came in, and I saw John Herncastle, with a torch in one hand, and a dagger dripping with blood in the other. A stone, set like a pommel, in the end of the dagger's handle, flashed in the torchlight, as he turned on me, like a gleam of fire. The dying Indian sank to his knees, pointed to the dagger in Herncastle's hand, and said, in his native language—"The Moonstone will have its vengeance yet on you and yours!" He spoke those words, and fell dead on the floor.

Before I could stir in the matter, the men who had followed me across the courtyard crowded in. My cousin rushed to meet them, like a madman. "Clear the room!" he shouted to me, "and set a guard on the door!" The men fell back as he threw himself on them with his torch and his dagger. I put two sentinels of my own company, on whom I could rely, to keep the door. Through the remainder of the night, I saw no more of my cousin.

Early in the morning, the plunder still going on, General Baird announced publicly by beat of drum, that any thief detected in the fact, be he whom he might, should be hung. The provost-marshal was in attendance, to prove that the General was in earnest; and in the throng that followed the proclamation, Herncastle and I met again.

He held out his hand, as usual, and said, "Good morning."

I waited before I gave him my hand in return.

"Tell me first," I said, "how the Indian in the armoury met his death, and what those last words meant, when he pointed to the dagger in your hand."

"The Indian met his death, as I suppose, by a mortal wound," said Herncastle. "What his last words meant I know no more than you do."

I looked at him narrowly. His frenzy of the previous day had all calmed down. I determined to give him another chance.

"Is that all you have to tell me?" I asked.

He answered, "That is all."

I turned my back on him; and we have not spoken since.

IV

I beg it to be understood that what I write here about my cousin (unless some necessity should arise for making it public) is for the information of the family only. Herncastle has said nothing that can justify me in speaking to our commanding officer. He has been taunted more than once about the Diamond, by those who recollect his angry outbreak before the assault; but, as may easily be imagined, his own remembrance of the circumstances under which I surprised him in the armoury has been enough to keep him silent. It is reported that he means to exchange into another regiment, avowedly for the purpose of separating himself from me.

Whether this be true or not, I cannot prevail upon myself to become his accuser—and I think with good reason. If I made the matter public, I have no evidence but moral evidence to bring forward. I have not only no proof that he killed the two men at the door; I cannot even declare that he killed the third man inside—for I cannot say that my own eyes saw the deed committed. It is true that I heard the dying Indian's words; but if those words were pronounced to be the ravings of delirium, how could I contradict the assertion from my own knowledge? Let our relatives, on either side, form their own opinion on what I have written, and decide for themselves whether the aversion I now feel towards this man is well or ill founded.

Although I attach no sort of credit to the fantastic Indian legend of the gem, I must acknowledge, before I conclude, that I am influenced by a certain superstition of my own in this matter. It is my conviction, or my delusion, no matter which, that crime brings its own fatality with it. I am not only persuaded of Herncastle's guilt; I am even fanciful enough to believe that he will live to regret it, if he keeps the Diamond; and that others will live to regret taking it from him, if he gives the Diamond away.

THE STORY
FIRST PERIOD
THE LOSS OF THE DIAMOND (1848)

The Events related by Gabriel Betteredge, house-steward in the service of Julia, Lady Verinder.

CHAPTER I

In the first part of Robinson Crusoe, at page one hundred and twenty-nine, you will find it thus written:

"Now I saw, though too late, the Folly of beginning a Work before we count the Cost, and before we judge rightly of our own Strength to go through with it."

Only yesterday, I opened my Robinson Crusoe at that place. Only this morning (May twenty-first, eighteen hundred and fifty), came my lady's nephew, Mr. Franklin Blake, and held a short conversation with me, as follows:—

"Betteredge," says Mr. Franklin, "I have been to the lawyer's about some family matters; and, among other things, we have been talking of the loss of the Indian Diamond, in my aunt's house in Yorkshire, two years since. Mr. Bruff thinks as I think, that the whole story ought, in the interests of truth, to be placed on record in writing—and the sooner the better."

Not perceiving his drift yet, and thinking it always desirable for the sake of peace and quietness to be on the lawyer's side, I said I thought so too. Mr. Franklin went on.

"In this matter of the Diamond," he said, "the characters of innocent people have suffered under suspicion already—as you know. The memories of innocent people may suffer, hereafter, for want of a record of the facts to which those who come after us can appeal. There can be no doubt that this strange family story of ours ought to be told. And I think, Betteredge, Mr. Bruff and I together have hit on the right way of telling it."

Very satisfactory to both of them, no doubt. But I failed to see what I myself had to do with it, so far.

The Moonstone

"We have certain events to relate," Mr. Franklin proceeded; "and we have certain persons concerned in those events who are capable of relating them. Starting from these plain facts, the idea is that we should all write the story of the Moonstone in turn—as far as our own personal experience extends, and no farther. We must begin by showing how the Diamond first fell into the hands of my uncle Herncastle, when he was serving in India fifty years since. This prefatory narrative I have already got by me in the form of an old family paper, which relates the necessary particulars on the authority of an eye-witness. The next thing to do is to tell how the Diamond found its way into my aunt's house in Yorkshire, two years ago, and how it came to be lost in little more than twelve hours afterwards. Nobody knows as much as you do, Betteredge, about what went on in the house at that time. So you must take the pen in hand, and start the story."

In those terms I was informed of what my personal concern was with the matter of the Diamond. If you are curious to know what course I took under the circumstances, I beg to inform you that I did what you would probably have done in my place. I modestly declared myself to be quite unequal to the task imposed upon me—and I privately felt, all the time, that I was quite clever enough to perform it, if I only gave my own abilities a fair chance. Mr. Franklin, I imagine, must have seen my private sentiments in my face. He declined to believe in my modesty; and he insisted on giving my abilities a fair chance.

Two hours have passed since Mr. Franklin left me. As soon as his back was turned, I went to my writing-desk to start the story. There I have sat helpless (in spite of my abilities) ever since; seeing what Robinson Crusoe saw, as quoted above—namely, the folly of beginning a work before we count the cost, and before we judge rightly of our own strength to go through with it. Please to remember, I opened the book by accident, at that bit, only the day before I rashly undertook the business now in hand; and, allow me to ask—if that isn't prophecy, what is?

I am not superstitious; I have read a heap of books in my time; I am a scholar in my own way. Though turned seventy, I possess an active memory, and legs to correspond. You are not to take it, if you please, as the saying of an ignorant man, when I express my opinion that such a book as Robinson Crusoe never was written, and never will be written again. I have tried that book for years—generally in combination with a pipe of tobacco—and I have found it my friend in need in all the necessities of this mortal life. When my spirits are bad—Robinson Crusoe. When I want advice—Robinson Crusoe. In past times when my wife plagued me; in present times when I have had a drop too much—Robinson Crusoe. I have worn out six stout Robinson Crusoes with hard work in my service. On my lady's last birthday she gave me a seventh. I took a drop too much on the strength of it; and Robinson Crusoe put me right again. Price four shillings and sixpence, bound in blue, with a picture into the bargain.

Still, this don't look much like starting the story of the Diamond—does it? I seem to be wandering off in search of Lord knows what, Lord knows where. We will take a new sheet of paper, if you please, and begin over again, with my best respects to you.

CHAPTER II

I spoke of my lady a line or two back. Now the Diamond could never have been in our house, where it was lost, if it had not been made a present of to my lady's daughter; and my lady's daughter would never have been in existence to have the present, if it had not been for my lady who (with pain and travail) produced her into the world. Consequently, if we begin with my lady, we are pretty sure of beginning far enough back. And that, let me tell you, when you have got such a job as mine in hand, is a real comfort at starting.

If you know anything of the fashionable world, you have heard tell of the three beautiful Miss Herncastles. Miss Adelaide; Miss Caroline; and Miss Julia — this last being the youngest and the best of the three sisters, in my opinion; and I had opportunities of judging, as you shall presently see. I went into the service of the old lord, their father (thank God, we have got nothing to do with him, in this business of the Diamond; he had the longest tongue and the shortest temper of any man, high or low, I ever met with) — I say, I went into the service of the old lord, as page-boy in waiting on the three honourable young ladies, at the age of fifteen years. There I lived till Miss Julia married the late Sir John Verinder. An excellent man, who only wanted somebody to manage him; and, between ourselves, he found somebody to do it; and what is more, he throve on it and grew fat on it, and lived happy and died easy on it, dating from the day when my lady took him to church to be married, to the day when she relieved him of his last breath, and closed his eyes for ever.

I have omitted to state that I went with the bride to the bride's husband's house and lands down here. "Sir John," she says, "I can't do without Gabriel Betteredge." "My lady," says Sir John, "I can't do without him, either." That was his way with her — and that was how I went into his service. It was all one to me where I went, so long as my mistress and I were together.

Seeing that my lady took an interest in the out-of-door work, and the farms, and such like, I took an interest in them too — with all the more reason that I was a small farmer's seventh son myself. My lady got me put under the bailiff, and I did my best, and gave satisfaction, and got promotion accordingly. Some years later, on the Monday as it might be, my lady says, "Sir John, your bailiff is a stupid old man. Pension him liberally, and let Gabriel Betteredge have his place." On the Tuesday as it might be, Sir John says, "My lady, the bailiff is pensioned liberally; and Gabriel Betteredge has got his place." You hear more than enough of married people living together miserably. Here is an example to the contrary. Let it be a warning to some of you, and an encouragement to others. In the meantime, I will go on with my story.

Well, there I was in clover, you will say. Placed in a position of trust and honour, with a little cottage of my own to live in, with my rounds on the estate to occupy me in the morning, and my accounts in the afternoon, and my pipe and my Robinson Crusoe in the evening—what more could I possibly want to make me happy? Remember what Adam wanted when he was alone in the Garden of Eden; and if you don't blame it in Adam, don't blame it in me.

The woman I fixed my eye on, was the woman who kept house for me at my cottage. Her name was Selina Goby. I agree with the late William Cobbett about picking a wife. See that she chews her food well and sets her foot down firmly on the ground when she walks, and you're all right. Selina Goby was all right in both these respects, which was one reason for marrying her. I had another reason, likewise, entirely of my own discovering. Selina, being a single woman, made me pay so much a week for her board and services. Selina, being my wife, couldn't charge for her board, and would have to give me her services for nothing. That was the point of view I looked at it from. Economy—with a dash of love. I put it to my mistress, as in duty bound, just as I had put it to myself.

"I have been turning Selina Goby over in my mind," I said, "and I think, my lady, it will be cheaper to marry her than to keep her."

My lady burst out laughing, and said she didn't know which to be most shocked at—my language or my principles. Some joke tickled her, I suppose, of the sort that you can't take unless you are a person of quality. Understanding nothing myself but that I was free to put it next to Selina, I went and put it accordingly. And what did Selina say? Lord! how little you must know of women, if you ask that. Of course she said, Yes.

The Moonstone

As my time drew nearer, and there got to be talk of my having a new coat for the ceremony, my mind began to misgive me. I have compared notes with other men as to what they felt while they were in my interesting situation; and they have all acknowledged that, about a week before it happened, they privately wished themselves out of it. I went a trifle further than that myself; I actually rose up, as it were, and tried to get out of it. Not for nothing! I was too just a man to expect she would let me off for nothing. Compensation to the woman when the man gets out of it, is one of the laws of England. In obedience to the laws, and after turning it over carefully in my mind, I offered Selina Goby a feather-bed and fifty shillings to be off the bargain. You will hardly believe it, but it is nevertheless true — she was fool enough to refuse.

After that it was all over with me, of course. I got the new coat as cheap as I could, and I went through all the rest of it as cheap as I could. We were not a happy couple, and not a miserable couple. We were six of one and half-a-dozen of the other. How it was I don't understand, but we always seemed to be getting, with the best of motives, in one another's way. When I wanted to go upstairs, there was my wife coming down; or when my wife wanted to go down, there was I coming up. That is married life, according to my experience of it.

After five years of misunderstandings on the stairs, it pleased an all-wise Providence to relieve us of each other by taking my wife. I was left with my little girl Penelope, and with no other child. Shortly afterwards Sir John died, and my lady was left with her little girl, Miss Rachel, and no other child. I have written to very poor purpose of my lady, if you require to be told that my little Penelope was taken care of, under my good mistress's own eye, and was sent to school and taught, and made a sharp girl, and promoted, when old enough, to be Miss Rachel's own maid.

As for me, I went on with my business as bailiff year after year up to Christmas 1847, when there came a change in my life. On that day, my lady invited herself to a cup of tea alone with me in my cottage. She remarked that, reckoning from the year when I started as page-boy in the time of the old lord, I had been more than fifty years in her service, and she put into my hands a beautiful waistcoat of wool that she had worked herself, to keep me warm in the bitter winter weather.

I received this magnificent present quite at a loss to find words to thank my mistress with for the honour she had done me. To my great astonishment, it turned out, however, that the waistcoat was not an honour, but a bribe. My lady had discovered that I was getting old before I had discovered it myself, and she had come to my cottage to wheedle me (if I may use such an expression) into giving up my hard out-of-door work as bailiff, and taking my ease for the rest of my days as steward in the house. I made as good a fight of it against the indignity of taking my ease as I could. But my mistress knew the weak side of me; she put it as a favour to herself. The dispute between us ended, after that, in my wiping my eyes, like an old fool, with my new woollen waistcoat, and saying I would think about it.

The perturbation in my mind, in regard to thinking about it, being truly dreadful after my lady had gone away, I applied the remedy which I have never yet found to fail me in cases of doubt and emergency. I smoked a pipe and took a turn at Robinson Crusoe. Before I had occupied myself with that extraordinary book five minutes, I came on a comforting bit (page one hundred and fifty-eight), as follows: "Today we love, what tomorrow we hate." I saw my way clear directly. Today I was all for continuing to be farm-bailiff; tomorrow, on the authority of Robinson Crusoe, I should be all the other way. Take myself tomorrow while in tomorrow's humour, and the thing was done. My mind being relieved in this manner, I went to sleep that night in the character of Lady Verinder's farm-bailiff, and I woke up the next morning in the character of Lady Verinder's house-steward. All quite comfortable, and all through Robinson Crusoe!

My daughter Penelope has just looked over my shoulder to see what I have done so far. She remarks that it is beautifully written, and every word of it true. But she points out one objection. She says what I have done so far isn't in the least what I was wanted to do. I am asked to tell the story of the Diamond and, instead of that, I have been telling the story of my own self. Curious, and quite beyond me to account for. I wonder whether the gentlemen who make a business and a living out of writing books, ever find their own selves getting in

The Moonstone

the way of their subjects, like me? If they do, I can feel for them. In the meantime, here is another false start, and more waste of good writing-paper. What's to be done now? Nothing that I know of, except for you to keep your temper, and for me to begin it all over again for the third time.

CHAPTER III

The question of how I am to start the story properly I have tried to settle in two ways. First, by scratching my head, which led to nothing. Second, by consulting my daughter Penelope, which has resulted in an entirely new idea.

Penelope's notion is that I should set down what happened, regularly day by day, beginning with the day when we got the news that Mr. Franklin Blake was expected on a visit to the house. When you come to fix your memory with a date in this way, it is wonderful what your memory will pick up for you upon that compulsion. The only difficulty is to fetch out the dates, in the first place. This Penelope offers to do for me by looking into her own diary, which she was taught to keep when she was at school, and which she has gone on keeping ever since. In answer to an improvement on this notion, devised by myself, namely, that she should tell the story instead of me, out of her own diary, Penelope observes, with a fierce look and a red face, that her journal is for her own private eye, and that no living creature shall ever know what is in it but herself. When I inquire what this means, Penelope says, "Fiddlesticks!" I say, Sweethearts.

Beginning, then, on Penelope's plan, I beg to mention that I was specially called one Wednesday morning into my lady's own sitting-room, the date being the twenty-fourth of May, eighteen hundred and forty-eight.

"Gabriel," says my lady, "here is news that will surprise you. Franklin Blake has come back from abroad. He has been staying with his father in London, and he is coming to us tomorrow to stop till next month, and keep Rachel's birthday."

If I had had a hat in my hand, nothing but respect would have prevented me from throwing that hat up to the ceiling. I had not seen Mr. Franklin since he was a boy, living along with us in this house. He was, out of all sight (as I remember him), the nicest boy that ever spun a top or broke a window. Miss Rachel, who was present, and to whom I made that remark, observed, in return, that she remembered him as the most atrocious tyrant that ever tortured a doll, and the hardest driver of an exhausted little girl in string harness that England could produce. "I burn with indignation, and I ache with fatigue," was the way Miss Rachel summed it up, "when I think of Franklin Blake."

Hearing what I now tell you, you will naturally ask how it was that Mr. Franklin should have passed all the years, from the time when he was a boy to the time when he was a man, out of his own country. I answer, because his father had the misfortune to be next heir to a Dukedom, and not to be able to prove it.

In two words, this was how the thing happened:

My lady's eldest sister married the celebrated Mr. Blake — equally famous for his great riches, and his great suit at law. How many years he went on worrying the tribunals of his country to turn out the Duke in possession, and to put himself in the Duke's place — how many lawyer's purses he filled to bursting, and how many otherwise harmless people he set by the ears together disputing whether he was right or wrong — is more by a great deal than I can reckon up. His wife died, and two of his three children died, before the tribunals could make up their minds to show him the door and take no more of his money. When it was all over, and the Duke in possession was left in possession, Mr. Blake discovered that the only way of being even with his country for the manner in which it had treated him, was not to let his country have the honour of educating his son. "How can I trust my native institutions," was the form in which he put it, "after the way in which my native institutions have behaved to me?" Add to this, that Mr. Blake disliked all boys, his own included, and you will admit that it could only end in one way. Master Franklin was taken from us in England, and was sent to institutions which his father could trust, in that superior country, Germany; Mr. Blake himself, you will observe, remaining snug in England, to improve his fellow-countrymen in the Parliament House, and to publish a statement on the subject of the Duke in possession, which has remained an unfinished statement from that day to this.

There! thank God, that's told! Neither you nor I need trouble our heads any more about Mr. Blake, senior. Leave him to the Dukedom; and let you and I stick to the Diamond.

The Diamond takes us back to Mr. Franklin, who was the innocent means of bringing that unlucky jewel into the house.

Our nice boy didn't forget us after he went abroad. He wrote every now and then; sometimes to my lady, sometimes to Miss Rachel, and sometimes to me. We had had a transaction together, before he left, which consisted in his borrowing of me a ball of string, a four-bladed knife, and seven-and-sixpence in money—the colour of which last I have not seen, and never expect to see again. His letters to me chiefly related to borrowing more. I heard, however, from my lady, how he got on abroad, as he grew in years and stature. After he had learnt what the institutions of Germany could teach him, he gave the French a turn next, and the Italians a turn after that. They made him among them a sort of universal genius, as well as I could understand it. He wrote a little; he painted a little; he sang and played and composed a little—borrowing, as I suspect, in all these cases, just as he had borrowed from me. His mother's fortune (seven hundred a year) fell to him when he came of age, and ran through him, as it might be through a sieve. The more money he had, the more he wanted; there was a hole in Mr. Franklin's pocket that nothing would sew up. Wherever he went, the lively, easy way of him made him welcome. He lived here, there, and everywhere; his address (as he used to put it himself) being "Post Office, Europe—to be left till called for." Twice over, he made up his mind to come back to England and see us; and twice over (saving your presence), some unmentionable woman stood in the way and stopped him. His third attempt succeeded, as you know already from what my lady told me. On Thursday the twenty-fifth of May, we were to see for the first time what our nice boy had grown to be as a man. He came of good blood; he had a high courage; and he was five-and-twenty years of age, by our reckoning. Now you know as much of Mr. Franklin Blake as I did—before Mr. Franklin Blake came down to our house.

The Thursday was as fine a summer's day as ever you saw: and my lady and Miss Rachel (not expecting Mr. Franklin till dinner-time) drove out to lunch with some friends in the neighbourhood.

When they were gone, I went and had a look at the bedroom which had been got ready for our guest, and saw that all was straight. Then, being butler in my lady's establishment, as well as steward (at my own particular request, mind, and because it vexed me to see anybody but myself in possession of the key of

The Moonstone

the late Sir John's cellar) — then, I say, I fetched up some of our famous Latour claret, and set it in the warm summer air to take off the chill before dinner. Concluding to set myself in the warm summer air next — seeing that what is good for old claret is equally good for old age — I took up my beehive chair to go out into the back court, when I was stopped by hearing a sound like the soft beating of a drum, on the terrace in front of my lady's residence.

Going round to the terrace, I found three mahogany-coloured Indians, in white linen frocks and trousers, looking up at the house.

The Indians, as I saw on looking closer, had small hand-drums slung in front of them. Behind them stood a little delicate-looking light-haired English boy carrying a bag. I judged the fellows to be strolling conjurors, and the boy with the bag to be carrying the tools of their trade. One of the three, who spoke English and who exhibited, I must own, the most elegant manners, presently informed me that my judgment was right. He requested permission to show his tricks in the presence of the lady of the house.

Now I am not a sour old man. I am generally all for amusement, and the last person in the world to distrust another person because he happens to be a few shades darker than myself. But the best of us have our weaknesses — and my weakness, when I know a family plate-basket to be out on a pantry-table, is to be instantly reminded of that basket by the sight of a strolling stranger whose manners are superior to my own. I accordingly informed the Indian that the lady of the house was out; and I warned him and his party off the premises. He made me a beautiful bow in return; and he and his party went off the premises. On my side, I returned to my beehive chair, and set myself down on the sunny side of the court, and fell (if the truth must be owned), not exactly into a sleep, but into the next best thing to it.

I was roused up by my daughter Penelope running out at me as if the house was on fire. What do you think she wanted? She wanted to have the three Indian jugglers instantly taken up; for this reason, namely, that they knew who was coming from London to visit us, and that they meant some mischief to Mr. Franklin Blake.

Mr. Franklin's name roused me. I opened my eyes, and made my girl explain herself.

It appeared that Penelope had just come from our lodge, where she had been having a gossip with the lodge-keeper's daughter. The two girls had seen the Indians pass out, after I had warned them off, followed by their little boy. Taking it into their heads that the boy was ill-used by the foreigners — for no reason that I could discover, except that he was pretty and delicate-looking — the two girls had stolen along the inner side of the hedge between us and the road, and had watched the proceedings of the foreigners on the outer side. Those proceedings resulted in the performance of the following extraordinary tricks.

They first looked up the road, and down the road, and made sure that they were alone. Then they all three faced about, and stared hard in the direction of our house. Then they jabbered and disputed in their own language, and looked at each other like men in doubt. Then they all turned to their little English boy, as if they expected him to help them. And then the chief Indian, who spoke English, said to the boy, "Hold out your hand."

On hearing those dreadful words, my daughter Penelope said she didn't know what prevented her heart from flying straight out of her. I thought privately that it might have been her stays. All I said, however, was, "You make my flesh creep." (Nota bene: Women like these little compliments.)

Well, when the Indian said, "Hold out your hand," the boy shrunk back, and shook his head, and said he didn't like it. The Indian, thereupon, asked him (not at all unkindly), whether he would like to be sent back to London, and left where they had found him, sleeping in an empty basket in a market — a hungry, ragged, and forsaken little boy. This, it seems, ended the difficulty. The little chap unwillingly held out his hand. Upon that, the Indian took a bottle from his bosom, and poured out of it some black stuff, like ink, into the palm of the boy's hand. The Indian — first touching the boy's head, and making signs over it in the air — then said, "Look." The boy became quite stiff, and stood like a statue, looking into the ink in the hollow of his hand.

The Moonstone

(So far, it seemed to me to be juggling, accompanied by a foolish waste of ink. I was beginning to feel sleepy again, when Penelope's next words stirred me up.)

The Indians looked up the road and down the road once more—and then the chief Indian said these words to the boy; "See the English gentleman from foreign parts."

The boy said, "I see him."

The Indian said, "Is it on the road to this house, and on no other, that the English gentleman will travel today?"

The boy said, "It is on the road to this house, and on no other, that the English gentleman will travel today."

The Indian put a second question—after waiting a little first. He said: "Has the English gentleman got It about him?"

The boy answered—also, after waiting a little first—"Yes."

The Indian put a third and last question: "Will the English gentleman come here, as he has promised to come, at the close of day?"

The boy said, "I can't tell."

The Indian asked why.

The boy said, "I am tired. The mist rises in my head, and puzzles me. I can see no more today."

With that the catechism ended. The chief Indian said something in his own language to the other two, pointing to the boy, and pointing towards the town, in which (as we afterwards discovered) they were lodged. He then, after making more signs on the boy's head, blew on his forehead, and so woke him up with a start. After that, they all went on their way towards the town, and the girls saw them no more.

Most things they say have a moral, if you only look for it. What was the moral of this?

The moral was, as I thought: First, that the chief juggler had heard Mr. Franklin's arrival talked of among the servants out-of-doors, and saw his way to making a little money by it. Second, that he and his men and boy (with a view to making the said money) meant to hang about till they saw my lady drive home, and then to come back, and foretell Mr. Franklin's arrival by magic. Third, that Penelope had heard them rehearsing their hocus-pocus, like actors rehearsing a play. Fourth, that I should do well to have an eye, that evening, on the plate-basket. Fifth, that Penelope would do well to cool down, and leave me, her father, to doze off again in the sun.

That appeared to me to be the sensible view. If you know anything of the ways of young women, you won't be surprised to hear that Penelope wouldn't take it. The moral of the thing was serious, according to my daughter. She particularly reminded me of the Indian's third question, Has the English gentleman got It about him? "Oh, father!" says Penelope, clasping her hands, "don't joke about this. What does 'It' mean?"

"We'll ask Mr. Franklin, my dear," I said, "if you can wait till Mr. Franklin comes." I winked to show I meant that in joke. Penelope took it quite seriously. My girl's earnestness tickled me. "What on earth should Mr. Franklin know about it?" I inquired. "Ask him," says Penelope. "And see whether he thinks it a laughing matter, too." With that parting shot, my daughter left me.

I settled it with myself, when she was gone, that I really would ask Mr. Franklin—mainly to set Penelope's mind at rest. What was said between us, when I did ask him, later on that same day, you will find set out fully in its proper place. But as I don't wish to raise your expectations and then disappoint them, I will take leave to warn you here—before we go any further—that you won't find the ghost of a joke in our conversation on the subject of the jugglers. To my great surprise, Mr. Franklin, like Penelope, took the thing seriously. How seriously, you will understand, when I tell you that, in his opinion, "It" meant the Moonstone.

CHAPTER IV

I am truly sorry to detain you over me and my beehive chair. A sleepy old man, in a sunny back yard, is not an interesting object, I am well aware. But things must be put down in their places, as things actually happened—and you must please to jog on a little while longer with me, in expectation of Mr. Franklin Blake's arrival later in the day.

Before I had time to doze off again, after my daughter Penelope had left me, I was disturbed by a rattling of plates and dishes in the servants' hall, which meant that dinner was ready. Taking my own meals in my own sitting-room, I had nothing to do with the servants' dinner, except to wish them a good stomach to it all round, previous to composing myself once more in my chair. I was just stretching my legs, when out bounced another woman on me. Not my daughter again; only Nancy, the kitchen-maid, this time. I was straight in her way out; and I observed, as she asked me to let her by, that she had a sulky face—a thing which, as head of the servants, I never allow, on principle, to pass me without inquiry.

"What are you turning your back on your dinner for?" I asked. "What's wrong now, Nancy?"

Nancy tried to push by, without answering; upon which I rose up, and took her by the ear. She is a nice plump young lass, and it is customary with me to adopt that manner of showing that I personally approve of a girl.

"What's wrong now?" I said once more.

"Rosanna's late again for dinner," says Nancy. "And I'm sent to fetch her in. All the hard work falls on my shoulders in this house. Let me alone, Mr. Betteredge!"

The person here mentioned as Rosanna was our second housemaid. Having a kind of pity for our second housemaid (why, you shall presently know), and seeing in Nancy's face, that she would fetch her fellow-servant in with more hard words than might be needful under the circumstances, it struck me that I had nothing particular to do, and that I might as well fetch Rosanna myself; giving her a hint to be punctual in future, which I knew she would take kindly from me.

"Where is Rosanna?" I inquired.

"At the sands, of course!" says Nancy, with a toss of her head. "She had another of her fainting fits this morning, and she asked to go out and get a breath of fresh air. I have no patience with her!"

"Go back to your dinner, my girl," I said. "I have patience with her, and I'll fetch her in."

Nancy (who has a fine appetite) looked pleased. When she looks pleased, she looks nice. When she looks nice, I chuck her under the chin. It isn't immorality—it's only habit.

Well, I took my stick, and set off for the sands.

No! it won't do to set off yet. I am sorry again to detain you; but you really must hear the story of the sands, and the story of Rosanna—for this reason, that the matter of the Diamond touches them both nearly. How hard I try to get on with my statement without stopping by the way, and how badly I succeed! But, there!—Persons and Things do turn up so vexatiously in this life, and will in a manner insist on being noticed. Let us take it easy, and let us take it short; we shall be in the thick of the mystery soon, I promise you!

Rosanna (to put the Person before the Thing, which is but common politeness) was the only new servant in our house. About four months before the time I am writing of, my lady had been in London, and had gone over a Reformatory, intended to save forlorn women from drifting back into bad ways, after they had got released from prison. The matron, seeing my lady took an interest in the place, pointed out a girl to her, named Rosanna Spearman, and told her a most miserable story, which I haven't the heart to repeat here; for I don't like to be made wretched without any use, and no more do you. The upshot of it was, that Rosanna Spearman had been a thief, and not being of the sort that get up Companies in the City, and rob from thousands, instead of only robbing from one, the law laid hold of her, and the prison and the reformatory followed the lead of the law. The matron's opinion of Rosanna was (in spite of what she had done) that the girl was one in a thousand, and that she only wanted a chance to prove herself worthy of any Christian woman's interest in her. My lady (being a Christian woman, if ever there was one yet) said to the matron, upon that, "Rosanna

Spearman shall have her chance, in my service." In a week afterwards, Rosanna Spearman entered this establishment as our second housemaid.

Not a soul was told the girl's story, excepting Miss Rachel and me. My lady, doing me the honour to consult me about most things, consulted me about Rosanna. Having fallen a good deal latterly into the late Sir John's way of always agreeing with my lady, I agreed with her heartily about Rosanna Spearman.

A fairer chance no girl could have had than was given to this poor girl of ours. None of the servants could cast her past life in her teeth, for none of the servants knew what it had been. She had her wages and her privileges, like the rest of them; and every now and then a friendly word from my lady, in private, to encourage her. In return, she showed herself, I am bound to say, well worthy of the kind treatment bestowed upon her. Though far from strong, and troubled occasionally with those fainting-fits already mentioned, she went about her work modestly and uncomplainingly, doing it carefully, and doing it well. But, somehow, she failed to make friends among the other women servants, excepting my daughter Penelope, who was always kind to Rosanna, though never intimate with her.

I hardly know what the girl did to offend them. There was certainly no beauty about her to make the others envious; she was the plainest woman in the house, with the additional misfortune of having one shoulder bigger than the other. What the servants chiefly resented, I think, was her silent tongue and her solitary ways. She read or worked in leisure hours when the rest gossiped. And when it came to her turn to go out, nine times out of ten she quietly put on her bonnet, and had her turn by herself. She never quarrelled, she never took offence; she only kept a certain distance, obstinately and civilly, between the rest of them and herself. Add to this that, plain as she was, there was just a dash of something that wasn't like a housemaid, and that was like a lady, about her. It might have been in her voice, or it might have been in her face. All I can say is, that the other women pounced on it like lightning the first day she came into the house, and said (which was most unjust) that Rosanna Spearman gave herself airs.

Having now told the story of Rosanna, I have only to notice one of the many queer ways of this strange girl to get on next to the story of the sands.

Our house is high up on the Yorkshire coast, and close by the sea. We have got beautiful walks all round us, in every direction but one. That one I acknowledge to be a horrid walk. It leads, for a quarter of a mile, through a melancholy plantation of firs, and brings you out between low cliffs on the loneliest and ugliest little bay on all our coast.

The sandhills here run down to the sea, and end in two spits of rock jutting out opposite each other, till you lose sight of them in the water. One is called the North Spit, and one the South. Between the two, shifting backwards and forwards at certain seasons of the year, lies the most horrible quicksand on the shores of Yorkshire. At the turn of the tide, something goes on in the unknown deeps below, which sets the whole face of the quicksand shivering and trembling in a manner most remarkable to see, and which has given to it, among the people in our parts, the name of the Shivering Sand. A great bank, half a mile out, nigh the mouth of the bay, breaks the force of the main ocean coming in from the offing. Winter and summer, when the tide flows over the quicksand, the sea seems to leave the waves behind it on the bank, and rolls its waters in smoothly with a heave, and covers the sand in silence. A lonesome and a horrid retreat, I can tell you! No boat ever ventures into this bay. No children from our fishing-village, called Cobb's Hole, ever come here to play. The very birds of the air, as it seems to me, give the Shivering Sand a wide berth. That a young woman, with dozens of nice walks to choose from, and company to go with her, if she only said "Come!", should prefer this place, and should sit and work or read in it, all alone, when it's her turn out, I grant you, passes belief. It's true, nevertheless, account for it as you may, that this was Rosanna Spearman's favourite walk, except when she went once or twice to Cobb's Hole, to see the only friend she had in our neighbourhood, of whom more anon. It's also true that I was now setting out for this same place, to fetch the girl in to dinner, which brings us round happily to our former point, and starts us fair again on our way to the sands.

I saw no sign of the girl in the plantation. When I got out, through the sandhills, on to the beach, there she was, in her little straw bonnet, and her plain grey cloak that she always wore to hide her deformed shoulder as much as might be—there she was, all alone, looking out on the quicksand and the sea.

She started when I came up with her, and turned her head away from me. Not looking me in the face being another of the proceedings, which, as head of the servants, I never allow, on principle, to pass without inquiry—I turned her round my way, and saw that she was crying. My bandanna handkerchief—one of six beauties given to me by my lady—was handy in my pocket. I took it out, and I said to Rosanna, "Come and sit down, my dear, on the slope of the beach along with me. I'll dry your eyes for you first, and then I'll make so bold as to ask what you have been crying about."

When you come to my age, you will find sitting down on the slope of a beach a much longer job than you think it now. By the time I was settled, Rosanna had dried her own eyes with a very inferior handkerchief to mine—cheap cambric. She looked very quiet, and very wretched; but she sat down by me like a good girl, when I told her. When you want to comfort a woman by the shortest way, take her on your knee. I thought of this golden rule. But there! Rosanna wasn't Nancy, and that's the truth of it!

"Now, tell me, my dear," I said, "what are you crying about?"

"About the years that are gone, Mr. Betteredge," says Rosanna quietly. "My past life still comes back to me sometimes."

"Come, come, my girl," I said, "your past life is all sponged out. Why can't you forget it?"

She took me by one of the lappets of my coat. I am a slovenly old man, and a good deal of my meat and drink gets splashed about on my clothes. Sometimes one of the women, and sometimes another, cleans me of my grease. The day before, Rosanna had taken out a spot for me on the lappet of my coat, with a new composition, warranted to remove anything. The grease was gone, but there was a little dull place left on the nap of the cloth where the grease had been. The girl pointed to that place, and shook her head.

"The stain is taken off," she said. "But the place shows, Mr.

Betteredge—the place shows!"

A remark which takes a man unawares by means of his own coat is not an easy remark to answer. Something in the girl herself, too, made me particularly sorry for her just then. She had nice brown eyes, plain as she was in other ways—and she looked at me with a sort of respect for my happy old age and my good character, as things for ever out of her own reach, which made my heart heavy for our second housemaid. Not feeling myself able to comfort her, there was only one other thing to do. That thing was—to take her in to dinner.

"Help me up," I said. "You're late for dinner, Rosanna—and I have come to fetch you in."

"You, Mr. Betteredge!" says she.

"They told Nancy to fetch you," I said. "But I thought you might like your scolding better, my dear, if it came from me."

Instead of helping me up, the poor thing stole her hand into mine, and gave it a little squeeze. She tried hard to keep from crying again, and succeeded—for which I respected her. "You're very kind, Mr. Betteredge," she said. "I don't want any dinner today—let me bide a little longer here."

"What makes you like to be here?" I asked. "What is it that brings you everlastingly to this miserable place?"

"Something draws me to it," says the girl, making images with her finger in the sand. "I try to keep away from it, and I can't. Sometimes," says she in a low voice, as if she was frightened at her own fancy, "sometimes, Mr. Betteredge, I think that my grave is waiting for me here."

"There's roast mutton and suet pudding waiting for you!" says I. "Go in to dinner directly. This is what comes, Rosanna, of thinking on an empty stomach!" I spoke severely, being naturally indignant (at my time of life) to hear a young woman of five-and-twenty talking about her latter end!

She didn't seem to hear me: she put her hand on my shoulder, and kept me where I was, sitting by her side.

"I think the place has laid a spell on me," she said. "I dream of it night after night; I think of it when I sit stitching at my work. You know I am grateful, Mr. Betteredge—you know I try to deserve your kindness, and my lady's confidence in me. But I wonder sometimes whether the life here is too quiet and too good for such a woman as I am, after all I have gone through, Mr. Betteredge—after all I have gone through. It's more lonely to me to be among the other servants, knowing I am not what they are, than it is to be here. My lady doesn't know, the matron at the reformatory doesn't know, what a dreadful reproach honest people are in themselves to a woman like me. Don't scold me, there's a dear good man. I do my work, don't I? Please not to tell my lady I am discontented—I am not. My mind's unquiet, sometimes, that's all." She snatched her hand off my shoulder, and suddenly pointed down to the quicksand. "Look!" she said "Isn't it wonderful? isn't it terrible? I have seen it dozens of times, and it's always as new to me as if I had never seen it before!"

I looked where she pointed. The tide was on the turn, and the horrid sand began to shiver. The broad brown face of it heaved slowly, and then dimpled and quivered all over. "Do you know what it looks like to me?" says Rosanna, catching me by the shoulder again. "It looks as if it had hundreds of suffocating people under it—all struggling to get to the surface, and all sinking lower and lower in the dreadful deeps! Throw a stone in, Mr. Betteredge! Throw a stone in, and let's see the sand suck it down!"

Here was unwholesome talk! Here was an empty stomach feeding on an unquiet mind! My answer—a pretty sharp one, in the poor girl's own interests, I promise you!—was at my tongue's end, when it was snapped short off on a sudden by a voice among the sandhills shouting for me by my name. "Betteredge!" cries the voice, "where are you?" "Here!" I shouted out in return, without a notion in my mind of who it was. Rosanna started to her feet, and stood looking towards the voice. I was just thinking of getting on my own legs next, when I was staggered by a sudden change in the girl's face.

Her complexion turned of a beautiful red, which I had never seen in it before; she brightened all over with a kind of speechless and breathless surprise. "Who is it?" I asked. Rosanna gave me back my own question. "Oh! who is it?" she said softly, more to herself than to me. I twisted round on the sand and looked behind me. There, coming out on us from among the hills, was a bright-eyed young gentleman, dressed in a beautiful fawn-coloured suit, with gloves and hat to match, with a rose in his button-hole, and a smile on his face that might have set the Shivering Sand itself smiling at him in return. Before I could get on my legs, he plumped down on the sand by the side of me, put his arm round my neck, foreign fashion, and gave me a hug that fairly squeezed the breath out of my body. "Dear old Betteredge!" says he. "I owe you seven-and-sixpence. Now do you know who I am?"

Lord bless us and save us! Here—four good hours before we expected him—was Mr. Franklin Blake!

Before I could say a word, I saw Mr. Franklin, a little surprised to all appearance, look up from me to Rosanna. Following his lead, I looked at the girl too. She was blushing of a deeper red than ever, seemingly at having caught Mr. Franklin's eye; and she turned and left us suddenly, in a confusion quite unaccountable to my mind, without either making her curtsey to the gentleman or saying a word to me. Very unlike her usual self: a civiller and better-behaved servant, in general, you never met with.

"That's an odd girl," says Mr. Franklin. "I wonder what she sees in me to surprise her?"

"I suppose, sir," I answered, drolling on our young gentleman's Continental education, "it's the varnish from foreign parts."

I set down here Mr. Franklin's careless question, and my foolish answer, as a consolation and encouragement to all stupid people—it being, as I have remarked, a great satisfaction to our inferior fellow-creatures to find that their betters are, on occasions, no brighter than they are. Neither Mr. Franklin, with his wonderful foreign training, nor I, with my age, experience, and natural mother-wit, had the ghost of an idea of what Rosanna Spearman's unaccountable behaviour really meant. She was out of our thoughts, poor soul, before we had seen the last flutter of her little grey cloak among the sandhills. And what of that? you will ask, naturally enough. Read on, good friend, as patiently as you can, and perhaps you will be as sorry for Rosanna Spearman as I was, when I found out the truth.

CHAPTER V

The first thing I did, after we were left together alone, was to make a third attempt to get up from my seat on the sand. Mr. Franklin stopped me.

"There is one advantage about this horrid place," he said; "we have got it all to ourselves. Stay where you are, Betteredge; I have something to say to you."

While he was speaking, I was looking at him, and trying to see something of the boy I remembered, in the man before me. The man put me out. Look as I might, I could see no more of his boy's rosy cheeks than of his boy's trim little jacket. His complexion had got pale: his face, at the lower part was covered, to my great surprise and disappointment, with a curly brown beard and moustachios. He had a lively touch-and-go way with him, very pleasant and engaging, I admit; but nothing to compare with his free-and-easy manners of other times. To make matters worse, he had promised to be tall, and had not kept his promise. He was neat, and slim, and well made; but he wasn't by an inch or two up to the middle height. In short, he baffled me altogether. The years that had passed had left nothing of his old self, except the bright, straightforward look in his eyes. There I found our nice boy again, and there I concluded to stop in my investigation.

"Welcome back to the old place, Mr. Franklin," I said. "All the more welcome, sir, that you have come some hours before we expected you."

"I have a reason for coming before you expected me," answered Mr. Franklin. "I suspect, Betteredge, that I have been followed and watched in London, for the last three or four days; and I have travelled by the morning instead of the afternoon train, because I wanted to give a certain dark-looking stranger the slip."

Those words did more than surprise me. They brought back to my mind, in a flash, the three jugglers, and Penelope's notion that they meant some mischief to Mr. Franklin Blake.

"Who's watching you, sir,—and why?" I inquired.

"Tell me about the three Indians you have had at the house

today," says Mr. Franklin, without noticing my question. "It's just possible, Betteredge, that my stranger and your three jugglers may turn out to be pieces of the same puzzle."

"How do you come to know about the jugglers, sir?" I asked, putting one question on the top of another, which was bad manners, I own. But you don't expect much from poor human nature—so don't expect much from me.

"I saw Penelope at the house," says Mr. Franklin; "and Penelope told me. Your daughter promised to be a pretty girl, Betteredge, and she has kept her promise. Penelope has got a small ear and a small foot. Did the late Mrs. Betteredge possess those inestimable advantages?"

"The late Mrs. Betteredge possessed a good many defects, sir," says I. "One of them (if you will pardon my mentioning it) was never keeping to the matter in hand. She was more like a fly than a woman: she couldn't settle on anything."

"She would just have suited me," says Mr. Franklin. "I never settle on anything either. Betteredge, your edge is better than ever. Your daughter said as much, when I asked for particulars about the jugglers. 'Father will tell you, sir. He's a wonderful man for his age; and he expresses himself beautifully.' Penelope's own words—blushing divinely. Not even my respect for you prevented me from—never mind; I knew her when she was a child, and she's none the worse for it. Let's be serious. What did the jugglers do?"

I was something dissatisfied with my daughter—not for letting Mr. Franklin kiss her; Mr. Franklin was welcome to that—but for forcing me to tell her foolish story at second hand. However, there was no help for it now but to mention the circumstances. Mr. Franklin's merriment all died away as I went on. He sat knitting his eyebrows, and twisting his beard. When I had done, he repeated after me two of the questions which the chief juggler had put to the boy—seemingly for the purpose of fixing them well in his mind.

"'Is it on the road to this house, and on no other, that the English gentleman will travel today?' 'Has the English gentleman got It about him?' I suspect," says Mr. Franklin, pulling a little sealed paper parcel out of his pocket, "that 'It' means this. And 'this,' Betteredge, means my uncle Herncastle's

The Moonstone

famous Diamond."

"Good Lord, sir!" I broke out, "how do you come to be in charge of the wicked Colonel's Diamond?"

"The wicked Colonel's will has left his Diamond as a birthday present to my cousin Rachel," says Mr. Franklin. "And my father, as the wicked Colonel's executor, has given it in charge to me to bring down here."

If the sea, then oozing in smoothly over the Shivering Sand, had been changed into dry land before my own eyes, I doubt if I could have been more surprised than I was when Mr. Franklin spoke those words.

"The Colonel's Diamond left to Miss Rachel!" says I. "And your father, sir, the Colonel's executor! Why, I would have laid any bet you like, Mr. Franklin, that your father wouldn't have touched the Colonel with a pair of tongs!"

"Strong language, Betteredge! What was there against the Colonel. He belonged to your time, not to mine. Tell me what you know about him, and I'll tell you how my father came to be his executor, and more besides. I have made some discoveries in London about my uncle Herncastle and his Diamond, which have rather an ugly look to my eyes; and I want you to confirm them. You called him the 'wicked Colonel' just now. Search your memory, my old friend, and tell me why."

I saw he was in earnest, and I told him.

Here follows the substance of what I said, written out entirely for your benefit. Pay attention to it, or you will be all abroad, when we get deeper into the story. Clear your mind of the children, or the dinner, or the new bonnet, or what not. Try if you can't forget politics, horses, prices in the City, and grievances at the club. I hope you won't take this freedom on my part amiss; it's only a way I have of appealing to the gentle reader. Lord! haven't I seen you with the greatest authors in your hands, and don't I know how ready your attention is to wander when it's a book that asks for it, instead of a person?

I spoke, a little way back, of my lady's father, the old lord with the short temper and the long tongue. He had five children in all. Two sons to begin with; then, after a long time, his wife broke out breeding again, and the three young ladies came briskly one after the other, as fast as the nature of things would permit; my mistress, as before mentioned, being the youngest and best of the three. Of the two sons, the eldest, Arthur, inherited the title and estates. The second, the Honourable John, got a fine fortune left him by a relative, and went into the army.

It's an ill bird, they say, that fouls its own nest. I look on the noble family of the Herncastles as being my nest; and I shall take it as a favour if I am not expected to enter into particulars on the subject of the Honourable John. He was, I honestly believe, one of the greatest blackguards that ever lived. I can hardly say more or less for him than that. He went into the army, beginning in the Guards. He had to leave the Guards before he was two-and-twenty—never mind why. They are very strict in the army, and they were too strict for the Honourable John. He went out to India to see whether they were equally strict there, and to try a little active service. In the matter of bravery (to give him his due), he was a mixture of bull-dog and game-cock, with a dash of the savage. He was at the taking of Seringapatam. Soon afterwards he changed into another regiment, and, in course of time, changed into a third. In the third he got his last step as lieutenant-colonel, and, getting that, got also a sunstroke, and came home to England.

He came back with a character that closed the doors of all his family against him, my lady (then just married) taking the lead, and declaring (with Sir John's approval, of course) that her brother should never enter any house of hers. There was more than one slur on the Colonel that made people shy of him; but the blot of the Diamond is all I need mention here.

It was said he had got possession of his Indian jewel by means which, bold as he was, he didn't dare acknowledge. He never attempted to sell it—not being in need of money, and not (to give him his due again) making money an object. He never gave it away; he never even showed it to any living soul. Some said he was afraid of its getting him into a difficulty with the military authorities; others (very ignorant indeed of the real nature of the man) said he was afraid, if he showed it, of its costing him his life.

There was perhaps a grain of truth mixed up with this last report. It was false to say that he was afraid; but it was a fact that his life had been twice threatened in India; and it was

The Moonstone

firmly believed that the Moonstone was at the bottom of it. When he came back to England, and found himself avoided by everybody, the Moonstone was thought to be at the bottom of it again. The mystery of the Colonel's life got in the Colonel's way, and outlawed him, as you may say, among his own people. The men wouldn't let him into their clubs; the women—more than one—whom he wanted to marry, refused him; friends and relations got too near-sighted to see him in the street.

Some men in this mess would have tried to set themselves right with the world. But to give in, even when he was wrong, and had all society against him, was not the way of the Honourable John. He had kept the Diamond, in flat defiance of assassination, in India. He kept the Diamond, in flat defiance of public opinion, in England. There you have the portrait of the man before you, as in a picture: a character that braved everything; and a face, handsome as it was, that looked possessed by the devil.

We heard different rumours about him from time to time. Sometimes they said he was given up to smoking opium and collecting old books; sometimes he was reported to be trying strange things in chemistry; sometimes he was seen carousing and amusing himself among the lowest people in the lowest slums of London. Anyhow, a solitary, vicious, underground life was the life the Colonel led. Once, and once only, after his return to England, I myself saw him, face to face.

About two years before the time of which I am now writing, and about a year and a half before the time of his death, the Colonel came unexpectedly to my lady's house in London. It was the night of Miss Rachel's birthday, the twenty-first of June; and there was a party in honour of it, as usual. I received a message from the footman to say that a gentleman wanted to see me. Going up into the hall, there I found the Colonel, wasted, and worn, and old, and shabby, and as wild and as wicked as ever.

"Go up to my sister," says he; "and say that I have called to wish my niece many happy returns of the day."

He had made attempts by letter, more than once already, to be reconciled with my lady, for no other purpose, I am firmly persuaded, than to annoy her. But this was the first time he had actually come to the house. I had it on the tip of my tongue to say that my mistress had a party that night. But the devilish look of him daunted me. I went upstairs with his message, and left him, by his own desire, waiting in the hall. The servants stood staring at him, at a distance, as if he was a walking engine of destruction, loaded with powder and shot, and likely to go off among them at a moment's notice.

My lady had a dash—no more—of the family temper. "Tell Colonel Herncastle," she said, when I gave her her brother's message, "that Miss Verinder is engaged, and that I decline to see him." I tried to plead for a civiller answer than that; knowing the Colonel's constitutional superiority to the restraints which govern gentlemen in general. Quite useless! The family temper flashed out at me directly. "When I want your advice," says my lady, "you know that I always ask for it. I don't ask for it now." I went downstairs with the message, of which I took the liberty of presenting a new and amended edition of my own contriving, as follows: "My lady and Miss Rachel regret that they are engaged, Colonel; and beg to be excused having the honour of seeing you."

I expected him to break out, even at that polite way of putting it. To my surprise he did nothing of the sort; he alarmed me by taking the thing with an unnatural quiet. His eyes, of a glittering bright grey, just settled on me for a moment; and he laughed, not out of himself, like other people, but into himself, in a soft, chuckling, horridly mischievous way. "Thank you, Betteredge," he said. "I shall remember my niece's birthday." With that, he turned on his heel, and walked out of the house.

The next birthday came round, and we heard he was ill in bed. Six months afterwards—that is to say, six months before the time I am now writing of—there came a letter from a highly respectable clergyman to my lady. It communicated two wonderful things in the way of family news. First, that the Colonel had forgiven his sister on his death-bed. Second, that he had forgiven everybody else, and had made a most edifying end. I have myself (in spite of the bishops and the clergy) an unfeigned respect for the Church; but I am firmly persuaded, at the same time, that the devil remained in undisturbed possession of the Honourable John, and that the last abominable act in the life of that abominable man was (saving your presence) to take the clergyman in!

This was the sum-total of what I had to tell Mr. Franklin. I remarked that he listened more and more eagerly the longer I went on. Also, that the story of the Colonel being sent away from his sister's door, on the occasion of his niece's birthday, seemed to strike Mr. Franklin like a shot that had hit the mark. Though he didn't acknowledge it, I saw that I had made him uneasy, plainly enough, in his face.

"You have said your say, Betteredge," he remarked. "It's my turn now. Before, however, I tell you what discoveries I have made in London, and how I came to be mixed up in this matter of the Diamond, I want to know one thing. You look, my old friend, as if you didn't quite understand the object to be answered by this consultation of ours. Do your looks belie you?"

"No, sir," I said. "My looks, on this occasion at any rate, tell the truth."

"In that case," says Mr. Franklin, "suppose I put you up to my point of view, before we go any further. I see three very serious questions involved in the Colonel's birthday-gift to my cousin Rachel. Follow me carefully, Betteredge; and count me off on your fingers, if it will help you," says Mr. Franklin, with a certain pleasure in showing how clear-headed he could be, which reminded me wonderfully of old times when he was a boy. "Question the first: Was the Colonel's Diamond the object of a conspiracy in India? Question the second: Has the conspiracy followed the Colonel's Diamond to England? Question the third: Did the Colonel know the conspiracy followed the Diamond; and has he purposely left a legacy of trouble and danger to his sister, through the innocent medium of his sister's child? That is what I am driving at, Betteredge. Don't let me frighten you."

It was all very well to say that, but he had frightened me.

If he was right, here was our quiet English house suddenly invaded by a devilish Indian Diamond—bringing after it a conspiracy of living rogues, set loose on us by the vengeance of a dead man. There was our situation as revealed to me in Mr. Franklin's last words! Who ever heard the like of it—in the nineteenth century, mind; in an age of progress, and in a country which rejoices in the blessings of the British constitution? Nobody ever heard the like of it, and, consequently, nobody can be expected to believe it. I shall go on with my story, however, in spite of that.

When you get a sudden alarm, of the sort that I had got now, nine times out of ten the place you feel it in is your stomach. When you feel it in your stomach, your attention wanders, and you begin to fidget. I fidgeted silently in my place on the sand. Mr. Franklin noticed me, contending with a perturbed stomach or mind—which you please; they mean the same thing—and, checking himself just as he was starting with his part of the story, said to me sharply, "What do you want?"

What did I want? I didn't tell him; but I'll tell you, in confidence. I wanted a whiff of my pipe, and a turn at Robinson Crusoe.

CHAPTER VI

Keeping my private sentiments to myself, I respectfully requested Mr. Franklin to go on. Mr. Franklin replied, "Don't fidget, Betteredge," and went on.

Our young gentleman's first words informed me that his discoveries, concerning the wicked Colonel and the Diamond, had begun with a visit which he had paid (before he came to us) to the family lawyer, at Hampstead. A chance word dropped by Mr. Franklin, when the two were alone, one day, after dinner, revealed that he had been charged by his father with a birthday present to be taken to Miss Rachel. One thing led to another; and it ended in the lawyer mentioning what the present really was, and how the friendly connexion between the late Colonel and Mr. Blake, senior, had taken its rise. The facts here are really so extraordinary, that I doubt if I can trust my own language to do justice to them. I prefer trying to report Mr. Franklin's discoveries, as nearly as may be, in Mr. Franklin's own words.

"You remember the time, Betteredge," he said, "when my father was trying to prove his title to that unlucky Dukedom? Well! that was also the time when my uncle Herncastle returned from India. My father discovered that his brother-in-law was in possession of certain papers which were likely to be of service to him in his lawsuit. He called on the Colonel, on pretence of welcoming him back to England. The Colonel was not to be deluded in that way. 'You want something,' he said, 'or you would never have compromised your reputation by calling on me.' My father saw that the one chance for him was to show his hand; he admitted, at once, that he wanted the papers. The Colonel asked for a day to consider his answer. His answer came in the shape of a most extraordinary letter, which my friend the lawyer showed me. The Colonel began by saying that he wanted something of my father, and that he begged to propose an exchange of friendly services between them. The fortune of war (that was the expression he used) had placed him in possession of one of the largest Diamonds in the world; and he had reason to believe that neither he nor his precious jewel was safe in any house, in any quarter of the globe, which they occupied together. Under these alarming circumstances, he had determined to place his Diamond in the keeping of another person. That person was not expected to run any risk. He might deposit the precious stone in any place especially guarded and set apart—like a banker's or jeweller's strongroom—for the safe custody of valuables of high price. His main personal responsibility in the matter was to be of the passive kind. He was to undertake either by himself, or by a trustworthy representative—to receive at a prearranged address, on certain prearranged days in every year, a note from the Colonel, simply stating the fact that he was a living man at that date. In the event of the date passing over without the note being received, the Colonel's silence might be taken as a sure token of the Colonel's death by murder. In that case, and in no other, certain sealed instructions relating to the disposal of the Diamond, and deposited with it, were to be opened, and followed implicitly. If my father chose to accept this strange charge, the Colonel's papers were at his disposal in return. That was the letter."

"What did your father do, sir?" I asked.

"Do?" says Mr. Franklin. "I'll tell you what he did. He brought the invaluable faculty, called common sense, to bear on the Colonel's letter. The whole thing, he declared, was simply absurd. Somewhere in his Indian wanderings, the Colonel had picked up with some wretched crystal which he took for a diamond. As for the danger of his being murdered, and the precautions devised to preserve his life and his piece of crystal, this was the nineteenth century, and any man in his senses had only to apply to the police. The Colonel had been a notorious opium-eater for years past; and, if the only way of getting at the valuable papers he possessed was by accepting a matter of opium as a matter of fact, my father was quite willing to take the ridiculous responsibility imposed on him—all the more readily that it involved no trouble to himself. The Diamond and the sealed instructions went into his banker's strongroom, and the Colonel's letters, periodically reporting him a living man, were received and opened by our family lawyer, Mr. Bruff, as my father's representative. No sensible person, in a similar position, could have viewed the matter in any other way. Nothing in this world, Betteredge, is probable unless it appeals to our own trumpery experience; and we only believe in a romance when we see it in a newspaper."

It was plain to me from this, that Mr. Franklin thought his father's notion about the Colonel hasty and wrong.

The Moonstone

"What is your own private opinion about the matter, sir?" I asked.

"Let's finish the story of the Colonel first," says Mr. Franklin. "There is a curious want of system, Betteredge, in the English mind; and your question, my old friend, is an instance of it. When we are not occupied in making machinery, we are (mentally speaking) the most slovenly people in the universe."

"So much," I thought to myself, "for a foreign education! He has learned that way of girding at us in France, I suppose."

Mr. Franklin took up the lost thread, and went on.

"My father," he said, "got the papers he wanted, and never saw his brother-in-law again from that time. Year after year, on the prearranged days, the prearranged letter came from the Colonel, and was opened by Mr. Bruff. I have seen the letters, in a heap, all of them written in the same brief, business-like form of words: 'Sir,—This is to certify that I am still a living man. Let the Diamond be. John Herncastle.' That was all he ever wrote, and that came regularly to the day; until some six or eight months since, when the form of the letter varied for the first time. It ran now: 'Sir,—They tell me I am dying. Come to me, and help me to make my will.' Mr. Bruff went, and found him, in the little suburban villa, surrounded by its own grounds, in which he had lived alone, ever since he had left India. He had dogs, cats, and birds to keep him company; but no human being near him, except the person who came daily to do the housework, and the doctor at the bedside. The will was a very simple matter. The Colonel had dissipated the greater part of his fortune in his chemical investigations. His will began and ended in three clauses, which he dictated from his bed, in perfect possession of his faculties. The first clause provided for the safe keeping and support of his animals. The second founded a professorship of experimental chemistry at a northern university. The third bequeathed the Moonstone as a birthday present to his niece, on condition that my father would act as executor. My father at first refused to act. On second thoughts, however, he gave way, partly because he was assured that the executorship would involve him in no trouble; partly because Mr. Bruff suggested, in Rachel's interest, that the Diamond might be worth something, after all."

"Did the Colonel give any reason, sir," I inquired, "why he left the Diamond to Miss Rachel?"

"He not only gave the reason—he had the reason written in his will," said Mr. Franklin. "I have got an extract, which you shall see presently. Don't be slovenly-minded, Betteredge! One thing at a time. You have heard about the Colonel's Will; now you must hear what happened after the Colonel's death. It was formally necessary to have the Diamond valued, before the Will could be proved. All the jewellers consulted, at once confirmed the Colonel's assertion that he possessed one of the largest diamonds in the world. The question of accurately valuing it presented some serious difficulties. Its size made it a phenomenon in the diamond market; its colour placed it in a category by itself; and, to add to these elements of uncertainty, there was a defect, in the shape of a flaw, in the very heart of the stone. Even with this last serious draw-back, however, the lowest of the various estimates given was twenty thousand pounds. Conceive my father's astonishment! He had been within a hair's-breadth of refusing to act as executor, and of allowing this magnificent jewel to be lost to the family. The interest he took in the matter now, induced him to open the sealed instructions which had been deposited with the Diamond. Mr. Bruff showed this document to me, with the other papers; and it suggests (to my mind) a clue to the nature of the conspiracy which threatened the Colonel's life."

"Then you do believe, sir," I said, "that there was a conspiracy?"

"Not possessing my father's excellent common sense," answered Mr. Franklin, "I believe the Colonel's life was threatened, exactly as the Colonel said. The sealed instructions, as I think, explain how it was that he died, after all, quietly in his bed. In the event of his death by violence (that is to say, in the absence of the regular letter from him at the appointed date), my father was then directed to send the Moonstone secretly to Amsterdam. It was to be deposited in that city with a famous diamond-cutter, and it was to be cut up into from four to six separate stones. The stones were then to be sold for what they would fetch, and the proceeds were to be applied to the founding of that professorship of experimental chemistry, which the Colonel has since endowed by his Will. Now,

The Moonstone

Betteredge, exert those sharp wits of yours, and observe the conclusion to which the Colonel's instructions point!"

I instantly exerted my wits. They were of the slovenly English sort; and they consequently muddled it all, until Mr. Franklin took them in hand, and pointed out what they ought to see.

"Remark," says Mr. Franklin, "that the integrity of the Diamond, as a whole stone, is here artfully made dependent on the preservation from violence of the Colonel's life. He is not satisfied with saying to the enemies he dreads, 'Kill me—and you will be no nearer to the Diamond than you are now; it is where you can't get at it—in the guarded strongroom of a bank.' He says instead, 'Kill me—and the Diamond will be the Diamond no longer; its identity will be destroyed.' What does that mean?"

Here I had (as I thought) a flash of the wonderful foreign brightness.

"I know," I said. "It means lowering the value of the stone, and cheating the rogues in that way!"

"Nothing of the sort," says Mr. Franklin. "I have inquired about that. The flawed Diamond, cut up, would actually fetch more than the Diamond as it now is; for this plain reason—that from four to six perfect brilliants might be cut from it, which would be, collectively, worth more money than the large—but imperfect single stone. If robbery for the purpose of gain was at the bottom of the conspiracy, the Colonel's instructions absolutely made the Diamond better worth stealing. More money could have been got for it, and the disposal of it in the diamond market would have been infinitely easier, if it had passed through the hands of the workmen of Amsterdam."

"Lord bless us, sir!" I burst out. "What was the plot, then?"

"A plot organised among the Indians who originally owned the jewel," says Mr. Franklin—"a plot with some old Hindoo superstition at the bottom of it. That is my opinion, confirmed by a family paper which I have about me at this moment."

I saw, now, why the appearance of the three Indian jugglers at our house had presented itself to Mr. Franklin in the light of a circumstance worth noting.

"I don't want to force my opinion on you," Mr. Franklin went on. "The idea of certain chosen servants of an old Hindoo superstition devoting themselves, through all difficulties and dangers, to watching the opportunity of recovering their sacred gem, appears to me to be perfectly consistent with everything that we know of the patience of Oriental races, and the influence of Oriental religions. But then I am an imaginative man; and the butcher, the baker, and the tax-gatherer, are not the only credible realities in existence to my mind. Let the guess I have made at the truth in this matter go for what it is worth, and let us get on to the only practical question that concerns us. Does the conspiracy against the Moonstone survive the Colonel's death? And did the Colonel know it, when he left the birthday gift to his niece?"

I began to see my lady and Miss Rachel at the end of it all, now. Not a word he said escaped me.

"I was not very willing, when I discovered the story of the Moonstone," said Mr. Franklin, "to be the means of bringing it here. But Mr. Bruff reminded me that somebody must put my cousin's legacy into my cousin's hands—and that I might as well do it as anybody else. After taking the Diamond out of the bank, I fancied I was followed in the streets by a shabby, dark-complexioned man. I went to my father's house to pick up my luggage, and found a letter there, which unexpectedly detained me in London. I went back to the bank with the Diamond, and thought I saw the shabby man again. Taking the Diamond once more out of the bank this morning, I saw the man for the third time, gave him the slip, and started (before he recovered the trace of me) by the morning instead of the afternoon train. Here I am, with the Diamond safe and sound—and what is the first news that meets me? I find that three strolling Indians have been at the house, and that my arrival from London, and something which I am expected to have about me, are two special objects of investigation to them when they believe themselves to be alone. I don't waste time and words on their pouring the ink into the boy's hand, and telling him to look in it for a man at a distance, and for something in that man's pocket. The thing (which I have often seen done in the East) is 'hocus-pocus' in my opinion, as it is in yours. The present question for us to decide is, whether I am wrongly attaching a meaning to a mere accident? or whether we really have evidence of the

The Moonstone

Indians being on the track of the Moonstone, the moment it is removed from the safe keeping of the bank?"

Neither he nor I seemed to fancy dealing with this part of the inquiry. We looked at each other, and then we looked at the tide, oozing in smoothly, higher and higher, over the Shivering Sand.

"What are you thinking of?" says Mr. Franklin, suddenly.

"I was thinking, sir," I answered, "that I should like to shy the Diamond into the quicksand, and settle the question in that way."

"If you have got the value of the stone in your pocket," answered Mr. Franklin, "say so, Betteredge, and in it goes!"

It's curious to note, when your mind's anxious, how very far in the way of relief a very small joke will go. We found a fund of merriment, at the time, in the notion of making away with Miss Rachel's lawful property, and getting Mr. Blake, as executor, into dreadful trouble—though where the merriment was, I am quite at a loss to discover now.

Mr. Franklin was the first to bring the talk back to the talk's proper purpose. He took an envelope out of his pocket, opened it, and handed to me the paper inside.

"Betteredge," he said, "we must face the question of the Colonel's motive in leaving this legacy to his niece, for my aunt's sake. Bear in mind how Lady Verinder treated her brother from the time when he returned to England, to the time when he told you he should remember his niece's birthday. And read that."

He gave me the extract from the Colonel's Will. I have got it by me while I write these words; and I copy it, as follows, for your benefit:

"Thirdly, and lastly, I give and bequeath to my niece, Rachel Verinder, daughter and only child of my sister, Julia Verinder, widow—if her mother, the said Julia Verinder, shall be living on the said Rachel Verinder's next Birthday after my death—the yellow Diamond belonging to me, and known in the East by the name of The Moonstone: subject to this condition, that her mother, the said Julia Verinder, shall be living at the time. And I hereby desire my executor to give my Diamond, either by his own hands or by the hands of some trustworthy representative whom he shall appoint, into the personal possession of my said niece Rachel, on her next birthday after my death, and in the presence, if possible, of my sister, the said Julia Verinder. And I desire that my said sister may be informed, by means of a true copy of this, the third and last clause of my Will, that I give the Diamond to her daughter Rachel, in token of my free forgiveness of the injury which her conduct towards me has been the means of inflicting on my reputation in my lifetime; and especially in proof that I pardon, as becomes a dying man, the insult offered to me as an officer and a gentleman, when her servant, by her orders, closed the door of her house against me, on the occasion of her daughter's birthday."

More words followed these, providing if my lady was dead, or if Miss Rachel was dead, at the time of the testator's decease, for the Diamond being sent to Holland, in accordance with the sealed instructions originally deposited with it. The proceeds of the sale were, in that case, to be added to the money already left by the Will for the professorship of chemistry at the university in the north.

I handed the paper back to Mr. Franklin, sorely troubled what to say to him. Up to that moment, my own opinion had been (as you know) that the Colonel had died as wickedly as he had lived. I don't say the copy from his Will actually converted me from that opinion: I only say it staggered me.

"Well," says Mr. Franklin, "now you have read the Colonel's own statement, what do you say? In bringing the Moonstone to my aunt's house, am I serving his vengeance blindfold, or am I vindicating him in the character of a penitent and Christian man?"

"It seems hard to say, sir," I answered, "that he died with a horrid revenge in his heart, and a horrid lie on his lips. God alone knows the truth. Don't ask me."

Mr. Franklin sat twisting and turning the extract from the Will in his fingers, as if he expected to squeeze the truth out of it in that manner. He altered quite remarkably, at the same time. From being brisk and bright, he now became, most unaccountably, a slow, solemn, and pondering young man.

The Moonstone

"This question has two sides," he said. "An Objective side, and a Subjective side. Which are we to take?"

He had had a German education as well as a French. One of the two had been in undisturbed possession of him (as I supposed) up to this time. And now (as well as I could make out) the other was taking its place. It is one of my rules in life, never to notice what I don't understand. I steered a middle course between the Objective side and the Subjective side. In plain English I stared hard, and said nothing.

"Let's extract the inner meaning of this," says Mr. Franklin. "Why did my uncle leave the Diamond to Rachel? Why didn't he leave it to my aunt?"

"That's not beyond guessing, sir, at any rate," I said. "Colonel Herncastle knew my lady well enough to know that she would have refused to accept any legacy that came to her from him."

"How did he know that Rachel might not refuse to accept it, too?"

"Is there any young lady in existence, sir, who could resist the temptation of accepting such a birthday present as The Moonstone?"

"That's the Subjective view," says Mr. Franklin. "It does you great credit, Betteredge, to be able to take the Subjective view. But there's another mystery about the Colonel's legacy which is not accounted for yet. How are we to explain his only giving Rachel her birthday present conditionally on her mother being alive?"

"I don't want to slander a dead man, sir," I answered. "But if he has purposely left a legacy of trouble and danger to his sister, by the means of her child, it must be a legacy made conditional on his sister's being alive to feel the vexation of it."

"Oh! That's your interpretation of his motive, is it? The Subjective interpretation again! Have you ever been in Germany, Betteredge?"

"No, sir. What's your interpretation, if you please?"

"I can see," says Mr. Franklin, "that the Colonel's object may, quite possibly, have been—not to benefit his niece, whom he had never even seen—but to prove to his sister that he had died forgiving her, and to prove it very prettily by means of a present made to her child. There is a totally different explanation from yours, Betteredge, taking its rise in a Subjective-Objective point of view. From all I can see, one interpretation is just as likely to be right as the other."

Having brought matters to this pleasant and comforting issue, Mr. Franklin appeared to think that he had completed all that was required of him. He laid down flat on his back on the sand, and asked what was to be done next.

He had been so clever, and clear-headed (before he began to talk the foreign gibberish), and had so completely taken the lead in the business up to the present time, that I was quite unprepared for such a sudden change as he now exhibited in this helpless leaning upon me. It was not till later that I learned—by assistance of Miss Rachel, who was the first to make the discovery—that these puzzling shifts and transformations in Mr. Franklin were due to the effect on him of his foreign training. At the age when we are all of us most apt to take our colouring, in the form of a reflection from the colouring of other people, he had been sent abroad, and had been passed on from one nation to another, before there was time for anyone colouring more than another to settle itself on him firmly. As a consequence of this, he had come back with so many different sides to his character, all more or less jarring with each other, that he seemed to pass his life in a state of perpetual contradiction with himself. He could be a busy man, and a lazy man; cloudy in the head, and clear in the head; a model of determination, and a spectacle of helplessness, all together. He had his French side, and his German side, and his Italian side—the original English foundation showing through, every now and then, as much as to say, "Here I am, sorely transmogrified, as you see, but there's something of me left at the bottom of him still." Miss Rachel used to remark that the Italian side of him was uppermost, on those occasions when he unexpectedly gave in, and asked you in his nice sweet-tempered way to take his own responsibilities on your shoulders. You will do him no injustice, I think, if you conclude that the Italian side of him was uppermost now.

"Isn't it your business, sir," I asked, "to know what to do

next? Surely it can't be mine?"

Mr. Franklin didn't appear to see the force of my question—not being in a position, at the time, to see anything but the sky over his head.

"I don't want to alarm my aunt without reason," he said. "And I don't want to leave her without what may be a needful warning. If you were in my place, Betteredge, tell me, in one word, what would you do?"

In one word, I told him: "Wait."

"With all my heart," says Mr. Franklin. "How long?"

I proceeded to explain myself.

"As I understand it, sir," I said, "somebody is bound to put this plaguy Diamond into Miss Rachel's hands on her birthday—and you may as well do it as another. Very good. This is the twenty-fifth of May, and the birthday is on the twenty-first of June. We have got close on four weeks before us. Let's wait and see what happens in that time; and let's warn my lady, or not, as the circumstances direct us."

"Perfect, Betteredge, as far as it goes!" says Mr. Franklin. "But between this and the birthday, what's to be done with the Diamond?"

"What your father did with it, to be sure, sir!" I answered. "Your father put it in the safe keeping of a bank in London. You put in the safe keeping of the bank at Frizinghall." (Frizinghall was our nearest town, and the Bank of England wasn't safer than the bank there.) "If I were you, sir," I added, "I would ride straight away with it to Frizinghall before the ladies come back."

The prospect of doing something—and, what is more, of doing that something on a horse—brought Mr. Franklin up like lightning from the flat of his back. He sprang to his feet, and pulled me up, without ceremony, on to mine. "Betteredge, you are worth your weight in gold," he said. "Come along, and saddle the best horse in the stables directly."

Here (God bless it!) was the original English foundation of him showing through all the foreign varnish at last! Here was the Master Franklin I remembered, coming out again in the good old way at the prospect of a ride, and reminding me of the good old times! Saddle a horse for him? I would have saddled a dozen horses, if he could only have ridden them all!

We went back to the house in a hurry; we had the fleetest horse in the stables saddled in a hurry; and Mr. Franklin rattled off in a hurry, to lodge the cursed Diamond once more in the strongroom of a bank. When I heard the last of his horse's hoofs on the drive, and when I turned about in the yard and found I was alone again, I felt half inclined to ask myself if I hadn't woke up from a dream.

CHAPTER VII

While I was in this bewildered frame of mind, sorely needing a little quiet time by myself to put me right again, my daughter Penelope got in my way (just as her late mother used to get in my way on the stairs), and instantly summoned me to tell her all that had passed at the conference between Mr. Franklin and me. Under present circumstances, the one thing to be done was to clap the extinguisher upon Penelope's curiosity on the spot. I accordingly replied that Mr. Franklin and I had both talked of foreign politics, till we could talk no longer, and had then mutually fallen asleep in the heat of the sun. Try that sort of answer when your wife or your daughter next worries you with an awkward question at an awkward time, and depend on the natural sweetness of women for kissing and making it up again at the next opportunity.

The afternoon wore on, and my lady and Miss Rachel came back.

Needless to say how astonished they were, when they heard that Mr. Franklin Blake had arrived, and had gone off again on horseback. Needless also to say, that they asked awkward questions directly, and that the "foreign politics" and the "falling asleep in the sun" wouldn't serve a second time over with them. Being at the end of my invention, I said Mr. Franklin's arrival by the early train was entirely attributable to one of Mr. Franklin's freaks. Being asked, upon that, whether his galloping off again on horseback was another of Mr. Franklin's freaks, I said, "Yes, it was;" and slipped out of it—I think very cleverly—in that way.

Having got over my difficulties with the ladies, I found more difficulties waiting for me when I went back to my own room. In came Penelope—with the natural sweetness of women—to kiss and make it up again; and—with the natural curiosity of women—to ask another question. This time she only wanted me to tell her what was the matter with our second housemaid, Rosanna Spearman.

After leaving Mr. Franklin and me at the Shivering Sand, Rosanna, it appeared, had returned to the house in a very unaccountable state of mind. She had turned (if Penelope was to be believed) all the colours of the rainbow. She had been merry without reason, and sad without reason. In one breath she asked hundreds of questions about Mr. Franklin Blake, and in another breath she had been angry with Penelope for presuming to suppose that a strange gentleman could possess any interest for her. She had been surprised, smiling, and scribbling Mr. Franklin's name inside her workbox. She had been surprised again, crying and looking at her deformed shoulder in the glass. Had she and Mr. Franklin known anything of each other before today? Quite impossible! Had they heard anything of each other? Impossible again! I could speak to Mr. Franklin's astonishment as genuine, when he saw how the girl stared at him. Penelope could speak to the girl's inquisitiveness as genuine, when she asked questions about Mr. Franklin. The conference between us, conducted in this way, was tiresome enough, until my daughter suddenly ended it by bursting out with what I thought the most monstrous supposition I had ever heard in my life.

"Father!" says Penelope, quite seriously, "there's only one explanation of it. Rosanna has fallen in love with Mr. Franklin Blake at first sight!"

You have heard of beautiful young ladies falling in love at first sight, and have thought it natural enough. But a housemaid out of a reformatory, with a plain face and a deformed shoulder, falling in love, at first sight, with a gentleman who comes on a visit to her mistress's house, match me that, in the way of an absurdity, out of any story-book in Christendom, if you can! I laughed till the tears rolled down my cheeks. Penelope resented my merriment, in rather a strange way. "I never knew you cruel before, father," she said, very gently, and went out.

My girl's words fell upon me like a splash of cold water. I was savage with myself, for feeling uneasy in myself the moment she had spoken them—but so it was. We will change the subject, if you please. I am sorry I drifted into writing about it; and not without reason, as you will see when we have gone on together a little longer.

The evening came, and the dressing-bell for dinner rang, before Mr. Franklin returned from Frizinghall. I took his hot water up to his room myself, expecting to hear, after this extraordinary delay, that something had happened. To my great disappointment (and no doubt to yours also), nothing had

The Moonstone

happened. He had not met with the Indians, either going or returning. He had deposited the Moonstone in the bank — describing it merely as a valuable of great price — and he had got the receipt for it safe in his pocket. I went downstairs, feeling that this was rather a flat ending, after all our excitement about the Diamond earlier in the day.

How the meeting between Mr. Franklin and his aunt and cousin went off, is more than I can tell you.

I would have given something to have waited at table that day. But, in my position in the household, waiting at dinner (except on high family festivals) was letting down my dignity in the eyes of the other servants — a thing which my lady considered me quite prone enough to do already, without seeking occasions for it. The news brought to me from the upper regions, that evening, came from Penelope and the footman. Penelope mentioned that she had never known Miss Rachel so particular about the dressing of her hair, and had never seen her look so bright and pretty as she did when she went down to meet Mr. Franklin in the drawing-room. The footman's report was, that the preservation of a respectful composure in the presence of his betters, and the waiting on Mr. Franklin Blake at dinner, were two of the hardest things to reconcile with each other that had ever tried his training in service. Later in the evening, we heard them singing and playing duets, Mr. Franklin piping high, Miss Rachel piping higher, and my lady, on the piano, following them as it were over hedge and ditch, and seeing them safe through it in a manner most wonderful and pleasant to hear through the open windows, on the terrace at night. Later still, I went to Mr. Franklin in the smoking-room, with the soda water and brandy, and found that Miss Rachel had put the Diamond clean out of his head. "She's the most charming girl I have seen since I came back to England!" was all I could extract from him, when I endeavoured to lead the conversation to more serious things.

Towards midnight, I went round the house to lock up, accompanied by my second in command (Samuel, the footman), as usual. When all the doors were made fast, except the side door that opened on the terrace, I sent Samuel to bed, and stepped out for a breath of fresh air before I too went to bed in my turn.

The night was still and close, and the moon was at the full in the heavens. It was so silent out of doors, that I heard from time to time, very faint and low, the fall of the sea, as the ground-swell heaved it in on the sand-bank near the mouth of our little bay. As the house stood, the terrace side was the dark side; but the broad moonlight showed fair on the gravel walk that ran along the next side to the terrace. Looking this way, after looking up at the sky, I saw the shadow of a person in the moonlight thrown forward from behind the corner of the house.

Being old and sly, I forbore to call out; but being also, unfortunately, old and heavy, my feet betrayed me on the gravel. Before I could steal suddenly round the corner, as I had proposed, I heard lighter feet than mine—and more than one pair of them as I thought—retreating in a hurry. By the time I had got to the corner, the trespassers, whoever they were, had run into the shrubbery at the off side of the walk, and were hidden from sight among the thick trees and bushes in that part of the grounds. From the shrubbery, they could easily make their way, over our fence into the road. If I had been forty years younger, I might have had a chance of catching them before they got clear of our premises. As it was, I went back to set a-going a younger pair of legs than mine. Without disturbing anybody, Samuel and I got a couple of guns, and went all round the house and through the shrubbery. Having made sure that no persons were lurking about anywhere in our grounds, we turned back. Passing over the walk where I had seen the shadow, I now noticed, for the first time, a little bright object, lying on the clean gravel, under the light of the moon. Picking the object up, I discovered it was a small bottle, containing a thick sweet-smelling liquor, as black as ink.

I said nothing to Samuel. But, remembering what Penelope had told me about the jugglers, and the pouring of the little pool of ink into the palm of the boy's hand, I instantly suspected that I had disturbed the three Indians, lurking about the house, and bent, in their heathenish way, on discovering the whereabouts of the Diamond that night.

CHAPTER VIII

Here, for one moment, I find it necessary to call a halt.

On summoning up my own recollections—and on getting Penelope to help me, by consulting her journal—I find that we may pass pretty rapidly over the interval between Mr. Franklin Blake's arrival and Miss Rachel's birthday. For the greater part of that time the days passed, and brought nothing with them worth recording. With your good leave, then, and with Penelope's help, I shall notice certain dates only in this place; reserving to myself to tell the story day by day, once more, as soon as we get to the time when the business of the Moonstone became the chief business of everybody in our house.

This said, we may now go on again—beginning, of course, with the bottle of sweet-smelling ink which I found on the gravel walk at night.

On the next morning (the morning of the twenty-sixth) I showed Mr. Franklin this article of jugglery, and told him what I have already told you. His opinion was, not only that the Indians had been lurking about after the Diamond, but also that they were actually foolish enough to believe in their own magic—meaning thereby the making of signs on a boy's head, and the pouring of ink into a boy's hand, and then expecting him to see persons and things beyond the reach of human vision. In our country, as well as in the East, Mr. Franklin informed me, there are people who practise this curious hocus-pocus (without the ink, however); and who call it by a French name, signifying something like brightness of sight. "Depend upon it," says Mr. Franklin, "the Indians took it for granted that we should keep the Diamond here; and they brought their clairvoyant boy to show them the way to it, if they succeeded in getting into the house last night."

"Do you think they'll try again, sir?" I asked.

"It depends," says Mr. Franklin, "on what the boy can really do. If he can see the Diamond through the iron safe of the bank at Frizinghall, we shall be troubled with no more visits from the Indians for the present. If he can't, we shall have another chance of catching them in the shrubbery, before many more nights are over our heads."

I waited pretty confidently for that latter chance; but, strange to relate, it never came.

Whether the jugglers heard, in the town, of Mr. Franklin having been seen at the bank, and drew their conclusions accordingly; or whether the boy really did see the Diamond where the Diamond was now lodged (which I, for one, flatly disbelieve); or whether, after all, it was a mere effect of chance, this at any rate is the plain truth—not the ghost of an Indian came near the house again, through the weeks that passed before Miss Rachel's birthday. The jugglers remained in and about the town plying their trade; and Mr. Franklin and I remained waiting to see what might happen, and resolute not to put the rogues on their guard by showing our suspicions of them too soon. With this report of the proceedings on either side, ends all that I have to say about the Indians for the present.

On the twenty-ninth of the month, Miss Rachel and Mr. Franklin hit on a new method of working their way together through the time which might otherwise have hung heavy on their hands. There are reasons for taking particular notice here of the occupation that amused them. You will find it has a bearing on something that is still to come.

Gentlefolks in general have a very awkward rock ahead in life—the rock ahead of their own idleness. Their lives being, for the most part, passed in looking about them for something to do, it is curious to see—especially when their tastes are of what is called the intellectual sort—how often they drift blindfold into some nasty pursuit. Nine times out of ten they take to torturing something, or to spoiling something—and they firmly believe they are improving their minds, when the plain truth is, they are only making a mess in the house. I have seen them (ladies, I am sorry to say, as well as gentlemen) go out, day after day, for example, with empty pill-boxes, and catch newts, and beetles, and spiders, and frogs, and come home and stick pins through the miserable wretches, or cut them up, without a pang of remorse, into little pieces. You see my young master, or my young mistress, poring over one of their spiders' insides with a magnifying-glass; or you meet one of their frogs walking downstairs without his head—and when you wonder what this cruel nastiness means, you are told that it means a taste in my young master or my young mistress for natural history.

Sometimes, again, you see them occupied for hours together in spoiling a pretty flower with pointed instruments, out of a stupid curiosity to know what the flower is made of. Is its colour any prettier, or its scent any sweeter, when you do know? But there! the poor souls must get through the time, you see—they must get through the time. You dabbled in nasty mud, and made pies, when you were a child; and you dabble in nasty science, and dissect spiders, and spoil flowers, when you grow up. In the one case and in the other, the secret of it is, that you have got nothing to think of in your poor empty head, and nothing to do with your poor idle hands. And so it ends in your spoiling canvas with paints, and making a smell in the house; or in keeping tadpoles in a glass box full of dirty water, and turning everybody's stomach in the house; or in chipping off bits of stone here, there, and everywhere, and dropping grit into all the victuals in the house; or in staining your fingers in the pursuit of photography, and doing justice without mercy on everybody's face in the house. It often falls heavy enough, no doubt, on people who are really obliged to get their living, to be forced to work for the clothes that cover them, the roof that shelters them, and the food that keeps them going. But compare the hardest day's work you ever did with the idleness that splits flowers and pokes its way into spiders' stomachs, and thank your stars that your head has got something it must think of, and your hands something that they must do.

As for Mr. Franklin and Miss Rachel, they tortured nothing, I am glad to say. They simply confined themselves to making a mess; and all they spoilt, to do them justice, was the panelling of a door.

Mr. Franklin's universal genius, dabbling in everything, dabbled in what he called "decorative painting." He had invented, he informed us, a new mixture to moisten paint with, which he described as a "vehicle." What it was made of, I don't know. What it did, I can tell you in two words—it stank. Miss Rachel being wild to try her hand at the new process, Mr. Franklin sent to London for the materials; mixed them up, with accompaniment of a smell which made the very dogs sneeze when they came into the room; put an apron and a bib over Miss Rachel's gown, and set her to work decorating her own little sitting-room—called, for want of English to name it in, her "boudoir." They began with the inside of the door. Mr. Franklin scraped off all the nice varnish with pumice-stone, and made what he described as a surface to work on. Miss Rachel then covered the surface, under his directions and with his help, with patterns and devices—griffins, birds, flowers, cupids, and such like—copied from designs made by a famous Italian painter, whose name escapes me: the one, I mean, who stocked the world with Virgin Maries, and had a sweetheart at the baker's. Viewed as work, this decoration was slow to do, and dirty to deal with. But our young lady and gentleman never seemed to tire of it. When they were not riding, or seeing company, or taking their meals, or piping their songs, there they were with their heads together, as busy as bees, spoiling the door. Who was the poet who said that Satan finds some mischief still for idle hands to do? If he had occupied my place in the family, and had seen Miss Rachel with her brush, and Mr. Franklin with his vehicle, he could have written nothing truer of either of them than that.

The next date worthy of notice is Sunday the fourth of June.

On that evening we, in the servants' hall, debated a domestic question for the first time, which, like the decoration of the door, has its bearing on something that is still to come.

Seeing the pleasure which Mr. Franklin and Miss Rachel took in each other's society, and noting what a pretty match they were in all personal respects, we naturally speculated on the chance of their putting their heads together with other objects in view besides the ornamenting of a door. Some of us said there would be a wedding in the house before the summer was over. Others (led by me) admitted it was likely enough Miss Rachel might be married; but we doubted (for reasons which will presently appear) whether her bridegroom would be Mr. Franklin Blake.

That Mr. Franklin was in love, on his side, nobody who saw and heard him could doubt. The difficulty was to fathom Miss Rachel. Let me do myself the honour of making you acquainted with her; after which, I will leave you to fathom for yourself—if you can.

My young lady's eighteenth birthday was the birthday now coming, on the twenty-first of June. If you happen to like dark women (who, I am informed, have gone out of fashion latterly

The Moonstone

in the gay world), and if you have no particular prejudice in favour of size, I answer for Miss Rachel as one of the prettiest girls your eyes ever looked on. She was small and slim, but all in fine proportion from top to toe. To see her sit down, to see her get up, and specially to see her walk, was enough to satisfy any man in his senses that the graces of her figure (if you will pardon me the expression) were in her flesh and not in her clothes. Her hair was the blackest I ever saw. Her eyes matched her hair. Her nose was not quite large enough, I admit. Her mouth and chin were (to quote Mr. Franklin) morsels for the gods; and her complexion (on the same undeniable authority) was as warm as the sun itself, with this great advantage over the sun, that it was always in nice order to look at. Add to the foregoing that she carried her head as upright as a dart, in a dashing, spirited, thoroughbred way—that she had a clear voice, with a ring of the right metal in it, and a smile that began very prettily in her eyes before it got to her lips—and there behold the portrait of her, to the best of my painting, as large as life!

And what about her disposition next? Had this charming creature no faults? She had just as many faults as you have, ma'am—neither more nor less.

To put it seriously, my dear pretty Miss Rachel, possessing a host of graces and attractions, had one defect, which strict impartiality compels me to acknowledge. She was unlike most other girls of her age, in this—that she had ideas of her own, and was stiff-necked enough to set the fashions themselves at defiance, if the fashions didn't suit her views. In trifles, this independence of hers was all well enough; but in matters of importance, it carried her (as my lady thought, and as I thought) too far. She judged for herself, as few women of twice her age judge in general; never asked your advice; never told you beforehand what she was going to do; never came with secrets and confidences to anybody, from her mother downwards. In little things and great, with people she loved, and people she hated (and she did both with equal heartiness), Miss Rachel always went on a way of her own, sufficient for herself in the joys and sorrows of her life. Over and over again I have heard my lady say, "Rachel's best friend and Rachel's worst enemy are, one and the other—Rachel herself."

The Moonstone

Add one thing more to this, and I have done.

With all her secrecy, and self-will, there was not so much as the shadow of anything false in her. I never remember her breaking her word; I never remember her saying No, and meaning Yes. I can call to mind, in her childhood, more than one occasion when the good little soul took the blame, and suffered the punishment, for some fault committed by a playfellow whom she loved. Nobody ever knew her to confess to it, when the thing was found out, and she was charged with it afterwards. But nobody ever knew her to lie about it, either. She looked you straight in the face, and shook her little saucy head, and said plainly, "I won't tell you!" Punished again for this, she would own to being sorry for saying "won't;" but, bread and water notwithstanding, she never told you. Self-willed—devilish self-willed sometimes—I grant; but the finest creature, nevertheless, that ever walked the ways of this lower world. Perhaps you think you see a certain contradiction here? In that case, a word in your ear. Study your wife closely, for the next four-and-twenty hours. If your good lady doesn't exhibit something in the shape of a contradiction in that time, Heaven help you!—you have married a monster.

I have now brought you acquainted with Miss Rachel, which you will find puts us face to face, next, with the question of that young lady's matrimonial views.

On June the twelfth, an invitation from my mistress was sent to a gentleman in London, to come and help to keep Miss Rachel's birthday. This was the fortunate individual on whom I believed her heart to be privately set! Like Mr. Franklin, he was a cousin of hers. His name was Mr. Godfrey Ablewhite.

My lady's second sister (don't be alarmed; we are not going very deep into family matters this time)—my lady's second sister, I say, had a disappointment in love; and taking a husband afterwards, on the neck or nothing principle, made what they call a misalliance. There was terrible work in the family when the Honourable Caroline insisted on marrying plain Mr. Ablewhite, the banker at Frizinghall. He was very rich and very respectable, and he begot a prodigious large family—all in his favour, so far. But he had presumed to raise himself from a low station in the world—and that was against him. However, Time and the progress of modern enlightenment put things right; and the misalliance passed muster very well. We are all getting liberal now; and (provided you can scratch me, if I scratch you) what do I care, in or out of Parliament, whether you are a Dustman or a Duke? That's the modern way of looking at it—and I keep up with the modern way. The Ablewhites lived in a fine house and grounds, a little out of Frizinghall. Very worthy people, and greatly respected in the neighbourhood. We shall not be much troubled with them in these pages—excepting Mr. Godfrey, who was Mr. Ablewhite's second son, and who must take his proper place here, if you please, for Miss Rachel's sake.

With all his brightness and cleverness and general good qualities, Mr. Franklin's chance of topping Mr. Godfrey in our young lady's estimation was, in my opinion, a very poor chance indeed.

In the first place, Mr. Godfrey was, in point of size, the finest man by far of the two. He stood over six feet high; he had a beautiful red and white colour; a smooth round face, shaved as bare as your hand; and a head of lovely long flaxen hair, falling negligently over the poll of his neck. But why do I try to give you this personal description of him? If you ever subscribed to a Ladies' Charity in London, you know Mr. Godfrey Ablewhite as well as I do. He was a barrister by profession; a ladies' man by temperament; and a good Samaritan by choice. Female benevolence and female destitution could do nothing without him. Maternal societies for confining poor women; Magdalen societies for rescuing poor women; strong-minded societies for putting poor women into poor men's places, and leaving the men to shift for themselves;—he was vice-president, manager, referee to them all. Wherever there was a table with a committee of ladies sitting round it in council there was Mr. Godfrey at the bottom of the board, keeping the temper of the committee, and leading the dear creatures along the thorny ways of business, hat in hand. I do suppose this was the most accomplished philanthropist (on a small independence) that England ever produced. As a speaker at charitable meetings the like of him for drawing your tears and your money was not easy to find. He was quite a public character. The last time I was in London, my mistress gave me two treats. She sent me to the theatre to see a dancing woman who was all the rage; and she sent me to Exeter Hall to hear Mr. Godfrey. The lady did it, with a band of music. The gentleman did it, with a handkerchief and a glass of water. Crowds at the performance with the legs. Ditto at the performance with the tongue. And with all this, the sweetest tempered person (I allude to Mr. Godfrey) — the simplest and pleasantest and easiest to please — you ever met with. He loved everybody. And everybody loved him. What chance had Mr. Franklin — what chance had anybody of average reputation and capacities — against such a man as this?

On the fourteenth, came Mr. Godfrey's answer.

He accepted my mistress's invitation, from the Wednesday of the birthday to the evening of Friday — when his duties to the Ladies' Charities would oblige him to return to town. He also enclosed a copy of verses on what he elegantly called his cousin's "natal day." Miss Rachel, I was informed, joined Mr. Franklin in making fun of the verses at dinner; and Penelope, who was all on Mr. Franklin's side, asked me, in great triumph, what I thought of that. "Miss Rachel has led you off on a false scent, my dear," I replied; "but my nose is not so easily mystified. Wait till Mr. Ablewhite's verses are followed by Mr. Ablewhite himself."

My daughter replied, that Mr. Franklin might strike in, and try his luck, before the verses were followed by the poet. In favour of this view, I must acknowledge that Mr. Franklin left no chance untried of winning Miss Rachel's good graces.

Though one of the most inveterate smokers I ever met with, he gave up his cigar, because she said, one day, she hated the stale smell of it in his clothes. He slept so badly, after this effort of self-denial, for want of the composing effect of the tobacco to which he was used, and came down morning after morning looking so haggard and worn, that Miss Rachel herself begged him to take to his cigars again. No! he would take to nothing again that could cause her a moment's annoyance; he would fight it out resolutely, and get back his sleep, sooner or later, by main force of patience in waiting for it. Such devotion as this, you may say (as some of them said downstairs), could never fail of producing the right effect on Miss Rachel — backed up, too, as it was, by the decorating work every day on the door. All very well — but she had a photograph of Mr. Godfrey in her bedroom; represented speaking at a public meeting, with all his hair blown out by the breath of his own eloquence, and his eyes,

The Moonstone

most lovely, charming the money out of your pockets. What do you say to that? Every morning — as Penelope herself owned to me — there was the man whom the women couldn't do without, looking on, in effigy, while Miss Rachel was having her hair combed. He would be looking on, in reality, before long — that was my opinion of it.

June the sixteenth brought an event which made Mr. Franklin's chance look, to my mind, a worse chance than ever.

A strange gentleman, speaking English with a foreign accent, came that morning to the house, and asked to see Mr. Franklin Blake on business. The business could not possibly have been connected with the Diamond, for these two reasons — first, that Mr. Franklin told me nothing about it; secondly, that he communicated it (when the gentleman had gone, as I suppose) to my lady. She probably hinted something about it next to her daughter. At any rate, Miss Rachel was reported to have said some severe things to Mr. Franklin, at the piano that evening, about the people he had lived among, and the principles he had adopted in foreign parts. The next day, for the first time, nothing was done towards the decoration of the door. I suspect some imprudence of Mr. Franklin's on the Continent — with a woman or a debt at the bottom of it — had followed him to England. But that is all guesswork. In this case, not only Mr. Franklin, but my lady too, for a wonder, left me in the dark.

On the seventeenth, to all appearance, the cloud passed away again. They returned to their decorating work on the door, and seemed to be as good friends as ever. If Penelope was to be believed, Mr. Franklin had seized the opportunity of the reconciliation to make an offer to Miss Rachel, and had neither been accepted nor refused. My girl was sure (from signs and tokens which I need not trouble you with) that her young mistress had fought Mr. Franklin off by declining to believe that he was in earnest, and had then secretly regretted treating him in that way afterwards. Though Penelope was admitted to more familiarity with her young mistress than maids generally are — for the two had been almost brought up together as children — still I knew Miss Rachel's reserved character too well to believe that she would show her mind to anybody in this way. What my daughter told me, on the present occasion, was, as I suspected, more what she wished than what she really knew.

On the nineteenth another event happened. We had the doctor in the house professionally. He was summoned to prescribe for a person whom I have had occasion to present to you in these pages—our second housemaid, Rosanna Spearman.

This poor girl—who had puzzled me, as you know already, at the Shivering Sand—puzzled me more than once again, in the interval time of which I am now writing. Penelope's notion that her fellow-servant was in love with Mr. Franklin (which my daughter, by my orders, kept strictly secret) seemed to be just as absurd as ever. But I must own that what I myself saw, and what my daughter saw also, of our second housemaid's conduct, began to look mysterious, to say the least of it.

For example, the girl constantly put herself in Mr. Franklin's way—very slyly and quietly, but she did it. He took about as much notice of her as he took of the cat; it never seemed to occur to him to waste a look on Rosanna's plain face. The poor thing's appetite, never much, fell away dreadfully; and her eyes in the morning showed plain signs of waking and crying at night. One day Penelope made an awkward discovery, which we hushed up on the spot. She caught Rosanna at Mr. Franklin's dressing-table, secretly removing a rose which Miss Rachel had given him to wear in his button-hole, and putting another rose like it, of her own picking, in its place. She was, after that, once or twice impudent to me, when I gave her a well-meant general hint to be careful in her conduct; and, worse still, she was not over-respectful now, on the few occasions when Miss Rachel accidentally spoke to her.

My lady noticed the change, and asked me what I thought about it. I tried to screen the girl by answering that I thought she was out of health; and it ended in the doctor being sent for, as already mentioned, on the nineteenth. He said it was her nerves, and doubted if she was fit for service. My lady offered to remove her for change of air to one of our farms, inland. She begged and prayed, with the tears in her eyes, to be let to stop; and, in an evil hour, I advised my lady to try her for a little longer. As the event proved, and as you will soon see, this was the worst advice I could have given. If I could only have looked a little way into the future, I would have taken Rosanna Spearman out of the house, then and there, with my own hand.

On the twentieth, there came a note from Mr. Godfrey. He

The Moonstone

had arranged to stop at Frizinghall that night, having occasion to consult his father on business. On the afternoon of the next day, he and his two eldest sisters would ride over to us on horseback, in good time before dinner. An elegant little casket in china accompanied the note, presented to Miss Rachel, with her cousin's love and best wishes. Mr. Franklin had only given her a plain locket not worth half the money. My daughter Penelope, nevertheless—such is the obstinacy of women—still backed him to win.

Thanks be to Heaven, we have arrived at the eve of the birthday at last! You will own, I think, that I have got you over the ground this time, without much loitering by the way. Cheer up! I'll ease you with another new chapter here—and, what is more, that chapter shall take you straight into the thick of the story.

CHAPTER IX

June twenty-first, the day of the birthday, was cloudy and unsettled at sunrise, but towards noon it cleared up bravely.

We, in the servants' hall, began this happy anniversary, as usual, by offering our little presents to Miss Rachel, with the regular speech delivered annually by me as the chief. I follow the plan adopted by the Queen in opening Parliament—namely, the plan of saying much the same thing regularly every year. Before it is delivered, my speech (like the Queen's) is looked for as eagerly as if nothing of the kind had ever been heard before. When it is delivered, and turns out not to be the novelty anticipated, though they grumble a little, they look forward hopefully to something newer next year. An easy people to govern, in the Parliament and in the Kitchen—that's the moral of it.

After breakfast, Mr. Franklin and I had a private conference on the subject of the Moonstone—the time having now come for removing it from the bank at Frizinghall, and placing it in Miss Rachel's own hands.

Whether he had been trying to make love to his cousin again, and had got a rebuff—or whether his broken rest, night after night, was aggravating the queer contradictions and uncertainties in his character—I don't know. But certain it is, that Mr. Franklin failed to show himself at his best on the morning of the birthday. He was in twenty different minds about the Diamond in as many minutes. For my part, I stuck fast by the plain facts as we knew them. Nothing had happened to justify us in alarming my lady on the subject of the jewel; and nothing could alter the legal obligation that now lay on Mr. Franklin to put it in his cousin's possession. That was my view of the matter; and, twist and turn it as he might, he was forced in the end to make it his view too. We arranged that he was to ride over, after lunch, to Frizinghall, and bring the Diamond back, with Mr. Godfrey and the two young ladies, in all probability, to keep him company on the way home again.

This settled, our young gentleman went back to Miss Rachel.

They consumed the whole morning, and part of the afternoon, in the everlasting business of decorating the door,

Penelope standing by to mix the colours, as directed; and my lady, as luncheon time drew near, going in and out of the room, with her handkerchief to her nose (for they used a deal of Mr. Franklin's vehicle that day), and trying vainly to get the two artists away from their work. It was three o'clock before they took off their aprons, and released Penelope (much the worse for the vehicle), and cleaned themselves of their mess. But they had done what they wanted — they had finished the door on the birthday, and proud enough they were of it. The griffins, cupids, and so on, were, I must own, most beautiful to behold; though so many in number, so entangled in flowers and devices, and so topsy-turvy in their actions and attitudes, that you felt them unpleasantly in your head for hours after you had done with the pleasure of looking at them. If I add that Penelope ended her part of the morning's work by being sick in the back-kitchen, it is in no unfriendly spirit towards the vehicle. No! no! It left off stinking when it dried; and if Art requires these sort of sacrifices — though the girl is my own daughter — I say, let Art have them!

Mr. Franklin snatched a morsel from the luncheon-table, and rode off to Frizinghall — to escort his cousins, as he told my lady. To fetch the Moonstone, as was privately known to himself and to me.

This being one of the high festivals on which I took my place at the side-board, in command of the attendance at table, I had plenty to occupy my mind while Mr. Franklin was away. Having seen to the wine, and reviewed my men and women who were to wait at dinner, I retired to collect myself before the company came. A whiff of — you know what, and a turn at a certain book which I have had occasion to mention in these pages, composed me, body and mind. I was aroused from what I am inclined to think must have been, not a nap, but a reverie, by the clatter of horses' hoofs outside; and, going to the door, received a cavalcade comprising Mr. Franklin and his three cousins, escorted by one of old Mr. Ablewhite's grooms.

Mr. Godfrey struck me, strangely enough, as being like Mr. Franklin in this respect — that he did not seem to be in his customary spirits. He kindly shook hands with me as usual, and was most politely glad to see his old friend Betteredge wearing so well. But there was a sort of cloud over him, which I couldn't at all account for; and when I asked how he had found his father in health, he answered rather shortly, "Much as usual." However, the two Miss Ablewhites were cheerful enough for twenty, which more than restored the balance. They were nearly as big as their brother; spanking, yellow-haired, rosy lasses, overflowing with super-abundant flesh and blood; bursting from head to foot with health and spirits. The legs of the poor horses trembled with carrying them; and when they jumped from their saddles (without waiting to be helped), I declare they bounced on the ground as if they were made of india-rubber. Everything the Miss Ablewhites said began with a large O; everything they did was done with a bang; and they giggled and screamed, in season and out of season, on the smallest provocation. Bouncers—that's what I call them.

Under cover of the noise made by the young ladies, I had an opportunity of saying a private word to Mr. Franklin in the hall.

"Have you got the Diamond safe, sir?"

He nodded, and tapped the breast-pocket of his coat.

"Have you seen anything of the Indians?"

"Not a glimpse." With that answer, he asked for my lady, and, hearing she was in the small drawing-room, went there straight. The bell rang, before he had been a minute in the room, and Penelope was sent to tell Miss Rachel that Mr. Franklin Blake wanted to speak to her.

Crossing the hall, about half an hour afterwards, I was brought to a sudden standstill by an outbreak of screams from the small drawing-room. I can't say I was at all alarmed; for I recognised in the screams the favourite large O of the Miss Ablewhites. However, I went in (on pretence of asking for instructions about the dinner) to discover whether anything serious had really happened.

There stood Miss Rachel at the table, like a person fascinated, with the Colonel's unlucky Diamond in her hand. There, on either side of her, knelt the two Bouncers, devouring the jewel with their eyes, and screaming with ecstasy every time it flashed on them in a new light. There, at the opposite side of the table, stood Mr. Godfrey, clapping his hands like a large child, and singing out softly, "Exquisite! exquisite!" There sat

The Moonstone

Mr. Franklin in a chair by the bookcase, tugging at his beard, and looking anxiously towards the window. And there, at the window, stood the object he was contemplating—my lady, having the extract from the Colonel's Will in her hand, and keeping her back turned on the whole of the company.

She faced me, when I asked for my instructions; and I saw the family frown gathering over her eyes, and the family temper twitching at the corners of her mouth.

"Come to my room in half an hour," she answered. "I shall have something to say to you then."

With those words, she went out. It was plain enough that she was posed by the same difficulty which had posed Mr. Franklin and me in our conference at the Shivering Sand. Was the legacy of the Moonstone a proof that she had treated her brother with cruel injustice? or was it a proof that he was worse than the worst she had ever thought of him? Serious questions those for my lady to determine, while her daughter, innocent of all knowledge of the Colonel's character, stood there with the Colonel's birthday gift in her hand.

Before I could leave the room in my turn, Miss Rachel, always considerate to the old servant who had been in the house when she was born, stopped me. "Look, Gabriel!" she said, and flashed the jewel before my eyes in a ray of sunlight that poured through the window.

Lord bless us! it was a Diamond! As large, or nearly, as a plover's egg! The light that streamed from it was like the light of the harvest moon. When you looked down into the stone, you looked into a yellow deep that drew your eyes into it so that they saw nothing else. It seemed unfathomable; this jewel, that you could hold between your finger and thumb, seemed unfathomable as the heavens themselves. We set it in the sun, and then shut the light out of the room, and it shone awfully out of the depths of its own brightness, with a moony gleam, in the dark. No wonder Miss Rachel was fascinated: no wonder her cousins screamed. The Diamond laid such a hold on me that I burst out with as large an "O" as the Bouncers themselves. The only one of us who kept his senses was Mr. Godfrey. He put an arm round each of his sister's waists, and, looking compassionately backwards and forwards between the

Diamond and me, said, "Carbon Betteredge! mere carbon, my good friend, after all!"

His object, I suppose, was to instruct me. All he did, however, was to remind me of the dinner. I hobbled off to my army of waiters downstairs. As I went out, Mr. Godfrey said, "Dear old Betteredge, I have the truest regard for him!" He was embracing his sisters, and ogling Miss Rachel, while he honoured me with that testimony of affection. Something like a stock of love to draw on there! Mr. Franklin was a perfect savage by comparison with him.

At the end of half an hour, I presented myself, as directed, in my lady's room.

What passed between my mistress and me, on this occasion, was, in the main, a repetition of what had passed between Mr. Franklin and me at the Shivering Sand — with this difference, that I took care to keep my own counsel about the jugglers, seeing that nothing had happened to justify me in alarming my lady on this head. When I received my dismissal, I could see that she took the blackest view possible of the Colonel's motives, and that she was bent on getting the Moonstone out of her daughter's possession at the first opportunity.

On my way back to my own part of the house, I was encountered by Mr. Franklin. He wanted to know if I had seen anything of his cousin Rachel. I had seen nothing of her. Could I tell him where his cousin Godfrey was? I didn't know; but I began to suspect that cousin Godfrey might not be far away from cousin Rachel. Mr. Franklin's suspicions apparently took the same turn. He tugged hard at his beard, and went and shut himself up in the library with a bang of the door that had a world of meaning in it.

I was interrupted no more in the business of preparing for the birthday dinner till it was time for me to smarten myself up for receiving the company. Just as I had got my white waistcoat on, Penelope presented herself at my toilet, on pretence of brushing what little hair I have got left, and improving the tie of my white cravat. My girl was in high spirits, and I saw she had something to say to me. She gave me a kiss on the top of my bald head, and whispered, "News for you, father! Miss Rachel has refused him."

"Who's 'him'?" I asked.

"The ladies' committee-man, father," says Penelope. "A nasty sly fellow! I hate him for trying to supplant Mr. Franklin!"

If I had had breath enough, I should certainly have protested against this indecent way of speaking of an eminent philanthropic character. But my daughter happened to be improving the tie of my cravat at that moment, and the whole strength of her feelings found its way into her fingers. I never was more nearly strangled in my life.

"I saw him take her away alone into the rose-garden," says Penelope. "And I waited behind the holly to see how they came back. They had gone out arm-in-arm, both laughing. They came back, walking separate, as grave as grave could be, and looking straight away from each other in a manner which there was no mistaking. I never was more delighted, father, in my life! There's one woman in the world who can resist Mr. Godfrey Ablewhite, at any rate; and, if I was a lady, I should be another!"

Here I should have protested again. But my daughter had got the hair-brush by this time, and the whole strength of her feelings had passed into that. If you are bald, you will understand how she sacrificed me. If you are not, skip this bit, and thank God you have got something in the way of a defence between your hair-brush and your head.

"Just on the other side of the holly," Penelope went on, "Mr. Godfrey came to a standstill. 'You prefer,' says he, 'that I should stop here as if nothing had happened?' Miss Rachel turned on him like lightning. 'You have accepted my mother's invitation,' she said; 'and you are here to meet her guests. Unless you wish to make a scandal in the house, you will remain, of course!' She went on a few steps, and then seemed to relent a little. 'Let us forget what has passed, Godfrey,' she said, 'and let us remain cousins still.' She gave him her hand. He kissed it, which I should have considered taking a liberty, and then she left him. He waited a little by himself, with his head down, and his heel grinding a hole slowly in the gravel walk; you never saw a man look more put out in your life. 'Awkward!' he said between his teeth, when he looked up, and went on to the house—'very awkward!' If that was his opinion of himself, he was quite right.

Awkward enough, I'm sure. And the end of it is, father, what I told you all along," cries Penelope, finishing me off with a last scarification, the hottest of all. "Mr. Franklin's the man!"

I got possession of the hair-brush, and opened my lips to administer the reproof which, you will own, my daughter's language and conduct richly deserved.

Before I could say a word, the crash of carriage-wheels outside struck in, and stopped me. The first of the dinner-company had come. Penelope instantly ran off. I put on my coat, and looked in the glass. My head was as red as a lobster; but, in other respects, I was as nicely dressed for the ceremonies of the evening as a man need be. I got into the hall just in time to announce the two first of the guests. You needn't feel particularly interested about them. Only the philanthropist's father and mother—Mr. and Mrs. Ablewhite.

CHAPTER X

One on the top of the other the rest of the company followed the Ablewhites, till we had the whole tale of them complete. Including the family, they were twenty-four in all. It was a noble sight to see, when they were settled in their places round the dinner-table, and the Rector of Frizinghall (with beautiful elocution) rose and said grace.

There is no need to worry you with a list of the guests. You will meet none of them a second time — in my part of the story, at any rate — with the exception of two.

Those two sat on either side of Miss Rachel, who, as queen of the day, was naturally the great attraction of the party. On this occasion she was more particularly the centre-point towards which everybody's eyes were directed; for (to my lady's secret annoyance) she wore her wonderful birthday present, which eclipsed all the rest — the Moonstone. It was without any setting when it had been placed in her hands; but that universal genius, Mr. Franklin, had contrived, with the help of his neat fingers and a little bit of silver wire, to fix it as a brooch in the bosom of her white dress. Everybody wondered at the prodigious size and beauty of the Diamond, as a matter of course. But the only two of the company who said anything out of the common way about it were those two guests I have mentioned, who sat by Miss Rachel on her right hand and her left.

The guest on her left was Mr. Candy, our doctor at Frizinghall.

This was a pleasant, companionable little man, with the drawback, however, I must own, of being too fond, in season and out of season, of his joke, and of his plunging in rather a headlong manner into talk with strangers, without waiting to feel his way first. In society, he was constantly making mistakes, and setting people unintentionally by the ears together. In his medical practice he was a more prudent man; picking up his discretion (as his enemies said) by a kind of instinct, and proving to be generally right where more carefully conducted doctors turned out to be wrong. What he said about the Diamond to Miss Rachel was said, as usual, by way of a mystification or joke. He gravely entreated her (in the interests of science) to let him take it home and burn it. "We will first heat it, Miss Rachel," says the doctor, "to such and such a degree; then we will expose it to a current of air; and, little by little — puff! — we evaporate the Diamond, and spare you a world of anxiety about the safe keeping of a valuable precious stone!" My lady, listening with rather a careworn expression on her face, seemed to wish that the doctor had been in earnest, and that he could have found Miss Rachel zealous enough in the cause of science to sacrifice her birthday gift.

The other guest, who sat on my young lady's right hand, was an eminent public character — being no other than the celebrated Indian traveller, Mr. Murthwaite, who, at risk of his life, had penetrated in disguise where no European had ever set foot before.

This was a long, lean, wiry, brown, silent man. He had a weary look, and a very steady, attentive eye. It was rumoured that he was tired of the humdrum life among the people in our parts, and longing to go back and wander off on the tramp again in the wild places of the East. Except what he said to Miss Rachel about her jewel, I doubt if he spoke six words or drank so much as a single glass of wine, all through the dinner. The Moonstone was the only object that interested him in the smallest degree. The fame of it seemed to have reached him, in some of those perilous Indian places where his wanderings had lain. After looking at it silently for so long a time that Miss Rachel began to get confused, he said to her in his cool immovable way, "If you ever go to India, Miss Verinder, don't take your uncle's birthday gift with you. A Hindoo diamond is sometimes part of a Hindoo religion. I know a certain city, and a certain temple in that city, where, dressed as you are now, your life would not be worth five minutes' purchase." Miss Rachel, safe in England, was quite delighted to hear of her danger in India. The Bouncers were more delighted still; they dropped their knives and forks with a crash, and burst out together vehemently, "O! how interesting!" My lady fidgeted in her chair, and changed the subject.

As the dinner got on, I became aware, little by little, that this festival was not prospering as other like festivals had prospered before it.

Looking back at the birthday now, by the light of what happened afterwards, I am half inclined to think that the cursed

The Moonstone

Diamond must have cast a blight on the whole company. I plied them well with wine; and being a privileged character, followed the unpopular dishes round the table, and whispered to the company confidentially, "Please to change your mind and try it; for I know it will do you good." Nine times out of ten they changed their minds—out of regard for their old original Betteredge, they were pleased to say—but all to no purpose. There were gaps of silence in the talk, as the dinner got on, that made me feel personally uncomfortable. When they did use their tongues again, they used them innocently, in the most unfortunate manner and to the worst possible purpose. Mr. Candy, the doctor, for instance, said more unlucky things than I ever knew him to say before. Take one sample of the way in which he went on, and you will understand what I had to put up with at the sideboard, officiating as I was in the character of a man who had the prosperity of the festival at heart.

One of our ladies present at dinner was worthy Mrs. Threadgall, widow of the late Professor of that name. Talking of her deceased husband perpetually, this good lady never mentioned to strangers that he was deceased. She thought, I suppose, that every able-bodied adult in England ought to know as much as that. In one of the gaps of silence, somebody mentioned the dry and rather nasty subject of human anatomy; whereupon good Mrs. Threadgall straightway brought in her late husband as usual, without mentioning that he was dead. Anatomy she described as the Professor's favourite recreation in his leisure hours. As ill-luck would have it, Mr. Candy, sitting opposite (who knew nothing of the deceased gentleman), heard her. Being the most polite of men, he seized the opportunity of assisting the Professor's anatomical amusements on the spot.

"They have got some remarkably fine skeletons lately at the College of Surgeons," says Mr. Candy, across the table, in a loud cheerful voice. "I strongly recommend the Professor, ma'am, when he next has an hour to spare, to pay them a visit."

You might have heard a pin fall. The company (out of respect to the Professor's memory) all sat speechless. I was behind Mrs. Threadgall at the time, plying her confidentially with a glass of hock. She dropped her head, and said in a very low voice, "My beloved husband is no more."

Unluckily Mr. Candy, hearing nothing, and miles away from

suspecting the truth, went on across the table louder and politer than ever.

"The Professor may not be aware," says he, "that the card of a member of the College will admit him, on any day but Sunday, between the hours of ten and four."

Mrs. Threadgall dropped her head right into her tucker, and, in a lower voice still, repeated the solemn words, "My beloved husband is no more."

I winked hard at Mr. Candy across the table. Miss Rachel touched his arm. My lady looked unutterable things at him. Quite useless! On he went, with a cordiality that there was no stopping anyhow. "I shall be delighted," says he, "to send the Professor my card, if you will oblige me by mentioning his present address."

"His present address, sir, is the grave," says Mrs. Threadgall, suddenly losing her temper, and speaking with an emphasis and fury that made the glasses ring again. "The Professor has been dead these ten years."

"Oh, good Heavens!" says Mr. Candy. Excepting the Bouncers, who burst out laughing, such a blank now fell on the company, that they might all have been going the way of the Professor, and hailing as he did from the direction of the grave.

So much for Mr. Candy. The rest of them were nearly as provoking in their different ways as the doctor himself. When they ought to have spoken, they didn't speak; or when they did speak they were perpetually at cross purposes. Mr. Godfrey, though so eloquent in public, declined to exert himself in private. Whether he was sulky, or whether he was bashful, after his discomfiture in the rose-garden, I can't say. He kept all his talk for the private ear of the lady (a member of our family) who sat next to him. She was one of his committee-women—a spiritually-minded person, with a fine show of collar-bone and a pretty taste in champagne; liked it dry, you understand, and plenty of it. Being close behind these two at the sideboard, I can testify, from what I heard pass between them, that the company lost a good deal of very improving conversation, which I caught up while drawing the corks, and carving the mutton, and so forth. What they said about their Charities I didn't hear. When I had time to listen to them, they had got a long way beyond their women to be confined, and their women to be rescued, and were disputing on serious subjects. Religion (I understand Mr. Godfrey to say, between the corks and the carving) meant love. And love meant religion. And earth was heaven a little the worse for wear. And heaven was earth, done up again to look like new. Earth had some very objectionable people in it; but, to make amends for that, all the women in heaven would be members of a prodigious committee that never quarrelled, with all the men in attendance on them as ministering angels. Beautiful! beautiful! But why the mischief did Mr. Godfrey keep it all to his lady and himself?

Mr. Franklin again—surely, you will say, Mr. Franklin stirred the company up into making a pleasant evening of it?

Nothing of the sort! He had quite recovered himself, and he was in wonderful force and spirits, Penelope having informed him, I suspect, of Mr. Godfrey's reception in the rose-garden. But, talk as he might, nine times out of ten he pitched on the wrong subject, or he addressed himself to the wrong person; the end of it being that he offended some, and puzzled all of them. That foreign training of his—those French and German and Italian sides of him, to which I have already alluded—came out, at my lady's hospitable board, in a most bewildering manner.

What do you think, for instance, of his discussing the lengths to which a married woman might let her admiration go for a man who was not her husband, and putting it in his clear-headed witty French way to the maiden aunt of the Vicar of Frizinghall? What do you think, when he shifted to the German side, of his telling the lord of the manor, while that great authority on cattle was quoting his experience in the breeding of bulls, that experience, properly understood counted for nothing, and that the proper way to breed bulls was to look deep into your own mind, evolve out of it the idea of a perfect bull, and produce him? What do you say, when our county member, growing hot, at cheese and salad time, about the spread of democracy in England, burst out as follows: "If we once lose our ancient safeguards, Mr. Blake, I beg to ask you, what have we got left?"—what do you say to Mr. Franklin answering, from the Italian point of view: "We have got three things left, sir— Love, Music, and Salad"? He not only terrified the company with such outbreaks as these, but, when the English side of him turned up in due course, he lost his foreign smoothness; and, getting on the subject of the medical profession, said such downright things in ridicule of doctors, that he actually put good-humoured little Mr. Candy in a rage.

The dispute between them began in Mr. Franklin being led — I forget how — to acknowledge that he had latterly slept very badly at night. Mr. Candy thereupon told him that his nerves were all out of order and that he ought to go through a course of medicine immediately. Mr. Franklin replied that a course of medicine, and a course of groping in the dark, meant, in his estimation, one and the same thing. Mr. Candy, hitting back smartly, said that Mr Franklin himself was, constitutionally speaking, groping in the dark after sleep, and that nothing but medicine could help him to find it. Mr. Franklin, keeping the ball up on his side, said he had often heard of the blind leading the blind, and now, for the first time, he knew what it meant. In this way, they kept it going briskly, cut and thrust, till they both of them got hot — Mr. Candy, in particular, so completely losing his self-control, in defence of his profession, that my lady was obliged to interfere, and forbid the dispute to go on. This necessary act of authority put the last extinguisher on the spirits of the company. The talk spurted up again here and there, for a minute or two at a time; but there was a miserable lack of life and sparkle in it. The Devil (or the Diamond) possessed that dinner-party; and it was a relief to everybody when my mistress rose, and gave the ladies the signal to leave the gentlemen over their wine.

I had just ranged the decanters in a row before old Mr. Ablewhite (who represented the master of the house), when there came a sound from the terrace which, startled me out of my company manners on the instant. Mr. Franklin and I looked at each other; it was the sound of the Indian drum. As I live by bread, here were the jugglers returning to us with the return of the Moonstone to the house!

As they rounded the corner of the terrace, and came in sight, I hobbled out to warn them off. But, as ill-luck would have it, the two Bouncers were beforehand with me. They whizzed out on to the terrace like a couple of skyrockets, wild to see the Indians exhibit their tricks. The other ladies followed; the gentlemen came out on their side. Before you could say, "Lord

The Moonstone

bless us!" the rogues were making their salaams; and the Bouncers were kissing the pretty little boy.

Mr. Franklin got on one side of Miss Rachel, and I put myself behind her. If our suspicions were right, there she stood, innocent of all knowledge of the truth, showing the Indians the Diamond in the bosom of her dress!

I can't tell you what tricks they performed, or how they did it. What with the vexation about the dinner, and what with the provocation of the rogues coming back just in the nick of time to see the jewel with their own eyes, I own I lost my head. The first thing that I remember noticing was the sudden appearance on the scene of the Indian traveller, Mr. Murthwaite. Skirting the half-circle in which the gentlefolks stood or sat, he came quietly behind the jugglers and spoke to them on a sudden in the language of their own country.

If he had pricked them with a bayonet, I doubt if the Indians could have started and turned on him with a more tigerish quickness than they did, on hearing the first words that passed his lips. The next moment they were bowing and salaaming to him in their most polite and snaky way. After a few words in the unknown tongue had passed on either side, Mr. Murthwaite withdrew as quietly as he had approached. The chief Indian, who acted as interpreter, thereupon wheeled about again towards the gentlefolks. I noticed that the fellow's coffee-coloured face had turned grey since Mr. Murthwaite had spoken to him. He bowed to my lady, and informed her that the exhibition was over. The Bouncers, indescribably disappointed, burst out with a loud "O!" directed against Mr. Murthwaite for stopping the performance. The chief Indian laid his hand humbly on his breast, and said a second time that the juggling was over. The little boy went round with the hat. The ladies withdrew to the drawing-room; and the gentlemen (excepting Mr. Franklin and Mr. Murthwaite) returned to their wine. I and the footman followed the Indians, and saw them safe off the premises.

Going back by way of the shrubbery, I smelt tobacco, and found Mr. Franklin and Mr. Murthwaite (the latter smoking a cheroot) walking slowly up and down among the trees. Mr. Franklin beckoned to me to join them.

"This," says Mr. Franklin, presenting me to the great traveller, "is Gabriel Betteredge, the old servant and friend of our family of whom I spoke to you just now. Tell him, if you please, what you have just told me."

Mr. Murthwaite took his cheroot out of his mouth, and leaned, in his weary way, against the trunk of a tree.

"Mr. Betteredge," he began, "those three Indians are no more jugglers than you and I are."

Here was a new surprise! I naturally asked the traveller if he had ever met with the Indians before.

"Never," says Mr. Murthwaite; "but I know what Indian juggling really is. All you have seen tonight is a very bad and clumsy imitation of it. Unless, after long experience, I am utterly mistaken, those men are high-caste Brahmins. I charged them with being disguised, and you saw how it told on them, clever as the Hindoo people are in concealing their feelings. There is a mystery about their conduct that I can't explain. They have doubly sacrificed their caste—first, in crossing the sea; secondly, in disguising themselves as jugglers. In the land they live in that is a tremendous sacrifice to make. There must be some very serious motive at the bottom of it, and some justification of no ordinary kind to plead for them, in recovery of their caste, when they return to their own country."

I was struck dumb. Mr. Murthwaite went on with his cheroot. Mr. Franklin, after what looked to me like a little private veering about between the different sides of his character, broke the silence as follows:

"I feel some hesitation, Mr. Murthwaite, in troubling you with family matters, in which you can have no interest and which I am not very willing to speak of out of our own circle. But, after what you have said, I feel bound, in the interests of Lady Verinder and her daughter, to tell you something which may possibly put the clue into your hands. I speak to you in confidence; you will oblige me, I am sure, by not forgetting that?"

With this preface, he told the Indian traveller all that he had told me at the Shivering Sand. Even the immovable Mr. Murthwaite was so interested in what he heard, that he let his cheroot go out.

"Now," says Mr. Franklin, when he had done, "what does your experience say?"

"My experience," answered the traveller, "says that you have had more narrow escapes of your life, Mr. Franklin Blake, than I have had of mine; and that is saying a great deal."

It was Mr. Franklin's turn to be astonished now.

"Is it really as serious as that?" he asked.

"In my opinion it is," answered Mr. Murthwaite. "I can't doubt, after what you have told me, that the restoration of the Moonstone to its place on the forehead of the Indian idol, is the motive and the justification of that sacrifice of caste which I alluded to just now. Those men will wait their opportunity with the patience of cats, and will use it with the ferocity of tigers. How you have escaped them I can't imagine," says the eminent traveller, lighting his cheroot again, and staring hard at Mr. Franklin. "You have been carrying the Diamond backwards and forwards, here and in London, and you are still a living man! Let us try and account for it. It was daylight, both times, I suppose, when you took the jewel out of the bank in London?"

"Broad daylight," says Mr. Franklin.

"And plenty of people in the streets?"

"Plenty."

"You settled, of course, to arrive at Lady Verinder's house at a certain time? It's a lonely country between this and the station. Did you keep your appointment?"

"No. I arrived four hours earlier than my appointment."

"I beg to congratulate you on that proceeding! When did you take the Diamond to the bank at the town here?"

"I took it an hour after I had brought it to this house—and three hours before anybody was prepared for seeing me in these parts."

"I beg to congratulate you again! Did you bring it back here alone?"

"No. I happened to ride back with my cousins and the

groom."

"I beg to congratulate you for the third time! If you ever feel inclined to travel beyond the civilised limits, Mr. Blake, let me know, and I will go with you. You are a lucky man."

Here I struck in. This sort of thing didn't at all square with my English ideas.

"You don't really mean to say, sir," I asked, "that they would have taken Mr. Franklin's life, to get their Diamond, if he had given them the chance?"

"Do you smoke, Mr. Betteredge?" says the traveller.

"Yes, sir.

"Do you care much for the ashes left in your pipe when you empty it?"

"No, sir."

"In the country those men came from, they care just as much about killing a man, as you care about emptying the ashes out of your pipe. If a thousand lives stood between them and the getting back of their Diamond—and if they thought they could destroy those lives without discovery—they would take them all. The sacrifice of caste is a serious thing in India, if you like. The sacrifice of life is nothing at all."

I expressed my opinion upon this, that they were a set of murdering thieves. Mr. Murthwaite expressed his opinion that they were a wonderful people. Mr. Franklin, expressing no opinion at all, brought us back to the matter in hand.

"They have seen the Moonstone on Miss Verinder's dress," he said. "What is to be done?"

"What your uncle threatened to do," answered Mr. Murthwaite. "Colonel Herncastle understood the people he had to deal with. Send the Diamond tomorrow (under guard of more than one man) to be cut up at Amsterdam. Make half a dozen diamonds of it, instead of one. There is an end of its sacred identity as The Moonstone—and there is an end of the conspiracy."

Mr. Franklin turned to me.

The Moonstone

"There is no help for it," he said. "We must speak to Lady Verinder tomorrow."

"What about tonight, sir?" I asked. "Suppose the Indians come back?"

Mr. Murthwaite answered me before Mr. Franklin could speak.

"The Indians won't risk coming back tonight," he said. "The direct way is hardly ever the way they take to anything—let alone a matter like this, in which the slightest mistake might be fatal to their reaching their end."

"But suppose the rogues are bolder than you think, sir?" I persisted.

"In that case," says Mr. Murthwaite, "let the dogs loose. Have you got any big dogs in the yard?"

"Two, sir. A mastiff and a bloodhound."

"They will do. In the present emergency, Mr. Betteredge, the mastiff and the bloodhound have one great merit—they are not likely to be troubled with your scruples about the sanctity of human life."

The strumming of the piano reached us from the drawing-room, as he fired that shot at me. He threw away his cheroot, and took Mr. Franklin's arm, to go back to the ladies. I noticed that the sky was clouding over fast, as I followed them to the house. Mr. Murthwaite noticed it too. He looked round at me, in his dry, droning way, and said:

"The Indians will want their umbrellas, Mr. Betteredge, tonight!"

It was all very well for him to joke. But I was not an eminent traveller—and my way in this world had not led me into playing ducks and drakes with my own life, among thieves and murderers in the outlandish places of the earth. I went into my own little room, and sat down in my chair in a perspiration, and wondered helplessly what was to be done next. In this anxious frame of mind, other men might have ended by working themselves up into a fever; I ended in a different way. I lit my pipe, and took a turn at Robinson Crusoe.

Before I had been at it five minutes, I came to this amazing bit—page one hundred and sixty-one—as follows:

"Fear of Danger is ten thousand times more terrifying than Danger itself, when apparent to the Eyes; and we find the Burthen of Anxiety greater, by much, than the Evil which we are anxious about."

The man who doesn't believe in Robinson Crusoe, after that, is a man with a screw loose in his understanding, or a man lost in the mist of his own self-conceit! Argument is thrown away upon him; and pity is better reserved for some person with a livelier faith.

I was far on with my second pipe, and still lost in admiration of that wonderful book, when Penelope (who had been handing round the tea) came in with her report from the drawing-room. She had left the Bouncers singing a duet—words beginning with a large "O," and music to correspond. She had observed that my lady made mistakes in her game of whist for the first time in our experience of her. She had seen the great traveller asleep in a corner. She had overheard Mr. Franklin sharpening his wits on Mr. Godfrey, at the expense of Ladies' Charities in general; and she had noticed that Mr. Godfrey hit him back again rather more smartly than became a gentleman of his benevolent character. She had detected Miss Rachel, apparently engaged in appeasing Mrs. Threadgall by showing her some photographs, and really occupied in stealing looks at Mr. Franklin, which no intelligent lady's maid could misinterpret for a single instant. Finally, she had missed Mr. Candy, the doctor, who had mysteriously disappeared from the drawing-room, and had then mysteriously returned, and entered into conversation with Mr. Godfrey. Upon the whole, things were prospering better than the experience of the dinner gave us any right to expect. If we could only hold on for another hour, old Father Time would bring up their carriages, and relieve us of them altogether.

Everything wears off in this world; and even the comforting effect of Robinson Crusoe wore off, after Penelope left me. I got fidgety again, and resolved on making a survey of the grounds before the rain came. Instead of taking the footman, whose nose was human, and therefore useless in any emergency, I took the bloodhound with me. His nose for a stranger was to be

The Moonstone

depended on. We went all round the premises, and out into the road — and returned as wise as we went, having discovered no such thing as a lurking human creature anywhere.

The arrival of the carriages was the signal for the arrival of the rain. It poured as if it meant to pour all night. With the exception of the doctor, whose gig was waiting for him, the rest of the company went home snugly, under cover, in close carriages. I told Mr. Candy that I was afraid he would get wet through. He told me, in return, that he wondered I had arrived at my time of life, without knowing that a doctor's skin was waterproof. So he drove away in the rain, laughing over his own little joke; and so we got rid of our dinner company.

The next thing to tell is the story of the night.

CHAPTER XI

When the last of the guests had driven away, I went back into the inner hall and found Samuel at the side-table, presiding over the brandy and soda water. My lady and Miss Rachel came out of the drawing-room, followed by the two gentlemen. Mr. Godfrey had some brandy and soda water, Mr. Franklin took nothing. He sat down, looking dead tired; the talking on this birthday occasion had, I suppose, been too much for him.

My lady, turning round to wish them good-night, looked hard at the wicked Colonel's legacy shining in her daughter's dress.

"Rachel," she asked, "where are you going to put your Diamond tonight?"

Miss Rachel was in high good spirits, just in that humour for talking nonsense, and perversely persisting in it as if it was sense, which you may sometimes have observed in young girls, when they are highly wrought up, at the end of an exciting day. First, she declared she didn't know where to put the Diamond. Then she said, "on her dressing-table, of course, along with her other things." Then she remembered that the Diamond might take to shining of itself, with its awful moony light in the dark — and that would terrify her in the dead of night. Then she bethought herself of an Indian cabinet which stood in her sitting-room; and instantly made up her mind to put the Indian diamond in the Indian cabinet, for the purpose of permitting two beautiful native productions to admire each other. Having let her little flow of nonsense run on as far as that point, her mother interposed and stopped her.

"My dear! your Indian cabinet has no lock to it," says my lady.

"Good Heavens, mamma!" cried Miss Rachel, "is this an hotel? Are there thieves in the house?"

Without taking notice of this fantastic way of talking, my lady wished the gentlemen good-night. She next turned to Miss Rachel, and kissed her. "Why not let me keep the Diamond for you tonight?" she asked.

Miss Rachel received that proposal as she might, ten years

The Moonstone

since, have received a proposal to part her from a new doll. My lady saw there was no reasoning with her that night. "Come into my room, Rachel, the first thing tomorrow morning," she said. "I shall have something to say to you." With those last words she left us slowly; thinking her own thoughts, and, to all appearance, not best pleased with the way by which they were leading her.

Miss Rachel was the next to say good-night. She shook hands first with Mr. Godfrey, who was standing at the other end of the hall, looking at a picture. Then she turned back to Mr. Franklin, still sitting weary and silent in a corner.

What words passed between them I can't say. But standing near the old oak frame which holds our large looking-glass, I saw her reflected in it, slyly slipping the locket which Mr. Franklin had given to her, out of the bosom of her dress, and showing it to him for a moment, with a smile which certainly meant something out of the common, before she tripped off to bed. This incident staggered me a little in the reliance I had previously felt on my own judgment. I began to think that Penelope might be right about the state of her young lady's affections, after all.

As soon as Miss Rachel left him eyes to see with, Mr. Franklin noticed me. His variable humour, shifting about everything, had shifted about the Indians already.

"Betteredge," he said, "I'm half inclined to think I took Mr. Murthwaite too seriously, when we had that talk in the shrubbery. I wonder whether he has been trying any of his traveller's tales on us? Do you really mean to let the dogs loose?"

"I'll relieve them of their collars, sir," I answered, "and leave them free to take a turn in the night, if they smell a reason for it."

"All right," says Mr. Franklin. "We'll see what is to be done tomorrow. I am not at all disposed to alarm my aunt, Betteredge, without a very pressing reason for it. Good-night."

He looked so worn and pale as he nodded to me, and took his candle to go upstairs, that I ventured to advise his having a drop of brandy-and-water, by way of night-cap. Mr. Godfrey, walking towards us from the other end of the hall, backed me. He pressed Mr. Franklin, in the friendliest manner, to take something, before he went to bed.

I only note these trifling circumstances, because, after all I had seen and heard, that day, it pleased me to observe that our two gentlemen were on just as good terms as ever. Their warfare of words (heard by Penelope in the drawing-room), and their rivalry for the best place in Miss Rachel's good graces, seemed to have set no serious difference between them. But there! they were both good-tempered, and both men of the world. And there is certainly this merit in people of station, that they are not nearly so quarrelsome among each other as people of no station at all.

Mr. Franklin declined the brandy-and-water, and went upstairs with Mr. Godfrey, their rooms being next door to each other. On the landing, however, either his cousin persuaded him, or he veered about and changed his mind as usual. "Perhaps I may want it in the night," he called down to me. "Send up some brandy-and-water into my room."

I sent up Samuel with the brandy-and-water; and then went out and unbuckled the dogs' collars. They both lost their heads with astonishment on being set loose at that time of night, and jumped upon me like a couple of puppies! However, the rain soon cooled them down again: they lapped a drop of water each, and crept back into their kennels. As I went into the house, I noticed signs in the sky which betokened a break in the weather for the better. For the present, it still poured heavily, and the ground was in a perfect sop.

Samuel and I went all over the house, and shut up as usual. I examined everything myself, and trusted nothing to my deputy on this occasion. All was safe and fast when I rested my old bones in bed, between midnight and one in the morning.

The worries of the day had been a little too much for me, I suppose. At any rate, I had a touch of Mr. Franklin's malady that night. It was sunrise before I fell off at last into a sleep. All the time I lay awake the house was as quiet as the grave. Not a sound stirred but the splash of the rain, and the sighing of the wind among the trees as a breeze sprang up with the morning.

About half-past seven I woke, and opened my window on a

The Moonstone

fine sunshiny day. The clock had struck eight, and I was just going out to chain up the dogs again, when I heard a sudden whisking of petticoats on the stairs behind me.

I turned about, and there was Penelope flying down after me like mad. "Father!" she screamed, "come upstairs, for God's sake! The Diamond is gone!"

"Are you out of your mind?" I asked her.

"Gone!" says Penelope. "Gone, nobody knows how! Come up and see."

She dragged me after her into our young lady's sitting-room, which opened into her bedroom. There, on the threshold of her bedroom door, stood Miss Rachel, almost as white in the face as the white dressing-gown that clothed her. There also stood the two doors of the Indian cabinet, wide open. One, of the drawers inside was pulled out as far as it would go.

"Look!" says Penelope. "I myself saw Miss Rachel put the Diamond into that drawer last night." I went to the cabinet. The drawer was empty.

"Is this true, miss?" I asked.

With a look that was not like herself, with a voice that was not like her own, Miss Rachel answered as my daughter had answered:

"The Diamond is gone!"

Having said those words, she withdrew into her bedroom, and shut and locked the door.

Before we knew which way to turn next, my lady came in, hearing my voice in her daughter's sitting-room, and wondering what had happened. The news of the loss of the Diamond seemed to petrify her. She went straight to Miss Rachel's bedroom, and insisted on being admitted. Miss Rachel let her in.

The alarm, running through the house like fire, caught the two gentlemen next.

Mr. Godfrey was the first to come out of his room. All he did when he heard what had happened was to hold up his hands in a state of bewilderment, which didn't say much for his natural strength of mind. Mr. Franklin, whose clear head I had confidently counted on to advise us, seemed to be as helpless as his cousin when he heard the news in his turn. For a wonder, he had had a good night's rest at last; and the unaccustomed luxury of sleep had, as he said himself, apparently stupefied him. However, when he had swallowed his cup of coffee — which he always took, on the foreign plan, some hours before he ate any breakfast — his brains brightened; the clear-headed side of him turned up, and he took the matter in hand, resolutely and cleverly, much as follows:

He first sent for the servants, and told them to leave all the lower doors and windows (with the exception of the front door, which I had opened) exactly as they had been left when we locked up over night. He next proposed to his cousin and to me to make quite sure, before we took any further steps, that the Diamond had not accidentally dropped somewhere out of sight — say at the back of the cabinet, or down behind the table on which the cabinet stood. Having searched in both places, and found nothing — having also questioned Penelope, and discovered from her no more than the little she had already told me — Mr. Franklin suggested next extending our inquiries to Miss Rachel, and sent Penelope to knock at her bedroom door.

My lady answered the knock, and closed the door behind her. The moment after we heard it locked inside by Miss Rachel. My mistress came out among us, looking sorely puzzled and distressed. "The loss of the Diamond seems to have quite overwhelmed Rachel," she said, in reply to Mr. Franklin. "She shrinks, in the strangest manner, from speaking of it, even to me. It is impossible you can see her for the present."

Having added to our perplexities by this account of Miss Rachel, my lady, after a little effort, recovered her usual composure, and acted with her usual decision.

"I suppose there is no help for it?" she said, quietly. "I suppose I have no alternative but to send for the police?"

"And the first thing for the police to do," added Mr. Franklin, catching her up, "is to lay hands on the Indian jugglers who performed here last night."

My lady and Mr. Godfrey (not knowing what Mr. Franklin and I knew) both started, and both looked surprised.

The Moonstone

"I can't stop to explain myself now," Mr. Franklin went on. "I can only tell you that the Indians have certainly stolen the Diamond. Give me a letter of introduction," says he, addressing my lady, "to one of the magistrates at Frizinghall—merely telling him that I represent your interests and wishes, and let me ride off with it instantly. Our chance of catching the thieves may depend on our not wasting one unnecessary minute." (Nota bene: Whether it was the French side or the English, the right side of Mr. Franklin seemed to be uppermost now. The only question was, How long would it last?)

He put pen, ink, and paper before his aunt, who (as it appeared to me) wrote the letter he wanted a little unwillingly. If it had been possible to overlook such an event as the loss of a jewel worth twenty thousand pounds, I believe—with my lady's opinion of her late brother, and her distrust of his birthday-gift—it would have been privately a relief to her to let the thieves get off with the Moonstone scot free.

I went out with Mr. Franklin to the stables, and took the opportunity of asking him how the Indians (whom I suspected, of course, as shrewdly as he did) could possibly have got into the house.

"One of them might have slipped into the hall, in the confusion, when the dinner company were going away," says Mr. Franklin. "The fellow may have been under the sofa while my aunt and Rachel were talking about where the Diamond was to be put for the night. He would only have to wait till the house was quiet, and there it would be in the cabinet, to be had for the taking." With those words, he called to the groom to open the gate, and galloped off.

This seemed certainly to be the only rational explanation. But how had the thief contrived to make his escape from the house? I had found the front door locked and bolted, as I had left it at night, when I went to open it, after getting up. As for the other doors and windows, there they were still, all safe and fast, to speak for themselves. The dogs, too? Suppose the thief had got away by dropping from one of the upper windows, how had he escaped the dogs? Had he come provided for them with drugged meat? As the doubt crossed my mind, the dogs themselves came galloping at me round a corner, rolling each other over on the wet grass, in such lively health and spirits that it was with no small difficulty I brought them to reason, and chained them up again. The more I turned it over in my mind, the less satisfactory Mr. Franklin's explanation appeared to be.

We had our breakfasts—whatever happens in a house, robbery or murder, it doesn't matter, you must have your breakfast. When we had done, my lady sent for me; and I found myself compelled to tell her all that I had hitherto concealed, relating to the Indians and their plot. Being a woman of a high courage, she soon got over the first startling effect of what I had to communicate. Her mind seemed to be far more perturbed about her daughter than about the heathen rogues and their conspiracy. "You know how odd Rachel is, and how differently she behaves sometimes from other girls," my lady said to me. "But I have never, in all my experience, seen her so strange and so reserved as she is now. The loss of her jewel seems almost to have turned her brain. Who would have thought that horrible Diamond could have laid such a hold on her in so short a time?"

It was certainly strange. Taking toys and trinkets in general, Miss Rachel was nothing like so mad after them as most young girls. Yet there she was, still locked up inconsolably in her bedroom. It is but fair to add that she was not the only one of us in the house who was thrown out of the regular groove. Mr. Godfrey, for instance—though professionally a sort of consoler-general—seemed to be at a loss where to look for his own resources. Having no company to amuse him, and getting no chance of trying what his experience of women in distress could do towards comforting Miss Rachel, he wandered hither and thither about the house and gardens in an aimless uneasy way. He was in two different minds about what it became him to do, after the misfortune that had happened to us. Ought he to relieve the family, in their present situation, of the responsibility of him as a guest, or ought he to stay on the chance that even his humble services might be of some use? He decided ultimately that the last course was perhaps the most customary and considerate course to take, in such a very peculiar case of family distress as this was. Circumstances try the metal a man is really made of. Mr. Godfrey, tried by circumstances, showed himself of weaker metal than I had thought him to be. As for the women-servants excepting Rosanna Spearman, who kept by herself—they took to whispering together in corners, and staring at nothing suspiciously, as is the manner of that weaker half of the human family, when anything extraordinary happens in a house. I myself acknowledge to have been fidgety and ill-tempered. The cursed Moonstone had turned us all upside down.

A little before eleven Mr. Franklin came back. The resolute side of him had, to all appearance, given way, in the interval since his departure, under the stress that had been laid on it. He had left us at a gallop; he came back to us at a walk. When he went away, he was made of iron. When he returned, he was stuffed with cotton, as limp as limp could be.

"Well," says my lady, "are the police coming?"

"Yes," says Mr. Franklin; "they said they would follow me in a fly. Superintendent Seegrave, of your local police force, and two of his men. A mere form! The case is hopeless."

"What! have the Indians escaped, sir?" I asked.

"The poor ill-used Indians have been most unjustly put in prison," says Mr. Franklin. "They are as innocent as the babe unborn. My idea that one of them was hidden in the house has ended, like all the rest of my ideas, in smoke. It's been proved," says Mr. Franklin, dwelling with great relish on his own incapacity, "to be simply impossible."

After astonishing us by announcing this totally new turn in the matter of the Moonstone, our young gentleman, at his aunt's request, took a seat, and explained himself.

It appeared that the resolute side of him had held out as far as Frizinghall. He had put the whole case plainly before the magistrate, and the magistrate had at once sent for the police. The first inquiries instituted about the Indians showed that they had not so much as attempted to leave the town. Further questions addressed to the police, proved that all three had been seen returning to Frizinghall with their boy, on the previous night between ten and eleven—which (regard being had to hours and distances) also proved that they had walked straight back after performing on our terrace. Later still, at midnight, the police, having occasion to search the common lodging-house where they lived, had seen them all three again, and their little boy with them, as usual. Soon after midnight I myself had safely shut up the house. Plainer evidence than this, in favour of the

Indians, there could not well be. The magistrate said there was not even a case of suspicion against them so far. But, as it was just possible, when the police came to investigate the matter, that discoveries affecting the jugglers might be made, he would contrive, by committing them as rogues and vagabonds, to keep them at our disposal, under lock and key, for a week. They had ignorantly done something (I forget what) in the town, which barely brought them within the operation of the law. Every human institution (justice included) will stretch a little, if you only pull it the right way. The worthy magistrate was an old friend of my lady's, and the Indians were "committed" for a week, as soon as the court opened that morning.

Such was Mr. Franklin's narrative of events at Frizinghall. The Indian clue to the mystery of the lost jewel was now, to all appearance, a clue that had broken in our hands. If the jugglers were innocent, who, in the name of wonder, had taken the Moonstone out of Miss Rachel's drawer?

Ten minutes later, to our infinite relief; Superintendent Seegrave arrived at the house. He reported passing Mr. Franklin on the terrace, sitting in the sun (I suppose with the Italian side of him uppermost), and warning the police, as they went by, that the investigation was hopeless, before the investigation had begun.

For a family in our situation, the Superintendent of the Frizinghall police was the most comforting officer you could wish to see. Mr. Seegrave was tall and portly, and military in his manners. He had a fine commanding voice, and a mighty resolute eye, and a grand frock-coat which buttoned beautifully up to his leather stock. "I'm the man you want!" was written all over his face; and he ordered his two inferior police men about with a severity which convinced us all that there was no trifling with him.

He began by going round the premises, outside and in; the result of that investigation proving to him that no thieves had broken in upon us from outside, and that the robbery, consequently, must have been committed by some person in the house. I leave you to imagine the state the servants were in when this official announcement first reached their ears. The Superintendent decided to begin by examining the boudoir, and, that done, to examine the servants next. At the same time,

The Moonstone

he posted one of his men on the staircase which led to the servants' bedrooms, with instructions to let nobody in the house pass him, till further orders.

At this latter proceeding, the weaker half of the human family went distracted on the spot. They bounced out of their corners, whisked upstairs in a body to Miss Rachel's room (Rosanna Spearman being carried away among them this time), burst in on Superintendent Seegrave, and, all looking equally guilty, summoned him to say which of them he suspected, at once.

Mr. Superintendent proved equal to the occasion; he looked at them with his resolute eye, and he cowed them with his military voice.

"Now, then, you women, go downstairs again, everyone of you; I won't have you here. Look!" says Mr. Superintendent, suddenly pointing to a little smear of the decorative painting on Miss Rachel's door, at the outer edge, just under the lock. "Look what mischief the petticoats of some of you have done already. Clear out! clear out!" Rosanna Spearman, who was nearest to him, and nearest to the little smear on the door, set the example of obedience, and slipped off instantly to her work. The rest followed her out. The Superintendent finished his examination of the room, and, making nothing of it, asked me who had first discovered the robbery. My daughter had first discovered it. My daughter was sent for.

Mr. Superintendent proved to be a little too sharp with Penelope at starting. "Now, young woman, attend to me, and mind you speak the truth." Penelope fired up instantly. "I've never been taught to tell lies Mr. Policeman!—and if father can stand there and hear me accused of falsehood and thieving, and my own bedroom shut against me, and my character taken away, which is all a poor girl has left, he's not the good father I take him for!" A timely word from me put Justice and Penelope on a pleasanter footing together. The questions and answers went swimmingly, and ended in nothing worth mentioning. My daughter had seen Miss Rachel put the Diamond in the drawer of the cabinet the last thing at night. She had gone in with Miss Rachel's cup of tea at eight the next morning, and had found the drawer open and empty. Upon that, she had alarmed the house—and there was an end of Penelope's evidence.

Mr. Superintendent next asked to see Miss Rachel herself. Penelope mentioned his request through the door. The answer reached us by the same road: "I have nothing to tell the policeman—I can't see anybody." Our experienced officer looked equally surprised and offended when he heard that reply. I told him my young lady was ill, and begged him to wait a little and see her later. We thereupon went downstairs again, and were met by Mr. Godfrey and Mr. Franklin crossing the hall.

The two gentlemen, being inmates of the house, were summoned to say if they could throw any light on the matter. Neither of them knew anything about it. Had they heard any suspicious noises during the previous night? They had heard nothing but the pattering of the rain. Had I, lying awake longer than either of them, heard nothing either? Nothing! Released from examination, Mr. Franklin, still sticking to the helpless view of our difficulty, whispered to me: "That man will be of no earthly use to us. Superintendent Seegrave is an ass." Released in his turn, Mr. Godfrey whispered to me—"Evidently a most competent person. Betteredge, I have the greatest faith in him!" Many men, many opinions, as one of the ancients said, before my time.

Mr. Superintendent's next proceeding took him back to the "boudoir" again, with my daughter and me at his heels. His object was to discover whether any of the furniture had been moved, during the night, out of its customary place—his previous investigation in the room having, apparently, not gone quite far enough to satisfy his mind on this point.

While we were still poking about among the chairs and tables, the door of the bedroom was suddenly opened. After having denied herself to everybody, Miss Rachel, to our astonishment, walked into the midst of us of her own accord. She took up her garden hat from a chair, and then went straight to Penelope with this question:—

"Mr. Franklin Blake sent you with a message to me this morning?"

"Yes, miss."

"He wished to speak to me, didn't he?"

"Yes, miss."

"Where is he now?"

Hearing voices on the terrace below, I looked out of window, and saw the two gentlemen walking up and down together. Answering for my daughter, I said, "Mr. Franklin is on the terrace, miss."

Without another word, without heeding Mr. Superintendent, who tried to speak to her, pale as death, and wrapped up strangely in her own thoughts, she left the room, and went down to her cousins on the terrace.

It showed a want of due respect, it showed a breach of good manners, on my part, but, for the life of me, I couldn't help looking out of window when Miss Rachel met the gentlemen outside. She went up to Mr. Franklin without appearing to notice Mr. Godfrey, who thereupon drew back and left them by themselves. What she said to Mr. Franklin appeared to be spoken vehemently. It lasted but for a short time, and, judging by what I saw of his face from the window, seemed to astonish him beyond all power of expression. While they were still together, my lady appeared on the terrace. Miss Rachel saw her—said a few last words to Mr. Franklin—and suddenly went back into the house again, before her mother came up with her. My lady surprised herself, and noticing Mr. Franklin's surprise, spoke to him. Mr. Godfrey joined them, and spoke also. Mr. Franklin walked away a little between the two, telling them what had happened I suppose, for they both stopped short, after taking a few steps, like persons struck with amazement. I had just seen as much as this, when the door of the sitting-room was opened violently. Miss Rachel walked swiftly through to her bedroom, wild and angry, with fierce eyes and flaming cheeks. Mr. Superintendent once more attempted to question her. She turned round on him at her bedroom door. "I have not sent for you!" she cried out vehemently. "I don't want you. My Diamond is lost. Neither you nor anybody else will ever find it!" With those words she went in, and locked the door in our faces. Penelope, standing nearest to it, heard her burst out crying the moment she was alone again.

In a rage, one moment; in tears, the next! What did it mean?

I told the Superintendent it meant that Miss Rachel's temper was upset by the loss of her jewel. Being anxious for the honour of the family, it distressed me to see my young lady forget herself—even with a police-officer—and I made the best excuse I could, accordingly. In my own private mind I was more puzzled by Miss Rachel's extraordinary language and conduct than words can tell. Taking what she had said at her bedroom door as a guide to guess by, I could only conclude that she was mortally offended by our sending for the police, and that Mr. Franklin's astonishment on the terrace was caused by her having expressed herself to him (as the person chiefly instrumental in fetching the police) to that effect. If this guess was right, why—having lost her Diamond—should she object to the presence in the house of the very people whose business it was to recover it for her? And how, in Heaven's name, could she know that the Moonstone would never be found again?

As things stood, at present, no answer to those questions was to be hoped for from anybody in the house. Mr. Franklin appeared to think it a point of honour to forbear repeating to a servant—even to so old a servant as I was—what Miss Rachel had said to him on the terrace. Mr. Godfrey, who, as a gentleman and a relative, had been probably admitted into Mr. Franklin's confidence, respected that confidence as he was bound to do. My lady, who was also in the secret no doubt, and who alone had access to Miss Rachel, owned openly that she could make nothing of her. "You madden me when you talk of the Diamond!" All her mother's influence failed to extract from her a word more than that.

Here we were, then, at a dead-lock about Miss Rachel—and at a dead-lock about the Moonstone. In the first case, my lady was powerless to help us. In the second (as you shall presently judge), Mr. Seegrave was fast approaching the condition of a superintendent at his wits' end.

Having ferreted about all over the "boudoir," without making any discoveries among the furniture, our experienced officer applied to me to know, whether the servants in general were or were not acquainted with the place in which the Diamond had been put for the night.

"I knew where it was put, sir," I said, "to begin with. Samuel, the footman, knew also—for he was present in the hall, when they were talking about where the Diamond was to be kept that night. My daughter knew, as she has already told you. She or Samuel may have mentioned the thing to the other servants—or the other servants may have heard the talk for themselves, through the side-door of the hall, which might have been open to the back staircase. For all I can tell, everybody in the house may have known where the jewel was, last night."

My answer presenting rather a wide field for Mr. Superintendent's suspicions to range over, he tried to narrow it by asking about the servants' characters next.

I thought directly of Rosanna Spearman. But it was neither my place nor my wish to direct suspicion against a poor girl, whose honesty had been above all doubt as long as I had known her. The matron at the Reformatory had reported her to my lady as a sincerely penitent and thoroughly trustworthy girl. It was the Superintendent's business to discover reason for suspecting her first—and then, and not till then, it would be my duty to tell him how she came into my lady's service. "All our people have excellent characters," I said. "And all have deserved the trust their mistress has placed in them." After that, there was but one thing left for Mr. Seegrave to do—namely, to set to work, and tackle the servants' characters himself.

One after another, they were examined. One after another, they proved to have nothing to say—and said it (so far as the women were concerned) at great length, and with a very angry sense of the embargo laid on their bedrooms. The rest of them being sent back to their places downstairs, Penelope was then summoned, and examined separately a second time.

My daughter's little outbreak of temper in the "boudoir," and her readiness to think herself suspected, appeared to have produced an unfavourable impression on Superintendent Seegrave. It seemed also to dwell a little on his mind, that she had been the last person who saw the Diamond at night. When the second questioning was over, my girl came back to me in a frenzy. There was no doubt of it any longer—the police-officer had almost as good as told her she was the thief! I could scarcely believe him (taking Mr. Franklin's view) to be quite such an ass as that. But, though he said nothing, the eye with which he looked at my daughter was not a very pleasant eye to see. I laughed it off with poor Penelope, as something too ridiculous to be treated seriously—which it certainly was.

Secretly, I am afraid I was foolish enough to be angry too. It was a little trying—it was, indeed. My girl sat down in a corner, with her apron over her head, quite broken-hearted. Foolish of her, you will say. She might have waited till he openly accused her. Well, being a man of just an equal temper, I admit that. Still Mr. Superintendent might have remembered—never mind what he might have remembered. The devil take him!

The next and last step in the investigation brought matters, as they say, to a crisis. The officer had an interview (at which I was present) with my lady. After informing her that the Diamond must have been taken by somebody in the house, he requested permission for himself and his men to search the servants' rooms and boxes on the spot. My good mistress, like the generous high-bred woman she was, refused to let us be treated like thieves. "I will never consent to make such a return as that," she said, "for all I owe to the faithful servants who are employed in my house."

Mr. Superintendent made his bow, with a look in my direction, which said plainly, "Why employ me, if you are to tie my hands in this way?" As head of the servants, I felt directly that we were bound, in justice to all parties, not to profit by our mistress's generosity. "We gratefully thank your ladyship," I said; "but we ask your permission to do what is right in this matter by giving up our keys. When Gabriel Betteredge sets the example," says I, stopping Superintendent Seegrave at the door, "the rest of the servants will follow, I promise you. There are my keys, to begin with!" My lady took me by the hand, and thanked me with the tears in her eyes. Lord! what would I not have given, at that moment, for the privilege of knocking Superintendent Seegrave down!

As I had promised for them, the other servants followed my lead, sorely against the grain, of course, but all taking the view that I took. The women were a sight to see, while the police-officers were rummaging among their things. The cook looked as if she could grill Mr. Superintendent alive on a furnace, and the other women looked as if they could eat him when he was done.

The search over, and no Diamond or sign of a Diamond being found, of course, anywhere, Superintendent Seegrave retired to my little room to consider with himself what he was

The Moonstone

to do next. He and his men had now been hours in the house, and had not advanced us one inch towards a discovery of how the Moonstone had been taken, or of whom we were to suspect as the thief.

While the police-officer was still pondering in solitude, I was sent for to see Mr. Franklin in the library. To my unutterable astonishment, just as my hand was on the door, it was suddenly opened from the inside, and out walked Rosanna Spearman!

After the library had been swept and cleaned in the morning, neither first nor second housemaid had any business in that room at any later period of the day. I stopped Rosanna Spearman, and charged her with a breach of domestic discipline on the spot.

"What might you want in the library at this time of day?" I inquired.

"Mr. Franklin Blake dropped one of his rings upstairs," says Rosanna; "and I have been into the library to give it to him." The girl's face was all in a flush as she made me that answer; and she walked away with a toss of her head and a look of self-importance which I was quite at a loss to account for. The proceedings in the house had doubtless upset all the women-servants more or less; but none of them had gone clean out of their natural characters, as Rosanna, to all appearance, had now gone out of hers.

I found Mr. Franklin writing at the library-table. He asked for a conveyance to the railway station the moment I entered the room. The first sound of his voice informed me that we now had the resolute side of him uppermost once more. The man made of cotton had disappeared; and the man made of iron sat before me again.

"Going to London, sir?" I asked.

"Going to telegraph to London," says Mr. Franklin. "I have convinced my aunt that we must have a cleverer head than Superintendent Seegrave's to help us; and I have got her permission to despatch a telegram to my father. He knows the Chief Commissioner of Police, and the Commissioner can lay his hand on the right man to solve the mystery of the Diamond. Talking of mysteries, by-the-bye," says Mr. Franklin, dropping his voice, "I have another word to say to you before you go to the stables. Don't breathe a word of it to anybody as yet; but either Rosanna Spearman's head is not quite right, or I am afraid she knows more about the Moonstone than she ought to know."

I can hardly tell whether I was more startled or distressed at hearing him say that. If I had been younger, I might have confessed as much to Mr. Franklin. But when you are old, you acquire one excellent habit. In cases where you don't see your way clearly, you hold your tongue.

"She came in here with a ring I dropped in my bedroom," Mr. Franklin went on. "When I had thanked her, of course I expected her to go. Instead of that, she stood opposite to me at the table, looking at me in the oddest manner—half frightened, and half familiar—I couldn't make it out. 'This is a strange thing about the Diamond, sir,' she said, in a curiously sudden, headlong way. I said, 'Yes, it was,' and wondered what was coming next. Upon my honour, Betteredge, I think she must be wrong in the head! She said, 'They will never find the Diamond, sir, will they? No! nor the person who took it—I'll answer for that.' She actually nodded and smiled at me! Before I could ask her what she meant, we heard your step outside. I suppose she was afraid of your catching her here. At any rate, she changed colour, and left the room. What on earth does it mean?"

I could not bring myself to tell him the girl's story, even then. It would have been almost as good as telling him that she was the thief. Besides, even if I had made a clean breast of it, and even supposing she was the thief, the reason why she should let out her secret to Mr. Franklin, of all the people in the world, would have been still as far to seek as ever.

"I can't bear the idea of getting the poor girl into a scrape, merely because she has a flighty way with her, and talks very strangely," Mr. Franklin went on. "And yet if she had said to the Superintendent what she said to me, fool as he is, I'm afraid——" He stopped there, and left the rest unspoken.

"The best way, sir," I said, "will be for me to say two words privately to my mistress about it at the first opportunity. My lady has a very friendly interest in Rosanna; and the girl may only have been forward and foolish, after all. When there's a

The Moonstone

mess of any kind in a house, sir, the women-servants like to look at the gloomy side — it gives the poor wretches a kind of importance in their own eyes. If there's anybody ill, trust the women for prophesying that the person will die. If it's a jewel lost, trust them for prophesying that it will never be found again."

This view (which I am bound to say, I thought a probable view myself, on reflection) seemed to relieve Mr. Franklin mightily: he folded up his telegram, and dismissed the subject. On my way to the stables, to order the pony-chaise, I looked in at the servants' hall, where they were at dinner. Rosanna Spearman was not among them. On inquiry, I found that she had been suddenly taken ill, and had gone upstairs to her own room to lie down.

"Curious! She looked well enough when I saw her last," I remarked.

Penelope followed me out. "Don't talk in that way before the rest of them, father," she said. "You only make them harder on Rosanna than ever. The poor thing is breaking her heart about Mr. Franklin Blake."

Here was another view of the girl's conduct. If it was possible for Penelope to be right, the explanation of Rosanna's strange language and behaviour might have been all in this — that she didn't care what she said, so long as she could surprise Mr. Franklin into speaking to her. Granting that to be the right reading of the riddle, it accounted, perhaps, for her flighty, self-conceited manner when she passed me in the hall. Though he had only said three words, still she had carried her point, and Mr. Franklin had spoken to her.

I saw the pony harnessed myself. In the infernal network of mysteries and uncertainties that now surrounded us, I declare it was a relief to observe how well the buckles and straps understood each other! When you had seen the pony backed into the shafts of the chaise, you had seen something there was no doubt about. And that, let me tell you, was becoming a treat of the rarest kind in our household.

Going round with the chaise to the front door, I found not only Mr. Franklin, but Mr. Godfrey and Superintendent Seegrave also waiting for me on the steps.

Mr. Superintendent's reflections (after failing to find the Diamond in the servants' rooms or boxes) had led him, it appeared, to an entirely new conclusion. Still sticking to his first text, namely, that somebody in the house had stolen the jewel, our experienced officer was now of the opinion that the thief (he was wise enough not to name poor Penelope, whatever he might privately think of her!) had been acting in concert with the Indians; and he accordingly proposed shifting his inquiries to the jugglers in the prison at Frizinghall. Hearing of this new move, Mr. Franklin had volunteered to take the Superintendent back to the town, from which he could telegraph to London as easily as from our station. Mr. Godfrey, still devoutly believing in Mr. Seegrave, and greatly interested in witnessing the examination of the Indians, had begged leave to accompany the officer to Frizinghall. One of the two inferior policemen was to be left at the house, in case anything happened. The other was to go back with the Superintendent to the town. So the four places in the pony-chaise were just filled.

Before he took the reins to drive off, Mr. Franklin walked me away a few steps out of hearing of the others.

"I will wait to telegraph to London," he said, "till I see what comes of our examination of the Indians. My own conviction is, that this muddle-headed local police-officer is as much in the dark as ever, and is simply trying to gain time. The idea of any of the servants being in league with the Indians is a preposterous absurdity, in my opinion. Keep about the house, Betteredge, till I come back, and try what you can make of Rosanna Spearman. I don't ask you to do anything degrading to your own self-respect, or anything cruel towards the girl. I only ask you to exercise your observation more carefully than usual. We will make as light of it as we can before my aunt—but this is a more important matter than you may suppose."

"It is a matter of twenty thousand pounds, sir," I said, thinking of the value of the Diamond.

"It's a matter of quieting Rachel's mind," answered Mr. Franklin gravely. "I am very uneasy about her."

He left me suddenly; as if he desired to cut short any further talk between us. I thought I understood why. Further talk might have let me into the secret of what Miss Rachel had said to him on the terrace.

So they drove away to Frizinghall. I was ready enough, in the girl's own interest, to have a little talk with Rosanna in private. But the needful opportunity failed to present itself. She only came downstairs again at tea-time. When she did appear, she was flighty and excited, had what they call an hysterical attack, took a dose of sal-volatile by my lady's order, and was sent back to her bed.

The day wore on to its end drearily and miserably enough, I can tell you. Miss Rachel still kept her room, declaring that she was too ill to come down to dinner that day. My lady was in such low spirits about her daughter, that I could not bring myself to make her additionally anxious, by reporting what Rosanna Spearman had said to Mr. Franklin. Penelope persisted in believing that she was to be forthwith tried, sentenced, and transported for theft. The other women took to their Bibles and hymn-books, and looked as sour as verjuice over their reading—a result, which I have observed, in my sphere of life, to follow generally on the performance of acts of piety at unaccustomed periods of the day. As for me, I hadn't even heart enough to open my Robinson Crusoe. I went out into the yard, and, being hard up for a little cheerful society, set my chair by the kennels, and talked to the dogs.

Half an hour before dinner-time, the two gentlemen came back from Frizinghall, having arranged with Superintendent Seegrave that he was to return to us the next day. They had called on Mr. Murthwaite, the Indian traveller, at his present residence, near the town. At Mr. Franklin's request, he had kindly given them the benefit of his knowledge of the language, in dealing with those two, out of the three Indians, who knew nothing of English. The examination, conducted carefully, and at great length, had ended in nothing; not the shadow of a reason being discovered for suspecting the jugglers of having tampered with any of our servants. On reaching that conclusion, Mr. Franklin had sent his telegraphic message to London, and there the matter now rested till tomorrow came.

So much for the history of the day that followed the birthday. Not a glimmer of light had broken in on us, so far. A day or two after, however, the darkness lifted a little. How, and with what result, you shall presently see.

CHAPTER XII

The Thursday night passed, and nothing happened. With the Friday morning came two pieces of news.

Item the first: the baker's man declared he had met Rosanna Spearman, on the previous afternoon, with a thick veil on, walking towards Frizinghall by the foot-path way over the moor. It seemed strange that anybody should be mistaken about Rosanna, whose shoulder marked her out pretty plainly, poor thing — but mistaken the man must have been; for Rosanna, as you know, had been all the Thursday afternoon ill upstairs in her room.

Item the second came through the postman. Worthy Mr. Candy had said one more of his many unlucky things, when he drove off in the rain on the birthday night, and told me that a doctor's skin was waterproof. In spite of his skin, the wet had got through him. He had caught a chill that night, and was now down with a fever. The last accounts, brought by the postman, represented him to be light-headed — talking nonsense as glibly, poor man, in his delirium as he often talked it in his sober senses. We were all sorry for the little doctor; but Mr. Franklin appeared to regret his illness, chiefly on Miss Rachel's account. From what he said to my lady, while I was in the room at breakfast-time, he appeared to think that Miss Rachel — if the suspense about the Moonstone was not soon set at rest — might stand in urgent need of the best medical advice at our disposal.

Breakfast had not been over long, when a telegram from Mr. Blake, the elder, arrived, in answer to his son. It informed us that he had laid hands (by help of his friend, the Commissioner) on the right man to help us. The name of him was Sergeant Cuff; and the arrival of him from London might be expected by the morning train.

At reading the name of the new police-officer, Mr. Franklin gave a start. It seems that he had heard some curious anecdotes about Sergeant Cuff, from his father's lawyer, during his stay in London.

"I begin to hope we are seeing the end of our anxieties already," he said. "If half the stories I have heard are true, when it comes to unravelling a mystery, there isn't the equal in

The Moonstone

England of Sergeant Cuff!"

We all got excited and impatient as the time drew near for the appearance of this renowned and capable character. Superintendent Seegrave, returning to us at his appointed time, and hearing that the Sergeant was expected, instantly shut himself up in a room, with pen, ink, and paper, to make notes of the Report which would be certainly expected from him. I should have liked to have gone to the station myself, to fetch the Sergeant. But my lady's carriage and horses were not to be thought of, even for the celebrated Cuff; and the pony-chaise was required later for Mr. Godfrey. He deeply regretted being obliged to leave his aunt at such an anxious time; and he kindly put off the hour of his departure till as late as the last train, for the purpose of hearing what the clever London police-officer thought of the case. But on Friday night he must be in town, having a Ladies' Charity, in difficulties, waiting to consult him on Saturday morning.

When the time came for the Sergeant's arrival, I went down to the gate to look out for him.

A fly from the railway drove up as I reached the lodge; and out got a grizzled, elderly man, so miserably lean that he looked as if he had not got an ounce of flesh on his bones in any part of him. He was dressed all in decent black, with a white cravat round his neck. His face was as sharp as a hatchet, and the skin of it was as yellow and dry and withered as an autumn leaf. His eyes, of a steely light grey, had a very disconcerting trick, when they encountered your eyes, of looking as if they expected something more from you than you were aware of yourself. His walk was soft; his voice was melancholy; his long lanky fingers were hooked like claws. He might have been a parson, or an undertaker — or anything else you like, except what he really was. A more complete opposite to Superintendent Seegrave than Sergeant Cuff, and a less comforting officer to look at, for a family in distress, I defy you to discover, search where you may.

"Is this Lady Verinder's?" he asked.

"Yes, sir."

"I am Sergeant Cuff."

"This way, sir, if you please."

On our road to the house, I mentioned my name and position in the family, to satisfy him that he might speak to me about the business on which my lady was to employ him. Not a word did he say about the business, however, for all that. He admired the grounds, and remarked that he felt the sea air very brisk and refreshing. I privately wondered, on my side, how the celebrated Cuff had got his reputation. We reached the house, in the temper of two strange dogs, coupled up together for the first time in their lives by the same chain.

Asking for my lady, and hearing that she was in one of the conservatories, we went round to the gardens at the back, and sent a servant to seek her. While we were waiting, Sergeant Cuff looked through the evergreen arch on our left, spied out our rosery, and walked straight in, with the first appearance of anything like interest that he had shown yet. To the gardener's astonishment, and to my disgust, this celebrated policeman proved to be quite a mine of learning on the trumpery subject of rose-gardens.

"Ah, you've got the right exposure here to the south and sou'-west," says the Sergeant, with a wag of his grizzled head, and a streak of pleasure in his melancholy voice. "This is the shape for a rosery—nothing like a circle set in a square. Yes, yes; with walks between all the beds. But they oughtn't to be gravel walks like these. Grass, Mr. Gardener—grass walks between your roses; gravel's too hard for them. That's a sweet pretty bed of white roses and blush roses. They always mix well together, don't they? Here's the white musk rose, Mr. Betteredge—our old English rose holding up its head along with the best and the newest of them. Pretty dear!" says the Sergeant, fondling the Musk Rose with his lanky fingers, and speaking to it as if he was speaking to a child.

This was a nice sort of man to recover Miss Rachel's Diamond, and to find out the thief who stole it!

"You seem to be fond of roses, Sergeant?" I remarked.

"I haven't much time to be fond of anything," says Sergeant Cuff. "But when I have a moment's fondness to bestow, most times, Mr. Betteredge, the roses get it. I began my life among them in my father's nursery garden, and I shall end my life among them, if I can. Yes. One of these days (please God) I shall retire from catching thieves, and try my hand at growing roses. There will be grass walks, Mr. Gardener, between my beds," says the Sergeant, on whose mind the gravel paths of our rosery seemed to dwell unpleasantly.

"It seems an odd taste, sir," I ventured to say, "for a man in your line of life."

"If you will look about you (which most people won't do)," says Sergeant Cuff, "you will see that the nature of a man's tastes is, most times, as opposite as possible to the nature of a man's business. Show me any two things more opposite one from the other than a rose and a thief; and I'll correct my tastes accordingly — if it isn't too late at my time of life. You find the damask rose a goodish stock for most of the tender sorts, don't you, Mr. Gardener? Ah! I thought so. Here's a lady coming. Is it Lady Verinder?"

He had seen her before either I or the gardener had seen her, though we knew which way to look, and he didn't. I began to think him rather a quicker man than he appeared to be at first sight.

The Sergeant's appearance, or the Sergeant's errand — one or both — seemed to cause my lady some little embarrassment. She was, for the first time in all my experience of her, at a loss what to say at an interview with a stranger. Sergeant Cuff put her at her ease directly. He asked if any other person had been employed about the robbery before we sent for him; and hearing that another person had been called in, and was now in the house, begged leave to speak to him before anything else was done.

My lady led the way back. Before he followed her, the Sergeant relieved his mind on the subject of the gravel walks by a parting word to the gardener. "Get her ladyship to try grass," he said, with a sour look at the paths. "No gravel! no gravel!"

Why Superintendent Seegrave should have appeared to be several sizes smaller than life, on being presented to Sergeant Cuff, I can't undertake to explain. I can only state the fact. They retired together; and remained a weary long time shut up from all mortal intrusion. When they came out, Mr. Superintendent was excited, and Mr. Sergeant was yawning.

"The Sergeant wishes to see Miss Verinder's sitting-room," says Mr. Seegrave, addressing me with great pomp and eagerness. "The Sergeant may have some questions to ask. Attend the Sergeant, if you please!"

While I was being ordered about in this way, I looked at the great Cuff. The great Cuff, on his side, looked at Superintendent Seegrave in that quietly expecting way which I have already noticed. I can't affirm that he was on the watch for his brother officer's speedy appearance in the character of an Ass—I can only say that I strongly suspected it.

I led the way upstairs. The Sergeant went softly all over the Indian cabinet and all round the "boudoir;" asking questions (occasionally only of Mr. Superintendent, and continually of me), the drift of which I believe to have been equally unintelligible to both of us. In due time, his course brought him to the door, and put him face to face with the decorative painting that you know of. He laid one lean inquiring finger on the small smear, just under the lock, which Superintendent Seegrave had already noticed, when he reproved the women-servants for all crowding together into the room.

"That's a pity," says Sergeant Cuff. "How did it happen?"

He put the question to me. I answered that the women-servants had crowded into the room on the previous morning, and that some of their petticoats had done the mischief, "Superintendent Seegrave ordered them out, sir," I added, "before they did any more harm."

"Right!" says Mr. Superintendent in his military way. "I ordered them out. The petticoats did it, Sergeant—the petticoats did it."

"Did you notice which petticoat did it?" asked Sergeant Cuff, still addressing himself, not to his brother-officer, but to me.

"No, sir."

He turned to Superintendent Seegrave upon that, and said, "You noticed, I suppose?"

Mr. Superintendent looked a little taken aback; but he made the best of it. "I can't charge my memory, Sergeant," he said, "a

The Moonstone

mere trifle—a mere trifle."

Sergeant Cuff looked at Mr. Seegrave, as he had looked at the gravel walks in the rosery, and gave us, in his melancholy way, the first taste of his quality which we had had yet.

"I made a private inquiry last week, Mr. Superintendent," he said. "At one end of the inquiry there was a murder, and at the other end there was a spot of ink on a table cloth that nobody could account for. In all my experience along the dirtiest ways of this dirty little world, I have never met with such a thing as a trifle yet. Before we go a step further in this business we must see the petticoat that made the smear, and we must know for certain when that paint was wet."

Mr. Superintendent—taking his set-down rather sulkily—asked if he should summon the women. Sergeant Cuff, after considering a minute, sighed, and shook his head.

"No," he said, "we'll take the matter of the paint first. It's a question of Yes or No with the paint—which is short. It's a question of petticoats with the women—which is long. What o'clock was it when the servants were in this room yesterday morning? Eleven o'clock—eh? Is there anybody in the house who knows whether that paint was wet or dry, at eleven yesterday morning?"

"Her ladyship's nephew, Mr. Franklin Blake, knows," I said.

"Is the gentleman in the house?"

Mr. Franklin was as close at hand as could be—waiting for his first chance of being introduced to the great Cuff. In half a minute he was in the room, and was giving his evidence as follows:

"That door, Sergeant," he said, "has been painted by Miss Verinder, under my inspection, with my help, and in a vehicle of my own composition. The vehicle dries whatever colours may be used with it, in twelve hours."

"Do you remember when the smeared bit was done, sir?" asked the Sergeant.

"Perfectly," answered Mr. Franklin. "That was the last morsel of the door to be finished. We wanted to get it done, on Wednesday last—and I myself completed it by three in the afternoon, or soon after."

"Today is Friday," said Sergeant Cuff, addressing himself to Superintendent Seegrave. "Let us reckon back, sir. At three on the Wednesday afternoon, that bit of the painting was completed. The vehicle dried it in twelve hours—that is to say, dried it by three o'clock on Thursday morning. At eleven on Thursday morning you held your inquiry here. Take three from eleven, and eight remains. That paint had been eight hours dry, Mr. Superintendent, when you supposed that the women-servants' petticoats smeared it."

First knock-down blow for Mr. Seegrave! If he had not suspected poor Penelope, I should have pitied him.

Having settled the question of the paint, Sergeant Cuff, from that moment, gave his brother-officer up as a bad job—and addressed himself to Mr. Franklin, as the more promising assistant of the two.

"It's quite on the cards, sir," he said, "that you have put the clue into our hands."

As the words passed his lips, the bedroom door opened, and Miss Rachel came out among us suddenly.

She addressed herself to the Sergeant, without appearing to notice (or to heed) that he was a perfect stranger to her.

"Did you say," she asked, pointing to Mr. Franklin, "that he had put the clue into your hands?"

("This is Miss Verinder," I whispered, behind the Sergeant.)

"That gentleman, miss," says the Sergeant—with his steely-grey eyes carefully studying my young lady's face—"has possibly put the clue into our hands."

She turned for one moment, and tried to look at Mr. Franklin. I say, tried, for she suddenly looked away again before their eyes met. There seemed to be some strange disturbance in her mind. She coloured up, and then she turned pale again. With the paleness, there came a new look into her face—a look which it startled me to see.

"Having answered your question, miss," says the Sergeant, "I beg leave to make an inquiry in my turn. There is a smear on the painting of your door, here. Do you happen to know when it was done? or who did it?"

Instead of making any reply, Miss Rachel went on with her questions, as if he had not spoken, or as if she had not heard him.

"Are you another police-officer?" she asked.

"I am Sergeant Cuff, miss, of the Detective Police."

"Do you think a young lady's advice worth having?"

"I shall be glad to hear it, miss."

"Do your duty by yourself—and don't allow Mr Franklin Blake to help you!"

She said those words so spitefully, so savagely, with such an extraordinary outbreak of ill-will towards Mr. Franklin, in her voice and in her look, that—though I had known her from a baby, though I loved and honoured her next to my lady herself—I was ashamed of Miss Rachel for the first time in my life.

Sergeant Cuff's immovable eyes never stirred from off her face. "Thank you, miss," he said. "Do you happen to know anything about the smear? Might you have done it by accident yourself?"

"I know nothing about the smear."

With that answer, she turned away, and shut herself up again in her bedroom. This time, I heard her—as Penelope had heard her before—burst out crying as soon as she was alone again.

I couldn't bring myself to look at the Sergeant—I looked at Mr. Franklin, who stood nearest to me. He seemed to be even more sorely distressed at what had passed than I was.

"I told you I was uneasy about her," he said. "And now you see why."

"Miss Verinder appears to be a little out of temper about the loss of her Diamond," remarked the Sergeant. "It's a valuable jewel. Natural enough! natural enough!"

Here was the excuse that I had made for her (when she

forgot herself before Superintendent Seegrave, on the previous day) being made for her over again, by a man who couldn't have had my interest in making it—for he was a perfect stranger! A kind of cold shudder ran through me, which I couldn't account for at the time. I know, now, that I must have got my first suspicion, at that moment, of a new light (and horrid light) having suddenly fallen on the case, in the mind of Sergeant Cuff—purely and entirely in consequence of what he had seen in Miss Rachel, and heard from Miss Rachel, at that first interview between them.

"A young lady's tongue is a privileged member, sir," says the Sergeant to Mr. Franklin. "Let us forget what has passed, and go straight on with this business. Thanks to you, we know when the paint was dry. The next thing to discover is when the paint was last seen without that smear. You have got a head on your shoulders—and you understand what I mean."

Mr. Franklin composed himself, and came back with an effort from Miss Rachel to the matter in hand.

"I think I do understand," he said. "The more we narrow the question of time, the more we also narrow the field of inquiry."

"That's it, sir," said the Sergeant. "Did you notice your work here, on the Wednesday afternoon, after you had done it?"

Mr. Franklin shook his head, and answered, "I can't say I did."

"Did you?" inquired Sergeant Cuff, turning to me.

"I can't say I did either, sir."

"Who was the last person in the room, the last thing on Wednesday night?"

"Miss Rachel, I suppose, sir."

Mr. Franklin struck in there, "Or possibly your daughter, Betteredge." He turned to Sergeant Cuff, and explained that my daughter was Miss Verinder's maid.

"Mr. Betteredge, ask your daughter to step up. Stop!" says the Sergeant, taking me away to the window, out of earshot, "Your Superintendent here," he went on, in a whisper, "has made a pretty full report to me of the manner in which he has managed this case. Among other things, he has, by his own confession, set the servants' backs up. It's very important to smooth them down again. Tell your daughter, and tell the rest of them, these two things, with my compliments: First, that I have no evidence before me, yet, that the Diamond has been stolen; I only know that the Diamond has been lost. Second, that my business here with the servants is simply to ask them to lay their heads together and help me to find it."

My experience of the women-servants, when Superintendent Seegrave laid his embargo on their rooms, came in handy here.

"May I make so bold, Sergeant, as to tell the women a third thing?" I asked. "Are they free (with your compliments) to fidget up and downstairs, and whisk in and out of their bedrooms, if the fit takes them?"

"Perfectly free," said the Sergeant.

"That will smooth them down, sir," I remarked, "from the cook to the scullion."

"Go, and do it at once, Mr. Betteredge."

I did it in less than five minutes. There was only one difficulty when I came to the bit about the bedrooms. It took a pretty stiff exertion of my authority, as chief, to prevent the whole of the female household from following me and Penelope upstairs, in the character of volunteer witnesses in a burning fever of anxiety to help Sergeant Cuff.

The Sergeant seemed to approve of Penelope. He became a trifle less dreary; and he looked much as he had looked when he noticed the white musk rose in the flower-garden. Here is my daughter's evidence, as drawn off from her by the Sergeant. She gave it, I think, very prettily—but, there! she is my child all over: nothing of her mother in her; Lord bless you, nothing of her mother in her!

Penelope examined: Took a lively interest in the painting on the door, having helped to mix the colours. Noticed the bit of work under the lock, because it was the last bit done. Had seen it, some hours afterwards, without a smear. Had left it, as late as twelve at night, without a smear. Had, at that hour, wished her young lady good-night in the bedroom; had heard the clock strike in the "boudoir"; had her hand at the time on the handle of the painted door; knew the paint was wet (having helped to mix the colours, as aforesaid); took particular pains not to touch it; could swear that she held up the skirts of her dress, and that there was no smear on the paint then; could not swear that her dress mightn't have touched it accidentally in going out; remembered the dress she had on, because it was new, a present from Miss Rachel; her father remembered, and could speak to it, too; could, and would, and did fetch it; dress recognised by her father as the dress she wore that night; skirts examined, a long job from the size of them; not the ghost of a paint-stain discovered anywhere. End of Penelope's evidence — and very pretty and convincing, too. Signed, Gabriel Betteredge.

The Sergeant's next proceeding was to question me about any large dogs in the house who might have got into the room, and done the mischief with a whisk of their tails. Hearing that this was impossible, he next sent for a magnifying-glass, and tried how the smear looked, seen that way. No skin-mark (as of a human hand) printed off on the paint. All the signs visible — signs which told that the paint had been smeared by some loose article of somebody's dress touching it in going by. That somebody (putting together Penelope's evidence and Mr. Franklin's evidence) must have been in the room, and done the mischief, between midnight and three o'clock on the Thursday morning.

Having brought his investigation to this point, Sergeant Cuff discovered that such a person as Superintendent Seegrave was still left in the room, upon which he summed up the proceedings for his brother-officer's benefit, as follows:

"This trifle of yours, Mr. Superintendent," says the Sergeant, pointing to the place on the door, "has grown a little in importance since you noticed it last. At the present stage of the inquiry there are, as I take it, three discoveries to make, starting from that smear. Find out (first) whether there is any article of dress in this house with the smear of the paint on it. Find out (second) who that dress belongs to. Find out (third) how the person can account for having been in this room, and smeared the paint, between midnight and three in the morning. If the person can't satisfy you, you haven't far to look for the hand that has got the Diamond. I'll work this by myself, if you please, and detain you no longer from your regular business in the

The Moonstone

town. You have got one of your men here, I see. Leave him here at my disposal, in case I want him—and allow me to wish you good morning."

Superintendent Seegrave's respect for the Sergeant was great; but his respect for himself was greater still. Hit hard by the celebrated Cuff, he hit back smartly, to the best of his ability, on leaving the room.

"I have abstained from expressing any opinion, so far," says Mr. Superintendent, with his military voice still in good working order. "I have now only one remark to offer on leaving this case in your hands. There is such a thing, Sergeant, as making a mountain out of a molehill. Good morning."

"There is also such a thing as making nothing out of a molehill, in consequence of your head being too high to see it." Having returned his brother-officer's compliments in those terms, Sergeant Cuff wheeled about, and walked away to the window by himself.

Mr. Franklin and I waited to see what was coming next. The Sergeant stood at the window with his hands in his pockets, looking out, and whistling the tune of "The Last Rose of Summer" softly to himself. Later in the proceedings, I discovered that he only forgot his manners so far as to whistle, when his mind was hard at work, seeing its way inch by inch to its own private ends, on which occasions "The Last Rose of Summer" evidently helped and encouraged him. I suppose it fitted in somehow with his character. It reminded him, you see, of his favourite roses, and, as he whistled it, it was the most melancholy tune going.

Turning from the window, after a minute or two, the Sergeant walked into the middle of the room, and stopped there, deep in thought, with his eyes on Miss Rachel's bedroom door. After a little he roused himself, nodded his head, as much as to say, "That will do," and, addressing me, asked for ten minutes' conversation with my mistress, at her ladyship's earliest convenience.

Leaving the room with this message, I heard Mr. Franklin ask the Sergeant a question, and stopped to hear the answer also at the threshold of the door.

"Can you guess yet," inquired Mr. Franklin, "who has stolen the Diamond?"

"Nobody has stolen the Diamond," answered Sergeant Cuff.

We both started at that extraordinary view of the case, and both earnestly begged him to tell us what he meant.

"Wait a little," said the Sergeant. "The pieces of the puzzle are not all put together yet."

CHAPTER XIII

I found my lady in her own sitting room. She started and looked annoyed when I mentioned that Sergeant Cuff wished to speak to her.

"Must I see him?" she asked. "Can't you represent me, Gabriel?"

I felt at a loss to understand this, and showed it plainly, I suppose, in my face. My lady was so good as to explain herself.

"I am afraid my nerves are a little shaken," she said. "There is something in that police-officer from London which I recoil from—I don't know why. I have a presentiment that he is bringing trouble and misery with him into the house. Very foolish, and very unlike me—but so it is."

I hardly knew what to say to this. The more I saw of Sergeant Cuff, the better I liked him. My lady rallied a little after having opened her heart to me—being, naturally, a woman of a high courage, as I have already told you.

"If I must see him, I must," she said. "But I can't prevail on myself to see him alone. Bring him in, Gabriel, and stay here as long as he stays."

This was the first attack of the megrims that I remembered in my mistress since the time when she was a young girl. I went back to the "boudoir." Mr. Franklin strolled out into the garden, and joined Mr. Godfrey, whose time for departure was now drawing near. Sergeant Cuff and I went straight to my mistress's room.

I declare my lady turned a shade paler at the sight of him! She commanded herself, however, in other respects, and asked the Sergeant if he had any objection to my being present. She was so good as to add, that I was her trusted adviser, as well as her old servant, and that in anything which related to the household I was the person whom it might be most profitable to consult. The Sergeant politely answered that he would take my presence as a favour, having something to say about the servants in general, and having found my experience in that quarter already of some use to him. My lady pointed to two chairs, and we set in for our conference immediately.

"I have already formed an opinion on this case," says Sergeant Cuff, "which I beg your ladyship's permission to keep to myself for the present. My business now is to mention what I have discovered upstairs in Miss Verinder's sitting-room, and what I have decided (with your ladyship's leave) on doing next."

He then went into the matter of the smear on the paint, and stated the conclusions he drew from it—just as he had stated them (only with greater respect of language) to Superintendent Seegrave. "One thing," he said, in conclusion, "is certain. The Diamond is missing out of the drawer in the cabinet. Another thing is next to certain. The marks from the smear on the door must be on some article of dress belonging to somebody in this house. We must discover that article of dress before we go a step further."

"And that discovery," remarked my mistress, "implies, I presume, the discovery of the thief?"

"I beg your ladyship's pardon—I don't say the Diamond is stolen. I only say, at present, that the Diamond is missing. The discovery of the stained dress may lead the way to finding it."

Her ladyship looked at me. "Do you understand this?" she said.

"Sergeant Cuff understands it, my lady," I answered.

"How do you propose to discover the stained dress?" inquired my mistress, addressing herself once more to the Sergeant. "My good servants, who have been with me for years, have, I am ashamed to say, had their boxes and rooms searched already by the other officer. I can't and won't permit them to be insulted in that way a second time!"

(There was a mistress to serve! There was a woman in ten thousand, if you like!)

"That is the very point I was about to put to your ladyship," said the Sergeant. "The other officer has done a world of harm to this inquiry, by letting the servants see that he suspected them. If I give them cause to think themselves suspected a second time, there's no knowing what obstacles they may not throw in my way—the women especially. At the same time, their boxes must be searched again—for this plain reason, that

The Moonstone

the first investigation only looked for the Diamond, and that the second investigation must look for the stained dress. I quite agree with you, my lady, that the servants' feelings ought to be consulted. But I am equally clear that the servants' wardrobes ought to be searched."

This looked very like a dead-lock. My lady said so, in choicer language than mine.

"I have got a plan to meet the difficulty," said Sergeant Cuff, "if your ladyship will consent to it. I propose explaining the case to the servants."

"The women will think themselves suspected directly," I said, interrupting him.

"The women won't, Mr. Betteredge," answered the Sergeant, "if I can tell them I am going to examine the wardrobes of everybody — from her ladyship downwards — who slept in the house on Wednesday night. It's a mere formality," he added, with a side look at my mistress; "but the servants will accept it as even dealing between them and their betters; and, instead of hindering the investigation, they will make a point of honour of assisting it."

I saw the truth of that. My lady, after her first surprise was over, saw the truth of it also.

"You are certain the investigation is necessary?" she said.

"It's the shortest way that I can see, my lady, to the end we have in view."

My mistress rose to ring the bell for her maid. "You shall speak to the servants," she said, "with the keys of my wardrobe in your hand."

Sergeant Cuff stopped her by a very unexpected question.

"Hadn't we better make sure first," he asked, "that the other ladies and gentlemen in the house will consent, too?"

"The only other lady in the house is Miss Verinder," answered my mistress, with a look of surprise. "The only gentlemen are my nephews, Mr. Blake and Mr. Ablewhite. There is not the least fear of a refusal from any of the three."

I reminded my lady here that Mr. Godfrey was going away.

As I said the words, Mr. Godfrey himself knocked at the door to say good-bye, and was followed in by Mr. Franklin, who was going with him to the station. My lady explained the difficulty. Mr. Godfrey settled it directly. He called to Samuel, through the window, to take his portmanteau upstairs again, and he then put the key himself into Sergeant Cuff's hand. "My luggage can follow me to London," he said, "when the inquiry is over." The Sergeant received the key with a becoming apology. "I am sorry to put you to any inconvenience, sir, for a mere formality; but the example of their betters will do wonders in reconciling the servants to this inquiry." Mr. Godfrey, after taking leave of my lady, in a most sympathising manner, left a farewell message for Miss Rachel, the terms of which made it clear to my mind that he had not taken No for an answer, and that he meant to put the marriage question to her once more, at the next opportunity. Mr. Franklin, on following his cousin out, informed the Sergeant that all his clothes were open to examination, and that nothing he possessed was kept under lock and key. Sergeant Cuff made his best acknowledgments. His views, you will observe, had been met with the utmost readiness by my lady, by Mr. Godfrey, and by Mr. Franklin. There was only Miss. Rachel now wanting to follow their lead, before we called the servants together, and began the search for the stained dress.

My lady's unaccountable objection to the Sergeant seemed to make our conference more distasteful to her than ever, as soon as we were left alone again. "If I send you down Miss Verinder's keys," she said to him, "I presume I shall have done all you want of me for the present?"

"I beg your ladyship's pardon," said Sergeant Cuff. "Before we begin, I should like, if convenient, to have the washing-book. The stained article of dress may be an article of linen. If the search leads to nothing, I want to be able to account next for all the linen in the house, and for all the linen sent to the wash. If there is an article missing, there will be at least a presumption that it has got the paint-stain on it, and that it has been purposely made away with, yesterday or today, by the person owning it. Superintendent Seegrave," added the Sergeant, turning to me, "pointed the attention of the women-servants to the smear, when they all crowded into the room on Thursday morning. That may turn out, Mr. Betteredge, to have been one more of Superintendent Seegrave's many mistakes."

The Moonstone

My lady desired me to ring the bell, and order the washing-book. She remained with us until it was produced, in case Sergeant Cuff had any further request to make of her after looking at it.

The washing-book was brought in by Rosanna Spearman. The girl had come down to breakfast that morning miserably pale and haggard, but sufficiently recovered from her illness of the previous day to do her usual work. Sergeant Cuff looked attentively at our second housemaid—at her face, when she came in; at her crooked shoulder, when she went out.

"Have you anything more to say to me?" asked my lady, still as eager as ever to be out of the Sergeant's society.

The great Cuff opened the washing-book, understood it perfectly in half a minute, and shut it up again. "I venture to trouble your ladyship with one last question," he said. "Has the young woman who brought us this book been in your employment as long as the other servants?"

"Why do you ask?" said my lady.

"The last time I saw her," answered the Sergeant, "she was in prison for theft."

After that, there was no help for it, but to tell him the truth. My mistress dwelt strongly on Rosanna's good conduct in her service, and on the high opinion entertained of her by the matron at the Reformatory. "You don't suspect her, I hope?" my lady added, in conclusion, very earnestly.

"I have already told your ladyship that I don't suspect any person in the house of thieving—up to the present time."

After that answer, my lady rose to go upstairs, and ask for Miss Rachel's keys. The Sergeant was beforehand with me in opening the door for her. He made a very low bow. My lady shuddered as she passed him.

We waited, and waited, and no keys appeared. Sergeant Cuff made no remark to me. He turned his melancholy face to the window; he put his lanky hands into his pockets; and he whistled "The Last Rose of Summer" softly to himself.

At last, Samuel came in, not with the keys, but with a morsel of paper for me. I got at my spectacles, with some fumbling and difficulty, feeling the Sergeant's dismal eyes fixed on me all the time. There were two or three lines on the paper, written in pencil by my lady. They informed me that Miss Rachel flatly refused to have her wardrobe examined. Asked for her reasons, she had burst out crying. Asked again, she had said: "I won't, because I won't. I must yield to force if you use it, but I will yield to nothing else." I understood my lady's disinclination to face Sergeant Cuff with such an answer from her daughter as that. If I had not been too old for the amiable weaknesses of youth, I believe I should have blushed at the notion of facing him myself.

"Any news of Miss Verinder's keys?" asked the Sergeant.

"My young lady refuses to have her wardrobe examined."

"Ah!" said the Sergeant.

His voice was not quite in such a perfect state of discipline as his face. When he said "Ah!" he said it in the tone of a man who had heard something which he expected to hear. He half angered and half frightened me—why, I couldn't tell, but he did it.

"Must the search be given up?" I asked.

"Yes," said the Sergeant, "the search must be given up, because your young lady refuses to submit to it like the rest. We must examine all the wardrobes in the house or none. Send Mr. Ablewhite's portmanteau to London by the next train, and return the washing-book, with my compliments and thanks, to the young woman who brought it in."

He laid the washing-book on the table, and taking out his penknife, began to trim his nails.

"You don't seem to be much disappointed," I said.

"No," said Sergeant Cuff; "I am not much disappointed."

I tried to make him explain himself.

"Why should Miss Rachel put an obstacle in your way?" I inquired. "Isn't it her interest to help you?"

"Wait a little, Mr. Betteredge—wait a little."

Cleverer heads than mine might have seen his drift. Or a

person less fond of Miss Rachel than I was, might have seen his drift. My lady's horror of him might (as I have since thought) have meant that she saw his drift (as the scripture says) "in a glass darkly." I didn't see it yet—that's all I know.

"What's to be done next?" I asked.

Sergeant Cuff finished the nail on which he was then at work, looked at it for a moment with a melancholy interest, and put up his penknife.

"Come out into the garden," he said, "and let's have a look at the roses."

CHAPTER XIV

The nearest way to the garden, on going out of my lady's sitting-room, was by the shrubbery path, which you already know of. For the sake of your better understanding of what is now to come, I may add to this, that the shrubbery path was Mr. Franklin's favourite walk. When he was out in the grounds, and when we failed to find him anywhere else, we generally found him here.

I am afraid I must own that I am rather an obstinate old man. The more firmly Sergeant Cuff kept his thoughts shut up from me, the more firmly I persisted in trying to look in at them. As we turned into the shrubbery path, I attempted to circumvent him in another way.

"As things are now," I said, "if I was in your place, I should be at my wits' end."

"If you were in my place," answered the Sergeant, "you would have formed an opinion—and, as things are now, any doubt you might previously have felt about your own conclusions would be completely set at rest. Never mind for the present what those conclusions are, Mr. Betteredge. I haven't brought you out here to draw me like a badger; I have brought you out here to ask for some information. You might have given it to me no doubt, in the house, instead of out of it. But doors and listeners have a knack of getting together; and, in my line of life, we cultivate a healthy taste for the open air."

Who was to circumvent this man? I gave in—and waited as patiently as I could to hear what was coming next.

"We won't enter into your young lady's motives," the Sergeant went on; "we will only say it's a pity she declines to assist me, because, by so doing, she makes this investigation more difficult than it might otherwise have been. We must now try to solve the mystery of the smear on the door—which, you may take my word for it, means the mystery of the Diamond also—in some other way. I have decided to see the servants, and to search their thoughts and actions, Mr. Betteredge, instead of searching their wardrobes. Before I begin, however, I want to ask you a question or two. You are an observant man—did you notice anything strange in any of the servants (making due allowance, of course, for fright and fluster), after the loss of the Diamond was found out? Any particular quarrel among them? Anyone of them not in his or her usual spirits? Unexpectedly out of temper, for instance? or unexpectedly taken ill?"

I had just time to think of Rosanna Spearman's sudden illness at yesterday's dinner—but not time to make any answer—when I saw Sergeant Cuff's eyes suddenly turn aside towards the shrubbery; and I heard him say softly to himself, "Hullo!"

"What's the matter?" I asked.

"A touch of the rheumatics in my back," said the Sergeant, in a loud voice, as if he wanted some third person to hear us. "We shall have a change in the weather before long."

A few steps further brought us to the corner of the house. Turning off sharp to the right, we entered on the terrace, and went down, by the steps in the middle, into the garden below. Sergeant Cuff stopped there, in the open space, where we could see round us on every side.

"About that young person, Rosanna Spearman?" he said. "It isn't very likely, with her personal appearance, that she has got a lover. But, for the girl's own sake, I must ask you at once whether she has provided herself with a sweetheart, poor wretch, like the rest of them?"

What on earth did he mean, under present circumstances, by putting such a question to me as that? I stared at him, instead of answering him.

"I saw Rosanna Spearman hiding in the shrubbery as we went by," said the Sergeant.

"When you said 'Hullo'?"

"Yes—when I said 'Hullo!' If there's a sweetheart in the case, the hiding doesn't much matter. If there isn't—as things are in this house—the hiding is a highly suspicious circumstance, and it will be my painful duty to act on it accordingly."

What, in God's name, was I to say to him? I knew the shrubbery was Mr. Franklin's favourite walk; I knew he would most likely turn that way when he came back from the station; I knew that Penelope had over and over again caught her fellow-servant hanging about there, and had always declared to me that Rosanna's object was to attract Mr. Franklin's attention. If my daughter was right, she might well have been lying in wait for Mr. Franklin's return when the Sergeant noticed her. I was put between the two difficulties of mentioning Penelope's fanciful notion as if it was mine, or of leaving an unfortunate creature to suffer the consequences, the very serious consequences, of exciting the suspicion of Sergeant Cuff. Out of pure pity for the girl—on my soul and my character, out of pure pity for the girl—I gave the Sergeant the necessary explanations, and told him that Rosanna had been mad enough to set her heart on Mr. Franklin Blake.

Sergeant Cuff never laughed. On the few occasions when anything amused him, he curled up a little at the corners of the lips, nothing more. He curled up now.

"Hadn't you better say she's mad enough to be an ugly girl and only a servant?" he asked. "The falling in love with a gentleman of Mr. Franklin Blake's manners and appearance doesn't seem to me to be the maddest part of her conduct by any means. However, I'm glad the thing is cleared up: it relieves one's mind to have things cleared up. Yes, I'll keep it a secret, Mr. Betteredge. I like to be tender to human infirmity—though I don't get many chances of exercising that virtue in my line of life. You think Mr. Franklin Blake hasn't got a suspicion of the girl's fancy for him? Ah! he would have found it out fast enough if she had been nice-looking. The ugly women have a bad time of it in this world; let's hope it will be made up to them in another. You have got a nice garden here, and a well-kept lawn. See for yourself how much better the flowers look with grass about them instead of gravel. No, thank you. I won't take a rose. It goes to my heart to break them off the stem. Just as it goes to your heart, you know, when there's something wrong in the servants' hall. Did you notice anything you couldn't account for in any of the servants when the loss of the Diamond was first found out?"

I had got on very fairly well with Sergeant Cuff so far. But the slyness with which he slipped in that last question put me on my guard. In plain English, I didn't at all relish the notion of helping his inquiries, when those inquiries took him (in the capacity of snake in the grass) among my fellow-servants.

"I noticed nothing," I said, "except that we all lost our heads together, myself included."

"Oh," says the Sergeant, "that's all you have to tell me, is it?"

I answered, with (as I flattered myself) an unmoved countenance, "That is all."

Sergeant Cuff's dismal eyes looked me hard in the face.

"Mr. Betteredge," he said, "have you any objection to oblige me by shaking hands? I have taken an extraordinary liking to you."

(Why he should have chosen the exact moment when I was deceiving him to give me that proof of his good opinion, is beyond all comprehension! I felt a little proud—I really did feel a little proud of having been one too many at last for the celebrated Cuff!)

We went back to the house; the Sergeant requesting that I would give him a room to himself, and then send in the servants (the indoor servants only), one after another, in the order of their rank, from first to last.

I showed Sergeant Cuff into my own room, and then called the servants together in the hall. Rosanna Spearman appeared among them, much as usual. She was as quick in her way as the Sergeant in his, and I suspect she had heard what he said to me about the servants in general, just before he discovered her. There she was, at any rate, looking as if she had never heard of such a place as the shrubbery in her life.

I sent them in, one by one, as desired. The cook was the first to enter the Court of Justice, otherwise my room. She remained but a short time. Report, on coming out: "Sergeant Cuff is depressed in his spirits; but Sergeant Cuff is a perfect gentleman." My lady's own maid followed. Remained much longer. Report, on coming out: "If Sergeant Cuff doesn't believe a respectable woman, he might keep his opinion to himself, at any rate!" Penelope went next. Remained only a moment or two. Report, on coming out: "Sergeant Cuff is much to be pitied. He must have been crossed in love, father, when he was a young man." The first housemaid followed Penelope. Remained, like my lady's maid, a long time. Report, on coming out: "I didn't enter her ladyship's service, Mr. Betteredge, to be doubted to my face by a low police-officer!" Rosanna Spearman went next. Remained longer than any of them. No report on coming out—dead silence, and lips as pale as ashes. Samuel, the footman, followed Rosanna. Remained a minute or two. Report, on coming out: "Whoever blacks Sergeant Cuff's boots ought to be ashamed of himself." Nancy, the kitchen-maid, went last. Remained a minute or two. Report, on coming out: "Sergeant Cuff has a heart; he doesn't cut jokes, Mr. Betteredge, with a poor hard-working girl."

Going into the Court of Justice, when it was all over, to hear if there were any further commands for me, I found the Sergeant at his old trick—looking out of window, and whistling "The Last Rose of Summer" to himself.

"Any discoveries, sir?" I inquired.

"If Rosanna Spearman asks leave to go out," said the Sergeant, "let the poor thing go; but let me know first."

I might as well have held my tongue about Rosanna and Mr. Franklin! It was plain enough; the unfortunate girl had fallen under Sergeant Cuff's suspicions, in spite of all I could do to prevent it.

"I hope you don't think Rosanna is concerned in the loss of the Diamond?" I ventured to say.

The corners of the Sergeant's melancholy mouth curled up, and he looked hard in my face, just as he had looked in the garden.

"I think I had better not tell you, Mr. Betteredge," he said. "You might lose your head, you know, for the second time."

I began to doubt whether I had been one too many for the celebrated Cuff, after all! It was rather a relief to me that we were interrupted here by a knock at the door, and a message from the cook. Rosanna Spearman had asked to go out, for the usual reason, that her head was bad, and she wanted a breath of fresh air. At a sign from the Sergeant, I said, Yes. "Which is the servants' way out?" he asked, when the messenger had gone. I showed him the servants' way out. "Lock the door of your room," says the Sergeant; "and if anybody asks for me, say I'm in there, composing my mind." He curled up again at the corners of the lips, and disappeared.

The Moonstone

Left alone, under those circumstances, a devouring curiosity pushed me on to make some discoveries for myself.

It was plain that Sergeant Cuff's suspicions of Rosanna had been roused by something that he had found out at his examination of the servants in my room. Now, the only two servants (excepting Rosanna herself) who had remained under examination for any length of time, were my lady's own maid and the first housemaid, those two being also the women who had taken the lead in persecuting their unfortunate fellow-servant from the first. Reaching these conclusions, I looked in on them, casually as it might be, in the servants' hall, and, finding tea going forward, instantly invited myself to that meal. (For, nota bene, a drop of tea is to a woman's tongue what a drop of oil is to a wasting lamp.)

My reliance on the tea-pot, as an ally, did not go unrewarded. In less than half an hour I knew as much as the Sergeant himself.

My lady's maid and the housemaid, had, it appeared, neither of them believed in Rosanna's illness of the previous day. These two devils—I ask your pardon; but how else can you describe a couple of spiteful women?—had stolen upstairs, at intervals during the Thursday afternoon; had tried Rosanna's door, and found it locked; had knocked, and not been answered; had listened, and not heard a sound inside. When the girl had come down to tea, and had been sent up, still out of sorts, to bed again, the two devils aforesaid had tried her door once more, and found it locked; had looked at the keyhole, and found it stopped up; had seen a light under the door at midnight, and had heard the crackling of a fire (a fire in a servant's bedroom in the month of June!) at four in the morning. All this they had told Sergeant Cuff, who, in return for their anxiety to enlighten him, had eyed them with sour and suspicious looks, and had shown them plainly that he didn't believe either one or the other. Hence, the unfavourable reports of him which these two women had brought out with them from the examination. Hence, also (without reckoning the influence of the tea-pot), their readiness to let their tongues run to any length on the subject of the Sergeant's ungracious behaviour to them.

Having had some experience of the great Cuff's roundabout

ways, and having last seen him evidently bent on following Rosanna privately when she went out for her walk, it seemed clear to me that he had thought it unadvisable to let the lady's maid and the housemaid know how materially they had helped him. They were just the sort of women, if he had treated their evidence as trustworthy, to have been puffed up by it, and to have said or done something which would have put Rosanna Spearman on her guard.

I walked out in the fine summer afternoon, very sorry for the poor girl, and very uneasy in my mind at the turn things had taken. Drifting towards the shrubbery, some time later, there I met Mr. Franklin. After returning from seeing his cousin off at the station, he had been with my lady, holding a long conversation with her. She had told him of Miss Rachel's unaccountable refusal to let her wardrobe be examined; and had put him in such low spirits about my young lady that he seemed to shrink from speaking on the subject. The family temper appeared in his face that evening, for the first time in my experience of him.

"Well, Betteredge," he said, "how does the atmosphere of mystery and suspicion in which we are all living now, agree with you? Do you remember that morning when I first came here with the Moonstone? I wish to God we had thrown it into the quicksand!"

After breaking out in that way, he abstained from speaking again until he had composed himself. We walked silently, side by side, for a minute or two, and then he asked me what had become of Sergeant Cuff. It was impossible to put Mr. Franklin off with the excuse of the Sergeant being in my room, composing his mind. I told him exactly what had happened, mentioning particularly what my lady's maid and the house-maid had said about Rosanna Spearman.

Mr. Franklin's clear head saw the turn the Sergeant's suspicions had taken, in the twinkling of an eye.

"Didn't you tell me this morning," he said, "that one of the tradespeople declared he had met Rosanna yesterday, on the footway to Frizinghall, when we supposed her to be ill in her room?"

"Yes, sir."

"If my aunt's maid and the other woman have spoken the truth, you may depend upon it the tradesman did meet her. The girl's attack of illness was a blind to deceive us. She had some guilty reason for going to the town secretly. The paint-stained dress is a dress of hers; and the fire heard crackling in her room at four in the morning was a fire lit to destroy it. Rosanna Spearman has stolen the Diamond. I'll go in directly, and tell my aunt the turn things have taken."

"Not just yet, if you please, sir," said a melancholy voice behind us.

We both turned about, and found ourselves face to face with Sergeant Cuff.

"Why not just yet?" asked Mr. Franklin.

"Because, sir, if you tell her ladyship, her ladyship will tell Miss Verinder."

"Suppose she does. What then?" Mr. Franklin said those words with a sudden heat and vehemence, as if the Sergeant had mortally offended him.

"Do you think it's wise, sir," said Sergeant Cuff, quietly, "to put such a question as that to me — at such a time as this?"

There was a moment's silence between them: Mr. Franklin walked close up to the Sergeant. The two looked each other straight in the face. Mr. Franklin spoke first, dropping his voice as suddenly as he had raised it.

"I suppose you know, Mr. Cuff," he said, "that you are treading on delicate ground?"

"It isn't the first time, by a good many hundreds, that I find myself treading on delicate ground," answered the other, as immovable as ever.

"I am to understand that you forbid me to tell my aunt what has happened?"

"You are to understand, if you please, sir, that I throw up the case, if you tell Lady Verinder, or tell anybody, what has happened, until I give you leave."

That settled it. Mr. Franklin had no choice but to submit. He turned away in anger — and left us.

I had stood there listening to them, all in a tremble; not knowing whom to suspect, or what to think next. In the midst of my confusion, two things, however, were plain to me. First, that my young lady was, in some unaccountable manner, at the bottom of the sharp speeches that had passed between them. Second, that they thoroughly understood each other, without having previously exchanged a word of explanation on either side.

"Mr. Betteredge," says the Sergeant, "you have done a very foolish thing in my absence. You have done a little detective business on your own account. For the future, perhaps you will be so obliging as to do your detective business along with me."

He took me by the arm, and walked me away with him along the road by which he had come. I dare say I had deserved his reproof—but I was not going to help him to set traps for Rosanna Spearman, for all that. Thief or no thief, legal or not legal, I don't care—I pitied her.

"What do you want of me?" I asked, shaking him off, and stopping short.

"Only a little information about the country round here," said the Sergeant.

I couldn't well object to improve Sergeant Cuff in his geography.

"Is there any path, in that direction, leading to the sea-beach from this house?" asked the Sergeant. He pointed, as he spoke, to the fir-plantation which led to the Shivering Sand.

"Yes," I said, "there is a path."

"Show it to me."

Side by side, in the grey of the summer evening, Sergeant Cuff and I set forth for the Shivering Sand.

CHAPTER XV

The Sergeant remained silent, thinking his own thoughts, till we entered the plantation of firs which led to the quicksand. There he roused himself, like a man whose mind was made up, and spoke to me again.

"Mr. Betteredge," he said, "as you have honoured me by taking an oar in my boat, and as you may, I think, be of some assistance to me before the evening is out, I see no use in our mystifying one another any longer, and I propose to set you an example of plain speaking on my side. You are determined to give me no information to the prejudice of Rosanna Spearman, because she has been a good girl to you, and because you pity her heartily. Those humane considerations do you a world of credit, but they happen in this instance to be humane considerations clean thrown away. Rosanna Spearman is not in the slightest danger of getting into trouble—no, not if I fix her with being concerned in the disappearance of the Diamond, on evidence which is as plain as the nose on your face!"

"Do you mean that my lady won't prosecute?" I asked.

"I mean that your lady can't prosecute," said the Sergeant. "Rosanna Spearman is simply an instrument in the hands of another person, and Rosanna Spearman will be held harmless for that other person's sake."

He spoke like a man in earnest—there was no denying that. Still, I felt something stirring uneasily against him in my mind. "Can't you give that other person a name?" I said.

"Can't you, Mr. Betteredge?"

"No."

Sergeant Cuff stood stock-still, and surveyed me with a look of melancholy interest.

"It's always a pleasure to me to be tender towards human infirmity," he said. "I feel particularly tender at the present moment, Mr. Betteredge, towards you. And you, with the same excellent motive, feel particularly tender towards Rosanna Spearman, don't you? Do you happen to know whether she has had a new outfit of linen lately?"

What he meant by slipping in this extraordinary question unawares, I was at a total loss to imagine. Seeing no possible injury to Rosanna if I owned the truth, I answered that the girl had come to us rather sparely provided with linen, and that my lady, in recompense for her good conduct (I laid a stress on her good conduct), had given her a new outfit not a fortnight since.

"This is a miserable world," says the Sergeant. "Human life, Mr. Betteredge, is a sort of target—misfortune is always firing at it, and always hitting the mark. But for that outfit, we should have discovered a new nightgown or petticoat among Rosanna's things, and have nailed her in that way. You're not at a loss to follow me, are you? You have examined the servants yourself, and you know what discoveries two of them made outside Rosanna's door. Surely you know what the girl was about yesterday, after she was taken ill? You can't guess? Oh dear me, it's as plain as that strip of light there, at the end of the trees. At eleven, on Thursday morning, Superintendent Seegrave (who is a mass of human infirmity) points out to all the women servants the smear on the door. Rosanna has her own reasons for suspecting her own things; she takes the first opportunity of getting to her room, finds the paint-stain on her night-gown, or petticoat, or what not, shams ill and slips away to the town, gets the materials for making a new petticoat or nightgown, makes it alone in her room on the Thursday night, lights a fire (not to destroy it; two of her fellow-servants are prying outside her door, and she knows better than to make a smell of burning, and to have a lot of tinder to get rid of)—lights a fire, I say, to dry and iron the substitute dress after wringing it out, keeps the stained dress hidden (probably on her), and is at this moment occupied in making away with it, in some convenient place, on that lonely bit of beach ahead of us. I have traced her this evening to your fishing village, and to one particular cottage, which we may possibly have to visit, before we go back. She stopped in the cottage for some time, and she came out with (as I believe) something hidden under her cloak. A cloak (on a woman's back) is an emblem of charity—it covers a multitude of sins. I saw her set off northwards along the coast, after leaving the cottage. Is your sea-shore here considered a fine specimen of marine landscape, Mr. Betteredge?"

I answered, "Yes," as shortly as might be.

The Moonstone

"Tastes differ," says Sergeant Cuff. "Looking at it from my point of view, I never saw a marine landscape that I admired less. If you happen to be following another person along your sea-coast, and if that person happens to look round, there isn't a scrap of cover to hide you anywhere. I had to choose between taking Rosanna in custody on suspicion, or leaving her, for the time being, with her little game in her own hands. For reasons which I won't trouble you with, I decided on making any sacrifice rather than give the alarm as soon as tonight to a certain person who shall be nameless between us. I came back to the house to ask you to take me to the north end of the beach by another way. Sand—in respect of its printing off people's footsteps—is one of the best detective officers I know. If we don't meet with Rosanna Spearman by coming round on her in this way, the sand may tell us what she has been at, if the light only lasts long enough. Here is the sand. If you will excuse my suggesting it—suppose you hold your tongue, and let me go first?"

If there is such a thing known at the doctor's shop as a detective-fever, that disease had now got fast hold of your humble servant. Sergeant Cuff went on between the hillocks of sand, down to the beach. I followed him (with my heart in my mouth); and waited at a little distance for what was to happen next.

As it turned out, I found myself standing nearly in the same place where Rosanna Spearman and I had been talking together when Mr. Franklin suddenly appeared before us, on arriving at our house from London. While my eyes were watching the Sergeant, my mind wandered away in spite of me to what had passed, on that former occasion, between Rosanna and me. I declare I almost felt the poor thing slip her hand again into mine, and give it a little grateful squeeze to thank me for speaking kindly to her. I declare I almost heard her voice telling me again that the Shivering Sand seemed to draw her to it against her own will, whenever she went out—almost saw her face brighten again, as it brightened when she first set eyes upon Mr. Franklin coming briskly out on us from among the hillocks. My spirits fell lower and lower as I thought of these things—and the view of the lonesome little bay, when I looked about to rouse myself, only served to make me feel more uneasy still.

The last of the evening light was fading away; and over all the desolate place there hung a still and awful calm. The heave of the main ocean on the great sandbank out in the bay, was a heave that made no sound. The inner sea lay lost and dim, without a breath of wind to stir it. Patches of nasty ooze floated, yellow-white, on the dead surface of the water. Scum and slime shone faintly in certain places, where the last of the light still caught them on the two great spits of rock jutting out, north and south, into the sea. It was now the time of the turn of the tide: and even as I stood there waiting, the broad brown face of the quicksand began to dimple and quiver—the only moving thing in all the horrid place.

I saw the Sergeant start as the shiver of the sand caught his eye. After looking at it for a minute or so, he turned and came back to me.

"A treacherous place, Mr. Betteredge," he said; "and no signs of Rosanna Spearman anywhere on the beach, look where you may."

He took me down lower on the shore, and I saw for myself that his footsteps and mine were the only footsteps printed off on the sand.

"How does the fishing village bear, standing where we are now?" asked Sergeant Cuff.

"Cobb's Hole," I answered (that being the name of the place), "bears as near as may be, due south."

"I saw the girl this evening, walking northward along the shore, from Cobb's Hole," said the Sergeant. "Consequently, she must have been walking towards this place. Is Cobb's Hole on the other side of that point of land there? And can we get to it—now it's low water—by the beach?"

I answered, "Yes," to both those questions.

"If you'll excuse my suggesting it, we'll step out briskly," said the Sergeant. "I want to find the place where she left the shore, before it gets dark."

We had walked, I should say, a couple of hundred yards towards Cobb's Hole, when Sergeant Cuff suddenly went down on his knees on the beach, to all appearance seized with a

The Moonstone

sudden frenzy for saying his prayers.

"There's something to be said for your marine landscape here, after all," remarked the Sergeant. "Here are a woman's footsteps, Mr. Betteredge! Let us call them Rosanna's footsteps, until we find evidence to the contrary that we can't resist. Very confused footsteps, you will please to observe—purposely confused, I should say. Ah, poor soul, she understands the detective virtues of sand as well as I do! But hasn't she been in rather too great a hurry to tread out the marks thoroughly? I think she has. Here's one footstep going from Cobb's Hole; and here is another going back to it. Isn't that the toe of her shoe pointing straight to the water's edge? And don't I see two heel-marks further down the beach, close at the water's edge also? I don't want to hurt your feelings, but I'm afraid Rosanna is sly. It looks as if she had determined to get to that place you and I have just come from, without leaving any marks on the sand to trace her by. Shall we say that she walked through the water from this point till she got to that ledge of rocks behind us, and came back the same way, and then took to the beach again where those two heel marks are still left? Yes, we'll say that. It seems to fit in with my notion that she had something under her cloak, when she left the cottage. No! not something to destroy—for, in that case, where would have been the need of all these precautions to prevent my tracing the place at which her walk ended? Something to hide is, I think, the better guess of the two. Perhaps, if we go on to the cottage, we may find out what that something is?"

At this proposal, my detective-fever suddenly cooled. "You don't want me," I said. "What good can I do?"

"The longer I know you, Mr. Betteredge," said the Sergeant, "the more virtues I discover. Modesty—oh dear me, how rare modesty is in this world! and how much of that rarity you possess! If I go alone to the cottage, the people's tongues will be tied at the first question I put to them. If I go with you, I go introduced by a justly respected neighbour, and a flow of conversation is the necessary result. It strikes me in that light; how does it strike you?"

Not having an answer of the needful smartness as ready as I could have wished, I tried to gain time by asking him what cottage he wanted to go to.

On the Sergeant describing the place, I recognised it as a cottage inhabited by a fisherman named Yolland, with his wife and two grown-up children, a son and a daughter. If you will look back, you will find that, in first presenting Rosanna Spearman to your notice, I have described her as occasionally varying her walk to the Shivering Sand, by a visit to some friends of hers at Cobb's Hole. Those friends were the Yollands—respectable, worthy people, a credit to the neighbourhood. Rosanna's acquaintance with them had begun by means of the daughter, who was afflicted with a misshapen foot, and who was known in our parts by the name of Limping Lucy. The two deformed girls had, I suppose, a kind of fellow-feeling for each other. Anyway, the Yollands and Rosanna always appeared to get on together, at the few chances they had of meeting, in a pleasant and friendly manner. The fact of Sergeant Cuff having traced the girl to their cottage, set the matter of my helping his inquiries in quite a new light. Rosanna had merely gone where she was in the habit of going; and to show that she had been in company with the fisherman and his family was as good as to prove that she had been innocently occupied so far, at any rate. It would be doing the girl a service, therefore, instead of an injury, if I allowed myself to be convinced by Sergeant Cuff's logic. I professed myself convinced by it accordingly.

We went on to Cobb's Hole, seeing the footsteps on the sand, as long as the light lasted.

On reaching the cottage, the fisherman and his son proved to be out in the boat; and Limping Lucy, always weak and weary, was resting on her bed upstairs. Good Mrs. Yolland received us alone in her kitchen. When she heard that Sergeant Cuff was a celebrated character in London, she clapped a bottle of Dutch gin and a couple of clean pipes on the table, and stared as if she could never see enough of him.

I sat quiet in a corner, waiting to hear how the Sergeant would find his way to the subject of Rosanna Spearman. His usual roundabout manner of going to work proved, on this occasion, to be more roundabout than ever. How he managed it is more than I could tell at the time, and more than I can tell now. But this is certain, he began with the Royal Family, the Primitive Methodists, and the price of fish; and he got from that

The Moonstone

(in his dismal, underground way) to the loss of the Moonstone, the spitefulness of our first house-maid, and the hard behaviour of the women-servants generally towards Rosanna Spearman. Having reached his subject in this fashion, he described himself as making his inquiries about the lost Diamond, partly with a view to find it, and partly for the purpose of clearing Rosanna from the unjust suspicions of her enemies in the house. In about a quarter of an hour from the time when we entered the kitchen, good Mrs. Yolland was persuaded that she was talking to Rosanna's best friend, and was pressing Sergeant Cuff to comfort his stomach and revive his spirits out of the Dutch bottle.

Being firmly persuaded that the Sergeant was wasting his breath to no purpose on Mrs. Yolland, I sat enjoying the talk between them, much as I have sat, in my time, enjoying a stage play. The great Cuff showed a wonderful patience; trying his luck drearily this way and that way, and firing shot after shot, as it were, at random, on the chance of hitting the mark. Everything to Rosanna's credit, nothing to Rosanna's prejudice—that was how it ended, try as he might; with Mrs. Yolland talking nineteen to the dozen, and placing the most entire confidence in him. His last effort was made, when we had looked at our watches, and had got on our legs previous to taking leave.

"I shall now wish you good-night, ma'am," says the Sergeant. "And I shall only say, at parting, that Rosanna Spearman has a sincere well-wisher in myself, your obedient servant. But, oh dear me! she will never get on in her present place; and my advice to her is—leave it."

"Bless your heart alive! she is going to leave it!" cries Mrs. Yolland. (Nota bene—I translate Mrs. Yolland out of the Yorkshire language into the English language. When I tell you that the all-accomplished Cuff was every now and then puzzled to understand her until I helped him, you will draw your own conclusions as to what your state of mind would be if I reported her in her native tongue.)

Rosanna Spearman going to leave us! I pricked up my ears at that. It seemed strange, to say the least of it, that she should have given no warning, in the first place, to my lady or to me. A certain doubt came up in my mind whether Sergeant Cuff's last random shot might not have hit the mark. I began to question whether my share in the proceedings was quite as harmless a one as I had thought it. It might be all in the way of the Sergeant's business to mystify an honest woman by wrapping her round in a network of lies but it was my duty to have remembered, as a good Protestant, that the father of lies is the Devil—and that mischief and the Devil are never far apart. Beginning to smell mischief in the air, I tried to take Sergeant Cuff out. He sat down again instantly, and asked for a little drop of comfort out of the Dutch bottle. Mrs Yolland sat down opposite to him, and gave him his nip. I went on to the door, excessively uncomfortable, and said I thought I must bid them good-night—and yet I didn't go.

"So she means to leave?" says the Sergeant. "What is she to do when she does leave? Sad, sad! The poor creature has got no friends in the world, except you and me."

"Ah, but she has though!" says Mrs. Yolland. "She came in here, as I told you, this evening; and, after sitting and talking a little with my girl Lucy and me she asked to go upstairs by herself, into Lucy's room. It's the only room in our place where there's pen and ink. 'I want to write a letter to a friend,' she says 'and I can't do it for the prying and peeping of the servants up at the house.' Who the letter was written to I can't tell you: it must have been a mortal long one, judging by the time she stopped upstairs over it. I offered her a postage-stamp when she came down. She hadn't got the letter in her hand, and she didn't accept the stamp. A little close, poor soul (as you know), about herself and her doings. But a friend she has got somewhere, I can tell you; and to that friend you may depend upon it, she will go."

"Soon?" asked the Sergeant.

"As soon as she can." says Mrs. Yolland.

Here I stepped in again from the door. As chief of my lady's establishment, I couldn't allow this sort of loose talk about a servant of ours going, or not going, to proceed any longer in my presence, without noticing it.

"You must be mistaken about Rosanna Spearman," I said. "If she had been going to leave her present situation, she would have mentioned it, in the first place, to me."

The Moonstone

"Mistaken?" cries Mrs. Yolland. "Why, only an hour ago she bought some things she wanted for travelling—of my own self, Mr. Betteredge, in this very room. And that reminds me," says the wearisome woman, suddenly beginning to feel in her pocket, "of something I have got it on my mind to say about Rosanna and her money. Are you either of you likely to see her when you go back to the house?"

"I'll take a message to the poor thing, with the greatest pleasure," answered Sergeant Cuff, before I could put in a word edgewise.

Mrs. Yolland produced out of her pocket, a few shillings and sixpences, and counted them out with a most particular and exasperating carefulness in the palm of her hand. She offered the money to the Sergeant, looking mighty loth to part with it all the while.

"Might I ask you to give this back to Rosanna, with my love and respects?" says Mrs. Yolland. "She insisted on paying me for the one or two things she took a fancy to this evening—and money's welcome enough in our house, I don't deny it. Still, I'm not easy in my mind about taking the poor thing's little savings. And to tell you the truth, I don't think my man would like to hear that I had taken Rosanna Spearman's money, when he comes back tomorrow morning from his work. Please say she's heartily welcome to the things she bought of me—as a gift. And don't leave the money on the table," says Mrs. Yolland, putting it down suddenly before the Sergeant, as if it burnt her fingers—"don't, there's a good man! For times are hard, and flesh is weak; and I might feel tempted to put it back in my pocket again."

"Come along!" I said, "I can't wait any longer: I must go back to the house."

"I'll follow you directly," says Sergeant Cuff.

For the second time, I went to the door; and, for the second time, try as I might, I couldn't cross the threshold.

"It's a delicate matter, ma'am," I heard the Sergeant say, "giving money back. You charged her cheap for the things, I'm sure?"

"Cheap!" says Mrs. Yolland. "Come and judge for yourself."

She took up the candle and led the Sergeant to a corner of the kitchen. For the life of me, I couldn't help following them. Shaken down in the corner was a heap of odds and ends (mostly old metal), which the fisherman had picked up at different times from wrecked ships, and which he hadn't found a market for yet, to his own mind. Mrs. Yolland dived into this rubbish, and brought up an old japanned tin case, with a cover to it, and a hasp to hang it up by — the sort of thing they use, on board ship, for keeping their maps and charts, and such-like, from the wet.

"There!" says she. "When Rosanna came in this evening, she bought the fellow to that. 'It will just do,' she says, 'to put my cuffs and collars in, and keep them from being crumpled in my box.' One and ninepence, Mr. Cuff. As I live by bread, not a halfpenny more!"

"Dirt cheap!" says the Sergeant, with a heavy sigh.

He weighed the case in his hand. I thought I heard a note or two of "The Last Rose of Summer" as he looked at it. There was no doubt now! He had made another discovery to the prejudice of Rosanna Spearman, in the place of all others where I thought her character was safest, and all through me! I leave you to imagine what I felt, and how sincerely I repented having been the medium of introduction between Mrs. Yolland and Sergeant Cuff.

"That will do," I said. "We really must go."

Without paying the least attention to me, Mrs. Yolland took another dive into the rubbish, and came up out of it, this time, with a dog-chain.

"Weigh it in your hand, sir," she said to the Sergeant. "We had three of these; and Rosanna has taken two of them. 'What can you want, my dear, with a couple of dog's chains?' says I. 'If I join them together they'll do round my box nicely,' says she. 'Rope's cheapest,' says I. 'Chain's surest,' says she. 'Who ever heard of a box corded with chain,' says I. 'Oh, Mrs. Yolland, don't make objections!' says she; 'let me have my chains!' A strange girl, Mr. Cuff — good as gold, and kinder than a sister to my Lucy — but always a little strange. There! I humoured her. Three and sixpence. On the word of an honest woman, three and sixpence, Mr. Cuff!"

The Moonstone

"Each?" says the Sergeant.

"Both together!" says Mrs. Yolland. "Three and sixpence for the two."

"Given away, ma'am," says the Sergeant, shaking his head. "Clean given away!"

"There's the money," says Mrs. Yolland, getting back sideways to the little heap of silver on the table, as if it drew her in spite of herself. "The tin case and the dog chains were all she bought, and all she took away. One and ninepence and three and sixpence—total, five and three. With my love and respects—and I can't find it in my conscience to take a poor girl's savings, when she may want them herself."

"I can't find it in my conscience, ma'am, to give the money back," says Sergeant Cuff. "You have as good as made her a present of the things—you have indeed."

"Is that your sincere opinion, sir?" says Mrs. Yolland brightening up wonderfully.

"There can't be a doubt about it," answered the Sergeant. "Ask Mr. Betteredge."

It was no use asking me. All they got out of me was, "Good-night."

"Bother the money!" says Mrs. Yolland. With these words, she appeared to lose all command over herself; and, making a sudden snatch at the heap of silver, put it back, holus-bolus, in her pocket. "It upsets one's temper, it does, to see it lying there, and nobody taking it," cries this unreasonable woman, sitting down with a thump, and looking at Sergeant Cuff, as much as to say, "It's in my pocket again now—get it out if you can!"

This time, I not only went to the door, but went fairly out on the road back. Explain it how you may, I felt as if one or both of them had mortally offended me. Before I had taken three steps down the village, I heard the Sergeant behind me.

"Thank you for your introduction, Mr. Betteredge," he said. "I am indebted to the fisherman's wife for an entirely new sensation. Mrs. Yolland has puzzled me."

It was on the tip of my tongue to have given him a sharp

145

answer, for no better reason than this—that I was out of temper with him, because I was out of temper with myself. But when he owned to being puzzled, a comforting doubt crossed my mind whether any great harm had been done after all. I waited in discreet silence to hear more.

"Yes," says the Sergeant, as if he was actually reading my thoughts in the dark. "Instead of putting me on the scent, it may console you to know, Mr. Betteredge (with your interest in Rosanna), that you have been the means of throwing me off. What the girl has done, tonight, is clear enough, of course. She has joined the two chains, and has fastened them to the hasp in the tin case. She has sunk the case, in the water or in the quicksand. She has made the loose end of the chain fast to some place under the rocks, known only to herself. And she will leave the case secure at its anchorage till the present proceedings have come to an end; after which she can privately pull it up again out of its hiding-place, at her own leisure and convenience. All perfectly plain, so far. But," says the Sergeant, with the first tone of impatience in his voice that I had heard yet, "the mystery is—what the devil has she hidden in the tin case?"

I thought to myself, "The Moonstone!" But I only said to Sergeant Cuff, "Can't you guess?"

"It's not the Diamond," says the Sergeant. "The whole experience of my life is at fault, if Rosanna Spearman has got the Diamond."

On hearing those words, the infernal detective-fever began, I suppose, to burn in me again. At any rate, I forgot myself in the interest of guessing this new riddle. I said rashly, "The stained dress!"

Sergeant Cuff stopped short in the dark, and laid his hand on my arm.

"Is anything thrown into that quicksand of yours, ever thrown up on the surface again?" he asked.

"Never," I answered. "Light or heavy whatever goes into the Shivering Sand is sucked down, and seen no more."

"Does Rosanna Spearman know that?"

"She knows it as well as I do."

"Then," says the Sergeant, "what on earth has she got to do but to tie up a bit of stone in the stained dress and throw it into the quicksand? There isn't the shadow of a reason why she should have hidden it—and yet she must have hidden it. Query," says the Sergeant, walking on again, "is the paint-stained dress a petticoat or a night-gown? or is it something else which there is a reason for preserving at any risk? Mr. Betteredge, if nothing occurs to prevent it, I must go to Frizinghall tomorrow, and discover what she bought in the town, when she privately got the materials for making the substitute dress. It's a risk to leave the house, as things are now—but it's a worse risk still to stir another step in this matter in the dark. Excuse my being a little out of temper; I'm degraded in my own estimation—I have let Rosanna Spearman puzzle me."

When we got back, the servants were at supper. The first person we saw in the outer yard was the policeman whom Superintendent Seegrave had left at the Sergeant's disposal. The Sergeant asked if Rosanna Spearman had returned. Yes. When? Nearly an hour since. What had she done? She had gone upstairs to take off her bonnet and cloak—and she was now at supper quietly with the rest.

Without making any remark, Sergeant Cuff walked on, sinking lower and lower in his own estimation, to the back of the house. Missing the entrance in the dark, he went on (in spite of my calling to him) till he was stopped by a wicket-gate which led into the garden. When I joined him to bring him back by the right way, I found that he was looking up attentively at one particular window, on the bedroom floor, at the back of the house.

Looking up, in my turn, I discovered that the object of his contemplation was the window of Miss Rachel's room, and that lights were passing backwards and forwards there as if something unusual was going on.

"Isn't that Miss Verinder's room?" asked Sergeant Cuff.

I replied that it was, and invited him to go in with me to supper. The Sergeant remained in his place, and said something about enjoying the smell of the garden at night. I left him to his enjoyment. Just as I was turning in at the door, I heard "The

Last Rose of Summer" at the wicket-gate. Sergeant Cuff had made another discovery! And my young lady's window was at the bottom of it this time!

The latter reflection took me back again to the Sergeant, with a polite intimation that I could not find it in my heart to leave him by himself. "Is there anything you don't understand up there?" I added, pointing to Miss Rachel's window.

Judging by his voice, Sergeant Cuff had suddenly risen again to the right place in his own estimation. "You are great people for betting in Yorkshire, are you not?" he asked.

"Well?" I said. "Suppose we are?"

"If I was a Yorkshireman," proceeded the Sergeant, taking my arm, "I would lay you an even sovereign, Mr. Betteredge, that your young lady has suddenly resolved to leave the house. If I won on that event, I should offer to lay another sovereign, that the idea has occurred to her within the last hour." The first of the Sergeant's guesses startled me. The second mixed itself up somehow in my head with the report we had heard from the policeman, that Rosanna Spearman had returned from the sands within the last hour. The two together had a curious effect on me as we went in to supper. I shook off Sergeant Cuff's arm, and, forgetting my manners, pushed by him through the door to make my own inquiries for myself.

Samuel, the footman, was the first person I met in the passage.

"Her ladyship is waiting to see you and Sergeant Cuff," he said, before I could put any questions to him.

"How long has she been waiting?" asked the Sergeant's voice behind me.

"For the last hour, sir."

There it was again! Rosanna had come back; Miss Rachel had taken some resolution out of the common; and my lady had been waiting to see the Sergeant—all within the last hour! It was not pleasant to find these very different persons and things linking themselves together in this way. I went on upstairs, without looking at Sergeant Cuff, or speaking to him. My hand took a sudden fit of trembling as I lifted it to knock at my mistress's door.

"I shouldn't be surprised," whispered the Sergeant over my shoulder, "if a scandal was to burst up in the house tonight. Don't be alarmed! I have put the muzzle on worse family difficulties than this, in my time."

As he said the words I heard my mistress's voice calling to us to come in.

CHAPTER XVI

We found my lady with no light in the room but the reading-lamp. The shade was screwed down so as to overshadow her face. Instead of looking up at us in her usual straightforward way, she sat close at the table, and kept her eyes fixed obstinately on an open book.

"Officer," she said, "is it important to the inquiry you are conducting, to know beforehand if any person now in this house wishes to leave it?"

"Most important, my lady."

"I have to tell you, then, that Miss Verinder proposes going to stay with her aunt, Mrs. Ablewhite, of Frizinghall. She has arranged to leave us the first thing tomorrow morning."

Sergeant Cuff looked at me. I made a step forward to speak to my mistress—and, feeling my heart fail me (if I must own it), took a step back again, and said nothing.

"May I ask your ladyship when Miss Verinder informed you that she was going to her aunt's?" inquired the Sergeant.

"About an hour since," answered my mistress.

Sergeant Cuff looked at me once more. They say old people's hearts are not very easily moved. My heart couldn't have thumped much harder than it did now, if I had been five-and-twenty again!

"I have no claim, my lady," says the Sergeant, "to control Miss Verinder's actions. All I can ask you to do is to put off her departure, if possible, till later in the day. I must go to Frizinghall myself tomorrow morning—and I shall be back by two o'clock, if not before. If Miss Verinder can be kept here till that time, I should wish to say two words to her—unexpectedly—before she goes."

My lady directed me to give the coachman her orders, that the carriage was not to come for Miss Rachel until two o'clock. "Have you more to say?" she asked of the Sergeant, when this had been done.

"Only one thing, your ladyship. If Miss Verinder is surprised at this change in the arrangements, please not to mention Me as being the cause of putting off her journey."

My mistress lifted her head suddenly from her book as if she was going to say something—checked herself by a great effort—and, looking back again at the open page, dismissed us with a sign of her hand.

"That's a wonderful woman," said Sergeant Cuff, when we were out in the hall again. "But for her self-control, the mystery that puzzles you, Mr. Betteredge, would have been at an end tonight."

At those words, the truth rushed at last into my stupid old head. For the moment, I suppose I must have gone clean out of my senses. I seized the Sergeant by the collar of his coat, and pinned him against the wall.

"Damn you!" I cried out, "there's something wrong about Miss Rachel—and you have been hiding it from me all this time!"

Sergeant Cuff looked up at me—flat against the wall—without stirring a hand, or moving a muscle of his melancholy face.

"Ah," he said, "you've guessed it at last."

My hand dropped from his collar, and my head sunk on my breast. Please to remember, as some excuse for my breaking out as I did, that I had served the family for fifty years. Miss Rachel had climbed upon my knees, and pulled my whiskers, many and many a time when she was a child. Miss Rachel, with all her faults, had been, to my mind, the dearest and prettiest and best young mistress that ever an old servant waited on, and loved. I begged Sergeant's Cuff's pardon, but I am afraid I did it with watery eyes, and not in a very becoming way.

"Don't distress yourself, Mr. Betteredge," says the Sergeant, with more kindness than I had any right to expect from him. "In my line of life if we were quick at taking offence, we shouldn't be worth salt to our porridge. If it's any comfort to you, collar me again. You don't in the least know how to do it; but I'll overlook your awkwardness in consideration of your feelings."

He curled up at the corners of his lips, and, in his own dreary way, seemed to think he had delivered himself of a very good joke.

I led him into my own little sitting-room, and closed the door.

"Tell me the truth, Sergeant," I said. "What do you suspect? It's no kindness to hide it from me now."

"I don't suspect," said Sergeant Cuff. "I know."

My unlucky temper began to get the better of me again.

"Do you mean to tell me, in plain English," I said, "that Miss Rachel has stolen her own Diamond?"

"Yes," says the Sergeant; "that is what I mean to tell you, in so many words. Miss Verinder has been in secret possession of the Moonstone from first to last; and she has taken Rosanna Spearman into her confidence, because she has calculated on our suspecting Rosanna Spearman of the theft. There is the whole case in a nutshell. Collar me again, Mr. Betteredge. If it's any vent to your feelings, collar me again."

God help me! my feelings were not to be relieved in that way. "Give me your reasons!" That was all I could say to him.

"You shall hear my reasons tomorrow," said the Sergeant. "If Miss Verinder refuses to put off her visit to her aunt (which you will find Miss Verinder will do), I shall be obliged to lay the whole case before your mistress tomorrow. And, as I don't know what may come of it, I shall request you to be present, and to hear what passes on both sides. Let the matter rest for tonight. No, Mr. Betteredge, you don't get a word more on the subject of the Moonstone out of me. There is your table spread for supper. That's one of the many human infirmities which I always treat tenderly. If you will ring the bell, I'll say grace. 'For what we are going to receive — —'"

"I wish you a good appetite to it, Sergeant," I said. "My appetite is gone. I'll wait and see you served, and then I'll ask you to excuse me, if I go away, and try to get the better of this by myself."

I saw him served with the best of everything — and I shouldn't have been sorry if the best of everything had choked him. The head gardener (Mr. Begbie) came in at the same time, with his weekly account. The Sergeant got on the subject of roses and the merits of grass walks and gravel walks immediately. I left the two together, and went out with a heavy heart. This was the first trouble I remember for many a long year which wasn't to be blown off by a whiff of tobacco, and which was even beyond the reach of Robinson Crusoe.

Being restless and miserable, and having no particular room to go to, I took a turn on the terrace, and thought it over in peace and quietness by myself. It doesn't much matter what my thoughts were. I felt wretchedly old, and worn out, and unfit for my place — and began to wonder, for the first time in my life, when it would please God to take me. With all this, I held firm, notwithstanding, to my belief in Miss Rachel. If Sergeant Cuff had been Solomon in all his glory, and had told me that my young lady had mixed herself up in a mean and guilty plot, I should have had but one answer for Solomon, wise as he was, "You don't know her; and I do."

My meditations were interrupted by Samuel. He brought me a written message from my mistress.

Going into the house to get a light to read it by, Samuel remarked that there seemed a change coming in the weather. My troubled mind had prevented me from noticing it before. But, now my attention was roused, I heard the dogs uneasy, and the wind moaning low. Looking up at the sky, I saw the rack of clouds getting blacker and blacker, and hurrying faster and faster over a watery moon. Wild weather coming — Samuel was right, wild weather coming.

The message from my lady informed me, that the magistrate at Frizinghall had written to remind her about the three Indians. Early in the coming week, the rogues must needs be released, and left free to follow their own devices. If we had any more questions to ask them, there was no time to lose. Having forgotten to mention this, when she had last seen Sergeant Cuff, my mistress now desired me to supply the omission. The Indians had gone clean out of my head (as they have, no doubt, gone clean out of yours). I didn't see much use in stirring that subject again. However, I obeyed my orders on the spot, as a matter of course.

I found Sergeant Cuff and the gardener, with a bottle of Scotch whisky between them, head over ears in an argument on the growing of roses. The Sergeant was so deeply interested that he held up his hand, and signed to me not to interrupt the discussion, when I came in. As far as I could understand it, the question between them was, whether the white moss rose did, or did not, require to be budded on the dog-rose to make it grow well. Mr. Begbie said, Yes; and Sergeant Cuff said, No. They appealed to me, as hotly as a couple of boys. Knowing nothing whatever about the growing of roses, I steered a middle course—just as her Majesty's judges do, when the scales of justice bother them by hanging even to a hair. "Gentlemen," I remarked, "there is much to be said on both sides." In the temporary lull produced by that impartial sentence, I laid my lady's written message on the table, under the eyes of Sergeant Cuff.

I had got by this time, as nearly as might be, to hate the Sergeant. But truth compels me to acknowledge that, in respect of readiness of mind, he was a wonderful man.

In half a minute after he had read the message, he had looked back into his memory for Superintendent Seegrave's report; had picked out that part of it in which the Indians were concerned; and was ready with his answer. A certain great traveller, who understood the Indians and their language, had figured in Mr. Seegrave's report, hadn't he? Very well. Did I know the gentleman's name and address? Very well again. Would I write them on the back of my lady's message? Much obliged to me. Sergeant Cuff would look that gentleman up, when he went to Frizinghall in the morning.

"Do you expect anything to come of it?" I asked. "Superintendent Seegrave found the Indians as innocent as the babe unborn."

"Superintendent Seegrave has been proved wrong, up to this time, in all his conclusions," answered the Sergeant. "It may be worth while to find out tomorrow whether Superintendent Seegrave was wrong about the Indians as well." With that he turned to Mr. Begbie, and took up the argument again exactly at the place where it had left off. "This question between us is a question of soils and seasons, and patience and pains, Mr. Gardener. Now let me put it to you from another point of view. You take your white moss rose——"

By that time, I had closed the door on them, and was out of hearing of the rest of the dispute.

In the passage, I met Penelope hanging about, and asked what she was waiting for.

She was waiting for her young lady's bell, when her young lady chose to call her back to go on with the packing for the next day's journey. Further inquiry revealed to me, that Miss Rachel had given it as a reason for wanting to go to her aunt at Frizinghall, that the house was unendurable to her, and that she could bear the odious presence of a policeman under the same roof with herself no longer. On being informed, half an hour since, that her departure would be delayed till two in the afternoon, she had flown into a violent passion. My lady, present at the time, had severely rebuked her, and then (having apparently something to say, which was reserved for her daughter's private ear) had sent Penelope out of the room. My girl was in wretchedly low spirits about the changed state of things in the house. "Nothing goes right, father; nothing is like what it used to be. I feel as if some dreadful misfortune was hanging over us all."

That was my feeling too. But I put a good face on it, before my daughter. Miss Rachel's bell rang while we were talking. Penelope ran up the back stairs to go on with the packing. I went by the other way to the hall, to see what the glass said about the change in the weather.

Just as I approached the swing-door leading into the hall from the servants' offices, it was violently opened from the other side, and Rosanna Spearman ran by me, with a miserable look of pain in her face, and one of her hands pressed hard over her heart, as if the pang was in that quarter. "What's the matter, my girl?" I asked, stopping her. "Are you ill?" "For God's sake, don't speak to me," she answered, and twisted herself out of my hands, and ran on towards the servants' staircase. I called to the cook (who was within hearing) to look after the poor girl. Two other persons proved to be within hearing, as well as the cook. Sergeant Cuff darted softly out of my room, and asked what was the matter. I answered, "Nothing." Mr. Franklin, on the other side, pulled open the swing-door, and beckoning me into the hall, inquired if I had seen anything of Rosanna Spearman.

"She has just passed me, sir, with a very disturbed face, and in a very odd manner."

"I am afraid I am innocently the cause of that disturbance, Betteredge."

"You, sir!"

"I can't explain it," says Mr. Franklin; "but, if the girl is concerned in the loss of the Diamond, I do really believe she was on the point of confessing everything—to me, of all the people in the world—not two minutes since."

Looking towards the swing-door, as he said those last words, I fancied I saw it opened a little way from the inner side.

Was there anybody listening? The door fell to, before I could get to it. Looking through, the moment after, I thought I saw the tails of Sergeant Cuff's respectable black coat disappearing round the corner of the passage. He knew, as well as I did, that he could expect no more help from me, now that I had discovered the turn which his investigations were really taking. Under those circumstances, it was quite in his character to help himself, and to do it by the underground way.

Not feeling sure that I had really seen the Sergeant—and not desiring to make needless mischief, where, Heaven knows, there was mischief enough going on already—I told Mr. Franklin that I thought one of the dogs had got into the house—and then begged him to describe what had happened between Rosanna and himself.

"Were you passing through the hall, sir?" I asked. "Did you meet her accidentally, when she spoke to you?"

Mr. Franklin pointed to the billiard-table.

"I was knocking the balls about," he said, "and trying to get this miserable business of the Diamond out of my mind. I happened to look up—and there stood Rosanna Spearman at the side of me, like a ghost! Her stealing on me in that way was so strange, that I hardly knew what to do at first. Seeing a very anxious expression in her face, I asked her if she wished to speak to me. She answered, 'Yes, if I dare.' Knowing what suspicion attached to her, I could only put one construction on such language as that. I confess it made me uncomfortable. I had no wish to invite the girl's confidence. At the same time, in the difficulties that now beset us, I could hardly feel justified in refusing to listen to her, if she was really bent on speaking to me. It was an awkward position; and I dare say I got out of it awkwardly enough. I said to her, 'I don't quite understand you. Is there anything you want me to do?' Mind, Betteredge, I didn't speak unkindly! The poor girl can't help being ugly—I felt that, at the time. The cue was still in my hand, and I went on knocking the balls about, to take off the awkwardness of the thing. As it turned out, I only made matters worse still. I'm afraid I mortified her without meaning it! She suddenly turned away. 'He looks at the billiard balls,' I heard her say. 'Anything rather than look at me!' Before I could stop her, she had left the hall. I am not quite easy about it, Betteredge. Would you mind telling Rosanna that I meant no unkindness? I have been a little hard on her, perhaps, in my own thoughts—I have almost hoped that the loss of the Diamond might be traced to her. Not from any ill-will to the poor girl: but——" He stopped there, and going back to the billiard-table, began to knock the balls about once more.

After what had passed between the Sergeant and me, I knew what it was that he had left unspoken as well as he knew it himself.

Nothing but the tracing of the Moonstone to our second housemaid could now raise Miss Rachel above the infamous suspicion that rested on her in the mind of Sergeant Cuff. It was no longer a question of quieting my young lady's nervous excitement; it was a question of proving her innocence. If Rosanna had done nothing to compromise herself, the hope which Mr. Franklin confessed to having felt would have been hard enough on her in all conscience. But this was not the case. She had pretended to be ill, and had gone secretly to Frizinghall. She had been up all night, making something or destroying something, in private. And she had been at the Shivering Sand, that evening, under circumstances which were highly suspicious, to say the least of them. For all these reasons (sorry as I was for Rosanna) I could not but think that Mr. Franklin's way of looking at the matter was neither unnatural nor unreasonable, in Mr. Franklin's position. I said a word to him to that effect.

"Yes, yes!" he said in return. "But there is just a chance—a very poor one, certainly—that Rosanna's conduct may admit of some explanation which we don't see at present. I hate hurting a woman's feelings, Betteredge! Tell the poor creature what I told you to tell her. And if she wants to speak to me—I don't care whether I get into a scrape or not—send her to me in the library." With those kind words he laid down the cue and left me.

Inquiry at the servants' offices informed me that Rosanna had retired to her own room. She had declined all offers of assistance with thanks, and had only asked to be left to rest in quiet. Here, therefore, was an end of any confession on her part (supposing she really had a confession to make) for that night. I reported the result to Mr. Franklin, who, thereupon, left the library, and went up to bed.

I was putting the lights out, and making the windows fast, when Samuel came in with news of the two guests whom I had left in my room.

The argument about the white moss rose had apparently come to an end at last. The gardener had gone home, and Sergeant Cuff was nowhere to be found in the lower regions of the house.

I looked into my room. Quite true—nothing was to be discovered there but a couple of empty tumblers and a strong smell of hot grog. Had the Sergeant gone of his own accord to the bedchamber that was prepared for him? I went upstairs to see.

After reaching the second landing, I thought I heard a sound of quiet and regular breathing on my left-hand side. My left-hand side led to the corridor which communicated with Miss Rachel's room. I looked in, and there, coiled up on three chairs placed right across the passage—there, with a red handkerchief tied round his grizzled head, and his respectable black coat rolled up for a pillow, lay and slept Sergeant Cuff!

He woke, instantly and quietly, like a dog, the moment I approached him.

"Good-night, Mr. Betteredge," he said. "And mind, if you ever take to growing roses, the white moss rose is all the better for not being budded on the dog-rose, whatever the gardener may say to the contrary!"

"What are you doing here?" I asked. "Why are you not in your proper bed?"

"I am not in my proper bed," answered the Sergeant, "because I am one of the many people in this miserable world who can't earn their money honestly and easily at the same time. There was a coincidence, this evening, between the period of Rosanna Spearman's return from the Sands and the period when Miss Verinder stated her resolution to leave the house. Whatever Rosanna may have hidden, it's clear to my mind that your young lady couldn't go away until she knew that it was hidden. The two must have communicated privately once already tonight. If they try to communicate again, when the house is quiet, I want to be in the way, and stop it. Don't blame me for upsetting your sleeping arrangements, Mr. Betteredge—blame the Diamond."

"I wish to God the Diamond had never found its way into this house!" I broke out.

Sergeant Cuff looked with a rueful face at the three chairs on which he had condemned himself to pass the night.

"So do I," he said, gravely.

CHAPTER XVII

Nothing happened in the night; and (I am happy to add) no attempt at communication between Miss Rachel and Rosanna rewarded the vigilance of Sergeant Cuff.

I had expected the Sergeant to set off for Frizinghall the first thing in the morning. He waited about, however, as if he had something else to do first. I left him to his own devices; and going into the grounds shortly after, met Mr. Franklin on his favourite walk by the shrubbery side.

Before we had exchanged two words, the Sergeant unexpectedly joined us. He made up to Mr. Franklin, who received him, I must own, haughtily enough. "Have you anything to say to me?" was all the return he got for politely wishing Mr. Franklin good morning.

"I have something to say to you, sir," answered the Sergeant, "on the subject of the inquiry I am conducting here. You detected the turn that inquiry was really taking, yesterday. Naturally enough, in your position, you are shocked and distressed. Naturally enough, also, you visit your own angry sense of your own family scandal upon Me."

"What do you want?" Mr. Franklin broke in, sharply enough.

"I want to remind you, sir, that I have at any rate, thus far, not been proved to be wrong. Bearing that in mind, be pleased to remember, at the same time, that I am an officer of the law acting here under the sanction of the mistress of the house. Under these circumstances, is it, or is it not, your duty as a good citizen, to assist me with any special information which you may happen to possess?"

"I possess no special information," says Mr. Franklin.

Sergeant Cuff put that answer by him, as if no answer had been made.

"You may save my time, sir, from being wasted on an inquiry at a distance," he went on, "if you choose to understand me and speak out."

"I don't understand you," answered Mr. Franklin; "and I

have nothing to say."

"One of the female servants (I won't mention names) spoke to you privately, sir, last night."

Once more Mr. Franklin cut him short; once more Mr. Franklin answered, "I have nothing to say."

Standing by in silence, I thought of the movement in the swing-door on the previous evening, and of the coat-tails which I had seen disappearing down the passage. Sergeant Cuff had, no doubt, just heard enough, before I interrupted him, to make him suspect that Rosanna had relieved her mind by confessing something to Mr. Franklin Blake.

This notion had barely struck me—when who should appear at the end of the shrubbery walk but Rosanna Spearman in her own proper person! She was followed by Penelope, who was evidently trying to make her retrace her steps to the house. Seeing that Mr. Franklin was not alone, Rosanna came to a standstill, evidently in great perplexity what to do next. Penelope waited behind her. Mr. Franklin saw the girls as soon as I saw them. The Sergeant, with his devilish cunning, took on not to have noticed them at all. All this happened in an instant. Before either Mr. Franklin or I could say a word, Sergeant Cuff struck in smoothly, with an appearance of continuing the previous conversation.

"You needn't be afraid of harming the girl, sir," he said to Mr. Franklin, speaking in a loud voice, so that Rosanna might hear him. "On the contrary, I recommend you to honour me with your confidence, if you feel any interest in Rosanna Spearman."

Mr. Franklin instantly took on not to have noticed the girls either. He answered, speaking loudly on his side:

"I take no interest whatever in Rosanna Spearman."

I looked towards the end of the walk. All I saw at the distance was that Rosanna suddenly turned round, the moment Mr. Franklin had spoken. Instead of resisting Penelope, as she had done the moment before, she now let my daughter take her by the arm and lead her back to the house.

The breakfast-bell rang as the two girls disappeared—and

even Sergeant Cuff was now obliged to give it up as a bad job! He said to me quietly, "I shall go to Frizinghall, Mr. Betteredge; and I shall be back before two." He went his way without a word more—and for some few hours we were well rid of him.

"You must make it right with Rosanna," Mr. Franklin said to me, when we were alone. "I seem to be fated to say or do something awkward, before that unlucky girl. You must have seen yourself that Sergeant Cuff laid a trap for both of us. If he could confuse me, or irritate her into breaking out, either she or I might have said something which would answer his purpose. On the spur of the moment, I saw no better way out of it than the way I took. It stopped the girl from saying anything, and it showed the Sergeant that I saw through him. He was evidently listening, Betteredge, when I was speaking to you last night."

He had done worse than listen, as I privately thought to myself. He had remembered my telling him that the girl was in love with Mr. Franklin; and he had calculated on that, when he appealed to Mr. Franklin's interest in Rosanna—in Rosanna's hearing.

"As to listening, sir," I remarked (keeping the other point to myself), "we shall all be rowing in the same boat if this sort of thing goes on much longer. Prying, and peeping, and listening are the natural occupations of people situated as we are. In another day or two, Mr. Franklin, we shall all be struck dumb together—for this reason, that we shall all be listening to surprise each other's secrets, and all know it. Excuse my breaking out, sir. The horrid mystery hanging over us in this house gets into my head like liquor, and makes me wild. I won't forget what you have told me. I'll take the first opportunity of making it right with Rosanna Spearman."

"You haven't said anything to her yet about last night, have you?" Mr. Franklin asked.

"No, sir."

"Then say nothing now. I had better not invite the girl's confidence, with the Sergeant on the look-out to surprise us together. My conduct is not very consistent, Betteredge—is it? I see no way out of this business, which isn't dreadful to think of, unless the Diamond is traced to Rosanna. And yet I can't, and won't, help Sergeant Cuff to find the girl out."

The Moonstone

Unreasonable enough, no doubt. But it was my state of mind as well. I thoroughly understood him. If you will, for once in your life, remember that you are mortal, perhaps you will thoroughly understand him too.

The state of things, indoors and out, while Sergeant Cuff was on his way to Frizinghall, was briefly this:

Miss Rachel waited for the time when the carriage was to take her to her aunt's, still obstinately shut up in her own room. My lady and Mr. Franklin breakfasted together. After breakfast, Mr. Franklin took one of his sudden resolutions, and went out precipitately to quiet his mind by a long walk. I was the only person who saw him go; and he told me he should be back before the Sergeant returned. The change in the weather, foreshadowed overnight, had come. Heavy rain had been followed soon after dawn, by high wind. It was blowing fresh, as the day got on. But though the clouds threatened more than once, the rain still held off. It was not a bad day for a walk, if you were young and strong, and could breast the great gusts of wind which came sweeping in from the sea.

I attended my lady after breakfast, and assisted her in the settlement of our household accounts. She only once alluded to the matter of the Moonstone, and that was in the way of forbidding any present mention of it between us. "Wait till that man comes back," she said, meaning the Sergeant. "We must speak of it then: we are not obliged to speak of it now."

After leaving my mistress, I found Penelope waiting for me in my room.

"I wish, father, you would come and speak to Rosanna," she said. "I am very uneasy about her."

I suspected what was the matter readily enough. But it is a maxim of mine that men (being superior creatures) are bound to improve women—if they can. When a woman wants me to do anything (my daughter, or not, it doesn't matter), I always insist on knowing why. The oftener you make them rummage their own minds for a reason, the more manageable you will find them in all the relations of life. It isn't their fault (poor wretches!) that they act first and think afterwards; it's the fault of the fools who humour them.

Penelope's reason why, on this occasion, may be given in her own words. "I am afraid, father," she said, "Mr. Franklin has hurt Rosanna cruelly, without intending it."

"What took Rosanna into the shrubbery walk?" I asked.

"Her own madness," says Penelope; "I can call it nothing else. She was bent on speaking to Mr. Franklin, this morning, come what might of it. I did my best to stop her; you saw that. If I could only have got her away before she heard those dreadful words——"

"There! there!" I said, "don't lose your head. I can't call to mind that anything happened to alarm Rosanna."

"Nothing to alarm her, father. But Mr. Franklin said he took no interest whatever in her—and, oh, he said it in such a cruel voice!"

"He said it to stop the Sergeant's mouth," I answered.

"I told her that," says Penelope. "But you see, father (though Mr. Franklin isn't to blame), he's been mortifying and disappointing her for weeks and weeks past; and now this comes on the top of it all! She has no right, of course, to expect him to take any interest in her. It's quite monstrous that she should forget herself and her station in that way. But she seems to have lost pride, and proper feeling, and everything. She frightened me, father, when Mr. Franklin said those words. They seemed to turn her into stone. A sudden quiet came over her, and she has gone about her work, ever since, like a woman in a dream."

I began to feel a little uneasy. There was something in the way Penelope put it which silenced my superior sense. I called to mind, now my thoughts were directed that way, what had passed between Mr. Franklin and Rosanna overnight. She looked cut to the heart on that occasion; and now, as ill-luck would have it, she had been unavoidably stung again, poor soul, on the tender place. Sad! sad!—all the more sad because the girl had no reason to justify her, and no right to feel it.

I had promised Mr. Franklin to speak to Rosanna, and this seemed the fittest time for keeping my word.

We found the girl sweeping the corridor outside the

bedrooms, pale and composed, and neat as ever in her modest print dress. I noticed a curious dimness and dullness in her eyes—not as if she had been crying but as if she had been looking at something too long. Possibly, it was a misty something raised by her own thoughts. There was certainly no object about her to look at which she had not seen already hundreds on hundreds of times.

"Cheer up, Rosanna!" I said. "You mustn't fret over your own fancies. I have got something to say to you from Mr. Franklin."

I thereupon put the matter in the right view before her, in the friendliest and most comforting words I could find. My principles, in regard to the other sex, are, as you may have noticed, very severe. But somehow or other, when I come face to face with the women, my practice (I own) is not conformable.

"Mr. Franklin is very kind and considerate. Please to thank him." That was all the answer she made me.

My daughter had already noticed that Rosanna went about her work like a woman in a dream. I now added to this observation, that she also listened and spoke like a woman in a dream. I doubted if her mind was in a fit condition to take in what I had said to her.

"Are you quite sure, Rosanna, that you understand me?" I asked.

"Quite sure."

She echoed me, not like a living woman, but like a creature moved by machinery. She went on sweeping all the time. I took away the broom as gently and as kindly as I could.

"Come, come, my girl!" I said, "this is not like yourself. You have got something on your mind. I'm your friend—and I'll stand your friend, even if you have done wrong. Make a clean breast of it, Rosanna—make a clean breast of it!"

The time had been, when my speaking to her in that way would have brought the tears into her eyes. I could see no change in them now.

"Yes," she said, "I'll make a clean breast of it."

"To my lady?" I asked.

"No."

"To Mr. Franklin?"

"Yes; to Mr. Franklin."

I hardly knew what to say to that. She was in no condition to understand the caution against speaking to him in private, which Mr. Franklin had directed me to give her. Feeling my way, little by little, I only told her Mr. Franklin had gone out for a walk.

"It doesn't matter," she answered. "I shan't trouble Mr. Franklin, today."

"Why not speak to my lady?" I said. "The way to relieve your mind is to speak to the merciful and Christian mistress who has always been kind to you."

She looked at me for a moment with a grave and steady attention, as if she was fixing what I said in her mind. Then she took the broom out of my hands and moved off with it slowly, a little way down the corridor.

"No," she said, going on with her sweeping, and speaking to herself; "I know a better way of relieving my mind than that."

"What is it?"

"Please to let me go on with my work."

Penelope followed her, and offered to help her.

She answered, "No. I want to do my work. Thank you, Penelope." She looked round at me. "Thank you, Mr. Betteredge."

There was no moving her—there was nothing more to be said. I signed to Penelope to come away with me. We left her, as we had found her, sweeping the corridor, like a woman in a dream.

"This is a matter for the doctor to look into," I said. "It's beyond me."

My daughter reminded me of Mr. Candy's illness, owing (as you may remember) to the chill he had caught on the night of the dinner-party. His assistant—a certain Mr. Ezra Jennings—was at our disposal, to be sure. But nobody knew much about him in our parts. He had been engaged by Mr. Candy under rather peculiar circumstances; and, right or wrong, we none of us liked him or trusted him. There were other doctors at Frizinghall. But they were strangers to our house; and Penelope doubted, in Rosanna's present state, whether strangers might not do her more harm than good.

I thought of speaking to my lady. But, remembering the heavy weight of anxiety which she already had on her mind, I hesitated to add to all the other vexations this new trouble. Still, there was a necessity for doing something. The girl's state was, to my thinking, downright alarming—and my mistress ought to be informed of it. Unwilling enough, I went to her sitting-room. No one was there. My lady was shut up with Miss Rachel. It was impossible for me to see her till she came out again.

I waited in vain till the clock on the front staircase struck the quarter to two. Five minutes afterwards, I heard my name called, from the drive outside the house. I knew the voice directly. Sergeant Cuff had returned from Frizinghall.

CHAPTER XVIII

Going down to the front door, I met the Sergeant on the steps.

It went against the grain with me, after what had passed between us, to show him that I felt any sort of interest in his proceedings. In spite of myself, however, I felt an interest that there was no resisting. My sense of dignity sank from under me, and out came the words: "What news from Frizinghall?"

"I have seen the Indians," answered Sergeant Cuff. "And I have found out what Rosanna bought privately in the town, on Thursday last. The Indians will be set free on Wednesday in next week. There isn't a doubt on my mind, and there isn't a doubt on Mr. Murthwaite's mind, that they came to this place to steal the Moonstone. Their calculations were all thrown out, of course, by what happened in the house on Wednesday night; and they have no more to do with the actual loss of the jewel than you have. But I can tell you one thing, Mr. Betteredge — if we don't find the Moonstone, they will. You have not heard the last of the three jugglers yet."

Mr. Franklin came back from his walk as the Sergeant said those startling words. Governing his curiosity better than I had governed mine, he passed us without a word, and went on into the house.

As for me, having already dropped my dignity, I determined to have the whole benefit of the sacrifice. "So much for the Indians," I said. "What about Rosanna next?"

Sergeant Cuff shook his head.

"The mystery in that quarter is thicker than ever," he said. "I have traced her to a shop at Frizinghall, kept by a linen draper named Maltby. She bought nothing whatever at any of the other drapers' shops, or at any milliners' or tailors' shops; and she bought nothing at Maltby's but a piece of long cloth. She was very particular in choosing a certain quality. As to quantity, she bought enough to make a nightgown."

"Whose nightgown?" I asked.

"Her own, to be sure. Between twelve and three, on the Thursday morning, she must have slipped down to your young

The Moonstone

lady's room, to settle the hiding of the Moonstone while all the rest of you were in bed. In going back to her own room, her nightgown must have brushed the wet paint on the door. She couldn't wash out the stain; and she couldn't safely destroy the night-gown without first providing another like it, to make the inventory of her linen complete."

"What proves that it was Rosanna's nightgown?" I objected.

"The material she bought for making the substitute dress," answered the Sergeant. "If it had been Miss Verinder's nightgown, she would have had to buy lace, and frilling, and Lord knows what besides; and she wouldn't have had time to make it in one night. Plain long cloth means a plain servant's nightgown. No, no, Mr. Betteredge — all that is clear enough. The pinch of the question is — why, after having provided the substitute dress, does she hide the smeared nightgown, instead of destroying it? If the girl won't speak out, there is only one way of settling the difficulty. The hiding-place at the Shivering Sand must be searched — and the true state of the case will be discovered there."

"How are you to find the place?" I inquired.

"I am sorry to disappoint you," said the Sergeant — "but that's a secret which I mean to keep to myself."

(Not to irritate your curiosity, as he irritated mine, I may here inform you that he had come back from Frizinghall provided with a search-warrant. His experience in such matters told him that Rosanna was in all probability carrying about her a memorandum of the hiding-place, to guide her, in case she returned to it, under changed circumstances and after a lapse of time. Possessed of this memorandum, the Sergeant would be furnished with all that he could desire.)

"Now, Mr. Betteredge," he went on, "suppose we drop speculation, and get to business. I told Joyce to have an eye on Rosanna. Where is Joyce?"

Joyce was the Frizinghall policeman, who had been left by Superintendent Seegrave at Sergeant Cuff's disposal. The clock struck two, as he put the question; and, punctual to the moment, the carriage came round to take Miss Rachel to her aunt's.

"One thing at a time," said the Sergeant, stopping me as I was about to send in search of Joyce. "I must attend to Miss Verinder first."

As the rain was still threatening, it was the close carriage that had been appointed to take Miss Rachel to Frizinghall. Sergeant Cuff beckoned Samuel to come down to him from the rumble behind.

"You will see a friend of mine waiting among the trees, on this side of the lodge gate," he said. "My friend, without stopping the carriage, will get up into the rumble with you. You have nothing to do but to hold your tongue, and shut your eyes. Otherwise, you will get into trouble."

With that advice, he sent the footman back to his place. What Samuel thought I don't know. It was plain, to my mind, that Miss Rachel was to be privately kept in view from the time when she left our house — if she did leave it. A watch set on my young lady! A spy behind her in the rumble of her mother's carriage! I could have cut my own tongue out for having forgotten myself so far as to speak to Sergeant Cuff.

The first person to come out of the house was my lady. She stood aside, on the top step, posting herself there to see what happened. Not a word did she say, either to the Sergeant or to me. With her lips closed, and her arms folded in the light garden cloak which she had wrapped round her on coming into the air, there she stood, as still as a statue, waiting for her daughter to appear.

In a minute more, Miss Rachel came downstairs — very nicely dressed in some soft yellow stuff, that set off her dark complexion, and clipped her tight (in the form of a jacket) round the waist. She had a smart little straw hat on her head, with a white veil twisted round it. She had primrose-coloured gloves that fitted her hands like a second skin. Her beautiful black hair looked as smooth as satin under her hat. Her little ears were like rosy shells — they had a pearl dangling from each of them. She came swiftly out to us, as straight as a lily on its stem, and as lithe and supple in every movement she made as a young cat. Nothing that I could discover was altered in her pretty face, but her eyes and her lips. Her eyes were brighter and fiercer than I liked to see; and her lips had so completely lost their colour and

The Moonstone

their smile that I hardly knew them again. She kissed her mother in a hasty and sudden manner on the cheek. She said, "Try to forgive me, mamma"—and then pulled down her veil over her face so vehemently that she tore it. In another moment she had run down the steps, and had rushed into the carriage as if it was a hiding-place.

Sergeant Cuff was just as quick on his side. He put Samuel back, and stood before Miss Rachel, with the open carriage-door in his hand, at the instant when she settled herself in her place.

"What do you want?" says Miss Rachel, from behind her veil.

"I want to say one word to you, miss," answered the Sergeant, "before you go. I can't presume to stop your paying a visit to your aunt. I can only venture to say that your leaving us, as things are now, puts an obstacle in the way of my recovering your Diamond. Please to understand that; and now decide for yourself whether you go or stay."

Miss Rachel never even answered him. "Drive on, James!" she called out to the coachman.

Without another word, the Sergeant shut the carriage-door. Just as he closed it, Mr. Franklin came running down the steps. "Good-bye, Rachel," he said, holding out his hand.

"Drive on!" cried Miss Rachel, louder than ever, and taking no more notice of Mr. Franklin than she had taken of Sergeant Cuff.

Mr. Franklin stepped back thunderstruck, as well he might be. The coachman, not knowing what to do, looked towards my lady, still standing immovable on the top step. My lady, with anger and sorrow and shame all struggling together in her face, made him a sign to start the horses, and then turned back hastily into the house. Mr. Franklin, recovering the use of his speech, called after her, as the carriage drove off, "Aunt! you were quite right. Accept my thanks for all your kindness—and let me go."

My lady turned as though to speak to him. Then, as if distrusting herself, waved her hand kindly. "Let me see you, before you leave us, Franklin," she said, in a broken voice—and went on to her own room.

"Do me a last favour, Betteredge," says Mr. Franklin, turning to me, with the tears in his eyes. "Get me away to the train as soon as you can!"

He too went his way into the house. For the moment, Miss Rachel had completely unmanned him. Judge from that, how fond he must have been of her!

Sergeant Cuff and I were left face to face, at the bottom of the steps. The Sergeant stood with his face set towards a gap in the trees, commanding a view of one of the windings of the drive which led from the house. He had his hands in his pockets, and he was softly whistling "The Last Rose of Summer" to himself.

"There's a time for everything," I said savagely enough. "This isn't a time for whistling."

At that moment, the carriage appeared in the distance, through the gap, on its way to the lodge-gate. There was another man, besides Samuel, plainly visible in the rumble behind.

"All right!" said the Sergeant to himself. He turned round to me. "It's no time for whistling, Mr. Betteredge, as you say. It's time to take this business in hand, now, without sparing anybody. We'll begin with Rosanna Spearman. Where is Joyce?"

We both called for Joyce, and received no answer. I sent one of the stable-boys to look for him.

"You heard what I said to Miss Verinder?" remarked the Sergeant, while we were waiting. "And you saw how she received it? I tell her plainly that her leaving us will be an obstacle in the way of my recovering her Diamond—and she leaves, in the face of that statement! Your young lady has got a travelling companion in her mother's carriage, Mr. Betteredge—and the name of it is, the Moonstone."

I said nothing. I only held on like death to my belief in Miss Rachel.

The stable-boy came back, followed—very unwillingly, as it appeared to me—by Joyce.

"Where is Rosanna Spearman?" asked Sergeant Cuff.

The Moonstone

"I can't account for it, sir," Joyce began; "and I am very sorry. But somehow or other — —"

"Before I went to Frizinghall," said the Sergeant, cutting him short, "I told you to keep your eyes on Rosanna Spearman, without allowing her to discover that she was being watched. Do you mean to tell me that you have let her give you the slip?"

"I am afraid, sir," says Joyce, beginning to tremble, "that I was perhaps a little too careful not to let her discover me. There are such a many passages in the lower parts of this house— —"

"How long is it since you missed her?"

"Nigh on an hour since, sir."

"You can go back to your regular business at Frizinghall," said the Sergeant, speaking just as composedly as ever, in his usual quiet and dreary way. "I don't think your talents are at all in our line, Mr. Joyce. Your present form of employment is a trifle beyond you. Good morning."

The man slunk off. I find it very difficult to describe how I was affected by the discovery that Rosanna Spearman was missing. I seemed to be in fifty different minds about it, all at the same time. In that state, I stood staring at Sergeant Cuff— and my powers of language quite failed me.

"No, Mr. Betteredge," said the Sergeant, as if he had discovered the uppermost thought in me, and was picking it out to be answered, before all the rest. "Your young friend, Rosanna, won't slip through my fingers so easy as you think. As long as I know where Miss Verinder is, I have the means at my disposal of tracing Miss Verinder's accomplice. I prevented them from communicating last night. Very good. They will get together at Frizinghall, instead of getting together here. The present inquiry must be simply shifted (rather sooner than I had anticipated) from this house, to the house at which Miss Verinder is visiting. In the meantime, I'm afraid I must trouble you to call the servants together again."

I went round with him to the servants' hall. It is very disgraceful, but it is not the less true, that I had another attack of the detective-fever, when he said those last words. I forgot that I hated Sergeant Cuff. I seized him confidentially by the arm. I said, "For goodness' sake, tell us what you are going to do with the servants now?"

The great Cuff stood stock-still, and addressed himself in a kind of melancholy rapture to the empty air.

"If this man," said the Sergeant (apparently meaning me), "only understood the growing of roses he would be the most completely perfect character on the face of creation!" After that strong expression of feeling, he sighed, and put his arm through mine. "This is how it stands," he said, dropping down again to business. "Rosanna has done one of two things. She has either gone direct to Frizinghall (before I can get there), or she has gone first to visit her hiding-place at the Shivering Sand. The first thing to find out is, which of the servants saw the last of her before she left the house."

On instituting this inquiry, it turned out that the last person who had set eyes on Rosanna was Nancy, the kitchenmaid.

Nancy had seen her slip out with a letter in her hand, and stop the butcher's man who had just been delivering some meat at the back door. Nancy had heard her ask the man to post the letter when he got back to Frizinghall. The man had looked at the address, and had said it was a roundabout way of delivering a letter directed to Cobb's Hole, to post it at Frizinghall—and that, moreover, on a Saturday, which would prevent the letter from getting to its destination until Monday morning, Rosanna had answered that the delivery of the letter being delayed till Monday was of no importance. The only thing she wished to be sure of was that the man would do what she told him. The man had promised to do it, and had driven away. Nancy had been called back to her work in the kitchen. And no other person had seen anything afterwards of Rosanna Spearman.

"Well?" I asked, when we were alone again.

"Well," says the Sergeant. "I must go to Frizinghall."

"About the letter, sir?"

"Yes. The memorandum of the hiding-place is in that letter. I must see the address at the post-office. If it is the address I suspect, I shall pay our friend, Mrs. Yolland, another visit on Monday next."

I went with the Sergeant to order the pony-chaise. In the stable-yard we got a new light thrown on the missing girl.

CHAPTER XIX

The news of Rosanna's disappearance had, as it appeared, spread among the out-of-door servants. They too had made their inquiries; and they had just laid hands on a quick little imp, nicknamed "Duffy"—who was occasionally employed in weeding the garden, and who had seen Rosanna Spearman as lately as half-an-hour since. Duffy was certain that the girl had passed him in the fir-plantation, not walking, but running, in the direction of the sea-shore.

"Does this boy know the coast hereabouts?" asked Sergeant Cuff.

"He has been born and bred on the coast," I answered.

"Duffy!" says the Sergeant, "do you want to earn a shilling? If you do, come along with me. Keep the pony-chaise ready, Mr. Betteredge, till I come back."

He started for the Shivering Sand, at a rate that my legs (though well enough preserved for my time of life) had no hope of matching. Little Duffy, as the way is with the young savages in our parts when they are in high spirits, gave a howl, and trotted off at the Sergeant's heels.

Here again, I find it impossible to give anything like a clear account of the state of my mind in the interval after Sergeant Cuff had left us. A curious and stupefying restlessness got possession of me. I did a dozen different needless things in and out of the house, not one of which I can now remember. I don't even know how long it was after the Sergeant had gone to the sands, when Duffy came running back with a message for me. Sergeant Cuff had given the boy a leaf torn out of his pocket-book, on which was written in pencil, "Send me one of Rosanna Spearman's boots, and be quick about it."

I despatched the first woman-servant I could find to Rosanna's room; and I sent the boy back to say that I myself would follow him with the boot.

This, I am well aware, was not the quickest way to take of obeying the directions which I had received. But I was resolved to see for myself what new mystification was going on before I trusted Rosanna's boot in the Sergeant's hands. My old notion of screening the girl, if I could, seemed to have come back on me again, at the eleventh hour. This state of feeling (to say nothing of the detective-fever) hurried me off, as soon as I had got the boot, at the nearest approach to a run which a man turned seventy can reasonably hope to make.

As I got near the shore, the clouds gathered black, and the rain came down, drifting in great white sheets of water before the wind. I heard the thunder of the sea on the sand-bank at the mouth of the bay. A little further on, I passed the boy crouching for shelter under the lee of the sandhills. Then I saw the raging sea, and the rollers tumbling in on the sand-bank, and the driven rain sweeping over the waters like a flying garment, and the yellow wilderness of the beach with one solitary black figure standing on it—the figure of Sergeant Cuff.

He waved his hand towards the north, when he first saw me. "Keep on that side!" he shouted. "And come on down here to me!"

I went down to him, choking for breath, with my heart leaping as if it was like to leap out of me. I was past speaking. I had a hundred questions to put to him; and not one of them would pass my lips. His face frightened me. I saw a look in his eyes which was a look of horror. He snatched the boot out of my hand, and set it in a footmark on the sand, bearing south from us as we stood, and pointing straight towards the rocky ledge called the South Spit. The mark was not yet blurred out by the rain—and the girl's boot fitted it to a hair.

The Sergeant pointed to the boot in the footmark, without saying a word.

I caught at his arm, and tried to speak to him, and failed as I had failed when I tried before. He went on, following the footsteps down and down to where the rocks and the sand joined. The South Spit was just awash with the flowing tide; the waters heaved over the hidden face of the Shivering Sand. Now this way and now that, with an obstinate patience that was dreadful to see, Sergeant Cuff tried the boot in the footsteps, and always found it pointing the same way—straight to the rocks. Hunt as he might, no sign could he find anywhere of the footsteps walking from them.

He gave it up at last. Still keeping silence, he looked again at

The Moonstone

me; and then he looked out at the waters before us, heaving in deeper and deeper over the quicksand. I looked where he looked—and I saw his thought in his face. A dreadful dumb trembling crawled all over me on a sudden. I fell upon my knees on the beach.

"She has been back at the hiding-place," I heard the Sergeant say to himself. "Some fatal accident has happened to her on those rocks."

The girl's altered looks, and words, and actions—the numbed, deadened way in which she listened to me, and spoke to me—when I had found her sweeping the corridor but a few hours since, rose up in my mind, and warned me, even as the Sergeant spoke, that his guess was wide of the dreadful truth. I tried to tell him of the fear that had frozen me up. I tried to say, "The death she has died, Sergeant, was a death of her own seeking." No! the words wouldn't come. The dumb trembling held me in its grip. I couldn't feel the driving rain. I couldn't see the rising tide. As in the vision of a dream, the poor lost creature came back before me. I saw her again as I had seen her in the past time—on the morning when I went to fetch her into the house. I heard her again, telling me that the Shivering Sand seemed to draw her to it against her will, and wondering whether her grave was waiting for her there. The horror of it struck at me, in some unfathomable way, through my own child. My girl was just her age. My girl, tried as Rosanna was tried, might have lived that miserable life, and died this dreadful death.

The Sergeant kindly lifted me up, and turned me away from the sight of the place where she had perished.

With that relief, I began to fetch my breath again, and to see things about me, as things really were. Looking towards the sandhills, I saw the men-servants from out-of-doors, and the fisherman, named Yolland, all running down to us together; and all, having taken the alarm, calling out to know if the girl had been found. In the fewest words, the Sergeant showed them the evidence of the footmarks, and told them that a fatal accident must have happened to her. He then picked out the fisherman from the rest, and put a question to him, turning about again towards the sea: "Tell me," he said. "Could a boat have taken her off, in such weather as this, from those rocks where her footmarks stop?"

The fisherman pointed to the rollers tumbling in on the sand-bank, and to the great waves leaping up in clouds of foam against the headlands on either side of us.

"No boat that ever was built," he answered, "could have got to her through that."

Sergeant Cuff looked for the last time at the foot-marks on the sand, which the rain was now fast blurring out.

"There," he said, "is the evidence that she can't have left this place by land. And here," he went on, looking at the fisherman, "is the evidence that she can't have got away by sea." He stopped, and considered for a minute. "She was seen running towards this place, half an hour before I got here from the house," he said to Yolland. "Some time has passed since then. Call it, altogether, an hour ago. How high would the water be, at that time, on this side of the rocks?" He pointed to the south side—otherwise, the side which was not filled up by the quicksand.

"As the tide makes today," said the fisherman, "there wouldn't have been water enough to drown a kitten on that side of the Spit, an hour since."

Sergeant Cuff turned about northward, towards the quicksand.

"How much on this side?" he asked.

"Less still," answered Yolland. "The Shivering Sand would have been just awash, and no more."

The Sergeant turned to me, and said that the accident must have happened on the side of the quicksand. My tongue was loosened at that. "No accident!" I told him. "When she came to this place, she came weary of her life, to end it here."

He started back from me. "How do you know?" he asked. The rest of them crowded round. The Sergeant recovered himself instantly. He put them back from me; he said I was an old man; he said the discovery had shaken me; he said, "Let him alone a little." Then he turned to Yolland, and asked, "Is there any chance of finding her, when the tide ebbs again?" And Yolland answered, "None. What the Sand gets, the Sand keeps for ever." Having said that, the fisherman came a step nearer, and addressed himself to me.

"Mr. Betteredge," he said, "I have a word to say to you about the young woman's death. Four foot out, broadwise, along the side of the Spit, there's a shelf of rock, about half fathom down under the sand. My question is—why didn't she strike that? If she slipped, by accident, from off the Spit, she fell in where there's foothold at the bottom, at a depth that would barely cover her to the waist. She must have waded out, or jumped out, into the Deeps beyond—or she wouldn't be missing now. No accident, sir! The Deeps of the Quicksand have got her. And they have got her by her own act."

After that testimony from a man whose knowledge was to be relied on, the Sergeant was silent. The rest of us, like him, held our peace. With one accord, we all turned back up the slope of the beach.

At the sandhillocks we were met by the under-groom, running to us from the house. The lad is a good lad, and has an honest respect for me. He handed me a little note, with a decent sorrow in his face. "Penelope sent me with this, Mr. Betteredge," he said. "She found it in Rosanna's room."

It was her last farewell word to the old man who had done his best—thank God, always done his best—to befriend her.

"You have often forgiven me, Mr. Betteredge, in past times. When you next see the Shivering Sand, try to forgive me once more. I have found my grave where my grave was waiting for me. I have lived, and died, sir, grateful for your kindness."

There was no more than that. Little as it was, I hadn't manhood enough to hold up against it. Your tears come easy, when you're young, and beginning the world. Your tears come easy, when you're old, and leaving it. I burst out crying.

Sergeant Cuff took a step nearer to me—meaning kindly, I don't doubt. I shrank back from him. "Don't touch me," I said. "It's the dread of you, that has driven her to it."

"You are wrong, Mr. Betteredge," he answered, quietly. "But there will be time enough to speak of it when we are indoors again."

I followed the rest of them, with the help of the groom's arm. Through the driving rain we went back — to meet the trouble and the terror that were waiting for us at the house.

CHAPTER XX

Those in front had spread the news before us. We found the servants in a state of panic. As we passed my lady's door, it was thrown open violently from the inner side. My mistress came out among us (with Mr. Franklin following, and trying vainly to compose her), quite beside herself with the horror of the thing.

"You are answerable for this!" she cried out, threatening the Sergeant wildly with her hand. "Gabriel! give that wretch his money—and release me from the sight of him!"

The Sergeant was the only one among us who was fit to cope with her—being the only one among us who was in possession of himself.

"I am no more answerable for this distressing calamity, my lady, than you are," he said. "If, in half an hour from this, you still insist on my leaving the house, I will accept your ladyship's dismissal, but not your ladyship's money."

It was spoken very respectfully, but very firmly at the same time—and it had its effect on my mistress as well as on me. She suffered Mr. Franklin to lead her back into the room. As the door closed on the two, the Sergeant, looking about among the women-servants in his observant way, noticed that while all the rest were merely frightened, Penelope was in tears. "When your father has changed his wet clothes," he said to her, "come and speak to us, in your father's room."

Before the half-hour was out, I had got my dry clothes on, and had lent Sergeant Cuff such change of dress as he required. Penelope came in to us to hear what the Sergeant wanted with her. I don't think I ever felt what a good dutiful daughter I had, so strongly as I felt it at that moment. I took her and sat her on my knee and I prayed God bless her. She hid her head on my bosom, and put her arms round my neck—and we waited a little while in silence. The poor dead girl must have been at the bottom of it, I think, with my daughter and with me. The Sergeant went to the window, and stood there looking out. I thought it right to thank him for considering us both in this way—and I did.

People in high life have all the luxuries to themselves— among others, the luxury of indulging their feelings. People in low life have no such privilege. Necessity, which spares our betters, has no pity on us. We learn to put our feelings back into ourselves, and to jog on with our duties as patiently as may be. I don't complain of this—I only notice it. Penelope and I were ready for the Sergeant, as soon as the Sergeant was ready on his side. Asked if she knew what had led her fellow-servant to destroy herself, my daughter answered (as you will foresee) that it was for love of Mr. Franklin Blake. Asked next, if she had mentioned this notion of hers to any other person, Penelope answered, "I have not mentioned it, for Rosanna's sake." I felt it necessary to add a word to this. I said, "And for Mr. Franklin's sake, my dear, as well. If Rosanna has died for love of him, it is not with his knowledge or by his fault. Let him leave the house today, if he does leave it, without the useless pain of knowing the truth." Sergeant Cuff said, "Quite right," and fell silent again; comparing Penelope's notion (as it seemed to me) with some other notion of his own which he kept to himself.

At the end of the half-hour, my mistress's bell rang.

On my way to answer it, I met Mr. Franklin coming out of his aunt's sitting-room. He mentioned that her ladyship was ready to see Sergeant Cuff—in my presence as before—and he added that he himself wanted to say two words to the Sergeant first. On our way back to my room, he stopped, and looked at the railway time-table in the hall.

"Are you really going to leave us, sir?" I asked. "Miss Rachel will surely come right again, if you only give her time?"

"She will come right again," answered Mr. Franklin, "when she hears that I have gone away, and that she will see me no more."

I thought he spoke in resentment of my young lady's treatment of him. But it was not so. My mistress had noticed, from the time when the police first came into the house, that the bare mention of him was enough to set Miss Rachel's temper in a flame. He had been too fond of his cousin to like to confess this to himself, until the truth had been forced on him, when she drove off to her aunt's. His eyes once opened in that cruel way which you know of, Mr. Franklin had taken his resolution—the one resolution which a man of any spirit could take—to leave the house.

What he had to say to the Sergeant was spoken in my presence. He described her ladyship as willing to acknowledge that she had spoken over-hastily. And he asked if Sergeant Cuff would consent—in that case—to accept his fee, and to leave the matter of the Diamond where the matter stood now. The Sergeant answered, "No, sir. My fee is paid me for doing my duty. I decline to take it, until my duty is done."

"I don't understand you," says Mr. Franklin.

"I'll explain myself, sir," says the Sergeant. "When I came here, I undertook to throw the necessary light on the matter of the missing Diamond. I am now ready, and waiting to redeem my pledge. When I have stated the case to Lady Verinder as the case now stands, and when I have told her plainly what course of action to take for the recovery of the Moonstone, the responsibility will be off my shoulders. Let her ladyship decide, after that, whether she does, or does not, allow me to go on. I shall then have done what I undertook to do—and I'll take my fee."

In those words Sergeant Cuff reminded us that, even in the Detective Police, a man may have a reputation to lose.

The view he took was so plainly the right one, that there was no more to be said. As I rose to conduct him to my lady's room, he asked if Mr. Franklin wished to be present. Mr. Franklin answered, "Not unless Lady Verinder desires it." He added, in a whisper to me, as I was following the Sergeant out, "I know what that man is going to say about Rachel; and I am too fond of her to hear it, and keep my temper. Leave me by myself."

I left him, miserable enough, leaning on the sill of my window, with his face hidden in his hands and Penelope peeping through the door, longing to comfort him. In Mr. Franklin's place, I should have called her in. When you are ill-used by one woman, there is great comfort in telling it to another—because, nine times out of ten, the other always takes your side. Perhaps, when my back was turned, he did call her in? In that case it is only doing my daughter justice to declare that she would stick at nothing, in the way of comforting Mr. Franklin Blake.

In the meantime, Sergeant Cuff and I proceeded to my lady's room.

At the last conference we had held with her, we had found her not over willing to lift her eyes from the book which she had on the table. On this occasion there was a change for the better. She met the Sergeant's eye with an eye that was as steady as his own. The family spirit showed itself in every line of her face; and I knew that Sergeant Cuff would meet his match, when a woman like my mistress was strung up to hear the worst he could say to her.

CHAPTER XXI

The first words, when we had taken our seats, were spoken by my lady.

"Sergeant Cuff," she said, "there was perhaps some excuse for the inconsiderate manner in which I spoke to you half an hour since. I have no wish, however, to claim that excuse. I say, with perfect sincerity, that I regret it, if I wronged you."

The grace of voice and manner with which she made him that atonement had its due effect on the Sergeant. He requested permission to justify himself—putting his justification as an act of respect to my mistress. It was impossible, he said, that he could be in any way responsible for the calamity, which had shocked us all, for this sufficient reason, that his success in bringing his inquiry to its proper end depended on his neither saying nor doing anything that could alarm Rosanna Spearman. He appealed to me to testify whether he had, or had not, carried that object out. I could, and did, bear witness that he had. And there, as I thought, the matter might have been judiciously left to come to an end.

Sergeant Cuff, however, took it a step further, evidently (as you shall now judge) with the purpose of forcing the most painful of all possible explanations to take place between her ladyship and himself.

"I have heard a motive assigned for the young woman's suicide," said the Sergeant, "which may possibly be the right one. It is a motive quite unconnected with the case which I am conducting here. I am bound to add, however, that my own opinion points the other way. Some unbearable anxiety in connexion with the missing Diamond, has, I believe, driven the poor creature to her own destruction. I don't pretend to know what that unbearable anxiety may have been. But I think (with your ladyship's permission) I can lay my hand on a person who is capable of deciding whether I am right or wrong."

"Is the person now in the house?" my mistress asked, after waiting a little.

"The person has left the house, my lady."

That answer pointed as straight to Miss Rachel as straight

could be. A silence dropped on us which I thought would never come to an end. Lord! how the wind howled, and how the rain drove at the window, as I sat there waiting for one or other of them to speak again!

"Be so good as to express yourself plainly," said my lady. "Do you refer to my daughter?"

"I do," said Sergeant Cuff, in so many words.

My mistress had her cheque-book on the table when we entered the room — no doubt to pay the Sergeant his fee. She now put it back in the drawer. It went to my heart to see how her poor hand trembled — the hand that had loaded her old servant with benefits; the hand that, I pray God, may take mine, when my time comes, and I leave my place for ever!

"I had hoped," said my lady, very slowly and quietly, "to have recompensed your services, and to have parted with you without Miss Verinder's name having been openly mentioned between us as it has been mentioned now. My nephew has probably said something of this, before you came into my room?"

"Mr. Blake gave his message, my lady. And I gave Mr. Blake a reason— —"

"It is needless to tell me your reason. After what you have just said, you know as well as I do that you have gone too far to go back. I owe it to myself, and I owe it to my child, to insist on your remaining here, and to insist on your speaking out."

The Sergeant looked at his watch.

"If there had been time, my lady," he answered, "I should have preferred writing my report, instead of communicating it by word of mouth. But, if this inquiry is to go on, time is of too much importance to be wasted in writing. I am ready to go into the matter at once. It is a very painful matter for me to speak of, and for you to hear."

There my mistress stopped him once more.

"I may possibly make it less painful to you, and to my good servant and friend here," she said, "if I set the example of speaking boldly, on my side. You suspect Miss Verinder of deceiving us all, by secreting the Diamond for some purpose of her own? Is that true?"

"Quite true, my lady."

"Very well. Now, before you begin, I have to tell you, as Miss Verinder's mother, that she is absolutely incapable of doing what you suppose her to have done. Your knowledge of her character dates from a day or two since. My knowledge of her character dates from the beginning of her life. State your suspicion of her as strongly as you please—it is impossible that you can offend me by doing so. I am sure, beforehand, that (with all your experience) the circumstances have fatally misled you in this case. Mind! I am in possession of no private information. I am as absolutely shut out of my daughter's confidence as you are. My one reason for speaking positively, is the reason you have heard already. I know my child."

She turned to me, and gave me her hand. I kissed it in silence. "You may go on," she said, facing the Sergeant again as steadily as ever.

Sergeant Cuff bowed. My mistress had produced but one effect on him. His hatchet-face softened for a moment, as if he was sorry for her. As to shaking him in his own conviction, it was plain to see that she had not moved him by a single inch. He settled himself in his chair; and he began his vile attack on Miss Rachel's character in these words:

"I must ask your ladyship," he said, "to look this matter in the face, from my point of view as well as from yours. Will you please to suppose yourself coming down here, in my place, and with my experience? and will you allow me to mention very briefly what that experience has been?"

My mistress signed to him that she would do this. The Sergeant went on:

"For the last twenty years," he said, "I have been largely employed in cases of family scandal, acting in the capacity of confidential man. The one result of my domestic practice which has any bearing on the matter now in hand, is a result which I may state in two words. It is well within my experience, that young ladies of rank and position do occasionally have private debts which they dare not acknowledge to their nearest relatives and friends. Sometimes, the milliner and the jeweller are at the bottom of it. Sometimes, the money is wanted for purposes which I don't suspect in this case, and which I won't shock you by mentioning. Bear in mind what I have said, my lady—and now let us see how events in this house have forced me back on my own experience, whether I liked it or not!"

He considered with himself for a moment, and went on—with a horrid clearness that obliged you to understand him; with an abominable justice that favoured nobody.

"My first information relating to the loss of the Moonstone," said the Sergeant, "came to me from Superintendent Seegrave. He proved to my complete satisfaction that he was perfectly incapable of managing the case. The one thing he said which struck me as worth listening to, was this—that Miss Verinder had declined to be questioned by him, and had spoken to him with a perfectly incomprehensible rudeness and contempt. I thought this curious—but I attributed it mainly to some clumsiness on the Superintendent's part which might have offended the young lady. After that, I put it by in my mind, and applied myself, single-handed, to the case. It ended, as you are aware, in the discovery of the smear on the door, and in Mr. Franklin Blake's evidence satisfying me, that this same smear, and the loss of the Diamond, were pieces of the same puzzle. So far, if I suspected anything, I suspected that the Moonstone had been stolen, and that one of the servants might prove to be the thief. Very good. In this state of things, what happens? Miss Verinder suddenly comes out of her room, and speaks to me. I observe three suspicious appearances in that young lady. She is still violently agitated, though more than four-and-twenty hours have passed since the Diamond was lost. She treats me as she has already treated Superintendent Seegrave. And she is mortally offended with Mr. Franklin Blake. Very good again. Here (I say to myself) is a young lady who has lost a valuable jewel—a young lady, also, as my own eyes and ears inform me, who is of an impetuous temperament. Under these circumstances, and with that character, what does she do? She betrays an incomprehensible resentment against Mr. Blake, Mr. Superintendent, and myself—otherwise, the very three people who have all, in their different ways, been trying to help her to recover her lost jewel. Having brought my inquiry to that point—then, my lady, and not till then, I begin to look back into my own mind for my own experience. My own experience

The Moonstone

explains Miss Verinder's otherwise incomprehensible conduct. It associates her with those other young ladies that I know of. It tells me she has debts she daren't acknowledge, that must be paid. And it sets me asking myself, whether the loss of the Diamond may not mean—that the Diamond must be secretly pledged to pay them. That is the conclusion which my experience draws from plain facts. What does your ladyship's experience say against it?"

"What I have said already," answered my mistress. "The circumstances have misled you."

I said nothing on my side. Robinson Crusoe—God knows how—had got into my muddled old head. If Sergeant Cuff had found himself, at that moment, transported to a desert island, without a man Friday to keep him company, or a ship to take him off—he would have found himself exactly where I wished him to be! (Nota bene:—I am an average good Christian, when you don't push my Christianity too far. And all the rest of you—which is a great comfort—are, in this respect, much the same as I am.)

Sergeant Cuff went on:

"Right or wrong, my lady," he said, "having drawn my conclusion, the next thing to do was to put it to the test. I suggested to your ladyship the examination of all the wardrobes in the house. It was a means of finding the article of dress which had, in all probability, made the smear; and it was a means of putting my conclusion to the test. How did it turn out? Your ladyship consented; Mr. Blake consented; Mr. Ablewhite consented. Miss Verinder alone stopped the whole proceeding by refusing point-blank. That result satisfied me that my view was the right one. If your ladyship and Mr. Betteredge persist in not agreeing with me, you must be blind to what happened before you this very day. In your hearing, I told the young lady that her leaving the house (as things were then) would put an obstacle in the way of my recovering her jewel. You saw yourselves that she drove off in the face of that statement. You saw yourself that, so far from forgiving Mr. Blake for having done more than all the rest of you to put the clue into my hands, she publicly insulted Mr. Blake, on the steps of her mother's house. What do these things mean? If Miss Verinder is not privy to the suppression of the Diamond, what do these things mean?"

This time he looked my way. It was downright frightful to hear him piling up proof after proof against Miss Rachel, and to know, while one was longing to defend her, that there was no disputing the truth of what he said. I am (thank God!) constitutionally superior to reason. This enabled me to hold firm to my lady's view, which was my view also. This roused my spirit, and made me put a bold face on it before Sergeant Cuff. Profit, good friends, I beseech you, by my example. It will save you from many troubles of the vexing sort. Cultivate a superiority to reason, and see how you pare the claws of all the sensible people when they try to scratch you for your own good!

Finding that I made no remark, and that my mistress made no remark, Sergeant Cuff proceeded. Lord! how it did enrage me to notice that he was not in the least put out by our silence!

"There is the case, my lady, as it stands against Miss Verinder alone," he said. "The next thing is to put the case as it stands against Miss Verinder and the deceased Rosanna Spearman taken together. We will go back for a moment, if you please, to your daughter's refusal to let her wardrobe be examined. My mind being made up, after that circumstance, I had two questions to consider next. First, as to the right method of conducting my inquiry. Second, as to whether Miss Verinder had an accomplice among the female servants in the house. After carefully thinking it over, I determined to conduct the inquiry in, what we should call at our office, a highly irregular manner. For this reason: I had a family scandal to deal with, which it was my business to keep within the family limits. The less noise made, and the fewer strangers employed to help me, the better. As to the usual course of taking people in custody on suspicion, going before the magistrate, and all the rest of it—nothing of the sort was to be thought of, when your ladyship's daughter was (as I believed) at the bottom of the whole business. In this case, I felt that a person of Mr. Betteredge's character and position in the house—knowing the servants as he did, and having the honour of the family at heart—would be safer to take as an assistant than any other person whom I could lay my hand on. I should have tried Mr. Blake as well—but for one obstacle in the way. He saw the drift of my proceedings at a very early date; and, with his interest in Miss Verinder, any mutual understanding was impossible between him and me. I trouble your ladyship with these particulars to show you that I have kept the family secret within the family circle. I am the only outsider who knows it—and my professional existence depends on holding my tongue."

Here I felt that my professional existence depended on not holding my tongue. To be held up before my mistress, in my old age, as a sort of deputy-policeman, was, once again, more than my Christianity was strong enough to bear.

"I beg to inform your ladyship," I said, "that I never, to my knowledge, helped this abominable detective business, in any way, from first to last; and I summon Sergeant Cuff to contradict me, if he dares!"

Having given vent in those words, I felt greatly relieved. Her ladyship honoured me by a little friendly pat on the shoulder. I looked with righteous indignation at the Sergeant, to see what he thought of such a testimony as that! The Sergeant looked back like a lamb, and seemed to like me better than ever.

My lady informed him that he might continue his statement. "I understand," she said, "that you have honestly done your best, in what you believe to be my interest. I am ready to hear what you have to say next."

"What I have to say next," answered Sergeant Cuff, "relates to Rosanna Spearman. I recognised the young woman, as your ladyship may remember, when she brought the washing-book into this room. Up to that time I was inclined to doubt whether Miss Verinder had trusted her secret to anyone. When I saw Rosanna, I altered my mind. I suspected her at once of being privy to the suppression of the Diamond. The poor creature has met her death by a dreadful end, and I don't want your ladyship to think, now she's gone, that I was unduly hard on her. If this had been a common case of thieving, I should have given Rosanna the benefit of the doubt just as freely as I should have given it to any of the other servants in the house. Our experience of the Reformatory woman is, that when tried in service—and when kindly and judiciously treated—they prove themselves in the majority of cases to be honestly penitent, and honestly worthy of the pains taken with them. But this was not a common case of thieving. It was a case—in my mind—of a deeply planned fraud, with the owner of the Diamond at the bottom of it. Holding this view, the first consideration which naturally presented itself to me, in connection with Rosanna, was this: Would Miss Verinder be satisfied (begging your ladyship's pardon) with leading us all to think that the Moonstone was merely lost? Or would she go a step further, and delude us into believing that the Moonstone was stolen? In the latter event there was Rosanna Spearman—with the character of a thief—ready to her hand; the person of all others to lead your ladyship off, and to lead me off, on a false scent."

Was it possible (I asked myself) that he could put his case against Miss Rachel and Rosanna in a more horrid point of view than this? It was possible, as you shall now see.

"I had another reason for suspecting the deceased woman," he said, "which appears to me to have been stronger still. Who would be the very person to help Miss Verinder in raising money privately on the Diamond? Rosanna Spearman. No young lady in Miss Verinder's position could manage such a risky matter as that by herself. A go-between she must have, and who so fit, I ask again, as Rosanna Spearman? Your ladyship's deceased housemaid was at the top of her profession when she was a thief. She had relations, to my certain knowledge, with one of the few men in London (in the money-lending line) who would advance a large sum on such a notable jewel as the Moonstone, without asking awkward questions, or insisting on awkward conditions. Bear this in mind, my lady; and now let me show you how my suspicions have been justified by Rosanna's own acts, and by the plain inferences to be drawn from them."

He thereupon passed the whole of Rosanna's proceedings under review. You are already as well acquainted with those proceedings as I am; and you will understand how unanswerably this part of his report fixed the guilt of being concerned in the disappearance of the Moonstone on the memory of the poor dead girl. Even my mistress was daunted by what he said now. She made him no answer when he had done. It didn't seem to matter to the Sergeant whether he was answered or not. On he went (devil take him!), just as steady as ever.

"Having stated the whole case as I understand it," he said, "I have only to tell your ladyship, now, what I propose to do next. I see two ways of bringing this inquiry successfully to an end. One of those ways I look upon as a certainty. The other, I admit, is a bold experiment, and nothing more. Your ladyship shall decide. Shall we take the certainty first?"

My mistress made him a sign to take his own way, and choose for himself.

"Thank you," said the Sergeant. "We'll begin with the certainty, as your ladyship is so good as to leave it to me. Whether Miss Verinder remains at Frizinghall, or whether she returns here, I propose, in either case, to keep a careful watch on all her proceedings—on the people she sees, on the rides and walks she may take, and on the letters she may write and receive."

"What next?" asked my mistress.

"I shall next," answered the Sergeant, "request your ladyship's leave to introduce into the house, as a servant in the place of Rosanna Spearman, a woman accustomed to private inquiries of this sort, for whose discretion I can answer."

"What next?" repeated my mistress.

"Next," proceeded the Sergeant, "and last, I propose to send one of my brother-officers to make an arrangement with that money-lender in London, whom I mentioned just now as formerly acquainted with Rosanna Spearman—and whose name and address, your ladyship may rely on it, have been communicated by Rosanna to Miss Verinder. I don't deny that the course of action I am now suggesting will cost money, and consume time. But the result is certain. We run a line round the Moonstone, and we draw that line closer and closer till we find it in Miss Verinder's possession, supposing she decides to keep it. If her debts press, and she decides on sending it away, then we have our man ready, and we meet the Moonstone on its arrival in London."

To hear her own daughter made the subject of such a proposal as this, stung my mistress into speaking angrily for the first time.

"Consider your proposal declined, in every particular," she

said. "And go on to your other way of bringing the inquiry to an end."

"My other way," said the Sergeant, going on as easy as ever, "is to try that bold experiment to which I have alluded. I think I have formed a pretty correct estimate of Miss Verinder's temperament. She is quite capable (according to my belief) of committing a daring fraud. But she is too hot and impetuous in temper, and too little accustomed to deceit as a habit, to act the hypocrite in small things, and to restrain herself under all provocations. Her feelings, in this case, have repeatedly got beyond her control, at the very time when it was plainly her interest to conceal them. It is on this peculiarity in her character that I now propose to act. I want to give her a great shock suddenly, under circumstances that will touch her to the quick. In plain English, I want to tell Miss Verinder, without a word of warning, of Rosanna's death—on the chance that her own better feelings will hurry her into making a clean breast of it. Does your ladyship accept that alternative?"

My mistress astonished me beyond all power of expression. She answered him on the instant:

"Yes; I do."

"The pony-chaise is ready," said the Sergeant. "I wish your ladyship good morning."

My lady held up her hand, and stopped him at the door.

"My daughter's better feelings shall be appealed to, as you propose," she said. "But I claim the right, as her mother, of putting her to the test myself. You will remain here, if you please; and I will go to Frizinghall."

For once in his life, the great Cuff stood speechless with amazement, like an ordinary man.

My mistress rang the bell, and ordered her waterproof things. It was still pouring with rain; and the close carriage had gone, as you know, with Miss Rachel to Frizinghall. I tried to dissuade her ladyship from facing the severity of the weather. Quite useless! I asked leave to go with her, and hold the umbrella. She wouldn't hear of it. The pony-chaise came round, with the groom in charge. "You may rely on two things," she said to Sergeant Cuff, in the hall. "I will try the experiment on

Miss Verinder as boldly as you could try it yourself. And I will inform you of the result, either personally or by letter, before the last train leaves for London tonight."

With that, she stepped into the chaise, and, taking the reins herself, drove off to Frizinghall.

CHAPTER XXII

My mistress having left us, I had leisure to think of Sergeant Cuff. I found him sitting in a snug corner of the hall, consulting his memorandum book, and curling up viciously at the corners of the lips.

"Making notes of the case?" I asked.

"No," said the Sergeant. "Looking to see what my next professional engagement is."

"Oh!" I said. "You think it's all over then, here?"

"I think," answered Sergeant Cuff, "that Lady Verinder is one of the cleverest women in England. I also think a rose much better worth looking at than a diamond. Where is the gardener, Mr. Betteredge?"

There was no getting a word more out of him on the matter of the Moonstone. He had lost all interest in his own inquiry; and he would persist in looking for the gardener. An hour afterwards, I heard them at high words in the conservatory, with the dog-rose once more at the bottom of the dispute.

In the meantime, it was my business to find out whether Mr. Franklin persisted in his resolution to leave us by the afternoon train. After having been informed of the conference in my lady's room, and of how it had ended, he immediately decided on waiting to hear the news from Frizinghall. This very natural alteration in his plans—which, with ordinary people, would have led to nothing in particular—proved, in Mr. Franklin's case, to have one objectionable result. It left him unsettled, with a legacy of idle time on his hands, and, in so doing, it let out all the foreign sides of his character, one on the top of another, like rats out of a bag.

Now as an Italian-Englishman, now as a German-Englishman, and now as a French-Englishman, he drifted in and out of all the sitting-rooms in the house, with nothing to talk of but Miss Rachel's treatment of him; and with nobody to address himself to but me. I found him (for example) in the library, sitting under the map of Modern Italy, and quite unaware of any other method of meeting his troubles, except the method of talking about them. "I have several worthy aspirations,

Betteredge; but what am I to do with them now? I am full of dormant good qualities, if Rachel would only have helped me to bring them out!" He was so eloquent in drawing the picture of his own neglected merits, and so pathetic in lamenting over it when it was done, that I felt quite at my wits' end how to console him, when it suddenly occurred to me that here was a case for the wholesome application of a bit of Robinson Crusoe. I hobbled out to my own room, and hobbled back with that immortal book. Nobody in the library! The map of Modern Italy stared at me; and I stared at the map of Modern Italy.

I tried the drawing-room. There was his handkerchief on the floor, to prove that he had drifted in. And there was the empty room to prove that he had drifted out again.

I tried the dining-room, and discovered Samuel with a biscuit and a glass of sherry, silently investigating the empty air. A minute since, Mr. Franklin had rung furiously for a little light refreshment. On its production, in a violent hurry, by Samuel, Mr. Franklin had vanished before the bell downstairs had quite done ringing with the pull he had given to it.

I tried the morning-room, and found him at last. There he was at the window, drawing hieroglyphics with his finger in the damp on the glass.

"Your sherry is waiting for you, sir," I said to him. I might as well have addressed myself to one of the four walls of the room; he was down in the bottomless deep of his own meditations, past all pulling up. "How do you explain Rachel's conduct, Betteredge?" was the only answer I received. Not being ready with the needful reply, I produced Robinson Crusoe, in which I am firmly persuaded some explanation might have been found, if we had only searched long enough for it. Mr. Franklin shut up Robinson Crusoe, and floundered into his German-English gibberish on the spot. "Why not look into it?" he said, as if I had personally objected to looking into it. "Why the devil lose your patience, Betteredge, when patience is all that's wanted to arrive at the truth? Don't interrupt me. Rachel's conduct is perfectly intelligible, if you will only do her the common justice to take the Objective view first, and the Subjective view next, and the Objective-Subjective view to wind up with. What do we know? We know that the loss of the Moonstone, on Thursday morning last, threw her into a state of nervous excitement, from which she has not recovered yet. Do you mean to deny the Objective view, so far? Very well, then—don't interrupt me. Now, being in a state of nervous excitement, how are we to expect that she should behave as she might otherwise have behaved to any of the people about her? Arguing in this way, from within-outwards, what do we reach? We reach the Subjective view. I defy you to controvert the Subjective view. Very well then—what follows? Good Heavens! the Objective-Subjective explanation follows, of course! Rachel, properly speaking, is not Rachel, but Somebody Else. Do I mind being cruelly treated by Somebody Else? You are unreasonable enough, Betteredge; but you can hardly accuse me of that. Then how does it end? It ends, in spite of your confounded English narrowness and prejudice, in my being perfectly happy and comfortable. Where's the sherry?"

My head was by this time in such a condition, that I was not quite sure whether it was my own head, or Mr. Franklin's. In this deplorable state, I contrived to do, what I take to have been, three Objective things. I got Mr. Franklin his sherry; I retired to my own room; and I solaced myself with the most composing pipe of tobacco I ever remember to have smoked in my life.

Don't suppose, however, that I was quit of Mr. Franklin on such easy terms as these. Drifting again, out of the morning-room into the hall, he found his way to the offices next, smelt my pipe, and was instantly reminded that he had been simple enough to give up smoking for Miss Rachel's sake. In the twinkling of an eye, he burst in on me with his cigar-case, and came out strong on the one everlasting subject, in his neat, witty, unbelieving, French way. "Give me a light, Betteredge. Is it conceivable that a man can have smoked as long as I have without discovering that there is a complete system for the treatment of women at the bottom of his cigar-case? Follow me carefully, and I will prove it in two words. You choose a cigar, you try it, and it disappoints you. What do you do upon that? You throw it away and try another. Now observe the application! You choose a woman, you try her, and she breaks your heart. Fool! take a lesson from your cigar-case. Throw her away, and try another!"

I shook my head at that. Wonderfully clever, I dare say, but my own experience was dead against it. "In the time of the late

Mrs. Betteredge," I said, "I felt pretty often inclined to try your philosophy, Mr. Franklin. But the law insists on your smoking your cigar, sir, when you have once chosen it." I pointed that observation with a wink. Mr. Franklin burst out laughing—and we were as merry as crickets, until the next new side of his character turned up in due course. So things went on with my young master and me; and so (while the Sergeant and the gardener were wrangling over the roses) we two spent the interval before the news came back from Frizinghall.

The pony-chaise returned a good half hour before I had ventured to expect it. My lady had decided to remain for the present, at her sister's house. The groom brought two letters from his mistress; one addressed to Mr. Franklin, and the other to me.

Mr. Franklin's letter I sent to him in the library—into which refuge his driftings had now taken him for the second time. My own letter, I read in my own room. A cheque, which dropped out when I opened it, informed me (before I had mastered the contents) that Sergeant Cuff's dismissal from the inquiry after the Moonstone was now a settled thing.

I sent to the conservatory to say that I wished to speak to the Sergeant directly. He appeared, with his mind full of the gardener and the dog-rose, declaring that the equal of Mr. Begbie for obstinacy never had existed yet, and never would exist again. I requested him to dismiss such wretched trifling as this from our conversation, and to give his best attention to a really serious matter. Upon that he exerted himself sufficiently to notice the letter in my hand. "Ah!" he said in a weary way, "you have heard from her ladyship. Have I anything to do with it, Mr. Betteredge?"

"You shall judge for yourself, Sergeant." I thereupon read him the letter (with my best emphasis and discretion), in the following words:

"MY GOOD GABRIEL,—I request that you will inform Sergeant Cuff, that I have performed the promise I made to him; with this result, so far as Rosanna Spearman is concerned. Miss Verinder solemnly declares, that she has never spoken a word in private to Rosanna, since that unhappy woman first entered my house. They never met, even accidentally, on the night when the Diamond was lost; and no communication of any sort whatever took place between them, from the Thursday morning when the alarm was first raised in the house, to this present Saturday afternoon, when Miss Verinder left us. After telling my daughter suddenly, and in so many words, of Rosanna Spearman's suicide—this is what has come of it."

Having reached that point, I looked up, and asked Sergeant Cuff what he thought of the letter, so far?

"I should only offend you if I expressed my opinion," answered the Sergeant. "Go on, Mr. Betteredge," he said, with the most exasperating resignation, "go on."

When I remembered that this man had had the audacity to complain of our gardener's obstinacy, my tongue itched to "go on" in other words than my mistress's. This time, however, my Christianity held firm. I proceeded steadily with her ladyship's letter:

"Having appealed to Miss Verinder in the manner which the officer thought most desirable, I spoke to her next in the manner which I myself thought most likely to impress her. On two different occasions, before my daughter left my roof, I privately warned her that she was exposing herself to suspicion of the most unendurable and most degrading kind. I have now told her, in the plainest terms, that my apprehensions have been realised.

"Her answer to this, on her own solemn affirmation, is as plain as words can be. In the first place, she owes no money privately to any living creature. In the second place, the Diamond is not now, and never has been, in her possession, since she put it into her cabinet on Wednesday night.

"The confidence which my daughter has placed in me goes no further than this. She maintains an obstinate silence, when I ask her if she can explain the disappearance of the Diamond. She refuses, with tears, when I appeal to her to speak out for my sake. 'The day will come when you will know why I am careless about being suspected, and why I am silent even to you. I have done much to make my mother pity me—nothing to make my mother blush for me.' Those are my daughter's own words.

"After what has passed between the officer and me, I think—

stranger as he is — that he should be made acquainted with what Miss Verinder has said, as well as you. Read my letter to him, and then place in his hands the cheque which I enclose. In resigning all further claim on his services, I have only to say that I am convinced of his honesty and his intelligence; but I am more firmly persuaded than ever, that the circumstances, in this case, have fatally misled him."

There the letter ended. Before presenting the cheque, I asked Sergeant Cuff if he had any remark to make.

"It's no part of my duty, Mr. Betteredge," he answered, "to make remarks on a case, when I have done with it."

I tossed the cheque across the table to him. "Do you believe in that part of her ladyship's letter?" I said, indignantly.

The Sergeant looked at the cheque, and lifted up his dismal eyebrows in acknowledgment of her ladyship's liberality.

"This is such a generous estimate of the value of my time," he said, "that I feel bound to make some return for it. I'll bear in mind the amount in this cheque, Mr. Betteredge, when the occasion comes round for remembering it."

"What do you mean?" I asked.

"Her ladyship has smoothed matters over for the present very cleverly," said the Sergeant. "But this family scandal is of the sort that bursts up again when you least expect it. We shall have more detective-business on our hands, sir, before the Moonstone is many months older."

If those words meant anything, and if the manner in which he spoke them meant anything — it came to this. My mistress's letter had proved, to his mind, that Miss Rachel was hardened enough to resist the strongest appeal that could be addressed to her, and that she had deceived her own mother (good God, under what circumstances!) by a series of abominable lies. How other people, in my place, might have replied to the Sergeant, I don't know. I answered what he said in these plain terms:

"Sergeant Cuff, I consider your last observation as an insult to my lady and her daughter!"

"Mr. Betteredge, consider it as a warning to yourself, and you will be nearer the mark."

Hot and angry as I was, the infernal confidence with which he gave me that answer closed my lips.

I walked to the window to compose myself. The rain had given over; and, who should I see in the court-yard, but Mr. Begbie, the gardener, waiting outside to continue the dog-rose controversy with Sergeant Cuff.

"My compliments to the Sairgent," said Mr. Begbie, the moment he set eyes on me. "If he's minded to walk to the station, I'm agreeable to go with him."

"What!" cries the Sergeant, behind me, "are you not convinced yet?"

"The de'il a bit I'm convinced!" answered Mr. Begbie.

"Then I'll walk to the station!" says the Sergeant.

"Then I'll meet you at the gate!" says Mr. Begbie.

I was angry enough, as you know—but how was any man's anger to hold out against such an interruption as this? Sergeant Cuff noticed the change in me, and encouraged it by a word in season. "Come! come!" he said, "why not treat my view of the case as her ladyship treats it? Why not say, the circumstances have fatally misled me?"

To take anything as her ladyship took it was a privilege worth enjoying—even with the disadvantage of its having been offered to me by Sergeant Cuff. I cooled slowly down to my customary level. I regarded any other opinion of Miss Rachel, than my lady's opinion or mine, with a lofty contempt. The only thing I could not do, was to keep off the subject of the Moonstone! My own good sense ought to have warned me, I know, to let the matter rest—but, there! the virtues which distinguish the present generation were not invented in my time. Sergeant Cuff had hit me on the raw, and, though I did look down upon him with contempt, the tender place still tingled for all that. The end of it was that I perversely led him back to the subject of her ladyship's letter. "I am quite satisfied myself," I said. "But never mind that! Go on, as if I was still open to conviction. You think Miss Rachel is not to be believed on her word; and you say we shall hear of the Moonstone again. Back your opinion, Sergeant," I concluded, in an airy way. "Back your opinion."

The Moonstone

Instead of taking offence, Sergeant Cuff seized my hand, and shook it till my fingers ached again.

"I declare to heaven," says this strange officer solemnly, "I would take to domestic service tomorrow, Mr. Betteredge, if I had a chance of being employed along with You! To say you are as transparent as a child, sir, is to pay the children a compliment which nine out of ten of them don't deserve. There! there! we won't begin to dispute again. You shall have it out of me on easier terms than that. I won't say a word more about her ladyship, or about Miss Verinder—I'll only turn prophet, for once in a way, and for your sake. I have warned you already that you haven't done with the Moonstone yet. Very well. Now I'll tell you, at parting, of three things which will happen in the future, and which, I believe, will force themselves on your attention, whether you like it or not."

"Go on!" I said, quite unabashed, and just as airy as ever.

"First," said the Sergeant, "you will hear something from the Yollands—when the postman delivers Rosanna's letter at Cobb's Hole, on Monday next."

If he had thrown a bucket of cold water over me, I doubt if I could have felt it much more unpleasantly than I felt those words. Miss Rachel's assertion of her innocence had left Rosanna's conduct—the making the new nightgown, the hiding the smeared nightgown, and all the rest of it—entirely without explanation. And this had never occurred to me, till Sergeant Cuff forced it on my mind all in a moment!

"In the second place," proceeded the Sergeant, "you will hear of the three Indians again. You will hear of them in the neighbourhood, if Miss Rachel remains in the neighbourhood. You will hear of them in London, if Miss Rachel goes to London."

Having lost all interest in the three jugglers, and having thoroughly convinced myself of my young lady's innocence, I took this second prophecy easily enough. "So much for two of the three things that are going to happen," I said. "Now for the third!"

"Third, and last," said Sergeant Cuff, "you will, sooner or later, hear something of that money-lender in London, whom I have twice taken the liberty of mentioning already. Give me your pocket-book, and I'll make a note for you of his name and address—so that there may be no mistake about it if the thing really happens."

He wrote accordingly on a blank leaf—"Mr. Septimus Luker, Middlesex-place, Lambeth, London."

"There," he said, pointing to the address, "are the last words, on the subject of the Moonstone, which I shall trouble you with for the present. Time will show whether I am right or wrong. In the meanwhile, sir, I carry away with me a sincere personal liking for you, which I think does honour to both of us. If we don't meet again before my professional retirement takes place, I hope you will come and see me in a little house near London, which I have got my eye on. There will be grass walks, Mr. Betteredge, I promise you, in my garden. And as for the white moss rose——"

"The de'il a bit ye'll get the white moss rose to grow, unless you bud him on the dogue-rose first," cried a voice at the window.

We both turned round. There was the everlasting Mr. Begbie, too eager for the controversy to wait any longer at the gate. The Sergeant wrung my hand, and darted out into the court-yard, hotter still on his side. "Ask him about the moss rose, when he comes back, and see if I have left him a leg to stand on!" cried the great Cuff, hailing me through the window in his turn. "Gentlemen, both!" I answered, moderating them again as I had moderated them once already. "In the matter of the moss rose there is a great deal to be said on both sides!" I might as well (as the Irish say) have whistled jigs to a milestone. Away they went together, fighting the battle of the roses without asking or giving quarter on either side. The last I saw of them, Mr. Begbie was shaking his obstinate head, and Sergeant Cuff had got him by the arm like a prisoner in charge. Ah, well! well! I own I couldn't help liking the Sergeant—though I hated him all the time.

Explain that state of mind, if you can. You will soon be rid, now, of me and my contradictions. When I have reported Mr. Franklin's departure, the history of the Saturday's events will be finished at last. And when I have next described certain strange things that happened in the course of the new week, I shall have done my part of the Story, and shall hand over the pen to the person who is appointed to follow my lead. If you are as tired of reading this narrative as I am of writing it—Lord, how we shall enjoy ourselves on both sides a few pages further on!

CHAPTER XXIII

I had kept the pony-chaise ready, in case Mr. Franklin persisted in leaving us by the train that night. The appearance of the luggage, followed downstairs by Mr. Franklin himself, informed me plainly enough that he had held firm to a resolution for once in his life.

"So you have really made up your mind, sir?" I said, as we met in the hall. "Why not wait a day or two longer, and give Miss Rachel another chance?"

The foreign varnish appeared to have all worn off Mr. Franklin, now that the time had come for saying good-bye. Instead of replying to me in words, he put the letter which her ladyship had addressed to him into my hand. The greater part of it said over again what had been said already in the other communication received by me. But there was a bit about Miss Rachel added at the end, which will account for the steadiness of Mr. Franklin's determination, if it accounts for nothing else.

"You will wonder, I dare say" (her ladyship wrote), "at my allowing my own daughter to keep me perfectly in the dark. A Diamond worth twenty thousand pounds has been lost—and I am left to infer that the mystery of its disappearance is no mystery to Rachel, and that some incomprehensible obligation of silence has been laid on her, by some person or persons utterly unknown to me, with some object in view at which I cannot even guess. Is it conceivable that I should allow myself to be trifled with in this way? It is quite conceivable, in Rachel's present state. She is in a condition of nervous agitation pitiable to see. I dare not approach the subject of the Moonstone again until time has done something to quiet her. To help this end, I have not hesitated to dismiss the police-officer. The mystery which baffles us, baffles him too. This is not a matter in which any stranger can help us. He adds to what I have to suffer; and he maddens Rachel if she only hears his name.

"My plans for the future are as well settled as they can be. My present idea is to take Rachel to London—partly to relieve her mind by a complete change, partly to try what may be done by consulting the best medical advice. Can I ask you to meet us in town? My dear Franklin, you, in your way, must imitate my patience, and wait, as I do, for a fitter time. The valuable assistance which you rendered to the inquiry after the lost jewel is still an unpardoned offence, in the present dreadful state of Rachel's mind. Moving blindfold in this matter, you have added to the burden of anxiety which she has had to bear, by innocently threatening her secret with discovery, through your exertions. It is impossible for me to excuse the perversity that holds you responsible for consequences which neither you nor I could imagine or foresee. She is not to be reasoned with—she can only be pitied. I am grieved to have to say it, but for the present, you and Rachel are better apart. The only advice I can offer you is, to give her time."

I handed the letter back, sincerely sorry for Mr. Franklin, for I knew how fond he was of my young lady; and I saw that her mother's account of her had cut him to the heart. "You know the proverb, sir," was all I said to him. "When things are at the worst, they're sure to mend. Things can't be much worse, Mr. Franklin, than they are now."

Mr. Franklin folded up his aunt's letter, without appearing to be much comforted by the remark which I had ventured on addressing to him.

"When I came here from London with that horrible Diamond," he said, "I don't believe there was a happier household in England than this. Look at the household now! Scattered, disunited—the very air of the place poisoned with mystery and suspicion! Do you remember that morning at the Shivering Sand, when we talked about my uncle Herncastle, and his birthday gift? The Moonstone has served the Colonel's vengeance, Betteredge, by means which the Colonel himself never dreamt of!"

With that he shook me by the hand, and went out to the pony-chaise.

I followed him down the steps. It was very miserable to see him leaving the old place, where he had spent the happiest years of his life, in this way. Penelope (sadly upset by all that had happened in the house) came round crying, to bid him good-bye. Mr. Franklin kissed her. I waved my hand as much as to say, "You're heartily welcome, sir." Some of the other female servants appeared, peeping after him round the corner. He was one of those men whom the women all like. At the last moment,

I stopped the pony-chaise, and begged as a favour that he would let us hear from him by letter. He didn't seem to heed what I said — he was looking round from one thing to another, taking a sort of farewell of the old house and grounds. "Tell us where you are going to, sir!" I said, holding on by the chaise, and trying to get at his future plans in that way. Mr. Franklin pulled his hat down suddenly over his eyes. "Going?" says he, echoing the word after me. "I am going to the devil!" The pony started at the word, as if he had felt a Christian horror of it. "God bless you, sir, go where you may!" was all I had time to say, before he was out of sight and hearing. A sweet and pleasant gentleman! With all his faults and follies, a sweet and pleasant gentleman! He left a sad gap behind him, when he left my lady's house.

It was dull and dreary enough, when the long summer evening closed in, on that Saturday night.

I kept my spirits from sinking by sticking fast to my pipe and my Robinson Crusoe. The women (excepting Penelope) beguiled the time by talking of Rosanna's suicide. They were all obstinately of opinion that the poor girl had stolen the Moonstone, and that she had destroyed herself in terror of being found out. My daughter, of course, privately held fast to what she had said all along. Her notion of the motive which was really at the bottom of the suicide failed, oddly enough, just where my young lady's assertion of her innocence failed also. It left Rosanna's secret journey to Frizinghall, and Rosanna's proceedings in the matter of the nightgown entirely unaccounted for. There was no use in pointing this out to Penelope; the objection made about as much impression on her as a shower of rain on a waterproof coat. The truth is, my daughter inherits my superiority to reason — and, in respect to that accomplishment, has got a long way ahead of her own father.

On the next day (Sunday), the close carriage, which had been kept at Mr. Ablewhite's, came back to us empty. The coachman brought a message for me, and written instructions for my lady's own maid and for Penelope.

The message informed me that my mistress had determined to take Miss Rachel to her house in London, on the Monday. The written instructions informed the two maids of the clothing that was wanted, and directed them to meet their mistresses in town at a given hour. Most of the other servants were to follow. My lady had found Miss Rachel so unwilling to return to the house, after what had happened in it, that she had decided on going to London direct from Frizinghall. I was to remain in the country, until further orders, to look after things indoors and out. The servants left with me were to be put on board wages.

Being reminded, by all this, of what Mr. Franklin had said about our being a scattered and disunited household, my mind was led naturally to Mr. Franklin himself. The more I thought of him, the more uneasy I felt about his future proceedings. It ended in my writing, by the Sunday's post, to his father's valet, Mr. Jeffco (whom I had known in former years) to beg he would let me know what Mr. Franklin had settled to do, on arriving in London.

The Sunday evening was, if possible, duller even than the Saturday evening. We ended the day of rest, as hundreds of thousands of people end it regularly, once a week, in these islands—that is to say, we all anticipated bedtime, and fell asleep in our chairs.

How the Monday affected the rest of the household I don't know. The Monday gave me a good shake up. The first of Sergeant Cuff's prophecies of what was to happen—namely, that I should hear from the Yollands—came true on that day.

I had seen Penelope and my lady's maid off in the railway with the luggage for London, and was pottering about the grounds, when I heard my name called. Turning round, I found myself face to face with the fisherman's daughter, Limping Lucy. Bating her lame foot and her leanness (this last a horrid draw-back to a woman, in my opinion), the girl had some pleasing qualities in the eye of a man. A dark, keen, clever face, and a nice clear voice, and a beautiful brown head of hair counted among her merits. A crutch appeared in the list of her misfortunes. And a temper reckoned high in the sum total of her defects.

"Well, my dear," I said, "what do you want with me?"

"Where's the man you call Franklin Blake?" says the girl, fixing me with a fierce look, as she rested herself on her crutch.

"That's not a respectful way to speak of any gentleman," I answered. "If you wish to inquire for my lady's nephew, you will please to mention him as Mr. Franklin Blake."

She limped a step nearer to me, and looked as if she could have eaten me alive. "Mr. Franklin Blake?" she repeated after me. "Murderer Franklin Blake would be a fitter name for him."

My practice with the late Mrs. Betteredge came in handy here. Whenever a woman tries to put you out of temper, turn the tables, and put her out of temper instead. They are generally prepared for every effort you can make in your own defence, but that. One word does it as well as a hundred; and one word did it with Limping Lucy. I looked her pleasantly in the face; and I said—"Pooh!"

The girl's temper flamed out directly. She poised herself on her sound foot, and she took her crutch, and beat it furiously three times on the ground. "He's a murderer! he's a murderer! he's a murderer! He has been the death of Rosanna Spearman!" She screamed that answer out at the top of her voice. One or two of the people at work in the grounds near us looked up—saw it was Limping Lucy—knew what to expect from that quarter—and looked away again.

"He has been the death of Rosanna Spearman?" I repeated. "What makes you say that, Lucy?"

"What do you care? What does any man care? Oh! if she had only thought of the men as I think, she might have been living now!"

"She always thought kindly of me, poor soul," I said; "and, to the best of my ability, I always tried to act kindly by her."

I spoke those words in as comforting a manner as I could. The truth is, I hadn't the heart to irritate the girl by another of my smart replies. I had only noticed her temper at first. I noticed her wretchedness now—and wretchedness is not uncommonly insolent, you will find, in humble life. My answer melted Limping Lucy. She bent her head down, and laid it on the top of her crutch.

"I loved her," the girl said softly. "She had lived a miserable life, Mr. Betteredge—vile people had ill-treated her and led her wrong—and it hadn't spoiled her sweet temper. She was an

The Moonstone

angel. She might have been happy with me. I had a plan for our going to London together like sisters, and living by our needles. That man came here, and spoilt it all. He bewitched her. Don't tell me he didn't mean it, and didn't know it. He ought to have known it. He ought to have taken pity on her. 'I can't live without him—and, oh, Lucy, he never even looks at me.' That's what she said. Cruel, cruel, cruel. I said, 'No man is worth fretting for in that way.' And she said, 'There are men worth dying for, Lucy, and he is one of them.' I had saved up a little money. I had settled things with father and mother. I meant to take her away from the mortification she was suffering here. We should have had a little lodging in London, and lived together like sisters. She had a good education, sir, as you know, and she wrote a good hand. She was quick at her needle. I have a good education, and I write a good hand. I am not as quick at my needle as she was—but I could have done. We might have got our living nicely. And, oh! what happens this morning? what happens this morning? Her letter comes and tells me that she has done with the burden of her life. Her letter comes, and bids me good-bye for ever. Where is he?" cries the girl, lifting her head from the crutch, and flaming out again through her tears. "Where's this gentleman that I mustn't speak of, except with respect? Ha, Mr. Betteredge, the day is not far off when the poor will rise against the rich. I pray Heaven they may begin with him. I pray Heaven they may begin with him."

Here was another of your average good Christians, and here was the usual break-down, consequent on that same average Christianity being pushed too far! The parson himself (though I own this is saying a great deal) could hardly have lectured the girl in the state she was in now. All I ventured to do was to keep her to the point—in the hope of something turning up which might be worth hearing.

"What do you want with Mr. Franklin Blake?" I asked.

"I want to see him."

"For anything particular?"

"I have got a letter to give him."

"From Rosanna Spearman?"

"Yes."

"Sent to you in your own letter?"

"Yes."

Was the darkness going to lift? Were all the discoveries that I was dying to make, coming and offering themselves to me of their own accord? I was obliged to wait a moment. Sergeant Cuff had left his infection behind him. Certain signs and tokens, personal to myself, warned me that the detective-fever was beginning to set in again.

"You can't see Mr. Franklin," I said.

"I must, and will, see him."

"He went to London last night."

Limping Lucy looked me hard in the face, and saw that I was speaking the truth. Without a word more, she turned about again instantly towards Cobb's Hole.

"Stop!" I said. "I expect news of Mr. Franklin Blake tomorrow. Give me your letter, and I'll send it on to him by the post."

Limping Lucy steadied herself on her crutch and looked back at me over her shoulder.

"I am to give it from my hands into his hands," she said. "And I am to give it to him in no other way."

"Shall I write, and tell him what you have said?"

"Tell him I hate him. And you will tell him the truth."

"Yes, yes. But about the letter——?"

"If he wants the letter, he must come back here, and get it from Me."

With those words she limped off on the way to Cobb's Hole. The detective-fever burnt up all my dignity on the spot. I followed her, and tried to make her talk. All in vain. It was my misfortune to be a man—and Limping Lucy enjoyed disappointing me. Later in the day, I tried my luck with her mother. Good Mrs. Yolland could only cry, and recommend a drop of comfort out of the Dutch bottle. I found the fisherman on the beach. He said it was "a bad job," and went on mending his net. Neither father nor mother knew more than I knew. The one way left to try was the chance, which might come with the morning, of writing to Mr. Franklin Blake.

I leave you to imagine how I watched for the postman on Tuesday morning. He brought me two letters. One, from Penelope (which I had hardly patience enough to read), announced that my lady and Miss Rachel were safely established in London. The other, from Mr. Jeffco, informed me that his master's son had left England already.

On reaching the metropolis, Mr. Franklin had, it appeared, gone straight to his father's residence. He arrived at an awkward time. Mr. Blake, the elder, was up to his eyes in the business of the House of Commons, and was amusing himself at home that night with the favourite parliamentary plaything which they call "a private bill." Mr. Jeffco himself showed Mr. Franklin into his father's study. "My dear Franklin! why do you surprise me in this way? Anything wrong?" "Yes; something wrong with Rachel; I am dreadfully distressed about it." "Grieved to hear it. But I can't listen to you now." "When can you listen?" "My dear boy! I won't deceive you. I can listen at the end of the session, not a moment before. Good-night." "Thank you, sir. Good-night."

Such was the conversation, inside the study, as reported to me by Mr. Jeffco. The conversation outside the study, was shorter still. "Jeffco, see what time the tidal train starts tomorrow morning." "At six-forty, Mr. Franklin." "Have me called at five." "Going abroad, sir?" "Going, Jeffco, wherever the railway chooses to take me." "Shall I tell your father, sir?" "Yes; tell him at the end of the session."

The next morning Mr. Franklin had started for foreign parts. To what particular place he was bound, nobody (himself included) could presume to guess. We might hear of him next in Europe, Asia, Africa, or America. The chances were as equally divided as possible, in Mr. Jeffco's opinion, among the four quarters of the globe.

This news — by closing up all prospects of my bringing Limping Lucy and Mr. Franklin together — at once stopped any further progress of mine on the way to discovery. Penelope's belief that her fellow-servant had destroyed herself through unrequited love for Mr. Franklin Blake, was confirmed — and that was all. Whether the letter which Rosanna had left to be given to him after her death did, or did not, contain the confession which Mr. Franklin had suspected her of trying to make to him in her life-time, it was impossible to say. It might be only a farewell word, telling nothing but the secret of her unhappy fancy for a person beyond her reach. Or it might own the whole truth about the strange proceedings in which Sergeant Cuff had detected her, from the time when the Moonstone was lost, to the time when she rushed to her own destruction at the Shivering Sand. A sealed letter it had been placed in Limping Lucy's hand, and a sealed letter it remained to me and to everyone about the girl, her own parents included. We all suspected her of having been in the dead woman's confidence; we all tried to make her speak; we all failed. Now one, and now another, of the servants — still holding to the belief that Rosanna had stolen the Diamond and had hidden it — peered and poked about the rocks to which she had been traced, and peered and poked in vain. The tide ebbed, and the tide flowed; the summer went on, and the autumn came. And the Quicksand, which hid her body, hid her secret too.

The news of Mr. Franklin's departure from England on the Sunday morning, and the news of my lady's arrival in London with Miss Rachel on the Monday afternoon, had reached me, as you are aware, by the Tuesday's post. The Wednesday came, and brought nothing. The Thursday produced a second budget of news from Penelope.

My girl's letter informed me that some great London doctor had been consulted about her young lady, and had earned a guinea by remarking that she had better be amused. Flower-shows, operas, balls — there was a whole round of gaieties in prospect; and Miss Rachel, to her mother's astonishment, eagerly took to it all. Mr. Godfrey had called; evidently as sweet as ever on his cousin, in spite of the reception he had met with, when he tried his luck on the occasion of the birthday. To Penelope's great regret, he had been most graciously received, and had added Miss Rachel's name to one of his Ladies' Charities on the spot. My mistress was reported to be out of spirits, and to have held two long interviews with her lawyer. Certain speculations followed, referring to a poor relation of the family — one Miss Clack, whom I have mentioned in my account of the birthday dinner, as sitting next to Mr. Godfrey, and having a pretty taste in champagne. Penelope was astonished to find that Miss Clack had not called yet. She would surely not be long before she fastened herself on my lady as usual—and so forth, and so forth, in the way women have of girding at each other, on and off paper. This would not have been worth mentioning, I admit, but for one reason. I hear you are likely to be turned over to Miss Clack, after parting with me. In that case, just do me the favour of not believing a word she says, if she speaks of your humble servant.

On Friday, nothing happened—except that one of the dogs showed signs of a breaking out behind the ears. I gave him a dose of syrup of buckthorn, and put him on a diet of pot-liquor and vegetables till further orders. Excuse my mentioning this. It has slipped in somehow. Pass it over please. I am fast coming to the end of my offences against your cultivated modern taste. Besides, the dog was a good creature, and deserved a good physicking; he did indeed.

Saturday, the last day of the week, is also the last day in my narrative.

The morning's post brought me a surprise in the shape of a London newspaper. The handwriting on the direction puzzled me. I compared it with the money-lender's name and address as recorded in my pocket-book, and identified it at once as the writing of Sergeant Cuff.

Looking through the paper eagerly enough, after this discovery, I found an ink-mark drawn round one of the police reports. Here it is, at your service. Read it as I read it, and you will set the right value on the Sergeant's polite attention in sending me the news of the day:

"LAMBETH—Shortly before the closing of the court, Mr. Septimus Luker, the well-known dealer in ancient gems, carvings, intagli, &c., &c., applied to the sitting magistrate for advice. The applicant stated that he had been annoyed, at intervals throughout the day, by the proceedings of some of those strolling Indians who infest the streets. The persons complained of were three in number. After having been sent away by the police, they had returned again and again, and had attempted to enter the house on pretence of asking for charity. Warned off in the front, they had been discovered again at the back of the premises. Besides the annoyance complained of, Mr. Luker expressed himself as being under some apprehension that robbery might be contemplated. His collection contained many unique gems, both classical and Oriental, of the highest value. He had only the day before been compelled to dismiss a skilled workman in ivory carving from his employment (a native of India, as we understood), on suspicion of attempted theft; and he felt by no means sure that this man and the street jugglers of whom he complained, might not be acting in concert. It might be their object to collect a crowd, and create a disturbance in the street, and, in the confusion thus caused, to obtain access to the house. In reply to the magistrate, Mr. Luker admitted that he had no evidence to produce of any attempt at robbery being in contemplation. He could speak positively to the annoyance and interruption caused by the Indians, but not to anything else. The magistrate remarked that, if the annoyance were repeated, the applicant could summon the Indians to that court, where they might easily be dealt with under the Act. As to the valuables in Mr. Luker's possession, Mr. Luker himself must take the best measures for their safe custody. He would do well perhaps to communicate with the police, and to adopt such additional precautions as their experience might suggest. The applicant thanked his worship, and withdrew."

One of the wise ancients is reported (I forget on what occasion) as having recommended his fellow-creatures to "look to the end." Looking to the end of these pages of mine, and wondering for some days past how I should manage to write it, I find my plain statement of facts coming to a conclusion, most appropriately, of its own self. We have gone on, in this matter of the Moonstone, from one marvel to another; and here we end with the greatest marvel of all—namely, the accomplishment of Sergeant Cuff's three predictions in less than a week from the time when he had made them.

After hearing from the Yollands on the Monday, I had now heard of the Indians, and heard of the money-lender, in the news from London—Miss Rachel herself remember, being also in London at the time. You see, I put things at their worst, even when they tell dead against my own view. If you desert me, and side with the Sergeant, on the evidence before you—if the only rational explanation you can see is, that Miss Rachel and Mr. Luker must have got together, and that the Moonstone must be now in pledge in the money-lender's house—I own, I can't blame you for arriving at that conclusion. In the dark, I have brought you thus far. In the dark I am compelled to leave you, with my best respects.

Why compelled? it may be asked. Why not take the persons who have gone along with me, so far, up into those regions of superior enlightenment in which I sit myself?

In answer to this, I can only state that I am acting under orders, and that those orders have been given to me (as I understand) in the interests of truth. I am forbidden to tell more in this narrative than I knew myself at the time. Or, to put it plainer, I am to keep strictly within the limits of my own experience, and am not to inform you of what other persons told me—for the very sufficient reason that you are to have the information from those other persons themselves, at first hand. In this matter of the Moonstone the plan is, not to present reports, but to produce witnesses. I picture to myself a member of the family reading these pages fifty years hence. Lord! what a compliment he will feel it, to be asked to take nothing on hearsay, and to be treated in all respects like a Judge on the bench.

At this place, then, we part—for the present, at least—after long journeying together, with a companionable feeling, I hope, on both sides. The devil's dance of the Indian Diamond has threaded its way to London; and to London you must go after it, leaving me at the country house. Please to excuse the faults of this composition—my talking so much of myself, and being too familiar, I am afraid, with you. I mean no harm; and I drink most respectfully (having just done dinner) to your health and prosperity, in a tankard of her ladyship's ale. May you find in these leaves of my writing, what Robinson Crusoe found in his experience on the desert island—namely, "something to comfort yourselves from, and to set in the Description of Good and Evil, on the Credit Side of the Account."—Farewell.

THE END OF THE FIRST PERIOD.

SECOND PERIOD.
THE DISCOVERY OF THE TRUTH.
(1848-1849.)

The Events related in several Narratives.

FIRST NARRATIVE.

Contributed by Miss Clack; niece of the late Sir John Verinder

CHAPTER I

I am indebted to my dear parents (both now in heaven) for having had habits of order and regularity instilled into me at a very early age.

In that happy bygone time, I was taught to keep my hair tidy at all hours of the day and night, and to fold up every article of my clothing carefully, in the same order, on the same chair, in the same place at the foot of the bed, before retiring to rest. An entry of the day's events in my little diary invariably preceded the folding up. The "Evening Hymn" (repeated in bed) invariably followed the folding up. And the sweet sleep of childhood invariably followed the "Evening Hymn."

In later life (alas!) the Hymn has been succeeded by sad and bitter meditations; and the sweet sleep has been but ill exchanged for the broken slumbers which haunt the uneasy pillow of care. On the other hand, I have continued to fold my clothes, and to keep my little diary. The former habit links me to my happy childhood—before papa was ruined. The latter habit—hitherto mainly useful in helping me to discipline the fallen nature which we all inherit from Adam—has unexpectedly proved important to my humble interests in quite another way. It has enabled poor Me to serve the caprice of a wealthy member of the family into which my late uncle married. I am fortunate enough to be useful to Mr. Franklin Blake.

I have been cut off from all news of my relatives by marriage for some time past. When we are isolated and poor, we are not infrequently forgotten. I am now living, for economy's sake, in a little town in Brittany, inhabited by a select circle of serious English friends, and possessed of the inestimable advantages of a Protestant clergyman and a cheap market.

In this retirement — a Patmos amid the howling ocean of popery that surrounds us — a letter from England has reached me at last. I find my insignificant existence suddenly remembered by Mr. Franklin Blake. My wealthy relative — would that I could add my spiritually-wealthy relative! — writes, without even an attempt at disguising that he wants something of me. The whim has seized him to stir up the deplorable scandal of the Moonstone: and I am to help him by writing the account of what I myself witnessed while visiting at Aunt Verinder's house in London. Pecuniary remuneration is offered to me — with the want of feeling peculiar to the rich. I am to re-open wounds that Time has barely closed; I am to recall the most intensely painful remembrances — and this done, I am to feel myself compensated by a new laceration, in the shape of Mr. Blake's cheque. My nature is weak. It cost me a hard struggle, before Christian humility conquered sinful pride, and self-denial accepted the cheque.

Without my diary, I doubt — pray let me express it in the grossest terms! — if I could have honestly earned my money. With my diary, the poor labourer (who forgives Mr. Blake for insulting her) is worthy of her hire. Nothing escaped me at the time I was visiting dear Aunt Verinder. Everything was entered (thanks to my early training) day by day as it happened; and everything down to the smallest particular, shall be told here. My sacred regard for truth is (thank God) far above my respect for persons. It will be easy for Mr. Blake to suppress what may not prove to be sufficiently flattering in these pages to the person chiefly concerned in them. He has purchased my time, but not even his wealth can purchase my conscience too.*

[*Note. Added by Franklin Blake. — Miss Clack may make her mind quite easy on this point. Nothing will be added, altered or removed, in her manuscript, or in any of the other manuscripts which pass through my hands. Whatever opinions any of the writers may express, whatever peculiarities of treatment may mark, and perhaps in a literary sense, disfigure the narratives which I am now collecting, not a line will be tampered with anywhere, from first to last. As genuine documents they are sent to me—and as genuine documents I shall preserve them, endorsed by the attestations of witnesses who can speak to the facts. It only remains to be added that "the person chiefly concerned" in Miss Clack's narrative, is happy enough at the present moment, not only to brave the smartest exercise of Miss Clack's pen, but even to recognise its unquestionable value as an instrument for the exhibition of Miss Clack's character.]

My diary informs me, that I was accidentally passing Aunt Verinder's house in Montagu Square, on Monday, 3rd July, 1848.

Seeing the shutters opened, and the blinds drawn up, I felt that it would be an act of polite attention to knock, and make inquiries. The person who answered the door, informed me that my aunt and her daughter (I really cannot call her my cousin!) had arrived from the country a week since, and meditated making some stay in London. I sent up a message at once, declining to disturb them, and only begging to know whether I could be of any use.

The person who answered the door, took my message in insolent silence, and left me standing in the hall. She is the daughter of a heathen old man named Betteredge—long, too long, tolerated in my aunt's family. I sat down in the hall to wait for my answer—and, having always a few tracts in my bag, I selected one which proved to be quite providentially applicable to the person who answered the door. The hall was dirty, and the chair was hard; but the blessed consciousness of returning good for evil raised me quite above any trifling considerations of that kind. The tract was one of a series addressed to young women on the sinfulness of dress. In style it was devoutly familiar. Its title was, "A Word With You On Your Cap-Ribbons."

"My lady is much obliged, and begs you will come and lunch tomorrow at two."

I passed over the manner in which she gave her message, and the dreadful boldness of her look. I thanked this young castaway; and I said, in a tone of Christian interest, "Will you favour me by accepting a tract?"

She looked at the title. "Is it written by a man or a woman,

Miss? If it's written by a woman, I had rather not read it on that account. If it's written by a man, I beg to inform him that he knows nothing about it." She handed me back the tract, and opened the door. We must sow the good seed somehow. I waited till the door was shut on me, and slipped the tract into the letter-box. When I had dropped another tract through the area railings, I felt relieved, in some small degree, of a heavy responsibility towards others.

We had a meeting that evening of the Select Committee of the Mothers'-Small-Clothes-Conversion-Society. The object of this excellent Charity is—as all serious people know—to rescue unredeemed fathers' trousers from the pawnbroker, and to prevent their resumption, on the part of the irreclaimable parent, by abridging them immediately to suit the proportions of the innocent son. I was a member, at that time, of the select committee; and I mention the Society here, because my precious and admirable friend, Mr. Godfrey Ablewhite, was associated with our work of moral and material usefulness. I had expected to see him in the boardroom, on the Monday evening of which I am now writing, and had proposed to tell him, when we met, of dear Aunt Verinder's arrival in London. To my great disappointment he never appeared. On my expressing a feeling of surprise at his absence, my sisters of the Committee all looked up together from their trousers (we had a great pressure of business that night), and asked in amazement, if I had not heard the news. I acknowledged my ignorance, and was then told, for the first time, of an event which forms, so to speak, the starting-point of this narrative. On the previous Friday, two gentlemen—occupying widely-different positions in society—had been the victims of an outrage which had startled all London. One of the gentlemen was Mr. Septimus Luker, of Lambeth. The other was Mr. Godfrey Ablewhite.

Living in my present isolation, I have no means of introducing the newspaper-account of the outrage into my narrative. I was also deprived, at the time, of the inestimable advantage of hearing the events related by the fervid eloquence of Mr. Godfrey Ablewhite. All I can do is to state the facts as they were stated, on that Monday evening, to me; proceeding on the plan which I have been taught from infancy to adopt in folding up my clothes. Everything shall be put neatly, and everything shall be put in its place. These lines are written by a poor weak woman. From a poor weak woman who will be cruel enough to expect more?

The date—thanks to my dear parents, no dictionary that ever was written can be more particular than I am about dates—was Friday, June 30th, 1848.

Early on that memorable day, our gifted Mr. Godfrey happened to be cashing a cheque at a banking-house in Lombard Street. The name of the firm is accidentally blotted in my diary, and my sacred regard for truth forbids me to hazard a guess in a matter of this kind. Fortunately, the name of the firm doesn't matter. What does matter is a circumstance that occurred when Mr. Godfrey had transacted his business. On gaining the door, he encountered a gentleman—a perfect stranger to him—who was accidentally leaving the office exactly at the same time as himself. A momentary contest of politeness ensued between them as to who should be the first to pass through the door of the bank. The stranger insisted on making Mr. Godfrey precede him; Mr. Godfrey said a few civil words; they bowed, and parted in the street.

Thoughtless and superficial people may say, Here is surely a very trumpery little incident related in an absurdly circumstantial manner. Oh, my young friends and fellow-sinners! beware of presuming to exercise your poor carnal reason. Oh, be morally tidy. Let your faith be as your stockings, and your stockings as your faith. Both ever spotless, and both ready to put on at a moment's notice!

I beg a thousand pardons. I have fallen insensibly into my Sunday-school style. Most inappropriate in such a record as this. Let me try to be worldly—let me say that trifles, in this case as in many others, led to terrible results. Merely premising that the polite stranger was Mr. Luker, of Lambeth, we will now follow Mr. Godfrey home to his residence at Kilburn.

He found waiting for him, in the hall, a poorly clad but delicate and interesting-looking little boy. The boy handed him a letter, merely mentioning that he had been entrusted with it by an old lady whom he did not know, and who had given him no instructions to wait for an answer. Such incidents as these were not uncommon in Mr. Godfrey's large experience as a promoter of public charities. He let the boy go, and opened the

The Moonstone

letter.

The handwriting was entirely unfamiliar to him. It requested his attendance, within an hour's time, at a house in Northumberland Street, Strand, which he had never had occasion to enter before. The object sought was to obtain from the worthy manager certain details on the subject of the Mothers'-Small-Clothes-Conversion-Society, and the information was wanted by an elderly lady who proposed adding largely to the resources of the charity, if her questions were met by satisfactory replies. She mentioned her name, and she added that the shortness of her stay in London prevented her from giving any longer notice to the eminent philanthropist whom she addressed.

Ordinary people might have hesitated before setting aside their own engagements to suit the convenience of a stranger. The Christian Hero never hesitates where good is to be done. Mr. Godfrey instantly turned back, and proceeded to the house in Northumberland Street. A most respectable though somewhat corpulent man answered the door, and, on hearing Mr. Godfrey's name, immediately conducted him into an empty apartment at the back, on the drawing-room floor. He noticed two unusual things on entering the room. One of them was a faint odour of musk and camphor. The other was an ancient Oriental manuscript, richly illuminated with Indian figures and devices, that lay open to inspection on a table.

He was looking at the book, the position of which caused him to stand with his back turned towards the closed folding doors communicating with the front room, when, without the slightest previous noise to warn him, he felt himself suddenly seized round the neck from behind. He had just time to notice that the arm round his neck was naked and of a tawny-brown colour, before his eyes were bandaged, his mouth was gagged, and he was thrown helpless on the floor by (as he judged) two men. A third rifled his pockets, and—if, as a lady, I may venture to use such an expression—searched him, without ceremony, through and through to his skin.

Here I should greatly enjoy saying a few cheering words on the devout confidence which could alone have sustained Mr. Godfrey in an emergency so terrible as this. Perhaps, however, the position and appearance of my admirable friend at the culminating period of the outrage (as above described) are hardly within the proper limits of female discussion. Let me pass over the next few moments, and return to Mr. Godfrey at the time when the odious search of his person had been completed. The outrage had been perpetrated throughout in dead silence. At the end of it some words were exchanged, among the invisible wretches, in a language which he did not understand, but in tones which were plainly expressive (to his cultivated ear) of disappointment and rage. He was suddenly lifted from the ground, placed in a chair, and bound there hand and foot. The next moment he felt the air flowing in from the open door, listened, and concluded that he was alone again in the room.

An interval elapsed, and he heard a sound below like the rustling sound of a woman's dress. It advanced up the stairs, and stopped. A female scream rent the atmosphere of guilt. A man's voice below exclaimed "Hullo!" A man's feet ascended the stairs. Mr. Godfrey felt Christian fingers unfastening his bandage, and extracting his gag. He looked in amazement at two respectable strangers, and faintly articulated, "What does it mean?" The two respectable strangers looked back, and said, "Exactly the question we were going to ask you."

The inevitable explanation followed. No! Let me be scrupulously particular. Sal volatile and water followed, to compose dear Mr. Godfrey's nerves. The explanation came next.

It appeared from the statement of the landlord and landlady of the house (persons of good repute in the neighbourhood), that their first and second floor apartments had been engaged, on the previous day, for a week certain, by a most respectable-looking gentleman — the same who has been already described as answering the door to Mr. Godfrey's knock. The gentleman had paid the week's rent and all the week's extras in advance, stating that the apartments were wanted for three Oriental noblemen, friends of his, who were visiting England for the first time. Early on the morning of the outrage, two of the Oriental strangers, accompanied by their respectable English friend, took possession of the apartments. The third was expected to join them shortly; and the luggage (reported as very bulky) was announced to follow when it had passed through the Custom-house, late in the afternoon. Not more than ten minutes previous to Mr. Godfrey's visit, the third foreigner had arrived. Nothing out of the common had happened, to the knowledge of the landlord and landlady downstairs, until within the last five minutes—when they had seen the three foreigners, accompanied by their respectable English friend, all leave the house together, walking quietly in the direction of the Strand. Remembering that a visitor had called, and not having seen the visitor also leave the house, the landlady had thought it rather strange that the gentleman should be left by himself upstairs. After a short discussion with her husband, she had considered it advisable to ascertain whether anything was wrong. The result had followed, as I have already attempted to describe it; and there the explanation of the landlord and the landlady came to an end.

An investigation was next made in the room. Dear Mr. Godfrey's property was found scattered in all directions. When the articles were collected, however, nothing was missing; his watch, chain, purse, keys, pocket-handkerchief, note-book, and all his loose papers had been closely examined, and had then been left unharmed to be resumed by the owner. In the same way, not the smallest morsel of property belonging to the proprietors of the house had been abstracted. The Oriental noblemen had removed their own illuminated manuscript, and had removed nothing else.

What did it mean? Taking the worldly point of view, it appeared to mean that Mr. Godfrey had been the victim of some incomprehensible error, committed by certain unknown men. A dark conspiracy was on foot in the midst of us; and our beloved and innocent friend had been entangled in its meshes. When the Christian hero of a hundred charitable victories plunges into a pitfall that has been dug for him by mistake, oh, what a warning it is to the rest of us to be unceasingly on our guard! How soon may our own evil passions prove to be Oriental noblemen who pounce on us unawares!

I could write pages of affectionate warning on this one theme, but (alas!) I am not permitted to improve—I am condemned to narrate. My wealthy relative's cheque—henceforth, the incubus of my existence—warns me that I have not done with this record of violence yet. We must leave Mr. Godfrey to recover in Northumberland Street, and must follow the proceedings of Mr. Luker at a later period of the day.

After leaving the bank, Mr. Luker had visited various parts of London on business errands. Returning to his own residence, he found a letter waiting for him, which was described as having been left a short time previously by a boy. In this case, as in Mr. Godfrey's case, the handwriting was strange; but the name mentioned was the name of one of Mr. Luker's customers. His correspondent announced (writing in the third person—apparently by the hand of a deputy) that he had been unexpectedly summoned to London. He had just established himself in lodgings in Alfred Place, Tottenham Court Road; and he desired to see Mr. Luker immediately, on the subject of a purchase which he contemplated making. The gentleman was an enthusiastic collector of Oriental antiquities, and had been for many years a liberal patron of the establishment in Lambeth. Oh, when shall we wean ourselves from the worship of Mammon! Mr. Luker called a cab, and drove off instantly to his liberal patron.

Exactly what had happened to Mr. Godfrey in Northumberland Street now happened to Mr. Luker in Alfred Place. Once more the respectable man answered the door, and showed the visitor upstairs into the back drawing-room. There, again, lay the illuminated manuscript on a table. Mr. Luker's attention was absorbed, as Mr. Godfrey's attention had been absorbed, by this beautiful work of Indian art. He too was aroused from his studies by a tawny naked arm round his throat, by a bandage over his eyes, and by a gag in his mouth. He too was thrown prostrate and searched to the skin. A longer interval had then elapsed than had passed in the experience of Mr. Godfrey; but it had ended as before, in the persons of the house suspecting something wrong, and going upstairs to see what had happened. Precisely the same explanation which the landlord in Northumberland Street had given to Mr. Godfrey, the landlord in Alfred Place now gave to Mr. Luker. Both had been imposed on in the same way by the plausible address and well-filled purse of the respectable stranger, who introduced himself as acting for his foreign friends. The one point of difference between the two cases occurred when the scattered contents of Mr. Luker's pockets were being collected from the floor. His watch and purse were safe, but (less fortunate than Mr. Godfrey) one of the loose papers that he carried about him had been taken away. The paper in question acknowledged the receipt of a valuable of great price which Mr. Luker had that day left in the care of his bankers. This document would be useless for purposes of fraud, inasmuch as it provided that the valuable should only be given up on the personal application of the owner. As soon as he recovered himself, Mr. Luker hurried to the bank, on the chance that the thieves who had robbed him might ignorantly present themselves with the receipt. Nothing had been seen of them when he arrived at the establishment, and nothing was seen of them afterwards. Their respectable English friend had (in the opinion of the bankers) looked the receipt over before they attempted to make use of it, and had given them the necessary warning in good time.

Information of both outrages was communicated to the police, and the needful investigations were pursued, I believe, with great energy. The authorities held that a robbery had been planned, on insufficient information received by the thieves. They had been plainly not sure whether Mr. Luker had, or had not, trusted the transmission of his precious gem to another person; and poor polite Mr. Godfrey had paid the penalty of having been seen accidentally speaking to him. Add to this, that Mr. Godfrey's absence from our Monday evening meeting had been occasioned by a consultation of the authorities, at which he was requested to assist—and all the explanations required being now given, I may proceed with the simpler story of my own little personal experiences in Montagu Square.

I was punctual to the luncheon hour on Tuesday. Reference to my diary shows this to have been a chequered day—much in it to be devoutly regretted, much in it to be devoutly thankful for.

Dear Aunt Verinder received me with her usual grace and kindness. But I noticed, after a little while, that something was wrong. Certain anxious looks escaped my aunt, all of which took the direction of her daughter. I never see Rachel myself without wondering how it can be that so insignificant-looking a person should be the child of such distinguished parents as Sir John and Lady Verinder. On this occasion, however, she not only disappointed—she really shocked me. There was an absence of all lady-like restraint in her language and manner most painful to see. She was possessed by some feverish excitement which made her distressingly loud when she laughed, and sinfully wasteful and capricious in what she ate and drank at lunch. I felt deeply for her poor mother, even before the true state of the case had been confidentially made known to me.

Luncheon over, my aunt said: "Remember what the doctor told you, Rachel, about quieting yourself with a book after taking your meals."

"I'll go into the library, mamma," she answered. "But if Godfrey calls, mind I am told of it. I am dying for more news of him, after his adventure in Northumberland Street." She kissed her mother on the forehead, and looked my way. "Good-bye, Clack," she said, carelessly. Her insolence roused no angry feeling in me; I only made a private memorandum to pray for her.

When we were left by ourselves, my aunt told me the whole horrible story of the Indian Diamond, which, I am happy to know, it is not necessary to repeat here. She did not conceal from me that she would have preferred keeping silence on the subject. But when her own servants all knew of the loss of the Moonstone, and when some of the circumstances had actually found their way into the newspapers—when strangers were speculating whether there was any connection between what had happened at Lady Verinder's country house, and what had happened in Northumberland Street and Alfred Place—concealment was not to be thought of; and perfect frankness became a necessity as well as a virtue.

Some persons, hearing what I now heard, would have been probably overwhelmed with astonishment. For my own part, knowing Rachel's spirit to have been essentially unregenerate from her childhood upwards, I was prepared for whatever my aunt could tell me on the subject of her daughter. It might have gone on from bad to worse till it ended in Murder; and I should still have said to myself, The natural result! oh, dear, dear, the natural result! The one thing that did shock me was the course my aunt had taken under the circumstances. Here surely was a case for a clergyman, if ever there was one yet! Lady Verinder had thought it a case for a physician. All my poor aunt's early life had been passed in her father's godless household. The natural result again! Oh, dear, dear, the natural result again!

"The doctors recommend plenty of exercise and amusement for Rachel, and strongly urge me to keep her mind as much as possible from dwelling on the past," said Lady Verinder.

"Oh, what heathen advice!" I thought to myself. "In this Christian country, what heathen advice!"

My aunt went on, "I do my best to carry out my instructions. But this strange adventure of Godfrey's happens at a most unfortunate time. Rachel has been incessantly restless and excited since she first heard of it. She left me no peace till I had written and asked my nephew Ablewhite to come here. She even feels an interest in the other person who was roughly used—Mr. Luker, or some such name—though the man is, of course, a total stranger to her."

"Your knowledge of the world, dear aunt, is superior to mine," I suggested diffidently. "But there must be a reason surely for this extraordinary conduct on Rachel's part. She is keeping a sinful secret from you and from everybody. May there not be something in these recent events which threatens her secret with discovery?"

"Discovery?" repeated my aunt. "What can you possibly mean? Discovery through Mr. Luker? Discovery through my nephew?"

As the word passed her lips, a special providence occurred. The servant opened the door, and announced Mr. Godfrey Ablewhite.

CHAPTER II

Mr. Godfrey followed the announcement of his name—as Mr. Godfrey does everything else—exactly at the right time. He was not so close on the servant's heels as to startle us. He was not so far behind as to cause us the double inconvenience of a pause and an open door. It is in the completeness of his daily life that the true Christian appears. This dear man was very complete.

"Go to Miss Verinder," said my aunt, addressing the servant, "and tell her Mr. Ablewhite is here."

We both inquired after his health. We both asked him together whether he felt like himself again, after his terrible adventure of the past week. With perfect tact, he contrived to answer us at the same moment. Lady Verinder had his reply in words. I had his charming smile.

"What," he cried, with infinite tenderness, "have I done to deserve all this sympathy? My dear aunt! my dear Miss Clack! I have merely been mistaken for somebody else. I have only been blindfolded; I have only been strangled; I have only been thrown flat on my back, on a very thin carpet, covering a particularly hard floor. Just think how much worse it might have been! I might have been murdered; I might have been robbed. What have I lost? Nothing but Nervous Force—which the law doesn't recognise as property; so that, strictly speaking, I have lost nothing at all. If I could have had my own way, I would have kept my adventure to myself—I shrink from all this fuss and publicity. But Mr. Luker made his injuries public, and my injuries, as the necessary consequence, have been proclaimed in their turn. I have become the property of the newspapers, until the gentle reader gets sick of the subject. I am very sick indeed of it myself. May the gentle reader soon be like me! And how is dear Rachel? Still enjoying the gaieties of London? So glad to hear it! Miss Clack, I need all your indulgence. I am sadly behind-hand with my Committee Work and my dear Ladies. But I really do hope to look in at the Mothers'-Small-Clothes next week. Did you make cheering progress at Monday's Committee? Was the Board hopeful about future prospects? And are we nicely off for Trousers?"

The heavenly gentleness of his smile made his apologies

irresistible. The richness of his deep voice added its own indescribable charm to the interesting business question which he had just addressed to me. In truth, we were almost too nicely off for Trousers; we were quite overwhelmed by them. I was just about to say so, when the door opened again, and an element of worldly disturbance entered the room, in the person of Miss Verinder.

She approached dear Mr. Godfrey at a most unladylike rate of speed, with her hair shockingly untidy, and her face, what I should call, unbecomingly flushed.

"I am charmed to see you, Godfrey," she said, addressing him, I grieve to add, in the off-hand manner of one young man talking to another. "I wish you had brought Mr. Luker with you. You and he (as long as our present excitement lasts) are the two most interesting men in all London. It's morbid to say this; it's unhealthy; it's all that a well-regulated mind like Miss Clack's most instinctively shudders at. Never mind that. Tell me the whole of the Northumberland Street story directly. I know the newspapers have left some of it out."

Even dear Mr. Godfrey partakes of the fallen nature which we all inherit from Adam—it is a very small share of our human legacy, but, alas! he has it. I confess it grieved me to see him take Rachel's hand in both of his own hands, and lay it softly on the left side of his waistcoat. It was a direct encouragement to her reckless way of talking, and her insolent reference to me.

"Dearest Rachel," he said, in the same voice which had thrilled me when he spoke of our prospects and our trousers, "the newspapers have told you everything—and they have told it much better than I can."

"Godfrey thinks we all make too much of the matter," my aunt remarked. "He has just been saying that he doesn't care to speak of it."

"Why?"

She put the question with a sudden flash in her eyes, and a sudden look up into Mr. Godfrey's face. On his side, he looked down at her with an indulgence so injudicious and so ill-deserved, that I really felt called on to interfere.

"Rachel, darling!" I remonstrated gently, "true greatness and true courage are ever modest."

"You are a very good fellow in your way, Godfrey," she said—not taking the smallest notice, observe, of me, and still speaking to her cousin as if she was one young man addressing another. "But I am quite sure you are not great; I don't believe you possess any extraordinary courage; and I am firmly persuaded—if you ever had any modesty—that your lady-worshippers relieved you of that virtue a good many years since. You have some private reason for not talking of your adventure in Northumberland Street; and I mean to know it."

"My reason is the simplest imaginable, and the most easily acknowledged," he answered, still bearing with her. "I am tired of the subject."

"You are tired of the subject? My dear Godfrey, I am going to make a remark."

"What is it?"

"You live a great deal too much in the society of women. And you have contracted two very bad habits in consequence. You have learnt to talk nonsense seriously, and you have got into a way of telling fibs for the pleasure of telling them. You can't go straight with your lady-worshippers. I mean to make you go straight with me. Come, and sit down. I am brimful of downright questions; and I expect you to be brimful of downright answers."

She actually dragged him across the room to a chair by the window, where the light would fall on his face. I deeply feel being obliged to report such language, and to describe such conduct. But, hemmed in, as I am, between Mr. Franklin Blake's cheque on one side and my own sacred regard for truth on the other, what am I to do? I looked at my aunt. She sat unmoved; apparently in no way disposed to interfere. I had never noticed this kind of torpor in her before. It was, perhaps, the reaction after the trying time she had had in the country. Not a pleasant symptom to remark, be it what it might, at dear Lady Verinder's age, and with dear Lady Verinder's autumnal exuberance of figure.

In the meantime, Rachel had settled herself at the window with our amiable and forbearing—our too forbearing—Mr.

The Moonstone

Godfrey. She began the string of questions with which she had threatened him, taking no more notice of her mother, or of myself, than if we had not been in the room.

"Have the police done anything, Godfrey?"

"Nothing whatever."

"It is certain, I suppose, that the three men who laid the trap for you were the same three men who afterwards laid the trap for Mr. Luker?"

"Humanly speaking, my dear Rachel, there can be no doubt of it."

"And not a trace of them has been discovered?"

"Not a trace."

"It is thought—is it not?—that these three men are the three Indians who came to our house in the country."

"Some people think so."

"Do you think so?"

"My dear Rachel, they blindfolded me before I could see their faces. I know nothing whatever of the matter. How can I offer an opinion on it?"

Even the angelic gentleness of Mr. Godfrey was, you see, beginning to give way at last under the persecution inflicted on him. Whether unbridled curiosity, or ungovernable dread, dictated Miss Verinder's questions I do not presume to inquire. I only report that, on Mr. Godfrey's attempting to rise, after giving her the answer just described, she actually took him by the two shoulders, and pushed him back into his chair—Oh, don't say this was immodest! don't even hint that the recklessness of guilty terror could alone account for such conduct as I have described! We must not judge others. My Christian friends, indeed, indeed, indeed, we must not judge others!

She went on with her questions, unabashed. Earnest Biblical students will perhaps be reminded—as I was reminded—of the blinded children of the devil, who went on with their orgies, unabashed, in the time before the Flood.

"I want to know something about Mr. Luker, Godfrey."

"I am again unfortunate, Rachel. No man knows less of Mr. Luker than I do."

"You never saw him before you and he met accidentally at the bank?"

"Never."

"You have seen him since?"

"Yes. We have been examined together, as well as separately, to assist the police."

"Mr. Luker was robbed of a receipt which he had got from his banker's—was he not? What was the receipt for?"

"For a valuable gem which he had placed in the safe keeping of the bank."

"That's what the newspapers say. It may be enough for the general reader; but it is not enough for me. The banker's receipt must have mentioned what the gem was?"

"The banker's receipt, Rachel—as I have heard it described—mentioned nothing of the kind. A valuable gem, belonging to Mr. Luker; deposited by Mr. Luker; sealed with Mr. Luker's seal; and only to be given up on Mr. Luker's personal application. That was the form, and that is all I know about it."

She waited a moment, after he had said that. She looked at her mother, and sighed. She looked back again at Mr. Godfrey, and went on.

"Some of our private affairs, at home," she said, "seem to have got into the newspapers?"

"I grieve to say, it is so."

"And some idle people, perfect strangers to us, are trying to trace a connexion between what happened at our house in Yorkshire and what has happened since, here in London?"

"The public curiosity, in certain quarters, is, I fear, taking that turn."

"The people who say that the three unknown men who ill-

The Moonstone

used you and Mr. Luker are the three Indians, also say that the valuable gem — —"

There she stopped. She had become gradually, within the last few moments, whiter and whiter in the face. The extraordinary blackness of her hair made this paleness, by contrast, so ghastly to look at, that we all thought she would faint, at the moment when she checked herself in the middle of her question. Dear Mr. Godfrey made a second attempt to leave his chair. My aunt entreated her to say no more. I followed my aunt with a modest medicinal peace-offering, in the shape of a bottle of salts. We none of us produced the slightest effect on her. "Godfrey, stay where you are. Mamma, there is not the least reason to be alarmed about me. Clack, you're dying to hear the end of it—I won't faint, expressly to oblige you."

Those were the exact words she used—taken down in my diary the moment I got home. But, oh, don't let us judge! My Christian friends, don't let us judge!

She turned once more to Mr. Godfrey. With an obstinacy dreadful to see, she went back again to the place where she had checked herself, and completed her question in these words:

"I spoke to you, a minute since, about what people were saying in certain quarters. Tell me plainly, Godfrey, do they any of them say that Mr. Luker's valuable gem is—the Moonstone?"

As the name of the Indian Diamond passed her lips, I saw a change come over my admirable friend. His complexion deepened. He lost the genial suavity of manner which is one of his greatest charms. A noble indignation inspired his reply.

"They do say it," he answered. "There are people who don't hesitate to accuse Mr. Luker of telling a falsehood to serve some private interests of his own. He has over and over again solemnly declared that, until this scandal assailed him, he had never even heard of the Moonstone. And these vile people reply, without a shadow of proof to justify them, He has his reasons for concealment; we decline to believe him on his oath. Shameful! shameful!"

Rachel looked at him very strangely—I can't well describe how—while he was speaking. When he had done, she said, "Considering that Mr. Luker is only a chance acquaintance of yours, you take up his cause, Godfrey, rather warmly."

My gifted friend made her one of the most truly evangelical answers I ever heard in my life.

"I hope, Rachel, I take up the cause of all oppressed people rather warmly," he said.

The tone in which those words were spoken might have melted a stone. But, oh dear, what is the hardness of stone? Nothing, compared to the hardness of the unregenerate human heart! She sneered. I blush to record it—she sneered at him to his face.

"Keep your noble sentiments for your Ladies' Committees, Godfrey. I am certain that the scandal which has assailed Mr. Luker, has not spared You."

Even my aunt's torpor was roused by those words.

"My dear Rachel," she remonstrated, "you have really no right to say that!"

"I mean no harm, mamma—I mean good. Have a moment's patience with me, and you will see."

She looked back at Mr. Godfrey, with what appeared to be a sudden pity for him. She went the length—the very unladylike length—of taking him by the hand.

"I am certain," she said, "that I have found out the true reason of your unwillingness to speak of this matter before my mother and before me. An unlucky accident has associated you in people's minds with Mr. Luker. You have told me what scandal says of him. What does scandal say of you?"

Even at the eleventh hour, dear Mr. Godfrey—always ready to return good for evil—tried to spare her.

"Don't ask me!" he said. "It's better forgotten, Rachel—it is, indeed."

"I will hear it!" she cried out, fiercely, at the top of her voice.

"Tell her, Godfrey!" entreated my aunt. "Nothing can do her such harm as your silence is doing now!"

Mr. Godfrey's fine eyes filled with tears. He cast one last appealing look at her—and then he spoke the fatal words:

"If you will have it, Rachel—scandal says that the Moonstone is in pledge to Mr. Luker, and that I am the man who has pawned it."

She started to her feet with a scream. She looked backwards and forwards from Mr. Godfrey to my aunt, and from my aunt to Mr. Godfrey, in such a frantic manner that I really thought she had gone mad.

"Don't speak to me! Don't touch me!" she exclaimed, shrinking back from all of us (I declare like some hunted animal!) into a corner of the room. "This is my fault! I must set it right. I have sacrificed myself—I had a right to do that, if I liked. But to let an innocent man be ruined; to keep a secret which destroys his character for life—Oh, good God, it's too horrible! I can't bear it!"

My aunt half rose from her chair, then suddenly sat down again. She called to me faintly, and pointed to a little phial in her work-box.

"Quick!" she whispered. "Six drops, in water. Don't let Rachel see."

Under other circumstances, I should have thought this strange. There was no time now to think—there was only time to give the medicine. Dear Mr. Godfrey unconsciously assisted me in concealing what I was about from Rachel, by speaking composing words to her at the other end of the room.

"Indeed, indeed, you exaggerate," I heard him say. "My reputation stands too high to be destroyed by a miserable passing scandal like this. It will be all forgotten in another week. Let us never speak of it again." She was perfectly inaccessible, even to such generosity as this. She went on from bad to worse.

"I must, and will, stop it," she said. "Mamma! hear what I say. Miss Clack! hear what I say. I know the hand that took the Moonstone. I know—" she laid a strong emphasis on the words; she stamped her foot in the rage that possessed her—"I know that Godfrey Ablewhite is innocent! Take me to the magistrate, Godfrey! Take me to the magistrate, and I will swear it!"

My aunt caught me by the hand, and whispered, "Stand between us for a minute or two. Don't let Rachel see me." I noticed a bluish tinge in her face which alarmed me. She saw I was startled. "The drops will put me right in a minute or two," she said, and so closed her eyes, and waited a little.

While this was going on, I heard dear Mr. Godfrey still gently remonstrating.

"You must not appear publicly in such a thing as this," he said. "Your reputation, dearest Rachel, is something too pure and too sacred to be trifled with."

"My reputation!" She burst out laughing. "Why, I am accused, Godfrey, as well as you. The best detective officer in England declares that I have stolen my own Diamond. Ask him what he thinks—and he will tell you that I have pledged the Moonstone to pay my private debts!" She stopped, ran across the room—and fell on her knees at her mother's feet. "Oh mamma! mamma! mamma! I must be mad—mustn't I?—not to own the truth now!" She was too vehement to notice her mother's condition—she was on her feet again, and back with Mr. Godfrey, in an instant. "I won't let you—I won't let any innocent man—be accused and disgraced through my fault. If you won't take me before the magistrate, draw out a declaration of your innocence on paper, and I will sign it. Do as I tell you, Godfrey, or I'll write it to the newspapers I'll go out, and cry it in the streets!"

We will not say this was the language of remorse—we will say it was the language of hysterics. Indulgent Mr. Godfrey pacified her by taking a sheet of paper, and drawing out the declaration. She signed it in a feverish hurry. "Show it everywhere—don't think of me," she said, as she gave it to him. "I am afraid, Godfrey, I have not done you justice, hitherto, in my thoughts. You are more unselfish—you are a better man than I believed you to be. Come here when you can, and I will try and repair the wrong I have done you."

She gave him her hand. Alas, for our fallen nature! Alas, for Mr. Godfrey! He not only forgot himself so far as to kiss her hand—he adopted a gentleness of tone in answering her which, in such a case, was little better than a compromise with sin. "I will come, dearest," he said, "on condition that we don't speak of this hateful subject again." Never had I seen and heard our Christian Hero to less advantage than on this occasion.

Before another word could be said by anybody, a

The Moonstone

thundering knock at the street door startled us all. I looked through the window, and saw the World, the Flesh, and the Devil waiting before the house—as typified in a carriage and horses, a powdered footman, and three of the most audaciously dressed women I ever beheld in my life.

Rachel started, and composed herself. She crossed the room to her mother.

"They have come to take me to the flower-show," she said. "One word, mamma, before I go. I have not distressed you, have I?"

(Is the bluntness of moral feeling which could ask such a question as that, after what had just happened, to be pitied or condemned? I like to lean towards mercy. Let us pity it.)

The drops had produced their effect. My poor aunt's complexion was like itself again. "No, no, my dear," she said. "Go with our friends, and enjoy yourself."

Her daughter stooped, and kissed her. I had left the window, and was near the door, when Rachel approached it to go out. Another change had come over her—she was in tears. I looked with interest at the momentary softening of that obdurate heart. I felt inclined to say a few earnest words. Alas! my well-meant sympathy only gave offence. "What do you mean by pitying me?" she asked in a bitter whisper, as she passed to the door. "Don't you see how happy I am? I'm going to the flower-show, Clack; and I've got the prettiest bonnet in London." She completed the hollow mockery of that address by blowing me a kiss—and so left the room.

I wish I could describe in words the compassion I felt for this miserable and misguided girl. But I am almost as poorly provided with words as with money. Permit me to say—my heart bled for her.

Returning to my aunt's chair, I observed dear Mr. Godfrey searching for something softly, here and there, in different parts of the room. Before I could offer to assist him he had found what he wanted. He came back to my aunt and me, with his declaration of innocence in one hand, and with a box of matches in the other.

"Dear aunt, a little conspiracy!" he said. "Dear Miss Clack, a pious fraud which even your high moral rectitude will excuse! Will you leave Rachel to suppose that I accept the generous self-sacrifice which has signed this paper? And will you kindly bear witness that I destroy it in your presence, before I leave the house?" He kindled a match, and, lighting the paper, laid it to burn in a plate on the table. "Any trifling inconvenience that I may suffer is as nothing," he remarked, "compared with the importance of preserving that pure name from the contaminating contact of the world. There! We have reduced it to a little harmless heap of ashes; and our dear impulsive Rachel will never know what we have done! How do you feel? My precious friends, how do you feel? For my poor part, I am as light-hearted as a boy!"

He beamed on us with his beautiful smile; he held out a hand to my aunt, and a hand to me. I was too deeply affected by his noble conduct to speak. I closed my eyes; I put his hand, in a kind of spiritual self-forgetfulness, to my lips. He murmured a soft remonstrance. Oh the ecstasy, the pure, unearthly ecstasy of that moment! I sat — I hardly know on what — quite lost in my own exalted feelings. When I opened my eyes again, it was like descending from heaven to earth. There was nobody but my aunt in the room. He had gone.

I should like to stop here — I should like to close my narrative with the record of Mr. Godfrey's noble conduct. Unhappily there is more, much more, which the unrelenting pecuniary pressure of Mr. Blake's cheque obliges me to tell. The painful disclosures which were to reveal themselves in my presence, during that Tuesday's visit to Montagu Square, were not at an end yet.

Finding myself alone with Lady Verinder, I turned naturally to the subject of her health; touching delicately on the strange anxiety which she had shown to conceal her indisposition, and the remedy applied to it, from the observation of her daughter.

My aunt's reply greatly surprised me.

"Drusilla," she said (if I have not already mentioned that my Christian name is Drusilla, permit me to mention it now), "you are touching quite innocently, I know — on a very distressing subject."

I rose immediately. Delicacy left me but one alternative — the alternative, after first making my apologies, of taking my leave. Lady Verinder stopped me, and insisted on my sitting down again.

"You have surprised a secret," she said, "which I had confided to my sister Mrs. Ablewhite, and to my lawyer Mr. Bruff, and to no one else. I can trust in their discretion; and I am sure, when I tell you the circumstances, I can trust in yours. Have you any pressing engagement, Drusilla? or is your time your own this afternoon?"

It is needless to say that my time was entirely at my aunt's disposal.

"Keep me company then," she said, "for another hour. I have something to tell you which I believe you will be sorry to hear. And I shall have a service to ask of you afterwards, if you don't object to assist me."

It is again needless to say that, so far from objecting, I was all eagerness to assist her.

"You can wait here," she went on, "till Mr. Bruff comes at five. And you can be one of the witnesses, Drusilla, when I sign my Will."

Her Will! I thought of the drops which I had seen in her work-box. I thought of the bluish tinge which I had noticed in her complexion. A light which was not of this world—a light shining prophetically from an unmade grave—dawned on my mind. My aunt's secret was a secret no longer.

CHAPTER III

Consideration for poor Lady Verinder forbade me even to hint that I had guessed the melancholy truth, before she opened her lips. I waited her pleasure in silence; and, having privately arranged to say a few sustaining words at the first convenient opportunity, felt prepared for any duty that could claim me, no matter how painful it might be.

"I have been seriously ill, Drusilla, for some time past," my aunt began. "And, strange to say, without knowing it myself."

I thought of the thousands and thousands of perishing human creatures who were all at that moment spiritually ill, without knowing it themselves. And I greatly feared that my poor aunt might be one of the number. "Yes, dear," I said, sadly. "Yes."

"I brought Rachel to London, as you know, for medical advice," she went on. "I thought it right to consult two doctors."

Two doctors! And, oh me (in Rachel's state), not one clergyman! "Yes, dear?" I said once more. "Yes?"

"One of the two medical men," proceeded my aunt, "was a stranger to me. The other had been an old friend of my husband's, and had always felt a sincere interest in me for my husband's sake. After prescribing for Rachel, he said he wished to speak to me privately in another room. I expected, of course, to receive some special directions for the management of my daughter's health. To my surprise, he took me gravely by the hand, and said, 'I have been looking at you, Lady Verinder, with a professional as well as a personal interest. You are, I am afraid, far more urgently in need of medical advice than your daughter.' He put some questions to me, which I was at first inclined to treat lightly enough, until I observed that my answers distressed him. It ended in his making an appointment to come and see me, accompanied by a medical friend, on the next day, at an hour when Rachel would not be at home. The result of that visit — most kindly and gently conveyed to me — satisfied both the physicians that there had been precious time lost, which could never be regained, and that my case had now passed beyond the reach of their art. For more than two years I have been suffering under an insidious form of heart disease,

The Moonstone

which, without any symptoms to alarm me, has, by little and little, fatally broken me down. I may live for some months, or I may die before another day has passed over my head—the doctors cannot, and dare not, speak more positively than this. It would be vain to say, my dear, that I have not had some miserable moments since my real situation has been made known to me. But I am more resigned than I was, and I am doing my best to set my worldly affairs in order. My one great anxiety is that Rachel should be kept in ignorance of the truth. If she knew it, she would at once attribute my broken health to anxiety about the Diamond, and would reproach herself bitterly, poor child, for what is in no sense her fault. Both the doctors agree that the mischief began two, if not three years since. I am sure you will keep my secret, Drusilla—for I am sure I see sincere sorrow and sympathy for me in your face."

Sorrow and sympathy! Oh, what Pagan emotions to expect from a Christian Englishwoman anchored firmly on her faith!

Little did my poor aunt imagine what a gush of devout thankfulness thrilled through me as she approached the close of her melancholy story. Here was a career of usefulness opened before me! Here was a beloved relative and perishing fellow-creature, on the eve of the great change, utterly unprepared; and led, providentially led, to reveal her situation to Me! How can I describe the joy with which I now remembered that the precious clerical friends on whom I could rely, were to be counted, not by ones or twos, but by tens and twenties. I took my aunt in my arms—my overflowing tenderness was not to be satisfied, now, with anything less than an embrace. "Oh!" I said to her, fervently, "the indescribable interest with which you inspire me! Oh! the good I mean to do you, dear, before we part!" After another word or two of earnest prefatory warning, I gave her her choice of three precious friends, all plying the work of mercy from morning to night in her own neighbourhood; all equally inexhaustible in exhortation; all affectionately ready to exercise their gifts at a word from me. Alas! the result was far from encouraging. Poor Lady Verinder looked puzzled and frightened, and met everything I could say to her with the purely worldly objection that she was not strong enough to face strangers. I yielded—for the moment only, of course. My large experience (as Reader and Visitor, under not less, first and last, than fourteen beloved clerical friends) informed me that this was another case for preparation by books. I possessed a little library of works, all suitable to the present emergency, all calculated to arouse, convince, prepare, enlighten, and fortify my aunt. "You will read, dear, won't you?" I said, in my most winning way. "You will read, if I bring you my own precious books? Turned down at all the right places, aunt. And marked in pencil where you are to stop and ask yourself, 'Does this apply to me?'" Even that simple appeal—so absolutely heathenising is the influence of the world—appeared to startle my aunt. She said, "I will do what I can, Drusilla, to please you," with a look of surprise, which was at once instructive and terrible to see. Not a moment was to be lost. The clock on the mantel-piece informed me that I had just time to hurry home; to provide myself with a first series of selected readings (say a dozen only); and to return in time to meet the lawyer, and witness Lady Verinder's Will. Promising faithfully to be back by five o'clock, I left the house on my errand of mercy.

When no interests but my own are involved, I am humbly content to get from place to place by the omnibus. Permit me to give an idea of my devotion to my aunt's interests by recording that, on this occasion, I committed the prodigality of taking a cab.

I drove home, selected and marked my first series of readings, and drove back to Montagu Square, with a dozen works in a carpet-bag, the like of which, I firmly believe, are not to be found in the literature of any other country in Europe. I paid the cabman exactly his fare. He received it with an oath; upon which I instantly gave him a tract. If I had presented a pistol at his head, this abandoned wretch could hardly have exhibited greater consternation. He jumped up on his box, and, with profane exclamations of dismay, drove off furiously. Quite useless, I am happy to say! I sowed the good seed, in spite of him, by throwing a second tract in at the window of the cab.

The servant who answered the door—not the person with the cap-ribbons, to my great relief, but the foot-man—informed me that the doctor had called, and was still shut up with Lady Verinder. Mr. Bruff, the lawyer, had arrived a minute since and was waiting in the library. I was shown into the library to wait too.

The Moonstone

Mr. Bruff looked surprised to see me. He is the family solicitor, and we had met more than once, on previous occasions, under Lady Verinder's roof. A man, I grieve to say, grown old and grizzled in the service of the world. A man who, in his hours of business, was the chosen prophet of Law and Mammon; and who, in his hours of leisure, was equally capable of reading a novel and of tearing up a tract.

"Have you come to stay here, Miss Clack?" he asked, with a look at my carpet-bag.

To reveal the contents of my precious bag to such a person as this would have been simply to invite an outburst of profanity. I lowered myself to his own level, and mentioned my business in the house.

"My aunt has informed me that she is about to sign her Will," I answered. "She has been so good as to ask me to be one of the witnesses."

"Aye? aye? Well, Miss Clack, you will do. You are over twenty-one, and you have not the slightest pecuniary interest in Lady Verinder's Will."

Not the slightest pecuniary interest in Lady Verinder's Will. Oh, how thankful I felt when I heard that! If my aunt, possessed of thousands, had remembered poor Me, to whom five pounds is an object—if my name had appeared in the Will, with a little comforting legacy attached to it—my enemies might have doubted the motive which had loaded me with the choicest treasures of my library, and had drawn upon my failing resources for the prodigal expenses of a cab. Not the cruellest scoffer of them all could doubt now. Much better as it was! Oh, surely, surely, much better as it was!

I was aroused from these consoling reflections by the voice of Mr. Bruff. My meditative silence appeared to weigh upon the spirits of this worldling, and to force him, as it were, into talking to me against his own will.

"Well, Miss Clack, what's the last news in the charitable circles? How is your friend Mr. Godfrey Ablewhite, after the mauling he got from the rogues in Northumberland Street? Egad! they're telling a pretty story about that charitable gentleman at my club!"

I had passed over the manner in which this person had remarked that I was more than twenty-one, and that I had no pecuniary interest in my aunt's Will. But the tone in which he alluded to dear Mr. Godfrey was too much for my forbearance. Feeling bound, after what had passed in my presence that afternoon, to assert the innocence of my admirable friend, whenever I found it called in question—I own to having also felt bound to include in the accomplishment of this righteous purpose, a stinging castigation in the case of Mr. Bruff.

"I live very much out of the world," I said; "and I don't possess the advantage, sir, of belonging to a club. But I happen to know the story to which you allude; and I also know that a viler falsehood than that story never was told."

"Yes, yes, Miss Clack—you believe in your friend. Natural enough. Mr. Godfrey Ablewhite, won't find the world in general quite so easy to convince as a committee of charitable ladies. Appearances are dead against him. He was in the house when the Diamond was lost. And he was the first person in the house to go to London afterwards. Those are ugly circumstances, ma'am, viewed by the light of later events."

I ought, I know, to have set him right before he went any farther. I ought to have told him that he was speaking in ignorance of a testimony to Mr. Godfrey's innocence, offered by the only person who was undeniably competent to speak from a positive knowledge of the subject. Alas! the temptation to lead the lawyer artfully on to his own discomfiture was too much for me. I asked what he meant by "later events"—with an appearance of the utmost innocence.

"By later events, Miss Clack, I mean events in which the Indians are concerned," proceeded Mr. Bruff, getting more and more superior to poor Me, the longer he went on. "What do the Indians do, the moment they are let out of the prison at Frizinghall? They go straight to London, and fix on Mr. Luker. What follows? Mr. Luker feels alarmed for the safety of 'a valuable of great price,' which he has got in the house. He lodges it privately (under a general description) in his bankers' strongroom. Wonderfully clever of him: but the Indians are just as clever on their side. They have their suspicions that the 'valuable of great price' is being shifted from one place to another; and they hit on a singularly bold and complete way of clearing those suspicions up. Whom do they seize and search? Not Mr. Luker only—which would be intelligible enough—but Mr. Godfrey Ablewhite as well. Why? Mr. Ablewhite's explanation is, that they acted on blind suspicion, after seeing him accidentally speaking to Mr. Luker. Absurd! Half-a-dozen other people spoke to Mr. Luker that morning. Why were they not followed home too, and decoyed into the trap? No! no! The plain inference is, that Mr. Ablewhite had his private interest in the 'valuable' as well as Mr. Luker, and that the Indians were so uncertain as to which of the two had the disposal of it, that there was no alternative but to search them both. Public opinion says that, Miss Clack. And public opinion, on this occasion, is not easily refuted."

He said those last words, looking so wonderfully wise in his own worldly conceit, that I really (to my shame be it spoken) could not resist leading him a little farther still, before I overwhelmed him with the truth.

"I don't presume to argue with a clever lawyer like you," I said. "But is it quite fair, sir, to Mr. Ablewhite to pass over the opinion of the famous London police officer who investigated this case? Not the shadow of a suspicion rested upon anybody but Miss Verinder, in the mind of Sergeant Cuff."

"Do you mean to tell me, Miss Clack, that you agree with the Sergeant?"

"I judge nobody, sir, and I offer no opinion."

"And I commit both those enormities, ma'am. I judge the Sergeant to have been utterly wrong; and I offer the opinion that, if he had known Rachel's character as I know it, he would have suspected everybody in the house but her. I admit that she has her faults—she is secret, and self-willed; odd and wild, and unlike other girls of her age. But true as steel, and high-minded and generous to a fault. If the plainest evidence in the world pointed one way, and if nothing but Rachel's word of honour pointed the other, I would take her word before the evidence, lawyer as I am! Strong language, Miss Clack; but I mean it."

"Would you object to illustrate your meaning, Mr. Bruff, so that I may be sure I understand it? Suppose you found Miss Verinder quite unaccountably interested in what has happened to Mr. Ablewhite and Mr. Luker? Suppose she asked the strangest questions about this dreadful scandal, and displayed the most ungovernable agitation when she found out the turn it was taking?"

"Suppose anything you please, Miss Clack, it wouldn't shake my belief in Rachel Verinder by a hair's-breadth."

"She is so absolutely to be relied on as that?"

"So absolutely to be relied on as that."

"Then permit me to inform you, Mr. Bruff, that Mr. Godfrey Ablewhite was in this house not two hours since, and that his entire innocence of all concern in the disappearance of the Moonstone was proclaimed by Miss Verinder herself, in the strongest language I ever heard used by a young lady in my life."

I enjoyed the triumph—the unholy triumph, I fear I must admit—of seeing Mr. Bruff utterly confounded and overthrown by a few plain words from Me. He started to his feet, and stared at me in silence. I kept my seat, undisturbed, and related the whole scene as it had occurred. "And what do you say about Mr. Ablewhite now?" I asked, with the utmost possible gentleness, as soon as I had done.

"If Rachel has testified to his innocence, Miss Clack, I don't scruple to say that I believe in his innocence as firmly as you do. I have been misled by appearances, like the rest of the world; and I will make the best atonement I can, by publicly contradicting the scandal which has assailed your friend wherever I meet with it. In the meantime, allow me to congratulate you on the masterly manner in which you have opened the full fire of your batteries on me at the moment when I least expected it. You would have done great things in my profession, ma'am, if you had happened to be a man."

With those words he turned away from me, and began walking irritably up and down the room.

I could see plainly that the new light I had thrown on the subject had greatly surprised and disturbed him. Certain expressions dropped from his lips, as he became more and more absorbed in his own thoughts, which suggested to my mind the abominable view that he had hitherto taken of the mystery of the lost Moonstone. He had not scrupled to suspect dear Mr.

Godfrey of the infamy of stealing the Diamond, and to attribute Rachel's conduct to a generous resolution to conceal the crime. On Miss Verinder's own authority—a perfectly unassailable authority, as you are aware, in the estimation of Mr. Bruff—that explanation of the circumstances was now shown to be utterly wrong. The perplexity into which I had plunged this high legal authority was so overwhelming that he was quite unable to conceal it from notice. "What a case!" I heard him say to himself, stopping at the window in his walk, and drumming on the glass with his fingers. "It not only defies explanation, it's even beyond conjecture."

There was nothing in these words which made any reply at all needful, on my part—and yet, I answered them! It seems hardly credible that I should not have been able to let Mr. Bruff alone, even now. It seems almost beyond mere mortal perversity that I should have discovered, in what he had just said, a new opportunity of making myself personally disagreeable to him. But—ah, my friends! nothing is beyond mortal perversity; and anything is credible when our fallen natures get the better of us!

"Pardon me for intruding on your reflections," I said to the unsuspecting Mr. Bruff. "But surely there is a conjecture to make which has not occurred to us yet."

"Maybe, Miss Clack. I own I don't know what it is."

"Before I was so fortunate, sir, as to convince you of Mr. Ablewhite's innocence, you mentioned it as one of the reasons for suspecting him, that he was in the house at the time when the Diamond was lost. Permit me to remind you that Mr. Franklin Blake was also in the house at the time when the Diamond was lost."

The old worldling left the window, took a chair exactly opposite to mine, and looked at me steadily, with a hard and vicious smile.

"You are not so good a lawyer, Miss Clack," he remarked in a meditative manner, "as I supposed. You don't know how to let well alone."

"I am afraid I fail to follow you, Mr. Bruff," I said, modestly.

"It won't do, Miss Clack—it really won't do a second time.

Franklin Blake is a prime favourite of mine, as you are well aware. But that doesn't matter. I'll adopt your view, on this occasion, before you have time to turn round on me. You're quite right, ma'am. I have suspected Mr. Ablewhite, on grounds which abstractedly justify suspecting Mr. Blake too. Very good — let's suspect them together. It's quite in his character, we will say, to be capable of stealing the Moonstone. The only question is, whether it was his interest to do so."

"Mr. Franklin Blake's debts," I remarked, "are matters of family notoriety."

"And Mr. Godfrey Ablewhite's debts have not arrived at that stage of development yet. Quite true. But there happen to be two difficulties in the way of your theory, Miss Clack. I manage Franklin Blake's affairs, and I beg to inform you that the vast majority of his creditors (knowing his father to be a rich man) are quite content to charge interest on their debts, and to wait for their money. There is the first difficulty — which is tough enough. You will find the second tougher still. I have it on the authority of Lady Verinder herself, that her daughter was ready to marry Franklin Blake, before that infernal Indian Diamond disappeared from the house. She had drawn him on and put him off again, with the coquetry of a young girl. But she had confessed to her mother that she loved cousin Franklin, and her mother had trusted cousin Franklin with the secret. So there he was, Miss Clack, with his creditors content to wait, and with the certain prospect before him of marrying an heiress. By all means consider him a scoundrel; but tell me, if you please, why he should steal the Moonstone?"

"The human heart is unsearchable," I said gently. "Who is to fathom it?"

"In other words, ma'am — though he hadn't the shadow of a reason for taking the Diamond — he might have taken it, nevertheless, through natural depravity. Very well. Say he did. Why the devil ——"

"I beg your pardon, Mr. Bruff. If I hear the devil referred to in that manner, I must leave the room."

"I beg your pardon, Miss Clack — I'll be more careful in my choice of language for the future. All I meant to ask was this. Why — even supposing he did take the Diamond — should

Franklin Blake make himself the most prominent person in the house in trying to recover it? You may tell me he cunningly did that to divert suspicion from himself. I answer that he had no need to divert suspicion—because nobody suspected him. He first steals the Moonstone (without the slightest reason) through natural depravity; and he then acts a part, in relation to the loss of the jewel, which there is not the slightest necessity to act, and which leads to his mortally offending the young lady who would otherwise have married him. That is the monstrous proposition which you are driven to assert, if you attempt to associate the disappearance of the Moonstone with Franklin Blake. No, no, Miss Clack! After what has passed here today, between us two, the dead-lock, in this case, is complete. Rachel's own innocence is (as her mother knows, and as I know) beyond a doubt. Mr. Ablewhite's innocence is equally certain—or Rachel would never have testified to it. And Franklin Blake's innocence, as you have just seen, unanswerably asserts itself. On the one hand, we are morally certain of all these things. And, on the other hand, we are equally sure that somebody has brought the Moonstone to London, and that Mr. Luker, or his banker, is in private possession of it at this moment. What is the use of my experience, what is the use of any person's experience, in such a case as that? It baffles me; it baffles you, it baffles everybody."

No—not everybody. It had not baffled Sergeant Cuff. I was about to mention this, with all possible mildness, and with every necessary protest against being supposed to cast a slur upon Rachel—when the servant came in to say that the doctor had gone, and that my aunt was waiting to receive us.

This stopped the discussion. Mr. Bruff collected his papers, looking a little exhausted by the demands which our conversation had made on him. I took up my bag-full of precious publications, feeling as if I could have gone on talking for hours. We proceeded in silence to Lady Verinder's room.

Permit me to add here, before my narrative advances to other events, that I have not described what passed between the lawyer and me, without having a definite object in view. I am ordered to include in my contribution to the shocking story of the Moonstone a plain disclosure, not only of the turn which suspicion took, but even of the names of the persons on whom suspicion rested, at the time when the Indian Diamond was believed to be in London. A report of my conversation in the library with Mr. Bruff appeared to me to be exactly what was wanted to answer this purpose—while, at the same time, it possessed the great moral advantage of rendering a sacrifice of sinful self-esteem essentially necessary on my part. I have been obliged to acknowledge that my fallen nature got the better of me. In making that humiliating confession, I get the better of my fallen nature. The moral balance is restored; the spiritual atmosphere feels clear once more. Dear friends, we may go on again.

CHAPTER IV

The signing of the Will was a much shorter matter than I had anticipated. It was hurried over, to my thinking, in indecent haste. Samuel, the footman, was sent for to act as second witness — and the pen was put at once into my aunt's hand. I felt strongly urged to say a few appropriate words on this solemn occasion. But Mr. Bruff's manner convinced me that it was wisest to check the impulse while he was in the room. In less than two minutes it was all over — and Samuel (unbenefited by what I might have said) had gone downstairs again.

Mr. Bruff folded up the Will, and then looked my way; apparently wondering whether I did or did not mean to leave him alone with my aunt. I had my mission of mercy to fulfil, and my bag of precious publications ready on my lap. He might as well have expected to move St. Paul's Cathedral by looking at it, as to move Me. There was one merit about him (due no doubt to his worldly training) which I have no wish to deny. He was quick at seeing things. I appeared to produce almost the same impression on him which I had produced on the cabman. He too uttered a profane expression, and withdrew in a violent hurry, and left me mistress of the field.

As soon as we were alone, my aunt reclined on the sofa, and then alluded, with some appearance of confusion, to the subject of her Will.

"I hope you won't think yourself neglected, Drusilla," she said. "I mean to give you your little legacy, my dear, with my own hand."

Here was a golden opportunity! I seized it on the spot. In other words, I instantly opened my bag, and took out the top publication. It proved to be an early edition — only the twenty-fifth — of the famous anonymous work (believed to be by precious Miss Bellows), entitled The Serpent at Home. The design of the book — with which the worldly reader may not be acquainted — is to show how the Evil One lies in wait for us in all the most apparently innocent actions of our daily lives. The chapters best adapted to female perusal are "Satan in the Hair Brush;" "Satan behind the Looking Glass;" "Satan under the Tea Table;" "Satan out of the Window" — and many others.

"Give your attention, dear aunt, to this precious book—and you will give me all I ask." With those words, I handed it to her open, at a marked passage—one continuous burst of burning eloquence! Subject: Satan among the Sofa Cushions.

Poor Lady Verinder (reclining thoughtlessly on her own sofa cushions) glanced at the book, and handed it back to me looking more confused than ever.

"I'm afraid, Drusilla," she said, "I must wait till I am a little better, before I can read that. The doctor——"

The moment she mentioned the doctor's name, I knew what was coming. Over and over again in my past experience among my perishing fellow-creatures, the members of the notoriously infidel profession of Medicine had stepped between me and my mission of mercy—on the miserable pretence that the patient wanted quiet, and that the disturbing influence of all others which they most dreaded, was the influence of Miss Clack and her Books. Precisely the same blinded materialism (working treacherously behind my back) now sought to rob me of the only right of property that my poverty could claim—my right of spiritual property in my perishing aunt.

"The doctor tells me," my poor misguided relative went on, "that I am not so well today. He forbids me to see any strangers; and he orders me, if I read at all, only to read the lightest and the most amusing books. 'Do nothing, Lady Verinder, to weary your head, or to quicken your pulse'—those were his last words, Drusilla, when he left me today."

There was no help for it but to yield again—for the moment only, as before. Any open assertion of the infinitely superior importance of such a ministry as mine, compared with the ministry of the medical man, would only have provoked the doctor to practise on the human weakness of his patient, and to threaten to throw up the case. Happily, there are more ways than one of sowing the good seed, and few persons are better versed in those ways than myself.

"You might feel stronger, dear, in an hour or two," I said. "Or you might wake, tomorrow morning, with a sense of something wanting, and even this unpretending volume might be able to supply it. You will let me leave the book, aunt? The doctor can hardly object to that!"

The Moonstone

I slipped it under the sofa cushions, half in, and half out, close by her handkerchief, and her smelling-bottle. Every time her hand searched for either of these, it would touch the book; and, sooner or later (who knows?) the book might touch her. After making this arrangement, I thought it wise to withdraw. "Let me leave you to repose, dear aunt; I will call again tomorrow." I looked accidentally towards the window as I said that. It was full of flowers, in boxes and pots. Lady Verinder was extravagantly fond of these perishable treasures, and had a habit of rising every now and then, and going to look at them and smell them. A new idea flashed across my mind. "Oh! may I take a flower?" I said—and got to the window unsuspected, in that way. Instead of taking away a flower, I added one, in the shape of another book from my bag, which I left, to surprise my aunt, among the geraniums and roses. The happy thought followed, "Why not do the same for her, poor dear, in every other room that she enters?" I immediately said good-bye; and, crossing the hall, slipped into the library. Samuel, coming up to let me out, and supposing I had gone, went downstairs again. On the library table I noticed two of the "amusing books" which the infidel doctor had recommended. I instantly covered them from sight with two of my own precious publications. In the breakfast-room I found my aunt's favourite canary singing in his cage. She was always in the habit of feeding the bird herself. Some groundsel was strewed on a table which stood immediately under the cage. I put a book among the groundsel. In the drawing-room I found more cheering opportunities of emptying my bag. My aunt's favourite musical pieces were on the piano. I slipped in two more books among the music. I disposed of another in the back drawing-room, under some unfinished embroidery, which I knew to be of Lady Verinder's working. A third little room opened out of the back drawing-room, from which it was shut off by curtains instead of a door. My aunt's plain old-fashioned fan was on the chimney-piece. I opened my ninth book at a very special passage, and put the fan in as a marker, to keep the place. The question then came, whether I should go higher still, and try the bedroom floor—at the risk, undoubtedly, of being insulted, if the person with the cap-ribbons happened to be in the upper regions of the house, and to find me out. But oh, what of that? It is a poor Christian that is afraid of being insulted. I went upstairs, prepared to bear anything. All was silent and solitary—it was the servants' tea-time, I suppose. My aunt's room was in front. The miniature of my late dear uncle, Sir John, hung on the wall opposite the bed. It seemed to smile at me; it seemed to say, "Drusilla! deposit a book." There were tables on either side of my aunt's bed. She was a bad sleeper, and wanted, or thought she wanted, many things at night. I put a book near the matches on one side, and a book under the box of chocolate drops on the other. Whether she wanted a light, or whether she wanted a drop, there was a precious publication to meet her eye, or to meet her hand, and to say with silent eloquence, in either case, "Come, try me! try me!" But one book was now left at the bottom of my bag, and but one apartment was still unexplored—the bath-room, which opened out of the bedroom. I peeped in; and the holy inner voice that never deceives, whispered to me, "You have met her, Drusilla, everywhere else; meet her at the bath, and the work is done." I observed a dressing-gown thrown across a chair. It had a pocket in it, and in that pocket I put my last book. Can words express my exquisite sense of duty done, when I had slipped out of the house, unsuspected by any of them, and when I found myself in the street with my empty bag under my arm? Oh, my worldly friends, pursuing the phantom, Pleasure, through the guilty mazes of Dissipation, how easy it is to be happy, if you will only be good!

When I folded up my things that night—when I reflected on the true riches which I had scattered with such a lavish hand, from top to bottom of the house of my wealthy aunt—I declare I felt as free from all anxiety as if I had been a child again. I was so light-hearted that I sang a verse of the Evening Hymn. I was so light-hearted that I fell asleep before I could sing another. Quite like a child again! quite like a child again!

So I passed that blissful night. On rising the next morning, how young I felt! I might add, how young I looked, if I were capable of dwelling on the concerns of my own perishable body. But I am not capable—and I add nothing.

Towards luncheon time—not for the sake of the creature-comforts, but for the certainty of finding dear aunt—I put on my bonnet to go to Montagu Square. Just as I was ready, the maid at the lodgings in which I then lived looked in at the door, and said, "Lady Verinder's servant, to see Miss Clack."

I occupied the parlour-floor, at that period of my residence in London. The front parlour was my sitting-room. Very small, very low in the ceiling, very poorly furnished—but, oh, so neat! I looked into the passage to see which of Lady Verinder's servants had asked for me. It was the young footman, Samuel—a civil fresh-coloured person, with a teachable look and a very obliging manner. I had always felt a spiritual interest in Samuel, and a wish to try him with a few serious words. On this occasion, I invited him into my sitting-room.

He came in, with a large parcel under his arm. When he put the parcel down, it appeared to frighten him. "My lady's love, Miss; and I was to say that you would find a letter inside." Having given that message, the fresh-coloured young footman surprised me by looking as if he would have liked to run away.

I detained him to make a few kind inquiries. Could I see my aunt, if I called in Montagu Square? No; she had gone out for a drive. Miss Rachel had gone with her, and Mr. Ablewhite had taken a seat in the carriage, too. Knowing how sadly dear Mr. Godfrey's charitable work was in arrear, I thought it odd that he should be going out driving, like an idle man. I stopped Samuel at the door, and made a few more kind inquiries. Miss Rachel was going to a ball that night, and Mr. Ablewhite had arranged to come to coffee, and go with her. There was a morning concert advertised for tomorrow, and Samuel was ordered to take places for a large party, including a place for Mr. Ablewhite. "All the tickets may be gone, Miss," said this innocent youth, "if I don't run and get them at once!" He ran as he said the words—and I found myself alone again, with some anxious thoughts to occupy me.

We had a special meeting of the Mothers'-Small-Clothes-Conversion Society that night, summoned expressly with a view to obtaining Mr. Godfrey's advice and assistance. Instead of sustaining our sisterhood, under an overwhelming flow of Trousers which quite prostrated our little community, he had arranged to take coffee in Montagu Square, and to go to a ball afterwards! The afternoon of the next day had been selected for the Festival of the British-Ladies'-Servants'-Sunday-Sweetheart-Supervision Society. Instead of being present, the life and soul of that struggling Institution, he had engaged to make one of a party of worldlings at a morning concert! I asked myself what did it mean? Alas! it meant that our Christian Hero was to reveal himself to me in a new character, and to become associated in my mind with one of the most awful backslidings of modern times.

To return, however, to the history of the passing day. On finding myself alone in my room, I naturally turned my attention to the parcel which appeared to have so strangely intimidated the fresh-coloured young footman. Had my aunt sent me my promised legacy? and had it taken the form of cast-off clothes, or worn-out silver spoons, or unfashionable jewellery, or anything of that sort? Prepared to accept all, and to resent nothing, I opened the parcel—and what met my view? The twelve precious publications which I had scattered through the house, on the previous day; all returned to me by the doctor's orders! Well might the youthful Samuel shrink when he brought his parcel into my room! Well might he run when he had performed his miserable errand! As to my aunt's letter, it simply amounted, poor soul, to this—that she dare not disobey her medical man.

What was to be done now? With my training and my principles, I never had a moment's doubt.

Once self-supported by conscience, once embarked on a career of manifest usefulness, the true Christian never yields. Neither public nor private influences produce the slightest effect on us, when we have once got our mission. Taxation may be the consequence of a mission; riots may be the consequence of a mission; wars may be the consequence of a mission: we go on with our work, irrespective of every human consideration which moves the world outside us. We are above reason; we are beyond ridicule; we see with nobody's eyes, we hear with nobody's ears, we feel with nobody's hearts, but our own. Glorious, glorious privilege! And how is it earned? Ah, my friends, you may spare yourselves the useless inquiry! We are the only people who can earn it—for we are the only people who are always right.

In the case of my misguided aunt, the form which pious perseverance was next to take revealed itself to me plainly enough.

Preparation by clerical friends had failed, owing to Lady Verinder's own reluctance. Preparation by books had failed, owing to the doctor's infidel obstinacy. So be it! What was the next thing to try? The next thing to try was—Preparation by Little Notes. In other words, the books themselves having been sent back, select extracts from the books, copied by different hands, and all addressed as letters to my aunt, were, some to be sent by post, and some to be distributed about the house on the plan I had adopted on the previous day. As letters they would excite no suspicion; as letters they would be opened—and, once opened, might be read. Some of them I wrote myself. "Dear aunt, may I ask your attention to a few lines?" &c. "Dear aunt, I was reading last night, and I chanced on the following passage," &c. Other letters were written for me by my valued fellow-workers, the sisterhood at the Mothers'-Small-Clothes. "Dear madam, pardon the interest taken in you by a true, though humble, friend." "Dear madam, may a serious person surprise you by saying a few cheering words?" Using these and other similar forms of courteous appeal, we reintroduced all my precious passages under a form which not even the doctor's watchful materialism could suspect. Before the shades of evening had closed around us, I had a dozen awakening letters for my aunt, instead of a dozen awakening books. Six I made immediate arrangements for sending through the post, and six I kept in my pocket for personal distribution in the house the next day.

Soon after two o'clock I was again on the field of pious conflict, addressing more kind inquiries to Samuel at Lady Verinder's door.

My aunt had had a bad night. She was again in the room in which I had witnessed her Will, resting on the sofa, and trying to get a little sleep.

I said I would wait in the library, on the chance of seeing her. In the fervour of my zeal to distribute the letters, it never occurred to me to inquire about Rachel. The house was quiet, and it was past the hour at which the musical performance began. I took it for granted that she and her party of pleasure-seekers (Mr. Godfrey, alas! included) were all at the concert, and eagerly devoted myself to my good work, while time and opportunity were still at my own disposal.

My aunt's correspondence of the morning—including the six awakening letters which I had posted overnight—was lying unopened on the library table. She had evidently not felt herself equal to dealing with a large mass of letters—and she might be daunted by the number of them, if she entered the library later in the day. I put one of my second set of six letters on the chimney-piece by itself; leaving it to attract her curiosity, by means of its solitary position, apart from the rest. A second letter I put purposely on the floor in the breakfast-room. The first servant who went in after me would conclude that my aunt had dropped it, and would be specially careful to restore it to her. The field thus sown on the basement story, I ran lightly upstairs to scatter my mercies next over the drawing-room floor.

Just as I entered the front room, I heard a double knock at the street-door—a soft, fluttering, considerate little knock. Before I could think of slipping back to the library (in which I was supposed to be waiting), the active young footman was in the hall, answering the door. It mattered little, as I thought. In my aunt's state of health, visitors in general were not admitted. To my horror and amazement, the performer of the soft little knock proved to be an exception to general rules. Samuel's voice below me (after apparently answering some questions which I did not hear) said, unmistakably, "Upstairs, if you please, sir." The next moment I heard footsteps—a man's footsteps—approaching the drawing-room floor. Who could this favoured male visitor possibly be? Almost as soon as I asked myself the question, the answer occurred to me. Who could it be but the doctor?

In the case of any other visitor, I should have allowed myself to be discovered in the drawing-room. There would have been nothing out of the common in my having got tired of the library, and having gone upstairs for a change. But my own self-respect stood in the way of my meeting the person who had insulted me by sending me back my books. I slipped into the little third room, which I have mentioned as communicating with the back drawing-room, and dropped the curtains which closed the open doorway. If I only waited there for a minute or two, the usual result in such cases would take place. That is to say, the doctor would be conducted to his patient's room.

I waited a minute or two, and more than a minute or two. I heard the visitor walking restlessly backwards and forwards. I

The Moonstone

also heard him talking to himself. I even thought I recognised the voice. Had I made a mistake? Was it not the doctor, but somebody else? Mr. Bruff, for instance? No! an unerring instinct told me it was not Mr. Bruff. Whoever he was, he was still talking to himself. I parted the heavy curtains the least little morsel in the world, and listened.

The words I heard were, "I'll do it today!" And the voice that spoke them was Mr. Godfrey Ablewhite's.

CHAPTER V

My hand dropped from the curtain. But don't suppose — oh, don't suppose — that the dreadful embarrassment of my situation was the uppermost idea in my mind! So fervent still was the sisterly interest I felt in Mr. Godfrey, that I never stopped to ask myself why he was not at the concert. No! I thought only of the words — the startling words — which had just fallen from his lips. He would do it today. He had said, in a tone of terrible resolution, he would do it today. What, oh what, would he do? Something even more deplorably unworthy of him than what he had done already? Would he apostatise from the faith? Would he abandon us at the Mothers'-Small-Clothes? Had we seen the last of his angelic smile in the committee-room? Had we heard the last of his unrivalled eloquence at Exeter Hall? I was so wrought up by the bare idea of such awful eventualities as these in connection with such a man, that I believe I should have rushed from my place of concealment, and implored him in the name of all the Ladies' Committees in London to explain himself — when I suddenly heard another voice in the room. It penetrated through the curtains; it was loud, it was bold, it was wanting in every female charm. The voice of Rachel Verinder.

"Why have you come up here, Godfrey?" she asked. "Why didn't you go into the library?"

He laughed softly, and answered, "Miss Clack is in the library."

"Clack in the library!" She instantly seated herself on the ottoman in the back drawing-room. "You are quite right, Godfrey. We had much better stop here."

I had been in a burning fever, a moment since, and in some doubt what to do next. I became extremely cold now, and felt no doubt whatever. To show myself, after what I had heard, was impossible. To retreat — except into the fireplace — was equally out of the question. A martyrdom was before me. In justice to myself, I noiselessly arranged the curtains so that I could both see and hear. And then I met my martyrdom, with the spirit of a primitive Christian.

"Don't sit on the ottoman," the young lady proceeded.

"Bring a chair, Godfrey. I like people to be opposite to me when I talk to them."

He took the nearest seat. It was a low chair. He was very tall, and many sizes too large for it. I never saw his legs to such disadvantage before.

"Well?" she went on. "What did you say to them?"

"Just what you said, dear Rachel, to me."

"That mamma was not at all well today? And that I didn't quite like leaving her to go to the concert?"

"Those were the words. They were grieved to lose you at the concert, but they quite understood. All sent their love; and all expressed a cheering belief that Lady Verinder's indisposition would soon pass away."

"You don't think it's serious, do you, Godfrey?"

"Far from it! In a few days, I feel quite sure, all will be well again."

"I think so, too. I was a little frightened at first, but I think so too. It was very kind to go and make my excuses for me to people who are almost strangers to you. But why not have gone with them to the concert? It seems very hard that you should miss the music too."

"Don't say that, Rachel! If you only knew how much happier I am—here, with you!"

He clasped his hands, and looked at her. In the position which he occupied, when he did that, he turned my way. Can words describe how I sickened when I noticed exactly the same pathetic expression on his face, which had charmed me when he was pleading for destitute millions of his fellow-creatures on the platform at Exeter Hall!

"It's hard to get over one's bad habits, Godfrey. But do try to get over the habit of paying compliments—do, to please me."

"I never paid you a compliment, Rachel, in my life. Successful love may sometimes use the language of flattery, I admit. But hopeless love, dearest, always speaks the truth."

He drew his chair close, and took her hand, when he said

"hopeless love." There was a momentary silence. He, who thrilled everybody, had doubtless thrilled her. I thought I now understood the words which had dropped from him when he was alone in the drawing-room, "I'll do it today." Alas! the most rigid propriety could hardly have failed to discover that he was doing it now.

"Have you forgotten what we agreed on, Godfrey, when you spoke to me in the country? We agreed that we were to be cousins, and nothing more."

"I break the agreement, Rachel, every time I see you."

"Then don't see me."

"Quite useless! I break the agreement every time I think of you. Oh, Rachel! how kindly you told me, only the other day, that my place in your estimation was a higher place than it had ever been yet! Am I mad to build the hopes I do on those dear words? Am I mad to dream of some future day when your heart may soften to me? Don't tell me so, if I am! Leave me my delusion, dearest! I must have that to cherish, and to comfort me, if I have nothing else!"

His voice trembled, and he put his white handkerchief to his eyes. Exeter Hall again! Nothing wanting to complete the parallel but the audience, the cheers, and the glass of water.

Even her obdurate nature was touched. I saw her lean a little nearer to him. I heard a new tone of interest in her next words.

"Are you really sure, Godfrey, that you are so fond of me as that?"

"Sure! You know what I was, Rachel. Let me tell you what I am. I have lost every interest in life, but my interest in you. A transformation has come over me which I can't account for, myself. Would you believe it? My charitable business is an unendurable nuisance to me; and when I see a Ladies' Committee now, I wish myself at the uttermost ends of the earth!"

If the annals of apostasy offer anything comparable to such a declaration as that, I can only say that the case in point is not producible from the stores of my reading. I thought of the Mothers'-Small-Clothes. I thought of the Sunday-Sweetheart-

Supervision. I thought of the other Societies, too numerous to mention, all built up on this man as on a tower of strength. I thought of the struggling Female Boards, who, so to speak, drew the breath of their business-life through the nostrils of Mr. Godfrey—of that same Mr. Godfrey who had just reviled our good work as a "nuisance"—and just declared that he wished he was at the uttermost ends of the earth when he found himself in our company! My young female friends will feel encouraged to persevere, when I mention that it tried even my discipline before I could devour my own righteous indignation in silence. At the same time, it is only justice to myself to add, that I didn't lose a syllable of the conversation. Rachel was the next to speak.

"You have made your confession," she said. "I wonder whether it would cure you of your unhappy attachment to me, if I made mine?"

He started. I confess I started too. He thought, and I thought, that she was about to divulge the mystery of the Moonstone.

"Would you think, to look at me," she went on, "that I am the wretchedest girl living? It's true, Godfrey. What greater wretchedness can there be than to live degraded in your own estimation? That is my life now."

"My dear Rachel! it's impossible you can have any reason to speak of yourself in that way!"

"How do you know I have no reason?"

"Can you ask me the question! I know it, because I know you. Your silence, dearest, has never lowered you in the estimation of your true friends. The disappearance of your precious birthday gift may seem strange; your unexplained connection with that event may seem stranger still——"

"Are you speaking of the Moonstone, Godfrey?"

"I certainly thought that you referred——"

"I referred to nothing of the sort. I can hear of the loss of the Moonstone, let who will speak of it, without feeling degraded in my own estimation. If the story of the Diamond ever comes to light, it will be known that I accepted a dreadful responsibility; it will be known that I involved myself in the keeping of a miserable secret—but it will be as clear as the sun at noon-day that I did nothing mean! You have misunderstood me, Godfrey. It's my fault for not speaking more plainly. Cost me what it may, I will be plainer now. Suppose you were not in love with me? Suppose you were in love with some other woman?"

"Yes?"

"Suppose you discovered that woman to be utterly unworthy of you? Suppose you were quite convinced that it was a disgrace to you to waste another thought on her? Suppose the bare idea of ever marrying such a person made your face burn, only with thinking of it."

"Yes?"

"And, suppose, in spite of all that—you couldn't tear her from your heart? Suppose the feeling she had roused in you (in the time when you believed in her) was not a feeling to be hidden? Suppose the love this wretch had inspired in you? Oh, how can I find words to say it in! How can I make a man understand that a feeling which horrifies me at myself, can be a feeling that fascinates me at the same time? It's the breath of my life, Godfrey, and it's the poison that kills me—both in one! Go away! I must be out of my mind to talk as I am talking now. No! you mustn't leave me—you mustn't carry away a wrong impression. I must say what is to be said in my own defence. Mind this! He doesn't know—he never will know, what I have told you. I will never see him—I don't care what happens—I will never, never, never see him again! Don't ask me his name! Don't ask me any more! Let's change the subject. Are you doctor enough, Godfrey, to tell me why I feel as if I was stifling for want of breath? Is there a form of hysterics that bursts into words instead of tears? I dare say! What does it matter? You will get over any trouble I have caused you, easily enough now. I have dropped to my right place in your estimation, haven't I? Don't notice me! Don't pity me! For God's sake, go away!"

She turned round on a sudden, and beat her hands wildly on the back of the ottoman. Her head dropped on the cushions; and she burst out crying. Before I had time to feel shocked, at this, I was horror-struck by an entirely unexpected proceeding on the part of Mr. Godfrey. Will it be credited that he fell on his knees at her feet?—on both knees, I solemnly declare! May modesty mention that he put his arms round her next? And may reluctant admiration acknowledge that he electrified her with two words?

"Noble creature!"

No more than that! But he did it with one of the bursts which have made his fame as a public speaker. She sat, either quite thunderstruck, or quite fascinated—I don't know which—without even making an effort to put his arms back where his arms ought to have been. As for me, my sense of propriety was completely bewildered. I was so painfully uncertain whether it was my first duty to close my eyes, or to stop my ears, that I did neither. I attribute my being still able to hold the curtain in the right position for looking and listening, entirely to suppressed hysterics. In suppressed hysterics, it is admitted, even by the doctors, that one must hold something.

"Yes," he said, with all the fascination of his evangelical voice and manner, "you are a noble creature! A woman who can speak the truth, for the truth's own sake—a woman who will sacrifice her pride, rather than sacrifice an honest man who loves her—is the most priceless of all treasures. When such a woman marries, if her husband only wins her esteem and regard, he wins enough to ennoble his whole life. You have spoken, dearest, of your place in my estimation. Judge what that place is—when I implore you on my knees, to let the cure of your poor wounded heart be my care. Rachel! will you honour me, will you bless me, by being my wife?"

By this time I should certainly have decided on stopping my ears, if Rachel had not encouraged me to keep them open, by answering him in the first sensible words I had ever heard fall from her lips.

"Godfrey!" she said, "you must be mad!"

"I never spoke more reasonably, dearest—in your interests, as well as in mine. Look for a moment to the future. Is your happiness to be sacrificed to a man who has never known how you feel towards him, and whom you are resolved never to see again? Is it not your duty to yourself to forget this ill-fated attachment? and is forgetfulness to be found in the life you are leading now? You have tried that life, and you are wearying of it already. Surround yourself with nobler interests than the wretched interests of the world. A heart that loves and honours you; a home whose peaceful claims and happy duties win gently on you day by day—try the consolation, Rachel, which is to be found there! I don't ask for your love—I will be content with your affection and regard. Let the rest be left, confidently left, to your husband's devotion, and to Time that heals even wounds as deep as yours."

She began to yield already. Oh, what a bringing-up she must have had! Oh, how differently I should have acted in her place!

"Don't tempt me, Godfrey," she said; "I am wretched enough and reckless enough as it is. Don't tempt me to be more wretched and more wreckless still!"

"One question, Rachel. Have you any personal objection to me?"

"I! I always liked you. After what you have just said to me, I should be insensible indeed if I didn't respect and admire you as well."

"Do you know many wives, my dear Rachel, who respect and admire their husbands? And yet they and their husbands get on very well. How many brides go to the altar with hearts that would bear inspection by the men who take them there? And yet it doesn't end unhappily—somehow or other the nuptial establishment jogs on. The truth is, that women try marriage as a Refuge, far more numerously than they are willing to admit; and, what is more, they find that marriage has justified their confidence in it. Look at your own case once again. At your age, and with your attractions, is it possible for you to sentence yourself to a single life? Trust my knowledge of the world—nothing is less possible. It is merely a question of time. You may marry some other man, some years hence. Or you may marry the man, dearest, who is now at your feet, and who prizes your respect and admiration above the love of any other woman on the face of the earth."

"Gently, Godfrey! you are putting something into my head which I never thought of before. You are tempting me with a new prospect, when all my other prospects are closed before me. I tell you again, I am miserable enough and desperate enough, if you say another word, to marry you on your own terms. Take the warning, and go!"

"I won't even rise from my knees, till you have said yes!"

"If I say yes you will repent, and I shall repent, when it is too late!"

"We shall both bless the day, darling, when I pressed, and when you yielded."

"Do you feel as confidently as you speak?"

"You shall judge for yourself. I speak from what I have seen in my own family. Tell me what you think of our household at Frizinghall. Do my father and mother live unhappily together?"

"Far from it—so far as I can see."

"When my mother was a girl, Rachel (it is no secret in the family), she had loved as you love—she had given her heart to a man who was unworthy of her. She married my father, respecting him, admiring him, but nothing more. Your own eyes have seen the result. Is there no encouragement in it for you and for me?"*

* See Betteredge's Narrative, chapter viii.

"You won't hurry me, Godfrey?"

"My time shall be yours."

"You won't ask me for more than I can give?"

"My angel! I only ask you to give me yourself."

"Take me!"

In those two words, she accepted him!

He had another burst—a burst of unholy rapture this time. He drew her nearer and nearer to him till her face touched his; and then—No! I really cannot prevail upon myself to carry this shocking disclosure any farther. Let me only say, that I tried to close my eyes before it happened, and that I was just one moment too late. I had calculated, you see, on her resisting. She submitted. To every right-feeling person of my own sex, volumes could say no more.

Even my innocence in such matters began to see its way to the end of the interview now. They understood each other so thoroughly by this time, that I fully expected to see them walk off together, arm in arm, to be married. There appeared, however, judging by Mr. Godfrey's next words, to be one more trifling formality which it was necessary to observe. He seated himself—unforbidden this time—on the ottoman by her side. "Shall I speak to your dear mother?" he asked. "Or will you?"

She declined both alternatives.

"Let my mother hear nothing from either of us, until she is better. I wish it to be kept a secret for the present, Godfrey. Go now, and come back this evening. We have been here alone together quite long enough."

She rose, and, in rising, looked for the first time towards the little room in which my martyrdom was going on.

"Who has drawn those curtains?" she exclaimed.

"The room is close enough, as it is, without keeping the air out of it in that way."

She advanced to the curtains. At the moment when she laid her hand on them—at the moment when the discovery of me appeared to be quite inevitable—the voice of the fresh-coloured young footman, on the stairs, suddenly suspended any further proceedings on her side or on mine. It was unmistakably the voice of a man in great alarm.

"Miss Rachel!" he called out, "where are you, Miss Rachel?"

She sprang back from the curtains, and ran to the door.

The footman came just inside the room. His ruddy colour was all gone. He said, "Please to come downstairs, Miss! My lady has fainted, and we can't bring her to again."

In a moment more I was alone, and free to go downstairs in my turn, quite unobserved.

Mr. Godfrey passed me in the hall, hurrying out, to fetch the doctor. "Go in, and help them!" he said, pointing to the room. I found Rachel on her knees by the sofa, with her mother's head on her bosom. One look at my aunt's face (knowing what I knew) was enough to warn me of the dreadful truth. I kept my thoughts to myself till the doctor came in. It was not long before he arrived. He began by sending Rachel out of the room—and then he told the rest of us that Lady Verinder was no more.

The Moonstone

Serious persons, in search of proofs of hardened scepticism, may be interested in hearing that he showed no signs of remorse when he looked at Me.

At a later hour I peeped into the breakfast-room, and the library. My aunt had died without opening one of the letters which I had addressed to her. I was so shocked at this, that it never occurred to me, until some days afterwards, that she had also died without giving me my little legacy.

CHAPTER VI

(1.) "Miss Clack presents her compliments to Mr. Franklin Blake; and, in sending him the fifth chapter of her humble narrative, begs to say that she feels quite unequal to enlarge as she could wish on an event so awful, under the circumstances, as Lady Verinder's death. She has, therefore, attached to her own manuscripts, copious Extracts from precious publications in her possession, all bearing on this terrible subject. And may those Extracts (Miss Clack fervently hopes) sound as the blast of a trumpet in the ears of her respected kinsman, Mr. Franklin Blake."

(2.) "Mr. Franklin Blake presents his compliments to Miss Clack, and begs to thank her for the fifth chapter of her narrative. In returning the extracts sent with it, he will refrain from mentioning any personal objection which he may entertain to this species of literature, and will merely say that the proposed additions to the manuscript are not necessary to the fulfilment of the purpose that he has in view."

(3.) "Miss Clack begs to acknowledge the return of her Extracts. She affectionately reminds Mr. Franklin Blake that she is a Christian, and that it is, therefore, quite impossible for him to offend her. Miss C. persists in feeling the deepest interest in Mr. Blake, and pledges herself, on the first occasion when sickness may lay him low, to offer him the use of her Extracts for the second time. In the meanwhile she would be glad to know, before beginning the final chapters of her narrative, whether she may be permitted to make her humble contribution complete, by availing herself of the light which later discoveries have thrown on the mystery of the Moonstone."

(4.) "Mr. Franklin Blake is sorry to disappoint Miss Clack. He can only repeat the instructions which he had the honour of giving her when she began her narrative. She is requested to limit herself to her own individual experience of persons and events, as recorded in her diary. Later discoveries she will be good enough to leave to the pens of those persons who can write in the capacity of actual witnesses."

(5.) "Miss Clack is extremely sorry to trouble Mr. Franklin Blake with another letter. Her Extracts have been returned, and the expression of her matured views on the subject of the

Moonstone has been forbidden. Miss Clack is painfully conscious that she ought (in the worldly phrase) to feel herself put down. But, no—Miss C. has learnt Perseverance in the School of Adversity. Her object in writing is to know whether Mr. Blake (who prohibits everything else) prohibits the appearance of the present correspondence in Miss Clack's narrative? Some explanation of the position in which Mr. Blake's interference has placed her as an authoress, seems due on the ground of common justice. And Miss Clack, on her side, is most anxious that her letters should be produced to speak for themselves."

(6.) "Mr. Franklin Blake agrees to Miss Clack's proposal, on the understanding that she will kindly consider this intimation of his consent as closing the correspondence between them."

(7.) "Miss Clack feels it an act of Christian duty (before the correspondence closes) to inform Mr. Franklin Blake that his last letter—evidently intended to offend her—has not succeeded in accomplishing the object of the writer. She affectionately requests Mr. Blake to retire to the privacy of his own room, and to consider with himself whether the training which can thus elevate a poor weak woman above the reach of insult, be not worthy of greater admiration than he is now disposed to feel for it. On being favoured with an intimation to that effect, Miss C. solemnly pledges herself to send back the complete series of her Extracts to Mr. Franklin Blake."

[To this letter no answer was received. Comment is needless.

(Signed) DRUSILLA CLACK.]

CHAPTER VII

The foregoing correspondence will sufficiently explain why no choice is left to me but to pass over Lady Verinder's death with the simple announcement of the fact which ends my fifth chapter.

Keeping myself for the future strictly within the limits of my own personal experience, I have next to relate that a month elapsed from the time of my aunt's decease before Rachel Verinder and I met again. That meeting was the occasion of my spending a few days under the same roof with her. In the course of my visit, something happened, relative to her marriage-engagement with Mr. Godfrey Ablewhite, which is important enough to require special notice in these pages. When this last of many painful family circumstances has been disclosed, my task will be completed; for I shall then have told all that I know, as an actual (and most unwilling) witness of events.

My aunt's remains were removed from London, and were buried in the little cemetery attached to the church in her own park. I was invited to the funeral with the rest of the family. But it was impossible (with my religious views) to rouse myself in a few days only from the shock which this death had caused me. I was informed, moreover, that the rector of Frizinghall was to read the service. Having myself in past times seen this clerical castaway making one of the players at Lady Verinder's whist-table, I doubt, even if I had been fit to travel, whether I should have felt justified in attending the ceremony.

Lady Verinder's death left her daughter under the care of her brother-in-law, Mr. Ablewhite the elder. He was appointed guardian by the will, until his niece married, or came of age. Under these circumstances, Mr. Godfrey informed his father, I suppose, of the new relation in which he stood towards Rachel. At any rate, in ten days from my aunt's death, the secret of the marriage-engagement was no secret at all within the circle of the family, and the grand question for Mr. Ablewhite senior — another confirmed castaway! — was how to make himself and his authority most agreeable to the wealthy young lady who was going to marry his son.

Rachel gave him some trouble at the outset, about the choice of a place in which she could be prevailed upon to reside. The house in Montagu Square was associated with the calamity of her mother's death. The house in Yorkshire was associated with the scandalous affair of the lost Moonstone. Her guardian's own residence at Frizinghall was open to neither of these objections. But Rachel's presence in it, after her recent bereavement, operated as a check on the gaieties of her cousins, the Miss Ablewhites—and she herself requested that her visit might be deferred to a more favourable opportunity. It ended in a proposal, emanating from old Mr. Ablewhite, to try a furnished house at Brighton. His wife, an invalid daughter, and Rachel were to inhabit it together, and were to expect him to join them later in the season. They would see no society but a few old friends, and they would have his son Godfrey, travelling backwards and forwards by the London train, always at their disposal.

I describe this aimless flitting about from one place of residence to another—this insatiate restlessness of body and appalling stagnation of soul—merely with the view to arriving at results. The event which (under Providence) proved to be the means of bringing Rachel Verinder and myself together again, was no other than the hiring of the house at Brighton.

My Aunt Ablewhite is a large, silent, fair-complexioned woman, with one noteworthy point in her character. From the hour of her birth she has never been known to do anything for herself. She has gone through life, accepting everybody's help, and adopting everybody's opinions. A more hopeless person, in a spiritual point of view, I have never met with—there is absolutely, in this perplexing case, no obstructive material to work upon. Aunt Ablewhite would listen to the Grand Lama of Thibet exactly as she listens to Me, and would reflect his views quite as readily as she reflects mine. She found the furnished house at Brighton by stopping at an hotel in London, composing herself on a sofa, and sending for her son. She discovered the necessary servants by breakfasting in bed one morning (still at the hotel), and giving her maid a holiday on condition that the girl "would begin enjoying herself by fetching Miss Clack." I found her placidly fanning herself in her dressing-gown at eleven o'clock. "Drusilla, dear, I want some servants. You are so clever—please get them for me." I looked round the untidy room. The church-bells were going for a week-day service; they suggested a word of affectionate remonstrance on my part. "Oh, aunt!" I said sadly. "Is this worthy of a Christian Englishwoman? Is the passage from time to eternity to be made in this manner?" My aunt answered, "I'll put on my gown, Drusilla, if you will be kind enough to help me." What was to be said after that? I have done wonders with murderesses—I have never advanced an inch with Aunt Ablewhite. "Where is the list," I asked, "of the servants whom you require?" My aunt shook her head; she hadn't even energy enough to keep the list. "Rachel has got it, dear," she said, "in the next room." I went into the next room, and so saw Rachel again for the first time since we had parted in Montagu Square.

She looked pitiably small and thin in her deep mourning. If I attached any serious importance to such a perishable trifle as personal appearance, I might be inclined to add that hers was one of those unfortunate complexions which always suffer when not relieved by a border of white next the skin. But what are our complexions and our looks? Hindrances and pitfalls, dear girls, which beset us on our way to higher things! Greatly to my surprise, Rachel rose when I entered the room, and came forward to meet me with outstretched hand.

"I am glad to see you," she said. "Drusilla, I have been in the habit of speaking very foolishly and very rudely to you, on former occasions. I beg your pardon. I hope you will forgive me."

My face, I suppose, betrayed the astonishment I felt at this. She coloured up for a moment, and then proceeded to explain herself.

"In my poor mother's lifetime," she went on, "her friends were not always my friends, too. Now I have lost her, my heart turns for comfort to the people she liked. She liked you. Try to be friends with me, Drusilla, if you can."

To any rightly-constituted mind, the motive thus acknowledged was simply shocking. Here in Christian England was a young woman in a state of bereavement, with so little idea of where to look for true comfort, that she actually expected to find it among her mother's friends! Here was a relative of mine, awakened to a sense of her shortcomings towards others, under the influence, not of conviction and duty, but of sentiment and impulse! Most deplorable to think of—but, still, suggestive of something hopeful, to a person of my experience in plying the good work. There could be no harm, I thought, in ascertaining the extent of the change which the loss of her mother had wrought in Rachel's character. I decided, as a useful test, to probe her on the subject of her marriage-engagement to Mr. Godfrey Ablewhite.

Having first met her advances with all possible cordiality, I sat by her on the sofa, at her own request. We discussed family affairs and future plans—always excepting that one future plan which was to end in her marriage. Try as I might to turn the conversation that way, she resolutely declined to take the hint. Any open reference to the question, on my part, would have been premature at this early stage of our reconciliation. Besides, I had discovered all I wanted to know. She was no longer the reckless, defiant creature whom I had heard and seen, on the occasion of my martyrdom in Montagu Square. This was, of itself, enough to encourage me to take her future conversion in hand—beginning with a few words of earnest warning directed against the hasty formation of the marriage tie, and so getting on to higher things. Looking at her, now, with this new interest—and calling to mind the headlong suddenness with which she had met Mr. Godfrey's matrimonial views—I felt the solemn duty of interfering with a fervour which assured me that I should achieve no common results. Rapidity of proceeding was, as I believed, of importance in this case. I went back at once to the question of the servants wanted for the furnished house.

"Where is the list, dear?"

Rachel produced it.

"Cook, kitchen-maid, housemaid, and footman," I read. "My dear Rachel, these servants are only wanted for a term—the term during which your guardian has taken the house. We shall have great difficulty in finding persons of character and capacity to accept a temporary engagement of that sort, if we try in London. Has the house in Brighton been found yet?"

"Yes. Godfrey has taken it; and persons in the house wanted him to hire them as servants. He thought they would hardly do for us, and came back having settled nothing."

"And you have no experience yourself in these matters,

Rachel?"

"None whatever."

"And Aunt Ablewhite won't exert herself?"

"No, poor dear. Don't blame her, Drusilla. I think she is the only really happy woman I have ever met with."

"There are degrees in happiness, darling. We must have a little talk, some day, on that subject. In the meantime I will undertake to meet the difficulty about the servants. Your aunt will write a letter to the people of the house——"

"She will sign a letter, if I write it for her, which comes to the same thing."

"Quite the same thing. I shall get the letter, and I will go to Brighton tomorrow."

"How extremely kind of you! We will join you as soon as you are ready for us. And you will stay, I hope, as my guest. Brighton is so lively; you are sure to enjoy it."

In those words the invitation was given, and the glorious prospect of interference was opened before me.

It was then the middle of the week. By Saturday afternoon the house was ready for them. In that short interval I had sifted, not the characters only, but the religious views as well, of all the disengaged servants who applied to me, and had succeeded in making a selection which my conscience approved. I also discovered, and called on two serious friends of mine, residents in the town, to whom I knew I could confide the pious object which had brought me to Brighton. One of them—a clerical friend—kindly helped me to take sittings for our little party in the church in which he himself ministered. The other—a single lady, like myself—placed the resources of her library (composed throughout of precious publications) entirely at my disposal. I borrowed half-a-dozen works, all carefully chosen with a view to Rachel. When these had been judiciously distributed in the various rooms she would be likely to occupy, I considered that my preparations were complete. Sound doctrine in the servants who waited on her; sound doctrine in the minister who preached to her; sound doctrine in the books that lay on her table—such was the treble welcome which my zeal had prepared for the motherless girl! A heavenly composure filled my mind, on that Saturday afternoon, as I sat at the window waiting the arrival of my relatives. The giddy throng passed and repassed before my eyes. Alas! how many of them felt my exquisite sense of duty done? An awful question. Let us not pursue it.

Between six and seven the travellers arrived. To my indescribable surprise, they were escorted, not by Mr. Godfrey (as I had anticipated), but by the lawyer, Mr. Bruff.

"How do you do, Miss Clack?" he said. "I mean to stay this time."

That reference to the occasion on which I had obliged him to postpone his business to mine, when we were both visiting in Montagu Square, satisfied me that the old worldling had come to Brighton with some object of his own in view. I had prepared quite a little Paradise for my beloved Rachel—and here was the Serpent already!

"Godfrey was very much vexed, Drusilla, not to be able to come with us," said my Aunt Ablewhite. "There was something in the way which kept him in town. Mr. Bruff volunteered to take his place, and make a holiday of it till Monday morning. By-the-bye, Mr. Bruff, I'm ordered to take exercise, and I don't like it. That," added Aunt Ablewhite, pointing out of window to an invalid going by in a chair on wheels, drawn by a man, "is my idea of exercise. If it's air you want, you get it in your chair. And if it's fatigue you want, I am sure it's fatigue enough to look at the man."

Rachel stood silent, at a window by herself, with her eyes fixed on the sea.

"Tired, love?" I inquired.

"No. Only a little out of spirits," she answered. "I have often seen the sea, on our Yorkshire coast, with that light on it. And I was thinking, Drusilla, of the days that can never come again."

Mr. Bruff remained to dinner, and stayed through the evening. The more I saw of him, the more certain I felt that he had some private end to serve in coming to Brighton. I watched him carefully. He maintained the same appearance of ease, and talked the same godless gossip, hour after hour, until it was time to take leave. As he shook hands with Rachel, I caught his hard and cunning eyes resting on her for a moment with a peculiar interest and attention. She was plainly concerned in the object that he had in view. He said nothing out of the common to her or to anyone on leaving. He invited himself to luncheon the next day, and then he went away to his hotel.

It was impossible the next morning to get my Aunt Ablewhite out of her dressing-gown in time for church. Her invalid daughter (suffering from nothing, in my opinion, but incurable laziness, inherited from her mother) announced that she meant to remain in bed for the day. Rachel and I went alone together to church. A magnificent sermon was preached by my gifted friend on the heathen indifference of the world to the sinfulness of little sins. For more than an hour his eloquence (assisted by his glorious voice) thundered through the sacred edifice. I said to Rachel, when we came out, "Has it found its way to your heart, dear?" And she answered, "No; it has only made my head ache." This might have been discouraging to some people; but, once embarked on a career of manifest usefulness, nothing discourages Me.

We found Aunt Ablewhite and Mr. Bruff at luncheon. When Rachel declined eating anything, and gave as a reason for it that she was suffering from a headache, the lawyer's cunning instantly saw, and seized, the chance that she had given him.

"There is only one remedy for a headache," said this horrible old man. "A walk, Miss Rachel, is the thing to cure you. I am entirely at your service, if you will honour me by accepting my arm."

"With the greatest pleasure. A walk is the very thing I was longing for."

"It's past two," I gently suggested. "And the afternoon service, Rachel, begins at three."

"How can you expect me to go to church again," she asked, petulantly, "with such a headache as mine?"

Mr. Bruff officiously opened the door for her. In another minute more they were both out of the house. I don't know when I have felt the solemn duty of interfering so strongly as I felt it at that moment. But what was to be done? Nothing was to

The Moonstone

be done but to interfere at the first opportunity, later in the day.

On my return from the afternoon service I found that they had just got back. One look at them told me that the lawyer had said what he wanted to say. I had never before seen Rachel so silent and so thoughtful. I had never before seen Mr. Bruff pay her such devoted attention, and look at her with such marked respect. He had (or pretended that he had) an engagement to dinner that day — and he took an early leave of us all; intending to go back to London by the first train the next morning.

"Are you sure of your own resolution?" he said to Rachel at the door.

"Quite sure," she answered — and so they parted.

The moment his back was turned, Rachel withdrew to her own room. She never appeared at dinner. Her maid (the person with the cap-ribbons) was sent downstairs to announce that her headache had returned. I ran up to her and made all sorts of sisterly offers through the door. It was locked, and she kept it locked. Plenty of obstructive material to work on here! I felt greatly cheered and stimulated by her locking the door.

When her cup of tea went up to her the next morning, I followed it in. I sat by her bedside and said a few earnest words. She listened with languid civility. I noticed my serious friend's precious publications huddled together on a table in a corner. Had she chanced to look into them? — I asked. Yes — and they had not interested her. Would she allow me to read a few passages of the deepest interest, which had probably escaped her eye? No, not now — she had other things to think of. She gave these answers, with her attention apparently absorbed in folding and refolding the frilling on her nightgown. It was plainly necessary to rouse her by some reference to those worldly interests which she still had at heart.

"Do you know, love," I said, "I had an odd fancy, yesterday, about Mr. Bruff? I thought, when I saw you after your walk with him, that he had been telling you some bad news."

Her fingers dropped from the frilling of her nightgown, and her fierce black eyes flashed at me.

"Quite the contrary!" she said. "It was news I was interested in hearing — and I am deeply indebted to Mr. Bruff for telling me of it."

"Yes?" I said, in a tone of gentle interest.

Her fingers went back to the frilling, and she turned her head sullenly away from me. I had been met in this manner, in the course of plying the good work, hundreds of times. She merely stimulated me to try again. In my dauntless zeal for her welfare, I ran the great risk, and openly alluded to her marriage engagement.

"News you were interested in hearing?" I repeated. "I suppose, my dear Rachel, that must be news of Mr. Godfrey Ablewhite?"

She started up in the bed, and turned deadly pale. It was evidently on the tip of her tongue to retort on me with the unbridled insolence of former times. She checked herself—laid her head back on the pillow—considered a minute—and then answered in these remarkable words:

"I shall never marry Mr. Godfrey Ablewhite."

It was my turn to start at that.

"What can you possibly mean?" I exclaimed. "The marriage is considered by the whole family as a settled thing!"

"Mr. Godfrey Ablewhite is expected here today," she said doggedly. "Wait till he comes—and you will see."

"But my dear Rachel——"

She rang the bell at the head of her bed. The person with the cap-ribbons appeared.

"Penelope! my bath."

Let me give her her due. In the state of my feelings at that moment, I do sincerely believe that she had hit on the only possible way of forcing me to leave the room.

By the mere worldly mind my position towards Rachel might have been viewed as presenting difficulties of no ordinary kind. I had reckoned on leading her to higher things by means of a little earnest exhortation on the subject of her marriage. And now, if she was to be believed, no such event as her marriage was to take place at all. But ah, my friends! a working Christian of my experience (with an evangelising prospect before her) takes broader views than these. Supposing Rachel really broke off the marriage, on which the Ablewhites, father and son, counted as a settled thing, what would be the result? It could only end, if she held firm, in an exchanging of hard words and bitter accusations on both sides. And what would be the effect on Rachel when the stormy interview was over? A salutary moral depression would be the effect. Her pride would be exhausted, her stubbornness would be exhausted, by the resolute resistance which it was in her character to make under the circumstances. She would turn for sympathy to the nearest person who had sympathy to offer. And I was that nearest person — brimful of comfort, charged to overflowing with seasonable and reviving words. Never had the evangelising prospect looked brighter, to my eyes, than it looked now.

She came down to breakfast, but she ate nothing, and hardly uttered a word.

After breakfast she wandered listlessly from room to room — then suddenly roused herself, and opened the piano. The music she selected to play was of the most scandalously profane sort, associated with performances on the stage which it curdles one's blood to think of. It would have been premature to interfere with her at such a time as this. I privately ascertained the hour at which Mr. Godfrey Ablewhite was expected, and then I escaped the music by leaving the house.

Being out alone, I took the opportunity of calling upon my two resident friends. It was an indescribable luxury to find myself indulging in earnest conversation with serious persons. Infinitely encouraged and refreshed, I turned my steps back again to the house, in excellent time to await the arrival of our expected visitor. I entered the dining-room, always empty at that hour of the day, and found myself face to face with Mr. Godfrey Ablewhite!

He made no attempt to fly the place. Quite the contrary. He advanced to meet me with the utmost eagerness.

"Dear Miss Clack, I have been only waiting to see you! Chance set me free of my London engagements today sooner than I had expected, and I have got here, in consequence, earlier than my appointed time."

Not the slightest embarrassment encumbered his explanation, though this was his first meeting with me after the scene in Montagu Square. He was not aware, it is true, of my having been a witness of that scene. But he knew, on the other hand, that my attendances at the Mothers' Small-Clothes, and my relations with friends attached to other charities, must have informed me of his shameless neglect of his Ladies and of his Poor. And yet there he was before me, in full possession of his charming voice and his irresistible smile!

"Have you seen Rachel yet?" I asked.

He sighed gently, and took me by the hand. I should certainly have snatched my hand away, if the manner in which he gave his answer had not paralysed me with astonishment.

"I have seen Rachel," he said with perfect tranquillity. "You are aware, dear friend, that she was engaged to me? Well, she has taken a sudden resolution to break the engagement. Reflection has convinced her that she will best consult her welfare and mine by retracting a rash promise, and leaving me free to make some happier choice elsewhere. That is the only reason she will give, and the only answer she will make to every question that I can ask of her."

"What have you done on your side?" I inquired. "Have you submitted."

"Yes," he said with the most unruffled composure, "I have submitted."

His conduct, under the circumstances, was so utterly inconceivable, that I stood bewildered with my hand in his. It is a piece of rudeness to stare at anybody, and it is an act of indelicacy to stare at a gentleman. I committed both those improprieties. And I said, as if in a dream, "What does it mean?"

"Permit me to tell you," he replied. "And suppose we sit down?"

He led me to a chair. I have an indistinct remembrance that he was very affectionate. I don't think he put his arm round my waist to support me—but I am not sure. I was quite helpless, and his ways with ladies were very endearing. At any rate, we sat down. I can answer for that, if I can answer for nothing more.

CHAPTER VIII

"I have lost a beautiful girl, an excellent social position, and a handsome income," Mr. Godfrey began; "and I have submitted to it without a struggle. What can be the motive for such extraordinary conduct as that? My precious friend, there is no motive."

"No motive?" I repeated.

"Let me appeal, my dear Miss Clack, to your experience of children," he went on. "A child pursues a certain course of conduct. You are greatly struck by it, and you attempt to get at the motive. The dear little thing is incapable of telling you its motive. You might as well ask the grass why it grows, or the birds why they sing. Well! in this matter, I am like the dear little thing—like the grass—like the birds. I don't know why I made a proposal of marriage to Miss Verinder. I don't know why I have shamefully neglected my dear Ladies. I don't know why I have apostatised from the Mothers' Small-Clothes. You say to the child, Why have you been naughty? And the little angel puts its finger into its mouth, and doesn't know. My case exactly, Miss Clack! I couldn't confess it to anybody else. I feel impelled to confess it to you!"

I began to recover myself. A mental problem was involved here. I am deeply interested in mental problems—and I am not, it is thought, without some skill in solving them.

"Best of friends, exert your intellect, and help me," he proceeded. "Tell me—why does a time come when these matrimonial proceedings of mine begin to look like something done in a dream? Why does it suddenly occur to me that my true happiness is in helping my dear Ladies, in going my modest round of useful work, in saying my few earnest words when called on by my Chairman? What do I want with a position? I have got a position! What do I want with an income? I can pay for my bread and cheese, and my nice little lodging, and my two coats a year. What do I want with Miss Verinder? She has told me with her own lips (this, dear lady, is between ourselves) that she loves another man, and that her only idea in marrying me is to try and put that other man out of her head. What a horrid union is this! Oh, dear me, what a horrid union is this! Such are my reflections, Miss Clack, on my way to

Brighton. I approach Rachel with the feeling of a criminal who is going to receive his sentence. When I find that she has changed her mind too—when I hear her propose to break the engagement—I experience (there is no sort of doubt about it) a most overpowering sense of relief. A month ago I was pressing her rapturously to my bosom. An hour ago, the happiness of knowing that I shall never press her again, intoxicates me like strong liquor. The thing seems impossible—the thing can't be. And yet there are the facts, as I had the honour of stating them when we first sat down together in these two chairs. I have lost a beautiful girl, an excellent social position, and a handsome income; and I have submitted to it without a struggle. Can you account for it, dear friend? It's quite beyond me."

His magnificent head sank on his breast, and he gave up his own mental problem in despair.

I was deeply touched. The case (if I may speak as a spiritual physician) was now quite plain to me. It is no uncommon event, in the experience of us all, to see the possessors of exalted ability occasionally humbled to the level of the most poorly-gifted people about them. The object, no doubt, in the wise economy of Providence, is to remind greatness that it is mortal and that the power which has conferred it can also take it away. It was now—to my mind—easy to discern one of these salutary humiliations in the deplorable proceedings on dear Mr. Godfrey's part, of which I had been the unseen witness. And it was equally easy to recognise the welcome reappearance of his own finer nature in the horror with which he recoiled from the idea of a marriage with Rachel, and in the charming eagerness which he showed to return to his Ladies and his Poor.

I put this view before him in a few simple and sisterly words. His joy was beautiful to see. He compared himself, as I went on, to a lost man emerging from the darkness into the light. When I answered for a loving reception of him at the Mothers' Small-Clothes, the grateful heart of our Christian Hero overflowed. He pressed my hands alternately to his lips. Overwhelmed by the exquisite triumph of having got him back among us, I let him do what he liked with my hands. I closed my eyes. I felt my head, in an ecstasy of spiritual self-forgetfulness, sinking on his shoulder. In a moment more I should certainly have swooned away in his arms, but for an interruption from the outer world, which brought me to myself again. A horrid rattling of knives and forks sounded outside the door, and the footman came in to lay the table for luncheon.

Mr. Godfrey started up, and looked at the clock on the mantelpiece.

"How time flies with you!" he exclaimed. "I shall barely catch the train."

I ventured on asking why he was in such a hurry to get back to town. His answer reminded me of family difficulties that were still to be reconciled, and of family disagreements that were yet to come.

"I have heard from my father," he said. "Business obliges him to leave Frizinghall for London today, and he proposes coming on here, either this evening or tomorrow. I must tell him what has happened between Rachel and me. His heart is set on our marriage—there will be great difficulty, I fear, in reconciling him to the breaking-off of the engagement. I must stop him, for all our sakes, from coming here till he is reconciled. Best and dearest of friends, we shall meet again!"

With those words he hurried out. In equal haste on my side, I ran upstairs to compose myself in my own room before meeting Aunt Ablewhite and Rachel at the luncheon-table.

I am well aware—to dwell for a moment yet on the subject of Mr. Godfrey—that the all-profaning opinion of the world has charged him with having his own private reasons for releasing Rachel from her engagement, at the first opportunity she gave him. It has also reached my ears, that his anxiety to recover his place in my estimation has been attributed in certain quarters, to a mercenary eagerness to make his peace (through me) with a venerable committee-woman at the Mothers' Small-Clothes, abundantly blessed with the goods of this world, and a beloved and intimate friend of my own. I only notice these odious slanders for the sake of declaring that they never had a moment's influence on my mind. In obedience to my instructions, I have exhibited the fluctuations in my opinion of our Christian Hero, exactly as I find them recorded in my diary. In justice to myself, let me here add that, once reinstated in his place in my estimation, my gifted friend never lost that place again. I write with the tears in my eyes, burning to say more.

The Moonstone

But no—I am cruelly limited to my actual experience of persons and things. In less than a month from the time of which I am now writing, events in the money-market (which diminished even my miserable little income) forced me into foreign exile, and left me with nothing but a loving remembrance of Mr. Godfrey which the slander of the world has assailed, and assailed in vain.

Let me dry my eyes, and return to my narrative.

I went downstairs to luncheon, naturally anxious to see how Rachel was affected by her release from her marriage engagement.

It appeared to me—but I own I am a poor authority in such matters—that the recovery of her freedom had set her thinking again of that other man whom she loved, and that she was furious with herself for not being able to control a revulsion of feeling of which she was secretly ashamed. Who was the man? I had my suspicions—but it was needless to waste time in idle speculation. When I had converted her, she would, as a matter of course, have no concealments from Me. I should hear all about the man; I should hear all about the Moonstone. If I had had no higher object in stirring her up to a sense of spiritual things, the motive of relieving her mind of its guilty secrets would have been enough of itself to encourage me to go on.

Aunt Ablewhite took her exercise in the afternoon in an invalid chair. Rachel accompanied her. "I wish I could drag the chair," she broke out, recklessly. "I wish I could fatigue myself till I was ready to drop."

She was in the same humour in the evening. I discovered in one of my friend's precious publications—the Life, Letters, and Labours of Miss Jane Ann Stamper, forty-fourth edition—passages which bore with a marvellous appropriateness on Rachel's present position. Upon my proposing to read them, she went to the piano. Conceive how little she must have known of serious people, if she supposed that my patience was to be exhausted in that way! I kept Miss Jane Ann Stamper by me, and waited for events with the most unfaltering trust in the future.

Old Mr. Ablewhite never made his appearance that night. But I knew the importance which his worldly greed attached to his son's marriage with Miss Verinder—and I felt a positive conviction (do what Mr. Godfrey might to prevent it) that we should see him the next day. With his interference in the matter, the storm on which I had counted would certainly come, and the salutary exhaustion of Rachel's resisting powers would as certainly follow. I am not ignorant that old Mr. Ablewhite has the reputation generally (especially among his inferiors) of being a remarkably good-natured man. According to my observation of him, he deserves his reputation as long as he has his own way, and not a moment longer.

The next day, exactly as I had foreseen, Aunt Ablewhite was as near to being astonished as her nature would permit, by the sudden appearance of her husband. He had barely been a minute in the house, before he was followed, to my astonishment this time, by an unexpected complication in the shape of Mr. Bruff.

I never remember feeling the presence of the lawyer to be more unwelcome than I felt it at that moment. He looked ready for anything in the way of an obstructive proceeding—capable even of keeping the peace with Rachel for one of the combatants!

"This is a pleasant surprise, sir," said Mr. Ablewhite, addressing himself with his deceptive cordiality to Mr. Bruff. "When I left your office yesterday, I didn't expect to have the honour of seeing you at Brighton today."

"I turned over our conversation in my mind, after you had gone," replied Mr. Bruff. "And it occurred to me that I might perhaps be of some use on this occasion. I was just in time to catch the train, and I had no opportunity of discovering the carriage in which you were travelling."

Having given that explanation, he seated himself by Rachel. I retired modestly to a corner—with Miss Jane Ann Stamper on my lap, in case of emergency. My aunt sat at the window; placidly fanning herself as usual. Mr. Ablewhite stood up in the middle of the room, with his bald head much pinker than I had ever seen it yet, and addressed himself in the most affectionate manner to his niece.

"Rachel, my dear," he said, "I have heard some very extraordinary news from Godfrey. And I am here to inquire about it. You have a sitting-room of your own in this house. Will you honour me by showing me the way to it?"

Rachel never moved. Whether she was determined to bring matters to a crisis, or whether she was prompted by some private sign from Mr. Bruff, is more than I can tell. She declined doing old Mr. Ablewhite the honour of conducting him into her sitting-room.

"Whatever you wish to say to me," she answered, "can be said here—in the presence of my relatives, and in the presence" (she looked at Mr. Bruff) "of my mother's trusted old friend."

"Just as you please, my dear," said the amiable Mr. Ablewhite. He took a chair. The rest of them looked at his face—as if they expected it, after seventy years of worldly training, to speak the truth. I looked at the top of his bald head; having noticed on other occasions that the temper which was really in him had a habit of registering itself there.

"Some weeks ago," pursued the old gentleman, "my son informed me that Miss Verinder had done him the honour to engage herself to marry him. Is it possible, Rachel, that he can have misinterpreted—or presumed upon—what you really said to him?"

"Certainly not," she replied. "I did engage myself to marry him."

"Very frankly answered!" said Mr. Ablewhite. "And most satisfactory, my dear, so far. In respect to what happened some weeks since, Godfrey has made no mistake. The error is evidently in what he told me yesterday. I begin to see it now. You and he have had a lovers' quarrel—and my foolish son has interpreted it seriously. Ah! I should have known better than that at his age."

The fallen nature in Rachel—the mother Eve, so to speak—began to chafe at this.

"Pray let us understand each other, Mr. Ablewhite," she said. "Nothing in the least like a quarrel took place yesterday between your son and me. If he told you that I proposed breaking off our marriage engagement, and that he agreed on his side—he told you the truth."

The self-registering thermometer at the top of Mr. Ablewhite's bald head began to indicate a rise of temper. His face was more amiable than ever—but there was the pink at the top of his face, a shade deeper already!

"Come, come, my dear!" he said, in his most soothing manner, "now don't be angry, and don't be hard on poor Godfrey! He has evidently said some unfortunate thing. He was always clumsy from a child—but he means well, Rachel, he means well!"

"Mr. Ablewhite, I have either expressed myself very badly, or you are purposely mistaking me. Once for all, it is a settled thing between your son and myself that we remain, for the rest of our lives, cousins and nothing more. Is that plain enough?"

The tone in which she said those words made it impossible, even for old Mr. Ablewhite, to mistake her any longer. His thermometer went up another degree, and his voice when he next spoke, ceased to be the voice which is appropriate to a notoriously good-natured man.

"I am to understand, then," he said, "that your marriage engagement is broken off?"

"You are to understand that, Mr. Ablewhite, if you please."

"I am also to take it as a matter of fact that the proposal to withdraw from the engagement came, in the first instance, from you?"

"It came, in the first instance, from me. And it met, as I have told you, with your son's consent and approval."

The thermometer went up to the top of the register. I mean, the pink changed suddenly to scarlet.

"My son is a mean-spirited hound!" cried this furious old worldling. "In justice to myself as his father—not in justice to him—I beg to ask you, Miss Verinder, what complaint you have to make of Mr. Godfrey Ablewhite?"

Here Mr. Bruff interfered for the first time.

"You are not bound to answer that question," he said to Rachel.

Old Mr. Ablewhite fastened on him instantly.

The Moonstone

"Don't forget, sir," he said, "that you are a self-invited guest here. Your interference would have come with a better grace if you had waited until it was asked for."

Mr. Bruff took no notice. The smooth varnish on his wicked old face never cracked. Rachel thanked him for the advice he had given to her, and then turned to old Mr. Ablewhite—preserving her composure in a manner which (having regard to her age and her sex) was simply awful to see.

"Your son put the same question to me which you have just asked," she said. "I had only one answer for him, and I have only one answer for you. I proposed that we should release each other, because reflection had convinced me that I should best consult his welfare and mine by retracting a rash promise, and leaving him free to make his choice elsewhere."

"What has my son done?" persisted Mr. Ablewhite. "I have a right to know that. What has my son done?"

She persisted just as obstinately on her side.

"You have had the only explanation which I think it necessary to give to you, or to him," she answered.

"In plain English, it's your sovereign will and pleasure, Miss Verinder, to jilt my son?"

Rachel was silent for a moment. Sitting close behind her, I heard her sigh. Mr. Bruff took her hand, and gave it a little squeeze. She recovered herself, and answered Mr. Ablewhite as boldly as ever.

"I have exposed myself to worse misconstruction than that," she said. "And I have borne it patiently. The time has gone by, when you could mortify me by calling me a jilt."

She spoke with a bitterness of tone which satisfied me that the scandal of the Moonstone had been in some way recalled to her mind. "I have no more to say," she added, wearily, not addressing the words to anyone in particular, and looking away from us all, out of the window that was nearest to her.

Mr. Ablewhite got upon his feet, and pushed away his chair so violently that it toppled over and fell on the floor.

"I have something more to say on my side," he announced,

bringing down the flat of his hand on the table with a bang. "I have to say that if my son doesn't feel this insult, I do!"

Rachel started, and looked at him in sudden surprise.

"Insult?" she repeated. "What do you mean?"

"Insult!" reiterated Mr. Ablewhite. "I know your motive, Miss Verinder, for breaking your promise to my son! I know it as certainly as if you had confessed it in so many words. Your cursed family pride is insulting Godfrey, as it insulted me when I married your aunt. Her family—her beggarly family—turned their backs on her for marrying an honest man, who had made his own place and won his own fortune. I had no ancestors. I wasn't descended from a set of cut-throat scoundrels who lived by robbery and murder. I couldn't point to the time when the Ablewhites hadn't a shirt to their backs, and couldn't sign their own names. Ha! ha! I wasn't good enough for the Herncastles, when I married. And now, it comes to the pinch, my son isn't good enough for you. I suspected it, all along. You have got the Herncastle blood in you, my young lady! I suspected it all along."

"A very unworthy suspicion," remarked Mr. Bruff. "I am astonished that you have the courage to acknowledge it."

Before Mr. Ablewhite could find words to answer in, Rachel spoke in a tone of the most exasperating contempt.

"Surely," she said to the lawyer, "this is beneath notice. If he can think in that way, let us leave him to think as he pleases."

From scarlet, Mr. Ablewhite was now becoming purple. He gasped for breath; he looked backwards and forwards from Rachel to Mr. Bruff in such a frenzy of rage with both of them that he didn't know which to attack first. His wife, who had sat impenetrably fanning herself up to this time, began to be alarmed, and attempted, quite uselessly, to quiet him. I had, throughout this distressing interview, felt more than one inward call to interfere with a few earnest words, and had controlled myself under a dread of the possible results, very unworthy of a Christian Englishwoman who looks, not to what is meanly prudent, but to what is morally right. At the point at which matters had now arrived, I rose superior to all considerations of mere expediency. If I had contemplated interposing any remonstrance of my own humble devising, I might possibly have still hesitated. But the distressing domestic emergency which now confronted me, was most marvellously and beautifully provided for in the Correspondence of Miss Jane Ann Stamper—Letter one thousand and one, on "Peace in Families." I rose in my modest corner, and I opened my precious book.

"Dear Mr. Ablewhite," I said, "one word!"

When I first attracted the attention of the company by rising, I could see that he was on the point of saying something rude to me. My sisterly form of address checked him. He stared at me in heathen astonishment.

"As an affectionate well-wisher and friend," I proceeded, "and as one long accustomed to arouse, convince, prepare, enlighten, and fortify others, permit me to take the most pardonable of all liberties—the liberty of composing your mind."

He began to recover himself; he was on the point of breaking out—he would have broken out, with anybody else. But my voice (habitually gentle) possesses a high note or so, in emergencies. In this emergency, I felt imperatively called upon to have the highest voice of the two.

I held up my precious book before him; I rapped the open page impressively with my forefinger. "Not my words!" I exclaimed, in a burst of fervent interruption. "Oh, don't suppose that I claim attention for My humble words! Manna in the wilderness, Mr. Ablewhite! Dew on the parched earth! Words of comfort, words of wisdom, words of love—the blessed, blessed, blessed words of Miss Jane Ann Stamper!"

I was stopped there by a momentary impediment of the breath. Before I could recover myself, this monster in human form shouted out furiously,

"Miss Jane Ann Stamper be — —!"

It is impossible for me to write the awful word, which is here represented by a blank. I shrieked as it passed his lips; I flew to my little bag on the side table; I shook out all my tracts; I seized the one particular tract on profane swearing, entitled, "Hush, for Heaven's Sake!"; I handed it to him with an expression of agonised entreaty. He tore it in two, and threw it back at me across the table. The rest of them rose in alarm, not knowing what might happen next. I instantly sat down again in my corner. There had once been an occasion, under somewhat similar circumstances, when Miss Jane Ann Stamper had been taken by the two shoulders and turned out of a room. I waited, inspired by her spirit, for a repetition of her martyrdom.

But no—it was not to be. His wife was the next person whom he addressed. "Who—who—who," he said, stammering with rage, "who asked this impudent fanatic into the house? Did you?"

Before Aunt Ablewhite could say a word, Rachel answered for her.

"Miss Clack is here," she said, "as my guest."

Those words had a singular effect on Mr. Ablewhite. They suddenly changed him from a man in a state of red-hot anger to a man in a state of icy-cold contempt. It was plain to everybody that Rachel had said something—short and plain as her answer had been—which gave him the upper hand of her at last.

"Oh?" he said. "Miss Clack is here as your guest—in my house?"

It was Rachel's turn to lose her temper at that. Her colour rose, and her eyes brightened fiercely. She turned to the lawyer, and, pointing to Mr. Ablewhite, asked haughtily, "What does he mean?"

Mr. Bruff interfered for the third time.

"You appear to forget," he said, addressing Mr. Ablewhite, "that you took this house as Miss Verinder's guardian, for Miss Verinder's use."

"Not quite so fast," interposed Mr. Ablewhite. "I have a last word to say, which I should have said some time since, if this——" He looked my way, pondering what abominable name he should call me—"if this Rampant Spinster had not interrupted us. I beg to inform you, sir, that, if my son is not good enough to be Miss Verinder's husband, I cannot presume to consider his father good enough to be Miss Verinder's guardian. Understand, if you please, that I refuse to accept the position which is offered to me by Lady Verinder's will. In your legal phrase, I decline to act. This house has necessarily been hired in my name. I take the entire responsibility of it on my shoulders. It is my house. I can keep it, or let it, just as I please. I have no wish to hurry Miss Verinder. On the contrary, I beg her to remove her guest and her luggage, at her own entire convenience." He made a low bow, and walked out of the room.

That was Mr. Ablewhite's revenge on Rachel, for refusing to marry his son!

The instant the door closed, Aunt Ablewhite exhibited a phenomenon which silenced us all. She became endowed with energy enough to cross the room!

"My dear," she said, taking Rachel by the hand, "I should be ashamed of my husband, if I didn't know that it is his temper which has spoken to you, and not himself. You," continued Aunt Ablewhite, turning on me in my corner with another endowment of energy, in her looks this time instead of her limbs—"you are the mischievous person who irritated him. I hope I shall never see you or your tracts again." She went back to Rachel and kissed her. "I beg your pardon, my dear," she said, "in my husband's name. What can I do for you?"

Consistently perverse in everything—capricious and unreasonable in all the actions of her life—Rachel melted into tears at those commonplace words, and returned her aunt's kiss in silence.

"If I may be permitted to answer for Miss Verinder," said Mr. Bruff, "might I ask you, Mrs. Ablewhite, to send Penelope down with her mistress's bonnet and shawl. Leave us ten minutes together," he added, in a lower tone, "and you may rely on my setting matters right, to your satisfaction as well as to Rachel's."

The trust of the family in this man was something wonderful to see. Without a word more, on her side, Aunt Ablewhite left the room.

"Ah!" said Mr. Bruff, looking after her. "The Herncastle blood has its drawbacks, I admit. But there is something in good breeding after all!"

Having made that purely worldly remark, he looked hard at

my corner, as if he expected me to go. My interest in Rachel—an infinitely higher interest than his—riveted me to my chair.

Mr. Bruff gave it up, exactly as he had given it up at Aunt Verinder's, in Montagu Square. He led Rachel to a chair by the window, and spoke to her there.

"My dear young lady," he said, "Mr. Ablewhite's conduct has naturally shocked you, and taken you by surprise. If it was worth while to contest the question with such a man, we might soon show him that he is not to have things all his own way. But it isn't worth while. You were quite right in what you said just now; he is beneath our notice."

He stopped, and looked round at my corner. I sat there quite immovable, with my tracts at my elbow and with Miss Jane Ann Stamper on my lap.

"You know," he resumed, turning back again to Rachel, "that it was part of your poor mother's fine nature always to see the best of the people about her, and never the worst. She named her brother-in-law your guardian because she believed in him, and because she thought it would please her sister. I had never liked Mr. Ablewhite myself, and I induced your mother to let me insert a clause in the will, empowering her executors, in certain events, to consult with me about the appointment of a new guardian. One of those events has happened today; and I find myself in a position to end all these dry business details, I hope agreeably, with a message from my wife. Will you honour Mrs. Bruff by becoming her guest? And will you remain under my roof, and be one of my family, until we wise people have laid our heads together, and have settled what is to be done next?"

At those words, I rose to interfere. Mr. Bruff had done exactly what I had dreaded he would do, when he asked Mrs. Ablewhite for Rachel's bonnet and shawl.

Before I could interpose a word, Rachel had accepted his invitation in the warmest terms. If I suffered the arrangement thus made between them to be carried out—if she once passed the threshold of Mr. Bruff's door—farewell to the fondest hope of my life, the hope of bringing my lost sheep back to the fold! The bare idea of such a calamity as this quite overwhelmed me. I cast the miserable trammels of worldly discretion to the winds, and spoke with the fervour that filled me, in the words that came first.

"Stop!" I said—"stop! I must be heard. Mr. Bruff! you are not related to her, and I am. I invite her—I summon the executors to appoint me guardian. Rachel, dearest Rachel, I offer you my modest home; come to London by the next train, love, and share it with me!"

Mr. Bruff said nothing. Rachel looked at me with a cruel astonishment which she made no effort to conceal.

"You are very kind, Drusilla," she said. "I shall hope to visit you whenever I happen to be in London. But I have accepted Mr. Bruff's invitation, and I think it will be best, for the present, if I remain under Mr. Bruff's care."

"Oh, don't say so!" I pleaded. "I can't part with you, Rachel—I can't part with you!"

I tried to fold her in my arms. But she drew back. My fervour did not communicate itself; it only alarmed her.

"Surely," she said, "this is a very unnecessary display of agitation? I don't understand it."

"No more do I," said Mr. Bruff.

Their hardness—their hideous, worldly hardness—revolted me.

"Oh, Rachel! Rachel!" I burst out. "Haven't you seen yet, that my heart yearns to make a Christian of you? Has no inner voice told you that I am trying to do for you, what I was trying to do for your dear mother when death snatched her out of my hands?"

Rachel advanced a step nearer, and looked at me very strangely.

"I don't understand your reference to my mother," she said. "Miss Clack, will you have the goodness to explain yourself?"

Before I could answer, Mr. Bruff came forward, and offering his arm to Rachel, tried to lead her out of the room.

"You had better not pursue the subject, my dear," he said. "And Miss Clack had better not explain herself."

If I had been a stock or a stone, such an interference as this must have roused me into testifying to the truth. I put Mr. Bruff aside indignantly with my own hand, and, in solemn and suitable language, I stated the view with which sound doctrine does not scruple to regard the awful calamity of dying unprepared.

Rachel started back from me—I blush to write—with a scream of horror.

"Come away!" she said to Mr. Bruff. "Come away, for God's sake, before that woman can say any more! Oh, think of my poor mother's harmless, useful, beautiful life! You were at the funeral, Mr. Bruff; you saw how everybody loved her; you saw the poor helpless people crying at her grave over the loss of their best friend. And that wretch stands there, and tries to make me doubt that my mother, who was an angel on earth, is an angel in heaven now! Don't stop to talk about it! Come away! It stifles me to breathe the same air with her! It frightens me to feel that we are in the same room together!"

Deaf to all remonstrance, she ran to the door.

At the same moment, her maid entered with her bonnet and shawl. She huddled them on anyhow. "Pack my things," she said, "and bring them to Mr. Bruff's." I attempted to approach her—I was shocked and grieved, but, it is needless to say, not offended. I only wished to say to her, "May your hard heart be softened! I freely forgive you!" She pulled down her veil, and tore her shawl away from my hand, and, hurrying out, shut the door in my face. I bore the insult with my customary fortitude. I remember it now with my customary superiority to all feeling of offence.

Mr. Bruff had his parting word of mockery for me, before he too hurried out, in his turn.

"You had better not have explained yourself, Miss Clack," he said, and bowed, and left the room.

The person with the cap-ribbons followed.

"It's easy to see who has set them all by the ears together," she said. "I'm only a poor servant—but I declare I'm ashamed of you!" She too went out, and banged the door after her.

I was left alone in the room. Reviled by them all, deserted by them all, I was left alone in the room.

Is there more to be added to this plain statement of facts — to this touching picture of a Christian persecuted by the world? No! my diary reminds me that one more of the many chequered chapters in my life ends here. From that day forth, I never saw Rachel Verinder again. She had my forgiveness at the time when she insulted me. She has had my prayerful good wishes ever since. And when I die — to complete the return on my part of good for evil — she will have the Life, Letters, and Labours of Miss Jane Ann Stamper left her as a legacy by my will.

SECOND NARRATIVE.

Contributed by Mathew Bruff, Solicitor, of Gray's Inn Square.

CHAPTER I

My fair friend, Miss Clack, having laid down the pen, there are two reasons for my taking it up next, in my turn.

In the first place, I am in a position to throw the necessary light on certain points of interest which have thus far been left in the dark. Miss Verinder had her own private reason for breaking her marriage engagement—and I was at the bottom of it. Mr. Godfrey Ablewhite had his own private reason for withdrawing all claim to the hand of his charming cousin—and I discovered what it was.

In the second place, it was my good or ill fortune, I hardly know which, to find myself personally involved—at the period of which I am now writing—in the mystery of the Indian Diamond. I had the honour of an interview, at my own office, with an Oriental stranger of distinguished manners, who was no other, unquestionably, than the chief of the three Indians. Add to this, that I met with the celebrated traveller, Mr. Murthwaite, the day afterwards, and that I held a conversation with him on the subject of the Moonstone, which has a very important bearing on later events. And there you have the statement of my claims to fill the position which I occupy in these pages.

The true story of the broken marriage engagement comes first in point of time, and must therefore take the first place in the present narrative. Tracing my way back along the chain of events, from one end to the other, I find it necessary to open the scene, oddly enough as you will think, at the bedside of my excellent client and friend, the late Sir John Verinder.

Sir John had his share—perhaps rather a large share—of the more harmless and amiable of the weaknesses incidental to humanity. Among these, I may mention as applicable to the matter in hand, an invincible reluctance—so long as he enjoyed his usual good health—to face the responsibility of making his will. Lady Verinder exerted her influence to rouse him to a sense of duty in this matter; and I exerted my influence. He admitted the justice of our views—but he went no further than that, until he found himself afflicted with the illness which ultimately brought him to his grave. Then, I was sent for at last, to take my client's instructions on the subject of his will. They proved to be the simplest instructions I had ever received in the whole of my professional career.

Sir John was dozing, when I entered the room. He roused himself at the sight of me.

"How do you do, Mr. Bruff?" he said. "I sha'n't be very long about this. And then I'll go to sleep again." He looked on with great interest while I collected pens, ink, and paper. "Are you ready?" he asked. I bowed and took a dip of ink, and waited for my instructions.

"I leave everything to my wife," said Sir John. "That's all." He turned round on his pillow, and composed himself to sleep again.

I was obliged to disturb him.

"Am I to understand," I asked, "that you leave the whole of the property, of every sort and description, of which you die possessed, absolutely to Lady Verinder?"

"Yes," said Sir John. "Only, I put it shorter. Why can't you put it shorter, and let me go to sleep again? Everything to my wife. That's my Will."

His property was entirely at his own disposal, and was of two kinds. Property in land (I purposely abstain from using technical language), and property in money. In the majority of cases, I am afraid I should have felt it my duty to my client to ask him to reconsider his Will. In the case of Sir John, I knew Lady Verinder to be, not only worthy of the unreserved trust which her husband had placed in her (all good wives are worthy of that)—but to be also capable of properly administering a trust (which, in my experience of the fair sex, not one in a thousand of them is competent to do). In ten minutes, Sir John's Will was drawn, and executed, and Sir John himself, good man, was finishing his interrupted nap.

Lady Verinder amply justified the confidence which her husband had placed in her. In the first days of her widowhood, she sent for me, and made her Will. The view she took of her position was so thoroughly sound and sensible, that I was relieved of all necessity for advising her. My responsibility began and ended with shaping her instructions into the proper legal form. Before Sir John had been a fortnight in his grave, the future of his daughter had been most wisely and most affectionately provided for.

The Will remained in its fireproof box at my office, through more years than I like to reckon up. It was not till the summer of eighteen hundred and forty-eight that I found occasion to look at it again under very melancholy circumstances.

At the date I have mentioned, the doctors pronounced the sentence on poor Lady Verinder, which was literally a sentence of death. I was the first person whom she informed of her situation; and I found her anxious to go over her Will again with me.

It was impossible to improve the provisions relating to her daughter. But, in the lapse of time, her wishes in regard to certain minor legacies, left to different relatives, had undergone some modification; and it became necessary to add three or four Codicils to the original document. Having done this at once, for fear of accident, I obtained her ladyship's permission to embody her recent instructions in a second Will. My object was to avoid certain inevitable confusions and repetitions which now disfigured the original document, and which, to own the truth, grated sadly on my professional sense of the fitness of things.

The execution of this second Will has been described by Miss Clack, who was so obliging as to witness it. So far as regarded Rachel Verinder's pecuniary interests, it was, word for word, the exact counterpart of the first Will. The only changes introduced related to the appointment of a guardian, and to certain provisions concerning that appointment, which were made under my advice. On Lady Verinder's death, the Will was placed in the hands of my proctor to be "proved" (as the phrase is) in the usual way.

In about three weeks from that time—as well as I can remember—the first warning reached me of something unusual going on under the surface. I happened to be looking in at my friend the proctor's office, and I observed that he received me with an appearance of greater interest than usual.

"I have some news for you," he said. "What do you think I

heard at Doctors' Commons this morning? Lady Verinder's Will has been asked for, and examined, already!"

This was news indeed! There was absolutely nothing which could be contested in the Will; and there was nobody I could think of who had the slightest interest in examining it. (I shall perhaps do well if I explain in this place, for the benefit of the few people who don't know it already, that the law allows all Wills to be examined at Doctors' Commons by anybody who applies, on the payment of a shilling fee.)

"Did you hear who asked for the Will?" I asked.

"Yes; the clerk had no hesitation in telling me. Mr. Smalley, of the firm of Skipp and Smalley, asked for it. The Will has not been copied yet into the great Folio Registers. So there was no alternative but to depart from the usual course, and to let him see the original document. He looked it over carefully, and made a note in his pocket-book. Have you any idea of what he wanted with it?"

I shook my head. "I shall find out," I answered, "before I am a day older." With that I went back at once to my own office.

If any other firm of solicitors had been concerned in this unaccountable examination of my deceased client's Will, I might have found some difficulty in making the necessary discovery. But I had a hold over Skipp and Smalley which made my course in this matter a comparatively easy one. My common-law clerk (a most competent and excellent man) was a brother of Mr. Smalley's; and, owing to this sort of indirect connection with me, Skipp and Smalley had, for some years past, picked up the crumbs that fell from my table, in the shape of cases brought to my office, which, for various reasons, I did not think it worth while to undertake. My professional patronage was, in this way, of some importance to the firm. I intended, if necessary, to remind them of that patronage, on the present occasion.

The moment I got back I spoke to my clerk; and, after telling him what had happened, I sent him to his brother's office, "with Mr. Bruff's compliments, and he would be glad to know why Messrs. Skipp and Smalley had found it necessary to examine Lady Verinder's will."

This message brought Mr. Smalley back to my office in company with his brother. He acknowledged that he had acted under instructions received from a client. And then he put it to me, whether it would not be a breach of professional confidence on his part to say more.

We had a smart discussion upon that. He was right, no doubt; and I was wrong. The truth is, I was angry and suspicious—and I insisted on knowing more. Worse still, I declined to consider any additional information offered me, as a secret placed in my keeping: I claimed perfect freedom to use my own discretion. Worse even than that, I took an unwarrantable advantage of my position. "Choose, sir," I said to Mr. Smalley, "between the risk of losing your client's business and the risk of losing Mine." Quite indefensible, I admit—an act of tyranny, and nothing less. Like other tyrants, I carried my point. Mr. Smalley chose his alternative, without a moment's hesitation.

He smiled resignedly, and gave up the name of his client:

Mr. Godfrey Ablewhite.

That was enough for me—I wanted to know no more.

Having reached this point in my narrative, it now becomes necessary to place the reader of these lines—so far as Lady Verinder's Will is concerned—on a footing of perfect equality, in respect of information, with myself.

Let me state, then, in the fewest possible words, that Rachel Verinder had nothing but a life-interest in the property. Her mother's excellent sense, and my long experience, had combined to relieve her of all responsibility, and to guard her from all danger of becoming the victim in the future of some needy and unscrupulous man. Neither she, nor her husband (if she married), could raise sixpence, either on the property in land, or on the property in money. They would have the houses in London and in Yorkshire to live in, and they would have the handsome income—and that was all.

When I came to think over what I had discovered, I was sorely perplexed what to do next.

Hardly a week had passed since I had heard (to my surprise and distress) of Miss Verinder's proposed marriage. I had the sincerest admiration and affection for her; and I had been inexpressibly grieved when I heard that she was about to throw herself away on Mr. Godfrey Ablewhite. And now, here was the man—whom I had always believed to be a smooth-tongued impostor—justifying the very worst that I had thought of him, and plainly revealing the mercenary object of the marriage, on his side! And what of that?—you may reply—the thing is done every day. Granted, my dear sir. But would you think of it quite as lightly as you do, if the thing was done (let us say) with your own sister?

The first consideration which now naturally occurred to me was this. Would Mr. Godfrey Ablewhite hold to his engagement, after what his lawyer had discovered for him?

It depended entirely on his pecuniary position, of which I knew nothing. If that position was not a desperate one, it would be well worth his while to marry Miss Verinder for her income alone. If, on the other hand, he stood in urgent need of realising a large sum by a given time, then Lady Verinder's Will would exactly meet the case, and would preserve her daughter from falling into a scoundrel's hands.

In the latter event, there would be no need for me to distress Miss Rachel, in the first days of her mourning for her mother, by an immediate revelation of the truth. In the former event, if I remained silent, I should be conniving at a marriage which would make her miserable for life.

My doubts ended in my calling at the hotel in London, at which I knew Mrs. Ablewhite and Miss Verinder to be staying. They informed me that they were going to Brighton the next day, and that an unexpected obstacle prevented Mr. Godfrey Ablewhite from accompanying them. I at once proposed to take his place. While I was only thinking of Rachel Verinder, it was possible to hesitate. When I actually saw her, my mind was made up directly, come what might of it, to tell her the truth.

I found my opportunity, when I was out walking with her, on the day after my arrival.

"May I speak to you," I asked, "about your marriage engagement?"

"Yes," she said, indifferently, "if you have nothing more

interesting to talk about."

"Will you forgive an old friend and servant of your family, Miss Rachel, if I venture on asking whether your heart is set on this marriage?"

"I am marrying in despair, Mr. Bruff—on the chance of dropping into some sort of stagnant happiness which may reconcile me to my life."

Strong language! and suggestive of something below the surface, in the shape of a romance. But I had my own object in view, and I declined (as we lawyers say) to pursue the question into its side issues.

"Mr. Godfrey Ablewhite can hardly be of your way of thinking," I said. "His heart must be set on the marriage at any rate?"

"He says so, and I suppose I ought to believe him. He would hardly marry me, after what I have owned to him, unless he was fond of me."

Poor thing! the bare idea of a man marrying her for his own selfish and mercenary ends had never entered her head. The task I had set myself began to look like a harder task than I had bargained for.

"It sounds strangely," I went on, "in my old-fashioned ears——"

"What sounds strangely?" she asked.

"To hear you speak of your future husband as if you were not quite sure of the sincerity of his attachment. Are you conscious of any reason in your own mind for doubting him?"

Her astonishing quickness of perception, detected a change in my voice, or my manner, when I put that question, which warned her that I had been speaking all along with some ulterior object in view. She stopped, and taking her arm out of mine, looked me searchingly in the face.

"Mr. Bruff," she said, "you have something to tell me about Godfrey Ablewhite. Tell it."

I knew her well enough to take her at her word. I told it.

The Moonstone

She put her arm again into mine, and walked on with me slowly. I felt her hand tightening its grasp mechanically on my arm, and I saw her getting paler and paler as I went on—but, not a word passed her lips while I was speaking. When I had done, she still kept silence. Her head drooped a little, and she walked by my side, unconscious of my presence, unconscious of everything about her; lost—buried, I might almost say—in her own thoughts.

I made no attempt to disturb her. My experience of her disposition warned me, on this, as on former occasions, to give her time.

The first instinct of girls in general, on being told of anything which interests them, is to ask a multitude of questions, and then to run off, and talk it all over with some favourite friend. Rachel Verinder's first instinct, under similar circumstances, was to shut herself up in her own mind, and to think it over by herself. This absolute self-dependence is a great virtue in a man. In a woman it has a serious drawback of morally separating her from the mass of her sex, and so exposing her to misconstruction by the general opinion. I strongly suspect myself of thinking as the rest of the world think in this matter—except in the case of Rachel Verinder. The self-dependence in her character, was one of its virtues in my estimation; partly, no doubt, because I sincerely admired and liked her; partly, because the view I took of her connexion with the loss of the Moonstone was based on my own special knowledge of her disposition. Badly as appearances might look, in the matter of the Diamond—shocking as it undoubtedly was to know that she was associated in any way with the mystery of an undiscovered theft—I was satisfied nevertheless that she had done nothing unworthy of her, because I was also satisfied that she had not stirred a step in the business, without shutting herself up in her own mind, and thinking it over first.

We had walked on, for nearly a mile I should say, before Rachel roused herself. She suddenly looked up at me with a faint reflection of her smile of happier times—the most irresistible smile I have ever seen on a woman's face.

"I owe much already to your kindness," she said. "And I feel more deeply indebted to it now than ever. If you hear any rumours of my marriage when you get back to London contradict them at once, on my authority."

"Have you resolved to break your engagement?" I asked.

"Can you doubt it?" she returned proudly, "after what you have told me!"

"My dear Miss Rachel, you are very young—and you may find more difficulty in withdrawing from your present position than you anticipate. Have you no one—I mean a lady, of course—whom you could consult?"

"No one," she answered.

It distressed me, it did indeed distress me, to hear her say that. She was so young and so lonely—and she bore it so well! The impulse to help her got the better of any sense of my own unfitness which I might have felt under the circumstances; and I stated such ideas on the subject as occurred to me on the spur of the moment, to the best of my ability. I have advised a prodigious number of clients, and have dealt with some exceedingly awkward difficulties, in my time. But this was the first occasion on which I had ever found myself advising a young lady how to obtain her release from a marriage engagement. The suggestion I offered amounted briefly to this. I recommended her to tell Mr. Godfrey Ablewhite—at a private interview, of course—that he had, to her certain knowledge, betrayed the mercenary nature of the motive on his side. She was then to add that their marriage, after what she had discovered, was a simple impossibility—and she was to put it to him, whether he thought it wisest to secure her silence by falling in with her views, or to force her, by opposing them, to make the motive under which she was acting generally known. If he attempted to defend himself, or to deny the facts, she was, in that event, to refer him to me.

Miss Verinder listened attentively till I had done. She then thanked me very prettily for my advice, but informed me at the same time that it was impossible for her to follow it.

"May I ask," I said, "what objection you see to following it?"

She hesitated—and then met me with a question on her side.

"Suppose you were asked to express your opinion of Mr. Godfrey Ablewhite's conduct?" she began.

"Yes?"

"What would you call it?"

"I should call it the conduct of a meanly deceitful man."

"Mr. Bruff! I have believed in that man. I have promised to marry that man. How can I tell him he is mean, how can I tell him he has deceived me, how can I disgrace him in the eyes of the world after that? I have degraded myself by ever thinking of him as my husband. If I say what you tell me to say to him—I am owning that I have degraded myself to his face. I can't do that. After what has passed between us, I can't do that! The shame of it would be nothing to him. But the shame of it would be unendurable to me."

Here was another of the marked peculiarities in her character disclosing itself to me without reserve. Here was her sensitive horror of the bare contact with anything mean, blinding her to every consideration of what she owed to herself, hurrying her into a false position which might compromise her in the estimation of all her friends! Up to this time, I had been a little diffident about the propriety of the advice I had given to her. But, after what she had just said, I had no sort of doubt that it was the best advice that could have been offered; and I felt no sort of hesitation in pressing it on her again.

She only shook her head, and repeated her objection in other words.

"He has been intimate enough with me to ask me to be his wife. He has stood high enough in my estimation to obtain my consent. I can't tell him to his face that he is the most contemptible of living creatures, after that!"

"But, my dear Miss Rachel," I remonstrated, "it's equally impossible for you to tell him that you withdraw from your engagement without giving some reason for it."

"I shall say that I have thought it over, and that I am satisfied it will be best for both of us if we part.

"No more than that?"

"No more."

"Have you thought of what he may say, on his side?"

"He may say what he pleases."

It was impossible not to admire her delicacy and her resolution, and it was equally impossible not to feel that she was putting herself in the wrong. I entreated her to consider her own position. I reminded her that she would be exposing herself to the most odious misconstruction of her motives. "You can't brave public opinion," I said, "at the command of private feeling."

"I can," she answered. "I have done it already."

"What do you mean?"

"You have forgotten the Moonstone, Mr. Bruff. Have I not braved public opinion, there, with my own private reasons for it?"

Her answer silenced me for the moment. It set me trying to trace the explanation of her conduct, at the time of the loss of the Moonstone, out of the strange avowal which had just escaped her. I might perhaps have done it when I was younger. I certainly couldn't do it now.

I tried a last remonstrance before we returned to the house. She was just as immovable as ever. My mind was in a strange conflict of feelings about her when I left her that day. She was obstinate; she was wrong. She was interesting; she was admirable; she was deeply to be pitied. I made her promise to write to me the moment she had any news to send. And I went back to my business in London, with a mind exceedingly ill at ease.

On the evening of my return, before it was possible for me to receive my promised letter, I was surprised by a visit from Mr. Ablewhite the elder, and was informed that Mr. Godfrey had got his dismissal—and had accepted it—that very day.

With the view I already took of the case, the bare fact stated in the words that I have underlined, revealed Mr. Godfrey Ablewhite's motive for submission as plainly as if he had acknowledged it himself. He needed a large sum of money; and he needed it by a given time. Rachel's income, which would have helped him to anything else, would not help him here; and Rachel had accordingly released herself, without encountering a moment's serious opposition on his part. If I am told that this is

The Moonstone

a mere speculation, I ask, in my turn, what other theory will account for his giving up a marriage which would have maintained him in splendour for the rest of his life?

Any exultation I might otherwise have felt at the lucky turn which things had now taken, was effectually checked by what passed at my interview with old Mr. Ablewhite.

He came, of course, to know whether I could give him any explanation of Miss Verinder's extraordinary conduct. It is needless to say that I was quite unable to afford him the information he wanted. The annoyance which I thus inflicted, following on the irritation produced by a recent interview with his son, threw Mr. Ablewhite off his guard. Both his looks and his language convinced me that Miss Verinder would find him a merciless man to deal with, when he joined the ladies at Brighton the next day.

I had a restless night, considering what I ought to do next. How my reflections ended, and how thoroughly well founded my distrust of Mr. Ablewhite proved to be, are items of information which (as I am told) have already been put tidily in their proper places, by that exemplary person, Miss Clack. I have only to add — in completion of her narrative — that Miss Verinder found the quiet and repose which she sadly needed, poor thing, in my house at Hampstead. She honoured us by making a long stay. My wife and daughters were charmed with her; and, when the executors decided on the appointment of a new guardian, I feel sincere pride and pleasure in recording that my guest and my family parted like old friends, on either side.

CHAPTER II

The next thing I have to do, is to present such additional information as I possess on the subject of the Moonstone, or, to speak more correctly, on the subject of the Indian plot to steal the Diamond. The little that I have to tell is (as I think I have already said) of some importance, nevertheless, in respect of its bearing very remarkably on events which are still to come.

About a week or ten days after Miss Verinder had left us, one of my clerks entered the private room at my office, with a card in his hand, and informed me that a gentleman was below, who wanted to speak to me.

I looked at the card. There was a foreign name written on it, which has escaped my memory. It was followed by a line written in English at the bottom of the card, which I remember perfectly well:

"Recommended by Mr. Septimus Luker."

The audacity of a person in Mr. Luker's position presuming to recommend anybody to me, took me so completely by surprise, that I sat silent for the moment, wondering whether my own eyes had not deceived me. The clerk, observing my bewilderment, favoured me with the result of his own observation of the stranger who was waiting downstairs.

"Here's rather a remarkable-looking man, sir. So dark in the complexion that we all set him down in the office for an Indian, or something of that sort."

Associating the clerk's idea with the line inscribed on the card in my hand, I thought it possible that the Moonstone might be at the bottom of Mr. Luker's recommendation, and of the stranger's visit at my office. To the astonishment of my clerk, I at once decided on granting an interview to the gentleman below.

In justification of the highly unprofessional sacrifice to mere curiosity which I thus made, permit me to remind anybody who may read these lines, that no living person (in England, at any rate) can claim to have had such an intimate connexion with the romance of the Indian Diamond as mine has been. I was trusted with the secret of Colonel Herncastle's plan for escaping assassination. I received the Colonel's letters, periodically reporting himself a living man. I drew his Will, leaving the Moonstone to Miss Verinder. I persuaded his executor to act, on the chance that the jewel might prove to be a valuable acquisition to the family. And, lastly, I combated Mr. Franklin Blake's scruples, and induced him to be the means of transporting the Diamond to Lady Verinder's house. If anyone can claim a prescriptive right of interest in the Moonstone, and in everything connected with it, I think it is hardly to be denied that I am the man.

The moment my mysterious client was shown in, I felt an inner conviction that I was in the presence of one of the three Indians — probably of the chief. He was carefully dressed in European costume. But his swarthy complexion, his long lithe figure, and his grave and graceful politeness of manner were enough to betray his Oriental origin to any intelligent eyes that looked at him.

I pointed to a chair, and begged to be informed of the nature of his business with me.

After first apologising — in an excellent selection of English words — for the liberty which he had taken in disturbing me, the Indian produced a small parcel the outer covering of which was of cloth of gold. Removing this and a second wrapping of some silken fabric, he placed a little box, or casket, on my table, most beautifully and richly inlaid in jewels, on an ebony ground.

"I have come, sir," he said, "to ask you to lend me some money. And I leave this as an assurance to you that my debt will be paid back."

I pointed to his card. "And you apply to me," I rejoined, "at Mr. Luker's recommendation?"

The Indian bowed.

"May I ask how it is that Mr. Luker himself did not advance the money that you require?"

"Mr. Luker informed me, sir, that he had no money to lend."

"And so he recommended you to come to me?"

The Indian, in his turn, pointed to the card. "It is written there," he said.

The Moonstone

Briefly answered, and thoroughly to the purpose! If the Moonstone had been in my possession, this Oriental gentleman would have murdered me, I am well aware, without a moment's hesitation. At the same time, and barring that slight drawback, I am bound to testify that he was the perfect model of a client. He might not have respected my life. But he did what none of my own countrymen had ever done, in all my experience of them — he respected my time.

"I am sorry," I said, "that you should have had the trouble of coming to me. Mr. Luker is quite mistaken in sending you here. I am trusted, like other men in my profession, with money to lend. But I never lend it to strangers, and I never lend it on such a security as you have produced."

Far from attempting, as other people would have done, to induce me to relax my own rules, the Indian only made me another bow, and wrapped up his box in its two coverings without a word of protest. He rose — this admirable assassin rose to go, the moment I had answered him!

"Will your condescension towards a stranger, excuse my asking one question," he said, "before I take my leave?"

I bowed on my side. Only one question at parting! The average in my experience was fifty.

"Supposing, sir, it had been possible (and customary) for you to lend me the money," he said, "in what space of time would it have been possible (and customary) for me to pay it back?"

"According to the usual course pursued in this country," I answered, "you would have been entitled to pay the money back (if you liked) in one year's time from the date at which it was first advanced to you."

The Indian made me a last bow, the lowest of all — and suddenly and softly walked out of the room.

It was done in a moment, in a noiseless, supple, cat-like way, which a little startled me, I own. As soon as I was composed enough to think, I arrived at one distinct conclusion in reference to the otherwise incomprehensible visitor who had favoured me with a call.

His face, voice, and manner—while I was in his company—were under such perfect control that they set all scrutiny at defiance. But he had given me one chance of looking under the smooth outer surface of him, for all that. He had not shown the slightest sign of attempting to fix anything that I had said to him in his mind, until I mentioned the time at which it was customary to permit the earliest repayment, on the part of a debtor, of money that had been advanced as a loan. When I gave him that piece of information, he looked me straight in the face, while I was speaking, for the first time. The inference I drew from this was—that he had a special purpose in asking me his last question, and a special interest in hearing my answer to it. The more carefully I reflected on what had passed between us, the more shrewdly I suspected the production of the casket, and the application for the loan, of having been mere formalities, designed to pave the way for the parting inquiry addressed to me.

I had satisfied myself of the correctness of this conclusion—and was trying to get on a step further, and penetrate the Indian's motives next—when a letter was brought to me, which proved to be from no less a person that Mr. Septimus Luker himself. He asked my pardon in terms of sickening servility, and assured me that he could explain matters to my satisfaction, if I would honour him by consenting to a personal interview.

I made another unprofessional sacrifice to mere curiosity. I honoured him by making an appointment at my office, for the next day.

Mr. Luker was, in every respect, such an inferior creature to the Indian—he was so vulgar, so ugly, so cringing, and so prosy—that he is quite unworthy of being reported, at any length, in these pages. The substance of what he had to tell me may be fairly stated as follows:

The day before I had received the visit of the Indian, Mr. Luker had been favoured with a call from that accomplished gentleman. In spite of his European disguise, Mr. Luker had instantly identified his visitor with the chief of the three Indians, who had formerly annoyed him by loitering about his house, and who had left him no alternative but to consult a magistrate. From this startling discovery he had rushed to the conclusion (naturally enough I own) that he must certainly be in the company of one of the three men, who had blindfolded him, gagged him, and robbed him of his banker's receipt. The result was that he became quite paralysed with terror, and that he firmly believed his last hour had come.

On his side, the Indian preserved the character of a perfect stranger. He produced the little casket, and made exactly the same application which he had afterwards made to me. As the speediest way of getting rid of him, Mr. Luker had at once declared that he had no money. The Indian had thereupon asked to be informed of the best and safest person to apply to for the loan he wanted. Mr. Luker had answered that the best and safest person, in such cases, was usually a respectable solicitor. Asked to name some individual of that character and profession, Mr. Luker had mentioned me—for the one simple reason that, in the extremity of his terror, mine was the first name which occurred to him. "The perspiration was pouring off me like rain, sir," the wretched creature concluded. "I didn't know what I was talking about. And I hope you'll look over it, Mr. Bruff, sir, in consideration of my having been really and truly frightened out of my wits."

I excused the fellow graciously enough. It was the readiest way of releasing myself from the sight of him. Before he left me, I detained him to make one inquiry.

Had the Indian said anything noticeable, at the moment of quitting Mr. Luker's house?

Yes! The Indian had put precisely the same question to Mr. Luker, at parting, which he had put to me; receiving of course, the same answer as the answer which I had given him.

What did it mean? Mr. Luker's explanation gave me no assistance towards solving the problem. My own unaided ingenuity, consulted next, proved quite unequal to grapple with the difficulty. I had a dinner engagement that evening; and I went upstairs, in no very genial frame of mind, little suspecting that the way to my dressing-room and the way to discovery, meant, on this particular occasion, one and the same thing.

CHAPTER III

The prominent personage among the guests at the dinner party I found to be Mr. Murthwaite.

On his appearance in England, after his wanderings, society had been greatly interested in the traveller, as a man who had passed through many dangerous adventures, and who had escaped to tell the tale. He had now announced his intention of returning to the scene of his exploits, and of penetrating into regions left still unexplored. This magnificent indifference to placing his safety in peril for the second time, revived the flagging interest of the worshippers in the hero. The law of chances was clearly against his escaping on this occasion. It is not every day that we can meet an eminent person at dinner, and feel that there is a reasonable prospect of the news of his murder being the news that we hear of him next.

When the gentlemen were left by themselves in the dining-room, I found myself sitting next to Mr. Murthwaite. The guests present being all English, it is needless to say that, as soon as the wholesome check exercised by the presence of the ladies was removed, the conversation turned on politics as a necessary result.

In respect to this all-absorbing national topic, I happen to be one of the most un-English Englishmen living. As a general rule, political talk appears to me to be of all talk the most dreary and the most profitless. Glancing at Mr. Murthwaite, when the bottles had made their first round of the table, I found that he was apparently of my way of thinking. He was doing it very dexterously — with all possible consideration for the feelings of his host — but it is not the less certain that he was composing himself for a nap. It struck me as an experiment worth attempting, to try whether a judicious allusion to the subject of the Moonstone would keep him awake, and, if it did, to see what he thought of the last new complication in the Indian conspiracy, as revealed in the prosaic precincts of my office.

"If I am not mistaken, Mr. Murthwaite," I began, "you were acquainted with the late Lady Verinder, and you took some interest in the strange succession of events which ended in the loss of the Moonstone?"

The eminent traveller did me the honour of waking up in an instant, and asking me who I was.

I informed him of my professional connection with the Herncastle family, not forgetting the curious position which I had occupied towards the Colonel and his Diamond in the bygone time.

Mr. Murthwaite shifted round in his chair, so as to put the rest of the company behind him (Conservatives and Liberals alike), and concentrated his whole attention on plain Mr. Bruff, of Gray's Inn Square.

"Have you heard anything, lately, of the Indians?" he asked.

"I have every reason to believe," I answered, "that one of them had an interview with me, in my office, yesterday."

Mr. Murthwaite was not an easy man to astonish; but that last answer of mine completely staggered him. I described what had happened to Mr. Luker, and what had happened to myself, exactly as I have described it here. "It is clear that the Indian's parting inquiry had an object," I added. "Why should he be so anxious to know the time at which a borrower of money is usually privileged to pay the money back?"

"Is it possible that you don't see his motive, Mr. Bruff?"

"I am ashamed of my stupidity, Mr. Murthwaite — but I certainly don't see it."

The great traveller became quite interested in sounding the immense vacuity of my dulness to its lowest depths.

"Let me ask you one question," he said. "In what position does the conspiracy to seize the Moonstone now stand?"

"I can't say," I answered. "The Indian plot is a mystery to me."

"The Indian plot, Mr. Bruff, can only be a mystery to you, because you have never seriously examined it. Shall we run it over together, from the time when you drew Colonel Herncastle's Will, to the time when the Indian called at your office? In your position, it may be of very serious importance to the interests of Miss Verinder, that you should be able to take a clear view of this matter in case of need. Tell me, bearing that in mind, whether you will penetrate the Indian's motive for yourself? or whether you wish me to save you the trouble of making any inquiry into it?"

It is needless to say that I thoroughly appreciated the practical purpose which I now saw that he had in view, and that the first of the two alternatives was the alternative I chose.

"Very good," said Mr. Murthwaite. "We will take the question of the ages of the three Indians first. I can testify that they all look much about the same age—and you can decide for yourself, whether the man whom you saw was, or was not, in the prime of life. Not forty, you think? My idea too. We will say not forty. Now look back to the time when Colonel Herncastle came to England, and when you were concerned in the plan he adopted to preserve his life. I don't want you to count the years. I will only say, it is clear that these present Indians, at their age, must be the successors of three other Indians (high caste Brahmins all of them, Mr. Bruff, when they left their native country!) who followed the Colonel to these shores. Very well. These present men of ours have succeeded to the men who were here before them. If they had only done that, the matter would not have been worth inquiring into. But they have done more. They have succeeded to the organisation which their predecessors established in this country. Don't start! The organisation is a very trumpery affair, according to our ideas, I have no doubt. I should reckon it up as including the command of money; the services, when needed, of that shady sort of Englishman, who lives in the byways of foreign life in London; and, lastly, the secret sympathy of such few men of their own country, and (formerly, at least) of their own religion, as happen to be employed in ministering to some of the multitudinous wants of this great city. Nothing very formidable, as you see! But worth notice at starting, because we may find occasion to refer to this modest little Indian organisation as we go on. Having now cleared the ground, I am going to ask you a question; and I expect your experience to answer it. What was the event which gave the Indians their first chance of seizing the Diamond?"

I understood the allusion to my experience.

"The first chance they got," I replied, "was clearly offered to them by Colonel Herncastle's death. They would be aware of his death, I suppose, as a matter of course?"

"As a matter of course. And his death, as you say, gave them their first chance. Up to that time the Moonstone was safe in the strongroom of the bank. You drew the Colonel's Will leaving his jewel to his niece; and the Will was proved in the usual way. As a lawyer, you can be at no loss to know what course the Indians would take (under English advice) after that."

"They would provide themselves with a copy of the Will from Doctors' Commons," I said.

"Exactly. One or other of those shady Englishmen to whom I have alluded, would get them the copy you have described. That copy would inform them that the Moonstone was bequeathed to the daughter of Lady Verinder, and that Mr. Blake the elder, or some person appointed by him, was to place it in her hands. You will agree with me that the necessary information about persons in the position of Lady Verinder and Mr. Blake, would be perfectly easy information to obtain. The one difficulty for the Indians would be to decide whether they should make their attempt on the Diamond when it was in course of removal from the keeping of the bank, or whether they should wait until it was taken down to Yorkshire to Lady Verinder's house. The second way would be manifestly the safest way — and there you have the explanation of the appearance of the Indians at Frizinghall, disguised as jugglers, and waiting their time. In London, it is needless to say, they had their organisation at their disposal to keep them informed of events. Two men would do it. One to follow anybody who went from Mr. Blake's house to the bank. And one to treat the lower men servants with beer, and to hear the news of the house. These commonplace precautions would readily inform them that Mr. Franklin Blake had been to the bank, and that Mr. Franklin Blake was the only person in the house who was going to visit Lady Verinder. What actually followed upon that discovery, you remember, no doubt, quite as correctly as I do."

I remembered that Franklin Blake had detected one of the spies, in the street — that he had, in consequence, advanced the time of his arrival in Yorkshire by some hours — and that (thanks to old Betteredge's excellent advice) he had lodged the Diamond in the bank at Frizinghall, before the Indians were so much as prepared to see him in the neighbourhood. All perfectly clear so far. But the Indians being ignorant of the precautions thus taken, how was it that they had made no attempt on Lady Verinder's house (in which they must have supposed the Diamond to be) through the whole of the interval that elapsed before Rachel's birthday?

In putting this difficulty to Mr. Murthwaite, I thought it right to add that I had heard of the little boy, and the drop of ink, and the rest of it, and that any explanation based on the theory of clairvoyance was an explanation which would carry no conviction whatever with it, to my mind.

"Nor to mine either," said Mr. Murthwaite. "The clairvoyance in this case is simply a development of the romantic side of the Indian character. It would be refreshment and an encouragement to those men—quite inconceivable, I grant you, to the English mind—to surround their wearisome and perilous errand in this country with a certain halo of the marvellous and the supernatural. Their boy is unquestionably a sensitive subject to the mesmeric influence—and, under that influence, he has no doubt reflected what was already in the mind of the person mesmerising him. I have tested the theory of clairvoyance—and I have never found the manifestations get beyond that point. The Indians don't investigate the matter in this way; the Indians look upon their boy as a Seer of things invisible to their eyes—and, I repeat, in that marvel they find the source of a new interest in the purpose that unites them. I only notice this as offering a curious view of human character, which must be quite new to you. We have nothing whatever to do with clairvoyance, or with mesmerism, or with anything else that is hard of belief to a practical man, in the inquiry that we are now pursuing. My object in following the Indian plot, step by step, is to trace results back, by rational means, to natural causes. Have I succeeded to your satisfaction so far?"

"Not a doubt of it, Mr. Murthwaite! I am waiting, however, with some anxiety, to hear the rational explanation of the difficulty which I have just had the honour of submitting to you."

Mr. Murthwaite smiled. "It's the easiest difficulty to deal with of all," he said. "Permit me to begin by admitting your statement of the case as a perfectly correct one. The Indians were undoubtedly not aware of what Mr. Franklin Blake had done with the Diamond—for we find them making their first mistake, on the first night of Mr. Blake's arrival at his aunt's house."

"Their first mistake?" I repeated.

"Certainly! The mistake of allowing themselves to be surprised, lurking about the terrace at night, by Gabriel Betteredge. However, they had the merit of seeing for themselves that they had taken a false step—for, as you say, again, with plenty of time at their disposal, they never came near the house for weeks afterwards."

"Why, Mr. Murthwaite? That's what I want to know! Why?"

"Because no Indian, Mr. Bruff, ever runs an unnecessary risk. The clause you drew in Colonel Herncastle's Will, informed them (didn't it?) that the Moonstone was to pass absolutely into Miss Verinder's possession on her birthday. Very well. Tell me which was the safest course for men in their position? To make their attempt on the Diamond while it was under the control of Mr. Franklin Blake, who had shown already that he could suspect and outwit them? Or to wait till the Diamond was at the disposal of a young girl, who would innocently delight in wearing the magnificent jewel at every possible opportunity? Perhaps you want a proof that my theory is correct? Take the conduct of the Indians themselves as the proof. They appeared at the house, after waiting all those weeks, on Miss Verinder's birthday; and they were rewarded for the patient accuracy of their calculations by seeing the Moonstone in the bosom of her dress! When I heard the story of the Colonel and the Diamond, later in the evening, I felt so sure about the risk Mr. Franklin Blake had run (they would have certainly attacked him, if he had not happened to ride back to Lady Verinder's in the company of other people); and I was so strongly convinced of the worse risk still, in store for Miss Verinder, that I recommended following the Colonel's plan, and destroying the identity of the gem by having it cut into separate stones. How its extraordinary disappearance that night, made my advice useless, and utterly defeated the Hindoo plot—and how all further action on the part of the Indians was paralysed the next day by their confinement in prison as rogues and vagabonds—you know as well as I do. The first act in the conspiracy closes there. Before we go on to the second, may I ask whether I have met your difficulty, with an explanation which is satisfactory to the mind of a practical man?"

It was impossible to deny that he had met my difficulty fairly; thanks to his superior knowledge of the Indian character—and thanks to his not having had hundreds of other Wills to think of since Colonel Herncastle's time!

"So far, so good," resumed Mr. Murthwaite. "The first chance the Indians had of seizing the Diamond was a chance lost, on the day when they were committed to the prison at Frizinghall. When did the second chance offer itself? The second chance offered itself—as I am in a condition to prove—while they were still in confinement."

He took out his pocket-book, and opened it at a particular leaf, before he went on.

"I was staying," he resumed, "with some friends at Frizinghall, at the time. A day or two before the Indians were set free (on a Monday, I think), the governor of the prison came to me with a letter. It had been left for the Indians by one Mrs. Macann, of whom they had hired the lodging in which they lived; and it had been delivered at Mrs. Macann's door, in ordinary course of post, on the previous morning. The prison authorities had noticed that the postmark was 'Lambeth,' and that the address on the outside, though expressed in correct English, was, in form, oddly at variance with the customary method of directing a letter. On opening it, they had found the contents to be written in a foreign language, which they rightly guessed at as Hindustani. Their object in coming to me was, of course, to have the letter translated to them. I took a copy in my pocket-book of the original, and of my translation—and there they are at your service."

He handed me the open pocket-book. The address on the letter was the first thing copied. It was all written in one paragraph, without any attempt at punctuation, thus: "To the three Indian men living with the lady called Macann at Frizinghall in Yorkshire." The Hindoo characters followed; and the English translation appeared at the end, expressed in these mysterious words:

"In the name of the Regent of the Night, whose seat is on the Antelope, whose arms embrace the four corners of the earth.

"Brothers, turn your faces to the south, and come to me in the street of many noises, which leads down to the muddy river.

"The reason is this.

"My own eyes have seen it."

There the letter ended, without either date or signature. I handed it back to Mr. Murthwaite, and owned that this curious specimen of Hindoo correspondence rather puzzled me.

"I can explain the first sentence to you," he said; "and the conduct of the Indians themselves will explain the rest. The god of the moon is represented, in the Hindoo mythology, as a four-armed deity, seated on an antelope; and one of his titles is the regent of the night. Here, then, to begin with, is something which looks suspiciously like an indirect reference to the Moonstone. Now, let us see what the Indians did, after the prison authorities had allowed them to receive their letter. On the very day when they were set free they went at once to the railway station, and took their places in the first train that started for London. We all thought it a pity at Frizinghall that their proceedings were not privately watched. But, after Lady Verinder had dismissed the police-officer, and had stopped all further inquiry into the loss of the Diamond, no one else could presume to stir in the matter. The Indians were free to go to London, and to London they went. What was the next news we heard of them, Mr. Bruff?"

"They were annoying Mr. Luker," I answered, "by loitering about the house at Lambeth."

"Did you read the report of Mr. Luker's application to the magistrate?"

"Yes."

"In the course of his statement he referred, if you remember, to a foreign workman in his employment, whom he had just dismissed on suspicion of attempted theft, and whom he also distrusted as possibly acting in collusion with the Indians who had annoyed him. The inference is pretty plain, Mr. Bruff, as to who wrote that letter which puzzled you just now, and as to which of Mr. Luker's Oriental treasures the workman had attempted to steal."

The inference (as I hastened to acknowledge) was too plain to need being pointed out. I had never doubted that the Moonstone had found its way into Mr. Luker's hands, at the time Mr. Murthwaite alluded to. My only question had been, How had the Indians discovered the circumstance? This question (the most difficult to deal with of all, as I had thought) had now received its answer, like the rest. Lawyer as I was, I began to feel that I might trust Mr. Murthwaite to lead me blindfold through the last windings of the labyrinth, along which he had guided me thus far. I paid him the compliment of telling him this, and found my little concession very graciously received.

"You shall give me a piece of information in your turn before we go on," he said. "Somebody must have taken the Moonstone from Yorkshire to London. And somebody must have raised money on it, or it would never have been in Mr. Luker's possession. Has there been any discovery made of who that person was?"

"None that I know of."

"There was a story (was there not?) about Mr. Godfrey Ablewhite. I am told he is an eminent philanthropist—which is decidedly against him, to begin with."

I heartily agreed in this with Mr. Murthwaite. At the same time, I felt bound to inform him (without, it is needless to say, mentioning Miss Verinder's name) that Mr. Godfrey Ablewhite had been cleared of all suspicion, on evidence which I could answer for as entirely beyond dispute.

"Very well," said Mr. Murthwaite, quietly, "let us leave it to time to clear the matter up. In the meanwhile, Mr. Bruff, we must get back again to the Indians, on your account. Their journey to London simply ended in their becoming the victims of another defeat. The loss of their second chance of seizing the Diamond is mainly attributable, as I think, to the cunning and foresight of Mr. Luker—who doesn't stand at the top of the prosperous and ancient profession of usury for nothing! By the prompt dismissal of the man in his employment, he deprived the Indians of the assistance which their confederate would have rendered them in getting into the house. By the prompt transport of the Moonstone to his banker's, he took the conspirators by surprise before they were prepared with a new plan for robbing him. How the Indians, in this latter case, suspected what he had done, and how they contrived to possess themselves of his banker's receipt, are events too recent to need dwelling on. Let it be enough to say that they know the Moonstone to be once more out of their reach; deposited (under the general description of 'a valuable of great price') in a banker's strong room. Now, Mr. Bruff, what is their third chance of seizing the Diamond? and when will it come?"

As the question passed his lips, I penetrated the motive of the Indian's visit to my office at last!

"I see it!" I exclaimed. "The Indians take it for granted, as we do, that the Moonstone has been pledged; and they want to be certainly informed of the earliest period at which the pledge can be redeemed — because that will be the earliest period at which the Diamond can be removed from the safe keeping of the bank!"

"I told you you would find it out for yourself, Mr. Bruff, if I only gave you a fair chance. In a year from the time when the Moonstone was pledged, the Indians will be on the watch for their third chance. Mr. Luker's own lips have told them how long they will have to wait, and your respectable authority has satisfied them that Mr. Luker has spoken the truth. When do we suppose, at a rough guess, that the Diamond found its way into the money-lender's hands?"

"Towards the end of last June," I answered, "as well as I can reckon it."

"And we are now in the year 'forty-eight. Very good. If the unknown person who has pledged the Moonstone can redeem it in a year, the jewel will be in that person's possession again at the end of June, 'forty-nine. I shall be thousands of miles from England and English news at that date. But it may be worth your while to take a note of it, and to arrange to be in London at the time."

"You think something serious will happen?" I said.

"I think I shall be safer," he answered, "among the fiercest fanatics of Central Asia than I should be if I crossed the door of the bank with the Moonstone in my pocket. The Indians have

The Moonstone

been defeated twice running, Mr. Bruff. It's my firm belief that they won't be defeated a third time."

Those were the last words he said on the subject. The coffee came in; the guests rose, and dispersed themselves about the room; and we joined the ladies of the dinner-party upstairs.

I made a note of the date, and it may not be amiss if I close my narrative by repeating that note here:

June, 'forty-nine. Expect news of the Indians, towards the end of the month.

And that done, I hand the pen, which I have now no further claim to use, to the writer who follows me next.

THIRD NARRATIVE.

Contributed by Franklin Blake.

CHAPTER I

In the spring of the year eighteen hundred and forty-nine I was wandering in the East, and had then recently altered the travelling plans which I had laid out some months before, and which I had communicated to my lawyer and my banker in London.

This change made it necessary for me to send one of my servants to obtain my letters and remittances from the English consul in a certain city, which was no longer included as one of my resting-places in my new travelling scheme. The man was to join me again at an appointed place and time. An accident, for which he was not responsible, delayed him on his errand. For a week I and my people waited, encamped on the borders of a desert. At the end of that time the missing man made his appearance, with the money and the letters, at the entrance of my tent.

"I am afraid I bring you bad news, sir," he said, and pointed to one of the letters, which had a mourning border round it, and the address on which was in the handwriting of Mr. Bruff.

I know nothing, in a case of this kind, so unendurable as suspense. The letter with the mourning border was the letter that I opened first.

It informed me that my father was dead, and that I was heir to his great fortune. The wealth which had thus fallen into my hands brought its responsibilities with it, and Mr. Bruff entreated me to lose no time in returning to England.

By daybreak the next morning, I was on my way back to my own country.

The picture presented of me, by my old friend Betteredge, at the time of my departure from England, is (as I think) a little overdrawn. He has, in his own quaint way, interpreted seriously one of his young mistress's many satirical references to my foreign education; and has persuaded himself that he actually saw those French, German, and Italian sides to my character, which my lively cousin only professed to discover in jest, and which never had any real existence, except in our good Betteredge's own brain. But, barring this drawback, I am bound to own that he has stated no more than the truth in representing me as wounded to the heart by Rachel's treatment, and as leaving England in the first keenness of suffering caused by the bitterest disappointment of my life.

I went abroad, resolved—if change and absence could help me—to forget her. It is, I am persuaded, no true view of human nature which denies that change and absence do help a man under these circumstances; they force his attention away from the exclusive contemplation of his own sorrow. I never forgot her; but the pang of remembrance lost its worst bitterness, little by little, as time, distance, and novelty interposed themselves more and more effectually between Rachel and me.

On the other hand, it is no less certain that, with the act of turning homeward, the remedy which had gained its ground so steadily, began now, just as steadily, to drop back. The nearer I drew to the country which she inhabited, and to the prospect of seeing her again, the more irresistibly her influence began to recover its hold on me. On leaving England she was the last person in the world whose name I would have suffered to pass my lips. On returning to England, she was the first person I inquired after, when Mr. Bruff and I met again.

I was informed, of course, of all that had happened in my absence; in other words, of all that has been related here in continuation of Betteredge's narrative—one circumstance only being excepted. Mr. Bruff did not, at that time, feel himself at liberty to inform me of the motives which had privately influenced Rachel and Godfrey Ablewhite in recalling the marriage promise, on either side. I troubled him with no embarrassing questions on this delicate subject. It was relief enough to me, after the jealous disappointment caused by hearing that she had ever contemplated being Godfrey's wife, to know that reflection had convinced her of acting rashly, and that she had effected her own release from her marriage engagement.

Having heard the story of the past, my next inquiries (still inquiries after Rachel!) advanced naturally to the present time. Under whose care had she been placed after leaving Mr. Bruff's house? and where was she living now?

She was living under the care of a widowed sister of the late Sir John Verinder—one Mrs. Merridew—whom her mother's executors had requested to act as guardian, and who had accepted the proposal. They were reported to me as getting on together admirably well, and as being now established, for the season, in Mrs. Merridew's house in Portland Place.

Half an hour after receiving this information, I was on my way to Portland Place—without having had the courage to own it to Mr. Bruff!

The man who answered the door was not sure whether Miss Verinder was at home or not. I sent him upstairs with my card, as the speediest way of setting the question at rest. The man came down again with an impenetrable face, and informed me that Miss Verinder was out.

I might have suspected other people of purposely denying themselves to me. But it was impossible to suspect Rachel. I left word that I would call again at six o'clock that evening.

At six o'clock I was informed for the second time that Miss Verinder was not at home. Had any message been left for me. No message had been left for me. Had Miss Verinder not received my card? The servant begged my pardon—Miss Verinder had received it.

The inference was too plain to be resisted. Rachel declined to see me.

On my side, I declined to be treated in this way, without making an attempt, at least, to discover a reason for it. I sent up my name to Mrs. Merridew, and requested her to favour me with a personal interview at any hour which it might be most convenient to her to name.

Mrs. Merridew made no difficulty about receiving me at once. I was shown into a comfortable little sitting-room, and found myself in the presence of a comfortable little elderly lady. She was so good as to feel great regret and much surprise, entirely on my account. She was at the same time, however, not in a position to offer me any explanation, or to press Rachel on a matter which appeared to relate to a question of private feeling alone. This was said over and over again, with a polite patience that nothing could tire; and this was all I gained by applying to Mrs. Merridew.

My last chance was to write to Rachel. My servant took a letter to her the next day, with strict instructions to wait for an answer.

The answer came back, literally in one sentence.

"Miss Verinder begs to decline entering into any correspondence with Mr. Franklin Blake."

Fond as I was of her, I felt indignantly the insult offered to me in that reply. Mr. Bruff came in to speak to me on business, before I had recovered possession of myself. I dismissed the business on the spot, and laid the whole case before him. He proved to be as incapable of enlightening me as Mrs. Merridew herself. I asked him if any slander had been spoken of me in Rachel's hearing. Mr. Bruff was not aware of any slander of which I was the object. Had she referred to me in any way while she was staying under Mr. Bruff's roof? Never. Had she not so much as asked, during all my long absence, whether I was living or dead? No such question had ever passed her lips. I took out of my pocket-book the letter which poor Lady Verinder had written to me from Frizinghall, on the day when I left her house in Yorkshire. And I pointed Mr. Bruff's attention to these two sentences in it:

"The valuable assistance which you rendered to the inquiry after the lost jewel is still an unpardoned offence, in the present dreadful state of Rachel's mind. Moving blindfold in this matter, you have added to the burden of anxiety which she has had to bear, by innocently threatening her secret with discovery through your exertions."

"Is it possible," I asked, "that the feeling towards me which is there described, is as bitter as ever against me now?"

Mr. Bruff looked unaffectedly distressed.

"If you insist on an answer," he said, "I own I can place no other interpretation on her conduct than that."

I rang the bell, and directed my servant to pack my portmanteau, and to send out for a railway guide. Mr. Bruff asked, in astonishment, what I was going to do.

"I am going to Yorkshire," I answered, "by the next train."

"May I ask for what purpose?"

"Mr. Bruff, the assistance I innocently rendered to the inquiry after the Diamond was an unpardoned offence, in Rachel's mind, nearly a year since; and it remains an unpardoned offence still. I won't accept that position! I am determined to find out the secret of her silence towards her mother, and her enmity towards me. If time, pains, and money can do it, I will lay my hand on the thief who took the Moonstone!"

The worthy old gentleman attempted to remonstrate—to induce me to listen to reason—to do his duty towards me, in short. I was deaf to everything that he could urge. No earthly consideration would, at that moment, have shaken the resolution that was in me.

"I shall take up the inquiry again," I went on, "at the point where I dropped it; and I shall follow it onwards, step by step, till I come to the present time. There are missing links in the evidence, as I left it, which Gabriel Betteredge can supply, and to Gabriel Betteredge I go!"

Towards sunset that evening I stood again on the well-remembered terrace, and looked once more at the peaceful old country house. The gardener was the first person whom I saw in the deserted grounds. He had left Betteredge, an hour since, sunning himself in the customary corner of the back yard. I knew it well; and I said I would go and seek him myself.

I walked round by the familiar paths and passages, and looked in at the open gate of the yard.

There he was—the dear old friend of the happy days that were never to come again—there he was in the old corner, on the old beehive chair, with his pipe in his mouth, and his Robinson Crusoe on his lap, and his two friends, the dogs, dozing on either side of him! In the position in which I stood, my shadow was projected in front of me by the last slanting rays of the sun. Either the dogs saw it, or their keen scent informed them of my approach; they started up with a growl. Starting in his turn, the old man quieted them by a word, and then shaded his failing eyes with his hand, and looked inquiringly at the figure at the gate.

My own eyes were full of tears. I was obliged to wait a moment before I could trust myself to speak to him.

CHAPTER II

"Betteredge!" I said, pointing to the well-remembered book on his knee, "has Robinson Crusoe informed you, this evening, that you might expect to see Franklin Blake?"

"By the lord Harry, Mr. Franklin!" cried the old man, "that's exactly what Robinson Crusoe has done!"

He struggled to his feet with my assistance, and stood for a moment, looking backwards and forwards between Robinson Crusoe and me, apparently at a loss to discover which of us had surprised him most. The verdict ended in favour of the book. Holding it open before him in both hands, he surveyed the wonderful volume with a stare of unutterable anticipation—as if he expected to see Robinson Crusoe himself walk out of the pages, and favour us with a personal interview.

"Here's the bit, Mr. Franklin!" he said, as soon as he had recovered the use of his speech. "As I live by bread, sir, here's the bit I was reading, the moment before you came in! Page one hundred and fifty-six as follows:—'I stood like one Thunderstruck, or as if I had seen an Apparition.' If that isn't as much as to say: 'Expect the sudden appearance of Mr. Franklin Blake'—there's no meaning in the English language!" said Betteredge, closing the book with a bang, and getting one of his hands free at last to take the hand which I offered him.

I had expected him, naturally enough under the circumstances, to overwhelm me with questions. But no—the hospitable impulse was the uppermost impulse in the old servant's mind, when a member of the family appeared (no matter how!) as a visitor at the house.

"Walk in, Mr. Franklin," he said, opening the door behind him, with his quaint old-fashioned bow. "I'll ask what brings you here afterwards—I must make you comfortable first. There have been sad changes, since you went away. The house is shut up, and the servants are gone. Never mind that! I'll cook your dinner; and the gardener's wife will make your bed—and if there's a bottle of our famous Latour claret left in the cellar, down your throat, Mr. Franklin, that bottle shall go. I bid you welcome, sir! I bid you heartily welcome!" said the poor old fellow, fighting manfully against the gloom of the deserted

The Moonstone

house, and receiving me with the sociable and courteous attention of the bygone time.

It vexed me to disappoint him. But the house was Rachel's house, now. Could I eat in it, or sleep in it, after what had happened in London? The commonest sense of self-respect forbade me—properly forbade me—to cross the threshold.

I took Betteredge by the arm, and led him out into the garden. There was no help for it. I was obliged to tell him the truth. Between his attachment to Rachel, and his attachment to me, he was sorely puzzled and distressed at the turn things had taken. His opinion, when he expressed it, was given in his usual downright manner, and was agreeably redolent of the most positive philosophy I know—the philosophy of the Betteredge school.

"Miss Rachel has her faults—I've never denied it," he began. "And riding the high horse, now and then, is one of them. She has been trying to ride over you—and you have put up with it. Lord, Mr. Franklin, don't you know women by this time better than that? You have heard me talk of the late Mrs. Betteredge?"

I had heard him talk of the late Mrs. Betteredge pretty often—invariably producing her as his one undeniable example of the inbred frailty and perversity of the other sex. In that capacity he exhibited her now.

"Very well, Mr. Franklin. Now listen to me. Different women have different ways of riding the high horse. The late Mrs. Betteredge took her exercise on that favourite female animal whenever I happened to deny her anything that she had set her heart on. So sure as I came home from my work on these occasions, so sure was my wife to call to me up the kitchen stairs, and to say that, after my brutal treatment of her, she hadn't the heart to cook me my dinner. I put up with it for some time—just as you are putting up with it now from Miss Rachel. At last my patience wore out. I went downstairs, and I took Mrs. Betteredge—affectionately, you understand—up in my arms, and carried her, holus-bolus, into the best parlour where she received her company. I said 'That's the right place for you, my dear,' and so went back to the kitchen. I locked myself in, and took off my coat, and turned up my shirt-sleeves, and cooked my own dinner. When it was done, I served it up in my best manner, and enjoyed it most heartily. I had my pipe and my drop of grog afterwards; and then I cleared the table, and washed the crockery, and cleaned the knives and forks, and put the things away, and swept up the hearth. When things were as bright and clean again, as bright and clean could be, I opened the door and let Mrs. Betteredge in. 'I've had my dinner, my dear,' I said; 'and I hope you will find that I have left the kitchen all that your fondest wishes can desire.' For the rest of that woman's life, Mr. Franklin, I never had to cook my dinner again! Moral: You have put up with Miss Rachel in London; don't put up with her in Yorkshire. Come back to the house!"

Quite unanswerable! I could only assure my good friend that even his powers of persuasion were, in this case, thrown away on me.

"It's a lovely evening," I said. "I shall walk to Frizinghall, and stay at the hotel, and you must come tomorrow morning and breakfast with me. I have something to say to you."

Betteredge shook his head gravely.

"I am heartily sorry for this," he said. "I had hoped, Mr. Franklin, to hear that things were all smooth and pleasant again between you and Miss Rachel. If you must have your own way, sir," he continued, after a moment's reflection, "there is no need to go to Frizinghall tonight for a bed. It's to be had nearer than that. There's Hotherstone's Farm, barely two miles from here. You can hardly object to that on Miss Rachel's account," the old man added slily. "Hotherstone lives, Mr. Franklin, on his own freehold."

I remembered the place the moment Betteredge mentioned it. The farm-house stood in a sheltered inland valley, on the banks of the prettiest stream in that part of Yorkshire: and the farmer had a spare bedroom and parlour, which he was accustomed to let to artists, anglers, and tourists in general. A more agreeable place of abode, during my stay in the neighbourhood, I could not have wished to find.

"Are the rooms to let?" I inquired.

"Mrs. Hotherstone herself, sir, asked for my good word to recommend the rooms, yesterday."

"I'll take them, Betteredge, with the greatest pleasure."

We went back to the yard, in which I had left my travelling-bag. After putting a stick through the handle, and swinging the bag over his shoulder, Betteredge appeared to relapse into the bewilderment which my sudden appearance had caused, when I surprised him in the beehive chair. He looked incredulously at the house, and then he wheeled about, and looked more incredulously still at me.

"I've lived a goodish long time in the world," said this best and dearest of all old servants—"but the like of this, I never did expect to see. There stands the house, and here stands Mr. Franklin Blake—and, Damme, if one of them isn't turning his back on the other, and going to sleep in a lodging!"

He led the way out, wagging his head and growling ominously. "There's only one more miracle that can happen," he said to me, over his shoulder. "The next thing you'll do, Mr. Franklin, will be to pay me back that seven-and-sixpence you borrowed of me when you were a boy."

This stroke of sarcasm put him in a better humour with himself and with me. We left the house, and passed through the lodge gates. Once clear of the grounds, the duties of hospitality (in Betteredge's code of morals) ceased, and the privileges of curiosity began.

He dropped back, so as to let me get on a level with him. "Fine evening for a walk, Mr. Franklin," he said, as if we had just accidentally encountered each other at that moment. "Supposing you had gone to the hotel at Frizinghall, sir?"

"Yes?"

"I should have had the honour of breakfasting with you, tomorrow morning."

"Come and breakfast with me at Hotherstone's Farm, instead."

"Much obliged to you for your kindness, Mr. Franklin. But it wasn't exactly breakfast that I was driving at. I think you mentioned that you had something to say to me? If it's no secret, sir," said Betteredge, suddenly abandoning the crooked way, and taking the straight one, "I'm burning to know what's brought you down here, if you please, in this sudden way."

"What brought me here before?" I asked.

"The Moonstone, Mr. Franklin. But what brings you now, sir?"

"The Moonstone again, Betteredge."

The old man suddenly stood still, and looked at me in the grey twilight as if he suspected his own ears of deceiving him.

"If that's a joke, sir," he said, "I'm afraid I'm getting a little dull in my old age. I don't take it."

"It's no joke," I answered. "I have come here to take up the inquiry which was dropped when I left England. I have come here to do what nobody has done yet—to find out who took the Diamond."

"Let the Diamond be, Mr. Franklin! Take my advice, and let the Diamond be! That cursed Indian jewel has misguided everybody who has come near it. Don't waste your money and your temper—in the fine spring time of your life, sir—by meddling with the Moonstone. How can you hope to succeed (saving your presence), when Sergeant Cuff himself made a mess of it? Sergeant Cuff!" repeated Betteredge, shaking his forefinger at me sternly. "The greatest policeman in England!"

"My mind is made up, my old friend. Even Sergeant Cuff doesn't daunt me. By-the-bye, I may want to speak to him, sooner or later. Have you heard anything of him lately?"

"The Sergeant won't help you, Mr. Franklin."

"Why not?"

"There has been an event, sir, in the police-circles, since you went away. The great Cuff has retired from business. He has got a little cottage at Dorking; and he's up to his eyes in the growing of roses. I have it in his own handwriting, Mr. Franklin. He has grown the white moss rose, without budding it on the dog-rose first. And Mr. Begbie the gardener is to go to Dorking, and own that the Sergeant has beaten him at last."

"It doesn't much matter," I said. "I must do without Sergeant Cuff's help. And I must trust to you, at starting."

It is likely enough that I spoke rather carelessly.

The Moonstone

At any rate, Betteredge seemed to be piqued by something in the reply which I had just made to him. "You might trust to worse than me, Mr. Franklin—I can tell you that," he said a little sharply.

The tone in which he retorted, and a certain disturbance, after he had spoken, which I detected in his manner, suggested to me that he was possessed of some information which he hesitated to communicate.

"I expect you to help me," I said, "in picking up the fragments of evidence which Sergeant Cuff has left behind him. I know you can do that. Can you do no more?"

"What more can you expect from me, sir?" asked Betteredge, with an appearance of the utmost humility.

"I expect more—from what you said just now."

"Mere boasting, Mr. Franklin," returned the old man obstinately. "Some people are born boasters, and they never get over it to their dying day. I'm one of them."

There was only one way to take with him. I appealed to his interest in Rachel, and his interest in me.

"Betteredge, would you be glad to hear that Rachel and I were good friends again?"

"I have served your family, sir, to mighty little purpose, if you doubt it!"

"Do you remember how Rachel treated me, before I left England?"

"As well as if it was yesterday! My lady herself wrote you a letter about it; and you were so good as to show the letter to me. It said that Miss Rachel was mortally offended with you, for the part you had taken in trying to recover her jewel. And neither my lady, nor you, nor anybody else could guess why.

"Quite true, Betteredge! And I come back from my travels, and find her mortally offended with me still. I knew that the Diamond was at the bottom of it, last year, and I know that the Diamond is at the bottom of it now. I have tried to speak to her, and she won't see me. I have tried to write to her, and she won't answer me. How, in Heaven's name, am I to clear the matter up? The chance of searching into the loss of the Moonstone, is the one chance of inquiry that Rachel herself has left me."

Those words evidently put the case before him, as he had not seen it yet. He asked a question which satisfied me that I had shaken him.

"There is no ill-feeling in this, Mr. Franklin, on your side—is there?"

"There was some anger," I answered, "when I left London. But that is all worn out now. I want to make Rachel come to an understanding with me—and I want nothing more."

"You don't feel any fear, sir—supposing you make any discoveries—in regard to what you may find out about Miss Rachel?"

I understood the jealous belief in his young mistress which prompted those words.

"I am as certain of her as you are," I answered. "The fullest disclosure of her secret will reveal nothing that can alter her place in your estimation, or in mine."

Betteredge's last-left scruples vanished at that.

"If I am doing wrong to help you, Mr. Franklin," he exclaimed, "all I can say is—I am as innocent of seeing it as the babe unborn! I can put you on the road to discovery, if you can only go on by yourself. You remember that poor girl of ours—Rosanna Spearman?"

"Of course!"

"You always thought she had some sort of confession in regard to this matter of the Moonstone, which she wanted to make to you?"

"I certainly couldn't account for her strange conduct in any other way."

"You may set that doubt at rest, Mr. Franklin, whenever you please."

It was my turn to come to a standstill now. I tried vainly, in the gathering darkness, to see his face. In the surprise of the moment, I asked a little impatiently what he meant.

The Moonstone

"Steady, sir!" proceeded Betteredge. "I mean what I say. Rosanna Spearman left a sealed letter behind her—a letter addressed to you."

"Where is it?"

"In the possession of a friend of hers, at Cobb's Hole. You must have heard tell, when you were here last, sir, of Limping Lucy—a lame girl with a crutch."

"The fisherman's daughter?"

"The same, Mr. Franklin."

"Why wasn't the letter forwarded to me?"

"Limping Lucy has a will of her own, sir. She wouldn't give it into any hands but yours. And you had left England before I could write to you."

"Let's go back, Betteredge, and get it at once!"

"Too late, sir, tonight. They're great savers of candles along our coast; and they go to bed early at Cobb's Hole."

"Nonsense! We might get there in half an hour."

"You might, sir. And when you did get there, you would find the door locked. He pointed to a light, glimmering below us; and, at the same moment, I heard through the stillness of the evening the bubbling of a stream. 'There's the Farm, Mr. Franklin! Make yourself comfortable for tonight, and come to me tomorrow morning if you'll be so kind?'"

"You will go with me to the fisherman's cottage?"

"Yes, sir."

"Early?"

"As early, Mr. Franklin, as you like."

We descended the path that led to the Farm.

CHAPTER III

I have only the most indistinct recollection of what happened at Hotherstone's Farm.

I remember a hearty welcome; a prodigious supper, which

would have fed a whole village in the East; a delightfully clean bedroom, with nothing in it to regret but that detestable product of the folly of our forefathers—a feather-bed; a restless night, with much kindling of matches, and many lightings of one little candle; and an immense sensation of relief when the sun rose, and there was a prospect of getting up.

It had been arranged over-night with Betteredge, that I was to call for him, on our way to Cobb's Hole, as early as I liked—which, interpreted by my impatience to get possession of the letter, meant as early as I could. Without waiting for breakfast at the Farm, I took a crust of bread in my hand, and set forth, in some doubt whether I should not surprise the excellent Betteredge in his bed. To my great relief he proved to be quite as excited about the coming event as I was. I found him ready, and waiting for me, with his stick in his hand.

"How are you this morning, Betteredge?"

"Very poorly, sir."

"Sorry to hear it. What do you complain of?"

"I complain of a new disease, Mr. Franklin, of my own inventing. I don't want to alarm you, but you're certain to catch it before the morning is out."

"The devil I am!"

"Do you feel an uncomfortable heat at the pit of your stomach, sir? and a nasty thumping at the top of your head? Ah! not yet? It will lay hold of you at Cobb's Hole, Mr. Franklin. I call it the detective-fever; and I first caught it in the company of Sergeant Cuff."

"Aye! aye! and the cure in this instance is to open Rosanna Spearman's letter, I suppose? Come along, and let's get it."

Early as it was, we found the fisherman's wife astir in her kitchen. On my presentation by Betteredge, good Mrs. Yolland performed a social ceremony, strictly reserved (as I afterwards learnt) for strangers of distinction. She put a bottle of Dutch gin and a couple of clean pipes on the table, and opened the conversation by saying, "What news from London, sir?"

Before I could find an answer to this immensely comprehensive question, an apparition advanced towards me, out of a dark corner of the kitchen. A wan, wild, haggard girl, with remarkably beautiful hair, and with a fierce keenness in her eyes, came limping up on a crutch to the table at which I was sitting, and looked at me as if I was an object of mingled interest and horror, which it quite fascinated her to see.

"Mr. Betteredge," she said, without taking her eyes off me, "mention his name again, if you please."

"This gentleman's name," answered Betteredge (with a strong emphasis on gentleman), "is Mr. Franklin Blake."

The girl turned her back on me, and suddenly left the room. Good Mrs. Yolland—as I believe—made some apologies for her daughter's odd behaviour, and Betteredge (probably) translated them into polite English. I speak of this in complete uncertainty. My attention was absorbed in following the sound of the girl's crutch. Thump-thump, up the wooden stairs; thump-thump across the room above our heads; thump-thump down the stairs again—and there stood the apparition at the open door, with a letter in its hand, beckoning me out!

I left more apologies in course of delivery behind me, and followed this strange creature—limping on before me, faster and faster—down the slope of the beach. She led me behind some boats, out of sight and hearing of the few people in the fishing-village, and then stopped, and faced me for the first time.

"Stand there," she said, "I want to look at you."

There was no mistaking the expression on her face. I inspired her with the strongest emotions of abhorrence and disgust. Let me not be vain enough to say that no woman had ever looked at me in this manner before. I will only venture on the more modest assertion that no woman had ever let me perceive it yet. There is a limit to the length of the inspection which a man can endure, under certain circumstances. I attempted to direct Limping Lucy's attention to some less revolting object than my face.

"I think you have got a letter to give me," I began. "Is it the letter there, in your hand?"

"Say that again," was the only answer I received.

I repeated the words, like a good child learning its lesson.

"No," said the girl, speaking to herself, but keeping her eyes still mercilessly fixed on me. "I can't find out what she saw in his face. I can't guess what she heard in his voice." She suddenly looked away from me, and rested her head wearily on the top of her crutch. "Oh, my poor dear!" she said, in the first soft tones which had fallen from her, in my hearing. "Oh, my lost darling! what could you see in this man?" She lifted her head again fiercely, and looked at me once more. "Can you eat and drink?" she asked.

I did my best to preserve my gravity, and answered, "Yes."

"Can you sleep?"

"Yes."

"When you see a poor girl in service, do you feel no remorse?"

"Certainly not. Why should I?"

She abruptly thrust the letter (as the phrase is) into my face.

"Take it!" she exclaimed furiously. "I never set eyes on you before. God Almighty forbid I should ever set eyes on you again."

With those parting words she limped away from me at the top of her speed. The one interpretation that I could put on her conduct has, no doubt, been anticipated by everybody. I could only suppose that she was mad.

Having reached that inevitable conclusion, I turned to the more interesting object of investigation which was presented to me by Rosanna Spearman's letter. The address was written as follows:—"For Franklin Blake, Esq. To be given into his own hands (and not to be trusted to anyone else), by Lucy Yolland."

I broke the seal. The envelope contained a letter: and this, in its turn, contained a slip of paper. I read the letter first:—

"Sir,—If you are curious to know the meaning of my behaviour to you, whilst you were staying in the house of my mistress, Lady Verinder, do what you are told to do in the memorandum enclosed with this—and do it without any person being present to overlook you. Your humble servant,

"ROSANNA SPEARMAN."

I turned to the slip of paper next. Here is the literal copy of it, word for word:

"Memorandum:—To go to the Shivering Sand at the turn of the tide. To walk out on the South Spit, until I get the South Spit Beacon, and the flagstaff at the Coast-guard station above Cobb's Hole in a line together. To lay down on the rocks, a stick, or any straight thing to guide my hand, exactly in the line of the beacon and the flagstaff. To take care, in doing this, that one end of the stick shall be at the edge of the rocks, on the side of them which overlooks the quicksand. To feel along the stick, among the seaweed (beginning from the end of the stick which points towards the beacon), for the Chain. To run my hand along the Chain, when found, until I come to the part of it which stretches over the edge of the rocks, down into the quicksand. And then, to pull the chain."

Just as I had read the last words—underlined in the original—I heard the voice of Betteredge behind me. The inventor of the detective-fever had completely succumbed to that irresistible malady. "I can't stand it any longer, Mr. Franklin. What does her letter say? For mercy's sake, sir, tell us, what does her letter say?"

I handed him the letter, and the memorandum. He read the first without appearing to be much interested in it. But the second—the memorandum—produced a strong impression on him.

"The Sergeant said it!" cried Betteredge. "From first to last, sir, the Sergeant said she had got a memorandum of the hiding-place. And here it is! Lord save us, Mr. Franklin, here is the secret that puzzled everybody, from the great Cuff downwards, ready and waiting, as one may say, to show itself to you! It's the ebb now, sir, as anybody may see for themselves. How long will it be till the turn of the tide?" He looked up, and observed a lad at work, at some little distance from us, mending a net. "Tammie Bright!" he shouted at the top of his voice.

"I hear you!" Tammie shouted back.

"When's the turn of the tide?"

"In an hour's time."

We both looked at our watches.

"We can go round by the coast, Mr. Franklin," said Betteredge; "and get to the quicksand in that way with plenty of time to spare. What do you say, sir?"

"Come along!"

On our way to the Shivering Sand, I applied to Betteredge to revive my memory of events (as affecting Rosanna Spearman) at the period of Sergeant Cuff's inquiry. With my old friend's help, I soon had the succession of circumstances clearly registered in my mind. Rosanna's journey to Frizinghall, when the whole household believed her to be ill in her own room—Rosanna's mysterious employment of the night-time with her door locked, and her candle burning till the morning—Rosanna's suspicious purchase of the japanned tin case, and the two dog's chains from Mrs. Yolland—the Sergeant's positive conviction that Rosanna had hidden something at the Shivering Sand, and the Sergeant's absolute ignorance as to what that something might be—all these strange results of the abortive inquiry into the loss of the Moonstone were clearly present to me again, when we reached the quicksand, and walked out together on the low ledge of rocks called the South Spit.

With Betteredge's help, I soon stood in the right position to see the Beacon and the Coast-guard flagstaff in a line together. Following the memorandum as our guide, we next laid my stick in the necessary direction, as neatly as we could, on the uneven surface of the rocks. And then we looked at our watches once more.

It wanted nearly twenty minutes yet of the turn of the tide. I suggested waiting through this interval on the beach, instead of on the wet and slippery surface of the rocks. Having reached the dry sand, I prepared to sit down; and, greatly to my surprise, Betteredge prepared to leave me.

"What are you going away for?" I asked.

"Look at the letter again, sir, and you will see."

A glance at the letter reminded me that I was charged, when I made my discovery, to make it alone.

"It's hard enough for me to leave you, at such a time as this,"

The Moonstone

said Betteredge. "But she died a dreadful death, poor soul—and I feel a kind of call on me, Mr. Franklin, to humour that fancy of hers. Besides," he added, confidentially, "there's nothing in the letter against your letting out the secret afterwards. I'll hang about in the fir-plantation, and wait till you pick me up. Don't be longer than you can help, sir. The detective-fever isn't an easy disease to deal with, under these circumstances."

With that parting caution, he left me.

The interval of expectation, short as it was when reckoned by the measure of time, assumed formidable proportions when reckoned by the measure of suspense. This was one of the occasions on which the invaluable habit of smoking becomes especially precious and consolatory. I lit a cigar, and sat down on the slope of the beach.

The sunlight poured its unclouded beauty on every object that I could see. The exquisite freshness of the air made the mere act of living and breathing a luxury. Even the lonely little bay welcomed the morning with a show of cheerfulness; and the bared wet surface of the quicksand itself, glittering with a golden brightness, hid the horror of its false brown face under a passing smile. It was the finest day I had seen since my return to England.

The turn of the tide came, before my cigar was finished. I saw the preliminary heaving of the Sand, and then the awful shiver that crept over its surface—as if some spirit of terror lived and moved and shuddered in the fathomless deeps beneath. I threw away my cigar, and went back again to the rocks.

My directions in the memorandum instructed me to feel along the line traced by the stick, beginning with the end which was nearest to the beacon.

I advanced, in this manner, more than half way along the stick, without encountering anything but the edges of the rocks. An inch or two further on, however, my patience was rewarded. In a narrow little fissure, just within reach of my forefinger, I felt the chain. Attempting, next, to follow it, by touch, in the direction of the quicksand, I found my progress stopped by a thick growth of seaweed—which had fastened itself into the fissure, no doubt, in the time that had elapsed since Rosanna

Spearman had chosen her hiding-place.

It was equally impossible to pull up the seaweed, or to force my hand through it. After marking the spot indicated by the end of the stick which was placed nearest to the quicksand, I determined to pursue the search for the chain on a plan of my own. My idea was to "sound" immediately under the rocks, on the chance of recovering the lost trace of the chain at the point at which it entered the sand. I took up the stick, and knelt down on the brink of the South Spit.

In this position, my face was within a few feet of the surface of the quicksand. The sight of it so near me, still disturbed at intervals by its hideous shivering fit, shook my nerves for the moment. A horrible fancy that the dead woman might appear on the scene of her suicide, to assist my search—an unutterable dread of seeing her rise through the heaving surface of the sand, and point to the place—forced itself into my mind, and turned me cold in the warm sunlight. I own I closed my eyes at the moment when the point of the stick first entered the quicksand.

The instant afterwards, before the stick could have been submerged more than a few inches, I was free from the hold of my own superstitious terror, and was throbbing with excitement from head to foot. Sounding blindfold, at my first attempt—at that first attempt I had sounded right! The stick struck the chain.

Taking a firm hold of the roots of the seaweed with my left hand, I laid myself down over the brink, and felt with my right hand under the overhanging edges of the rock. My right hand found the chain.

I drew it up without the slightest difficulty. And there was the japanned tin case fastened to the end of it.

The action of the water had so rusted the chain, that it was impossible for me to unfasten it from the hasp which attached it to the case. Putting the case between my knees and exerting my utmost strength, I contrived to draw off the cover. Some white substance filled the whole interior when I looked in. I put in my hand, and found it to be linen.

In drawing out the linen, I also drew out a letter crumpled up with it. After looking at the direction, and discovering that it bore my name, I put the letter in my pocket, and completely removed the linen. It came out in a thick roll, moulded, of course, to the shape of the case in which it had been so long confined, and perfectly preserved from any injury by the sea.

I carried the linen to the dry sand of the beach, and there unrolled and smoothed it out. There was no mistaking it as an article of dress. It was a nightgown.

The uppermost side, when I spread it out, presented to view innumerable folds and creases, and nothing more. I tried the undermost side, next—and instantly discovered the smear of the paint from the door of Rachel's boudoir!

My eyes remained riveted on the stain, and my mind took me back at a leap from present to past. The very words of Sergeant Cuff recurred to me, as if the man himself was at my side again, pointing to the unanswerable inference which he drew from the smear on the door.

"Find out whether there is any article of dress in this house with the stain of paint on it. Find out who that dress belongs to. Find out how the person can account for having been in the room, and smeared the paint between midnight and three in the morning. If the person can't satisfy you, you haven't far to look for the hand that took the Diamond."

One after another those words travelled over my memory, repeating themselves again and again with a wearisome, mechanical reiteration. I was roused from what felt like a trance of many hours—from what was really, no doubt, the pause of a few moments only—by a voice calling to me. I looked up, and saw that Betteredge's patience had failed him at last. He was just visible between the sandhills, returning to the beach.

The old man's appearance recalled me, the moment I perceived it, to my sense of present things, and reminded me that the inquiry which I had pursued thus far still remained incomplete. I had discovered the smear on the nightgown. To whom did the nightgown belong?

My first impulse was to consult the letter in my pocket—the letter which I had found in the case.

As I raised my hand to take it out, I remembered that there was a shorter way to discovery than this. The nightgown itself would reveal the truth, for, in all probability, the nightgown was marked with its owner's name.

I took it up from the sand, and looked for the mark.

I found the mark, and read—MY OWN NAME.

There were the familiar letters which told me that the nightgown was mine. I looked up from them. There was the sun; there were the glittering waters of the bay; there was old Betteredge, advancing nearer and nearer to me. I looked back again at the letters. My own name. Plainly confronting me—my own name.

"If time, pains, and money can do it, I will lay my hand on the thief who took the Moonstone."—I had left London, with those words on my lips. I had penetrated the secret which the quicksand had kept from every other living creature. And, on the unanswerable evidence of the paint-stain, I had discovered Myself as the Thief.

CHAPTER IV

I have not a word to say about my own sensations.

My impression is that the shock inflicted on me completely suspended my thinking and feeling power. I certainly could not have known what I was about when Betteredge joined me—for I have it on his authority that I laughed, when he asked what was the matter, and putting the nightgown into his hands, told him to read the riddle for himself.

Of what was said between us on the beach, I have not the faintest recollection. The first place in which I can now see myself again plainly is the plantation of firs. Betteredge and I are walking back together to the house; and Betteredge is telling me that I shall be able to face it, and he will be able to face it, when we have had a glass of grog.

The scene shifts from the plantation, to Betteredge's little sitting-room. My resolution not to enter Rachel's house is forgotten. I feel gratefully the coolness and shadiness and quiet of the room. I drink the grog (a perfectly new luxury to me, at that time of day), which my good old friend mixes with icy-cold water from the well. Under any other circumstances, the drink would simply stupefy me. As things are, it strings up my nerves. I begin to "face it," as Betteredge has predicted. And Betteredge, on his side, begins to "face it," too.

The picture which I am now presenting of myself, will, I suspect, be thought a very strange one, to say the least of it. Placed in a situation which may, I think, be described as entirely without parallel, what is the first proceeding to which I resort? Do I seclude myself from all human society? Do I set my mind to analyse the abominable impossibility which, nevertheless, confronts me as an undeniable fact? Do I hurry back to London by the first train to consult the highest authorities, and to set a searching inquiry on foot immediately? No. I accept the shelter of a house which I had resolved never to degrade myself by entering again; and I sit, tippling spirits and water in the company of an old servant, at ten o'clock in the morning. Is this the conduct that might have been expected from a man placed in my horrible position? I can only answer that the sight of old Betteredge's familiar face was an inexpressible comfort to me, and that the drinking of old Betteredge's grog helped me, as I believe nothing else would have helped me, in the state of complete bodily and mental prostration into which I had fallen. I can only offer this excuse for myself; and I can only admire that invariable preservation of dignity, and that strictly logical consistency of conduct which distinguish every man and woman who may read these lines, in every emergency of their lives from the cradle to the grave.

"Now, Mr. Franklin, there's one thing certain, at any rate," said Betteredge, throwing the nightgown down on the table between us, and pointing to it as if it was a living creature that could hear him. "He's a liar, to begin with."

This comforting view of the matter was not the view that presented itself to my mind.

"I am as innocent of all knowledge of having taken the Diamond as you are," I said. "But there is the witness against me! The paint on the nightgown, and the name on the nightgown are facts."

Betteredge lifted my glass, and put it persuasively into my hand.

"Facts?" he repeated. "Take a drop more grog, Mr. Franklin, and you'll get over the weakness of believing in facts! Foul play, sir!" he continued, dropping his voice confidentially. "That is how I read the riddle. Foul play somewhere—and you and I must find it out. Was there nothing else in the tin case, when you put your hand into it?"

The question instantly reminded me of the letter in my pocket. I took it out, and opened it. It was a letter of many pages, closely written. I looked impatiently for the signature at the end. "Rosanna Spearman."

As I read the name, a sudden remembrance illuminated my mind, and a sudden suspicion rose out of the new light.

"Stop!" I exclaimed. "Rosanna Spearman came to my aunt out of a reformatory? Rosanna Spearman had once been a thief?"

"There's no denying that, Mr. Franklin. What of it now, if you please?"

"What of it now? How do we know she may not have stolen

the Diamond after all? How do we know she may not have smeared my nightgown purposely with the paint?"

Betteredge laid his hand on my arm, and stopped me before I could say any more.

"You will be cleared of this, Mr. Franklin, beyond all doubt. But I hope you won't be cleared in that way. See what the letter says, sir. In justice to the girl's memory, see what it says."

I felt the earnestness with which he spoke—felt it as a friendly rebuke to me. "You shall form your own judgment on her letter," I said. "I will read it out."

I began—and read these lines:

"Sir—I have something to own to you. A confession which means much misery, may sometimes be made in very few words. This confession can be made in three words. I love you."

The letter dropped from my hand. I looked at Betteredge. "In the name of Heaven," I said, "what does it mean?"

He seemed to shrink from answering the question.

"You and Limping Lucy were alone together this morning, sir," he said. "Did she say nothing about Rosanna Spearman?"

"She never even mentioned Rosanna Spearman's name."

"Please to go back to the letter, Mr. Franklin. I tell you plainly, I can't find it in my heart to distress you, after what you have had to bear already. Let her speak for herself, sir. And get on with your grog. For your own sake, get on with your grog."

I resumed the reading of the letter.

"It would be very disgraceful to me to tell you this, if I was a living woman when you read it. I shall be dead and gone, sir, when you find my letter. It is that which makes me bold. Not even my grave will be left to tell of me. I may own the truth— with the quicksand waiting to hide me when the words are written.

"Besides, you will find your nightgown in my hiding-place, with the smear of the paint on it; and you will want to know how it came to be hidden by me? and why I said nothing to you about it in my life-time? I have only one reason to give. I did these strange things, because I loved you.

"I won't trouble you with much about myself, or my life, before you came to my lady's house. Lady Verinder took me out of a reformatory. I had gone to the reformatory from the prison. I was put in the prison, because I was a thief. I was a thief, because my mother went on the streets when I was quite a little girl. My mother went on the streets, because the gentleman who was my father deserted her. There is no need to tell such a common story as this, at any length. It is told quite often enough in the newspapers.

"Lady Verinder was very kind to me, and Mr. Betteredge was very kind to me. Those two, and the matron at the reformatory, are the only good people I have ever met with in all my life. I might have got on in my place — not happily — but I might have got on, if you had not come visiting. I don't blame you, sir. It's my fault — all my fault.

"Do you remember when you came out on us from among the sandhills, that morning, looking for Mr. Betteredge? You were like a prince in a fairy-story. You were like a lover in a dream. You were the most adorable human creature I had ever seen. Something that felt like the happy life I had never led yet, leapt up in me at the instant I set eyes on you. Don't laugh at this if you can help it. Oh, if I could only make you feel how serious it is to me!

"I went back to the house, and wrote your name and mine in my work-box, and drew a true lovers' knot under them. Then, some devil — no, I ought to say some good angel — whispered to me, 'Go and look in the glass.' The glass told me — never mind what. I was too foolish to take the warning. I went on getting fonder and fonder of you, just as if I was a lady in your own rank of life, and the most beautiful creature your eyes ever rested on. I tried — oh, dear, how I tried — to get you to look at me. If you had known how I used to cry at night with the misery and the mortification of your never taking any notice of me, you would have pitied me perhaps, and have given me a look now and then to live on.

"It would have been no very kind look, perhaps, if you had known how I hated Miss Rachel. I believe I found out you were in love with her, before you knew it yourself. She used to give

The Moonstone

you roses to wear in your button-hole. Ah, Mr. Franklin, you wore my roses oftener than either you or she thought! The only comfort I had at that time, was putting my rose secretly in your glass of water, in place of hers—and then throwing her rose away.

"If she had been really as pretty as you thought her, I might have borne it better. No; I believe I should have been more spiteful against her still. Suppose you put Miss Rachel into a servant's dress, and took her ornaments off? I don't know what is the use of my writing in this way. It can't be denied that she had a bad figure; she was too thin. But who can tell what the men like? And young ladies may behave in a manner which would cost a servant her place. It's no business of mine. I can't expect you to read my letter, if I write it in this way. But it does stir one up to hear Miss Rachel called pretty, when one knows all the time that it's her dress does it, and her confidence in herself.

"Try not to lose patience with me, sir. I will get on as fast as I can to the time which is sure to interest you—the time when the Diamond was lost.

"But there is one thing which I have got it on my mind to tell you first.

"My life was not a very hard life to bear, while I was a thief. It was only when they had taught me at the reformatory to feel my own degradation, and to try for better things, that the days grew long and weary. Thoughts of the future forced themselves on me now. I felt the dreadful reproach that honest people—even the kindest of honest people—were to me in themselves. A heart-breaking sensation of loneliness kept with me, go where I might, and do what I might, and see what persons I might. It was my duty, I know, to try and get on with my fellow-servants in my new place. Somehow, I couldn't make friends with them. They looked (or I thought they looked) as if they suspected what I had been. I don't regret, far from it, having been roused to make the effort to be a reformed woman—but, indeed, indeed it was a weary life. You had come across it like a beam of sunshine at first—and then you too failed me. I was mad enough to love you; and I couldn't even attract your notice. There was great misery—there really was great misery in that.

"Now I am coming to what I wanted to tell you. In those days of bitterness, I went two or three times, when it was my turn to go out, to my favourite place—the beach above the Shivering Sand. And I said to myself, 'I think it will end here. When I can bear it no longer, I think it will end here.' You will understand, sir, that the place had laid a kind of spell on me before you came. I had always had a notion that something would happen to me at the quicksand. But I had never looked at it, with the thought of its being the means of my making away with myself, till the time came of which I am now writing. Then I did think that here was a place which would end all my troubles for me in a moment or two—and hide me for ever afterwards.

"This is all I have to say about myself, reckoning from the morning when I first saw you, to the morning when the alarm was raised in the house that the Diamond was lost.

"I was so aggravated by the foolish talk among the women servants, all wondering who was to be suspected first; and I was so angry with you (knowing no better at that time) for the pains you took in hunting for the jewel, and sending for the police, that I kept as much as possible away by myself, until later in the day, when the officer from Frizinghall came to the house.

"Mr. Seegrave began, as you may remember, by setting a guard on the women's bedrooms; and the women all followed him upstairs in a rage, to know what he meant by the insult he had put on them. I went with the rest, because if I had done anything different from the rest, Mr. Seegrave was the sort of man who would have suspected me directly. We found him in Miss Rachel's room. He told us he wouldn't have a lot of women there; and he pointed to the smear on the painted door, and said some of our petticoats had done the mischief, and sent us all downstairs again.

"After leaving Miss Rachel's room, I stopped a moment on one of the landings, by myself, to see if I had got the paint-stain by any chance on my gown. Penelope Betteredge (the only one of the women with whom I was on friendly terms) passed, and noticed what I was about.

"'You needn't trouble yourself, Rosanna,' she said. 'The paint on Miss Rachel's door has been dry for hours. If Mr.

The Moonstone

Seegrave hadn't set a watch on our bedrooms, I might have told him as much. I don't know what you think—I was never so insulted before in my life!'

"Penelope was a hot-tempered girl. I quieted her, and brought her back to what she had said about the paint on the door having been dry for hours.

"'How do you know that?' I asked.

"'I was with Miss Rachel, and Mr. Franklin, all yesterday morning,' Penelope said, 'mixing the colours, while they finished the door. I heard Miss Rachel ask whether the door would be dry that evening, in time for the birthday company to see it. And Mr. Franklin shook his head, and said it wouldn't be dry in less than twelve hours. It was long past luncheon-time—it was three o'clock before they had done. What does your arithmetic say, Rosanna? Mine says the door was dry by three this morning.'

"'Did some of the ladies go upstairs yesterday evening to see it?' I asked. 'I thought I heard Miss Rachel warning them to keep clear of the door.'

"'None of the ladies made the smear,' Penelope answered. 'I left Miss Rachel in bed at twelve last night. And I noticed the door, and there was nothing wrong with it then.'

"'Oughtn't you to mention this to Mr. Seegrave, Penelope?'

"'I wouldn't say a word to help Mr. Seegrave for anything that could be offered to me!'

"She went to her work, and I went to mine."

"My work, sir, was to make your bed, and to put your room tidy. It was the happiest hour I had in the whole day. I used to kiss the pillow on which your head had rested all night. No matter who has done it since, you have never had your clothes folded as nicely as I folded them for you. Of all the little knick-knacks in your dressing-case, there wasn't one that had so much as a speck on it. You never noticed it, any more than you noticed me. I beg your pardon; I am forgetting myself. I will make haste, and go on again.

"Well, I went in that morning to do my work in your room. There was your nightgown tossed across the bed, just as you had thrown it off. I took it up to fold it—and I saw the stain of the paint from Miss Rachel's door!

"I was so startled by the discovery that I ran out with the nightgown in my hand, and made for the back stairs, and locked myself into my own room, to look at it in a place where nobody could intrude and interrupt me.

"As soon as I got my breath again, I called to mind my talk with Penelope, and I said to myself, 'Here's the proof that he was in Miss Rachel's sitting-room between twelve last night, and three this morning!'

"I shall not tell you in plain words what was the first suspicion that crossed my mind, when I had made that discovery. You would only be angry—and, if you were angry, you might tear my letter up and read no more of it.

"Let it be enough, if you please, to say only this. After thinking it over to the best of my ability, I made it out that the thing wasn't likely, for a reason that I will tell you. If you had been in Miss Rachel's sitting-room, at that time of night, with Miss Rachel's knowledge (and if you had been foolish enough to forget to take care of the wet door) she would have reminded you—she would never have let you carry away such a witness against her, as the witness I was looking at now! At the same time, I own I was not completely certain in my own mind that I had proved my own suspicion to be wrong. You will not have forgotten that I have owned to hating Miss Rachel. Try to think, if you can, that there was a little of that hatred in all this. It ended in my determining to keep the nightgown, and to wait, and watch, and see what use I might make of it. At that time, please to remember, not the ghost of an idea entered my head that you had stolen the Diamond."

There, I broke off in the reading of the letter for the second time.

I had read those portions of the miserable woman's confession which related to myself, with unaffected surprise, and, I can honestly add, with sincere distress. I had regretted, truly regretted, the aspersion which I had thoughtlessly cast on her memory, before I had seen a line of her letter. But when I had advanced as far as the passage which is quoted above, I own I felt my mind growing bitterer and bitterer against

The Moonstone

Rosanna Spearman as I went on. "Read the rest for yourself," I said, handing the letter to Betteredge across the table. "If there is anything in it that I must look at, you can tell me as you go on."

"I understand you, Mr. Franklin," he answered. "It's natural, sir, in you. And, God help us all!" he added, in a lower tone, "it's no less natural in her."

I proceed to copy the continuation of the letter from the original, in my own possession:—

"Having determined to keep the nightgown, and to see what use my love, or my revenge (I hardly know which) could turn it to in the future, the next thing to discover was how to keep it without the risk of being found out.

"There was only one way—to make another nightgown exactly like it, before Saturday came, and brought the laundry-woman and her inventory to the house.

"I was afraid to put it off till next day (the Friday); being in doubt lest some accident might happen in the interval. I determined to make the new nightgown on that same day (the Thursday), while I could count, if I played my cards properly, on having my time to myself. The first thing to do (after locking up your nightgown in my drawer) was to go back to your bedroom—not so much to put it to rights (Penelope would have done that for me, if I had asked her) as to find out whether you had smeared off any of the paint-stain from your nightgown, on the bed, or on any piece of furniture in the room.

"I examined everything narrowly, and at last, I found a few streaks of the paint on the inside of your dressing-gown—not the linen dressing-gown you usually wore in that summer season, but a flannel dressing-gown which you had with you also. I suppose you felt chilly after walking to and fro in nothing but your nightdress, and put on the warmest thing you could find. At any rate, there were the stains, just visible, on the inside of the dressing-gown. I easily got rid of these by scraping away the stuff of the flannel. This done, the only proof left against you was the proof locked up in my drawer.

"I had just finished your room when I was sent for to be questioned by Mr. Seegrave, along with the rest of the servants. Next came the examination of all our boxes. And then followed the most extraordinary event of the day—to me—since I had found the paint on your nightgown. This event came out of the second questioning of Penelope Betteredge by Superintendent Seegrave.

"Penelope returned to us quite beside herself with rage at the manner in which Mr. Seegrave had treated her. He had hinted, beyond the possibility of mistaking him, that he suspected her of being the thief. We were all equally astonished at hearing this, and we all asked, Why?

"'Because the Diamond was in Miss Rachel's sitting-room,' Penelope answered. "And because I was the last person in the sitting-room at night!'

"Almost before the words had left her lips, I remembered that another person had been in the sitting-room later than Penelope. That person was yourself. My head whirled round, and my thoughts were in dreadful confusion. In the midst of it all, something in my mind whispered to me that the smear on your nightgown might have a meaning entirely different to the meaning which I had given to it up to that time. 'If the last person who was in the room is the person to be suspected,' I thought to myself, 'the thief is not Penelope, but Mr. Franklin Blake!'

"In the case of any other gentleman, I believe I should have been ashamed of suspecting him of theft, almost as soon as the suspicion had passed through my mind.

"But the bare thought that you had let yourself down to my level, and that I, in possessing myself of your nightgown, had also possessed myself of the means of shielding you from being discovered, and disgraced for life—I say, sir, the bare thought of this seemed to open such a chance before me of winning your good will, that I passed blindfold, as one may say, from suspecting to believing. I made up my mind, on the spot, that you had shown yourself the busiest of anybody in fetching the police, as a blind to deceive us all; and that the hand which had taken Miss Rachel's jewel could by no possibility be any other hand than yours.

"The excitement of this new discovery of mine must, I think, have turned my head for a while. I felt such a devouring eagerness to see you—to try you with a word or two about the

The Moonstone

Diamond, and to make you look at me, and speak to me, in that way—that I put my hair tidy, and made myself as nice as I could, and went to you boldly in the library where I knew you were writing.

"You had left one of your rings upstairs, which made as good an excuse for my intrusion as I could have desired. But, oh, sir! if you have ever loved, you will understand how it was that all my courage cooled, when I walked into the room, and found myself in your presence. And then, you looked up at me so coldly, and you thanked me for finding your ring in such an indifferent manner, that my knees trembled under me, and I felt as if I should drop on the floor at your feet. When you had thanked me, you looked back, if you remember, at your writing. I was so mortified at being treated in this way, that I plucked up spirit enough to speak. I said, 'This is a strange thing about the Diamond, sir.' And you looked up again, and said, 'Yes, it is!' You spoke civilly (I can't deny that); but still you kept a distance—a cruel distance between us. Believing, as I did, that you had got the lost Diamond hidden about you, while you were speaking, your coolness so provoked me that I got bold enough, in the heat of the moment, to give you a hint. I said, 'They will never find the Diamond, sir, will they? No! nor the person who took it—I'll answer for that.' I nodded, and smiled at you, as much as to say, 'I know!' This time, you looked up at me with something like interest in your eyes; and I felt that a few more words on your side and mine might bring out the truth. Just at that moment, Mr. Betteredge spoilt it all by coming to the door. I knew his footstep, and I also knew that it was against his rules for me to be in the library at that time of day—let alone being there along with you. I had only just time to get out of my own accord, before he could come in and tell me to go. I was angry and disappointed; but I was not entirely without hope for all that. The ice, you see, was broken between us—and I thought I would take care, on the next occasion, that Mr. Betteredge was out of the way.

"When I got back to the servants' hall, the bell was going for our dinner. Afternoon already! and the materials for making the new nightgown were still to be got! There was but one chance of getting them. I shammed ill at dinner; and so secured the whole of the interval from then till tea-time to my own use.

"What I was about, while the household believed me to be lying down in my own room; and how I spent the night, after shamming ill again at tea-time, and having been sent up to bed, there is no need to tell you. Sergeant Cuff discovered that much, if he discovered nothing more. And I can guess how. I was detected (though I kept my veil down) in the draper's shop at Frizinghall. There was a glass in front of me, at the counter where I was buying the longcloth; and—in that glass—I saw one of the shopmen point to my shoulder and whisper to another. At night again, when I was secretly at work, locked into my room, I heard the breathing of the women servants who suspected me, outside my door.

"It didn't matter then; it doesn't matter now. On the Friday morning, hours before Sergeant Cuff entered the house, there was the new nightgown—to make up your number in place of the nightgown that I had got—made, wrung out, dried, ironed, marked, and folded as the laundry woman folded all the others, safe in your drawer. There was no fear (if the linen in the house was examined) of the newness of the nightgown betraying me. All your underclothing had been renewed, when you came to our house—I suppose on your return home from foreign parts.

"The next thing was the arrival of Sergeant Cuff; and the next great surprise was the announcement of what he thought about the smear on the door.

"I had believed you to be guilty (as I have owned), more because I wanted you to be guilty than for any other reason. And now, the Sergeant had come round by a totally different way to the same conclusion (respecting the nightgown) as mine! And I had got the dress that was the only proof against you! And not a living creature knew it—yourself included! I am afraid to tell you how I felt when I called these things to mind— you would hate my memory for ever afterwards."

At that place, Betteredge looked up from the letter.

"Not a glimmer of light so far, Mr. Franklin," said the old man, taking off his heavy tortoiseshell spectacles, and pushing Rosanna Spearman's confession a little away from him. "Have you come to any conclusion, sir, in your own mind, while I have been reading?"

"Finish the letter first, Betteredge; there may be something to enlighten us at the end of it. I shall have a word or two to say to you after that."

"Very good, sir. I'll just rest my eyes, and then I'll go on again. In the meantime, Mr. Franklin—I don't want to hurry you—but would you mind telling me, in one word, whether you see your way out of this dreadful mess yet?"

"I see my way back to London," I said, "to consult Mr. Bruff. If he can't help me——"

"Yes, sir?"

"And if the Sergeant won't leave his retirement at Dorking——"

"He won't, Mr. Franklin!"

"Then, Betteredge—as far as I can see now—I am at the end of my resources. After Mr. Bruff and the Sergeant, I don't know of a living creature who can be of the slightest use to me."

As the words passed my lips, some person outside knocked at the door of the room.

Betteredge looked surprised as well as annoyed by the interruption.

"Come in," he called out, irritably, "whoever you are!"

The door opened, and there entered to us, quietly, the most remarkable-looking man that I had ever seen. Judging him by his figure and his movements, he was still young. Judging him by his face, and comparing him with Betteredge, he looked the elder of the two. His complexion was of a gipsy darkness; his fleshless cheeks had fallen into deep hollows, over which the bone projected like a penthouse. His nose presented the fine shape and modelling so often found among the ancient people of the East, so seldom visible among the newer races of the West. His forehead rose high and straight from the brow. His marks and wrinkles were innumerable. From this strange face, eyes, stranger still, of the softest brown—eyes dreamy and mournful, and deeply sunk in their orbits—looked out at you, and (in my case, at least) took your attention captive at their will. Add to this a quantity of thick closely-curling hair, which, by some freak of Nature, had lost its colour in the most startlingly partial and capricious manner. Over the top of his head it was still of the deep black which was its natural colour. Round the sides of his head—without the slightest gradation of grey to break the force of the extraordinary contrast—it had turned completely white. The line between the two colours preserved no sort of regularity. At one place, the white hair ran up into the black; at another, the black hair ran down into the white. I looked at the man with a curiosity which, I am ashamed to say, I found it quite impossible to control. His soft brown eyes looked back at me gently; and he met my involuntary rudeness in staring at him, with an apology which I was conscious that I had not deserved.

"I beg your pardon," he said. "I had no idea that Mr. Betteredge was engaged." He took a slip of paper from his pocket, and handed it to Betteredge. "The list for next week," he said. His eyes just rested on me again—and he left the room as quietly as he had entered it.

"Who is that?" I asked.

"Mr. Candy's assistant," said Betteredge. "By-the-bye, Mr. Franklin, you will be sorry to hear that the little doctor has never recovered that illness he caught, going home from the birthday dinner. He's pretty well in health; but he lost his memory in the fever, and he has never recovered more than the wreck of it since. The work all falls on his assistant. Not much of it now, except among the poor. They can't help themselves, you know. They must put up with the man with the piebald hair, and the gipsy complexion—or they would get no doctoring at all."

"You don't seem to like him, Betteredge?"

"Nobody likes him, sir."

"Why is he so unpopular?"

"Well, Mr. Franklin, his appearance is against him, to begin with. And then there's a story that Mr. Candy took him with a very doubtful character. Nobody knows who he is—and he hasn't a friend in the place. How can you expect one to like him, after that?"

"Quite impossible, of course! May I ask what he wanted with you, when he gave you that bit of paper?"

"Only to bring me the weekly list of the sick people about here, sir, who stand in need of a little wine. My lady always had a regular distribution of good sound port and sherry among the infirm poor; and Miss Rachel wishes the custom to be kept up. Times have changed! times have changed! I remember when Mr. Candy himself brought the list to my mistress. Now it's Mr. Candy's assistant who brings the list to me. I'll go on with the letter, if you will allow me, sir," said Betteredge, drawing Rosanna Spearman's confession back to him. "It isn't lively reading, I grant you. But, there! it keeps me from getting sour with thinking of the past." He put on his spectacles, and wagged his head gloomily. "There's a bottom of good sense, Mr. Franklin, in our conduct to our mothers, when they first start us on the journey of life. We are all of us more or less unwilling to be brought into the world. And we are all of us right."

Mr. Candy's assistant had produced too strong an impression on me to be immediately dismissed from my thoughts. I passed over the last unanswerable utterance of the Betteredge philosophy; and returned to the subject of the man with the piebald hair.

"What is his name?" I asked.

"As ugly a name as need be," Betteredge answered gruffly. "Ezra Jennings."

CHAPTER V

Having told me the name of Mr. Candy's assistant, Betteredge appeared to think that we had wasted enough of our time on an insignificant subject. He resumed the perusal of Rosanna Spearman's letter.

On my side, I sat at the window, waiting until he had done. Little by little, the impression produced on me by Ezra Jennings—it seemed perfectly unaccountable, in such a situation as mine, that any human being should have produced an impression on me at all!—faded from my mind. My thoughts flowed back into their former channel. Once more, I forced myself to look my own incredible position resolutely in the face. Once more, I reviewed in my own mind the course which I had at last summoned composure enough to plan out for the future.

To go back to London that day; to put the whole case before Mr. Bruff; and, last and most important, to obtain (no matter by what means or at what sacrifice) a personal interview with Rachel—this was my plan of action, so far as I was capable of forming it at the time. There was more than an hour still to spare before the train started. And there was the bare chance that Betteredge might discover something in the unread portion of Rosanna Spearman's letter, which it might be useful for me to know before I left the house in which the Diamond had been lost. For that chance I was now waiting.

The letter ended in these terms:

"You have no need to be angry, Mr. Franklin, even if I did feel some little triumph at knowing that I held all your prospects in life in my own hands. Anxieties and fears soon came back to me. With the view Sergeant Cuff took of the loss of the Diamond, he would be sure to end in examining our linen and our dresses. There was no place in my room—there was no place in the house—which I could feel satisfied would be safe from him. How to hide the nightgown so that not even the Sergeant could find it? and how to do that without losing one moment of precious time?—these were not easy questions to answer. My uncertainties ended in my taking a way that may make you laugh. I undressed, and put the nightgown on me. You had worn it—and I had another little moment of pleasure in wearing it after you.

"The next news that reached us in the servants' hall showed that I had not made sure of the nightgown a moment too soon. Sergeant Cuff wanted to see the washing-book.

"I found it, and took it to him in my lady's sitting-room. The Sergeant and I had come across each other more than once in former days. I was certain he would know me again—and I was not certain of what he might do when he found me employed as servant in a house in which a valuable jewel had been lost. In this suspense, I felt it would be a relief to me to get the meeting between us over, and to know the worst of it at once.

"He looked at me as if I was a stranger, when I handed him the washing-book; and he was very specially polite in thanking me for bringing it. I thought those were both bad signs. There was no knowing what he might say of me behind my back; there was no knowing how soon I might not find myself taken in custody on suspicion, and searched. It was then time for your return from seeing Mr. Godfrey Ablewhite off by the railway; and I went to your favourite walk in the shrubbery, to try for another chance of speaking to you—the last chance, for all I knew to the contrary, that I might have.

"You never appeared; and, what was worse still, Mr. Betteredge and Sergeant Cuff passed by the place where I was hiding—and the Sergeant saw me.

"I had no choice, after that, but to return to my proper place and my proper work, before more disasters happened to me. Just as I was going to step across the path, you came back from the railway. You were making straight for the shrubbery, when you saw me—I am certain, sir, you saw me—and you turned away as if I had got the plague, and went into the house.*

* NOTE; by Franklin Blake.—The writer is entirely mistaken, poor creature. I never noticed her. My intention was certainly to have taken a turn in the shrubbery. But, remembering at the same moment that my aunt might wish to see me, after my return from the railway, I altered my mind, and went into the house.

"I made the best of my way indoors again, returning by the servants' entrance. There was nobody in the laundry-room at that time; and I sat down there alone. I have told you already of the thoughts which the Shivering Sand put into my head. Those thoughts came back to me now. I wondered in myself which it would be harder to do, if things went on in this manner—to bear Mr. Franklin Blake's indifference to me, or to jump into the quicksand and end it for ever in that way?

"It's useless to ask me to account for my own conduct, at this time. I try—and I can't understand it myself.

"Why didn't I stop you, when you avoided me in that cruel manner? Why didn't I call out, 'Mr. Franklin, I have got something to say to you; it concerns yourself, and you must, and shall, hear it?' You were at my mercy—I had got the whip-hand of you, as they say. And better than that, I had the means (if I could only make you trust me) of being useful to you in the future. Of course, I never supposed that you—a gentleman—had stolen the Diamond for the mere pleasure of stealing it. No. Penelope had heard Miss Rachel, and I had heard Mr. Betteredge, talk about your extravagance and your debts. It was plain enough to me that you had taken the Diamond to sell it, or pledge it, and so to get the money of which you stood in need. Well! I could have told you of a man in London who would have advanced a good large sum on the jewel, and who would have asked no awkward questions about it either.

"Why didn't I speak to you! why didn't I speak to you!

"I wonder whether the risks and difficulties of keeping the nightgown were as much as I could manage, without having other risks and difficulties added to them? This might have been the case with some women—but how could it be the case with me? In the days when I was a thief, I had run fifty times greater risks, and found my way out of difficulties to which this difficulty was mere child's play. I had been apprenticed, as you may say, to frauds and deceptions—some of them on such a grand scale, and managed so cleverly, that they became famous, and appeared in the newspapers. Was such a little thing as the keeping of the nightgown likely to weigh on my spirits, and to set my heart sinking within me, at the time when I ought to have spoken to you? What nonsense to ask the question! The thing couldn't be.

"Where is the use of my dwelling in this way on my own folly? The plain truth is plain enough, surely? Behind your back, I loved you with all my heart and soul. Before your face—

The Moonstone

there's no denying it—I was frightened of you; frightened of making you angry with me; frightened of what you might say to me (though you had taken the Diamond) if I presumed to tell you that I had found it out. I had gone as near to it as I dared when I spoke to you in the library. You had not turned your back on me then. You had not started away from me as if I had got the plague. I tried to provoke myself into feeling angry with you, and to rouse up my courage in that way. No! I couldn't feel anything but the misery and the mortification of it. You're a plain girl; you have got a crooked shoulder; you're only a housemaid—what do you mean by attempting to speak to Me?" You never uttered a word of that, Mr. Franklin; but you said it all to me, nevertheless! Is such madness as this to be accounted for? No. There is nothing to be done but to confess it, and let it be.

"I ask your pardon, once more, for this wandering of my pen. There is no fear of its happening again. I am close at the end now.

"The first person who disturbed me by coming into the empty room was Penelope. She had found out my secret long since, and she had done her best to bring me to my senses—and done it kindly too.

"'Ah!' she said, 'I know why you're sitting here, and fretting, all by yourself. The best thing that can happen for your advantage, Rosanna, will be for Mr. Franklin's visit here to come to an end. It's my belief that he won't be long now before he leaves the house.'

"In all my thoughts of you I had never thought of your going away. I couldn't speak to Penelope. I could only look at her.

"'I've just left Miss Rachel,' Penelope went on. 'And a hard matter I have had of it to put up with her temper. She says the house is unbearable to her with the police in it; and she's determined to speak to my lady this evening, and to go to her Aunt Ablewhite tomorrow. If she does that, Mr. Franklin will be the next to find a reason for going away, you may depend on it!'

"I recovered the use of my tongue at that. 'Do you mean to say Mr. Franklin will go with her?' I asked.

"'Only too gladly, if she would let him; but she won't. He has been made to feel her temper; he is in her black books too—and that after having done all he can to help her, poor fellow! No! no! If they don't make it up before tomorrow, you will see Miss Rachel go one way, and Mr. Franklin another. Where he may betake himself to I can't say. But he will never stay here, Rosanna, after Miss Rachel has left us.'

"I managed to master the despair I felt at the prospect of your going away. To own the truth, I saw a little glimpse of hope for myself if there was really a serious disagreement between Miss Rachel and you. 'Do you know,' I asked, 'what the quarrel is between them?'

"'It is all on Miss Rachel's side,' Penelope said. 'And, for anything I know to the contrary, it's all Miss Rachel's temper, and nothing else. I am loth to distress you, Rosanna; but don't run away with the notion that Mr. Franklin is ever likely to quarrel with her. He's a great deal too fond of her for that!'

"She had only just spoken those cruel words when there came a call to us from Mr. Betteredge. All the indoor servants were to assemble in the hall. And then we were to go in, one by one, and be questioned in Mr. Betteredge's room by Sergeant Cuff.

"It came to my turn to go in, after her ladyship's maid and the upper housemaid had been questioned first. Sergeant Cuff's inquiries—though he wrapped them up very cunningly—soon showed me that those two women (the bitterest enemies I had in the house) had made their discoveries outside my door, on the Tuesday afternoon, and again on the Thursday night. They had told the Sergeant enough to open his eyes to some part of the truth. He rightly believed me to have made a new nightgown secretly, but he wrongly believed the paint-stained nightgown to be mine. I felt satisfied of another thing, from what he said, which it puzzled me to understand. He suspected me, of course, of being concerned in the disappearance of the Diamond. But, at the same time, he let me see—purposely, as I thought—that he did not consider me as the person chiefly answerable for the loss of the jewel. He appeared to think that I had been acting under the direction of somebody else. Who that person might be, I couldn't guess then, and can't guess now.

"In this uncertainty, one thing was plain—that Sergeant Cuff was miles away from knowing the whole truth. You were safe as long as the nightgown was safe—and not a moment longer.

"I quite despair of making you understand the distress and terror which pressed upon me now. It was impossible for me to risk wearing your nightgown any longer. I might find myself taken off, at a moment's notice, to the police court at Frizinghall, to be charged on suspicion, and searched accordingly. While Sergeant Cuff still left me free, I had to choose—and at once— between destroying the nightgown, or hiding it in some safe place, at some safe distance from the house.

"If I had only been a little less fond of you, I think I should have destroyed it. But oh! how could I destroy the only thing I had which proved that I had saved you from discovery? If we did come to an explanation together, and if you suspected me of having some bad motive, and denied it all, how could I win upon you to trust me, unless I had the nightgown to produce? Was it wronging you to believe, as I did and do still, that you might hesitate to let a poor girl like me be the sharer of your secret, and your accomplice in the theft which your money-troubles had tempted you to commit? Think of your cold behaviour to me, sir, and you will hardly wonder at my unwillingness to destroy the only claim on your confidence and your gratitude which it was my fortune to possess.

"I determined to hide it; and the place I fixed on was the place I knew best—the Shivering Sand.

"As soon as the questioning was over, I made the first excuse that came into my head, and got leave to go out for a breath of fresh air. I went straight to Cobb's Hole, to Mr. Yolland's cottage. His wife and daughter were the best friends I had. Don't suppose I trusted them with your secret—I have trusted nobody. All I wanted was to write this letter to you, and to have a safe opportunity of taking the nightgown off me. Suspected as I was, I could do neither of those things with any sort of security, at the house.

"And now I have nearly got through my long letter, writing it alone in Lucy Yolland's bedroom. When it is done, I shall go downstairs with the nightgown rolled up, and hidden under my cloak. I shall find the means I want for keeping it safe and dry in its hiding-place, among the litter of old things in Mrs. Yolland's kitchen. And then I shall go to the Shivering Sand—don't be afraid of my letting my footmarks betray me!—and hide the nightgown down in the sand, where no living creature can find it without being first let into the secret by myself.

"And, when that's done, what then?

"Then, Mr. Franklin, I shall have two reasons for making another attempt to say the words to you which I have not said yet. If you leave the house, as Penelope believes you will leave it, and if I haven't spoken to you before that, I shall lose my opportunity forever. That is one reason. Then, again, there is the comforting knowledge—if my speaking does make you angry—that I have got the nightgown ready to plead my cause for me as nothing else can. That is my other reason. If these two together don't harden my heart against the coldness which has hitherto frozen it up (I mean the coldness of your treatment of me), there will be the end of my efforts—and the end of my life.

"Yes. If I miss my next opportunity—if you are as cruel as ever, and if I feel it again as I have felt it already—good-bye to the world which has grudged me the happiness that it gives to others. Good-bye to life, which nothing but a little kindness from you can ever make pleasurable to me again. Don't blame yourself, sir, if it ends in this way. But try—do try—to feel some forgiving sorrow for me! I shall take care that you find out what I have done for you, when I am past telling you of it myself. Will you say something kind of me then—in the same gentle way that you have when you speak to Miss Rachel? If you do that, and if there are such things as ghosts, I believe my ghost will hear it, and tremble with the pleasure of it.

"It's time I left off. I am making myself cry. How am I to see my way to the hiding-place if I let these useless tears come and blind me?

"Besides, why should I look at the gloomy side? Why not believe, while I can, that it will end well after all? I may find you in a good humour tonight—or, if not, I may succeed better tomorrow morning. I sha'n't improve my plain face by fretting—shall I? Who knows but I may have filled all these weary long pages of paper for nothing? They will go, for safety's sake (never mind now for what other reason) into the hiding-place along with the nightgown. It has been hard, hard work writing my letter. Oh! if we only end in understanding each other, how I shall enjoy tearing it up!

"I beg to remain, sir, your true lover and humble servant,

"ROSANNA SPEARMAN."

The reading of the letter was completed by Betteredge in silence. After carefully putting it back in the envelope, he sat thinking, with his head bowed down, and his eyes on the ground.

"Betteredge," I said, "is there any hint to guide me at the end of the letter?"

He looked up slowly, with a heavy sigh.

"There is nothing to guide you, Mr. Franklin," he answered. "If you take my advice you will keep the letter in the cover till these present anxieties of yours have come to an end. It will sorely distress you, whenever you read it. Don't read it now."

I put the letter away in my pocket-book.

A glance back at the sixteenth and seventeenth chapters of Betteredge's Narrative will show that there really was a reason for my thus sparing myself, at a time when my fortitude had been already cruelly tried. Twice over, the unhappy woman had made her last attempt to speak to me. And twice over, it had been my misfortune (God knows how innocently!) to repel the advances she had made to me. On the Friday night, as Betteredge truly describes it, she had found me alone at the billiard-table. Her manner and language suggested to me and would have suggested to any man, under the circumstances—that she was about to confess a guilty knowledge of the disappearance of the Diamond. For her own sake, I had purposely shown no special interest in what was coming; for her own sake, I had purposely looked at the billiard-balls, instead of looking at her—and what had been the result? I had sent her away from me, wounded to the heart! On the Saturday again—on the day when she must have foreseen, after what Penelope had told her, that my departure was close at hand—the same fatality still pursued us. She had once more attempted to meet me in the shrubbery walk, and she had found me there in company with Betteredge and Sergeant Cuff. In her hearing, the Sergeant, with his own underhand object in view, had appealed to my interest in Rosanna Spearman. Again for the poor creature's own sake, I had met the police-officer with a flat denial, and had declared—loudly declared, so that she might hear me too—that I felt "no interest whatever in Rosanna Spearman." At those words, solely designed to warn her against attempting to gain my private ear, she had turned away and left the place: cautioned of her danger, as I then believed; self-doomed to destruction, as I know now. From that point, I have already traced the succession of events which led me to the astounding discovery at the quicksand. The retrospect is now complete. I may leave the miserable story of Rosanna Spearman—to which, even at this distance of time, I cannot revert without a pang of distress—to suggest for itself all that is here purposely left unsaid. I may pass from the suicide at the Shivering Sand, with its strange and terrible influence on my present position and future prospects, to interests which concern the living people of this narrative, and to events which were already paving my way for the slow and toilsome journey from the darkness to the light.

CHAPTER VI

I walked to the railway station accompanied, it is needless to say, by Gabriel Betteredge. I had the letter in my pocket, and the nightgown safely packed in a little bag—both to be submitted, before I slept that night, to the investigation of Mr. Bruff.

We left the house in silence. For the first time in my experience of him, I found old Betteredge in my company without a word to say to me. Having something to say on my side, I opened the conversation as soon as we were clear of the lodge gates.

"Before I go to London," I began, "I have two questions to ask you. They relate to myself, and I believe they will rather surprise you."

"If they will put that poor creature's letter out of my head, Mr. Franklin, they may do anything else they like with me. Please to begin surprising me, sir, as soon as you can."

"My first question, Betteredge, is this. Was I drunk on the night of Rachel's Birthday?"

"You drunk!" exclaimed the old man. "Why it's the great defect of your character, Mr. Franklin that you only drink with your dinner, and never touch a drop of liquor afterwards!"

"But the birthday was a special occasion. I might have abandoned my regular habits, on that night of all others."

Betteredge considered for a moment.

"You did go out of your habits, sir," he said. "And I'll tell you how. You looked wretchedly ill—and we persuaded you to have a drop of brandy and water to cheer you up a little."

"I am not used to brandy and water. It is quite possible——"

"Wait a bit, Mr. Franklin. I knew you were not used, too. I poured you out half a wineglass-full of our fifty year old Cognac; and (more shame for me!) I drowned that noble liquor in nigh on a tumbler-full of cold water. A child couldn't have got drunk on it—let alone a grown man!"

I knew I could depend on his memory, in a matter of this kind. It was plainly impossible that I could have been intoxicated. I passed on to the second question.

"Before I was sent abroad, Betteredge, you saw a great deal of me when I was a boy? Now tell me plainly, do you remember anything strange of me, after I had gone to bed at night? Did you ever discover me walking in my sleep?"

Betteredge stopped, looked at me for a moment, nodded his head, and walked on again.

"I see your drift now, Mr. Franklin!" he said "You're trying to account for how you got the paint on your nightgown, without knowing it yourself. It won't do, sir. You're miles away still from getting at the truth. Walk in your sleep? You never did such a thing in your life!"

Here again, I felt that Betteredge must be right. Neither at home nor abroad had my life ever been of the solitary sort. If I had been a sleep-walker, there were hundreds on hundreds of people who must have discovered me, and who, in the interest of my own safety, would have warned me of the habit, and have taken precautions to restrain it.

Still, admitting all this, I clung—with an obstinacy which was surely natural and excusable, under the circumstances—to one or other of the only two explanations that I could see which accounted for the unendurable position in which I then stood. Observing that I was not yet satisfied, Betteredge shrewdly adverted to certain later events in the history of the Moonstone; and scattered both my theories to the wind at once and for ever.

"Let's try it another way, sir," he said. "Keep your own opinion, and see how far it will take you towards finding out the truth. If we are to believe the nightgown—which I don't for one—you not only smeared off the paint from the door, without knowing it, but you also took the Diamond without knowing it. Is that right, so far?"

"Quite right. Go on."

"Very good, sir. We'll say you were drunk, or walking in your sleep, when you took the jewel. That accounts for the night and morning, after the birthday. But how does it account for what has happened since that time? The Diamond has been taken to London, since that time. The Diamond has been pledged to Mr. Luker, since that time. Did you do those two things, without knowing it, too? Were you drunk when I saw you off in the pony-chaise on that Saturday evening? And did you walk in your sleep to Mr. Luker's, when the train had brought you to your journey's end? Excuse me for saying it, Mr. Franklin, but this business has so upset you, that you're not fit yet to judge for yourself. The sooner you lay your head alongside Mr. Bruff's head, the sooner you will see your way out of the dead-lock that has got you now."

We reached the station, with only a minute or two to spare.

I hurriedly gave Betteredge my address in London, so that he might write to me, if necessary; promising, on my side, to inform him of any news which I might have to communicate. This done, and just as I was bidding him farewell, I happened to glance towards the book-and-newspaper stall. There was Mr. Candy's remarkable-looking assistant again, speaking to the keeper of the stall! Our eyes met at the same moment. Ezra Jennings took off his hat to me. I returned the salute, and got into a carriage just as the train started. It was a relief to my mind, I suppose, to dwell on any subject which appeared to be, personally, of no sort of importance to me. At all events, I began the momentous journey back which was to take me to Mr. Bruff, wondering—absurdly enough, I admit—that I should have seen the man with the piebald hair twice in one day!

The hour at which I arrived in London precluded all hope of my finding Mr. Bruff at his place of business. I drove from the railway to his private residence at Hampstead, and disturbed the old lawyer dozing alone in his dining-room, with his favourite pug-dog on his lap, and his bottle of wine at his elbow.

I shall best describe the effect which my story produced on the mind of Mr. Bruff by relating his proceedings when he had heard it to the end. He ordered lights, and strong tea, to be taken into his study; and he sent a message to the ladies of his family, forbidding them to disturb us on any pretence whatever. These preliminaries disposed of, he first examined the nightgown, and then devoted himself to the reading of Rosanna Spearman's letter.

The reading completed, Mr. Bruff addressed me for the first time since we had been shut up together in the seclusion of his own room.

"Franklin Blake," said the old gentleman, "this is a very serious matter, in more respects than one. In my opinion, it concerns Rachel quite as nearly as it concerns you. Her extraordinary conduct is no mystery now. She believes you have stolen the Diamond."

I had shrunk from reasoning my own way fairly to that revolting conclusion. But it had forced itself on me, nevertheless. My resolution to obtain a personal interview with Rachel, rested really and truly on the ground just stated by Mr. Bruff.

"The first step to take in this investigation," the lawyer proceeded, "is to appeal to Rachel. She has been silent all this time, from motives which I (who know her character) can readily understand. It is impossible, after what has happened, to submit to that silence any longer. She must be persuaded to tell us, or she must be forced to tell us, on what grounds she bases her belief that you took the Moonstone. The chances are, that the whole of this case, serious as it seems now, will tumble to pieces, if we can only break through Rachel's inveterate reserve, and prevail upon her to speak out."

"That is a very comforting opinion for me," I said. "I own I should like to know — —"

"You would like to know how I can justify it," interposed Mr. Bruff. "I can tell you in two minutes. Understand, in the first place, that I look at this matter from a lawyer's point of view. It's a question of evidence, with me. Very well. The evidence breaks down, at the outset, on one important point."

"On what point?"

"You shall hear. I admit that the mark of the name proves the nightgown to be yours. I admit that the mark of the paint proves the nightgown to have made the smear on Rachel's door. But what evidence is there to prove that you are the person who wore it, on the night when the Diamond was lost?"

The objection struck me, all the more forcibly that it reflected an objection which I had felt myself.

"As to this," pursued the lawyer taking up Rosanna

Spearman's confession, "I can understand that the letter is a distressing one to you. I can understand that you may hesitate to analyse it from a purely impartial point of view. But I am not in your position. I can bring my professional experience to bear on this document, just as I should bring it to bear on any other. Without alluding to the woman's career as a thief, I will merely remark that her letter proves her to have been an adept at deception, on her own showing; and I argue from that, that I am justified in suspecting her of not having told the whole truth. I won't start any theory, at present, as to what she may or may not have done. I will only say that, if Rachel has suspected you on the evidence of the nightgown only, the chances are ninety-nine to a hundred that Rosanna Spearman was the person who showed it to her. In that case, there is the woman's letter, confessing that she was jealous of Rachel, confessing that she changed the roses, confessing that she saw a glimpse of hope for herself, in the prospect of a quarrel between Rachel and you. I don't stop to ask who took the Moonstone (as a means to her end, Rosanna Spearman would have taken fifty Moonstones) — I only say that the disappearance of the jewel gave this reclaimed thief who was in love with you, an opportunity of setting you and Rachel at variance for the rest of your lives. She had not decided on destroying herself, then, remember; and, having the opportunity, I distinctly assert that it was in her character, and in her position at the time, to take it. What do you say to that?"

"Some such suspicion," I answered, "crossed my own mind, as soon as I opened the letter."

"Exactly! And when you had read the letter, you pitied the poor creature, and couldn't find it in your heart to suspect her. Does you credit, my dear sir — does you credit!"

"But suppose it turns out that I did wear the nightgown? What then?"

"I don't see how the fact can be proved," said Mr. Bruff. "But assuming the proof to be possible, the vindication of your innocence would be no easy matter. We won't go into that, now. Let us wait and see whether Rachel hasn't suspected you on the evidence of the nightgown only."

"Good God, how coolly you talk of Rachel suspecting me!" I broke out. "What right has she to suspect Me, on any evidence, of being a thief?"

"A very sensible question, my dear sir. Rather hotly put—but well worth considering for all that. What puzzles you, puzzles me too. Search your memory, and tell me this. Did anything happen while you were staying at the house—not, of course, to shake Rachel's belief in your honour—but, let us say, to shake her belief (no matter with how little reason) in your principles generally?"

I started, in ungovernable agitation, to my feet. The lawyer's question reminded me, for the first time since I had left England, that something had happened.

In the eighth chapter of Betteredge's Narrative, an allusion will be found to the arrival of a foreigner and a stranger at my aunt's house, who came to see me on business. The nature of his business was this.

I had been foolish enough (being, as usual, straitened for money at the time) to accept a loan from the keeper of a small restaurant in Paris, to whom I was well known as a customer. A time was settled between us for paying the money back; and when the time came, I found it (as thousands of other honest men have found it) impossible to keep my engagement. I sent the man a bill. My name was unfortunately too well known on such documents: he failed to negotiate it. His affairs had fallen into disorder, in the interval since I had borrowed of him; bankruptcy stared him in the face; and a relative of his, a French lawyer, came to England to find me, and to insist upon the payment of my debt. He was a man of violent temper; and he took the wrong way with me. High words passed on both sides; and my aunt and Rachel were unfortunately in the next room, and heard us. Lady Verinder came in, and insisted on knowing what was the matter. The Frenchman produced his credentials, and declared me to be responsible for the ruin of a poor man, who had trusted in my honour. My aunt instantly paid him the money, and sent him off. She knew me better of course than to take the Frenchman's view of the transaction. But she was shocked at my carelessness, and justly angry with me for placing myself in a position, which, but for her interference, might have become a very disgraceful one. Either her mother told her, or Rachel heard what passed—I can't say which. She took her own romantic, high-flown view of the matter. I was "heartless"; I was "dishonourable"; I had "no principle"; there was "no knowing what I might do next" — in short, she said some of the severest things to me which I had ever heard from a young lady's lips. The breach between us lasted for the whole of the next day. The day after, I succeeded in making my peace, and thought no more of it. Had Rachel reverted to this unlucky accident, at the critical moment when my place in her estimation was again, and far more seriously, assailed? Mr. Bruff, when I had mentioned the circumstances to him, answered the question at once in the affirmative.

"It would have its effect on her mind," he said gravely. "And I wish, for your sake, the thing had not happened. However, we have discovered that there was a predisposing influence against you — and there is one uncertainty cleared out of our way, at any rate. I see nothing more that we can do now. Our next step in this inquiry must be the step that takes us to Rachel."

He rose, and began walking thoughtfully up and down the room. Twice, I was on the point of telling him that I had determined on seeing Rachel personally; and twice, having regard to his age and his character, I hesitated to take him by surprise at an unfavourable moment.

"The grand difficulty is," he resumed, "how to make her show her whole mind in this matter, without reserve. Have you any suggestions to offer?"

"I have made up my mind, Mr. Bruff, to speak to Rachel myself."

"You!" He suddenly stopped in his walk, and looked at me as if he thought I had taken leave of my senses. "You, of all the people in the world!" He abruptly checked himself, and took another turn in the room. "Wait a little," he said. "In cases of this extraordinary kind, the rash way is sometimes the best way." He considered the question for a moment or two, under that new light, and ended boldly by a decision in my favour. "Nothing venture, nothing have," the old gentleman resumed. "You have a chance in your favour which I don't possess — and you shall be the first to try the experiment."

"A chance in my favour?" I repeated, in the greatest surprise.

Mr. Bruff's face softened, for the first time, into a smile.

"This is how it stands," he said. "I tell you fairly, I don't trust your discretion, and I don't trust your temper. But I do trust in Rachel's still preserving, in some remote little corner of her heart, a certain perverse weakness for you. Touch that—and trust to the consequences for the fullest disclosures that can flow from a woman's lips! The question is—how are you to see her?"

"She has been a guest of yours at this house," I answered. "May I venture to suggest—if nothing was said about me beforehand—that I might see her here?"

"Cool!" said Mr. Bruff. With that one word of comment on the reply that I had made to him, he took another turn up and down the room.

"In plain English," he said, "my house is to be turned into a trap to catch Rachel; with a bait to tempt her, in the shape of an invitation from my wife and daughters. If you were anybody else but Franklin Blake, and if this matter was one atom less serious than it really is, I should refuse point-blank. As things are, I firmly believe Rachel will live to thank me for turning traitor to her in my old age. Consider me your accomplice. Rachel shall be asked to spend the day here; and you shall receive due notice of it."

"When? Tomorrow?"

"Tomorrow won't give us time enough to get her answer. Say the day after."

"How shall I hear from you?"

"Stay at home all the morning and expect me to call on you."

I thanked him for the inestimable assistance which he was rendering to me, with the gratitude that I really felt; and, declining a hospitable invitation to sleep that night at Hampstead, returned to my lodgings in London.

Of the day that followed, I have only to say that it was the longest day of my life. Innocent as I knew myself to be, certain as I was that the abominable imputation which rested on me must sooner or later be cleared off, there was nevertheless a sense of self-abasement in my mind which instinctively disinclined me to see any of my friends. We often hear (almost invariably, however, from superficial observers) that guilt can look like innocence. I believe it to be infinitely the truer axiom of the two that innocence can look like guilt. I caused myself to be denied all day, to every visitor who called; and I only ventured out under cover of the night.

The next morning, Mr. Bruff surprised me at the breakfast-table. He handed me a large key, and announced that he felt ashamed of himself for the first time in his life.

"Is she coming?"

"She is coming today, to lunch and spend the afternoon with my wife and my girls."

"Are Mrs. Bruff, and your daughters, in the secret?"

"Inevitably. But women, as you may have observed, have no principles. My family don't feel my pangs of conscience. The end being to bring you and Rachel together again, my wife and daughters pass over the means employed to gain it, as composedly as if they were Jesuits."

"I am infinitely obliged to them. What is this key?"

"The key of the gate in my back-garden wall. Be there at three this afternoon. Let yourself into the garden, and make your way in by the conservatory door. Cross the small drawing-room, and open the door in front of you which leads into the music-room. There, you will find Rachel—and find her, alone."

"How can I thank you!"

"I will tell you how. Don't blame me for what happens afterwards."

With those words, he went out.

I had many weary hours still to wait through. To while away the time, I looked at my letters. Among them was a letter from Betteredge.

I opened it eagerly. To my surprise and disappointment, it began with an apology warning me to expect no news of any importance. In the next sentence the everlasting Ezra Jennings appeared again! He had stopped Betteredge on the way out of the station, and had asked who I was. Informed on this point, he had mentioned having seen me to his master Mr. Candy. Mr.

Candy hearing of this, had himself driven over to Betteredge, to express his regret at our having missed each other. He had a reason for wishing particularly to speak to me; and when I was next in the neighbourhood of Frizinghall, he begged I would let him know. Apart from a few characteristic utterances of the Betteredge philosophy, this was the sum and substance of my correspondent's letter. The warm-hearted, faithful old man acknowledged that he had written "mainly for the pleasure of writing to me."

I crumpled up the letter in my pocket, and forgot it the moment after, in the all-absorbing interest of my coming interview with Rachel.

As the clock of Hampstead church struck three, I put Mr. Bruff's key into the lock of the door in the wall. When I first stepped into the garden, and while I was securing the door again on the inner side, I own to having felt a certain guilty doubtfulness about what might happen next. I looked furtively on either side of me; suspicious of the presence of some unexpected witness in some unknown corner of the garden. Nothing appeared, to justify my apprehensions. The walks were, one and all, solitudes; and the birds and the bees were the only witnesses.

I passed through the garden; entered the conservatory; and crossed the small drawing-room. As I laid my hand on the door opposite, I heard a few plaintive chords struck on the piano in the room within. She had often idled over the instrument in this way, when I was staying at her mother's house. I was obliged to wait a little, to steady myself. The past and present rose side by side, at that supreme moment—and the contrast shook me.

After the lapse of a minute, I roused my manhood, and opened the door.

CHAPTER VII

At the moment when I showed myself in the doorway, Rachel rose from the piano.

I closed the door behind me. We confronted each other in silence, with the full length of the room between us. The movement she had made in rising appeared to be the one exertion of which she was capable. All use of every other faculty, bodily or mental, seemed to be merged in the mere act of looking at me.

A fear crossed my mind that I had shown myself too suddenly. I advanced a few steps towards her. I said gently, "Rachel!"

The sound of my voice brought the life back to her limbs, and the colour to her face. She advanced, on her side, still without speaking. Slowly, as if acting under some influence independent of her own will, she came nearer and nearer to me; the warm dusky colour flushing her cheeks, the light of reviving intelligence brightening every instant in her eyes. I forgot the object that had brought me into her presence; I forgot the vile suspicion that rested on my good name; I forgot every consideration, past, present, and future, which I was bound to remember. I saw nothing but the woman I loved coming nearer and nearer to me. She trembled; she stood irresolute. I could resist it no longer—I caught her in my arms, and covered her face with kisses.

There was a moment when I thought the kisses were returned; a moment when it seemed as if she, too might have forgotten. Almost before the idea could shape itself in my mind, her first voluntary action made me feel that she remembered. With a cry which was like a cry of horror—with a strength which I doubt if I could have resisted if I had tried—she thrust me back from her. I saw merciless anger in her eyes; I saw merciless contempt on her lips. She looked me over, from head to foot, as she might have looked at a stranger who had insulted her.

"You coward!" she said. "You mean, miserable, heartless coward!"

Those were her first words! The most unendurable reproach

that a woman can address to a man, was the reproach that she picked out to address to Me.

"I remember the time, Rachel," I said, "when you could have told me that I had offended you, in a worthier way than that. I beg your pardon."

Something of the bitterness that I felt may have communicated itself to my voice. At the first words of my reply, her eyes, which had been turned away the moment before, looked back at me unwillingly. She answered in a low tone, with a sullen submission of manner which was quite new in my experience of her.

"Perhaps there is some excuse for me," she said. "After what you have done, is it a manly action, on your part, to find your way to me as you have found it today? It seems a cowardly experiment, to try an experiment on my weakness for you. It seems a cowardly surprise, to surprise me into letting you kiss me. But that is only a woman's view. I ought to have known it couldn't be your view. I should have done better if I had controlled myself, and said nothing."

The apology was more unendurable than the insult. The most degraded man living would have felt humiliated by it.

"If my honour was not in your hands," I said, "I would leave you this instant, and never see you again. You have spoken of what I have done. What have I done?"

"What have you done! You ask that question of me?"

"I ask it."

"I have kept your infamy a secret," she answered. "And I have suffered the consequences of concealing it. Have I no claim to be spared the insult of your asking me what you have done? Is all sense of gratitude dead in you? You were once a gentleman. You were once dear to my mother, and dearer still to me— —"

Her voice failed her. She dropped into a chair, and turned her back on me, and covered her face with her hands.

I waited a little before I trusted myself to say any more. In that moment of silence, I hardly know which I felt most keenly—the sting which her contempt had planted in me, or the proud resolution which shut me out from all community with her distress.

"If you will not speak first," I said, "I must. I have come here with something serious to say to you. Will you do me the common justice of listening while I say it?"

She neither moved, nor answered. I made no second appeal to her; I never advanced an inch nearer to her chair. With a pride which was as obstinate as her pride, I told her of my discovery at the Shivering Sand, and of all that had led to it. The narrative, of necessity, occupied some little time. From beginning to end, she never looked round at me, and she never uttered a word.

I kept my temper. My whole future depended, in all probability, on my not losing possession of myself at that moment. The time had come to put Mr. Bruff's theory to the test. In the breathless interest of trying that experiment, I moved round so as to place myself in front of her.

"I have a question to ask you," I said. "It obliges me to refer again to a painful subject. Did Rosanna Spearman show you the nightgown. Yes, or No?"

She started to her feet; and walked close up to me of her own accord. Her eyes looked me searchingly in the face, as if to read something there which they had never read yet.

"Are you mad?" she asked.

I still restrained myself. I said quietly, "Rachel, will you answer my question?"

She went on, without heeding me.

"Have you some object to gain which I don't understand? Some mean fear about the future, in which I am concerned? They say your father's death has made you a rich man. Have you come here to compensate me for the loss of my Diamond? And have you heart enough left to feel ashamed of your errand? Is that the secret of your pretence of innocence, and your story about Rosanna Spearman? Is there a motive of shame at the bottom of all the falsehood, this time?"

I stopped her there. I could control myself no longer.

"You have done me an infamous wrong!" I broke out hotly. "You suspect me of stealing your Diamond. I have a right to know, and I will know, the reason why!"

"Suspect you!" she exclaimed, her anger rising with mine. "You villain, I saw you take the Diamond with my own eyes!"

The revelation which burst upon me in those words, the overthrow which they instantly accomplished of the whole view of the case on which Mr. Bruff had relied, struck me helpless. Innocent as I was, I stood before her in silence. To her eyes, to any eyes, I must have looked like a man overwhelmed by the discovery of his own guilt.

She drew back from the spectacle of my humiliation and of her triumph. The sudden silence that had fallen upon me seemed to frighten her. "I spared you, at the time," she said. "I would have spared you now, if you had not forced me to speak." She moved away as if to leave the room—and hesitated before she got to the door. "Why did you come here to humiliate yourself?" she asked. "Why did you come here to humiliate me?" She went on a few steps, and paused once more. "For God's sake, say something!" she exclaimed, passionately. "If you have any mercy left, don't let me degrade myself in this way! Say something—and drive me out of the room!"

I advanced towards her, hardly conscious of what I was doing. I had possibly some confused idea of detaining her until she had told me more. From the moment when I knew that the evidence on which I stood condemned in Rachel's mind, was the evidence of her own eyes, nothing—not even my conviction of my own innocence—was clear to my mind. I took her by the hand; I tried to speak firmly and to the purpose. All I could say was, "Rachel, you once loved me."

She shuddered, and looked away from me. Her hand lay powerless and trembling in mine. "Let go of it," she said faintly.

My touch seemed to have the same effect on her which the sound of my voice had produced when I first entered the room. After she had said the word which called me a coward, after she had made the avowal which branded me as a thief—while her hand lay in mine I was her master still!

I drew her gently back into the middle of the room. I seated her by the side of me. "Rachel," I said, "I can't explain the contradiction in what I am going to tell you. I can only speak the truth as you have spoken it. You saw me—with your own eyes, you saw me take the Diamond. Before God who hears us, I declare that I now know I took it for the first time! Do you doubt me still?"

She had neither heeded nor heard me. "Let go of my hand," she repeated faintly. That was her only answer. Her head sank on my shoulder; and her hand unconsciously closed on mine, at the moment when she asked me to release it.

I refrained from pressing the question. But there my forbearance stopped. My chance of ever holding up my head again among honest men depended on my chance of inducing her to make her disclosure complete. The one hope left for me was the hope that she might have overlooked something in the chain of evidence—some mere trifle, perhaps, which might nevertheless, under careful investigation, be made the means of vindicating my innocence in the end. I own I kept possession of her hand. I own I spoke to her with all that I could summon back of the sympathy and confidence of the bygone time.

"I want to ask you something," I said. "I want you to tell me everything that happened, from the time when we wished each other good-night, to the time when you saw me take the Diamond."

She lifted her head from my shoulder, and made an effort to release her hand. "Oh, why go back to it!" she said. "Why go back to it!"

"I will tell you why, Rachel. You are the victim, and I am the victim, of some monstrous delusion which has worn the mask of truth. If we look at what happened on the night of your birthday together, we may end in understanding each other yet."

Her head dropped back on my shoulder. The tears gathered in her eyes, and fell slowly over her cheeks. "Oh!" she said, "have I never had that hope? Have I not tried to see it, as you are trying now?"

"You have tried by yourself," I answered. "You have not tried with me to help you."

Those words seemed to awaken in her something of the hope which I felt myself when I uttered them. She replied to my questions with more than docility—she exerted her intelligence; she willingly opened her whole mind to me.

"Let us begin," I said, "with what happened after we had wished each other good-night. Did you go to bed? or did you sit up?"

"I went to bed."

"Did you notice the time? Was it late?"

"Not very. About twelve o'clock, I think."

"Did you fall asleep?"

"No. I couldn't sleep that night."

"You were restless?"

"I was thinking of you."

The answer almost unmanned me. Something in the tone, even more than in the words, went straight to my heart. It was only after pausing a little first that I was able to go on.

"Had you any light in your room?" I asked.

"None—until I got up again, and lit my candle."

"How long was that, after you had gone to bed?"

"About an hour after, I think. About one o'clock."

"Did you leave your bedroom?"

"I was going to leave it. I had put on my dressing-gown; and I was going into my sitting-room to get a book——"

"Had you opened your bedroom door?"

"I had just opened it."

"But you had not gone into the sitting-room?"

"No—I was stopped from going into it."

"What stopped you?

"I saw a light, under the door; and I heard footsteps approaching it."

The Moonstone

"Were you frightened?"

"Not then. I knew my poor mother was a bad sleeper; and I remembered that she had tried hard, that evening, to persuade me to let her take charge of my Diamond. She was unreasonably anxious about it, as I thought; and I fancied she was coming to me to see if I was in bed, and to speak to me about the Diamond again, if she found that I was up."

"What did you do?"

"I blew out my candle, so that she might think I was in bed. I was unreasonable, on my side—I was determined to keep my Diamond in the place of my own choosing."

"After blowing out the candle, did you go back to bed?"

"I had no time to go back. At the moment when I blew the candle out, the sitting-room door opened, and I saw——"

"You saw?"

"You."

"Dressed as usual?"

"No."

"In my nightgown?"

"In your nightgown—with your bedroom candle in your hand."

"Alone?"

"Alone."

"Could you see my face?"

"Yes."

"Plainly?"

"Quite plainly. The candle in your hand showed it to me."

"Were my eyes open?"

"Yes."

"Did you notice anything strange in them? Anything like a fixed, vacant expression?"

"Nothing of the sort. Your eyes were bright—brighter than usual. You looked about in the room, as if you knew you were where you ought not to be, and as if you were afraid of being found out."

"Did you observe one thing when I came into the room—did you observe how I walked?"

"You walked as you always do. You came in as far as the middle of the room—and then you stopped and looked about you."

"What did I do, on first seeing me?"

"I could do nothing. I was petrified. I couldn't speak, I couldn't call out, I couldn't even move to shut my door."

"Could I see you, where you stood?"

"You might certainly have seen me. But you never looked towards me. It's useless to ask the question. I am sure you never saw me."

"How are you sure?"

"Would you have taken the Diamond? would you have acted as you did afterwards? would you be here now—if you had seen that I was awake and looking at you? Don't make me talk of that part of it! I want to answer you quietly. Help me to keep as calm as I can. Go on to something else."

She was right—in every way, right. I went on to other things.

"What did I do, after I had got to the middle of the room, and had stopped there?"

"You turned away, and went straight to the corner near the window—where my Indian cabinet stands."

"When I was at the cabinet, my back must have been turned towards you. How did you see what I was doing?"

"When you moved, I moved."

"So as to see what I was about with my hands?"

"There are three glasses in my sitting-room. As you stood there, I saw all that you did, reflected in one of them."

The Moonstone

"What did you see?"

"You put your candle on the top of the cabinet. You opened, and shut, one drawer after another, until you came to the drawer in which I had put my Diamond. You looked at the open drawer for a moment. And then you put your hand in, and took the Diamond out."

"How do you know I took the Diamond out?"

"I saw your hand go into the drawer. And I saw the gleam of the stone between your finger and thumb, when you took your hand out."

"Did my hand approach the drawer again—to close it, for instance?"

"No. You had the Diamond in your right hand; and you took the candle from the top of the cabinet with your left hand."

"Did I look about me again, after that?"

"No."

"Did I leave the room immediately?"

"No. You stood quite still, for what seemed a long time. I saw your face sideways in the glass. You looked like a man thinking, and dissatisfied with his own thoughts."

"What happened next?"

"You roused yourself on a sudden, and you went straight out of the room."

"Did I close the door after me?"

"No. You passed out quickly into the passage, and left the door open."

"And then?"

"Then, your light disappeared, and the sound of your steps died away, and I was left alone in the dark."

"Did nothing happen—from that time, to the time when the whole house knew that the Diamond was lost?"

"Nothing."

"Are you sure of that? Might you not have been asleep a part of the time?"

"I never slept. I never went back to my bed. Nothing happened until Penelope came in, at the usual time in the morning."

I dropped her hand, and rose, and took a turn in the room. Every question that I could put had been answered. Every detail that I could desire to know had been placed before me. I had even reverted to the idea of sleep-walking, and the idea of intoxication; and, again, the worthlessness of the one theory and the other had been proved — on the authority, this time, of the witness who had seen me. What was to be said next? what was to be done next? There rose the horrible fact of the Theft — the one visible, tangible object that confronted me, in the midst of the impenetrable darkness which enveloped all besides! Not a glimpse of light to guide me, when I had possessed myself of Rosanna Spearman's secret at the Shivering Sand. And not a glimpse of light now, when I had appealed to Rachel herself, and had heard the hateful story of the night from her own lips.

She was the first, this time, to break the silence.

"Well?" she said, "you have asked, and I have answered. You have made me hope something from all this, because you hoped something from it. What have you to say now?"

The tone in which she spoke warned me that my influence over her was a lost influence once more.

"We were to look at what happened on my birthday night, together," she went on; "and we were then to understand each other. Have we done that?"

She waited pitilessly for my reply. In answering her I committed a fatal error — I let the exasperating helplessness of my situation get the better of my self-control. Rashly and uselessly, I reproached her for the silence which had kept me until that moment in ignorance of the truth.

"If you had spoken when you ought to have spoken," I began; "if you had done me the common justice to explain yourself — —"

She broke in on me with a cry of fury. The few words I had

said seemed to have lashed her on the instant into a frenzy of rage.

"Explain myself!" she repeated. "Oh! is there another man like this in the world? I spare him, when my heart is breaking; I screen him when my own character is at stake; and he—of all human beings, he—turns on me now, and tells me that I ought to have explained myself! After believing in him as I did, after loving him as I did, after thinking of him by day, and dreaming of him by night—he wonders I didn't charge him with his disgrace the first time we met: 'My heart's darling, you are a Thief! My hero whom I love and honour, you have crept into my room under cover of the night, and stolen my Diamond!' That is what I ought to have said. You villain, you mean, mean, mean villain, I would have lost fifty diamonds, rather than see your face lying to me, as I see it lying now!"

I took up my hat. In mercy to her—yes! I can honestly say it—in mercy to her, I turned away without a word, and opened the door by which I had entered the room.

She followed, and snatched the door out of my hand; she closed it, and pointed back to the place that I had left.

"No!" she said. "Not yet! It seems that I owe a justification of my conduct to you. You shall stay and hear it. Or you shall stoop to the lowest infamy of all, and force your way out."

It wrung my heart to see her; it wrung my heart to hear her. I answered by a sign—it was all I could do—that I submitted myself to her will.

The crimson flush of anger began to fade out of her face, as I went back, and took my chair in silence. She waited a little, and steadied herself. When she went on, but one sign of feeling was discernible in her. She spoke without looking at me. Her hands were fast clasped in her lap, and her eyes were fixed on the ground.

"I ought to have done you the common justice to explain myself," she said, repeating my own words. "You shall see whether I did try to do you justice, or not. I told you just now that I never slept, and never returned to my bed, after you had left my sitting-room. It's useless to trouble you by dwelling on what I thought—you would not understand my thoughts—I will only tell you what I did, when time enough had passed to help me to recover myself. I refrained from alarming the house, and telling everybody what had happened—as I ought to have done. In spite of what I had seen, I was fond enough of you to believe—no matter what!—any impossibility, rather than admit it to my own mind that you were deliberately a thief. I thought and thought—and I ended in writing to you."

"I never received the letter."

"I know you never received it. Wait a little, and you shall hear why. My letter would have told you nothing openly. It would not have ruined you for life, if it had fallen into some other person's hands. It would only have said—in a manner which you yourself could not possibly have mistaken—that I had reason to know you were in debt, and that it was in my experience and in my mother's experience of you, that you were not very discreet, or very scrupulous about how you got money when you wanted it. You would have remembered the visit of the French lawyer, and you would have known what I referred to. If you had read on with some interest after that, you would have come to an offer I had to make to you—the offer, privately (not a word, mind, to be said openly about it between us!), of the loan of as large a sum of money as I could get.—And I would have got it!" she exclaimed, her colour beginning to rise again, and her eyes looking up at me once more. "I would have pledged the Diamond myself, if I could have got the money in no other way! In those words I wrote to you. Wait! I did more than that. I arranged with Penelope to give you the letter when nobody was near. I planned to shut myself into my bedroom, and to have the sitting-room left open and empty all the morning. And I hoped—with all my heart and soul I hoped!—that you would take the opportunity, and put the Diamond back secretly in the drawer."

I attempted to speak. She lifted her hand impatiently, and stopped me. In the rapid alternations of her temper, her anger was beginning to rise again. She got up from her chair, and approached me.

"I know what you are going to say," she went on. "You are going to remind me again that you never received my letter. I can tell you why. I tore it up.

"For what reason?" I asked.

"For the best of reasons. I preferred tearing it up to throwing it away upon such a man as you! What was the first news that reached me in the morning? Just as my little plan was complete, what did I hear? I heard that you—you!!!—were the foremost person in the house in fetching the police. You were the active man; you were the leader; you were working harder than any of them to recover the jewel! You even carried your audacity far enough to ask to speak to me about the loss of the Diamond—the Diamond which you yourself had stolen; the Diamond which was all the time in your own hands! After that proof of your horrible falseness and cunning, I tore up my letter. But even then—even when I was maddened by the searching and questioning of the policeman, whom you had sent in—even then, there was some infatuation in my mind which wouldn't let me give you up. I said to myself, 'He has played his vile farce before everybody else in the house. Let me try if he can play it before me.' Somebody told me you were on the terrace. I went down to the terrace. I forced myself to look at you; I forced myself to speak to you. Have you forgotten what I said?"

I might have answered that I remembered every word of it. But what purpose, at that moment, would the answer have served?

How could I tell her that what she had said had astonished me, had distressed me, had suggested to me that she was in a state of dangerous nervous excitement, had even roused a moment's doubt in my mind whether the loss of the jewel was as much a mystery to her as to the rest of us—but had never once given me so much as a glimpse at the truth? Without the shadow of a proof to produce in vindication of my innocence, how could I persuade her that I knew no more than the veriest stranger could have known of what was really in her thoughts when she spoke to me on the terrace?

"It may suit your convenience to forget; it suits my convenience to remember," she went on. "I know what I said—for I considered it with myself, before I said it. I gave you one opportunity after another of owning the truth. I left nothing unsaid that I could say—short of actually telling you that I knew you had committed the theft. And all the return you made, was to look at me with your vile pretence of astonishment, and your false face of innocence—just as you have looked at me today; just as you are looking at me now! I left you, that morning, knowing you at last for what you were—for what you are—as base a wretch as ever walked the earth!"

"If you had spoken out at the time, you might have left me, Rachel, knowing that you had cruelly wronged an innocent man."

"If I had spoken out before other people," she retorted, with another burst of indignation, "you would have been disgraced for life! If I had spoken out to no ears but yours, you would have denied it, as you are denying it now! Do you think I should have believed you? Would a man hesitate at a lie, who had done what I saw you do—who had behaved about it afterwards, as I saw you behave? I tell you again, I shrank from the horror of hearing you lie, after the horror of seeing you thieve. You talk as if this was a misunderstanding which a few words might have set right! Well! the misunderstanding is at an end. Is the thing set right? No! the thing is just where it was. I don't believe you now! I don't believe you found the nightgown, I don't believe in Rosanna Spearman's letter, I don't believe a word you have said. You stole it—I saw you! You affected to help the police—I saw you! You pledged the Diamond to the money-lender in London—I am sure of it! You cast the suspicion of your disgrace (thanks to my base silence!) on an innocent man! You fled to the Continent with your plunder the next morning! After all that vileness, there was but one thing more you could do. You could come here with a last falsehood on your lips—you could come here, and tell me that I have wronged you!"

If I had stayed a moment more, I know not what words might have escaped me which I should have remembered with vain repentance and regret. I passed by her, and opened the door for the second time. For the second time—with the frantic perversity of a roused woman—she caught me by the arm, and barred my way out.

"Let me go, Rachel" I said. "It will be better for both of us. Let me go."

The hysterical passion swelled in her bosom—her quickened convulsive breathing almost beat on my face, as she held me back at the door.

"Why did you come here?" she persisted, desperately. "I ask you again—why did you come here? Are you afraid I shall expose you? Now you are a rich man, now you have got a place in the world, now you may marry the best lady in the land—are you afraid I shall say the words which I have never said yet to anybody but you? I can't say the words! I can't expose you! I am worse, if worse can be, than you are yourself." Sobs and tears burst from her. She struggled with them fiercely; she held me more and more firmly. "I can't tear you out of my heart," she said, "even now! You may trust in the shameful, shameful weakness which can only struggle against you in this way!" She suddenly let go of me—she threw up her hands, and wrung them frantically in the air. "Any other woman living would shrink from the disgrace of touching him!" she exclaimed. "Oh, God! I despise myself even more heartily than I despise him!"

The tears were forcing their way into my eyes in spite of me—the horror of it was to be endured no longer.

"You shall know that you have wronged me, yet," I said. "Or you shall never see me again!"

With those words, I left her. She started up from the chair on which she had dropped the moment before: she started up—the noble creature!—and followed me across the outer room, with a last merciful word at parting.

"Franklin!" she said, "I forgive you! Oh, Franklin, Franklin! we shall never meet again. Say you forgive me!"

I turned, so as to let my face show her that I was past speaking—I turned, and waved my hand, and saw her dimly, as in a vision, through the tears that had conquered me at last.

The next moment, the worst bitterness of it was over. I was out in the garden again. I saw her, and heard her, no more.

CHAPTER VIII

Late that evening, I was surprised at my lodgings by a visit from Mr. Bruff.

There was a noticeable change in the lawyer's manner. It had lost its usual confidence and spirit. He shook hands with me, for the first time in his life, in silence.

"Are you going back to Hampstead?" I asked, by way of saying something.

"I have just left Hampstead," he answered. "I know, Mr. Franklin, that you have got at the truth at last. But, I tell you plainly, if I could have foreseen the price that was to be paid for it, I should have preferred leaving you in the dark."

"You have seen Rachel?"

"I have come here after taking her back to Portland Place; it was impossible to let her return in the carriage by herself. I can hardly hold you responsible—considering that you saw her in my house and by my permission—for the shock that this unlucky interview has inflicted on her. All I can do is to provide against a repetition of the mischief. She is young—she has a resolute spirit—she will get over this, with time and rest to help her. I want to be assured that you will do nothing to hinder her recovery. May I depend on your making no second attempt to see her—except with my sanction and approval?"

"After what she has suffered, and after what I have suffered," I said, "you may rely on me."

"I have your promise?"

"You have my promise."

Mr. Bruff looked relieved. He put down his hat, and drew his chair nearer to mine.

"That's settled!" he said. "Now, about the future—your future, I mean. To my mind, the result of the extraordinary turn which the matter has now taken is briefly this. In the first place, we are sure that Rachel has told you the whole truth, as plainly as words can tell it. In the second place—though we know that there must be some dreadful mistake somewhere—we can hardly blame her for believing you to be guilty, on the evidence of her own senses; backed, as that evidence has been, by circumstances which appear, on the face of them, to tell dead against you."

There I interposed. "I don't blame Rachel," I said. "I only regret that she could not prevail on herself to speak more plainly to me at the time."

"You might as well regret that Rachel is not somebody else," rejoined Mr. Bruff. "And even then, I doubt if a girl of any delicacy, whose heart had been set on marrying you, could have brought herself to charge you to your face with being a thief. Anyhow, it was not in Rachel's nature to do it. In a very different matter to this matter of yours—which placed her, however, in a position not altogether unlike her position towards you—I happen to know that she was influenced by a similar motive to the motive which actuated her conduct in your case. Besides, as she told me herself, on our way to town this evening, if she had spoken plainly, she would no more have believed your denial then than she believes it now. What answer can you make to that? There is no answer to be made to it. Come, come, Mr. Franklin! my view of the case has been proved to be all wrong, I admit—but, as things are now, my advice may be worth having for all that. I tell you plainly, we shall be wasting our time, and cudgelling our brains to no purpose, if we attempt to try back, and unravel this frightful complication from the beginning. Let us close our minds resolutely to all that happened last year at Lady Verinder's country house; and let us look to what we can discover in the future, instead of to what we can not discover in the past."

"Surely you forget," I said, "that the whole thing is essentially a matter of the past—so far as I am concerned?"

"Answer me this," retorted Mr. Bruff. "Is the Moonstone at the bottom of all the mischief—or is it not?"

"It is—of course."

"Very good. What do we believe was done with the Moonstone, when it was taken to London?"

"It was pledged to Mr. Luker."

"We know that you are not the person who pledged it. Do we know who did?"

"No."

"Where do we believe the Moonstone to be now?"

"Deposited in the keeping of Mr. Luker's bankers."

"Exactly. Now observe. We are already in the month of June. Towards the end of the month (I can't be particular to a day) a year will have elapsed from the time when we believe the jewel to have been pledged. There is a chance—to say the least—that the person who pawned it, may be prepared to redeem it when the year's time has expired. If he redeems it, Mr. Luker must himself—according to the terms of his own arrangement—take the Diamond out of his banker's hands. Under these circumstances, I propose setting a watch at the bank, as the present month draws to an end, and discovering who the person is to whom Mr. Luker restores the Moonstone. Do you see it now?"

I admitted (a little unwillingly) that the idea was a new one, at any rate.

"It's Mr. Murthwaite's idea quite as much as mine," said Mr. Bruff. "It might have never entered my head, but for a conversation we had together some time since. If Mr. Murthwaite is right, the Indians are likely to be on the lookout at the bank, towards the end of the month too—and something serious may come of it. What comes of it doesn't matter to you and me except as it may help us to lay our hands on the mysterious Somebody who pawned the Diamond. That person, you may rely on it, is responsible (I don't pretend to know how) for the position in which you stand at this moment; and that person alone can set you right in Rachel's estimation."

"I can't deny," I said, "that the plan you propose meets the difficulty in a way that is very daring, and very ingenious, and very new. But——"

"But you have an objection to make?"

"Yes. My objection is, that your proposal obliges us to wait."

"Granted. As I reckon the time, it requires you to wait about a fortnight—more or less. Is that so very long?"

"It's a life-time, Mr. Bruff, in such a situation as mine. My existence will be simply unendurable to me, unless I do something towards clearing my character at once."

"Well, well, I understand that. Have you thought yet of what you can do?"

"I have thought of consulting Sergeant Cuff."

"He has retired from the police. It's useless to expect the Sergeant to help you."

"I know where to find him; and I can but try."

"Try," said Mr. Bruff, after a moment's consideration. "The case has assumed such an extraordinary aspect since Sergeant Cuff's time, that you may revive his interest in the inquiry. Try, and let me hear the result. In the meanwhile," he continued, rising, "if you make no discoveries between this, and the end of the month, am I free to try, on my side, what can be done by keeping a lookout at the bank?"

"Certainly," I answered — "unless I relieve you of all necessity for trying the experiment in the interval."

Mr. Bruff smiled, and took up his hat.

"Tell Sergeant Cuff," he rejoined, "that I say the discovery of the truth depends on the discovery of the person who pawned the Diamond. And let me hear what the Sergeant's experience says to that."

So we parted.

Early the next morning, I set forth for the little town of Dorking — the place of Sergeant Cuff's retirement, as indicated to me by Betteredge.

Inquiring at the hotel, I received the necessary directions for finding the Sergeant's cottage. It was approached by a quiet bye-road, a little way out of the town, and it stood snugly in the middle of its own plot of garden ground, protected by a good brick wall at the back and the sides, and by a high quickset hedge in front. The gate, ornamented at the upper part by smartly-painted trellis-work, was locked. After ringing at the bell, I peered through the trellis-work, and saw the great Cuff's favourite flower everywhere; blooming in his garden, clustering over his door, looking in at his windows. Far from the crimes and the mysteries of the great city, the illustrious thief-taker was placidly living out the last Sybarite years of his life, smothered in roses!

A decent elderly woman opened the gate to me, and at once annihilated all the hopes I had built on securing the assistance of Sergeant Cuff. He had started, only the day before, on a journey to Ireland.

"Has he gone there on business?" I asked.

The woman smiled. "He has only one business now, sir," she said; "and that's roses. Some great man's gardener in Ireland has found out something new in the growing of roses—and Mr. Cuff's away to inquire into it."

"Do you know when he will be back?"

"It's quite uncertain, sir. Mr. Cuff said he should come back directly, or be away some time, just according as he found the new discovery worth nothing, or worth looking into. If you have any message to leave for him, I'll take care, sir, that he gets it."

I gave her my card, having first written on it in pencil: "I have something to say about the Moonstone. Let me hear from you as soon as you get back." That done, there was nothing left but to submit to circumstances, and return to London.

In the irritable condition of my mind, at the time of which I am now writing, the abortive result of my journey to the Sergeant's cottage simply aggravated the restless impulse in me to be doing something. On the day of my return from Dorking, I determined that the next morning should find me bent on a new effort at forcing my way, through all obstacles, from the darkness to the light.

What form was my next experiment to take?

If the excellent Betteredge had been present while I was considering that question, and if he had been let into the secret of my thoughts, he would, no doubt, have declared that the German side of me was, on this occasion, my uppermost side. To speak seriously, it is perhaps possible that my German training was in some degree responsible for the labyrinth of useless speculations in which I now involved myself. For the greater part of the night, I sat smoking, and building up theories, one more profoundly improbable than another. When I did get to sleep, my waking fancies pursued me in dreams. I rose the next morning, with Objective-Subjective and Subjective-Objective inextricably entangled together in my mind; and I began the day which was to witness my next effort at practical action of some kind, by doubting whether I had any sort of right (on purely philosophical grounds) to consider any sort of thing (the Diamond included) as existing at all.

How long I might have remained lost in the mist of my own metaphysics, if I had been left to extricate myself, it is impossible for me to say. As the event proved, accident came to my rescue, and happily delivered me. I happened to wear, that morning, the same coat which I had worn on the day of my interview with Rachel. Searching for something else in one of the pockets, I came upon a crumpled piece of paper, and, taking it out, found Betteredge's forgotten letter in my hand.

It seemed hard on my good old friend to leave him without a reply. I went to my writing-table, and read his letter again.

A letter which has nothing of the slightest importance in it, is not always an easy letter to answer. Betteredge's present effort at corresponding with me came within this category. Mr. Candy's assistant, otherwise Ezra Jennings, had told his master that he had seen me; and Mr. Candy, in his turn, wanted to see me and say something to me, when I was next in the neighbourhood of Frizinghall. What was to be said in answer to that, which would be worth the paper it was written on? I sat idly drawing likenesses from memory of Mr. Candy's remarkable-looking assistant, on the sheet of paper which I had vowed to dedicate to Betteredge—until it suddenly occurred to me that here was the irrepressible Ezra Jennings getting in my way again! I threw a dozen portraits, at least, of the man with the piebald hair (the hair in every case, remarkably like), into the waste-paper basket—and then and there, wrote my answer to Betteredge. It was a perfectly commonplace letter—but it had one excellent effect on me. The effort of writing a few sentences, in plain English, completely cleared my mind of the cloudy nonsense which had filled it since the previous day.

Devoting myself once more to the elucidation of the impenetrable puzzle which my own position presented to me, I now tried to meet the difficulty by investigating it from a plainly practical point of view. The events of the memorable night being still unintelligible to me, I looked a little farther back, and searched my memory of the earlier hours of the birthday for any incident which might prove of some assistance to me in finding the clue.

Had anything happened while Rachel and I were finishing the painted door? or, later, when I rode over to Frizinghall? or afterwards, when I went back with Godfrey Ablewhite and his sisters? or, later again, when I put the Moonstone into Rachel's hands? or, later still, when the company came, and we all assembled round the dinner-table? My memory disposed of that string of questions readily enough, until I came to the last. Looking back at the social event of the birthday dinner, I found myself brought to a standstill at the outset of the inquiry. I was not even capable of accurately remembering the number of the guests who had sat at the same table with me.

To feel myself completely at fault here, and to conclude, thereupon, that the incidents of the dinner might especially repay the trouble of investigating them, formed parts of the same mental process, in my case. I believe other people, in a similar situation, would have reasoned as I did. When the pursuit of our own interests causes us to become objects of inquiry to ourselves, we are naturally suspicious of what we don't know. Once in possession of the names of the persons who had been present at the dinner, I resolved—as a means of enriching the deficient resources of my own memory—to appeal to the memory of the rest of the guests; to write down all that they could recollect of the social events of the birthday; and to test the result, thus obtained, by the light of what had happened afterwards, when the company had left the house.

This last and newest of my many contemplated experiments in the art of inquiry—which Betteredge would probably have attributed to the clear-headed, or French, side of me being uppermost for the moment—may fairly claim record here, on its own merits. Unlikely as it may seem, I had now actually groped my way to the root of the matter at last. All I wanted was a hint to guide me in the right direction at starting. Before another day had passed over my head, that hint was given me by one of the company who had been present at the birthday feast!

With the plan of proceeding which I now had in view, it was

first necessary to possess the complete list of the guests. This I could easily obtain from Gabriel Betteredge. I determined to go back to Yorkshire on that day, and to begin my contemplated investigation the next morning.

It was just too late to start by the train which left London before noon. There was no alternative but to wait, nearly three hours, for the departure of the next train. Was there anything I could do in London, which might usefully occupy this interval of time?

My thoughts went back again obstinately to the birthday dinner.

Though I had forgotten the numbers, and, in many cases, the names of the guests, I remembered readily enough that by far the larger proportion of them came from Frizinghall, or from its neighbourhood. But the larger proportion was not all. Some few of us were not regular residents in the country. I myself was one of the few. Mr. Murthwaite was another. Godfrey Ablewhite was a third. Mr. Bruff — no: I called to mind that business had prevented Mr. Bruff from making one of the party. Had any ladies been present, whose usual residence was in London? I could only remember Miss Clack as coming within this latter category. However, here were three of the guests, at any rate, whom it was clearly advisable for me to see before I left town. I drove off at once to Mr. Bruff's office; not knowing the addresses of the persons of whom I was in search, and thinking it probable that he might put me in the way of finding them.

Mr. Bruff proved to be too busy to give me more than a minute of his valuable time. In that minute, however, he contrived to dispose — in the most discouraging manner — of all the questions I had to put to him.

In the first place, he considered my newly-discovered method of finding a clue to the mystery as something too purely fanciful to be seriously discussed. In the second, third, and fourth places, Mr. Murthwaite was now on his way back to the scene of his past adventures; Miss Clack had suffered losses, and had settled, from motives of economy, in France; Mr. Godfrey Ablewhite might, or might not, be discoverable somewhere in London. Suppose I inquired at his club? And suppose I excused Mr. Bruff, if he went back to his business and wished me good morning?

The field of inquiry in London, being now so narrowed as only to include the one necessity of discovering Godfrey's address, I took the lawyer's hint, and drove to his club.

In the hall, I met with one of the members, who was an old friend of my cousin's, and who was also an acquaintance of my own. This gentleman, after enlightening me on the subject of Godfrey's address, told me of two recent events in his life, which were of some importance in themselves, and which had not previously reached my ears.

It appeared that Godfrey, far from being discouraged by Rachel's withdrawal from her engagement to him had made matrimonial advances soon afterwards to another young lady, reputed to be a great heiress. His suit had prospered, and his marriage had been considered as a settled and certain thing. But, here again, the engagement had been suddenly and unexpectedly broken off—owing, it was said, on this occasion, to a serious difference of opinion between the bridegroom and the lady's father, on the question of settlements.

As some compensation for this second matrimonial disaster, Godfrey had soon afterwards found himself the object of fond pecuniary remembrance, on the part of one of his many admirers. A rich old lady—highly respected at the Mothers'-Small-Clothes-Conversion-Society, and a great friend of Miss Clack's (to whom she left nothing but a mourning ring)—had bequeathed to the admirable and meritorious Godfrey a legacy of five thousand pounds. After receiving this handsome addition to his own modest pecuniary resources, he had been heard to say that he felt the necessity of getting a little respite from his charitable labours, and that his doctor prescribed "a run on the Continent, as likely to be productive of much future benefit to his health." If I wanted to see him, it would be advisable to lose no time in paying my contemplated visit.

I went, then and there, to pay my visit.

The same fatality which had made me just one day too late in calling on Sergeant Cuff, made me again one day too late in calling on Godfrey. He had left London, on the previous morning, by the tidal train, for Dover. He was to cross to Ostend; and his servant believed he was going on to Brussels.

The time of his return was rather uncertain; but I might be sure he would be away at least three months.

I went back to my lodgings a little depressed in spirits. Three of the guests at the birthday dinner—and those three all exceptionally intelligent people—were out of my reach, at the very time when it was most important to be able to communicate with them. My last hopes now rested on Betteredge, and on the friends of the late Lady Verinder whom I might still find living in the neighbourhood of Rachel's country house.

On this occasion, I travelled straight to Frizinghall—the town being now the central point in my field of inquiry. I arrived too late in the evening to be able to communicate with Betteredge. The next morning, I sent a messenger with a letter, requesting him to join me at the hotel, at his earliest convenience.

Having taken the precaution—partly to save time, partly to accommodate Betteredge—of sending my messenger in a fly, I had a reasonable prospect, if no delays occurred, of seeing the old man within less than two hours from the time when I had sent for him. During this interval, I arranged to employ myself in opening my contemplated inquiry, among the guests present at the birthday dinner who were personally known to me, and who were easily within my reach. These were my relatives, the Ablewhites, and Mr. Candy. The doctor had expressed a special wish to see me, and the doctor lived in the next street. So to Mr. Candy I went first.

After what Betteredge had told me, I naturally anticipated finding traces in the doctor's face of the severe illness from which he had suffered. But I was utterly unprepared for such a change as I saw in him when he entered the room and shook hands with me. His eyes were dim; his hair had turned completely grey; his face was wizen; his figure had shrunk. I looked at the once lively, rattlepated, humorous little doctor—associated in my remembrance with the perpetration of incorrigible social indiscretions and innumerable boyish jokes—and I saw nothing left of his former self, but the old tendency to vulgar smartness in his dress. The man was a wreck; but his clothes and his jewellery—in cruel mockery of the change in him—were as gay and as gaudy as ever.

"I have often thought of you, Mr. Blake," he said; "and I am heartily glad to see you again at last. If there is anything I can do for you, pray command my services, sir — pray command my services!"

He said those few commonplace words with needless hurry and eagerness, and with a curiosity to know what had brought me to Yorkshire, which he was perfectly — I might say childishly — incapable of concealing from notice.

With the object that I had in view, I had of course foreseen the necessity of entering into some sort of personal explanation, before I could hope to interest people, mostly strangers to me, in doing their best to assist my inquiry. On the journey to Frizinghall I had arranged what my explanation was to be — and I seized the opportunity now offered to me of trying the effect of it on Mr. Candy.

"I was in Yorkshire, the other day, and I am in Yorkshire again now, on rather a romantic errand," I said. "It is a matter, Mr. Candy, in which the late Lady Verinder's friends all took some interest. You remember the mysterious loss of the Indian Diamond, now nearly a year since? Circumstances have lately happened which lead to the hope that it may yet be found — and I am interesting myself, as one of the family, in recovering it. Among the obstacles in my way, there is the necessity of collecting again all the evidence which was discovered at the time, and more if possible. There are peculiarities in this case which make it desirable to revive my recollection of everything that happened in the house, on the evening of Miss Verinder's birthday. And I venture to appeal to her late mother's friends who were present on that occasion, to lend me the assistance of their memories — —"

I had got as far as that in rehearsing my explanatory phrases, when I was suddenly checked by seeing plainly in Mr. Candy's face that my experiment on him was a total failure.

The little doctor sat restlessly picking at the points of his fingers all the time I was speaking. His dim watery eyes were fixed on my face with an expression of vacant and wistful inquiry very painful to see. What he was thinking of, it was impossible to divine. The one thing clearly visible was that I had failed, after the first two or three words, in fixing his attention.

The Moonstone

The only chance of recalling him to himself appeared to lie in changing the subject. I tried a new topic immediately.

"So much," I said, gaily, "for what brings me to Frizinghall! Now, Mr. Candy, it's your turn. You sent me a message by Gabriel Betteredge——"

He left off picking at his fingers, and suddenly brightened up.

"Yes! yes! yes!" he exclaimed eagerly. "That's it! I sent you a message!"

"And Betteredge duly communicated it by letter," I went on. "You had something to say to me, the next time I was in your neighbourhood. Well, Mr. Candy, here I am!"

"Here you are!" echoed the doctor. "And Betteredge was quite right. I had something to say to you. That was my message. Betteredge is a wonderful man. What a memory! At his age, what a memory!"

He dropped back into silence, and began picking at his fingers again. Recollecting what I had heard from Betteredge about the effect of the fever on his memory, I went on with the conversation, in the hope that I might help him at starting.

"It's a long time since we met," I said. "We last saw each other at the last birthday dinner my poor aunt was ever to give."

"That's it!" cried Mr. Candy. "The birthday dinner!" He started impulsively to his feet, and looked at me. A deep flush suddenly overspread his faded face, and he abruptly sat down again, as if conscious of having betrayed a weakness which he would fain have concealed. It was plain, pitiably plain, that he was aware of his own defect of memory, and that he was bent on hiding it from the observation of his friends.

Thus far he had appealed to my compassion only. But the words he had just said — few as they were — roused my curiosity instantly to the highest pitch. The birthday dinner had already become the one event in the past, at which I looked back with strangely-mixed feelings of hope and distrust. And here was the birthday dinner unmistakably proclaiming itself as the subject on which Mr. Candy had something important to say to me!

I attempted to help him out once more. But, this time, my own interests were at the bottom of my compassionate motive, and they hurried me on a little too abruptly, to the end I had in view.

"It's nearly a year now," I said, "since we sat at that pleasant table. Have you made any memorandum—in your diary, or otherwise—of what you wanted to say to me?"

Mr. Candy understood the suggestion, and showed me that he understood it, as an insult.

"I require no memorandum, Mr. Blake," he said, stiffly enough. "I am not such a very old man, yet—and my memory (thank God) is to be thoroughly depended on!"

It is needless to say that I declined to understand that he was offended with me.

"I wish I could say the same of my memory," I answered. "When I try to think of matters that are a year old, I seldom find my remembrance as vivid as I could wish it to be. Take the dinner at Lady Verinder's, for instance——"

Mr. Candy brightened up again, the moment the allusion passed my lips.

"Ah! the dinner, the dinner at Lady Verinder's!" he exclaimed, more eagerly than ever. "I have got something to say to you about that."

His eyes looked at me again with the painful expression of inquiry, so wistful, so vacant, so miserably helpless to see. He was evidently trying hard, and trying in vain, to recover the lost recollection. "It was a very pleasant dinner," he burst out suddenly, with an air of saying exactly what he wanted to say. "A very pleasant dinner, Mr. Blake, wasn't it?" He nodded and smiled, and appeared to think, poor fellow, that he had succeeded in concealing the total failure of his memory, by a well-timed exertion of his own presence of mind.

It was so distressing that I at once shifted the talk—deeply as I was interested in his recovering the lost remembrance—to topics of local interest.

Here, he got on glibly enough. Trumpery little scandals and quarrels in the town, some of them as much as a month old,

The Moonstone

appeared to recur to his memory readily. He chattered on, with something of the smooth gossiping fluency of former times. But there were moments, even in the full flow of his talkativeness, when he suddenly hesitated—looked at me for a moment with the vacant inquiry once more in his eyes—controlled himself—and went on again. I submitted patiently to my martyrdom (it is surely nothing less than martyrdom to a man of cosmopolitan sympathies, to absorb in silent resignation the news of a country town?) until the clock on the chimney-piece told me that my visit had been prolonged beyond half an hour. Having now some right to consider the sacrifice as complete, I rose to take leave. As we shook hands, Mr. Candy reverted to the birthday festival of his own accord.

"I am so glad we have met again," he said. "I had it on my mind—I really had it on my mind, Mr. Blake, to speak to you. About the dinner at Lady Verinder's, you know? A pleasant dinner—really a pleasant dinner now, wasn't it?"

On repeating the phrase, he seemed to feel hardly as certain of having prevented me from suspecting his lapse of memory, as he had felt on the first occasion. The wistful look clouded his face again: and, after apparently designing to accompany me to the street door, he suddenly changed his mind, rang the bell for the servant, and remained in the drawing-room.

I went slowly down the doctor's stairs, feeling the disheartening conviction that he really had something to say which it was vitally important to me to hear, and that he was morally incapable of saying it. The effort of remembering that he wanted to speak to me was, but too evidently, the only effort that his enfeebled memory was now able to achieve.

Just as I reached the bottom of the stairs, and had turned a corner on my way to the outer hall, a door opened softly somewhere on the ground floor of the house, and a gentle voice said behind me:—

"I am afraid, sir, you find Mr. Candy sadly changed?"

I turned round, and found myself face to face with Ezra Jennings.

CHAPTER IX

The doctor's pretty housemaid stood waiting for me, with the street door open in her hand. Pouring brightly into the hall, the morning light fell full on the face of Mr. Candy's assistant when I turned, and looked at him.

It was impossible to dispute Betteredge's assertion that the appearance of Ezra Jennings, speaking from a popular point of view, was against him. His gipsy-complexion, his fleshless cheeks, his gaunt facial bones, his dreamy eyes, his extraordinary parti-coloured hair, the puzzling contradiction between his face and figure which made him look old and young both together — were all more or less calculated to produce an unfavourable impression of him on a stranger's mind. And yet — feeling this as I certainly did — it is not to be denied that Ezra Jennings made some inscrutable appeal to my sympathies, which I found it impossible to resist. While my knowledge of the world warned me to answer the question which he had put, acknowledging that I did indeed find Mr. Candy sadly changed, and then to proceed on my way out of the house — my interest in Ezra Jennings held me rooted to the place, and gave him the opportunity of speaking to me in private about his employer, for which he had been evidently on the watch.

"Are you walking my way, Mr. Jennings?" I said, observing that he held his hat in his hand. "I am going to call on my aunt, Mrs. Ablewhite."

Ezra Jennings replied that he had a patient to see, and that he was walking my way.

We left the house together. I observed that the pretty servant girl — who was all smiles and amiability, when I wished her good morning on my way out — received a modest little message from Ezra Jennings, relating to the time at which he might be expected to return, with pursed-up lips, and with eyes which ostentatiously looked anywhere rather than look in his face. The poor wretch was evidently no favourite in the house. Out of the house, I had Betteredge's word for it that he was unpopular everywhere. "What a life!" I thought to myself, as we descended the doctor's doorsteps.

The Moonstone

Having already referred to Mr. Candy's illness on his side, Ezra Jennings now appeared determined to leave it to me to resume the subject. His silence said significantly, "It's your turn now." I, too, had my reasons for referring to the doctor's illness: and I readily accepted the responsibility of speaking first.

"Judging by the change I see in him," I began, "Mr. Candy's illness must have been far more serious than I had supposed?"

"It is almost a miracle," said Ezra Jennings, "that he lived through it."

"Is his memory never any better than I have found it today? He has been trying to speak to me— —"

"Of something which happened before he was taken ill?" asked the assistant, observing that I hesitated.

"Yes."

"His memory of events, at that past time, is hopelessly enfeebled," said Ezra Jennings. "It is almost to be deplored, poor fellow, that even the wreck of it remains. While he remembers dimly plans that he formed—things, here and there, that he had to say or do before his illness—he is perfectly incapable of recalling what the plans were, or what the thing was that he had to say or do. He is painfully conscious of his own deficiency, and painfully anxious, as you must have seen, to hide it from observation. If he could only have recovered in a complete state of oblivion as to the past, he would have been a happier man. Perhaps we should all be happier," he added, with a sad smile, "if we could but completely forget!"

"There are some events surely in all men's lives," I replied, "the memory of which they would be unwilling entirely to lose?"

"That is, I hope, to be said of most men, Mr. Blake. I am afraid it cannot truly be said of all. Have you any reason to suppose that the lost remembrance which Mr. Candy tried to recover—while you were speaking to him just now—was a remembrance which it was important to you that he should recall?"

In saying those words, he had touched, of his own accord, on the very point upon which I was anxious to consult him. The interest I felt in this strange man had impelled me, in the first instance, to give him the opportunity of speaking to me; reserving what I might have to say, on my side, in relation to his employer, until I was first satisfied that he was a person in whose delicacy and discretion I could trust. The little that he had said, thus far, had been sufficient to convince me that I was speaking to a gentleman. He had what I may venture to describe as the unsought self-possession, which is a sure sign of good breeding, not in England only, but everywhere else in the civilised world. Whatever the object which he had in view, in putting the question that he had just addressed to me, I felt no doubt that I was justified—so far—in answering him without reserve.

"I believe I have a strong interest," I said, "in tracing the lost remembrance which Mr. Candy was unable to recall. May I ask whether you can suggest to me any method by which I might assist his memory?"

Ezra Jennings looked at me, with a sudden flash of interest in his dreamy brown eyes.

"Mr. Candy's memory is beyond the reach of assistance," he said. "I have tried to help it often enough since his recovery, to be able to speak positively on that point."

This disappointed me; and I owned it.

"I confess you led me to hope for a less discouraging answer than that," I said.

Ezra Jennings smiled. "It may not, perhaps, be a final answer, Mr. Blake. It may be possible to trace Mr. Candy's lost recollection, without the necessity of appealing to Mr. Candy himself."

"Indeed? Is it an indiscretion, on my part, to ask how?"

"By no means. My only difficulty in answering your question, is the difficulty of explaining myself. May I trust to your patience, if I refer once more to Mr. Candy's illness: and if I speak of it this time without sparing you certain professional details?"

"Pray go on! You have interested me already in hearing the details."

My eagerness seemed to amuse—perhaps, I might rather say, to please him. He smiled again. We had by this time left the last houses in the town behind us. Ezra Jennings stopped for a moment, and picked some wild flowers from the hedge by the roadside. "How beautiful they are!" he said, simply, showing his little nosegay to me. "And how few people in England seem to admire them as they deserve!"

"You have not always been in England?" I said.

"No. I was born, and partly brought up, in one of our colonies. My father was an Englishman; but my mother—We are straying away from our subject, Mr. Blake; and it is my fault. The truth is, I have associations with these modest little hedgeside flowers—It doesn't matter; we were speaking of Mr. Candy. To Mr. Candy let us return."

Connecting the few words about himself which thus reluctantly escaped him, with the melancholy view of life which led him to place the conditions of human happiness in complete oblivion of the past, I felt satisfied that the story which I had read in his face was, in two particulars at least, the story that it really told. He had suffered as few men suffer; and there was the mixture of some foreign race in his English blood.

"You have heard, I dare say, of the original cause of Mr. Candy's illness?" he resumed. "The night of Lady Verinder's dinner-party was a night of heavy rain. My employer drove home through it in his gig, and reached the house wetted to the skin. He found an urgent message from a patient, waiting for him; and he most unfortunately went at once to visit the sick person, without stopping to change his clothes. I was myself professionally detained, that night, by a case at some distance from Frizinghall. When I got back the next morning, I found Mr. Candy's groom waiting in great alarm to take me to his master's room. By that time the mischief was done; the illness had set in."

"The illness has only been described to me, in general terms, as a fever," I said.

"I can add nothing which will make the description more accurate," answered Ezra Jennings. "From first to last the fever assumed no specific form. I sent at once to two of Mr. Candy's medical friends in the town, both physicians, to come and give me their opinion of the case. They agreed with me that it looked serious; but they both strongly dissented from the view I took of the treatment. We differed entirely in the conclusions which we drew from the patient's pulse. The two doctors, arguing from the rapidity of the beat, declared that a lowering treatment was the only treatment to be adopted. On my side, I admitted the rapidity of the pulse, but I also pointed to its alarming feebleness as indicating an exhausted condition of the system, and as showing a plain necessity for the administration of stimulants. The two doctors were for keeping him on gruel, lemonade, barley-water, and so on. I was for giving him champagne, or brandy, ammonia, and quinine. A serious difference of opinion, as you see! A difference between two physicians of established local repute, and a stranger who was only an assistant in the house. For the first few days, I had no choice but to give way to my elders and betters; the patient steadily sinking all the time. I made a second attempt to appeal to the plain, undeniably plain, evidence of the pulse. Its rapidity was unchecked, and its feebleness had increased. The two doctors took offence at my obstinacy. They said, 'Mr. Jennings, either we manage this case, or you manage it. Which is it to be?' I said, 'Gentlemen, give me five minutes to consider, and that plain question shall have a plain reply.' When the time expired, I was ready with my answer. I said, 'You positively refuse to try the stimulant treatment?' They refused in so many words. 'I mean to try it at once, gentlemen.' — 'Try it, Mr. Jennings, and we withdraw from the case.' I sent down to the cellar for a bottle of champagne; and I administered half a tumbler-full of it to the patient with my own hand. The two physicians took up their hats in silence, and left the house."

"You had assumed a serious responsibility," I said. "In your place, I am afraid I should have shrunk from it."

"In my place, Mr. Blake, you would have remembered that Mr. Candy had taken you into his employment, under circumstances which made you his debtor for life. In my place, you would have seen him sinking, hour by hour; and you would have risked anything, rather than let the one man on earth who had befriended you, die before your eyes. Don't suppose that I had no sense of the terrible position in which I had placed myself! There were moments when I felt all the misery of my friendlessness, all the peril of my dreadful responsibility. If I had been a happy man, if I had led a prosperous life, I believe I should have sunk under the task I had imposed on myself. But I had no happy time to look back at, no past peace of mind to force itself into contrast with my present anxiety and suspense—and I held firm to my resolution through it all. I took an interval in the middle of the day, when my patient's condition was at its best, for the repose I needed. For the rest of the four-and-twenty hours, as long as his life was in danger, I never left his bedside. Towards sunset, as usual in such cases, the delirium incidental to the fever came on. It lasted more or less through the night; and then intermitted, at that terrible time in the early morning—from two o'clock to five—when the vital energies even of the healthiest of us are at their lowest. It is then that Death gathers in his human harvest most abundantly. It was then that Death and I fought our fight over the bed, which should have the man who lay on it. I never hesitated in pursuing the treatment on which I had staked everything. When wine failed, I tried brandy. When the other stimulants lost their influence, I doubled the dose. After an interval of suspense—the like of which I hope to God I shall never feel again—there came a day when the rapidity of the pulse slightly, but appreciably, diminished; and, better still, there came also a change in the beat—an unmistakable change to steadiness and strength. Then, I knew that I had saved him; and then I own I broke down. I laid the poor fellow's wasted hand back on the bed, and burst out crying. An hysterical relief, Mr. Blake—nothing more! Physiology says, and says truly, that some men are born with female constitutions—and I am one of them!"

He made that bitterly professional apology for his tears, speaking quietly and unaffectedly, as he had spoken throughout. His tone and manner, from beginning to end, showed him to be especially, almost morbidly, anxious not to set himself up as an object of interest to me.

"You may well ask, why I have wearied you with all these details?" he went on. "It is the only way I can see, Mr. Blake, of properly introducing to you what I have to say next. Now you know exactly what my position was, at the time of Mr. Candy's illness, you will the more readily understand the sore need I had of lightening the burden on my mind by giving it, at intervals, some sort of relief. I have had the presumption to occupy my leisure, for some years past, in writing a book, addressed to the members of my profession—a book on the intricate and delicate subject of the brain and the nervous system. My work will probably never be finished; and it will certainly never be published. It has none the less been the friend of many lonely hours; and it helped me to while away the anxious time—the time of waiting, and nothing else—at Mr. Candy's bedside. I told you he was delirious, I think? And I mentioned the time at which his delirium came on?"

"Yes."

"Well, I had reached a section of my book, at that time, which touched on this same question of delirium. I won't trouble you at any length with my theory on the subject—I will confine myself to telling you only what it is your present interest to know. It has often occurred to me in the course of my medical practice, to doubt whether we can justifiably infer—in cases of delirium—that the loss of the faculty of speaking connectedly, implies of necessity the loss of the faculty of thinking connectedly as well. Poor Mr. Candy's illness gave me an opportunity of putting this doubt to the test. I understand the art of writing in shorthand; and I was able to take down the patient's 'wanderings', exactly as they fell from his lips.—Do you see, Mr. Blake, what I am coming to at last?"

I saw it clearly, and waited with breathless interest to hear more.

"At odds and ends of time," Ezra Jennings went on, "I reproduced my shorthand notes, in the ordinary form of writing—leaving large spaces between the broken phrases, and even the single words, as they had fallen disconnectedly from Mr. Candy's lips. I then treated the result thus obtained, on something like the principle which one adopts in putting together a child's 'puzzle.' It is all confusion to begin with; but it may be all brought into order and shape, if you can only find the right way. Acting on this plan, I filled in each blank space on the paper, with what the words or phrases on either side of it suggested to me as the speaker's meaning; altering over and over again, until my additions followed naturally on the spoken words which came before them, and fitted naturally into the spoken words which came after them. The result was, that I not only occupied in this way many vacant and anxious hours, but that I arrived at something which was (as it seemed to me) a confirmation of the theory that I held. In plainer words, after putting the broken sentences together I found the superior faculty of thinking going on, more or less connectedly, in my patient's mind, while the inferior faculty of expression was in a state of almost complete incapacity and confusion."

"One word!" I interposed eagerly. "Did my name occur in any of his wanderings?"

"You shall hear, Mr. Blake. Among my written proofs of the assertion which I have just advanced—or, I ought to say, among the written experiments, tending to put my assertion to the proof—there is one, in which your name occurs. For nearly the whole of one night, Mr. Candy's mind was occupied with something between himself and you. I have got the broken words, as they dropped from his lips, on one sheet of paper. And I have got the links of my own discovering which connect those words together, on another sheet of paper. The product (as the arithmeticians would say) is an intelligible statement—first, of something actually done in the past; secondly, of something which Mr. Candy contemplated doing in the future, if his illness had not got in the way, and stopped him. The question is whether this does, or does not, represent the lost recollection which he vainly attempted to find when you called on him this morning?"

"Not a doubt of it!" I answered. "Let us go back directly, and look at the papers!"

"Quite impossible, Mr. Blake."

"Why?"

"Put yourself in my position for a moment," said Ezra Jennings. "Would you disclose to another person what had dropped unconsciously from the lips of your suffering patient and your helpless friend, without first knowing that there was a necessity to justify you in opening your lips?"

I felt that he was unanswerable, here; but I tried to argue the question, nevertheless.

"My conduct in such a delicate matter as you describe," I replied, "would depend greatly on whether the disclosure was of a nature to compromise my friend or not."

"I have disposed of all necessity for considering that side of the question, long since," said Ezra Jennings. "Wherever my notes included anything which Mr. Candy might have wished to keep secret, those notes have been destroyed. My manuscript experiments at my friend's bedside, include nothing, now, which he would have hesitated to communicate to others, if he had recovered the use of his memory. In your case, I have every reason to suppose that my notes contain something which he actually wished to say to you."

"And yet, you hesitate?"

"And yet, I hesitate. Remember the circumstances under which I obtained the information which I possess! Harmless as it is, I cannot prevail upon myself to give it up to you, unless you first satisfy me that there is a reason for doing so. He was so miserably ill, Mr. Blake! and he was so helplessly dependent upon Me! Is it too much to ask, if I request you only to hint to me what your interest is in the lost recollection—or what you believe that lost recollection to be?"

To have answered him with the frankness which his language and his manner both claimed from me, would have been to commit myself to openly acknowledging that I was suspected of the theft of the Diamond. Strongly as Ezra Jennings had intensified the first impulsive interest which I had felt in him, he had not overcome my unconquerable reluctance to disclose the degrading position in which I stood. I took refuge once more in the explanatory phrases with which I had prepared myself to meet the curiosity of strangers.

This time I had no reason to complain of a want of attention on the part of the person to whom I addressed myself. Ezra Jennings listened patiently, even anxiously, until I had done.

"I am sorry to have raised your expectations, Mr. Blake, only to disappoint them," he said. "Throughout the whole period of Mr. Candy's illness, from first to last, not one word about the Diamond escaped his lips. The matter with which I heard him connect your name has, I can assure you, no discoverable relation whatever with the loss or the recovery of Miss Verinder's jewel."

We arrived, as he said those words, at a place where the highway along which we had been walking branched off into

The Moonstone

two roads. One led to Mr. Ablewhite's house, and the other to a moorland village some two or three miles off. Ezra Jennings stopped at the road which led to the village.

"My way lies in this direction," he said. "I am really and truly sorry, Mr. Blake, that I can be of no use to you."

His voice told me that he spoke sincerely. His soft brown eyes rested on me for a moment with a look of melancholy interest. He bowed, and went, without another word, on his way to the village.

For a minute or more I stood and watched him, walking farther and farther away from me; carrying farther and farther away with him what I now firmly believed to be the clue of which I was in search. He turned, after walking on a little way, and looked back. Seeing me still standing at the place where we had parted, he stopped, as if doubting whether I might not wish to speak to him again. There was no time for me to reason out my own situation—to remind myself that I was losing my opportunity, at what might be the turning point of my life, and all to flatter nothing more important than my own self-esteem! There was only time to call him back first, and to think afterwards. I suspect I am one of the rashest of existing men. I called him back—and then I said to myself, "Now there is no help for it. I must tell him the truth!"

He retraced his steps directly. I advanced along the road to meet him.

"Mr. Jennings," I said. "I have not treated you quite fairly. My interest in tracing Mr. Candy's lost recollection is not the interest of recovering the Moonstone. A serious personal matter is at the bottom of my visit to Yorkshire. I have but one excuse for not having dealt frankly with you in this matter. It is more painful to me than I can say, to mention to anybody what my position really is."

Ezra Jennings looked at me with the first appearance of embarrassment which I had seen in him yet.

"I have no right, Mr. Blake, and no wish," he said, "to intrude myself into your private affairs. Allow me to ask your pardon, on my side, for having (most innocently) put you to a painful test."

"You have a perfect right," I rejoined, "to fix the terms on which you feel justified in revealing what you heard at Mr. Candy's bedside. I understand and respect the delicacy which influences you in this matter. How can I expect to be taken into your confidence if I decline to admit you into mine? You ought to know, and you shall know, why I am interested in discovering what Mr. Candy wanted to say to me. If I turn out to be mistaken in my anticipations, and if you prove unable to help me when you are really aware of what I want, I shall trust to your honour to keep my secret—and something tells me that I shall not trust in vain."

"Stop, Mr. Blake. I have a word to say, which must be said before you go any farther."

I looked at him in astonishment. The grip of some terrible emotion seemed to have seized him, and shaken him to the soul. His gipsy complexion had altered to a livid greyish paleness; his eyes had suddenly become wild and glittering; his voice had dropped to a tone—low, stern, and resolute—which I now heard for the first time. The latent resources in the man, for good or for evil—it was hard, at that moment, to say which—leapt up in him and showed themselves to me, with the suddenness of a flash of light.

"Before you place any confidence in me," he went on, "you ought to know, and you must know, under what circumstances I have been received into Mr. Candy's house. It won't take long. I don't profess, sir, to tell my story (as the phrase is) to any man. My story will die with me. All I ask, is to be permitted to tell you, what I have told Mr. Candy. If you are still in the mind, when you have heard that, to say what you have proposed to say, you will command my attention and command my services. Shall we walk on?"

The suppressed misery in his face silenced me. I answered his question by a sign. We walked on.

After advancing a few hundred yards, Ezra Jennings stopped at a gap in the rough stone wall which shut off the moor from the road, at this part of it.

"Do you mind resting a little, Mr. Blake?" he asked. "I am not what I was—and some things shake me."

I agreed of course. He led the way through the gap to a patch of turf on the heathy ground, screened by bushes and dwarf trees on the side nearest to the road, and commanding in the opposite direction a grandly desolate view over the broad brown wilderness of the moor. The clouds had gathered, within the last half hour. The light was dull; the distance was dim. The lovely face of Nature met us, soft and still colourless—met us without a smile.

We sat down in silence. Ezra Jennings laid aside his hat, and passed his hand wearily over his forehead, wearily through his startling white and black hair. He tossed his little nosegay of wild flowers away from him, as if the remembrances which it recalled were remembrances which hurt him now.

"Mr. Blake!" he said, suddenly. "You are in bad company. The cloud of a horrible accusation has rested on me for years. I tell you the worst at once. I am a man whose life is a wreck, and whose character is gone."

I attempted to speak. He stopped me.

"No," he said. "Pardon me; not yet. Don't commit yourself to expressions of sympathy which you may afterwards wish to recall. I have mentioned an accusation which has rested on me for years. There are circumstances in connexion with it that tell against me. I cannot bring myself to acknowledge what the accusation is. And I am incapable, perfectly incapable, of proving my innocence. I can only assert my innocence. I assert it, sir, on my oath, as a Christian. It is useless to appeal to my honour as a man."

He paused again. I looked round at him. He never looked at me in return. His whole being seemed to be absorbed in the agony of recollecting, and in the effort to speak.

"There is much that I might say," he went on, "about the merciless treatment of me by my own family, and the merciless enmity to which I have fallen a victim. But the harm is done; the wrong is beyond all remedy. I decline to weary or distress you, sir, if I can help it. At the outset of my career in this country, the vile slander to which I have referred struck me down at once and for ever. I resigned my aspirations in my profession— obscurity was the only hope left for me. I parted with the woman I loved—how could I condemn her to share my disgrace? A medical assistant's place offered itself, in a remote corner of England. I got the place. It promised me peace; it promised me obscurity, as I thought. I was wrong. Evil report, with time and chance to help it, travels patiently, and travels far. The accusation from which I had fled followed me. I got warning of its approach. I was able to leave my situation voluntarily, with the testimonials that I had earned. They got me another situation in another remote district. Time passed again; and again the slander that was death to my character found me out. On this occasion I had no warning. My employer said, 'Mr. Jennings, I have no complaint to make against you; but you must set yourself right, or leave me.' I had but one choice—I left him. It's useless to dwell on what I suffered after that. I am only forty years old now. Look at my face, and let it tell for me the story of some miserable years. It ended in my drifting to this place, and meeting with Mr. Candy. He wanted an assistant. I referred him, on the question of capacity, to my last employer. The question of character remained. I told him what I have told you—and more. I warned him that there were difficulties in the way, even if he believed me. 'Here, as elsewhere,' I said 'I scorn the guilty evasion of living under an assumed name: I am no safer at Frizinghall than at other places from the cloud that follows me, go where I may.' He answered, 'I don't do things by halves—I believe you, and I pity you. If you will risk what may happen, I will risk it too.' God Almighty bless him! He has given me shelter, he has given me employment, he has given me rest of mind—and I have the certain conviction (I have had it for some months past) that nothing will happen now to make him regret it."

"The slander has died out?" I said.

"The slander is as active as ever. But when it follows me here, it will come too late."

"You will have left the place?"

"No, Mr. Blake—I shall be dead. For ten years past I have suffered from an incurable internal complaint. I don't disguise from you that I should have let the agony of it kill me long since, but for one last interest in life, which makes my existence of some importance to me still. I want to provide for a person— very dear to me—whom I shall never see again. My own little patrimony is hardly sufficient to make her independent of the

The Moonstone

world. The hope, if I could only live long enough, of increasing it to a certain sum, has impelled me to resist the disease by such palliative means as I could devise. The one effectual palliative in my case, is—opium. To that all-potent and all-merciful drug I am indebted for a respite of many years from my sentence of death. But even the virtues of opium have their limit. The progress of the disease has gradually forced me from the use of opium to the abuse of it. I am feeling the penalty at last. My nervous system is shattered; my nights are nights of horror. The end is not far off now. Let it come—I have not lived and worked in vain. The little sum is nearly made up; and I have the means of completing it, if my last reserves of life fail me sooner than I expect. I hardly know how I have wandered into telling you this. I don't think I am mean enough to appeal to your pity. Perhaps, I fancy you may be all the readier to believe me, if you know that what I have said to you, I have said with the certain knowledge in me that I am a dying man. There is no disguising, Mr. Blake, that you interest me. I have attempted to make my poor friend's loss of memory the means of bettering my acquaintance with you. I have speculated on the chance of your feeling a passing curiosity about what he wanted to say, and of my being able to satisfy it. Is there no excuse for my intruding myself on you? Perhaps there is some excuse. A man who has lived as I have lived has his bitter moments when he ponders over human destiny. You have youth, health, riches, a place in the world, a prospect before you. You, and such as you, show me the sunny side of human life, and reconcile me with the world that I am leaving, before I go. However this talk between us may end, I shall not forget that you have done me a kindness in doing that. It rests with you, sir, to say what you proposed saying, or to wish me good morning."

I had but one answer to make to that appeal. Without a moment's hesitation I told him the truth, as unreservedly as I have told it in these pages.

He started to his feet, and looked at me with breathless eagerness as I approached the leading incident of my story.

"It is certain that I went into the room," I said; "it is certain that I took the Diamond. I can only meet those two plain facts by declaring that, do what I might, I did it without my own knowledge——"

Ezra Jennings caught me excitedly by the arm.

"Stop!" he said. "You have suggested more to me than you suppose. Have you ever been accustomed to the use of opium?"

"I never tasted it in my life."

"Were your nerves out of order, at this time last year? Were you unusually restless and irritable?"

"Yes."

"Did you sleep badly?"

"Wretchedly. Many nights I never slept at all."

"Was the birthday night an exception? Try, and remember. Did you sleep well on that one occasion?"

"I do remember! I slept soundly."

He dropped my arm as suddenly as he had taken it—and looked at me with the air of a man whose mind was relieved of the last doubt that rested on it.

"This is a marked day in your life, and in mine," he said, gravely. "I am absolutely certain, Mr. Blake, of one thing—I have got what Mr. Candy wanted to say to you this morning, in the notes that I took at my patient's bedside. Wait! that is not all. I am firmly persuaded that I can prove you to have been unconscious of what you were about, when you entered the room and took the Diamond. Give me time to think, and time to question you. I believe the vindication of your innocence is in my hands!"

"Explain yourself, for God's sake! What do you mean?"

In the excitement of our colloquy, we had walked on a few steps, beyond the clump of dwarf trees which had hitherto screened us from view. Before Ezra Jennings could answer me, he was hailed from the high road by a man, in great agitation, who had been evidently on the look-out for him.

"I am coming," he called back; "I am coming as fast as I can!" He turned to me. "There is an urgent case waiting for me at the village yonder; I ought to have been there half an hour since—I must attend to it at once. Give me two hours from this time, and call at Mr. Candy's again—and I will engage to be ready for you."

"How am I to wait!" I exclaimed, impatiently. "Can't you quiet my mind by a word of explanation before we part?"

"This is far too serious a matter to be explained in a hurry, Mr. Blake. I am not wilfully trying your patience—I should only be adding to your suspense, if I attempted to relieve it as things are now. At Frizinghall, sir, in two hours' time!"

The man on the high road hailed him again. He hurried away, and left me.

CHAPTER X

How the interval of suspense in which I was now condemned might have affected other men in my position, I cannot pretend to say. The influence of the two hours' probation upon my temperament was simply this. I felt physically incapable of remaining still in any one place, and morally incapable of speaking to any one human being, until I had first heard all that Ezra Jennings had to say to me.

In this frame of mind, I not only abandoned my contemplated visit to Mrs. Ablewhite—I even shrank from encountering Gabriel Betteredge himself.

Returning to Frizinghall, I left a note for Betteredge, telling him that I had been unexpectedly called away for a few hours, but that he might certainly expect me to return towards three o'clock in the afternoon. I requested him, in the interval, to order his dinner at the usual hour, and to amuse himself as he pleased. He had, as I well knew, hosts of friends in Frizinghall; and he would be at no loss how to fill up his time until I returned to the hotel.

This done, I made the best of my way out of the town again, and roamed the lonely moorland country which surrounds Frizinghall, until my watch told me that it was time, at last, to return to Mr. Candy's house.

I found Ezra Jennings ready and waiting for me.

He was sitting alone in a bare little room, which communicated by a glazed door with a surgery. Hideous coloured diagrams of the ravages of hideous diseases decorated the barren buff-coloured walls. A bookcase filled with dingy medical works, and ornamented at the top with a skull, in place of the customary bust; a large deal table copiously splashed with ink; wooden chairs of the sort that are seen in kitchens and cottages; a threadbare drugget in the middle of the floor; a sink of water, with a basin and waste-pipe roughly let into the wall, horribly suggestive of its connection with surgical operations—comprised the entire furniture of the room. The bees were humming among a few flowers placed in pots outside the window; the birds were singing in the garden, and the faint intermittent jingle of a tuneless piano in some neighbouring

The Moonstone

house forced itself now and again on the ear. In any other place, these everyday sounds might have spoken pleasantly of the everyday world outside. Here, they came in as intruders on a silence which nothing but human suffering had the privilege to disturb. I looked at the mahogany instrument case, and at the huge roll of lint, occupying places of their own on the bookshelves, and shuddered inwardly as I thought of the sounds, familiar and appropriate to the everyday use of Ezra Jennings' room.

"I make no apology, Mr. Blake, for the place in which I am receiving you," he said. "It is the only room in the house, at this hour of the day, in which we can feel quite sure of being left undisturbed. Here are my papers ready for you; and here are two books to which we may have occasion to refer, before we have done. Bring your chair to the table, and we shall be able to consult them together."

I drew up to the table; and Ezra Jennings handed me his manuscript notes. They consisted of two large folio leaves of paper. One leaf contained writing which only covered the surface at intervals. The other presented writing, in red and black ink, which completely filled the page from top to bottom. In the irritated state of my curiosity, at that moment, I laid aside the second sheet of paper in despair.

"Have some mercy on me!" I said. "Tell me what I am to expect, before I attempt to read this."

"Willingly, Mr. Blake! Do you mind my asking you one or two more questions?"

"Ask me anything you like!"

He looked at me with the sad smile on his lips, and the kindly interest in his soft brown eyes.

"You have already told me," he said, "that you have never—to your knowledge—tasted opium in your life."

"To my knowledge," I repeated.

"You will understand directly why I speak with that reservation. Let us go on. You are not aware of ever having taken opium. At this time, last year, you were suffering from nervous irritation, and you slept wretchedly at night. On the night of the birthday, however, there was an exception to the rule—you slept soundly. Am I right, so far?"

"Quite right!"

"Can you assign any cause for the nervous suffering, and your want of sleep?"

"I can assign no cause. Old Betteredge made a guess at the cause, I remember. But that is hardly worth mentioning."

"Pardon me. Anything is worth mentioning in such a case as this. Betteredge attributed your sleeplessness to something. To what?"

"To my leaving off smoking."

"Had you been an habitual smoker?"

"Yes."

"Did you leave off the habit suddenly?"

"Yes."

"Betteredge was perfectly right, Mr. Blake. When smoking is a habit a man must have no common constitution who can leave it off suddenly without some temporary damage to his nervous system. Your sleepless nights are accounted for, to my mind. My next question refers to Mr. Candy. Do you remember having entered into anything like a dispute with him—at the birthday dinner, or afterwards—on the subject of his profession?"

The question instantly awakened one of my dormant remembrances in connection with the birthday festival. The foolish wrangle which took place, on that occasion, between Mr. Candy and myself, will be found described at much greater length than it deserves in the tenth chapter of Betteredge's Narrative. The details there presented of the dispute—so little had I thought of it afterwards—entirely failed to recur to my memory. All that I could now recall, and all that I could tell Ezra Jennings was, that I had attacked the art of medicine at the dinner-table with sufficient rashness and sufficient pertinacity to put even Mr. Candy out of temper for the moment. I also remembered that Lady Verinder had interfered to stop the dispute, and that the little doctor and I had "made it up again," as the children say, and had become as good friends as ever, before we shook hands that night.

"There is one thing more," said Ezra Jennings, "which it is very important I should know. Had you any reason for feeling any special anxiety about the Diamond, at this time last year?"

"I had the strongest reasons for feeling anxiety about the Diamond. I knew it to be the object of a conspiracy; and I was warned to take measures for Miss Verinder's protection, as the possessor of the stone."

"Was the safety of the Diamond the subject of conversation between you and any other person, immediately before you retired to rest on the birthday night?"

"It was the subject of a conversation between Lady Verinder and her daughter——"

"Which took place in your hearing?"

"Yes."

Ezra Jennings took up his notes from the table, and placed them in my hands.

"Mr. Blake," he said, "if you read those notes now, by the light which my questions and your answers have thrown on them, you will make two astounding discoveries concerning yourself. You will find:—First, that you entered Miss Verinder's sitting-room and took the Diamond, in a state of trance, produced by opium. Secondly, that the opium was given to you by Mr. Candy—without your own knowledge—as a practical refutation of the opinions which you had expressed to him at the birthday dinner."

I sat with the papers in my hand completely stupefied.

"Try and forgive poor Mr. Candy," said the assistant gently. "He has done dreadful mischief, I own; but he has done it innocently. If you will look at the notes, you will see that—but for his illness—he would have returned to Lady Verinder's the morning after the party, and would have acknowledged the trick that he had played you. Miss Verinder would have heard of it, and Miss Verinder would have questioned him—and the truth which has laid hidden for a year would have been discovered in a day."

I began to regain my self-possession. "Mr. Candy is beyond the reach of my resentment," I said angrily. "But the trick that he played me is not the less an act of treachery, for all that. I may forgive, but I shall not forget it."

"Every medical man commits that act of treachery, Mr. Blake, in the course of his practice. The ignorant distrust of opium (in England) is by no means confined to the lower and less cultivated classes. Every doctor in large practice finds himself, every now and then, obliged to deceive his patients, as Mr. Candy deceived you. I don't defend the folly of playing you a trick under the circumstances. I only plead with you for a more accurate and more merciful construction of motives."

"How was it done?" I asked. "Who gave me the laudanum, without my knowing it myself?"

"I am not able to tell you. Nothing relating to that part of the matter dropped from Mr. Candy's lips, all through his illness. Perhaps your own memory may point to the person to be suspected."

"No."

"It is useless, in that case, to pursue the inquiry. The laudanum was secretly given to you in some way. Let us leave it there, and go on to matters of more immediate importance. Read my notes, if you can. Familiarise your mind with what has happened in the past. I have something very bold and very startling to propose to you, which relates to the future."

Those last words roused me.

I looked at the papers, in the order in which Ezra Jennings had placed them in my hands. The paper which contained the smaller quantity of writing was the uppermost of the two. On this, the disconnected words, and fragments of sentences, which had dropped from Mr. Candy in his delirium, appeared as follows:

"... Mr. Franklin Blake ... and agreeable ... down a peg ... medicine ... confesses ... sleep at night ... tell him ... out of order . .. medicine ... he tells me ... and groping in the dark mean one and the same thing ... all the company at the dinner-table ... I say ... groping after sleep ... nothing but medicine ... he says ... leading the blind ... know what it means ... witty ... a night's rest

The Moonstone

in spite of his teeth ... wants sleep ... Lady Verinder's medicine chest ... five-and-twenty minims ... without his knowing it ... tomorrow morning ... Well, Mr. Blake ... medicine today ... never ... without it ... out, Mr. Candy ... excellent ... without it ... down on him ... truth ... something besides ... excellent ... dose of laudanum, sir ... bed ... what ... medicine now."

There, the first of the two sheets of paper came to an end. I handed it back to Ezra Jennings.

"That is what you heard at his bedside?" I said.

"Literally and exactly what I heard," he answered—"except that the repetitions are not transferred here from my short-hand notes. He reiterated certain words and phrases a dozen times over, fifty times over, just as he attached more or less importance to the idea which they represented. The repetitions, in this sense, were of some assistance to me in putting together those fragments. Don't suppose," he added, pointing to the second sheet of paper, "that I claim to have reproduced the expressions which Mr. Candy himself would have used if he had been capable of speaking connectedly. I only say that I have penetrated through the obstacle of the disconnected expression, to the thought which was underlying it connectedly all the time. Judge for yourself."

I turned to the second sheet of paper, which I now knew to be the key to the first.

Once more, Mr. Candy's wanderings appeared, copied in black ink; the intervals between the phrases being filled up by Ezra Jennings in red ink. I reproduce the result here, in one plain form; the original language and the interpretation of it coming close enough together in these pages to be easily compared and verified.

"... Mr. Franklin Blake is clever and agreeable, but he wants taking down a peg when he talks of medicine. He confesses that he has been suffering from want of sleep at night. I tell him that his nerves are out of order, and that he ought to take medicine. He tells me that taking medicine and groping in the dark mean one and the same thing. This before all the company at the dinner-table. I say to him, you are groping after sleep, and nothing but medicine can help you to find it. He says to me, I have heard of the blind leading the blind, and now I know what it means. Witty—but I can give him a night's rest in spite of his teeth. He really wants sleep; and Lady Verinder's medicine chest is at my disposal. Give him five-and-twenty minims of laudanum tonight, without his knowing it; and then call tomorrow morning. 'Well, Mr. Blake, will you try a little medicine today? You will never sleep without it.'—'There you are out, Mr. Candy: I have had an excellent night's rest without it.' Then, come down on him with the truth! 'You have had something besides an excellent night's rest; you had a dose of laudanum, sir, before you went to bed. What do you say to the art of medicine, now?'"

Admiration of the ingenuity which had woven this smooth and finished texture out of the ravelled skein was naturally the first impression that I felt, on handing the manuscript back to Ezra Jennings. He modestly interrupted the first few words in which my sense of surprise expressed itself, by asking me if the conclusion which he had drawn from his notes was also the conclusion at which my own mind had arrived.

"Do you believe as I believe," he said, "that you were acting under the influence of the laudanum in doing all that you did, on the night of Miss Verinder's birthday, in Lady Verinder's house?"

"I am too ignorant of the influence of laudanum to have an opinion of my own," I answered. "I can only follow your opinion, and feel convinced that you are right."

"Very well. The next question is this. You are convinced; and I am convinced—how are we to carry our conviction to the minds of other people?"

I pointed to the two manuscripts, lying on the table between us. Ezra Jennings shook his head.

"Useless, Mr. Blake! Quite useless, as they stand now for three unanswerable reasons. In the first place, those notes have been taken under circumstances entirely out of the experience of the mass of mankind. Against them, to begin with! In the second place, those notes represent a medical and metaphysical theory. Against them, once more! In the third place, those notes are of my making; there is nothing but my assertion to the contrary, to guarantee that they are not fabrications. Remember what I told you on the moor—and ask yourself what my assertion is worth. No! my notes have but one value, looking to the verdict of the world outside. Your innocence is to be vindicated; and they show how it can be done. We must put our conviction to the proof—and You are the man to prove it!"

"How?" I asked.

He leaned eagerly nearer to me across the table that divided us.

"Are you willing to try a bold experiment?"

"I will do anything to clear myself of the suspicion that rests on me now."

"Will you submit to some personal inconvenience for a time?"

"To any inconvenience, no matter what it may be."

"Will you be guided implicitly by my advice? It may expose you to the ridicule of fools; it may subject you to the remonstrances of friends whose opinions you are bound to respect."

"Tell me what to do!" I broke out impatiently. "And, come what may, I'll do it."

"You shall do this, Mr. Blake," he answered. "You shall steal the Diamond, unconsciously, for the second time, in the presence of witnesses whose testimony is beyond dispute."

I started to my feet. I tried to speak. I could only look at him.

"I believe it can be done," he went on. "And it shall be done—if you will only help me. Try to compose yourself—sit down, and hear what I have to say to you. You have resumed the habit of smoking; I have seen that for myself. How long have you resumed it."

"For nearly a year."

"Do you smoke more or less than you did?"

"More."

"Will you give up the habit again? Suddenly, mind!—as you gave it up before."

I began dimly to see his drift. "I will give it up, from this moment," I answered.

"If the same consequences follow, which followed last June," said Ezra Jennings—"if you suffer once more as you suffered then, from sleepless nights, we shall have gained our first step. We shall have put you back again into something assimilating to your nervous condition on the birthday night. If we can next revive, or nearly revive, the domestic circumstances which surrounded you; and if we can occupy your mind again with the various questions concerning the Diamond which formerly agitated it, we shall have replaced you, as nearly as possible in the same position, physically and morally, in which the opium found you last year. In that case we may fairly hope that a repetition of the dose will lead, in a greater or lesser degree, to a repetition of the result. There is my proposal, expressed in a few hasty words. You shall now see what reasons I have to justify me in making it."

He turned to one of the books at his side, and opened it at a place marked by a small slip of paper.

"Don't suppose that I am going to weary you with a lecture on physiology," he said. "I think myself bound to prove, in justice to both of us, that I am not asking you to try this experiment in deference to any theory of my own devising. Admitted principles, and recognised authorities, justify me in the view that I take. Give me five minutes of your attention; and I will undertake to show you that Science sanctions my proposal, fanciful as it may seem. Here, in the first place, is the physiological principle on which I am acting, stated by no less a person than Dr. Carpenter. Read it for yourself."

He handed me the slip of paper which had marked the place in the book. It contained a few lines of writing, as follows:—

"There seems much ground for the belief, that every sensory impression which has once been recognised by the perceptive consciousness, is registered (so to speak) in the brain, and may be reproduced at some subsequent time, although there may be no consciousness of its existence in the mind during the whole intermediate period."

"Is that plain, so far?" asked Ezra Jennings.

"Perfectly plain."

He pushed the open book across the table to me, and pointed to a passage, marked by pencil lines.

"Now," he said, "read that account of a case, which has — as I believe — a direct bearing on your own position, and on the experiment which I am tempting you to try. Observe, Mr. Blake, before you begin, that I am now referring you to one of the greatest of English physiologists. The book in your hand is Doctor Elliotson's Human Physiology; and the case which the doctor cites rests on the well-known authority of Mr. Combe."

The passage pointed out to me was expressed in these terms:

"Dr. Abel informed me," says Mr. Combe, "of an Irish porter to a warehouse, who forgot, when sober, what he had done when drunk; but, being drunk, again recollected the transactions of his former state of intoxication. On one occasion, being drunk, he had lost a parcel of some value, and in his sober moments could give no account of it. Next time he was intoxicated, he recollected that he had left the parcel at a certain house, and there being no address on it, it had remained there safely, and was got on his calling for it."

"Plain again?" asked Ezra Jennings.

"As plain as need be."

He put back the slip of paper in its place, and closed the book.

"Are you satisfied that I have not spoken without good authority to support me?" he asked. "If not, I have only to go to those bookshelves, and you have only to read the passages which I can point out to you."

"I am quite satisfied," I said, "without reading a word more."

"In that case, we may return to your own personal interest in this matter. I am bound to tell you that there is something to be said against the experiment as well as for it. If we could, this year, exactly reproduce, in your case, the conditions as they existed last year, it is physiologically certain that we should arrive at exactly the same result. But this — there is no denying it—is simply impossible. We can only hope to approximate to the conditions; and if we don't succeed in getting you nearly enough back to what you were, this venture of ours will fail. If we do succeed—and I am myself hopeful of success—you may at least so far repeat your proceedings on the birthday night, as to satisfy any reasonable person that you are guiltless, morally speaking, of the theft of the Diamond. I believe, Mr. Blake, I have now stated the question, on both sides of it, as fairly as I can, within the limits that I have imposed on myself. If there is anything that I have not made clear to you, tell me what it is—and if I can enlighten you, I will."

"All that you have explained to me," I said, "I understand perfectly. But I own I am puzzled on one point, which you have not made clear to me yet."

"What is the point?"

"I don't understand the effect of the laudanum on me. I don't understand my walking downstairs, and along corridors, and my opening and shutting the drawers of a cabinet, and my going back again to my own room. All these are active proceedings. I thought the influence of opium was first to stupefy you, and then to send you to sleep."

"The common error about opium, Mr. Blake! I am, at this moment, exerting my intelligence (such as it is) in your service, under the influence of a dose of laudanum, some ten times larger than the dose Mr. Candy administered to you. But don't trust to my authority—even on a question which comes within my own personal experience. I anticipated the objection you have just made: and I have again provided myself with independent testimony which will carry its due weight with it in your own mind, and in the minds of your friends."

He handed me the second of the two books which he had by him on the table.

"There," he said, "are the far-famed Confessions of an English Opium Eater! Take the book away with you, and read it. At the passage which I have marked, you will find that when De Quincey had committed what he calls 'a debauch of opium,' he either went to the gallery at the Opera to enjoy the music, or he wandered about the London markets on Saturday night, and interested himself in observing all the little shifts and bargainings of the poor in providing their Sunday's dinner. So much for the capacity of a man to occupy himself actively, and to move about from place to place under the influence of opium."

"I am answered so far," I said; "but I am not answered yet as to the effect produced by the opium on myself."

"I will try to answer you in a few words," said Ezra Jennings. "The action of opium is comprised, in the majority of cases, in two influences—a stimulating influence first, and a sedative influence afterwards. Under the stimulating influence, the latest and most vivid impressions left on your mind—namely, the impressions relating to the Diamond—would be likely, in your morbidly sensitive nervous condition, to become intensified in your brain, and would subordinate to themselves your judgment and your will exactly as an ordinary dream subordinates to itself your judgment and your will. Little by little, under this action, any apprehensions about the safety of the Diamond which you might have felt during the day would be liable to develop themselves from the state of doubt to the state of certainty—would impel you into practical action to preserve the jewel—would direct your steps, with that motive in view, into the room which you entered—and would guide your hand to the drawers of the cabinet, until you had found the drawer which held the stone. In the spiritualised intoxication of opium, you would do all that. Later, as the sedative action began to gain on the stimulant action, you would slowly become inert and stupefied. Later still you would fall into a deep sleep. When the morning came, and the effect of the opium had been all slept off, you would wake as absolutely ignorant of what you had done in the night as if you had been living at the Antipodes. Have I made it tolerably clear to you so far?"

"You have made it so clear," I said, "that I want you to go farther. You have shown me how I entered the room, and how I came to take the Diamond. But Miss Verinder saw me leave the room again, with the jewel in my hand. Can you trace my proceedings from that moment? Can you guess what I did next?"

"That is the very point I was coming to," he rejoined. "It is a question with me whether the experiment which I propose as a means of vindicating your innocence, may not also be made a means of recovering the lost Diamond as well. When you left Miss Verinder's sitting-room, with the jewel in your hand, you went back in all probability to your own room— —"

"Yes? and what then?"

"It is possible, Mr. Blake—I dare not say more—that your idea of preserving the Diamond led, by a natural sequence, to the idea of hiding the Diamond, and that the place in which you hid it was somewhere in your bedroom. In that event, the case of the Irish porter may be your case. You may remember, under the influence of the second dose of opium, the place in which you hid the Diamond under the influence of the first."

It was my turn, now, to enlighten Ezra Jennings. I stopped him, before he could say any more.

"You are speculating," I said, "on a result which cannot possibly take place. The Diamond is, at this moment, in London."

He started, and looked at me in great surprise.

"In London?" he repeated. "How did it get to London from Lady Verinder's house?"

"Nobody knows."

"You removed it with your own hand from Miss Verinder's room. How was it taken out of your keeping?"

"I have no idea how it was taken out of my keeping."

"Did you see it, when you woke in the morning?"

"No."

"Has Miss Verinder recovered possession of it?"

"No."

"Mr. Blake! there seems to be something here which wants clearing up. May I ask how you know that the Diamond is, at this moment, in London?"

I had put precisely the same question to Mr. Bruff when I made my first inquiries about the Moonstone, on my return to England. In answering Ezra Jennings, I accordingly repeated

The Moonstone

what I had myself heard from the lawyer's own lips—and what is already familiar to the readers of these pages.

He showed plainly that he was not satisfied with my reply.

"With all deference to you," he said, "and with all deference to your legal adviser, I maintain the opinion which I expressed just now. It rests, I am well aware, on a mere assumption. Pardon me for reminding you, that your opinion also rests on a mere assumption as well."

The view he took of the matter was entirely new to me. I waited anxiously to hear how he would defend it.

"I assume," pursued Ezra Jennings, "that the influence of the opium—after impelling you to possess yourself of the Diamond, with the purpose of securing its safety—might also impel you, acting under the same influence and the same motive, to hide it somewhere in your own room. You assume that the Hindoo conspirators could by no possibility commit a mistake. The Indians went to Mr. Luker's house after the Diamond—and, therefore, in Mr. Luker's possession the Diamond must be! Have you any evidence to prove that the Moonstone was taken to London at all? You can't even guess how, or by whom, it was removed from Lady Verinder's house! Have you any evidence that the jewel was pledged to Mr. Luker? He declares that he never heard of the Moonstone; and his bankers' receipt acknowledges nothing but the deposit of a valuable of great price. The Indians assume that Mr. Luker is lying—and you assume again that the Indians are right. All I say, in differing with you, is—that my view is possible. What more, Mr. Blake, either logically, or legally, can be said for yours?"

It was put strongly; but there was no denying that it was put truly as well.

"I confess you stagger me," I replied. "Do you object to my writing to Mr. Bruff, and telling him what you have said?"

"On the contrary, I shall be glad if you will write to Mr. Bruff. If we consult his experience, we may see the matter under a new light. For the present, let us return to our experiment with the opium. We have decided that you leave off the habit of smoking from this moment."

"From this moment?"

"That is the first step. The next step is to reproduce, as nearly as we can, the domestic circumstances which surrounded you last year."

How was this to be done? Lady Verinder was dead. Rachel and I, so long as the suspicion of theft rested on me, were parted irrevocably. Godfrey Ablewhite was away travelling on the Continent. It was simply impossible to reassemble the people who had inhabited the house, when I had slept in it last. The statement of this objection did not appear to embarrass Ezra Jennings. He attached very little importance, he said, to reassembling the same people—seeing that it would be vain to expect them to reassume the various positions which they had occupied towards me in the past times. On the other hand, he considered it essential to the success of the experiment, that I should see the same objects about me which had surrounded me when I was last in the house.

"Above all things," he said, "you must sleep in the room which you slept in, on the birthday night, and it must be furnished in the same way. The stairs, the corridors, and Miss Verinder's sitting-room, must also be restored to what they were when you saw them last. It is absolutely necessary, Mr. Blake, to replace every article of furniture in that part of the house which may now be put away. The sacrifice of your cigars will be useless, unless we can get Miss Verinder's permission to do that."

"Who is to apply to her for permission?" I asked.

"Is it not possible for you to apply?"

"Quite out of the question. After what has passed between us on the subject of the lost Diamond, I can neither see her, nor write to her, as things are now."

Ezra Jennings paused, and considered for a moment.

"May I ask you a delicate question?" he said.

I signed to him to go on.

"Am I right, Mr. Blake, in fancying (from one or two things which have dropped from you) that you felt no common interest in Miss Verinder, in former times?"

"Quite right."

"Was the feeling returned?"

"It was."

"Do you think Miss Verinder would be likely to feel a strong interest in the attempt to prove your innocence?"

"I am certain of it."

"In that case, I will write to Miss Verinder—if you will give me leave."

"Telling her of the proposal that you have made to me?"

"Telling her of everything that has passed between us today."

It is needless to say that I eagerly accepted the service which he had offered to me.

"I shall have time to write by today's post," he said, looking at his watch. "Don't forget to lock up your cigars, when you get back to the hotel! I will call tomorrow morning and hear how you have passed the night."

I rose to take leave of him; and attempted to express the grateful sense of his kindness which I really felt.

He pressed my hand gently. "Remember what I told you on the moor," he answered. "If I can do you this little service, Mr. Blake, I shall feel it like a last gleam of sunshine, falling on the evening of a long and clouded day."

We parted. It was then the fifteenth of June. The events of the next ten days—everyone of them more or less directly connected with the experiment of which I was the passive object—are all placed on record, exactly as they happened, in the Journal habitually kept by Mr. Candy's assistant. In the pages of Ezra Jennings nothing is concealed, and nothing is forgotten. Let Ezra Jennings tell how the venture with the opium was tried, and how it ended.

FOURTH NARRATIVE.

Extracted from the Journal of Ezra Jennings.

1849.—June 15.... With some interruption from patients, and some interruption from pain, I finished my letter to Miss Verinder in time for today's post. I failed to make it as short a letter as I could have wished. But I think I have made it plain. It leaves her entirely mistress of her own decision. If she consents to assist the experiment, she consents of her own free will, and not as a favour to Mr. Franklin Blake or to me.

June 16th.—Rose late, after a dreadful night; the vengeance of yesterday's opium, pursuing me through a series of frightful dreams. At one time I was whirling through empty space with the phantoms of the dead, friends and enemies together. At another, the one beloved face which I shall never see again, rose at my bedside, hideously phosphorescent in the black darkness, and glared and grinned at me. A slight return of the old pain, at the usual time in the early morning, was welcome as a change. It dispelled the visions—and it was bearable because it did that.

My bad night made it late in the morning, before I could get to Mr. Franklin Blake. I found him stretched on the sofa, breakfasting on brandy and soda water, and a dry biscuit.

"I am beginning, as well as you could possibly wish," he said. "A miserable, restless night; and a total failure of appetite this morning. Exactly what happened last year, when I gave up my cigars. The sooner I am ready for my second dose of laudanum, the better I shall be pleased."

"You shall have it on the earliest possible day," I answered. "In the meantime, we must be as careful of your health as we can. If we allow you to become exhausted, we shall fail in that way. You must get an appetite for your dinner. In other words, you must get a ride or a walk this morning, in the fresh air."

"I will ride, if they can find me a horse here. By-the-bye, I wrote to Mr. Bruff, yesterday. Have you written to Miss Verinder?"

"Yes—by last night's post."

"Very good. We shall have some news worth hearing, to tell each other tomorrow. Don't go yet! I have a word to say to you.

The Moonstone

You appeared to think, yesterday, that our experiment with the opium was not likely to be viewed very favourably by some of my friends. You were quite right. I call old Gabriel Betteredge one of my friends; and you will be amused to hear that he protested strongly when I saw him yesterday. 'You have done a wonderful number of foolish things in the course of your life, Mr. Franklin, but this tops them all!' There is Betteredge's opinion! You will make allowance for his prejudices, I am sure, if you and he happen to meet?"

I left Mr. Blake, to go my rounds among my patients; feeling the better and the happier even for the short interview that I had had with him.

What is the secret of the attraction that there is for me in this man? Does it only mean that I feel the contrast between the frankly kind manner in which he has allowed me to become acquainted with him, and the merciless dislike and distrust with which I am met by other people? Or is there really something in him which answers to the yearning that I have for a little human sympathy—the yearning, which has survived the solitude and persecution of many years; which seems to grow keener and keener, as the time comes nearer and nearer when I shall endure and feel no more? How useless to ask these questions! Mr. Blake has given me a new interest in life. Let that be enough, without seeking to know what the new interest is.

June 17th.—Before breakfast, this morning, Mr. Candy informed me that he was going away for a fortnight, on a visit to a friend in the south of England. He gave me as many special directions, poor fellow, about the patients, as if he still had the large practice which he possessed before he was taken ill. The practice is worth little enough now! Other doctors have superseded him; and nobody who can help it will employ me.

It is perhaps fortunate that he is to be away just at this time. He would have been mortified if I had not informed him of the experiment which I am going to try with Mr. Blake. And I hardly know what undesirable results might not have happened, if I had taken him into my confidence. Better as it is. Unquestionably, better as it is.

The post brought me Miss Verinder's answer, after Mr. Candy had left the house.

A charming letter! It gives me the highest opinion of her. There is no attempt to conceal the interest that she feels in our proceedings. She tells me, in the prettiest manner, that my letter has satisfied her of Mr. Blake's innocence, without the slightest need (so far as she is concerned) of putting my assertion to the proof. She even upbraids herself—most undeservedly, poor thing!—for not having divined at the time what the true solution of the mystery might really be. The motive underlying all this proceeds evidently from something more than a generous eagerness to make atonement for a wrong which she has innocently inflicted on another person. It is plain that she has loved him, throughout the estrangement between them. In more than one place the rapture of discovering that he has deserved to be loved, breaks its way innocently through the stoutest formalities of pen and ink, and even defies the stronger restraint still of writing to a stranger. Is it possible (I ask myself, in reading this delightful letter) that I, of all men in the world, am chosen to be the means of bringing these two young people together again? My own happiness has been trampled under foot; my own love has been torn from me. Shall I live to see a happiness of others, which is of my making—a love renewed, which is of my bringing back? Oh merciful Death, let me see it before your arms enfold me, before your voice whispers to me, "Rest at last!"

There are two requests contained in the letter. One of them prevents me from showing it to Mr. Franklin Blake. I am authorised to tell him that Miss Verinder willingly consents to place her house at our disposal; and, that said, I am desired to add no more.

So far, it is easy to comply with her wishes. But the second request embarrasses me seriously.

Not content with having written to Mr. Betteredge, instructing him to carry out whatever directions I may have to give, Miss Verinder asks leave to assist me, by personally superintending the restoration of her own sitting-room. She only waits a word of reply from me to make the journey to Yorkshire, and to be present as one of the witnesses on the night when the opium is tried for the second time.

Here, again, there is a motive under the surface; and, here again, I fancy that I can find it out.

The Moonstone

What she has forbidden me to tell Mr. Franklin Blake, she is (as I interpret it) eager to tell him with her own lips, before he is put to the test which is to vindicate his character in the eyes of other people. I understand and admire this generous anxiety to acquit him, without waiting until his innocence may, or may not, be proved. It is the atonement that she is longing to make, poor girl, after having innocently and inevitably wronged him. But the thing cannot be done. I have no sort of doubt that the agitation which a meeting between them would produce on both sides—reviving dormant feelings, appealing to old memories, awakening new hopes—would, in their effect on the mind of Mr. Blake, be almost certainly fatal to the success of our experiment. It is hard enough, as things are, to reproduce in him the conditions as they existed, or nearly as they existed, last year. With new interests and new emotions to agitate him, the attempt would be simply useless.

And yet, knowing this, I cannot find it in my heart to disappoint her. I must try if I can discover some new arrangement, before post-time, which will allow me to say Yes to Miss Verinder, without damage to the service which I have bound myself to render to Mr. Franklin Blake.

Two o'clock.—I have just returned from my round of medical visits; having begun, of course, by calling at the hotel.

Mr. Blake's report of the night is the same as before. He has had some intervals of broken sleep, and no more. But he feels it less today, having slept after yesterday's dinner. This after-dinner sleep is the result, no doubt, of the ride which I advised him to take. I fear I shall have to curtail his restorative exercise in the fresh air. He must not be too well; he must not be too ill. It is a case (as a sailor would say) of very fine steering.

He has not heard yet from Mr. Bruff. I found him eager to know if I had received any answer from Miss Verinder.

I told him exactly what I was permitted to tell, and no more. It was quite needless to invent excuses for not showing him the letter. He told me bitterly enough, poor fellow, that he understood the delicacy which disinclined me to produce it. "She consents, of course, as a matter of common courtesy and common justice," he said. "But she keeps her own opinion of me, and waits to see the result." I was sorely tempted to hint that he was now wronging her as she had wronged him. On reflection, I shrank from forestalling her in the double luxury of surprising and forgiving him.

My visit was a very short one. After the experience of the other night, I have been compelled once more to give up my dose of opium. As a necessary result, the agony of the disease that is in me has got the upper hand again. I felt the attack coming on, and left abruptly, so as not to alarm or distress him. It only lasted a quarter of an hour this time, and it left me strength enough to go on with my work.

Five o'clock. — I have written my reply to Miss Verinder.

The arrangement I have proposed reconciles the interests on both sides, if she will only consent to it. After first stating the objections that there are to a meeting between Mr. Blake and herself, before the experiment is tried, I have suggested that she should so time her journey as to arrive at the house privately, on the evening when we make the attempt. Travelling by the afternoon train from London, she would delay her arrival until nine o'clock. At that hour, I have undertaken to see Mr. Blake safely into his bedchamber; and so to leave Miss Verinder free to occupy her own rooms until the time comes for administering the laudanum. When that has been done, there can be no objection to her watching the result, with the rest of us. On the next morning, she shall show Mr. Blake (if she likes) her correspondence with me, and shall satisfy him in that way that he was acquitted in her estimation, before the question of his innocence was put to the proof.

In that sense, I have written to her. This is all that I can do today. Tomorrow I must see Mr. Betteredge, and give the necessary directions for re-opening the house.

June 18th. — Late again, in calling on Mr. Franklin Blake. More of that horrible pain in the early morning; followed, this time, by complete prostration, for some hours. I foresee, in spite of the penalties which it exacts from me, that I shall have to return to the opium for the hundredth time. If I had only myself to think of, I should prefer the sharp pains to the frightful dreams. But the physical suffering exhausts me. If I let myself sink, it may end in my becoming useless to Mr. Blake at the time when he wants me most.

It was nearly one o'clock before I could get to the hotel today. The visit, even in my shattered condition, proved to be a most amusing one—thanks entirely to the presence on the scene of Gabriel Betteredge.

I found him in the room, when I went in. He withdrew to the window and looked out, while I put my first customary question to my patient. Mr. Blake had slept badly again, and he felt the loss of rest this morning more than he had felt it yet.

I asked next if he had heard from Mr. Bruff.

A letter had reached him that morning. Mr. Bruff expressed the strongest disapproval of the course which his friend and client was taking under my advice. It was mischievous—for it excited hopes that might never be realised. It was quite unintelligible to his mind, except that it looked like a piece of trickery, akin to the trickery of mesmerism, clairvoyance, and the like. It unsettled Miss Verinder's house, and it would end in unsettling Miss Verinder herself. He had put the case (without mentioning names) to an eminent physician; and the eminent physician had smiled, had shaken his head, and had said— nothing. On these grounds, Mr. Bruff entered his protest, and left it there.

My next inquiry related to the subject of the Diamond. Had the lawyer produced any evidence to prove that the jewel was in London?

No, the lawyer had simply declined to discuss the question. He was himself satisfied that the Moonstone had been pledged to Mr. Luker. His eminent absent friend, Mr. Murthwaite (whose consummate knowledge of the Indian character no one could deny), was satisfied also. Under these circumstances, and with the many demands already made on him, he must decline entering into any disputes on the subject of evidence. Time would show; and Mr. Bruff was willing to wait for time.

It was quite plain—even if Mr. Blake had not made it plainer still by reporting the substance of the letter, instead of reading what was actually written—that distrust of me was at the bottom of all this. Having myself foreseen that result, I was neither mortified nor surprised. I asked Mr. Blake if his friend's protest had shaken him. He answered emphatically, that it had not produced the slightest effect on his mind. I was free after that to dismiss Mr. Bruff from consideration—and I did dismiss him accordingly.

A pause in the talk between us, followed—and Gabriel Betteredge came out from his retirement at the window.

"Can you favour me with your attention, sir?" he inquired, addressing himself to me.

"I am quite at your service," I answered.

Betteredge took a chair and seated himself at the table. He produced a huge old-fashioned leather pocket-book, with a pencil of dimensions to match. Having put on his spectacles, he opened the pocket-book, at a blank page, and addressed himself to me once more.

"I have lived," said Betteredge, looking at me sternly, "nigh on fifty years in the service of my late lady. I was page-boy before that, in the service of the old lord, her father. I am now somewhere between seventy and eighty years of age—never mind exactly where! I am reckoned to have got as pretty a knowledge and experience of the world as most men. And what does it all end in? It ends, Mr. Ezra Jennings, in a conjuring trick being performed on Mr. Franklin Blake, by a doctor's assistant with a bottle of laudanum—and by the living jingo, I'm appointed, in my old age, to be conjurer's boy!"

Mr. Blake burst out laughing. I attempted to speak. Betteredge held up his hand, in token that he had not done yet.

"Not a word, Mr. Jennings!" he said, "It don't want a word, sir, from you. I have got my principles, thank God. If an order comes to me, which is own brother to an order come from Bedlam, it don't matter. So long as I get it from my master or mistress, as the case may be, I obey it. I may have my own opinion, which is also, you will please to remember, the opinion of Mr. Bruff—the Great Mr. Bruff!" said Betteredge, raising his voice, and shaking his head at me solemnly. "It don't matter; I withdraw my opinion, for all that. My young lady says, 'Do it.' And I say, 'Miss, it shall be done.' Here I am, with my book and my pencil—the latter not pointed so well as I could wish, but when Christians take leave of their senses, who is to expect that pencils will keep their points? Give me your orders, Mr. Jennings. I'll have them in writing, sir. I'm determined not to be behind 'em, or before 'em, by so much as a hair's breadth. I'm a blind agent—that's what I am. A blind agent!" repeated Betteredge, with infinite relish of his own description of himself.

"I am very sorry," I began, "that you and I don't agree——"

"Don't bring me, into it!" interposed Betteredge. "This is not a matter of agreement, it's a matter of obedience. Issue your directions, sir—issue your directions!"

Mr. Blake made me a sign to take him at his word. I "issued my directions" as plainly and as gravely as I could.

"I wish certain parts of the house to be re-opened," I said, "and to be furnished, exactly as they were furnished at this time last year."

Betteredge gave his imperfectly-pointed pencil a preliminary lick with his tongue. "Name the parts, Mr. Jennings!" he said loftily.

"First, the inner hall, leading to the chief staircase."

"'First, the inner hall,'" Betteredge wrote. "Impossible to furnish that, sir, as it was furnished last year—to begin with."

"Why?"

"Because there was a stuffed buzzard, Mr. Jennings, in the hall last year. When the family left, the buzzard was put away with the other things. When the buzzard was put away—he burst."

"We will except the buzzard then."

Betteredge took a note of the exception. "'The inner hall to be furnished again, as furnished last year. A burst buzzard alone excepted.' Please to go on, Mr. Jennings."

"The carpet to be laid down on the stairs, as before."

"'The carpet to be laid down on the stairs, as before.' Sorry to disappoint you, sir. But that can't be done either."

"Why not?"

"Because the man who laid that carpet down is dead, Mr. Jennings—and the like of him for reconciling together a carpet and a corner, is not to be found in all England, look where you may."

"Very well. We must try the next best man in England."

Betteredge took another note; and I went on issuing my directions.

"Miss Verinder's sitting-room to be restored exactly to what it was last year. Also, the corridor leading from the sitting-room to the first landing. Also, the second corridor, leading from the second landing to the best bedrooms. Also, the bedroom occupied last June by Mr. Franklin Blake."

Betteredge's blunt pencil followed me conscientiously, word by word. "Go on, sir," he said, with sardonic gravity. "There's a deal of writing left in the point of this pencil yet."

I told him that I had no more directions to give. "Sir," said Betteredge, "in that case, I have a point or two to put on my own behalf." He opened the pocket-book at a new page, and gave the inexhaustible pencil another preliminary lick.

"I wish to know," he began, "whether I may, or may not, wash my hands— —"

"You may decidedly," said Mr. Blake. "I'll ring for the waiter."

"— —of certain responsibilities," pursued Betteredge, impenetrably declining to see anybody in the room but himself and me. "As to Miss Verinder's sitting-room, to begin with. When we took up the carpet last year, Mr. Jennings, we found a surprising quantity of pins. Am I responsible for putting back the pins?"

"Certainly not."

Betteredge made a note of that concession, on the spot.

"As to the first corridor next," he resumed. "When we moved the ornaments in that part, we moved a statue of a fat naked child—profanely described in the catalogue of the house as 'Cupid, god of Love.' He had two wings last year, in the fleshy part of his shoulders. My eye being off him, for the moment, he lost one of them. Am I responsible for Cupid's wing?"

I made another concession, and Betteredge made another

note.

"As to the second corridor," he went on. "There having been nothing in it, last year, but the doors of the rooms (to everyone of which I can swear, if necessary), my mind is easy, I admit, respecting that part of the house only. But, as to Mr. Franklin's bedroom (if that is to be put back to what it was before), I want to know who is responsible for keeping it in a perpetual state of litter, no matter how often it may be set right—his trousers here, his towels there, and his French novels everywhere. I say, who is responsible for untidying the tidiness of Mr. Franklin's room, him or me?"

Mr. Blake declared that he would assume the whole responsibility with the greatest pleasure. Betteredge obstinately declined to listen to any solution of the difficulty, without first referring it to my sanction and approval. I accepted Mr. Blake's proposal; and Betteredge made a last entry in the pocket-book to that effect.

"Look in when you like, Mr. Jennings, beginning from tomorrow," he said, getting on his legs. "You will find me at work, with the necessary persons to assist me. I respectfully beg to thank you, sir, for overlooking the case of the stuffed buzzard, and the other case of the Cupid's wing—as also for permitting me to wash my hands of all responsibility in respect of the pins on the carpet, and the litter in Mr. Franklin's room. Speaking as a servant, I am deeply indebted to you. Speaking as a man, I consider you to be a person whose head is full of maggots, and I take up my testimony against your experiment as a delusion and a snare. Don't be afraid, on that account, of my feelings as a man getting in the way of my duty as a servant! You shall be obeyed. The maggots notwithstanding, sir, you shall be obeyed. If it ends in your setting the house on fire, Damme if I send for the engines, unless you ring the bell and order them first!"

With that farewell assurance, he made me a bow, and walked out of the room.

"Do you think we can depend on him?" I asked.

"Implicitly," answered Mr. Blake. "When we go to the house, we shall find nothing neglected, and nothing forgotten."

June 19th.—Another protest against our contemplated proceedings! From a lady this time.

The morning's post brought me two letters. One from Miss Verinder, consenting, in the kindest manner, to the arrangement that I have proposed. The other from the lady under whose care she is living—one Mrs. Merridew.

Mrs. Merridew presents her compliments, and does not pretend to understand the subject on which I have been corresponding with Miss Verinder, in its scientific bearings. Viewed in its social bearings, however, she feels free to pronounce an opinion. I am probably, Mrs. Merridew thinks, not aware that Miss Verinder is barely nineteen years of age. To allow a young lady, at her time of life, to be present (without a "chaperone") in a house full of men among whom a medical experiment is being carried on, is an outrage on propriety which Mrs. Merridew cannot possibly permit. If the matter is allowed to proceed, she will feel it to be her duty—at a serious sacrifice of her own personal convenience—to accompany Miss Verinder to Yorkshire. Under these circumstances, she ventures to request that I will kindly reconsider the subject; seeing that Miss Verinder declines to be guided by any opinion but mine. Her presence cannot possibly be necessary; and a word from me, to that effect, would relieve both Mrs. Merridew and myself of a very unpleasant responsibility.

Translated from polite commonplace into plain English, the meaning of this is, as I take it, that Mrs. Merridew stands in mortal fear of the opinion of the world. She has unfortunately appealed to the very last man in existence who has any reason to regard that opinion with respect. I won't disappoint Miss Verinder; and I won't delay a reconciliation between two young people who love each other, and who have been parted too long already. Translated from plain English into polite commonplace, this means that Mr. Jennings presents his compliments to Mrs. Merridew, and regrets that he cannot feel justified in interfering any farther in the matter.

Mr. Blake's report of himself, this morning, was the same as before. We determined not to disturb Betteredge by overlooking him at the house today. Tomorrow will be time enough for our first visit of inspection.

The Moonstone

June 20th.—Mr. Blake is beginning to feel his continued restlessness at night. The sooner the rooms are refurnished, now, the better.

On our way to the house, this morning, he consulted me, with some nervous impatience and irresolution, about a letter (forwarded to him from London) which he had received from Sergeant Cuff.

The Sergeant writes from Ireland. He acknowledges the receipt (through his housekeeper) of a card and message which Mr. Blake left at his residence near Dorking, and announces his return to England as likely to take place in a week or less. In the meantime, he requests to be favoured with Mr. Blake's reasons for wishing to speak to him (as stated in the message) on the subject of the Moonstone. If Mr. Blake can convict him of having made any serious mistake, in the course of his last year's inquiry concerning the Diamond, he will consider it a duty (after the liberal manner in which he was treated by the late Lady Verinder) to place himself at that gentleman's disposal. If not, he begs permission to remain in his retirement, surrounded by the peaceful horticultural attractions of a country life.

After reading the letter, I had no hesitation in advising Mr. Blake to inform Sergeant Cuff, in reply, of all that had happened since the inquiry was suspended last year, and to leave him to draw his own conclusions from the plain facts.

On second thoughts I also suggested inviting the Sergeant to be present at the experiment, in the event of his returning to England in time to join us. He would be a valuable witness to have, in any case; and, if I proved to be wrong in believing the Diamond to be hidden in Mr. Blake's room, his advice might be of great importance, at a future stage of the proceedings over which I could exercise no control. This last consideration appeared to decide Mr. Blake. He promised to follow my advice.

The sound of the hammer informed us that the work of refurnishing was in full progress, as we entered the drive that led to the house.

Betteredge, attired for the occasion in a fisherman's red cap, and an apron of green baize, met us in the outer hall. The moment he saw me, he pulled out the pocket-book and pencil, and obstinately insisted on taking notes of everything that I said to him. Look where we might, we found, as Mr. Blake had foretold that the work was advancing as rapidly and as intelligently as it was possible to desire. But there was still much to be done in the inner hall, and in Miss Verinder's room. It seemed doubtful whether the house would be ready for us before the end of the week.

Having congratulated Betteredge on the progress that he had made (he persisted in taking notes every time I opened my lips; declining, at the same time, to pay the slightest attention to anything said by Mr. Blake); and having promised to return for a second visit of inspection in a day or two, we prepared to leave the house, going out by the back way. Before we were clear of the passages downstairs, I was stopped by Betteredge, just as I was passing the door which led into his own room.

"Could I say two words to you in private?" he asked, in a mysterious whisper.

I consented of course. Mr. Blake walked on to wait for me in the garden, while I accompanied Betteredge into his room. I fully anticipated a demand for certain new concessions, following the precedent already established in the cases of the stuffed buzzard, and the Cupid's wing. To my great surprise, Betteredge laid his hand confidentially on my arm, and put this extraordinary question to me:

"Mr. Jennings, do you happen to be acquainted with Robinson Crusoe?"

I answered that I had read Robinson Crusoe when I was a child.

"Not since then?" inquired Betteredge.

"Not since then."

He fell back a few steps, and looked at me with an expression of compassionate curiosity, tempered by superstitious awe.

"He has not read Robinson Crusoe since he was a child," said Betteredge, speaking to himself—not to me. "Let's try how Robinson Crusoe strikes him now!"

He unlocked a cupboard in a corner, and produced a dirty

and dog's-eared book, which exhaled a strong odour of stale tobacco as he turned over the leaves. Having found a passage of which he was apparently in search, he requested me to join him in the corner; still mysteriously confidential, and still speaking under his breath.

"In respect to this hocus-pocus of yours, sir, with the laudanum and Mr. Franklin Blake," he began. "While the workpeople are in the house, my duty as a servant gets the better of my feelings as a man. When the workpeople are gone, my feelings as a man get the better of my duty as a servant. Very good. Last night, Mr. Jennings, it was borne in powerfully on my mind that this new medical enterprise of yours would end badly. If I had yielded to that secret Dictate, I should have put all the furniture away again with my own hand, and have warned the workmen off the premises when they came the next morning."

"I am glad to find, from what I have seen upstairs," I said, "that you resisted the secret Dictate."

"Resisted isn't the word," answered Betteredge. "Wrostled is the word. I wrostled, sir, between the silent orders in my bosom pulling me one way, and the written orders in my pocket-book pushing me the other, until (saving your presence) I was in a cold sweat. In that dreadful perturbation of mind and laxity of body, to what remedy did I apply? To the remedy, sir, which has never failed me yet for the last thirty years and more—to This Book!"

He hit the book a sounding blow with his open hand, and struck out of it a stronger smell of stale tobacco than ever.

"What did I find here," pursued Betteredge, "at the first page I opened? This awful bit, sir, page one hundred and seventy-eight, as follows:—'Upon these, and many like Reflections, I afterwards made it a certain rule with me, That whenever I found those secret Hints or Pressings of my Mind, to doing, or not doing any Thing that presented; or to going this Way, or that Way, I never failed to obey the secret Dictate.' As I live by bread, Mr. Jennings, those were the first words that met my eye, exactly at the time when I myself was setting the secret Dictate at defiance! You don't see anything at all out of the common in that, do you, sir?"

"I see a coincidence—nothing more."

"You don't feel at all shaken, Mr. Jennings, in respect to this medical enterprise of yours?

"Not the least in the world."

Betteredge stared hard at me, in dead silence. He closed the book with great deliberation; he locked it up again in the cupboard with extraordinary care; he wheeled round, and stared hard at me once more. Then he spoke.

"Sir," he said gravely, "there are great allowances to be made for a man who has not read Robinson Crusoe since he was a child. I wish you good morning."

He opened his door with a low bow, and left me at liberty to find my own way into the garden. I met Mr. Blake returning to the house.

"You needn't tell me what has happened," he said. "Betteredge has played his last card: he has made another prophetic discovery in Robinson Crusoe. Have you humoured his favourite delusion? No? You have let him see that you don't believe in Robinson Crusoe? Mr. Jennings! you have fallen to the lowest possible place in Betteredge's estimation. Say what you like, and do what you like, for the future. You will find that he won't waste another word on you now."

June 21st.—A short entry must suffice in my journal today.

Mr. Blake has had the worst night that he has passed yet. I have been obliged, greatly against my will, to prescribe for him. Men of his sensitive organisation are fortunately quick in feeling the effect of remedial measures. Otherwise, I should be inclined to fear that he will be totally unfit for the experiment when the time comes to try it.

As for myself, after some little remission of my pains for the last two days I had an attack this morning, of which I shall say nothing but that it has decided me to return to the opium. I shall close this book, and take my full dose—five hundred drops.

June 22nd.—Our prospects look better today. Mr. Blake's nervous suffering is greatly allayed. He slept a little last night. My night, thanks to the opium, was the night of a man who is stunned. I can't say that I woke this morning; the fitter expression would be, that I recovered my senses.

We drove to the house to see if the refurnishing was done. It will be completed tomorrow—Saturday. As Mr. Blake foretold, Betteredge raised no further obstacles. From first to last, he was ominously polite, and ominously silent.

My medical enterprise (as Betteredge calls it) must now, inevitably, be delayed until Monday next. Tomorrow evening the workmen will be late in the house. On the next day, the established Sunday tyranny which is one of the institutions of this free country, so times the trains as to make it impossible to ask anybody to travel to us from London. Until Monday comes, there is nothing to be done but to watch Mr. Blake carefully, and to keep him, if possible, in the same state in which I find him today.

In the meanwhile, I have prevailed on him to write to Mr. Bruff, making a point of it that he shall be present as one of the witnesses. I especially choose the lawyer, because he is strongly prejudiced against us. If we convince him, we place our victory beyond the possibility of dispute.

Mr. Blake has also written to Sergeant Cuff; and I have sent a line to Miss Verinder. With these, and with old Betteredge (who is really a person of importance in the family) we shall have witnesses enough for the purpose—without including Mrs. Merridew, if Mrs. Merridew persists in sacrificing herself to the opinion of the world.

June 23rd.—The vengeance of the opium overtook me again last night. No matter; I must go on with it now till Monday is past and gone.

Mr. Blake is not so well again today. At two this morning, he confesses that he opened the drawer in which his cigars are put away. He only succeeded in locking it up again by a violent effort. His next proceeding, in case of temptation, was to throw the key out of window. The waiter brought it in this morning, discovered at the bottom of an empty cistern—such is Fate! I have taken possession of the key until Tuesday next.

June 24th.—Mr. Blake and I took a long drive in an open carriage. We both felt beneficially the blessed influence of the soft summer air. I dined with him at the hotel. To my great relief—for I found him in an over-wrought, over-excited state this morning—he had two hours' sound sleep on the sofa after dinner. If he has another bad night, now—I am not afraid of the consequences.

June 25th, Monday.—The day of the experiment! It is five o'clock in the afternoon. We have just arrived at the house.

The first and foremost question, is the question of Mr. Blake's health.

So far as it is possible for me to judge, he promises (physically speaking) to be quite as susceptible to the action of the opium tonight as he was at this time last year. He is, this afternoon, in a state of nervous sensitiveness which just stops short of nervous irritation. He changes colour readily; his hand is not quite steady; and he starts at chance noises, and at unexpected appearances of persons and things.

These results have all been produced by deprivation of sleep, which is in its turn the nervous consequence of a sudden cessation in the habit of smoking, after that habit has been carried to an extreme. Here are the same causes at work again, which operated last year; and here are, apparently, the same effects. Will the parallel still hold good, when the final test has been tried? The events of the night must decide.

While I write these lines, Mr. Blake is amusing himself at the billiard table in the inner hall, practising different strokes in the game, as he was accustomed to practise them when he was a guest in this house in June last. I have brought my journal here, partly with a view to occupying the idle hours which I am sure to have on my hands between this and tomorrow morning; partly in the hope that something may happen which it may be worth my while to place on record at the time.

Have I omitted anything, thus far? A glance at yesterday's entry shows me that I have forgotten to note the arrival of the morning's post. Let me set this right before I close these leaves for the present, and join Mr. Blake.

I received a few lines then, yesterday, from Miss Verinder. She has arranged to travel by the afternoon train, as I recommended. Mrs. Merridew has insisted on accompanying her. The note hints that the old lady's generally excellent temper is a little ruffled, and requests all due indulgence for her, in consideration of her age and her habits. I will endeavour, in my relations with Mrs. Merridew, to emulate the moderation which Betteredge displays in his relations with me. He received us today, portentously arrayed in his best black suit, and his stiffest white cravat. Whenever he looks my way, he remembers that I have not read Robinson Crusoe since I was a child, and he respectfully pities me.

Yesterday, also, Mr. Blake had the lawyer's answer. Mr. Bruff accepts the invitation—under protest. It is, he thinks, clearly necessary that a gentleman possessed of the average allowance of common sense, should accompany Miss Verinder to the scene of, what we will venture to call, the proposed exhibition. For want of a better escort, Mr. Bruff himself will be that gentleman.—So here is poor Miss Verinder provided with two "chaperones." It is a relief to think that the opinion of the world must surely be satisfied with this!

Nothing has been heard of Sergeant Cuff. He is no doubt still in Ireland. We must not expect to see him tonight.

Betteredge has just come in, to say that Mr. Blake has asked for me. I must lay down my pen for the present.

Seven o'clock.—We have been all over the refurnished rooms and staircases again; and we have had a pleasant stroll in the shrubbery, which was Mr. Blake's favourite walk when he was here last. In this way, I hope to revive the old impressions of places and things as vividly as possible in his mind.

We are now going to dine, exactly at the hour at which the birthday dinner was given last year. My object, of course, is a purely medical one in this case. The laudanum must find the process of digestion, as nearly as may be, where the laudanum found it last year.

At a reasonable time after dinner I propose to lead the conversation back again—as inartificially as I can—to the subject of the Diamond, and of the Indian conspiracy to steal it. When I have filled his mind with these topics, I shall have done all that it is in my power to do, before the time comes for giving him the second dose.

Half-past eight.—I have only this moment found an

opportunity of attending to the most important duty of all; the duty of looking in the family medicine chest, for the laudanum which Mr. Candy used last year.

Ten minutes since, I caught Betteredge at an unoccupied moment, and told him what I wanted. Without a word of objection, without so much as an attempt to produce his pocket-book, he led the way (making allowances for me at every step) to the store-room in which the medicine chest is kept.

I discovered the bottle, carefully guarded by a glass stopper tied over with leather. The preparation which it contained was, as I had anticipated, the common Tincture of Opium. Finding the bottle still well filled, I have resolved to use it, in preference to employing either of the two preparations with which I had taken care to provide myself, in case of emergency.

The question of the quantity which I am to administer presents certain difficulties. I have thought it over, and have decided on increasing the dose.

My notes inform me that Mr. Candy only administered twenty-five minims. This is a small dose to have produced the results which followed—even in the case of a person so sensitive as Mr. Blake. I think it highly probable that Mr. Candy gave more than he supposed himself to have given—knowing, as I do, that he has a keen relish of the pleasures of the table, and that he measured out the laudanum on the birthday, after dinner. In any case, I shall run the risk of enlarging the dose to forty minims. On this occasion, Mr. Blake knows beforehand that he is going to take the laudanum—which is equivalent, physiologically speaking, to his having (unconsciously to himself) a certain capacity in him to resist the effects. If my view is right, a larger quantity is therefore imperatively required, this time, to repeat the results which the smaller quantity produced, last year.

Ten o'clock.—The witnesses, or the company (which shall I call them?) reached the house an hour since.

A little before nine o'clock, I prevailed on Mr. Blake to accompany me to his bedroom; stating, as a reason, that I wished him to look round it, for the last time, in order to make quite sure that nothing had been forgotten in the refurnishing of the room. I had previously arranged with Betteredge, that the bedchamber prepared for Mr. Bruff should be the next room to Mr. Blake's, and that I should be informed of the lawyer's arrival by a knock at the door. Five minutes after the clock in the hall had struck nine, I heard the knock; and, going out immediately, met Mr. Bruff in the corridor.

My personal appearance (as usual) told against me. Mr. Bruff's distrust looked at me plainly enough out of Mr. Bruff's eyes. Being well used to producing this effect on strangers, I did not hesitate a moment in saying what I wanted to say, before the lawyer found his way into Mr. Blake's room.

"You have travelled here, I believe, in company with Mrs. Merridew and Miss Verinder?" I said.

"Yes," answered Mr. Bruff, as drily as might be.

"Miss Verinder has probably told you, that I wish her presence in the house (and Mrs. Merridew's presence of course) to be kept a secret from Mr. Blake, until my experiment on him has been tried first?"

"I know that I am to hold my tongue, sir!" said Mr. Bruff, impatiently. "Being habitually silent on the subject of human folly, I am all the readier to keep my lips closed on this occasion. Does that satisfy you?"

I bowed, and left Betteredge to show him to his room. Betteredge gave me one look at parting, which said, as if in so many words, "You have caught a Tartar, Mr. Jennings—and the name of him is Bruff."

It was next necessary to get the meeting over with the two ladies. I descended the stairs—a little nervously, I confess—on my way to Miss Verinder's sitting-room.

The gardener's wife (charged with looking after the accommodation of the ladies) met me in the first-floor corridor. This excellent woman treats me with an excessive civility which is plainly the offspring of down-right terror. She stares, trembles, and curtseys, whenever I speak to her. On my asking for Miss Verinder, she stared, trembled, and would no doubt have curtseyed next, if Miss Verinder herself had not cut that ceremony short, by suddenly opening her sitting-room door.

"Is that Mr. Jennings?" she asked.

Before I could answer, she came out eagerly to speak to me in the corridor. We met under the light of a lamp on a bracket. At the first sight of me, Miss Verinder stopped, and hesitated. She recovered herself instantly, coloured for a moment—and then, with a charming frankness, offered me her hand.

"I can't treat you like a stranger, Mr. Jennings," she said. "Oh, if you only knew how happy your letters have made me!"

She looked at my ugly wrinkled face, with a bright gratitude so new to me in my experience of my fellow-creatures, that I was at a loss how to answer her. Nothing had prepared me for her kindness and her beauty. The misery of many years has not hardened my heart, thank God. I was as awkward and as shy with her, as if I had been a lad in my teens.

"Where is he now?" she asked, giving free expression to her one dominant interest—the interest in Mr. Blake. "What is he doing? Has he spoken of me? Is he in good spirits? How does he bear the sight of the house, after what happened in it last year? When are you going to give him the laudanum? May I see you pour it out? I am so interested; I am so excited—I have ten thousand things to say to you, and they all crowd together so that I don't know what to say first. Do you wonder at the interest I take in this?"

"No," I said. "I venture to think that I thoroughly understand it."

She was far above the paltry affectation of being confused. She answered me as she might have answered a brother or a father.

"You have relieved me of indescribable wretchedness; you have given me a new life. How can I be ungrateful enough to have any concealment from you? I love him," she said simply, "I have loved him from first to last—even when I was wronging him in my own thoughts; even when I was saying the hardest and the cruellest words to him. Is there any excuse for me, in that? I hope there is—I am afraid it is the only excuse I have. When tomorrow comes, and he knows that I am in the house, do you think— —"

She stopped again, and looked at me very earnestly.

"When tomorrow comes," I said, "I think you have only to

tell him what you have just told me."

Her face brightened; she came a step nearer to me. Her fingers trifled nervously with a flower which I had picked in the garden, and which I had put into the button-hole of my coat.

"You have seen a great deal of him lately," she said. "Have you, really and truly, seen that?"

"Really and truly," I answered. "I am quite certain of what will happen tomorrow. I wish I could feel as certain of what will happen tonight."

At that point in the conversation, we were interrupted by the appearance of Betteredge with the tea-tray. He gave me another significant look as he passed on into the sitting-room. "Aye! aye! make your hay while the sun shines. The Tartar's upstairs, Mr. Jennings—the Tartar's upstairs!"

We followed him into the room. A little old lady, in a corner, very nicely dressed, and very deeply absorbed over a smart piece of embroidery, dropped her work in her lap, and uttered a faint little scream at the first sight of my gipsy complexion and my piebald hair.

"Mrs. Merridew," said Miss Verinder, "this is Mr. Jennings."

"I beg Mr. Jennings's pardon," said the old lady, looking at Miss Verinder, and speaking at me. "Railway travelling always makes me nervous. I am endeavouring to quiet my mind by occupying myself as usual. I don't know whether my embroidery is out of place, on this extraordinary occasion. If it interferes with Mr. Jennings's medical views, I shall be happy to put it away of course."

I hastened to sanction the presence of the embroidery, exactly as I had sanctioned the absence of the burst buzzard and the Cupid's wing. Mrs. Merridew made an effort—a grateful effort—to look at my hair. No! it was not to be done. Mrs. Merridew looked back again at Miss Verinder.

"If Mr. Jennings will permit me," pursued the old lady, "I should like to ask a favour. Mr. Jennings is about to try a scientific experiment tonight. I used to attend scientific experiments when I was a girl at school. They invariably ended in an explosion. If Mr. Jennings will be so very kind, I should like to be warned of the explosion this time. With a view to getting it over, if possible, before I go to bed."

I attempted to assure Mrs. Merridew that an explosion was not included in the programme on this occasion.

"No," said the old lady. "I am much obliged to Mr. Jennings—I am aware that he is only deceiving me for my own good. I prefer plain dealing. I am quite resigned to the explosion—but I do want to get it over, if possible, before I go to bed."

Here the door opened, and Mrs. Merridew uttered another little scream. The advent of the explosion? No: only the advent of Betteredge.

"I beg your pardon, Mr. Jennings," said Betteredge, in his most elaborately confidential manner. "Mr. Franklin wishes to know where you are. Being under your orders to deceive him, in respect to the presence of my young lady in the house, I have said I don't know. That you will please to observe, was a lie. Having one foot already in the grave, sir, the fewer lies you expect me to tell, the more I shall be indebted to you, when my conscience pricks me and my time comes."

There was not a moment to be wasted on the purely speculative question of Betteredge's conscience. Mr. Blake might make his appearance in search of me, unless I went to him at once in his own room. Miss Verinder followed me out into the corridor.

"They seem to be in a conspiracy to persecute you," she said. "What does it mean?"

"Only the protest of the world, Miss Verinder—on a very small scale—against anything that is new."

"What are we to do with Mrs. Merridew?"

"Tell her the explosion will take place at nine tomorrow morning."

"So as to send her to bed?"

"Yes—so as to send her to bed."

Miss Verinder went back to the sitting-room, and I went upstairs to Mr. Blake.

The Moonstone

To my surprise I found him alone; restlessly pacing his room, and a little irritated at being left by himself.

"Where is Mr. Bruff?" I asked.

He pointed to the closed door of communication between the two rooms. Mr. Bruff had looked in on him, for a moment; had attempted to renew his protest against our proceedings; and had once more failed to produce the smallest impression on Mr. Blake. Upon this, the lawyer had taken refuge in a black leather bag, filled to bursting with professional papers. "The serious business of life," he admitted, "was sadly out of place on such an occasion as the present. But the serious business of life must be carried on, for all that. Mr. Blake would perhaps kindly make allowance for the old-fashioned habits of a practical man. Time was money—and, as for Mr. Jennings, he might depend on it that Mr. Bruff would be forthcoming when called upon." With that apology, the lawyer had gone back to his own room, and had immersed himself obstinately in his black bag.

I thought of Mrs. Merridew and her embroidery, and of Betteredge and his conscience. There is a wonderful sameness in the solid side of the English character—just as there is a wonderful sameness in the solid expression of the English face.

"When are you going to give me the laudanum?" asked Mr. Blake impatiently.

"You must wait a little longer," I said. "I will stay and keep you company till the time comes."

It was then not ten o'clock. Inquiries which I had made, at various times, of Betteredge and Mr. Blake, had led me to the conclusion that the dose of laudanum given by Mr. Candy could not possibly have been administered before eleven. I had accordingly determined not to try the second dose until that time.

We talked a little; but both our minds were preoccupied by the coming ordeal. The conversation soon flagged—then dropped altogether. Mr. Blake idly turned over the books on his bedroom table. I had taken the precaution of looking at them, when we first entered the room. The Guardian; The Tatler; Richardson's Pamela; Mackenzie's Man of Feeling; Roscoe's Lorenzo de' Medici; and Robertson's Charles the Fifth—all classical works; all (of course) immeasurably superior to anything produced in later times; and all (from my present point of view) possessing the one great merit of enchaining nobody's interest, and exciting nobody's brain. I left Mr. Blake to the composing influence of Standard Literature, and occupied myself in making this entry in my journal.

My watch informs me that it is close on eleven o'clock. I must shut up these leaves once more.

Two o'clock A.M.—The experiment has been tried. With what result, I am now to describe.

At eleven o'clock, I rang the bell for Betteredge, and told Mr. Blake that he might at last prepare himself for bed.

I looked out of the window at the night. It was mild and rainy, resembling, in this respect, the night of the birthday—the twenty-first of June, last year. Without professing to believe in omens, it was at least encouraging to find no direct nervous influences—no stormy or electric perturbations—in the atmosphere. Betteredge joined me at the window, and mysteriously put a little slip of paper into my hand. It contained these lines:

"Mrs. Merridew has gone to bed, on the distinct understanding that the explosion is to take place at nine tomorrow morning, and that I am not to stir out of this part of the house until she comes and sets me free. She has no idea that the chief scene of the experiment is my sitting-room—or she would have remained in it for the whole night! I am alone, and very anxious. Pray let me see you measure out the laudanum; I want to have something to do with it, even in the unimportant character of a mere looker-on.—R.V."

I followed Betteredge out of the room, and told him to remove the medicine-chest into Miss Verinder's sitting-room.

The order appeared to take him completely by surprise. He looked as if he suspected me of some occult medical design on Miss Verinder! "Might I presume to ask," he said, "what my young lady and the medicine-chest have got to do with each other?"

"Stay in the sitting-room, and you will see."

Betteredge appeared to doubt his own unaided capacity to superintend me effectually, on an occasion when a medicine-chest was included in the proceedings.

"Is there any objection, sir" he asked, "to taking Mr. Bruff into this part of the business?"

"Quite the contrary! I am now going to ask Mr. Bruff to accompany me downstairs."

Betteredge withdrew to fetch the medicine-chest, without another word. I went back into Mr. Blake's room, and knocked at the door of communication. Mr. Bruff opened it, with his papers in his hand—immersed in Law; impenetrable to Medicine.

"I am sorry to disturb you," I said. "But I am going to prepare the laudanum for Mr. Blake; and I must request you to be present, and to see what I do."

"Yes?" said Mr. Bruff, with nine-tenths of his attention riveted on his papers, and with one-tenth unwillingly accorded to me. "Anything else?"

"I must trouble you to return here with me, and to see me administer the dose."

"Anything else?"

"One thing more. I must put you to the inconvenience of remaining in Mr. Blake's room, and of waiting to see what happens."

"Oh, very good!" said Mr. Bruff. "My room, or Mr. Blake's room—it doesn't matter which; I can go on with my papers anywhere. Unless you object, Mr. Jennings, to my importing that amount of common sense into the proceedings?"

Before I could answer, Mr. Blake addressed himself to the lawyer, speaking from his bed.

"Do you really mean to say that you don't feel any interest in what we are going to do?" he asked. "Mr. Bruff, you have no more imagination than a cow!"

"A cow is a very useful animal, Mr. Blake," said the lawyer. With that reply he followed me out of the room, still keeping his papers in his hand.

We found Miss Verinder, pale and agitated, restlessly pacing her sitting-room from end to end. At a table in a corner stood Betteredge, on guard over the medicine-chest. Mr. Bruff sat down on the first chair that he could find, and (emulating the usefulness of the cow) plunged back again into his papers on the spot.

Miss Verinder drew me aside, and reverted instantly to her one all-absorbing interest—her interest in Mr. Blake.

"How is he now?" she asked. "Is he nervous? is he out of temper? Do you think it will succeed? Are you sure it will do no harm?"

"Quite sure. Come, and see me measure it out."

"One moment! It is past eleven now. How long will it be before anything happens?"

"It is not easy to say. An hour perhaps."

"I suppose the room must be dark, as it was last year?"

"Certainly."

"I shall wait in my bedroom—just as I did before. I shall keep the door a little way open. It was a little way open last year. I will watch the sitting-room door; and the moment it moves, I will blow out my light. It all happened in that way, on my birthday night. And it must all happen again in the same way, musn't it?"

"Are you sure you can control yourself, Miss Verinder?"

"In his interests, I can do anything!" she answered fervently.

One look at her face told me that I could trust her. I addressed myself again to Mr. Bruff.

"I must trouble you to put your papers aside for a moment," I said.

"Oh, certainly!" He got up with a start—as if I had disturbed him at a particularly interesting place—and followed me to the medicine-chest. There, deprived of the breathless excitement incidental to the practice of his profession, he looked at Betteredge—and yawned wearily.

Miss Verinder joined me with a glass jug of cold water,

The Moonstone

which she had taken from a side-table. "Let me pour out the water," she whispered. "I must have a hand in it!"

I measured out the forty minims from the bottle, and poured the laudanum into a medicine glass. "Fill it till it is three parts full," I said, and handed the glass to Miss Verinder. I then directed Betteredge to lock up the medicine chest; informing him that I had done with it now. A look of unutterable relief overspread the old servant's countenance. He had evidently suspected me of a medical design on his young lady!

After adding the water as I had directed, Miss Verinder seized a moment—while Betteredge was locking the chest, and while Mr. Bruff was looking back to his papers—and slyly kissed the rim of the medicine glass. "When you give it to him," said the charming girl, "give it to him on that side!"

I took the piece of crystal which was to represent the Diamond from my pocket, and gave it to her.

"You must have a hand in this, too," I said. "You must put it where you put the Moonstone last year."

She led the way to the Indian cabinet, and put the mock Diamond into the drawer which the real Diamond had occupied on the birthday night. Mr. Bruff witnessed this proceeding, under protest, as he had witnessed everything else. But the strong dramatic interest which the experiment was now assuming, proved (to my great amusement) to be too much for Betteredge's capacity of self-restraint. His hand trembled as he held the candle, and he whispered anxiously, "Are you sure, miss, it's the right drawer?"

I led the way out again, with the laudanum and water in my hand. At the door, I stopped to address a last word to Miss Verinder.

"Don't be long in putting out the lights," I said.

"I will put them out at once," she answered. "And I will wait in my bedroom, with only one candle alight."

She closed the sitting-room door behind us. Followed by Mr. Bruff and Betteredge, I went back to Mr. Blake's room.

We found him moving restlessly from side to side of the bed, and wondering irritably whether he was to have the laudanum that night. In the presence of the two witnesses, I gave him the dose, and shook up his pillows, and told him to lie down again quietly and wait.

His bed, provided with light chintz curtains, was placed, with the head against the wall of the room, so as to leave a good open space on either side of it. On one side, I drew the curtains completely—and in the part of the room thus screened from his view, I placed Mr. Bruff and Betteredge, to wait for the result. At the bottom of the bed I half drew the curtains—and placed my own chair at a little distance, so that I might let him see me or not see me, speak to me or not speak to me, just as the circumstances might direct. Having already been informed that he always slept with a light in the room, I placed one of the two lighted candles on a little table at the head of the bed, where the glare of the light would not strike on his eyes. The other candle I gave to Mr. Bruff; the light, in this instance, being subdued by the screen of the chintz curtains. The window was open at the top, so as to ventilate the room. The rain fell softly, the house was quiet. It was twenty minutes past eleven, by my watch, when the preparations were completed, and I took my place on the chair set apart at the bottom of the bed.

Mr. Bruff resumed his papers, with every appearance of being as deeply interested in them as ever. But looking towards him now, I saw certain signs and tokens which told me that the Law was beginning to lose its hold on him at last. The suspended interest of the situation in which we were now placed was slowly asserting its influence even on his unimaginative mind. As for Betteredge, consistency of principle and dignity of conduct had become, in his case, mere empty words. He forgot that I was performing a conjuring trick on Mr. Franklin Blake; he forgot that I had upset the house from top to bottom; he forgot that I had not read Robinson Crusoe since I was a child. "For the Lord's sake, sir," he whispered to me, "tell us when it will begin to work."

"Not before midnight," I whispered back. "Say nothing, and sit still."

Betteredge dropped to the lowest depth of familiarity with me, without a struggle to save himself. He answered by a wink!

Looking next towards Mr. Blake, I found him as restless as

ever in his bed; fretfully wondering why the influence of the laudanum had not begun to assert itself yet. To tell him, in his present humour, that the more he fidgeted and wondered, the longer he would delay the result for which we were now waiting, would have been simply useless. The wiser course to take was to dismiss the idea of the opium from his mind, by leading him insensibly to think of something else.

With this view, I encouraged him to talk to me; contriving so to direct the conversation, on my side, as to lead it back again to the subject which had engaged us earlier in the evening — the subject of the Diamond. I took care to revert to those portions of the story of the Moonstone, which related to the transport of it from London to Yorkshire; to the risk which Mr. Blake had run in removing it from the bank at Frizinghall; and to the unexpected appearance of the Indians at the house, on the evening of the birthday. And I purposely assumed, in referring to these events, to have misunderstood much of what Mr. Blake himself had told me a few hours since. In this way, I set him talking on the subject with which it was now vitally important to fill his mind — without allowing him to suspect that I was making him talk for a purpose. Little by little, he became so interested in putting me right that he forgot to fidget in the bed. His mind was far away from the question of the opium, at the all-important time when his eyes first told me that the opium was beginning to lay its hold on his brain.

I looked at my watch. It wanted five minutes to twelve, when the premonitory symptoms of the working of the laudanum first showed themselves to me.

At this time, no unpractised eyes would have detected any change in him. But, as the minutes of the new morning wore away, the swiftly-subtle progress of the influence began to show itself more plainly. The sublime intoxication of opium gleamed in his eyes; the dew of a stealthy perspiration began to glisten on his face. In five minutes more, the talk which he still kept up with me, failed in coherence. He held steadily to the subject of the Diamond; but he ceased to complete his sentences. A little later, the sentences dropped to single words. Then, there was an interval of silence. Then, he sat up in bed. Then, still busy with the subject of the Diamond, he began to talk again — not to me, but to himself. That change told me that the first stage in the experiment was reached. The stimulant influence of the opium had got him.

The time, now, was twenty-three minutes past twelve. The next half hour, at most, would decide the question of whether he would, or would not, get up from his bed, and leave the room.

In the breathless interest of watching him—in the unutterable triumph of seeing the first result of the experiment declare itself in the manner, and nearly at the time, which I had anticipated—I had utterly forgotten the two companions of my night vigil. Looking towards them now, I saw the Law (as represented by Mr. Bruff's papers) lying unheeded on the floor. Mr. Bruff himself was looking eagerly through a crevice left in the imperfectly-drawn curtains of the bed. And Betteredge, oblivious of all respect for social distinctions, was peeping over Mr. Bruff's shoulder.

They both started back, on finding that I was looking at them, like two boys caught out by their schoolmaster in a fault. I signed to them to take off their boots quietly, as I was taking off mine. If Mr. Blake gave us the chance of following him, it was vitally necessary to follow him without noise.

Ten minutes passed—and nothing happened. Then, he suddenly threw the bed-clothes off him. He put one leg out of bed. He waited.

"I wish I had never taken it out of the bank," he said to himself. "It was safe in the bank."

My heart throbbed fast; the pulses at my temples beat furiously. The doubt about the safety of the Diamond was, once more, the dominant impression in his brain! On that one pivot, the whole success of the experiment turned. The prospect thus suddenly opened before me was too much for my shattered nerves. I was obliged to look away from him—or I should have lost my self-control.

There was another interval of silence.

When I could trust myself to look back at him he was out of his bed, standing erect at the side of it. The pupils of his eyes were now contracted; his eyeballs gleamed in the light of the candle as he moved his head slowly to and fro. He was

The Moonstone

thinking; he was doubting—he spoke again.

"How do I know?" he said. "The Indians may be hidden in the house."

He stopped, and walked slowly to the other end of the room. He turned—waited—came back to the bed.

"It's not even locked up," he went on. "It's in the drawer of her cabinet. And the drawer doesn't lock."

He sat down on the side of the bed. "Anybody might take it," he said.

He rose again restlessly, and reiterated his first words.

"How do I know? The Indians may be hidden in the house."

He waited again. I drew back behind the half curtain of the bed. He looked about the room, with a vacant glitter in his eyes. It was a breathless moment. There was a pause of some sort. A pause in the action of the opium? a pause in the action of the brain? Who could tell? Everything depended, now, on what he did next.

He laid himself down again on the bed!

A horrible doubt crossed my mind. Was it possible that the sedative action of the opium was making itself felt already? It was not in my experience that it should do this. But what is experience, where opium is concerned? There are probably no two men in existence on whom the drug acts in exactly the same manner. Was some constitutional peculiarity in him, feeling the influence in some new way? Were we to fail on the very brink of success?

No! He got up again abruptly. "How the devil am I to sleep," he said, "with this on my mind?"

He looked at the light, burning on the table at the head of his bed. After a moment, he took the candle in his hand.

I blew out the second candle, burning behind the closed curtains. I drew back, with Mr. Bruff and Betteredge, into the farthest corner by the bed. I signed to them to be silent, as if their lives had depended on it.

We waited—seeing and hearing nothing. We waited, hidden

from him by the curtains.

The light which he was holding on the other side of us moved suddenly. The next moment he passed us, swift and noiseless, with the candle in his hand.

He opened the bedroom door, and went out.

We followed him along the corridor. We followed him down the stairs. We followed him along the second corridor. He never looked back; he never hesitated.

He opened the sitting-room door, and went in, leaving it open behind him.

The door was hung (like all the other doors in the house) on large old-fashioned hinges. When it was opened, a crevice was opened between the door and the post. I signed to my two companions to look through this, so as to keep them from showing themselves. I placed myself — outside the door also — on the opposite side. A recess in the wall was at my left hand, in which I could instantly hide myself, if he showed any signs of looking back into the corridor.

He advanced to the middle of the room, with the candle still in his hand: he looked about him — but he never looked back.

I saw the door of Miss Verinder's bedroom, standing ajar. She had put out her light. She controlled herself nobly. The dim white outline of her summer dress was all that I could see. Nobody who had not known it beforehand would have suspected that there was a living creature in the room. She kept back, in the dark: not a word, not a movement escaped her.

It was now ten minutes past one. I heard, through the dead silence, the soft drip of the rain and the tremulous passage of the night air through the trees.

After waiting irresolute, for a minute or more, in the middle of the room, he moved to the corner near the window, where the Indian cabinet stood.

He put his candle on the top of the cabinet. He opened, and shut, one drawer after another, until he came to the drawer in which the mock Diamond was put. He looked into the drawer for a moment. Then he took the mock Diamond out with his right hand. With the other hand, he took the candle from the top of the cabinet.

He walked back a few steps towards the middle of the room, and stood still again.

Thus far, he had exactly repeated what he had done on the birthday night. Would his next proceeding be the same as the proceeding of last year? Would he leave the room? Would he go back now, as I believed he had gone back then, to his bedchamber? Would he show us what he had done with the Diamond, when he had returned to his own room?

His first action, when he moved once more, proved to be an action which he had not performed, when he was under the influence of the opium for the first time. He put the candle down on a table, and wandered on a little towards the farther end of the room. There was a sofa there. He leaned heavily on the back of it, with his left hand — then roused himself, and returned to the middle of the room. I could now see his eyes. They were getting dull and heavy; the glitter in them was fast dying out.

The suspense of the moment proved too much for Miss Verinder's self-control. She advanced a few steps — then stopped again. Mr. Bruff and Betteredge looked across the open doorway at me for the first time. The prevision of a coming disappointment was impressing itself on their minds as well as on mine.

Still, so long as he stood where he was, there was hope. We waited, in unutterable expectation, to see what would happen next.

The next event was decisive. He let the mock Diamond drop out of his hand.

It fell on the floor, before the doorway — plainly visible to him, and to everyone. He made no effort to pick it up: he looked down at it vacantly, and, as he looked, his head sank on his breast. He staggered — roused himself for an instant — walked back unsteadily to the sofa — and sat down on it. He made a last effort; he tried to rise, and sank back. His head fell on the sofa cushions. It was then twenty-five minutes past one o'clock. Before I had put my watch back in my pocket, he was asleep.

It was all over now. The sedative influence had got him; the experiment was at an end.

I entered the room, telling Mr. Bruff and Betteredge that they might follow me. There was no fear of disturbing him. We were free to move and speak.

"The first thing to settle," I said, "is the question of what we are to do with him. He will probably sleep for the next six or seven hours, at least. It is some distance to carry him back to his own room. When I was younger, I could have done it alone. But my health and strength are not what they were—I am afraid I must ask you to help me."

Before they could answer, Miss Verinder called to me softly. She met me at the door of her room, with a light shawl, and with the counterpane from her own bed.

"Do you mean to watch him while he sleeps?" she asked.

"Yes, I am not sure enough of the action of the opium in his case to be willing to leave him alone."

She handed me the shawl and the counterpane.

"Why should you disturb him?" she whispered. "Make his bed on the sofa. I can shut my door, and keep in my room."

It was infinitely the simplest and the safest way of disposing of him for the night. I mentioned the suggestion to Mr. Bruff and Betteredge—who both approved of my adopting it. In five minutes I had laid him comfortably on the sofa, and had covered him lightly with the counterpane and the shawl. Miss Verinder wished us good-night, and closed the door. At my request, we three then drew round the table in the middle of the room, on which the candle was still burning, and on which writing materials were placed.

"Before we separate," I began, "I have a word to say about the experiment which has been tried tonight. Two distinct objects were to be gained by it. The first of these objects was to prove, that Mr. Blake entered this room, and took the Diamond, last year, acting unconsciously and irresponsibly, under the influence of opium. After what you have both seen, are you both satisfied, so far?"

They answered me in the affirmative, without a moment's hesitation.

"The second object," I went on, "was to discover what he did with the Diamond, after he was seen by Miss Verinder to leave her sitting-room with the jewel in his hand, on the birthday night. The gaining of this object depended, of course, on his still continuing exactly to repeat his proceedings of last year. He has failed to do that; and the purpose of the experiment is defeated accordingly. I can't assert that I am not disappointed at the result—but I can honestly say that I am not surprised by it. I told Mr. Blake from the first, that our complete success in this matter depended on our completely reproducing in him the physical and moral conditions of last year—and I warned him that this was the next thing to a downright impossibility. We have only partially reproduced the conditions, and the experiment has been only partially successful in consequence. It is also possible that I may have administered too large a dose of laudanum. But I myself look upon the first reason that I have given, as the true reason why we have to lament a failure, as well as to rejoice over a success."

After saying those words, I put the writing materials before Mr. Bruff, and asked him if he had any objection—before we separated for the night—to draw out, and sign, a plain statement of what he had seen. He at once took the pen, and produced the statement with the fluent readiness of a practised hand.

"I owe you this," he said, signing the paper, "as some atonement for what passed between us earlier in the evening. I beg your pardon, Mr. Jennings, for having doubted you. You have done Franklin Blake an inestimable service. In our legal phrase, you have proved your case."

Betteredge's apology was characteristic of the man.

"Mr. Jennings," he said, "when you read Robinson Crusoe again (which I strongly recommend you to do), you will find that he never scruples to acknowledge it, when he turns out to have been in the wrong. Please to consider me, sir, as doing what Robinson Crusoe did, on the present occasion." With those words he signed the paper in his turn.

Mr. Bruff took me aside, as we rose from the table.

"One word about the Diamond," he said. "Your theory is that Franklin Blake hid the Moonstone in his room. My theory is, that the Moonstone is in the possession of Mr. Luker's bankers in London. We won't dispute which of us is right. We will only ask, which of us is in a position to put his theory to the test?"

"The test, in my case," I answered, "has been tried tonight, and has failed."

"The test, in my case," rejoined Mr. Bruff, "is still in process of trial. For the last two days I have had a watch set for Mr. Luker at the bank; and I shall cause that watch to be continued until the last day of the month. I know that he must take the Diamond himself out of his bankers' hands—and I am acting on the chance that the person who has pledged the Diamond may force him to do this by redeeming the pledge. In that case I may be able to lay my hand on the person. If I succeed, I clear up the mystery, exactly at the point where the mystery baffles us now! Do you admit that, so far?"

I admitted it readily.

"I am going back to town by the morning train," pursued the lawyer. "I may hear, when I return, that a discovery has been made—and it may be of the greatest importance that I should have Franklin Blake at hand to appeal to, if necessary. I intend to tell him, as soon as he wakes, that he must return with me to London. After all that has happened, may I trust to your influence to back me?"

"Certainly!" I said.

Mr. Bruff shook hands with me, and left the room. Betteredge followed him out.

I went to the sofa to look at Mr. Blake. He had not moved since I had laid him down and made his bed—he lay locked in a deep and quiet sleep.

While I was still looking at him, I heard the bedroom door softly opened. Once more, Miss Verinder appeared on the threshold, in her pretty summer dress.

"Do me a last favour?" she whispered. "Let me watch him with you."

I hesitated—not in the interests of propriety; only in the interest of her night's rest. She came close to me, and took my

The Moonstone

hand.

"I can't sleep; I can't even sit still, in my own room," she said. "Oh, Mr. Jennings, if you were me, only think how you would long to sit and look at him. Say, yes! Do!"

Is it necessary to mention that I gave way? Surely not!

She drew a chair to the foot of the sofa. She looked at him in a silent ecstasy of happiness, till the tears rose in her eyes. She dried her eyes, and said she would fetch her work. She fetched her work, and never did a single stitch of it. It lay in her lap—she was not even able to look away from him long enough to thread her needle. I thought of my own youth; I thought of the gentle eyes which had once looked love at me. In the heaviness of my heart I turned to my Journal for relief, and wrote in it what is written here.

So we kept our watch together in silence. One of us absorbed in his writing; the other absorbed in her love.

Hour after hour he lay in his deep sleep. The light of the new day grew and grew in the room, and still he never moved.

Towards six o'clock, I felt the warning which told me that my pains were coming back. I was obliged to leave her alone with him for a little while. I said I would go upstairs, and fetch another pillow for him out of his room. It was not a long attack, this time. In a little while I was able to venture back, and let her see me again.

I found her at the head of the sofa, when I returned. She was just touching his forehead with her lips. I shook my head as soberly as I could, and pointed to her chair. She looked back at me with a bright smile, and a charming colour in her face. "You would have done it," she whispered, "in my place!"

It is just eight o'clock. He is beginning to move for the first time.

Miss Verinder is kneeling by the side of the sofa. She has so placed herself that when his eyes first open, they must open on her face.

Shall I leave them together?

Yes!

Eleven o'clock.—The house is empty again. They have arranged it among themselves; they have all gone to London by the ten o'clock train. My brief dream of happiness is over. I have awakened again to the realities of my friendless and lonely life.

I dare not trust myself to write down, the kind words that have been said to me especially by Miss Verinder and Mr. Blake. Besides, it is needless. Those words will come back to me in my solitary hours, and will help me through what is left of the end of my life. Mr. Blake is to write, and tell me what happens in London. Miss Verinder is to return to Yorkshire in the autumn (for her marriage, no doubt); and I am to take a holiday, and be a guest in the house. Oh me, how I felt, as the grateful happiness looked at me out of her eyes, and the warm pressure of her hand said, "This is your doing!"

My poor patients are waiting for me. Back again, this morning, to the old routine! Back again, tonight, to the dreadful alternative between the opium and the pain!

God be praised for His mercy! I have seen a little sunshine—I have had a happy time.

FIFTH NARRATIVE.

The Story resumed by Franklin Blake.

CHAPTER I

But few words are needed, on my part, to complete the narrative that has been presented in the Journal of Ezra Jennings.

Of myself, I have only to say that I awoke on the morning of the twenty-sixth, perfectly ignorant of all that I had said and done under the influence of the opium—from the time when the drug first laid its hold on me, to the time when I opened my eyes, in Rachel's sitting-room.

Of what happened after my waking, I do not feel called upon to render an account in detail. Confining myself merely to results, I have to report that Rachel and I thoroughly understood each other, before a single word of explanation had passed on either side. I decline to account, and Rachel declines to account, for the extraordinary rapidity of our reconciliation. Sir and Madam, look back at the time when you were passionately attached to each other—and you will know what happened, after Ezra Jennings had shut the door of the sitting-room, as well as I know it myself.

I have, however, no objection to add, that we should have been certainly discovered by Mrs. Merridew, but for Rachel's presence of mind. She heard the sound of the old lady's dress in the corridor, and instantly ran out to meet her; I heard Mrs. Merridew say, "What is the matter?" and I heard Rachel answer, "The explosion!" Mrs. Merridew instantly permitted herself to be taken by the arm, and led into the garden, out of the way of the impending shock. On her return to the house, she met me in the hall, and expressed herself as greatly struck by the vast improvement in Science, since the time when she was a girl at school. "Explosions, Mr. Blake, are infinitely milder than they were. I assure you, I barely heard Mr. Jennings's explosion from the garden. And no smell afterwards, that I can detect, now we have come back to the house! I must really apologise to your medical friend. It is only due to him to say that he has managed it beautifully!"

So, after vanquishing Betteredge and Mr. Bruff, Ezra

Jennings vanquished Mrs. Merridew herself. There is a great deal of undeveloped liberal feeling in the world, after all!

At breakfast, Mr. Bruff made no secret of his reasons for wishing that I should accompany him to London by the morning train. The watch kept at the bank, and the result which might yet come of it, appealed so irresistibly to Rachel's curiosity, that she at once decided (if Mrs. Merridew had no objection) on accompanying us back to town—so as to be within reach of the earliest news of our proceedings.

Mrs. Merridew proved to be all pliability and indulgence, after the truly considerate manner in which the explosion had conducted itself; and Betteredge was accordingly informed that we were all four to travel back together by the morning train. I fully expected that he would have asked leave to accompany us. But Rachel had wisely provided her faithful old servant with an occupation that interested him. He was charged with completing the refurnishing of the house, and was too full of his domestic responsibilities to feel the "detective-fever" as he might have felt it under other circumstances.

Our one subject of regret, in going to London, was the necessity of parting, more abruptly than we could have wished, with Ezra Jennings. It was impossible to persuade him to accompany us. I could only promise to write to him—and Rachel could only insist on his coming to see her when she returned to Yorkshire. There was every prospect of our meeting again in a few months—and yet there was something very sad in seeing our best and dearest friend left standing alone on the platform, as the train moved out of the station.

On our arrival in London, Mr. Bruff was accosted at the terminus by a small boy, dressed in a jacket and trousers of threadbare black cloth, and personally remarkable in virtue of the extraordinary prominence of his eyes. They projected so far, and they rolled about so loosely, that you wondered uneasily why they remained in their sockets. After listening to the boy, Mr. Bruff asked the ladies whether they would excuse our accompanying them back to Portland Place. I had barely time to promise Rachel that I would return, and tell her everything that had happened, before Mr. Bruff seized me by the arm, and hurried me into a cab. The boy with the ill-secured eyes took his place on the box by the driver, and the driver was directed to go

The Moonstone

to Lombard Street.

"News from the bank?" I asked, as we started.

"News of Mr. Luker," said Mr. Bruff. "An hour ago, he was seen to leave his house at Lambeth, in a cab, accompanied by two men, who were recognised by my men as police officers in plain clothes. If Mr. Luker's dread of the Indians is at the bottom of this precaution, the inference is plain enough. He is going to take the Diamond out of the bank."

"And we are going to the bank to see what comes of it?"

"Yes — or to hear what has come of it, if it is all over by this time. Did you notice my boy — on the box, there?"

"I noticed his eyes."

Mr. Bruff laughed. "They call the poor little wretch 'Gooseberry' at the office," he said. "I employ him to go on errands — and I only wish my clerks who have nick-named him were as thoroughly to be depended on as he is. Gooseberry is one of the sharpest boys in London, Mr. Blake, in spite of his eyes."

It was twenty minutes to five when we drew up before the bank in Lombard Street. Gooseberry looked longingly at his master, as he opened the cab door.

"Do you want to come in too?" asked Mr. Bruff kindly. "Come in then, and keep at my heels till further orders. He's as quick as lightning," pursued Mr. Bruff, addressing me in a whisper. "Two words will do with Gooseberry, where twenty would be wanted with another boy."

We entered the bank. The outer office — with the long counter, behind which the cashiers sat — was crowded with people; all waiting their turn to take money out, or to pay money in, before the bank closed at five o'clock.

Two men among the crowd approached Mr. Bruff, as soon as he showed himself.

"Well," asked the lawyer. "Have you seen him?"

"He passed us here half an hour since, sir, and went on into the inner office."

"Has he not come out again yet?"

"No, sir."

Mr. Bruff turned to me. "Let us wait," he said.

I looked round among the people about me for the three Indians. Not a sign of them was to be seen anywhere. The only person present with a noticeably dark complexion was a tall man in a pilot coat, and a round hat, who looked like a sailor. Could this be one of them in disguise? Impossible! The man was taller than any of the Indians; and his face, where it was not hidden by a bushy black beard, was twice the breadth of any of their faces at least.

"They must have their spy somewhere," said Mr. Bruff, looking at the dark sailor in his turn. "And he may be the man."

Before he could say more, his coat-tail was respectfully pulled by his attendant sprite with the gooseberry eyes. Mr. Bruff looked where the boy was looking. "Hush!" he said. "Here is Mr. Luker!"

The money-lender came out from the inner regions of the bank, followed by his two guardian policemen in plain clothes.

"Keep your eye on him," whispered Mr. Bruff. "If he passes the Diamond to anybody, he will pass it here."

Without noticing either of us, Mr. Luker slowly made his way to the door—now in the thickest, now in the thinnest part of the crowd. I distinctly saw his hand move, as he passed a short, stout man, respectably dressed in a suit of sober grey. The man started a little, and looked after him. Mr. Luker moved on slowly through the crowd. At the door his guard placed themselves on either side of him. They were all three followed by one of Mr. Bruff's men—and I saw them no more.

I looked round at the lawyer, and then looked significantly towards the man in the suit of sober grey. "Yes!" whispered Mr. Bruff, "I saw it too!" He turned about, in search of his second man. The second man was nowhere to be seen. He looked behind him for his attendant sprite. Gooseberry had disappeared.

"What the devil does it mean?" said Mr. Bruff angrily. "They have both left us at the very time when we want them most."

The Moonstone

It came to the turn of the man in the grey suit to transact his business at the counter. He paid in a cheque—received a receipt for it—and turned to go out.

"What is to be done?" asked Mr. Bruff. "We can't degrade ourselves by following him."

"I can!" I said. "I wouldn't lose sight of that man for ten thousand pounds!"

"In that case," rejoined Mr. Bruff, "I wouldn't lose sight of you, for twice the money. A nice occupation for a man in my position," he muttered to himself, as we followed the stranger out of the bank. "For Heaven's sake don't mention it. I should be ruined if it was known."

The man in the grey suit got into an omnibus, going westward. We got in after him. There were latent reserves of youth still left in Mr. Bruff. I assert it positively—when he took his seat in the omnibus, he blushed!

The man in the grey suit stopped the omnibus, and got out in Oxford Street. We followed him again. He went into a chemist's shop.

Mr. Bruff started. "My chemist!" he exclaimed. "I am afraid we have made a mistake."

We entered the shop. Mr. Bruff and the proprietor exchanged a few words in private. The lawyer joined me again, with a very crestfallen face.

"It's greatly to our credit," he said, as he took my arm, and led me out—"that's one comfort!"

"What is to our credit?" I asked.

"Mr. Blake! you and I are the two worst amateur detectives that ever tried their hands at the trade. The man in the grey suit has been thirty years in the chemist's service. He was sent to the bank to pay money to his master's account—and he knows no more of the Moonstone than the babe unborn."

I asked what was to be done next.

"Come back to my office," said Mr. Bruff. "Gooseberry, and my second man, have evidently followed somebody else. Let us hope that they had their eyes about them at any rate!"

When we reached Gray's Inn Square, the second man had arrived there before us. He had been waiting for more than a quarter of an hour.

"Well!" asked Mr. Bruff. "What's your news?"

"I am sorry to say, sir," replied the man, "that I have made a mistake. I could have taken my oath that I saw Mr. Luker pass something to an elderly gentleman, in a light-coloured paletot. The elderly gentleman turns out, sir, to be a most respectable master iron-monger in Eastcheap."

"Where is Gooseberry?" asked Mr. Bruff resignedly.

The man stared. "I don't know, sir. I have seen nothing of him since I left the bank."

Mr. Bruff dismissed the man. "One of two things," he said to me. "Either Gooseberry has run away, or he is hunting on his own account. What do you say to dining here, on the chance that the boy may come back in an hour or two? I have got some good wine in the cellar, and we can get a chop from the coffee-house."

We dined at Mr. Bruff's chambers. Before the cloth was removed, "a person" was announced as wanting to speak to the lawyer. Was the person Gooseberry? No: only the man who had been employed to follow Mr. Luker when he left the bank.

The report, in this case, presented no feature of the slightest interest. Mr. Luker had gone back to his own house, and had there dismissed his guard. He had not gone out again afterwards. Towards dusk, the shutters had been put up, and the doors had been bolted. The street before the house, and the alley behind the house, had been carefully watched. No signs of the Indians had been visible. No person whatever had been seen loitering about the premises. Having stated these facts, the man waited to know whether there were any further orders. Mr. Bruff dismissed him for the night.

"Do you think Mr. Luker has taken the Moonstone home with him?" I asked.

"Not he," said Mr. Bruff. "He would never have dismissed his two policemen, if he had run the risk of keeping the Diamond in his own house again."

The Moonstone

We waited another half-hour for the boy, and waited in vain. It was then time for Mr. Bruff to go to Hampstead, and for me to return to Rachel in Portland Place. I left my card, in charge of the porter at the chambers, with a line written on it to say that I should be at my lodgings at half past ten, that night. The card was to be given to the boy, if the boy came back.

Some men have a knack of keeping appointments; and other men have a knack of missing them. I am one of the other men. Add to this, that I passed the evening at Portland Place, on the same seat with Rachel, in a room forty feet long, with Mrs. Merridew at the further end of it. Does anybody wonder that I got home at half past twelve instead of half past ten? How thoroughly heartless that person must be! And how earnestly I hope I may never make that person's acquaintance!

My servant handed me a morsel of paper when he let me in.

I read, in a neat legal handwriting, these words—"If you please, sir, I am getting sleepy. I will come back tomorrow morning, between nine and ten." Inquiry proved that a boy, with very extraordinary-looking eyes, had called, and presented my card and message, had waited an hour, had done nothing but fall asleep and wake up again, had written a line for me, and had gone home—after gravely informing the servant that "he was fit for nothing unless he got his night's rest."

At nine, the next morning, I was ready for my visitor. At half past nine, I heard steps outside my door. "Come in, Gooseberry!" I called out. "Thank you, sir," answered a grave and melancholy voice. The door opened. I started to my feet, and confronted—Sergeant Cuff!

"I thought I would look in here, Mr. Blake, on the chance of your being in town, before I wrote to Yorkshire," said the Sergeant.

He was as dreary and as lean as ever. His eyes had not lost their old trick (so subtly noticed in Betteredge's Narrative) of "looking as if they expected something more from you than you were aware of yourself." But, so far as dress can alter a man, the great Cuff was changed beyond all recognition. He wore a broad-brimmed white hat, a light shooting jacket, white trousers, and drab gaiters. He carried a stout oak stick. His whole aim and object seemed to be to look as if he had lived in the country all his life. When I complimented him on his Metamorphosis, he declined to take it as a joke. He complained, quite gravely, of the noises and the smells of London. I declare I am far from sure that he did not speak with a slightly rustic accent! I offered him breakfast. The innocent countryman was quite shocked. His breakfast hour was half-past six—and he went to bed with the cocks and hens!

"I only got back from Ireland last night," said the Sergeant, coming round to the practical object of his visit, in his own impenetrable manner. "Before I went to bed, I read your letter, telling me what has happened since my inquiry after the Diamond was suspended last year. There's only one thing to be said about the matter on my side. I completely mistook my case. How any man living was to have seen things in their true light, in such a situation as mine was at the time, I don't profess to know. But that doesn't alter the facts as they stand. I own that I made a mess of it. Not the first mess, Mr. Blake, which has distinguished my professional career! It's only in books that the officers of the detective force are superior to the weakness of making a mistake."

"You have come in the nick of time to recover your reputation," I said.

"I beg your pardon, Mr. Blake," rejoined the Sergeant. "Now I have retired from business, I don't care a straw about my reputation. I have done with my reputation, thank God! I am here, sir, in grateful remembrance of the late Lady Verinder's liberality to me. I will go back to my old work—if you want me, and if you will trust me—on that consideration, and on no other. Not a farthing of money is to pass, if you please, from you to me. This is on honour. Now tell me, Mr. Blake, how the case stands since you wrote to me last."

I told him of the experiment with the opium, and of what had occurred afterwards at the bank in Lombard Street. He was greatly struck by the experiment—it was something entirely new in his experience. And he was particularly interested in the theory of Ezra Jennings, relating to what I had done with the Diamond, after I had left Rachel's sitting-room, on the birthday night.

"I don't hold with Mr. Jennings that you hid the

The Moonstone

Moonstone," said Sergeant Cuff. "But I agree with him, that you must certainly have taken it back to your own room."

"Well?" I asked. "And what happened then?"

"Have you no suspicion yourself of what happened, sir?"

"None whatever."

"Has Mr. Bruff no suspicion?"

"No more than I have."

Sergeant Cuff rose, and went to my writing-table. He came back with a sealed envelope. It was marked "Private;" it was addressed to me; and it had the Sergeant's signature in the corner.

"I suspected the wrong person, last year," he said: "and I may be suspecting the wrong person now. Wait to open the envelope, Mr. Blake, till you have got at the truth. And then compare the name of the guilty person, with the name that I have written in that sealed letter."

I put the letter into my pocket—and then asked for the Sergeant's opinion of the measures which we had taken at the bank.

"Very well intended, sir," he answered, "and quite the right thing to do. But there was another person who ought to have been looked after besides Mr. Luker."

"The person named in the letter you have just given to me?"

"Yes, Mr. Blake, the person named in the letter. It can't be helped now. I shall have something to propose to you and Mr. Bruff, sir, when the time comes. Let's wait, first, and see if the boy has anything to tell us that is worth hearing."

It was close on ten o'clock, and the boy had not made his appearance. Sergeant Cuff talked of other matters. He asked after his old friend Betteredge, and his old enemy the gardener. In a minute more, he would no doubt have got from this, to the subject of his favourite roses, if my servant had not interrupted us by announcing that the boy was below.

On being brought into the room, Gooseberry stopped at the threshold of the door, and looked distrustfully at the stranger who was in my company. I told the boy to come to me.

"You may speak before this gentleman," I said. "He is here to assist me; and he knows all that has happened. Sergeant Cuff," I added, "this is the boy from Mr. Bruff's office."

In our modern system of civilisation, celebrity (no matter of what kind) is the lever that will move anything. The fame of the great Cuff had even reached the ears of the small Gooseberry. The boy's ill-fixed eyes rolled, when I mentioned the illustrious name, till I thought they really must have dropped on the carpet.

"Come here, my lad," said the Sergeant, "and let's hear what you have got to tell us."

The notice of the great man—the hero of many a famous story in every lawyer's office in London—appeared to fascinate the boy. He placed himself in front of Sergeant Cuff, and put his hands behind him, after the approved fashion of a neophyte who is examined in his catechism.

"What is your name?" said the Sergeant, beginning with the first question in the catechism.

"Octavius Guy," answered the boy. "They call me Gooseberry at the office because of my eyes."

"Octavius Guy, otherwise Gooseberry," pursued the Sergeant, with the utmost gravity, "you were missed at the bank yesterday. What were you about?"

"If you please, sir, I was following a man."

"Who was he?"

"A tall man, sir, with a big black beard, dressed like a sailor."

"I remember the man!" I broke in. "Mr. Bruff and I thought he was a spy employed by the Indians."

Sergeant Cuff did not appear to be much impressed by what Mr. Bruff and I had thought. He went on catechising Gooseberry.

"Well?" he said—"and why did you follow the sailor?"

"If you please, sir, Mr. Bruff wanted to know whether Mr.

496

Luker passed anything to anybody on his way out of the bank. I saw Mr. Luker pass something to the sailor with the black beard."

"Why didn't you tell Mr. Bruff what you saw?"

"I hadn't time to tell anybody, sir, the sailor went out in such a hurry."

"And you ran out after him—eh?"

"Yes, sir."

"Gooseberry," said the Sergeant, patting his head, "you have got something in that small skull of yours—and it isn't cotton-wool. I am greatly pleased with you, so far."

The boy blushed with pleasure. Sergeant Cuff went on.

"Well? and what did the sailor do, when he got into the street?"

"He called a cab, sir."

"And what did you do?"

"Held on behind, and run after it."

Before the Sergeant could put his next question, another visitor was announced—the head clerk from Mr. Bruff's office.

Feeling the importance of not interrupting Sergeant Cuff's examination of the boy, I received the clerk in another room. He came with bad news of his employer. The agitation and excitement of the last two days had proved too much for Mr. Bruff. He had awoke that morning with an attack of gout; he was confined to his room at Hampstead; and, in the present critical condition of our affairs, he was very uneasy at being compelled to leave me without the advice and assistance of an experienced person. The chief clerk had received orders to hold himself at my disposal, and was willing to do his best to replace Mr. Bruff.

I wrote at once to quiet the old gentleman's mind, by telling him of Sergeant Cuff's visit: adding that Gooseberry was at that moment under examination; and promising to inform Mr. Bruff, either personally, or by letter, of whatever might occur later in the day. Having despatched the clerk to Hampstead with my note, I returned to the room which I had left, and found Sergeant Cuff at the fireplace, in the act of ringing the bell.

"I beg your pardon, Mr. Blake," said the Sergeant. "I was just going to send word by your servant that I wanted to speak to you. There isn't a doubt on my mind that this boy—this most meritorious boy," added the Sergeant, patting Gooseberry on the head, "has followed the right man. Precious time has been lost, sir, through your unfortunately not being at home at half past ten last night. The only thing to do, now, is to send for a cab immediately."

In five minutes more, Sergeant Cuff and I (with Gooseberry on the box to guide the driver) were on our way eastward, towards the City.

"One of these days," said the Sergeant, pointing through the front window of the cab, "that boy will do great things in my late profession. He is the brightest and cleverest little chap I have met with, for many a long year past. You shall hear the substance, Mr. Blake, of what he told me while you were out of the room. You were present, I think, when he mentioned that he held on behind the cab, and ran after it?"

"Yes."

"Well, sir, the cab went from Lombard Street to the Tower Wharf. The sailor with the black beard got out, and spoke to the steward of the Rotterdam steamboat, which was to start next morning. He asked if he could be allowed to go on board at once, and sleep in his berth over-night. The steward said, No. The cabins, and berths, and bedding were all to have a thorough cleaning that evening, and no passenger could be allowed to come on board, before the morning. The sailor turned round, and left the wharf. When he got into the street again, the boy noticed for the first time, a man dressed like a respectable mechanic, walking on the opposite side of the road, and apparently keeping the sailor in view. The sailor stopped at an eating-house in the neighbourhood, and went in. The boy—not being able to make up his mind, at the moment—hung about among some other boys, staring at the good things in the eating-house window. He noticed the mechanic waiting, as he himself was waiting—but still on the opposite side of the street. After a minute, a cab came by slowly, and stopped where the mechanic was standing. The boy could only see plainly one person in the cab, who leaned forward at the window to speak to the mechanic. He described that person, Mr. Blake, without any prompting from me, as having a dark face, like the face of an Indian."

It was plain, by this time, that Mr. Bruff and I had made another mistake. The sailor with the black beard was clearly not a spy in the service of the Indian conspiracy. Was he, by any possibility, the man who had got the Diamond?

"After a little," pursued the Sergeant, "the cab moved on slowly down the street. The mechanic crossed the road, and went into the eating-house. The boy waited outside till he was hungry and tired—and then went into the eating-house, in his turn. He had a shilling in his pocket; and he dined sumptuously, he tells me, on a black-pudding, an eel-pie, and a bottle of ginger-beer. What can a boy not digest? The substance in question has never been found yet."

"What did he see in the eating-house?" I asked.

"Well, Mr. Blake, he saw the sailor reading the newspaper at one table, and the mechanic reading the newspaper at another. It was dusk before the sailor got up, and left the place. He looked about him suspiciously when he got out into the street. The boy—being a boy—passed unnoticed. The mechanic had not come out yet. The sailor walked on, looking about him, and apparently not very certain of where he was going next. The mechanic appeared once more, on the opposite side of the road. The sailor went on, till he got to Shore Lane, leading into Lower Thames Street. There he stopped before a public-house, under the sign of 'The Wheel of Fortune,' and, after examining the place outside, went in. Gooseberry went in too. There were a great many people, mostly of the decent sort, at the bar. 'The Wheel of Fortune' is a very respectable house, Mr. Blake; famous for its porter and pork-pies."

The Sergeant's digressions irritated me. He saw it; and confined himself more strictly to Gooseberry's evidence when he went on.

"The sailor," he resumed, "asked if he could have a bed. The landlord said 'No; they were full.' The barmaid corrected him, and said 'Number Ten was empty.' A waiter was sent for to show the sailor to Number Ten. Just before that, Gooseberry had noticed the mechanic among the people at the bar. Before the waiter had answered the call, the mechanic had vanished. The sailor was taken off to his room. Not knowing what to do next, Gooseberry had the wisdom to wait and see if anything happened. Something did happen. The landlord was called for. Angry voices were heard upstairs. The mechanic suddenly made his appearance again, collared by the landlord, and exhibiting, to Gooseberry's great surprise, all the signs and tokens of being drunk. The landlord thrust him out at the door, and threatened him with the police if he came back. From the altercation between them, while this was going on, it appeared that the man had been discovered in Number Ten, and had declared with drunken obstinacy that he had taken the room. Gooseberry was so struck by this sudden intoxication of a previously sober person, that he couldn't resist running out after the mechanic into the street. As long as he was in sight of the public-house, the man reeled about in the most disgraceful manner. The moment he turned the corner of the street, he recovered his balance instantly, and became as sober a member of society as you could wish to see. Gooseberry went back to 'The Wheel of Fortune' in a very bewildered state of mind. He waited about again, on the chance of something happening. Nothing happened; and nothing more was to be heard, or seen, of the sailor. Gooseberry decided on going back to the office. Just as he came to this conclusion, who should appear, on the opposite side of the street as usual, but the mechanic again! He looked up at one particular window at the top of the public-house, which was the only one that had a light in it. The light seemed to relieve his mind. He left the place directly. The boy made his way back to Gray's Inn—got your card and message—called—and failed to find you. There you have the state of the case, Mr. Blake, as it stands at the present time."

"What is your own opinion of the case, Sergeant?"

"I think it's serious, sir. Judging by what the boy saw, the Indians are in it, to begin with."

"Yes. And the sailor is evidently the person to whom Mr. Luker passed the Diamond. It seems odd that Mr. Bruff, and I, and the man in Mr. Bruff's employment, should all have been mistaken about who the person was."

"Not at all, Mr. Blake. Considering the risk that person ran, it's likely enough that Mr. Luker purposely misled you, by previous arrangement between them."

"Do you understand the proceedings at the public-house?" I asked. "The man dressed like a mechanic was acting of course in the employment of the Indians. But I am as much puzzled to account for his sudden assumption of drunkenness as Gooseberry himself."

"I think I can give a guess at what it means, sir," said the Sergeant. "If you will reflect, you will see that the man must have had some pretty strict instructions from the Indians. They were far too noticeable themselves to risk being seen at the bank, or in the public-house—they were obliged to trust everything to their deputy. Very good. Their deputy hears a certain number named in the public-house, as the number of the room which the sailor is to have for the night—that being also the room (unless our notion is all wrong) which the Diamond is to have for the night, too. Under those circumstances, the Indians, you may rely on it, would insist on having a description of the room—of its position in the house, of its capability of being approached from the outside, and so on. What was the man to do, with such orders as these? Just what he did! He ran upstairs to get a look at the room, before the sailor was taken into it. He was found there, making his observations—and he shammed drunk, as the easiest way of getting out of the difficulty. That's how I read the riddle. After he was turned out of the public-house, he probably went with his report to the place where his employers were waiting for him. And his employers, no doubt, sent him back to make sure that the sailor was really settled at the public-house till the next morning. As for what happened at 'The Wheel of Fortune,' after the boy left—we ought to have discovered that last night. It's eleven in the morning, now. We must hope for the best, and find out what we can."

In a quarter of an hour more, the cab stopped in Shore Lane, and Gooseberry opened the door for us to get out.

"All right?" asked the Sergeant.

"All right," answered the boy.

The moment we entered "The Wheel of Fortune" it was

plain even to my inexperienced eyes that there was something wrong in the house.

The only person behind the counter at which the liquors were served, was a bewildered servant girl, perfectly ignorant of the business. One or two customers, waiting for their morning drink, were tapping impatiently on the counter with their money. The barmaid appeared from the inner regions of the parlour, excited and preoccupied. She answered Sergeant Cuff's inquiry for the landlord, by telling him sharply that her master was upstairs, and was not to be bothered by anybody.

"Come along with me, sir," said Sergeant Cuff, coolly leading the way upstairs, and beckoning to the boy to follow him.

The barmaid called to her master, and warned him that strangers were intruding themselves into the house. On the first floor we were encountered by the landlord, hurrying down, in a highly irritated state, to see what was the matter.

"Who the devil are you? and what do you want here?" he asked.

"Keep your temper," said the Sergeant, quietly. "I'll tell you who I am to begin with. I am Sergeant Cuff."

The illustrious name instantly produced its effect. The angry landlord threw open the door of a sitting-room, and asked the Sergeant's pardon.

"I am annoyed and out of sorts, sir—that's the truth," he said. "Something unpleasant has happened in the house this morning. A man in my way of business has a deal to upset his temper, Sergeant Cuff."

"Not a doubt of it," said the Sergeant. "I'll come at once, if you will allow me, to what brings us here. This gentleman and I want to trouble you with a few inquiries, on a matter of some interest to both of us."

"Relating to what, sir?" asked the landlord.

"Relating to a dark man, dressed like a sailor, who slept here last night."

"Good God! that's the man who is upsetting the whole

The Moonstone

house at this moment!" exclaimed the landlord. "Do you, or does this gentleman know anything about him?"

"We can't be certain till we see him," answered the Sergeant.

"See him?" echoed the landlord. "That's the one thing that nobody has been able to do since seven o'clock this morning. That was the time when he left word, last night, that he was to be called. He was called—and there was no getting an answer from him, and no opening his door to see what was the matter. They tried again at eight, and they tried again at nine. No use! There was the door still locked—and not a sound to be heard in the room! I have been out this morning—and I only got back a quarter of an hour ago. I have hammered at the door myself—and all to no purpose. The potboy has gone to fetch a carpenter. If you can wait a few minutes, gentlemen, we will have the door opened, and see what it means."

"Was the man drunk last night?" asked Sergeant Cuff.

"Perfectly sober, sir—or I would never have let him sleep in my house."

"Did he pay for his bed beforehand?"

"No."

"Could he leave the room in any way, without going out by the door?"

"The room is a garret," said the landlord. "But there's a trap-door in the ceiling, leading out on to the roof—and a little lower down the street, there's an empty house under repair. Do you think, Sergeant, the blackguard has got off in that way, without paying?"

"A sailor," said Sergeant Cuff, "might have done it—early in the morning, before the street was astir. He would be used to climbing, and his head wouldn't fail him on the roofs of the houses."

As he spoke, the arrival of the carpenter was announced. We all went upstairs, at once, to the top story. I noticed that the Sergeant was unusually grave, even for him. It also struck me as odd that he told the boy (after having previously encouraged him to follow us), to wait in the room below till we came down again.

The carpenter's hammer and chisel disposed of the resistance of the door in a few minutes. But some article of furniture had been placed against it inside, as a barricade. By pushing at the door, we thrust this obstacle aside, and so got admission to the room. The landlord entered first; the Sergeant second; and I third. The other persons present followed us.

We all looked towards the bed, and all started.

The man had not left the room. He lay, dressed, on the bed — with a white pillow over his face, which completely hid it from view.

"What does that mean?" said the landlord, pointing to the pillow.

Sergeant Cuff led the way to the bed, without answering, and removed the pillow.

The man's swarthy face was placid and still; his black hair and beard were slightly, very slightly, discomposed. His eyes stared wide-open, glassy and vacant, at the ceiling. The filmy look and the fixed expression of them horrified me. I turned away, and went to the open window. The rest of them remained, where Sergeant Cuff remained, at the bed.

"He's in a fit!" I heard the landlord say.

"He's dead," the Sergeant answered. "Send for the nearest doctor, and send for the police."

The waiter was despatched on both errands. Some strange fascination seemed to hold Sergeant Cuff to the bed. Some strange curiosity seemed to keep the rest of them waiting, to see what the Sergeant would do next.

I turned again to the window. The moment afterwards, I felt a soft pull at my coat-tails, and a small voice whispered, "Look here, sir!"

Gooseberry had followed us into the room. His loose eyes rolled frightfully — not in terror, but in exultation. He had made a detective-discovery on his own account. "Look here, sir," he repeated — and led me to a table in the corner of the room.

On the table stood a little wooden box, open, and empty. On one side of the box lay some jewellers' cotton. On the other side,

The Moonstone

was a torn sheet of white paper, with a seal on it, partly destroyed, and with an inscription in writing, which was still perfectly legible. The inscription was in these words:

"Deposited with Messrs. Bushe, Lysaught, and Bushe, by Mr. Septimus Luker, of Middlesex Place, Lambeth, a small wooden box, sealed up in this envelope, and containing a valuable of great price. The box, when claimed, to be only given up by Messrs. Bushe and Co. on the personal application of Mr. Luker."

Those lines removed all further doubt, on one point at least. The sailor had been in possession of the Moonstone, when he had left the bank on the previous day.

I felt another pull at my coat-tails. Gooseberry had not done with me yet.

"Robbery!" whispered the boy, pointing, in high delight, to the empty box.

"You were told to wait downstairs," I said. "Go away!"

"And Murder!" added Gooseberry, pointing, with a keener relish still, to the man on the bed.

There was something so hideous in the boy's enjoyment of the horror of the scene, that I took him by the two shoulders and put him out of the room.

At the moment when I crossed the threshold of the door, I heard Sergeant Cuff's voice, asking where I was. He met me, as I returned into the room, and forced me to go back with him to the bedside.

"Mr. Blake!" he said. "Look at the man's face. It is a face disguised—and here's the proof of it!"

He traced with his finger a thin line of livid white, running backward from the dead man's forehead, between the swarthy complexion, and the slightly-disturbed black hair. "Let's see what is under this," said the Sergeant, suddenly seizing the black hair, with a firm grip of his hand.

My nerves were not strong enough to bear it. I turned away again from the bed.

The first sight that met my eyes, at the other end of the

room, was the irrepressible Gooseberry, perched on a chair, and looking with breathless interest, over the heads of his elders, at the Sergeant's proceedings.

"He's pulling off his wig!" whispered Gooseberry, compassionating my position, as the only person in the room who could see nothing.

There was a pause—and then a cry of astonishment among the people round the bed.

"He's pulled off his beard!" cried Gooseberry.

There was another pause—Sergeant Cuff asked for something. The landlord went to the wash-hand-stand, and returned to the bed with a basin of water and a towel.

Gooseberry danced with excitement on the chair. "Come up here, along with me, sir! He's washing off his complexion now!"

The Sergeant suddenly burst his way through the people about him, and came, with horror in his face, straight to the place where I was standing.

"Come back to the bed, sir!" he began. He looked at me closer, and checked himself "No!" he resumed. "Open the sealed letter first—the letter I gave you this morning."

I opened the letter.

"Read the name, Mr. Blake, that I have written inside."

I read the name that he had written. It was—Godfrey Ablewhite.

"Now," said the Sergeant, "come with me, and look at the man on the bed."

I went with him, and looked at the man on the bed.

GODFREY ABLEWHITE!
SIXTH NARRATIVE.

Contributed by Sergeant Cuff.

I

Dorking, Surrey, July 30th, 1849. To Franklin Blake, Esq. Sir, —I beg to apologise for the delay that has occurred in the production of the Report, with which I engaged to furnish you. I have waited to make it a complete Report; and I have been met, here and there, by obstacles which it was only possible to remove by some little expenditure of patience and time.

The object which I proposed to myself has now, I hope, been attained. You will find, in these pages, answers to the greater part—if not all—of the questions, concerning the late Mr. Godfrey Ablewhite, which occurred to your mind when I last had the honour of seeing you.

I propose to tell you—in the first place—what is known of the manner in which your cousin met his death; appending to the statement such inferences and conclusions as we are justified (according to my opinion) in drawing from the facts.

I shall then endeavour—in the second place—to put you in possession of such discoveries as I have made, respecting the proceedings of Mr. Godfrey Ablewhite, before, during and after the time, when you and he met as guests at the late Lady Verinder's country house.

II

As to your cousin's death, then, first.

It appears to be established, beyond any reasonable doubt, that he was killed (while he was asleep, or immediately on his waking) by being smothered with a pillow from his bed—that the persons guilty of murdering him are the three Indians—and that the object contemplated (and achieved) by the crime, was to obtain possession of the diamond, called the Moonstone.

The facts from which this conclusion is drawn, are derived partly from an examination of the room at the tavern; and partly from the evidence obtained at the Coroner's Inquest.

On forcing the door of the room, the deceased gentleman was discovered, dead, with the pillow of the bed over his face. The medical man who examined him, being informed of this circumstance, considered the post-mortem appearances as being perfectly compatible with murder by smothering—that is to say, with murder committed by some person, or persons, pressing the pillow over the nose and mouth of the deceased, until death resulted from congestion of the lungs.

Next, as to the motive for the crime.

A small box, with a sealed paper torn off from it (the paper containing an inscription) was found open, and empty, on a table in the room. Mr. Luker has himself personally identified the box, the seal, and the inscription. He has declared that the box did actually contain the diamond, called the Moonstone; and he has admitted having given the box (thus sealed up) to Mr. Godfrey Ablewhite (then concealed under a disguise), on the afternoon of the twenty-sixth of June last. The fair inference from all this is, that the stealing of the Moonstone was the motive of the crime.

Next, as to the manner in which the crime was committed.

On examination of the room (which is only seven feet high), a trap-door in the ceiling, leading out on to the roof of the house, was discovered open. The short ladder, used for obtaining access to the trap-door (and kept under the bed), was found placed at the opening, so as to enable any person or persons, in the room, to leave it again easily. In the trap-door itself was found a square aperture cut in the wood, apparently with some exceedingly sharp instrument, just behind the bolt which fastened the door on the inner side. In this way, any person from the outside could have drawn back the bolt, and opened the door, and have dropped (or have been noiselessly lowered by an accomplice) into the room—its height, as already observed, being only seven feet. That some person, or persons, must have got admission in this way, appears evident from the fact of the aperture being there. As to the manner in which he (or they) obtained access to the roof of the tavern, it is to be remarked that the third house, lower down in the street, was empty, and under repair—that a long ladder was left by the workmen, leading from the pavement to the top of the house— and that, on returning to their work, on the morning of the 27th,

The Moonstone

the men found the plank which they had tied to the ladder, to prevent anyone from using it in their absence, removed, and lying on the ground. As to the possibility of ascending by this ladder, passing over the roofs of the houses, passing back, and descending again, unobserved—it is discovered, on the evidence of the night policeman, that he only passes through Shore Lane twice in an hour, when out on his beat. The testimony of the inhabitants also declares, that Shore Lane, after midnight, is one of the quietest and loneliest streets in London. Here again, therefore, it seems fair to infer that—with ordinary caution, and presence of mind—any man, or men, might have ascended by the ladder, and might have descended again, unobserved. Once on the roof of the tavern, it has been proved, by experiment, that a man might cut through the trap-door, while lying down on it, and that in such a position, the parapet in front of the house would conceal him from the view of anyone passing in the street.

Lastly, as to the person, or persons, by whom the crime was committed.

It is known (1) that the Indians had an interest in possessing themselves of the Diamond. (2) It is at least probable that the man looking like an Indian, whom Octavius Guy saw at the window of the cab, speaking to the man dressed like a mechanic, was one of the three Hindoo conspirators. (3) It is certain that this same man dressed like a mechanic, was seen keeping Mr. Godfrey Ablewhite in view, all through the evening of the 26th, and was found in the bedroom (before Mr. Ablewhite was shown into it) under circumstances which lead to the suspicion that he was examining the room. (4) A morsel of torn gold thread was picked up in the bedroom, which persons expert in such matters, declare to be of Indian manufacture, and to be a species of gold thread not known in England. (5) On the morning of the 27th, three men, answering to the description of the three Indians, were observed in Lower Thames Street, were traced to the Tower Wharf, and were seen to leave London by the steamer bound for Rotterdam.

There is here, moral, if not legal, evidence, that the murder was committed by the Indians.

Whether the man personating a mechanic was, or was not, an accomplice in the crime, it is impossible to say. That he could have committed the murder alone, seems beyond the limits of probability. Acting by himself, he could hardly have smothered Mr. Ablewhite—who was the taller and stronger man of the two—without a struggle taking place, or a cry being heard. A servant girl, sleeping in the next room, heard nothing. The landlord, sleeping in the room below, heard nothing. The whole evidence points to the inference that more than one man was concerned in this crime—and the circumstances, I repeat, morally justify the conclusion that the Indians committed it.

I have only to add, that the verdict at the Coroner's Inquest was Wilful Murder against some person, or persons, unknown. Mr. Ablewhite's family have offered a reward, and no effort has been left untried to discover the guilty persons. The man dressed like a mechanic has eluded all inquiries. The Indians have been traced. As to the prospect of ultimately capturing these last, I shall have a word to say to you on that head, when I reach the end of the present Report.

In the meanwhile, having now written all that is needful on the subject of Mr. Godfrey Ablewhite's death, I may pass next to the narrative of his proceedings before, during, and after the time, when you and he met at the late Lady Verinder's house.

III

With regard to the subject now in hand, I may state, at the outset, that Mr. Godfrey Ablewhite's life had two sides to it.

The side turned up to the public view, presented the spectacle of a gentleman, possessed of considerable reputation as a speaker at charitable meetings, and endowed with administrative abilities, which he placed at the disposal of various Benevolent Societies, mostly of the female sort. The side kept hidden from the general notice, exhibited this same gentleman in the totally different character of a man of pleasure, with a villa in the suburbs which was not taken in his own name, and with a lady in the villa, who was not taken in his own name, either.

My investigations in the villa have shown me several fine pictures and statues; furniture tastefully selected, and admirably made; and a conservatory of the rarest flowers, the match of which it would not be easy to find in all London. My investigation of the lady has resulted in the discovery of jewels which are worthy to take rank with the flowers, and of carriages and horses which have (deservedly) produced a sensation in the Park, among persons well qualified to judge of the build of the one, and the breed of the others.

All this is, so far, common enough. The villa and the lady are such familiar objects in London life, that I ought to apologise for introducing them to notice. But what is not common and not familiar (in my experience), is that all these fine things were not only ordered, but paid for. The pictures, the statues, the flowers, the jewels, the carriages, and the horses—inquiry proved, to my indescribable astonishment, that not a sixpence of debt was owing on any of them. As to the villa, it had been bought, out and out, and settled on the lady.

I might have tried to find the right reading of this riddle, and tried in vain—but for Mr. Godfrey Ablewhite's death, which caused an inquiry to be made into the state of his affairs.

The inquiry elicited these facts:—

That Mr. Godfrey Ablewhite was entrusted with the care of a sum of twenty thousand pounds—as one of two Trustees for a young gentleman, who was still a minor in the year eighteen hundred and forty-eight. That the Trust was to lapse, and that the young gentleman was to receive the twenty thousand pounds on the day when he came of age, in the month of February, eighteen hundred and fifty. That, pending the arrival of this period, an income of six hundred pounds was to be paid to him by his two Trustees, half-yearly—at Christmas and Midsummer Day. That this income was regularly paid by the active Trustee, Mr. Godfrey Ablewhite. That the twenty thousand pounds (from which the income was supposed to be derived) had every farthing of it been sold out of the Funds, at different periods, ending with the end of the year eighteen hundred and forty-seven. That the power of attorney, authorising the bankers to sell out the stock, and the various written orders telling them what amounts to sell out, were formally signed by both the Trustees. That the signature of the second Trustee (a retired army officer, living in the country) was a signature forged, in every case, by the active Trustee— otherwise Mr. Godfrey Ablewhite.

In these facts lies the explanation of Mr. Godfrey's honourable conduct, in paying the debts incurred for the lady and the villa—and (as you will presently see) of more besides.

We may now advance to the date of Miss Verinder's birthday (in the year eighteen hundred and forty-eight)—the twenty-first of June.

On the day before, Mr. Godfrey Ablewhite arrived at his father's house, and asked (as I know from Mr. Ablewhite, senior, himself) for a loan of three hundred pounds. Mark the sum; and remember at the same time, that the half-yearly payment to the young gentleman was due on the twenty-fourth of the month. Also, that the whole of the young gentleman's fortune had been spent by his Trustee, by the end of the year 'forty-seven.

Mr. Ablewhite, senior, refused to lend his son a farthing.

The next day Mr. Godfrey Ablewhite rode over, with you, to Lady Verinder's house. A few hours afterwards, Mr. Godfrey (as you yourself have told me) made a proposal of marriage to Miss Verinder. Here, he saw his way no doubt—if accepted—to the end of all his money anxieties, present and future. But, as events actually turned out, what happened? Miss Verinder refused him.

On the night of the birthday, therefore, Mr. Godfrey Ablewhite's pecuniary position was this. He had three hundred pounds to find on the twenty-fourth of the month, and twenty thousand pounds to find in February eighteen hundred and fifty. Failing to raise these sums, at these times, he was a ruined man.

Under those circumstances, what takes place next?

You exasperate Mr. Candy, the doctor, on the sore subject of his profession; and he plays you a practical joke, in return, with a dose of laudanum. He trusts the administration of the dose, prepared in a little phial, to Mr. Godfrey Ablewhite—who has himself confessed the share he had in the matter, under circumstances which shall presently be related to you. Mr. Godfrey is all the readier to enter into the conspiracy, having himself suffered from your sharp tongue in the course of the evening. He joins Betteredge in persuading you to drink a little brandy and water before you go to bed. He privately drops the dose of laudanum into your cold grog. And you drink the mixture.

Let us now shift the scene, if you please to Mr. Luker's house at Lambeth. And allow me to remark, by way of preface, that Mr. Bruff and I, together, have found a means of forcing the money-lender to make a clean breast of it. We have carefully sifted the statement he has addressed to us; and here it is at your service.

IV

Late on the evening of Friday, the twenty-third of June ('forty-eight), Mr. Luker was surprised by a visit from Mr. Godfrey Ablewhite. He was more than surprised, when Mr. Godfrey produced the Moonstone. No such Diamond (according to Mr. Luker's experience) was in the possession of any private person in Europe.

Mr. Godfrey Ablewhite had two modest proposals to make, in relation to this magnificent gem. First, Would Mr. Luker be so good as to buy it? Secondly, Would Mr. Luker (in default of seeing his way to the purchase) undertake to sell it on commission, and to pay a sum down, on the anticipated result?

Mr. Luker tested the Diamond, weighed the Diamond and estimated the value of the Diamond, before he answered a word. His estimate (allowing for the flaw in the stone) was thirty thousand pounds.

Having reached that result, Mr. Luker opened his lips, and put a question: "How did you come by this?" Only six words! But what volumes of meaning in them!

Mr. Godfrey Ablewhite began a story. Mr. Luker opened his lips again, and only said three words, this time. "That won't do!"

Mr. Godfrey Ablewhite began another story. Mr. Luker wasted no more words on him. He got up, and rang the bell for the servant to show the gentleman out.

Upon this compulsion, Mr. Godfrey made an effort, and came out with a new and amended version of the affair, to the following effect.

After privately slipping the laudanum into your brandy and water, he wished you good-night, and went into his own room. It was the next room to yours; and the two had a door of communication between them. On entering his own room Mr. Godfrey (as he supposed) closed his door. His money troubles kept him awake. He sat, in his dressing-gown and slippers, for nearly an hour, thinking over his position. Just as he was preparing to get into bed, he heard you, talking to yourself, in your own room, and going to the door of communication, found that he had not shut it as he supposed.

He looked into your room to see what was the matter. He discovered you with the candle in your hand, just leaving your bedchamber. He heard you say to yourself, in a voice quite unlike your own voice, "How do I know? The Indians may be hidden in the house."

Up to that time, he had simply supposed himself (in giving you the laudanum) to be helping to make you the victim of a harmless practical joke. It now occurred to him, that the laudanum had taken some effect on you, which had not been foreseen by the doctor, any more than by himself. In the fear of an accident happening he followed you softly to see what you would do.

He followed you to Miss Verinder's sitting-room, and saw you go in. You left the door open. He looked through the crevice thus produced, between the door and the post, before he ventured into the room himself.

In that position, he not only detected you in taking the Diamond out of the drawer—he also detected Miss Verinder, silently watching you from her bedroom, through her open door. His own eyes satisfied him that she saw you take the Diamond, too.

Before you left the sitting-room again, you hesitated a little. Mr. Godfrey took advantage of this hesitation to get back again to his bedroom before you came out, and discovered him. He had barely got back, before you got back too. You saw him (as he supposes) just as he was passing through the door of communication. At any rate, you called to him in a strange, drowsy voice.

He came back to you. You looked at him in a dull sleepy

The Moonstone

way. You put the Diamond into his hand. You said to him, "Take it back, Godfrey, to your father's bank. It's safe there—it's not safe here." You turned away unsteadily, and put on your dressing-gown. You sat down in the large arm-chair in your room. You said, "I can't take it back to the bank. My head's like lead—and I can't feel my feet under me." Your head sank on the back of the chair—you heaved a heavy sigh—and you fell asleep.

Mr. Godfrey Ablewhite went back, with the Diamond, into his own room. His statement is, that he came to no conclusion, at that time—except that he would wait, and see what happened in the morning.

When the morning came, your language and conduct showed that you were absolutely ignorant of what you had said and done overnight. At the same time, Miss Verinder's language and conduct showed that she was resolved to say nothing (in mercy to you) on her side. If Mr. Godfrey Ablewhite chose to keep the Diamond, he might do so with perfect impunity. The Moonstone stood between him and ruin. He put the Moonstone into his pocket.

V

This was the story told by your cousin (under pressure of necessity) to Mr. Luker.

Mr. Luker believed the story to be, as to all main essentials, true—on this ground, that Mr. Godfrey Ablewhite was too great a fool to have invented it. Mr. Bruff and I agree with Mr. Luker, in considering this test of the truth of the story to be a perfectly reliable one.

The next question, was the question of what Mr. Luker would do in the matter of the Moonstone. He proposed the following terms, as the only terms on which he would consent to mix himself up with, what was (even in his line of business) a doubtful and dangerous transaction.

Mr. Luker would consent to lend Mr. Godfrey Ablewhite the sum of two thousand pounds, on condition that the Moonstone was to be deposited with him as a pledge. If, at the expiration of one year from that date, Mr. Godfrey Ablewhite paid three thousand pounds to Mr. Luker, he was to receive back the

Diamond, as a pledge redeemed. If he failed to produce the money at the expiration of the year, the pledge (otherwise the Moonstone) was to be considered as forfeited to Mr. Luker— who would, in this latter case, generously make Mr. Godfrey a present of certain promissory notes of his (relating to former dealings) which were then in the money-lender's possession.

It is needless to say, that Mr. Godfrey indignantly refused to listen to these monstrous terms. Mr. Luker thereupon, handed him back the Diamond, and wished him good-night.

Your cousin went to the door, and came back again. How was he to be sure that the conversation of that evening would be kept strictly secret between his friend and himself?

Mr. Luker didn't profess to know how. If Mr. Godfrey had accepted his terms, Mr. Godfrey would have made him an accomplice, and might have counted on his silence as on a certainty. As things were, Mr. Luker must be guided by his own interests. If awkward inquiries were made, how could he be expected to compromise himself, for the sake of a man who had declined to deal with him?

Receiving this reply, Mr. Godfrey Ablewhite did, what all animals (human and otherwise) do, when they find themselves caught in a trap. He looked about him in a state of helpless despair. The day of the month, recorded on a neat little card in a box on the money-lender's chimney-piece, happened to attract his eye. It was the twenty-third of June. On the twenty-fourth he had three hundred pounds to pay to the young gentleman for whom he was trustee, and no chance of raising the money, except the chance that Mr. Luker had offered to him. But for this miserable obstacle, he might have taken the Diamond to Amsterdam, and have made a marketable commodity of it, by having it cut up into separate stones. As matters stood, he had no choice but to accept Mr. Luker's terms. After all, he had a year at his disposal, in which to raise the three thousand pounds—and a year is a long time.

Mr. Luker drew out the necessary documents on the spot. When they were signed, he gave Mr. Godfrey Ablewhite two cheques. One, dated June 23rd, for three hundred pounds. Another, dated a week on, for the remaining balance seventeen hundred pounds.

The Moonstone

How the Moonstone was trusted to the keeping of Mr Luker's bankers, and how the Indians treated Mr. Luker and Mr. Godfrey (after that had been done) you know already.

The next event in your cousin's life refers again to Miss Verinder. He proposed marriage to her for the second time — and (after having being accepted) he consented, at her request, to consider the marriage as broken off. One of his reasons for making this concession has been penetrated by Mr. Bruff. Miss Verinder had only a life interest in her mother's property — and there was no raising the twenty thousand pounds on that.

But you will say, he might have saved the three thousand pounds, to redeem the pledged Diamond, if he had married. He might have done so certainly — supposing neither his wife, nor her guardians and trustees, objected to his anticipating more than half of the income at his disposal, for some unknown purpose, in the first year of his marriage. But even if he got over this obstacle, there was another waiting for him in the background. The lady at the Villa, had heard of his contemplated marriage. A superb woman, Mr. Blake, of the sort that are not to be trifled with — the sort with the light complexion and the Roman nose. She felt the utmost contempt for Mr. Godfrey Ablewhite. It would be silent contempt, if he made a handsome provision for her. Otherwise, it would be contempt with a tongue to it. Miss Verinder's life interest allowed him no more hope of raising the "provision" than of raising the twenty thousand pounds. He couldn't marry — he really couldn't marry, under all the circumstances.

How he tried his luck again with another lady, and how that marriage also broke down on the question of money, you know already. You also know of the legacy of five thousand pounds, left to him shortly afterwards, by one of those many admirers among the soft sex whose good graces this fascinating man had contrived to win. That legacy (as the event has proved) led him to his death.

I have ascertained that when he went abroad, on getting his five thousand pounds, he went to Amsterdam. There he made all the necessary arrangements for having the Diamond cut into separate stones. He came back (in disguise), and redeemed the Moonstone, on the appointed day. A few days were allowed to elapse (as a precaution agreed to by both parties) before the jewel was actually taken out of the bank. If he had got safe with it to Amsterdam, there would have been just time between July 'forty-nine, and February 'fifty (when the young gentleman came of age) to cut the Diamond, and to make a marketable commodity (polished or unpolished) of the separate stones. Judge from this, what motives he had to run the risk which he actually ran. It was "neck or nothing" with him—if ever it was "neck or nothing" with a man yet.

I have only to remind you, before closing this Report, that there is a chance of laying hands on the Indians, and of recovering the Moonstone yet. They are now (there is every reason to believe) on their passage to Bombay, in an East Indiaman. The ship (barring accidents) will touch at no other port on her way out; and the authorities at Bombay (already communicated with by letter, overland) will be prepared to board the vessel, the moment she enters the harbour.

I have the honour to remain, dear sir, your obedient servant, RICHARD CUFF (late sergeant in the Detective Force, Scotland Yard, London).*

* NOTE.—Wherever the Report touches on the events of the birthday, or of the three days that followed it, compare with Betteredge's Narrative, chapters viii. to xiii.

SEVENTH NARRATIVE.

In a Letter from Mr. Candy.

Frizinghall, Wednesday, September 26th, 1849. — Dear Mr. Franklin Blake, you will anticipate the sad news I have to tell you, on finding your letter to Ezra Jennings returned to you, unopened, in this enclosure. He died in my arms, at sunrise, on Wednesday last.

I am not to blame for having failed to warn you that his end was at hand. He expressly forbade me to write to you. "I am indebted to Mr. Franklin Blake," he said, "for having seen some happy days. Don't distress him, Mr. Candy — don't distress him."

His sufferings, up to the last six hours of his life, were terrible to see. In the intervals of remission, when his mind was clear, I entreated him to tell me of any relatives of his to whom I might write. He asked to be forgiven for refusing anything to me. And then he said — not bitterly — that he would die as he had lived, forgotten and unknown. He maintained that resolution to the last. There is no hope now of making any discoveries concerning him. His story is a blank.

The day before he died, he told me where to find all his papers. I brought them to him on his bed. There was a little bundle of old letters which he put aside. There was his unfinished book. There was his Diary — in many locked volumes. He opened the volume for this year, and tore out, one by one, the pages relating to the time when you and he were together. "Give those," he said, "to Mr. Franklin Blake. In years to come, he may feel an interest in looking back at what is written there." Then he clasped his hands, and prayed God fervently to bless you, and those dear to you. He said he should like to see you again. But the next moment he altered his mind. "No," he answered when I offered to write. "I won't distress him! I won't distress him!"

At his request I next collected the other papers — that is to say, the bundle of letters, the unfinished book and the volumes of the Diary — and enclosed them all in one wrapper, sealed with my own seal. "Promise," he said, "that you will put this into my coffin with your own hand; and that you will see that no other hand touches it afterwards."

I gave him my promise. And the promise has been performed.

He asked me to do one other thing for him — which it cost me a hard struggle to comply with. He said, "Let my grave be forgotten. Give me your word of honour that you will allow no monument of any sort — not even the commonest tombstone — to mark the place of my burial. Let me sleep, nameless. Let me rest, unknown." When I tried to plead with him to alter his resolution, he became for the first, and only time, violently agitated. I could not bear to see it; and I gave way. Nothing but a little grass mound marks the place of his rest. In time, the tombstones will rise round it. And the people who come after us will look and wonder at the nameless grave.

As I have told you, for six hours before his death his sufferings ceased. He dozed a little. I think he dreamed. Once or twice he smiled. A woman's name, as I suppose — the name of "Ella" — was often on his lips at this time. A few minutes before the end he asked me to lift him on his pillow, to see the sun rise through the window. He was very weak. His head fell on my shoulder. He whispered, "It's coming!" Then he said, "Kiss me!" I kissed his forehead. On a sudden he lifted his head. The sunlight touched his face. A beautiful expression, an angelic expression, came over it. He cried out three times, "Peace! peace! peace!" His head sank back again on my shoulder, and the long trouble of his life was at an end.

So he has gone from us. This was, as I think, a great man — though the world never knew him. He had the sweetest temper I have ever met with. The loss of him makes me feel very lonely. Perhaps I have never been quite myself since my illness. Sometimes, I think of giving up my practice, and going away, and trying what some of the foreign baths and waters will do for me.

It is reported here, that you and Miss Verinder are to be married next month. Please to accept my best congratulations.

The pages of my poor friend's Journal are waiting for you at my house — sealed up, with your name on the wrapper. I was afraid to trust them to the post.

My best respects and good wishes attend Miss Verinder. I remain, dear Mr. Franklin Blake, truly yours,

THOMAS CANDY.

EIGHTH NARRATIVE.

Contributed by Gabriel Betteredge.

I am the person (as you remember no doubt) who led the way in these pages, and opened the story. I am also the person who is left behind, as it were, to close the story up.

Let nobody suppose that I have any last words to say here concerning the Indian Diamond. I hold that unlucky jewel in abhorrence—and I refer you to other authority than mine, for such news of the Moonstone as you may, at the present time, be expected to receive. My purpose, in this place, is to state a fact in the history of the family, which has been passed over by everybody, and which I won't allow to be disrespectfully smothered up in that way. The fact to which I allude is—the marriage of Miss Rachel and Mr. Franklin Blake. This interesting event took place at our house in Yorkshire, on Tuesday, October ninth, eighteen hundred and forty-nine. I had a new suit of clothes on the occasion. And the married couple went to spend the honeymoon in Scotland.

Family festivals having been rare enough at our house, since my poor mistress's death, I own—on this occasion of the wedding—to having (towards the latter part of the day) taken a drop too much on the strength of it.

If you have ever done the same sort of thing yourself you will understand and feel for me. If you have not, you will very likely say, "Disgusting old man! why does he tell us this?" The reason why is now to come.

Having, then, taken my drop (bless you! you have got your favourite vice, too; only your vice isn't mine, and mine isn't yours), I next applied the one infallible remedy—that remedy being, as you know, Robinson Crusoe. Where I opened that unrivalled book, I can't say. Where the lines of print at last left off running into each other, I know, however, perfectly well. It was at page three hundred and eighteen—a domestic bit concerning Robinson Crusoe's marriage, as follows:

"With those Thoughts, I considered my new Engagement, that I had a Wife"—(Observe! so had Mr. Franklin!)—"one Child born"—(Observe again! that might yet be Mr. Franklin's case, too!)—"and my Wife then"—What Robinson Crusoe's wife

The Moonstone

did, or did not do, "then," I felt no desire to discover. I scored the bit about the Child with my pencil, and put a morsel of paper for a mark to keep the place; "Lie you there," I said, "till the marriage of Mr. Franklin and Miss Rachel is some months older — and then we'll see!"

The months passed (more than I had bargained for), and no occasion presented itself for disturbing that mark in the book. It was not till this present month of November, eighteen hundred and fifty, that Mr. Franklin came into my room, in high good spirits, and said, "Betteredge! I have got some news for you! Something is going to happen in the house, before we are many months older."

"Does it concern the family, sir?" I asked.

"It decidedly concerns the family," says Mr. Franklin.

"Has your good lady anything to do with it, if you please, sir?"

"She has a great deal to do with it," says Mr. Franklin, beginning to look a little surprised.

"You needn't say a word more, sir," I answered. "God bless you both! I'm heartily glad to hear it."

Mr. Franklin stared like a person thunderstruck. "May I venture to inquire where you got your information?" he asked. "I only got mine (imparted in the strictest secrecy) five minutes since."

Here was an opportunity of producing Robinson Crusoe! Here was a chance of reading that domestic bit about the child which I had marked on the day of Mr. Franklin's marriage! I read those miraculous words with an emphasis which did them justice, and then I looked him severely in the face. "Now, sir, do you believe in Robinson Crusoe?" I asked, with a solemnity, suitable to the occasion.

"Betteredge!" says Mr. Franklin, with equal solemnity, "I'm convinced at last." He shook hands with me — and I felt that I had converted him.

With the relation of this extraordinary circumstance, my reappearance in these pages comes to an end. Let nobody laugh at the unique anecdote here related. You are welcome to be as merry as you please over everything else I have written. But when I write of Robinson Crusoe, by the Lord it's serious—and I request you to take it accordingly!

When this is said, all is said. Ladies and gentlemen, I make my bow, and shut up the story.

EPILOGUE.

THE FINDING OF THE DIAMOND.

I

THE STATEMENT OF SERGEANT CUFF'S MAN. (1849.)

On the twenty-seventh of June last, I received instructions from Sergeant Cuff to follow three men; suspected of murder, and described as Indians. They had been seen on the Tower Wharf that morning, embarking on board the steamer bound for Rotterdam.

I left London by a steamer belonging to another company, which sailed on the morning of Thursday the twenty-eighth. Arriving at Rotterdam, I succeeded in finding the commander of the Wednesday's steamer. He informed me that the Indians had certainly been passengers on board his vessel—but as far as Gravesend only. Off that place, one of the three had inquired at what time they would reach Calais. On being informed that the steamer was bound to Rotterdam, the spokesman of the party expressed the greatest surprise and distress at the mistake which he and his two friends had made. They were all willing (he said) to sacrifice their passage money, if the commander of the steamer would only put them ashore. Commiserating their position, as foreigners in a strange land, and knowing no reason for detaining them, the commander signalled for a shore boat, and the three men left the vessel.

This proceeding of the Indians having been plainly resolved on beforehand, as a means of preventing their being traced, I lost no time in returning to England. I left the steamer at Gravesend, and discovered that the Indians had gone from that place to London. Thence, I again traced them as having left for Plymouth. Inquiries made at Plymouth proved that they had sailed, forty-eight hours previously, in the Bewley Castle, East Indiaman, bound direct to Bombay.

On receiving this intelligence, Sergeant Cuff caused the authorities at Bombay to be communicated with, overland—so that the vessel might be boarded by the police immediately on her entering the port. This step having been taken, my connection with the matter came to an end. I have heard nothing more of it since that time.

II

THE STATEMENT OF THE CAPTAIN. (1849.)

I am requested by Sergeant Cuff to set in writing certain facts, concerning three men (believed to be Hindoos) who were passengers, last summer, in the ship Bewley Castle, bound for Bombay direct, under my command.

The Hindoos joined us at Plymouth. On the passage out I heard no complaint of their conduct. They were berthed in the forward part of the vessel. I had but few occasions myself of personally noticing them.

In the latter part of the voyage, we had the misfortune to be becalmed for three days and nights, off the coast of India. I have not got the ship's journal to refer to, and I cannot now call to mind the latitude and longitude. As to our position, therefore, I am only able to state generally that the currents drifted us in towards the land, and that when the wind found us again, we reached our port in twenty-four hours afterwards.

The discipline of a ship (as all seafaring persons know) becomes relaxed in a long calm. The discipline of my ship became relaxed. Certain gentlemen among the passengers got some of the smaller boats lowered, and amused themselves by rowing about, and swimming, when the sun at evening time was cool enough to let them divert themselves in that way. The boats when done with ought to have been slung up again in their places. Instead of this they were left moored to the ship's side. What with the heat, and what with the vexation of the weather, neither officers nor men seemed to be in heart for their duty while the calm lasted.

On the third night, nothing unusual was heard or seen by the watch on deck. When the morning came, the smallest of the boats was missing—and the three Hindoos were next reported to be missing, too.

If these men had stolen the boat shortly after dark (which I have no doubt they did), we were near enough to the land to make it vain to send in pursuit of them, when the discovery was made in the morning. I have no doubt they got ashore, in that calm weather (making all due allowance for fatigue and clumsy rowing), before day-break.

On reaching our port, I there learnt, for the first time, the reason these passengers had for seizing their opportunity of escaping from the ship. I could only make the same statement to the authorities which I have made here. They considered me to blame for allowing the discipline of the vessel to be relaxed. I have expressed my regret on this score to them, and to my owners.

Since that time, nothing has been heard to my knowledge of the three Hindoos. I have no more to add to what is here written.

III

THE STATEMENT OF MR. MURTHWAITE. (1850.)

(In a letter to Mr. Bruff.)

Have you any recollection, my dear sir, of a semi-savage person whom you met out at dinner, in London, in the autumn of 'forty-eight? Permit me to remind you that the person's name was Murthwaite, and that you and he had a long conversation together after dinner. The talk related to an Indian Diamond, called the Moonstone, and to a conspiracy then in existence to get possession of the gem.

Since that time, I have been wandering in Central Asia. Thence I have drifted back to the scene of some of my past adventures in the north and north-west of India. About a fortnight since, I found myself in a certain district or province (but little known to Europeans) called Kattiawar.

Here an adventure befell me, in which (incredible as it may appear) you are personally interested.

In the wild regions of Kattiawar (and how wild they are, you will understand, when I tell you that even the husbandmen plough the land, armed to the teeth), the population is fanatically devoted to the old Hindoo religion — to the ancient worship of Bramah and Vishnu. The few Mahometan families, thinly scattered about the villages in the interior, are afraid to taste meat of any kind. A Mahometan even suspected of killing that sacred animal, the cow, is, as a matter of course, put to death without mercy in these parts by the pious Hindoo neighbours who surround him. To strengthen the religious enthusiasm of the people, two of the most famous shrines of Hindoo pilgrimage are contained within the boundaries of Kattiawar. One of them is Dwarka, the birthplace of the god Krishna. The other is the sacred city of Somnauth—sacked, and destroyed as long since as the eleventh century, by the Mahometan conqueror, Mahmoud of Ghizni.

Finding myself, for the second time, in these romantic regions, I resolved not to leave Kattiawar, without looking once more on the magnificent desolation of Somnauth. At the place where I planned to do this, I was (as nearly as I could calculate it) some three days distant, journeying on foot, from the sacred city.

I had not been long on the road, before I noticed that other people—by twos and threes—appeared to be travelling in the same direction as myself.

To such of these as spoke to me, I gave myself out as a Hindoo-Boodhist, from a distant province, bound on a pilgrimage. It is needless to say that my dress was of the sort to carry out this description. Add, that I know the language as well as I know my own, and that I am lean enough and brown enough to make it no easy matter to detect my European origin—and you will understand that I passed muster with the people readily: not as one of themselves, but as a stranger from a distant part of their own country.

On the second day, the number of Hindoos travelling in my direction had increased to fifties and hundreds. On the third day, the throng had swollen to thousands; all slowly converging to one point—the city of Somnauth.

A trifling service which I was able to render to one of my fellow-pilgrims, during the third day's journey, proved the means of introducing me to certain Hindoos of the higher caste. From these men I learnt that the multitude was on its way to a great religious ceremony, which was to take place on a hill at a little distance from Somnauth. The ceremony was in honour of

The Moonstone

the god of the Moon; and it was to be held at night.

The crowd detained us as we drew near to the place of celebration. By the time we reached the hill the moon was high in the heaven. My Hindoo friends possessed some special privileges which enabled them to gain access to the shrine. They kindly allowed me to accompany them. When we arrived at the place, we found the shrine hidden from our view by a curtain hung between two magnificent trees. Beneath the trees a flat projection of rock jutted out, and formed a species of natural platform. Below this, I stood, in company with my Hindoo friends.

Looking back down the hill, the view presented the grandest spectacle of Nature and Man, in combination, that I have ever seen. The lower slopes of the eminence melted imperceptibly into a grassy plain, the place of the meeting of three rivers. On one side, the graceful winding of the waters stretched away, now visible, now hidden by trees, as far as the eye could see. On the other, the waveless ocean slept in the calm of the night. People this lovely scene with tens of thousands of human creatures, all dressed in white, stretching down the sides of the hill, overflowing into the plain, and fringing the nearer banks of the winding rivers. Light this halt of the pilgrims by the wild red flames of cressets and torches, streaming up at intervals from every part of the innumerable throng. Imagine the moonlight of the East, pouring in unclouded glory over all — and you will form some idea of the view that met me when I looked forth from the summit of the hill.

A strain of plaintive music, played on stringed instruments and flutes, recalled my attention to the hidden shrine.

I turned, and saw on the rocky platform the figures of three men. In the central figure of the three I recognised the man to whom I had spoken in England, when the Indians appeared on the terrace at Lady Verinder's house. The other two who had been his companions on that occasion were no doubt his companions also on this.

One of the spectators, near whom I was standing, saw me start. In a whisper, he explained to me the apparition of the three figures on the platform of rock.

They were Brahmins (he said) who had forfeited their caste

in the service of the god. The god had commanded that their purification should be the purification by pilgrimage. On that night, the three men were to part. In three separate directions, they were to set forth as pilgrims to the shrines of India. Never more were they to look on each other's faces. Never more were they to rest on their wanderings, from the day which witnessed their separation, to the day which witnessed their death.

As those words were whispered to me, the plaintive music ceased. The three men prostrated themselves on the rock, before the curtain which hid the shrine. They rose—they looked on one another—they embraced. Then they descended separately among the people. The people made way for them in dead silence. In three different directions I saw the crowd part, at one and the same moment. Slowly the grand white mass of the people closed together again. The track of the doomed men through the ranks of their fellow mortals was obliterated. We saw them no more.

A new strain of music, loud and jubilant, rose from the hidden shrine. The crowd around me shuddered, and pressed together.

The curtain between the trees was drawn aside, and the shrine was disclosed to view.

There, raised high on a throne—seated on his typical antelope, with his four arms stretching towards the four corners of the earth—there, soared above us, dark and awful in the mystic light of heaven, the god of the Moon. And there, in the forehead of the deity, gleamed the yellow Diamond, whose splendour had last shone on me in England, from the bosom of a woman's dress!

Yes! after the lapse of eight centuries, the Moonstone looks forth once more, over the walls of the sacred city in which its story first began. How it has found its way back to its wild native land—by what accident, or by what crime, the Indians regained possession of their sacred gem, may be in your knowledge, but is not in mine. You have lost sight of it in England, and (if I know anything of this people) you have lost sight of it for ever.

So the years pass, and repeat each other; so the same events revolve in the cycles of time. What will be the next adventures

The Moonstone

of the Moonstone? Who can tell?

FINIS

Carmilla

By Joseph Sheridan Le Fanu

PROLOGUE

Upon a paper attached to the Narrative which follows, Doctor Hesselius has written a rather elaborate note, which he accompanies with a reference to his Essay on the strange subject which the MS. illuminates.

This mysterious subject he treats, in that Essay, with his usual learning and acumen, and with remarkable directness and condensation. It will form but one volume of the series of that extraordinary man's collected papers.

As I publish the case, in this volume, simply to interest the "laity," I shall forestall the intelligent lady, who relates it, in nothing; and after due consideration, I have determined, therefore, to abstain from presenting any précis of the learned Doctor's reasoning, or extract from his statement on a subject which he describes as "involving, not improbably, some of the profoundest arcana of our dual existence, and its intermediates."

I was anxious on discovering this paper, to reopen the correspondence commenced by Doctor Hesselius, so many years before, with a person so clever and careful as his informant seems to have been. Much to my regret, however, I found that she had died in the interval.

She, probably, could have added little to the Narrative which she communicates in the following pages, with, so far as I can pronounce, such conscientious particularity.

I.

An Early Fright

In Styria, we, though by no means magnificent people, inhabit a castle, or schloss. A small income, in that part of the world, goes a great way. Eight or nine hundred a year does wonders. Scantily enough ours would have answered among wealthy people at home. My father is English, and I bear an English name, although I never saw England. But here, in this lonely and primitive place, where everything is so marvelously cheap, I really don't see how ever so much more money would at all materially add to our comforts, or even luxuries.

My father was in the Austrian service, and retired upon a pension and his patrimony, and purchased this feudal residence, and the small estate on which it stands, a bargain.

Nothing can be more picturesque or solitary. It stands on a slight eminence in a forest. The road, very old and narrow, passes in front of its drawbridge, never raised in my time, and its moat, stocked with perch, and sailed over by many swans, and floating on its surface white fleets of water lilies.

Over all this the schloss shows its many-windowed front; its towers, and its Gothic chapel.

The forest opens in an irregular and very picturesque glade before its gate, and at the right a steep Gothic bridge carries the road over a stream that winds in deep shadow through the wood. I have said that this is a very lonely place. Judge whether I say truth. Looking from the hall door towards the road, the forest in which our castle stands extends fifteen miles to the right, and twelve to the left. The nearest inhabited village is about seven of your English miles to the left. The nearest inhabited schloss of any historic associations, is that of old General Spielsdorf, nearly twenty miles away to the right.

I have said "the nearest inhabited village," because there is, only three miles westward, that is to say in the direction of General Spielsdorf's schloss, a ruined village, with its quaint little church, now roofless, in the aisle of which are the moldering tombs of the proud family of Karnstein, now extinct, who once owned the equally desolate chateau which, in the thick of the forest, overlooks the silent ruins of the town.

Respecting the cause of the desertion of this striking and melancholy spot, there is a legend which I shall relate to you another time.

I must tell you now, how very small is the party who constitute the inhabitants of our castle. I don't include servants, or those dependents who occupy rooms in the buildings attached to the schloss. Listen, and wonder! My father, who is the kindest man on earth, but growing old; and I, at the date of my story, only nineteen. Eight years have passed since then.

I and my father constituted the family at the schloss. My mother, a Styrian lady, died in my infancy, but I had a good-natured governess, who had been with me from, I might almost say, my infancy. I could not remember the time when her fat, benignant face was not a familiar picture in my memory.

This was Madame Perrodon, a native of Berne, whose care and good nature now in part supplied to me the loss of my mother, whom I do not even remember, so early I lost her. She made a third at our little dinner party. There was a fourth, Mademoiselle De Lafontaine, a lady such as you term, I believe, a "finishing governess." She spoke French and German, Madame Perrodon French and broken English, to which my father and I added English, which, partly to prevent its becoming a lost language among us, and partly from patriotic motives, we spoke every day. The consequence was a Babel, at which strangers used to laugh, and which I shall make no attempt to reproduce in this narrative. And there were two or three young lady friends besides, pretty nearly of my own age, who were occasional visitors, for longer or shorter terms; and these visits I sometimes returned.

These were our regular social resources; but of course there were chance visits from "neighbors" of only five or six leagues distance. My life was, notwithstanding, rather a solitary one, I can assure you.

My gouvernantes had just so much control over me as you might conjecture such sage persons would have in the case of a rather spoiled girl, whose only parent allowed her pretty nearly her own way in everything.

Carmilla

The first occurrence in my existence, which produced a terrible impression upon my mind, which, in fact, never has been effaced, was one of the very earliest incidents of my life which I can recollect. Some people will think it so trifling that it should not be recorded here. You will see, however, by-and-by, why I mention it. The nursery, as it was called, though I had it all to myself, was a large room in the upper story of the castle, with a steep oak roof. I can't have been more than six years old, when one night I awoke, and looking round the room from my bed, failed to see the nursery maid. Neither was my nurse there; and I thought myself alone. I was not frightened, for I was one of those happy children who are studiously kept in ignorance of ghost stories, of fairy tales, and of all such lore as makes us cover up our heads when the door cracks suddenly, or the flicker of an expiring candle makes the shadow of a bedpost dance upon the wall, nearer to our faces. I was vexed and insulted at finding myself, as I conceived, neglected, and I began to whimper, preparatory to a hearty bout of roaring; when to my surprise, I saw a solemn, but very pretty face looking at me from the side of the bed. It was that of a young lady who was kneeling, with her hands under the coverlet. I looked at her with a kind of pleased wonder, and ceased whimpering. She caressed me with her hands, and lay down beside me on the bed, and drew me towards her, smiling; I felt immediately delightfully soothed, and fell asleep again. I was wakened by a sensation as if two needles ran into my breast very deep at the same moment, and I cried loudly. The lady started back, with her eyes fixed on me, and then slipped down upon the floor, and, as I thought, hid herself under the bed.

I was now for the first time frightened, and I yelled with all my might and main. Nurse, nursery maid, housekeeper, all came running in, and hearing my story, they made light of it, soothing me all they could meanwhile. But, child as I was, I could perceive that their faces were pale with an unwonted look of anxiety, and I saw them look under the bed, and about the room, and peep under tables and pluck open cupboards; and the housekeeper whispered to the nurse: "Lay your hand along that hollow in the bed; someone did lie there, so sure as you did not; the place is still warm."

I remember the nursery maid petting me, and all three examining my chest, where I told them I felt the puncture, and pronouncing that there was no sign visible that any such thing had happened to me.

The housekeeper and the two other servants who were in charge of the nursery, remained sitting up all night; and from that time a servant always sat up in the nursery until I was about fourteen.

I was very nervous for a long time after this. A doctor was called in, he was pallid and elderly. How well I remember his long saturnine face, slightly pitted with smallpox, and his chestnut wig. For a good while, every second day, he came and gave me medicine, which of course I hated.

The morning after I saw this apparition I was in a state of terror, and could not bear to be left alone, daylight though it was, for a moment.

I remember my father coming up and standing at the bedside, and talking cheerfully, and asking the nurse a number of questions, and laughing very heartily at one of the answers; and patting me on the shoulder, and kissing me, and telling me not to be frightened, that it was nothing but a dream and could not hurt me.

But I was not comforted, for I knew the visit of the strange woman was not a dream; and I was awfully frightened.

I was a little consoled by the nursery maid's assuring me that it was she who had come and looked at me, and lain down beside me in the bed, and that I must have been half-dreaming not to have known her face. But this, though supported by the nurse, did not quite satisfy me.

I remembered, in the course of that day, a venerable old man, in a black cassock, coming into the room with the nurse and housekeeper, and talking a little to them, and very kindly to me; his face was very sweet and gentle, and he told me they were going to pray, and joined my hands together, and desired me to say, softly, while they were praying, "Lord hear all good prayers for us, for Jesus' sake." I think these were the very words, for I often repeated them to myself, and my nurse used for years to make me say them in my prayers.

I remembered so well the thoughtful sweet face of that white-haired old man, in his black cassock, as he stood in that

Carmilla

rude, lofty, brown room, with the clumsy furniture of a fashion three hundred years old about him, and the scanty light entering its shadowy atmosphere through the small lattice. He kneeled, and the three women with him, and he prayed aloud with an earnest quavering voice for, what appeared to me, a long time. I forget all my life preceding that event, and for some time after it is all obscure also, but the scenes I have just described stand out vivid as the isolated pictures of the phantasmagoria surrounded by darkness.

II.

A Guest

I am now going to tell you something so strange that it will require all your faith in my veracity to believe my story. It is not only true, nevertheless, but truth of which I have been an eyewitness.

It was a sweet summer evening, and my father asked me, as he sometimes did, to take a little ramble with him along that beautiful forest vista which I have mentioned as lying in front of the schloss.

"General Spielsdorf cannot come to us so soon as I had hoped," said my father, as we pursued our walk.

He was to have paid us a visit of some weeks, and we had expected his arrival next day. He was to have brought with him a young lady, his niece and ward, Mademoiselle Rheinfeldt, whom I had never seen, but whom I had heard described as a very charming girl, and in whose society I had promised myself many happy days. I was more disappointed than a young lady living in a town, or a bustling neighborhood can possibly imagine. This visit, and the new acquaintance it promised, had furnished my day dream for many weeks.

"And how soon does he come?" I asked.

"Not till autumn. Not for two months, I dare say," he answered. "And I am very glad now, dear, that you never knew Mademoiselle Rheinfeldt."

"And why?" I asked, both mortified and curious.

"Because the poor young lady is dead," he replied. "I quite forgot I had not told you, but you were not in the room when I received the General's letter this evening."

I was very much shocked. General Spielsdorf had mentioned in his first letter, six or seven weeks before, that she was not so well as he would wish her, but there was nothing to suggest the remotest suspicion of danger.

"Here is the General's letter," he said, handing it to me. "I am afraid he is in great affliction; the letter appears to me to have been written very nearly in distraction."

We sat down on a rude bench, under a group of magnificent lime trees. The sun was setting with all its melancholy splendor behind the sylvan horizon, and the stream that flows beside our home, and passes under the steep old bridge I have mentioned, wound through many a group of noble trees, almost at our feet, reflecting in its current the fading crimson of the sky. General Spielsdorf's letter was so extraordinary, so vehement, and in some places so self-contradictory, that I read it twice over—the second time aloud to my father—and was still unable to account for it, except by supposing that grief had unsettled his mind.

It said "I have lost my darling daughter, for as such I loved her. During the last days of dear Bertha's illness I was not able to write to you.

Before then I had no idea of her danger. I have lost her, and now learn all, too late. She died in the peace of innocence, and in the glorious hope of a blessed futurity. The fiend who betrayed our infatuated hospitality has done it all. I thought I was receiving into my house innocence, gaiety, a charming companion for my lost Bertha. Heavens! what a fool have I been!

I thank God my child died without a suspicion of the cause of her sufferings. She is gone without so much as conjecturing the nature of her illness, and the accursed passion of the agent of all this misery. I devote my remaining days to tracking and extinguishing a monster. I am told I may hope to accomplish my righteous and merciful purpose. At present there is scarcely a gleam of light to guide me. I curse my conceited incredulity, my despicable affectation of superiority, my blindness, my obstinacy—all—too late. I cannot write or talk collectedly now. I am distracted. So soon as I shall have a little recovered, I mean to devote myself for a time to enquiry, which may possibly lead me as far as Vienna. Some time in the autumn, two months hence, or earlier if I live, I will see you—that is, if you permit me; I will then tell you all that I scarce dare put upon paper now. Farewell. Pray for me, dear friend."

In these terms ended this strange letter. Though I had never seen Bertha Rheinfeldt my eyes filled with tears at the sudden intelligence; I was startled, as well as profoundly disappointed.

The sun had now set, and it was twilight by the time I had returned the General's letter to my father.

It was a soft clear evening, and we loitered, speculating upon the possible meanings of the violent and incoherent sentences which I had just been reading. We had nearly a mile to walk before reaching the road that passes the schloss in front, and by that time the moon was shining brilliantly. At the drawbridge we met Madame Perrodon and Mademoiselle De Lafontaine, who had come out, without their bonnets, to enjoy the exquisite moonlight.

We heard their voices gabbling in animated dialogue as we approached. We joined them at the drawbridge, and turned about to admire with them the beautiful scene.

The glade through which we had just walked lay before us. At our left the narrow road wound away under clumps of lordly trees, and was lost to sight amid the thickening forest. At the right the same road crosses the steep and picturesque bridge, near which stands a ruined tower which once guarded that pass; and beyond the bridge an abrupt eminence rises, covered with trees, and showing in the shadows some grey ivy-clustered rocks.

Over the sward and low grounds a thin film of mist was stealing like smoke, marking the distances with a transparent veil; and here and there we could see the river faintly flashing in the moonlight.

No softer, sweeter scene could be imagined. The news I had just heard made it melancholy; but nothing could disturb its character of profound serenity, and the enchanted glory and vagueness of the prospect.

My father, who enjoyed the picturesque, and I, stood looking in silence over the expanse beneath us. The two good governesses, standing a little way behind us, discoursed upon the scene, and were eloquent upon the moon.

Madame Perrodon was fat, middle-aged, and romantic, and talked and sighed poetically. Mademoiselle De Lafontaine — in right of her father who was a German, assumed to be psychological, metaphysical, and something of a mystic — now declared that when the moon shone with a light so intense it was well known that it indicated a special spiritual activity. The effect of the full moon in such a state of brilliancy was manifold. It acted on dreams, it acted on lunacy, it acted on nervous people, it had marvelous physical influences connected with life. Mademoiselle related that her cousin, who was mate of a merchant ship, having taken a nap on deck on such a night, lying on his back, with his face full in the light on the moon, had wakened, after a dream of an old woman clawing him by the cheek, with his features horribly drawn to one side; and his countenance had never quite recovered its equilibrium.

"The moon, this night," she said, "is full of idyllic and magnetic influence — and see, when you look behind you at the front of the schloss how all its windows flash and twinkle with that silvery splendor, as if unseen hands had lighted up the rooms to receive fairy guests."

There are indolent styles of the spirits in which, indisposed to talk ourselves, the talk of others is pleasant to our listless ears; and I gazed on, pleased with the tinkle of the ladies' conversation.

"I have got into one of my moping moods tonight," said my father, after a silence, and quoting Shakespeare, whom, by way of keeping up our English, he used to read aloud, he said:

"'In truth I know not why I am so sad.

It wearies me: you say it wearies you;

But how I got it — came by it.'

"I forget the rest. But I feel as if some great misfortune were hanging over us. I suppose the poor General's afflicted letter has had something to do with it."

At this moment the unwonted sound of carriage wheels and many hoofs upon the road, arrested our attention.

They seemed to be approaching from the high ground overlooking the bridge, and very soon the equipage emerged from that point. Two horsemen first crossed the bridge, then came a carriage drawn by four horses, and two men rode behind.

It seemed to be the traveling carriage of a person of rank; and we were all immediately absorbed in watching that very unusual spectacle. It became, in a few moments, greatly more interesting, for just as the carriage had passed the summit of the steep bridge, one of the leaders, taking fright, communicated his panic to the rest, and after a plunge or two, the whole team broke into a wild gallop together, and dashing between the horsemen who rode in front, came thundering along the road towards us with the speed of a hurricane.

The excitement of the scene was made more painful by the clear, long-drawn screams of a female voice from the carriage window.

We all advanced in curiosity and horror; me rather in silence, the rest with various ejaculations of terror.

Our suspense did not last long. Just before you reach the castle drawbridge, on the route they were coming, there stands by the roadside a magnificent lime tree, on the other stands an ancient stone cross, at sight of which the horses, now going at a pace that was perfectly frightful, swerved so as to bring the wheel over the projecting roots of the tree.

I knew what was coming. I covered my eyes, unable to see it out, and turned my head away; at the same moment I heard a cry from my lady friends, who had gone on a little.

Curiosity opened my eyes, and I saw a scene of utter confusion. Two of the horses were on the ground, the carriage lay upon its side with two wheels in the air; the men were busy removing the traces, and a lady with a commanding air and figure had got out, and stood with clasped hands, raising the handkerchief that was in them every now and then to her eyes.

Through the carriage door was now lifted a young lady, who appeared to be lifeless. My dear old father was already beside the elder lady, with his hat in his hand, evidently tendering his aid and the resources of his schloss. The lady did not appear to hear him, or to have eyes for anything but the slender girl who was being placed against the slope of the bank.

I approached; the young lady was apparently stunned, but she was certainly not dead. My father, who piqued himself on being something of a physician, had just had his fingers on her wrist and assured the lady, who declared herself her mother, that her pulse, though faint and irregular, was undoubtedly still distinguishable. The lady clasped her hands and looked upward, as if in a momentary transport of gratitude; but immediately she broke out again in that theatrical way which is, I believe, natural to some people.

She was what is called a fine looking woman for her time of life, and must have been handsome; she was tall, but not thin, and dressed in black velvet, and looked rather pale, but with a proud and commanding countenance, though now agitated strangely.

"Who was ever being so born to calamity?" I heard her say, with clasped hands, as I came up. "Here am I, on a journey of life and death, in prosecuting which to lose an hour is possibly to lose all. My child will not have recovered sufficiently to resume her route for who can say how long. I must leave her: I cannot, dare not, delay. How far on, sir, can you tell, is the nearest village? I must leave her there; and shall not see my darling, or even hear of her till my return, three months hence."

I plucked my father by the coat, and whispered earnestly in his ear: "Oh! papa, pray ask her to let her stay with us — it would be so delightful. Do, pray."

"If Madame will entrust her child to the care of my daughter, and of her good gouvernante, Madame Perrodon, and permit her to remain as our guest, under my charge, until her return, it will confer a distinction and an obligation upon us, and we shall treat her with all the care and devotion which so sacred a trust deserves."

"I cannot do that, sir, it would be to task your kindness and chivalry too cruelly," said the lady, distractedly.

"It would, on the contrary, be to confer on us a very great kindness at the moment when we most need it. My daughter has just been disappointed by a cruel misfortune, in a visit from which she had long anticipated a great deal of happiness. If you confide this young lady to our care it will be her best consolation. The nearest village on your route is distant, and affords no such inn as you could think of placing your daughter at; you cannot allow her to continue her journey for any considerable distance without danger. If, as you say, you cannot suspend your journey, you must part with her tonight, and nowhere could you do so with more honest assurances of care and tenderness than here."

There was something in this lady's air and appearance so distinguished and even imposing, and in her manner so engaging, as to impress one, quite apart from the dignity of her equipage, with a conviction that she was a person of consequence.

By this time the carriage was replaced in its upright position, and the horses, quite tractable, in the traces again.

The lady threw on her daughter a glance which I fancied was not quite so affectionate as one might have anticipated from the beginning of the scene; then she beckoned slightly to my father, and withdrew two or three steps with him out of hearing; and talked to him with a fixed and stern countenance, not at all like that with which she had hitherto spoken.

I was filled with wonder that my father did not seem to perceive the change, and also unspeakably curious to learn what it could be that she was speaking, almost in his ear, with so much earnestness and rapidity.

Two or three minutes at most I think she remained thus employed, then she turned, and a few steps brought her to where her daughter lay, supported by Madame Perrodon. She kneeled beside her for a moment and whispered, as Madame supposed, a little benediction in her ear; then hastily kissing her she stepped into her carriage, the door was closed, the footmen in stately liveries jumped up behind, the outriders spurred on, the postilions cracked their whips, the horses plunged and broke suddenly into a furious canter that threatened soon again to become a gallop, and the carriage whirled away, followed at the same rapid pace by the two horsemen in the rear.

III.
We Compare Notes

We followed the cortege with our eyes until it was swiftly lost to sight in the misty wood; and the very sound of the hoofs and the wheels died away in the silent night air.

Nothing remained to assure us that the adventure had not been an illusion of a moment but the young lady, who just at that moment opened her eyes. I could not see, for her face was turned from me, but she raised her head, evidently looking about her, and I heard a very sweet voice ask complainingly, "Where is mamma?"

Our good Madame Perrodon answered tenderly, and added some comfortable assurances.

I then heard her ask:

"Where am I? What is this place?" and after that she said, "I don't see the carriage; and Matska, where is she?"

Madame answered all her questions in so far as she understood them; and gradually the young lady remembered how the misadventure came about, and was glad to hear that no one in, or in attendance on, the carriage was hurt; and on learning that her mamma had left her here, till her return in about three months, she wept.

I was going to add my consolations to those of Madame Perrodon when Mademoiselle De Lafontaine placed her hand upon my arm, saying:

"Don't approach, one at a time is as much as she can at present converse with; a very little excitement would possibly overpower her now."

As soon as she is comfortably in bed, I thought, I will run up to her room and see her.

My father in the meantime had sent a servant on horseback for the physician, who lived about two leagues away; and a bedroom was being prepared for the young lady's reception.

The stranger now rose, and leaning on Madame's arm, walked slowly over the drawbridge and into the castle gate.

In the hall, servants waited to receive her, and she was conducted forthwith to her room. The room we usually sat in as our drawing room is long, having four windows, that looked over the moat and drawbridge, upon the forest scene I have just described.

It is furnished in old carved oak, with large carved cabinets, and the chairs are cushioned with crimson Utrecht velvet. The walls are covered with tapestry, and surrounded with great gold frames, the figures being as large as life, in ancient and very curious costume, and the subjects represented are hunting, hawking, and generally festive. It is not too stately to be extremely comfortable; and here we had our tea, for with his usual patriotic leanings he insisted that the national beverage should make its appearance regularly with our coffee and chocolate.

We sat here this night, and with candles lighted, were talking over the adventure of the evening.

Madame Perrodon and Mademoiselle De Lafontaine were both of our party. The young stranger had hardly lain down in her bed when she sank into a deep sleep; and those ladies had left her in the care of a servant.

"How do you like our guest?" I asked, as soon as Madame entered. "Tell me all about her?"

"I like her extremely," answered Madame, "she is, I almost think, the prettiest creature I ever saw; about your age, and so gentle and nice."

"She is absolutely beautiful," threw in Mademoiselle, who had peeped for a moment into the stranger's room.

"And such a sweet voice!" added Madame Perrodon.

"Did you remark a woman in the carriage, after it was set up again, who did not get out," inquired Mademoiselle, "but only looked from the window?"

"No, we had not seen her."

Then she described a hideous black woman, with a sort of colored turban on her head, and who was gazing all the time from the carriage window, nodding and grinning derisively towards the ladies, with gleaming eyes and large white eyeballs, and her teeth set as if in fury.

"Did you remark what an ill-looking pack of men the servants were?" asked Madame.

"Yes," said my father, who had just come in, "ugly, hang-dog looking fellows as ever I beheld in my life. I hope they mayn't rob the poor lady in the forest. They are clever rogues, however; they got everything to rights in a minute."

"I dare say they are worn out with too long traveling," said Madame.

"Besides looking wicked, their faces were so strangely lean, and dark, and sullen. I am very curious, I own; but I dare say the young lady will tell you all about it tomorrow, if she is sufficiently recovered."

"I don't think she will," said my father, with a mysterious smile, and a little nod of his head, as if he knew more about it than he cared to tell us.

This made us all the more inquisitive as to what had passed between him and the lady in the black velvet, in the brief but earnest interview that had immediately preceded her departure.

We were scarcely alone, when I entreated him to tell me. He did not need much pressing.

"There is no particular reason why I should not tell you. She expressed a reluctance to trouble us with the care of her daughter, saying she was in delicate health, and nervous, but not subject to any kind of seizure—she volunteered that—nor to any illusion; being, in fact, perfectly sane."

"How very odd to say all that!" I interpolated. "It was so unnecessary."

"At all events it was said," he laughed, "and as you wish to know all that passed, which was indeed very little, I tell you. She then said, 'I am making a long journey of vital importance—she emphasized the word—rapid and secret; I shall return for my child in three months; in the meantime, she will be silent as to who we are, whence we come, and whither we are traveling.' That is all she said. She spoke very pure French. When she said the word 'secret,' she paused for a few seconds, looking sternly, her eyes fixed on mine. I fancy she makes a great point of that. You saw how quickly she was gone. I hope I have not done a very foolish thing, in taking charge of the young lady."

For my part, I was delighted. I was longing to see and talk to her; and only waiting till the doctor should give me leave. You, who live in towns, can have no idea how great an event the introduction of a new friend is, in such a solitude as surrounded us.

The doctor did not arrive till nearly one o'clock; but I could no more have gone to my bed and slept, than I could have overtaken, on foot, the carriage in which the princess in black velvet had driven away.

When the physician came down to the drawing room, it was to report very favorably upon his patient. She was now sitting up, her pulse quite regular, apparently perfectly well. She had sustained no injury, and the little shock to her nerves had passed away quite harmlessly. There could be no harm certainly in my seeing her, if we both wished it; and, with this permission I sent, forthwith, to know whether she would allow me to visit her for a few minutes in her room.

The servant returned immediately to say that she desired nothing more.

You may be sure I was not long in availing myself of this permission.

Our visitor lay in one of the handsomest rooms in the schloss. It was, perhaps, a little stately. There was a somber piece of tapestry opposite the foot of the bed, representing Cleopatra with the asps to her bosom; and other solemn classic scenes were displayed, a little faded, upon the other walls. But there was gold carving, and rich and varied color enough in the other decorations of the room, to more than redeem the gloom of the old tapestry.

There were candles at the bedside. She was sitting up; her slender pretty figure enveloped in the soft silk dressing gown, embroidered with flowers, and lined with thick quilted silk, which her mother had thrown over her feet as she lay upon the ground.

What was it that, as I reached the bedside and had just begun my little greeting, struck me dumb in a moment, and made me recoil a step or two from before her? I will tell you.

I saw the very face which had visited me in my childhood at night, which remained so fixed in my memory, and on which I had for so many years so often ruminated with horror, when no one suspected of what I was thinking.

It was pretty, even beautiful; and when I first beheld it, wore the same melancholy expression.

But this almost instantly lighted into a strange fixed smile of recognition.

There was a silence of fully a minute, and then at length she spoke; I could not.

"How wonderful!" she exclaimed. "Twelve years ago, I saw your face in a dream, and it has haunted me ever since."

"Wonderful indeed!" I repeated, overcoming with an effort the horror that had for a time suspended my utterances. "Twelve years ago, in vision or reality, I certainly saw you. I could not forget your face. It has remained before my eyes ever since."

Her smile had softened. Whatever I had fancied strange in it, was gone, and it and her dimpling cheeks were now delightfully pretty and intelligent.

I felt reassured, and continued more in the vein which hospitality indicated, to bid her welcome, and to tell her how much pleasure her accidental arrival had given us all, and especially what a happiness it was to me.

I took her hand as I spoke. I was a little shy, as lonely people are, but the situation made me eloquent, and even bold. She pressed my hand, she laid hers upon it, and her eyes glowed, as, looking hastily into mine, she smiled again, and blushed.

She answered my welcome very prettily. I sat down beside her, still wondering; and she said:

"I must tell you my vision about you; it is so very strange that you and I should have had, each of the other so vivid a dream, that each should have seen, I you and you me, looking as we do now, when of course we both were mere children. I was a child, about six years old, and I awoke from a confused and troubled dream, and found myself in a room, unlike my nursery, wainscoted clumsily in some dark wood, and with cupboards and bedsteads, and chairs, and benches placed about it. The beds were, I thought, all empty, and the room itself without anyone but myself in it; and I, after looking about me for some time, and admiring especially an iron candlestick with two branches, which I should certainly know again, crept under one of the beds to reach the window; but as I got from under the bed, I heard someone crying; and looking up, while I was still upon my knees, I saw you—most assuredly you—as I see you now; a beautiful young lady, with golden hair and large blue eyes, and lips—your lips—you as you are here.

"Your looks won me; I climbed on the bed and put my arms about you, and I think we both fell asleep. I was aroused by a scream; you were sitting up screaming. I was frightened, and slipped down upon the ground, and, it seemed to me, lost consciousness for a moment; and when I came to myself, I was again in my nursery at home. Your face I have never forgotten since. I could not be misled by mere resemblance. You are the lady whom I saw then."

It was now my turn to relate my corresponding vision, which I did, to the undisguised wonder of my new acquaintance.

"I don't know which should be most afraid of the other," she said, again smiling—"If you were less pretty I think I should be very much afraid of you, but being as you are, and you and I both so young, I feel only that I have made your acquaintance twelve years ago, and have already a right to your intimacy; at all events it does seem as if we were destined, from our earliest childhood, to be friends. I wonder whether you feel as strangely drawn towards me as I do to you; I have never had a friend— shall I find one now?" She sighed, and her fine dark eyes gazed passionately on me.

Now the truth is, I felt rather unaccountably towards the beautiful stranger. I did feel, as she said, "drawn towards her," but there was also something of repulsion. In this ambiguous feeling, however, the sense of attraction immensely prevailed. She interested and won me; she was so beautiful and so indescribably engaging.

I perceived now something of languor and exhaustion stealing over her, and hastened to bid her good night.

"The doctor thinks," I added, "that you ought to have a maid to sit up with you tonight; one of ours is waiting, and you will find her a very useful and quiet creature."

"How kind of you, but I could not sleep, I never could with an attendant in the room. I shan't require any assistance—and, shall I confess my weakness, I am haunted with a terror of robbers. Our house was robbed once, and two servants murdered, so I always lock my door. It has become a habit—and you look so kind I know you will forgive me. I see there is a key in the lock."

She held me close in her pretty arms for a moment and whispered in my ear, "Good night, darling, it is very hard to part with you, but good night; tomorrow, but not early, I shall see you again."

She sank back on the pillow with a sigh, and her fine eyes followed me with a fond and melancholy gaze, and she murmured again "Good night, dear friend."

Young people like, and even love, on impulse. I was flattered by the evident, though as yet undeserved, fondness she showed me. I liked the confidence with which she at once received me. She was determined that we should be very near friends.

Next day came and we met again. I was delighted with my companion; that is to say, in many respects.

Her looks lost nothing in daylight—she was certainly the most beautiful creature I had ever seen, and the unpleasant remembrance of the face presented in my early dream, had lost the effect of the first unexpected recognition.

She confessed that she had experienced a similar shock on seeing me, and precisely the same faint antipathy that had mingled with my admiration of her. We now laughed together over our momentary horrors.

IV.
Her Habits — A Saunter

I told you that I was charmed with her in most particulars.

There were some that did not please me so well.

She was above the middle height of women. I shall begin by describing her.

She was slender, and wonderfully graceful. Except that her movements were languid — very languid — indeed, there was nothing in her appearance to indicate an invalid. Her complexion was rich and brilliant; her features were small and beautifully formed; her eyes large, dark, and lustrous; her hair was quite wonderful, I never saw hair so magnificently thick and long when it was down about her shoulders; I have often placed my hands under it, and laughed with wonder at its weight. It was exquisitely fine and soft, and in color a rich very dark brown, with something of gold. I loved to let it down, tumbling with its own weight, as, in her room, she lay back in her chair talking in her sweet low voice, I used to fold and braid it, and spread it out and play with it. Heavens! If I had but known all!

I said there were particulars which did not please me. I have told you that her confidence won me the first night I saw her; but I found that she exercised with respect to herself, her mother, her history, everything in fact connected with her life, plans, and people, an ever wakeful reserve. I dare say I was unreasonable, perhaps I was wrong; I dare say I ought to have respected the solemn injunction laid upon my father by the stately lady in black velvet. But curiosity is a restless and unscrupulous passion, and no one girl can endure, with patience, that hers should be baffled by another. What harm could it do anyone to tell me what I so ardently desired to know? Had she no trust in my good sense or honor? Why would she not believe me when I assured her, so solemnly, that I would not divulge one syllable of what she told me to any mortal breathing.

There was a coldness, it seemed to me, beyond her years, in her smiling melancholy persistent refusal to afford me the least ray of light.

I cannot say we quarreled upon this point, for she would not quarrel upon any. It was, of course, very unfair of me to press her, very ill-bred, but I really could not help it; and I might just as well have let it alone.

What she did tell me amounted, in my unconscionable estimation—to nothing.

It was all summed up in three very vague disclosures:

First—Her name was Carmilla.

Second—Her family was very ancient and noble.

Third—Her home lay in the direction of the west.

She would not tell me the name of her family, nor their armorial bearings, nor the name of their estate, nor even that of the country they lived in.

You are not to suppose that I worried her incessantly on these subjects. I watched opportunity, and rather insinuated than urged my inquiries. Once or twice, indeed, I did attack her more directly. But no matter what my tactics, utter failure was invariably the result. Reproaches and caresses were all lost upon her. But I must add this, that her evasion was conducted with so pretty a melancholy and deprecation, with so many, and even passionate declarations of her liking for me, and trust in my honor, and with so many promises that I should at last know all, that I could not find it in my heart long to be offended with her.

She used to place her pretty arms about my neck, draw me to her, and laying her cheek to mine, murmur with her lips near my ear, "Dearest, your little heart is wounded; think me not cruel because I obey the irresistible law of my strength and weakness; if your dear heart is wounded, my wild heart bleeds with yours. In the rapture of my enormous humiliation I live in your warm life, and you shall die—die, sweetly die—into mine. I cannot help it; as I draw near to you, you, in your turn, will draw near to others, and learn the rapture of that cruelty, which yet is love; so, for a while, seek to know no more of me and mine, but trust me with all your loving spirit."

And when she had spoken such a rhapsody, she would press me more closely in her trembling embrace, and her lips in soft kisses gently glow upon my cheek.

Her agitations and her language were unintelligible to me.

From these foolish embraces, which were not of very frequent occurrence, I must allow, I used to wish to extricate myself; but my energies seemed to fail me. Her murmured words sounded like a lullaby in my ear, and soothed my resistance into a trance, from which I only seemed to recover myself when she withdrew her arms.

In these mysterious moods I did not like her. I experienced a strange tumultuous excitement that was pleasurable, ever and anon, mingled with a vague sense of fear and disgust. I had no distinct thoughts about her while such scenes lasted, but I was conscious of a love growing into adoration, and also of abhorrence. This I know is paradox, but I can make no other attempt to explain the feeling.

I now write, after an interval of more than ten years, with a trembling hand, with a confused and horrible recollection of certain occurrences and situations, in the ordeal through which I was unconsciously passing; though with a vivid and very sharp remembrance of the main current of my story.

But, I suspect, in all lives there are certain emotional scenes, those in which our passions have been most wildly and terribly roused, that are of all others the most vaguely and dimly remembered.

Sometimes after an hour of apathy, my strange and beautiful companion would take my hand and hold it with a fond pressure, renewed again and again; blushing softly, gazing in my face with languid and burning eyes, and breathing so fast that her dress rose and fell with the tumultuous respiration. It was like the ardor of a lover; it embarrassed me; it was hateful and yet over-powering; and with gloating eyes she drew me to her, and her hot lips traveled along my cheek in kisses; and she would whisper, almost in sobs, "You are mine, you shall be mine, you and I are one for ever." Then she had thrown herself back in her chair, with her small hands over her eyes, leaving me trembling.

"Are we related," I used to ask; "what can you mean by all this? I remind you perhaps of someone whom you love; but you must not, I hate it; I don't know you — I don't know myself when you look so and talk so."

She used to sigh at my vehemence, then turn away and drop my hand.

Respecting these very extraordinary manifestations I strove in vain to form any satisfactory theory — I could not refer them to affection or trick. It was unmistakably the momentary breaking out of suppressed instinct and emotion. Was she, notwithstanding her mother's volunteered denial, subject to brief visitations of insanity; or was there here a disguise and a romance? I had read in old storybooks of such things. What if a boyish lover had found his way into the house, and sought to prosecute his suit in masquerade, with the assistance of a clever old adventuress. But there were many things against this hypothesis, highly interesting as it was to my vanity.

I could boast of no little attentions such as masculine gallantry delights to offer. Between these passionate moments there were long intervals of commonplace, of gaiety, of brooding melancholy, during which, except that I detected her eyes so full of melancholy fire, following me, at times I might have been as nothing to her. Except in these brief periods of mysterious excitement her ways were girlish; and there was always a languor about her, quite incompatible with a masculine system in a state of health.

In some respects her habits were odd. Perhaps not so singular in the opinion of a town lady like you, as they appeared to us rustic people. She used to come down very late, generally not till one o'clock, she would then take a cup of chocolate, but eat nothing; we then went out for a walk, which was a mere saunter, and she seemed, almost immediately, exhausted, and either returned to the schloss or sat on one of the benches that were placed, here and there, among the trees. This was a bodily languor in which her mind did not sympathize. She was always an animated talker, and very intelligent.

She sometimes alluded for a moment to her own home, or mentioned an adventure or situation, or an early recollection, which indicated a people of strange manners, and described customs of which we knew nothing. I gathered from these

Carmilla

chance hints that her native country was much more remote than I had at first fancied.

As we sat thus one afternoon under the trees a funeral passed us by. It was that of a pretty young girl, whom I had often seen, the daughter of one of the rangers of the forest. The poor man was walking behind the coffin of his darling; she was his only child, and he looked quite heartbroken.

Peasants walking two-and-two came behind, they were singing a funeral hymn.

I rose to mark my respect as they passed, and joined in the hymn they were very sweetly singing.

My companion shook me a little roughly, and I turned surprised.

She said brusquely, "Don't you perceive how discordant that is?"

"I think it very sweet, on the contrary," I answered, vexed at the interruption, and very uncomfortable, lest the people who composed the little procession should observe and resent what was passing.

I resumed, therefore, instantly, and was again interrupted. "You pierce my ears," said Carmilla, almost angrily, and stopping her ears with her tiny fingers. "Besides, how can you tell that your religion and mine are the same; your forms wound me, and I hate funerals. What a fuss! Why you must die—everyone must die; and all are happier when they do. Come home."

"My father has gone on with the clergyman to the churchyard. I thought you knew she was to be buried today."

"She? I don't trouble my head about peasants. I don't know who she is," answered Carmilla, with a flash from her fine eyes.

"She is the poor girl who fancied she saw a ghost a fortnight ago, and has been dying ever since, till yesterday, when she expired."

"Tell me nothing about ghosts. I shan't sleep tonight if you do."

"I hope there is no plague or fever coming; all this looks very like it," I continued. "The swineherd's young wife died only a week ago, and she thought something seized her by the throat as she lay in her bed, and nearly strangled her. Papa says such horrible fancies do accompany some forms of fever. She was quite well the day before. She sank afterwards, and died before a week."

"Well, her funeral is over, I hope, and her hymn sung; and our ears shan't be tortured with that discord and jargon. It has made me nervous. Sit down here, beside me; sit close; hold my hand; press it hard-hard-harder."

We had moved a little back, and had come to another seat.

She sat down. Her face underwent a change that alarmed and even terrified me for a moment. It darkened, and became horribly livid; her teeth and hands were clenched, and she frowned and compressed her lips, while she stared down upon the ground at her feet, and trembled all over with a continued shudder as irrepressible as ague. All her energies seemed strained to suppress a fit, with which she was then breathlessly tugging; and at length a low convulsive cry of suffering broke from her, and gradually the hysteria subsided. "There! That comes of strangling people with hymns!" she said at last. "Hold me, hold me still. It is passing away."

And so gradually it did; and perhaps to dissipate the somber impression which the spectacle had left upon me, she became unusually animated and chatty; and so we got home.

This was the first time I had seen her exhibit any definable symptoms of that delicacy of health which her mother had spoken of. It was the first time, also, I had seen her exhibit anything like temper.

Both passed away like a summer cloud; and never but once afterwards did I witness on her part a momentary sign of anger. I will tell you how it happened.

She and I were looking out of one of the long drawing room windows, when there entered the courtyard, over the drawbridge, a figure of a wanderer whom I knew very well. He used to visit the schloss generally twice a year.

It was the figure of a hunchback, with the sharp lean features that generally accompany deformity. He wore a pointed black beard, and he was smiling from ear to ear, showing his white fangs. He was dressed in buff, black, and scarlet, and crossed with more straps and belts than I could count, from which hung all manner of things. Behind, he carried a magic lantern, and two boxes, which I well knew, in one of which was a salamander, and in the other a mandrake. These monsters used to make my father laugh. They were compounded of parts of monkeys, parrots, squirrels, fish, and hedgehogs, dried and stitched together with great neatness and startling effect. He had a fiddle, a box of conjuring apparatus, a pair of foils and masks attached to his belt, several other mysterious cases dangling about him, and a black staff with copper ferrules in his hand. His companion was a rough spare dog, that followed at his heels, but stopped short, suspiciously at the drawbridge, and in a little while began to howl dismally.

In the meantime, the mountebank, standing in the midst of the courtyard, raised his grotesque hat, and made us a very ceremonious bow, paying his compliments very volubly in execrable French, and German not much better.

Then, disengaging his fiddle, he began to scrape a lively air to which he sang with a merry discord, dancing with ludicrous airs and activity, that made me laugh, in spite of the dog's howling.

Then he advanced to the window with many smiles and salutations, and his hat in his left hand, his fiddle under his arm, and with a fluency that never took breath, he gabbled a long advertisement of all his accomplishments, and the resources of the various arts which he placed at our service, and the curiosities and entertainments which it was in his power, at our bidding, to display.

"Will your ladyships be pleased to buy an amulet against the oupire, which is going like the wolf, I hear, through these woods," he said dropping his hat on the pavement. "They are dying of it right and left and here is a charm that never fails; only pinned to the pillow, and you may laugh in his face."

These charms consisted of oblong slips of vellum, with

cabalistic ciphers and diagrams upon them.

Carmilla instantly purchased one, and so did I.

He was looking up, and we were smiling down upon him, amused; at least, I can answer for myself. His piercing black eye, as he looked up in our faces, seemed to detect something that fixed for a moment his curiosity,

In an instant he unrolled a leather case, full of all manner of odd little steel instruments.

"See here, my lady," he said, displaying it, and addressing me, "I profess, among other things less useful, the art of dentistry. Plague take the dog!" he interpolated. "Silence, beast! He howls so that your ladyships can scarcely hear a word. Your noble friend, the young lady at your right, has the sharpest tooth,—long, thin, pointed, like an awl, like a needle; ha, ha! With my sharp and long sight, as I look up, I have seen it distinctly; now if it happens to hurt the young lady, and I think it must, here am I, here are my file, my punch, my nippers; I will make it round and blunt, if her ladyship pleases; no longer the tooth of a fish, but of a beautiful young lady as she is. Hey? Is the young lady displeased? Have I been too bold? Have I offended her?"

The young lady, indeed, looked very angry as she drew back from the window.

"How dares that mountebank insult us so? Where is your father? I shall demand redress from him. My father would have had the wretch tied up to the pump, and flogged with a cart whip, and burnt to the bones with the cattle brand!"

She retired from the window a step or two, and sat down, and had hardly lost sight of the offender, when her wrath subsided as suddenly as it had risen, and she gradually recovered her usual tone, and seemed to forget the little hunchback and his follies.

My father was out of spirits that evening. On coming in he told us that there had been another case very similar to the two fatal ones which had lately occurred. The sister of a young peasant on his estate, only a mile away, was very ill, had been, as she described it, attacked very nearly in the same way, and was now slowly but steadily sinking.

"All this," said my father, "is strictly referable to natural causes. These poor people infect one another with their superstitions, and so repeat in imagination the images of terror that have infested their neighbors."

"But that very circumstance frightens one horribly," said Carmilla.

"How so?" inquired my father.

"I am so afraid of fancying I see such things; I think it would be as bad as reality."

"We are in God's hands: nothing can happen without his permission, and all will end well for those who love him. He is our faithful creator; He has made us all, and will take care of us."

"Creator! Nature!" said the young lady in answer to my gentle father. "And this disease that invades the country is natural. Nature. All things proceed from Nature—don't they? All things in the heaven, in the earth, and under the earth, act and live as Nature ordains? I think so."

"The doctor said he would come here today," said my father, after a silence. "I want to know what he thinks about it, and what he thinks we had better do."

"Doctors never did me any good," said Carmilla.

"Then you have been ill?" I asked.

"More ill than ever you were," she answered.

"Long ago?"

"Yes, a long time. I suffered from this very illness; but I forget all but my pain and weakness, and they were not so bad as are suffered in other diseases."

"You were very young then?"

"I dare say, let us talk no more of it. You would not wound a friend?"

She looked languidly in my eyes, and passed her arm round my waist lovingly, and led me out of the room. My father was busy over some papers near the window.

"Why does your papa like to frighten us?" said the pretty girl with a sigh and a little shudder.

"He doesn't, dear Carmilla, it is the very furthest thing from his mind."

"Are you afraid, dearest?"

"I should be very much if I fancied there was any real danger of my being attacked as those poor people were."

"You are afraid to die?"

"Yes, every one is."

"But to die as lovers may — to die together, so that they may live together.

Girls are caterpillars while they live in the world, to be finally butterflies when the summer comes; but in the meantime there are grubs and larvae, don't you see — each with their peculiar propensities, necessities and structure. So says Monsieur Buffon, in his big book, in the next room."

Later in the day the doctor came, and was closeted with papa for some time.

He was a skilful man, of sixty and upwards, he wore powder, and shaved his pale face as smooth as a pumpkin. He and papa emerged from the room together, and I heard papa laugh, and say as they came out:

"Well, I do wonder at a wise man like you. What do you say to hippogriffs and dragons?"

The doctor was smiling, and made answer, shaking his head —

"Nevertheless life and death are mysterious states, and we

Carmilla

know little of the resources of either."

And so they walked on, and I heard no more. I did not then know what the doctor had been broaching, but I think I guess it now.

V.
A Wonderful Likeness

This evening there arrived from Gratz the grave, dark-faced son of the picture cleaner, with a horse and cart laden with two large packing cases, having many pictures in each. It was a journey of ten leagues, and whenever a messenger arrived at the schloss from our little capital of Gratz, we used to crowd about him in the hall, to hear the news.

This arrival created in our secluded quarters quite a sensation. The cases remained in the hall, and the messenger was taken charge of by the servants till he had eaten his supper. Then with assistants, and armed with hammer, ripping chisel, and turnscrew, he met us in the hall, where we had assembled to witness the unpacking of the cases.

Carmilla sat looking listlessly on, while one after the other the old pictures, nearly all portraits, which had undergone the process of renovation, were brought to light. My mother was of an old Hungarian family, and most of these pictures, which were about to be restored to their places, had come to us through her.

My father had a list in his hand, from which he read, as the artist rummaged out the corresponding numbers. I don't know that the pictures were very good, but they were, undoubtedly, very old, and some of them very curious also. They had, for the most part, the merit of being now seen by me, I may say, for the first time; for the smoke and dust of time had all but obliterated them.

"There is a picture that I have not seen yet," said my father. "In one corner, at the top of it, is the name, as well as I could read, 'Marcia Karnstein,' and the date '1698'; and I am curious to see how it has turned out."

I remembered it; it was a small picture, about a foot and a half high, and nearly square, without a frame; but it was so blackened by age that I could not make it out.

The artist now produced it, with evident pride. It was quite beautiful; it was startling; it seemed to live. It was the effigy of Carmilla!

"Carmilla, dear, here is an absolute miracle. Here you are, living, smiling, ready to speak, in this picture. Isn't it beautiful, Papa? And see, even the little mole on her throat."

My father laughed, and said "Certainly it is a wonderful likeness," but he looked away, and to my surprise seemed but little struck by it, and went on talking to the picture cleaner, who was also something of an artist, and discoursed with intelligence about the portraits or other works, which his art had just brought into light and color, while I was more and more lost in wonder the more I looked at the picture.

"Will you let me hang this picture in my room, papa?" I asked.

"Certainly, dear," said he, smiling, "I'm very glad you think it so like.

It must be prettier even than I thought it, if it is."

The young lady did not acknowledge this pretty speech, did not seem to hear it. She was leaning back in her seat, her fine eyes under their long lashes gazing on me in contemplation, and she smiled in a kind of rapture.

"And now you can read quite plainly the name that is written in the corner.

It is not Marcia; it looks as if it was done in gold. The name is Mircalla, Countess Karnstein, and this is a little coronet over and underneath A.D.

1698. I am descended from the Karnsteins; that is, mamma was."

"Ah!" said the lady, languidly, "so am I, I think, a very long descent, very ancient. Are there any Karnsteins living now?"

"None who bear the name, I believe. The family were ruined, I believe, in some civil wars, long ago, but the ruins of the castle are only about three miles away."

"How interesting!" she said, languidly. "But see what beautiful moonlight!" She glanced through the hall door, which stood a little open. "Suppose you take a little ramble round the court, and look down at the road and river."

"It is so like the night you came to us," I said.

She sighed; smiling.

She rose, and each with her arm about the other's waist, we walked out upon the pavement.

In silence, slowly we walked down to the drawbridge, where the beautiful landscape opened before us.

"And so you were thinking of the night I came here?" she almost whispered.

"Are you glad I came?"

"Delighted, dear Carmilla," I answered.

"And you asked for the picture you think like me, to hang in your room," she murmured with a sigh, as she drew her arm closer about my waist, and let her pretty head sink upon my shoulder. "How romantic you are, Carmilla," I said. "Whenever you tell me your story, it will be made up chiefly of some one great romance."

She kissed me silently.

"I am sure, Carmilla, you have been in love; that there is, at this moment, an affair of the heart going on."

"I have been in love with no one, and never shall," she whispered, "unless it should be with you."

How beautiful she looked in the moonlight!

Shy and strange was the look with which she quickly hid her face in my neck and hair, with tumultuous sighs, that seemed almost to sob, and pressed in mine a hand that trembled.

Her soft cheek was glowing against mine. "Darling, darling," she murmured, "I live in you; and you would die for me, I love you so."

I started from her.

Carmilla

She was gazing on me with eyes from which all fire, all meaning had flown, and a face colorless and apathetic.

"Is there a chill in the air, dear?" she said drowsily. "I almost shiver; have I been dreaming? Let us come in. Come; come; come in."

"You look ill, Carmilla; a little faint. You certainly must take some wine," I said.

"Yes. I will. I'm better now. I shall be quite well in a few minutes. Yes, do give me a little wine," answered Carmilla, as we approached the door.

"Let us look again for a moment; it is the last time, perhaps, I shall see the moonlight with you."

"How do you feel now, dear Carmilla? Are you really better?" I asked.

I was beginning to take alarm, lest she should have been stricken with the strange epidemic that they said had invaded the country about us.

"Papa would be grieved beyond measure," I added, "if he thought you were ever so little ill, without immediately letting us know. We have a very skilful doctor near us, the physician who was with papa today."

"I'm sure he is. I know how kind you all are; but, dear child, I am quite well again. There is nothing ever wrong with me, but a little weakness.

People say I am languid; I am incapable of exertion; I can scarcely walk as far as a child of three years old: and every now and then the little strength I have falters, and I become as you have just seen me. But after all I am very easily set up again; in a moment I am perfectly myself. See how I have recovered."

So, indeed, she had; and she and I talked a great deal, and very animated she was; and the remainder of that evening passed without any recurrence of what I called her infatuations. I mean her crazy talk and looks, which embarrassed, and even frightened me.

But there occurred that night an event which gave my thoughts quite a new turn, and seemed to startle even Carmilla's languid nature into momentary energy.

VI.

A Very Strange Agony

When we got into the drawing room, and had sat down to our coffee and chocolate, although Carmilla did not take any, she seemed quite herself again, and Madame, and Mademoiselle De Lafontaine, joined us, and made a little card party, in the course of which papa came in for what he called his "dish of tea."

When the game was over he sat down beside Carmilla on the sofa, and asked her, a little anxiously, whether she had heard from her mother since her arrival.

She answered "No."

He then asked whether she knew where a letter would reach her at present.

"I cannot tell," she answered ambiguously, "but I have been thinking of leaving you; you have been already too hospitable and too kind to me. I have given you an infinity of trouble, and I should wish to take a carriage tomorrow, and post in pursuit of her; I know where I shall ultimately find her, although I dare not yet tell you."

"But you must not dream of any such thing," exclaimed my father, to my great relief. "We can't afford to lose you so, and I won't consent to your leaving us, except under the care of your mother, who was so good as to consent to your remaining with us till she should herself return. I should be quite happy if I knew that you heard from her: but this evening the accounts of the progress of the mysterious disease that has invaded our neighborhood, grow even more alarming; and my beautiful guest, I do feel the responsibility, unaided by advice from your mother, very much. But I shall do my best; and one thing is certain, that you must not think of leaving us without her distinct direction to that effect. We should suffer too much in parting from you to consent to it easily."

"Thank you, sir, a thousand times for your hospitality," she answered, smiling bashfully. "You have all been too kind to me; I have seldom been so happy in all my life before, as in your beautiful chateau, under your care, and in the society of your dear daughter."

So he gallantly, in his old-fashioned way, kissed her hand, smiling and pleased at her little speech.

I accompanied Carmilla as usual to her room, and sat and chatted with her while she was preparing for bed.

"Do you think," I said at length, "that you will ever confide fully in me?"

She turned round smiling, but made no answer, only continued to smile on me.

"You won't answer that?" I said. "You can't answer pleasantly; I ought not to have asked you."

"You were quite right to ask me that, or anything. You do not know how dear you are to me, or you could not think any confidence too great to look for.

But I am under vows, no nun half so awfully, and I dare not tell my story yet, even to you. The time is very near when you shall know everything. You will think me cruel, very selfish, but love is always selfish; the more ardent the more selfish. How jealous I am you cannot know. You must come with me, loving me, to death; or else hate me and still come with me. and hating me through death and after. There is no such word as indifference in my apathetic nature."

"Now, Carmilla, you are going to talk your wild nonsense again," I said hastily.

"Not I, silly little fool as I am, and full of whims and fancies; for your sake I'll talk like a sage. Were you ever at a ball?"

"No; how you do run on. What is it like? How charming it must be."

"I almost forget, it is years ago."

I laughed.

"You are not so old. Your first ball can hardly be forgotten yet."

"I remember everything about it—with an effort. I see it all, as divers see what is going on above them, through a medium, dense, rippling, but transparent. There occurred that night what has confused the picture, and made its colours faint. I was all but assassinated in my bed, wounded here," she touched her breast, "and never was the same since."

"Were you near dying?"

"Yes, very—a cruel love—strange love, that would have taken my life. Love will have its sacrifices. No sacrifice without blood. Let us go to sleep now; I feel so lazy. How can I get up just now and lock my door?"

She was lying with her tiny hands buried in her rich wavy hair, under her cheek, her little head upon the pillow, and her glittering eyes followed me wherever I moved, with a kind of shy smile that I could not decipher.

I bid her good night, and crept from the room with an uncomfortable sensation.

I often wondered whether our pretty guest ever said her prayers. I certainly had never seen her upon her knees. In the morning she never came down until long after our family prayers were over, and at night she never left the drawing room to attend our brief evening prayers in the hall.

If it had not been that it had casually come out in one of our careless talks that she had been baptised, I should have doubted her being a Christian. Religion was a subject on which I had never heard her speak a word. If I had known the world better, this particular neglect or antipathy would not have so much surprised me.

The precautions of nervous people are infectious, and persons of a like temperament are pretty sure, after a time, to imitate them. I had adopted Carmilla's habit of locking her bedroom door, having taken into my head all her whimsical alarms about midnight invaders and prowling assassins. I had also adopted her precaution of making a brief search through her room, to satisfy herself that no lurking assassin or robber was "ensconced."

These wise measures taken, I got into my bed and fell asleep.

A light was burning in my room. This was an old habit, of very early date, and which nothing could have tempted me to dispense with.

Thus fortifed I might take my rest in peace. But dreams come through stone walls, light up dark rooms, or darken light ones, and their persons make their exits and their entrances as they please, and laugh at locksmiths.

I had a dream that night that was the beginning of a very strange agony.

I cannot call it a nightmare, for I was quite conscious of being asleep.

But I was equally conscious of being in my room, and lying in bed, precisely as I actually was. I saw, or fancied I saw, the room and its furniture just as I had seen it last, except that it was very dark, and I saw something moving round the foot of the bed, which at first I could not accurately distinguish. But I soon saw that it was a sooty-black animal that resembled a monstrous cat. It appeared to me about four or five feet long for it measured fully the length of the hearthrug as it passed over it; and it continued to-ing and fro-ing with the lithe, sinister restlessness of a beast in a cage. I could not cry out, although as you may suppose, I was terrified. Its pace was growing faster, and the room rapidly darker and darker, and at length so dark that I could no longer see anything of it but its eyes. I felt it spring lightly on the bed. The two broad eyes approached my face, and suddenly I felt a stinging pain as if two large needles darted, an inch or two apart, deep into my breast. I waked with a scream. The room was lighted by the candle that burnt there all through the night, and I saw a female figure standing at the foot of the bed, a little at the right side. It was in a dark loose dress, and its hair was down and covered its shoulders. A block of stone could not have been more still. There was not the slightest stir of respiration. As I stared at it, the figure appeared to have changed its place, and was now nearer the door; then, close to it, the door opened, and it passed out.

I was now relieved, and able to breathe and move. My first thought was that Carmilla had been playing me a trick, and that I had forgotten to secure my door. I hastened to it, and found it locked as usual on the inside. I was afraid to open it—I was horrified. I sprang into my bed and covered my head up in the bedclothes, and lay there more dead than alive till morning.

VII.

Descending

It would be vain my attempting to tell you the horror with which, even now, I recall the occurrence of that night. It was no such transitory terror as a dream leaves behind it. It seemed to deepen by time, and communicated itself to the room and the very furniture that had encompassed the apparition.

I could not bear next day to be alone for a moment. I should have told papa, but for two opposite reasons. At one time I thought he would laugh at my story, and I could not bear its being treated as a jest; and at another I thought he might fancy that I had been attacked by the mysterious complaint which had invaded our neighborhood. I had myself no misgiving of the kind, and as he had been rather an invalid for some time, I was afraid of alarming him.

I was comfortable enough with my good-natured companions, Madame Perrodon, and the vivacious Mademoiselle Lafontaine. They both perceived that I was out of spirits and nervous, and at length I told them what lay so heavy at my heart.

Mademoiselle laughed, but I fancied that Madame Perrodon looked anxious.

"By-the-by," said Mademoiselle, laughing, "the long lime tree walk, behind Carmilla's bedroom window, is haunted!"

"Nonsense!" exclaimed Madame, who probably thought the theme rather inopportune, "and who tells that story, my dear?"

"Martin says that he came up twice, when the old yard gate was being repaired, before sunrise, and twice saw the same female figure walking down the lime tree avenue."

"So he well might, as long as there are cows to milk in the river fields," said Madame.

"I daresay; but Martin chooses to be frightened, and never did I see fool more frightened."

"You must not say a word about it to Carmilla, because she

can see down that walk from her room window," I interposed, "and she is, if possible, a greater coward than I."

Carmilla came down rather later than usual that day.

"I was so frightened last night," she said, so soon as were together, "and I am sure I should have seen something dreadful if it had not been for that charm I bought from the poor little hunchback whom I called such hard names. I had a dream of something black coming round my bed, and I awoke in a perfect horror, and I really thought, for some seconds, I saw a dark figure near the chimneypiece, but I felt under my pillow for my charm, and the moment my fingers touched it, the figure disappeared, and I felt quite certain, only that I had it by me, that something frightful would have made its appearance, and, perhaps, throttled me, as it did those poor people we heard of.

"Well, listen to me," I began, and recounted my adventure, at the recital of which she appeared horrified.

"And had you the charm near you?" she asked, earnestly.

"No, I had dropped it into a china vase in the drawing room, but I shall certainly take it with me tonight, as you have so much faith in it."

At this distance of time I cannot tell you, or even understand, how I overcame my horror so effectually as to lie alone in my room that night. I remember distinctly that I pinned the charm to my pillow. I fell asleep almost immediately, and slept even more soundly than usual all night.

Next night I passed as well. My sleep was delightfully deep and dreamless.

But I wakened with a sense of lassitude and melancholy, which, however, did not exceed a degree that was almost luxurious.

"Well, I told you so," said Carmilla, when I described my quiet sleep, "I had such delightful sleep myself last night; I pinned the charm to the breast of my nightdress. It was too far away the night before. I am quite sure it was all fancy, except the dreams. I used to think that evil spirits made dreams, but our doctor told me it is no such thing. Only a fever passing by, or some other malady, as they often do, he said, knocks at the door, and not being able to get in, passes on, with that alarm."

"And what do you think the charm is?" said I.

"It has been fumigated or immersed in some drug, and is an antidote against the malaria," she answered.

"Then it acts only on the body?"

"Certainly; you don't suppose that evil spirits are frightened by bits of ribbon, or the perfumes of a druggist's shop? No, these complaints, wandering in the air, begin by trying the nerves, and so infect the brain, but before they can seize upon you, the antidote repels them. That I am sure is what the charm has done for us. It is nothing magical, it is simply natural.

I should have been happier if I could have quite agreed with Carmilla, but I did my best, and the impression was a little losing its force.

For some nights I slept profoundly; but still every morning I felt the same lassitude, and a languor weighed upon me all day. I felt myself a changed girl. A strange melancholy was stealing over me, a melancholy that I would not have interrupted. Dim thoughts of death began to open, and an idea that I was slowly sinking took gentle, and, somehow, not unwelcome, possession of me. If it was sad, the tone of mind which this induced was also sweet.

Whatever it might be, my soul acquiesced in it.

I would not admit that I was ill, I would not consent to tell my papa, or to have the doctor sent for.

Carmilla became more devoted to me than ever, and her strange paroxysms of languid adoration more frequent. She used to gloat on me with increasing ardor the more my strength and spirits waned. This always shocked me like a momentary glare of insanity.

Without knowing it, I was now in a pretty advanced stage of the strangest illness under which mortal ever suffered. There was an unaccountable fascination in its earlier symptoms that more than reconciled me to the incapacitating effect of that stage of the malady. This fascination increased for a time, until it reached a certain point, when gradually a sense of the horrible mingled itself with it, deepening, as you shall hear, until it discolored and perverted the whole state of my life.

The first change I experienced was rather agreeable. It was very near the turning point from which began the descent of Avernus.

Certain vague and strange sensations visited me in my sleep. The prevailing one was of that pleasant, peculiar cold thrill which we feel in bathing, when we move against the current of a river. This was soon accompanied by dreams that seemed interminable, and were so vague that I could never recollect their scenery and persons, or any one connected portion of their action. But they left an awful impression, and a sense of exhaustion, as if I had passed through a long period of great mental exertion and danger.

After all these dreams there remained on waking a remembrance of having been in a place very nearly dark, and of having spoken to people whom I could not see; and especially of one clear voice, of a female's, very deep, that spoke as if at a distance, slowly, and producing always the same sensation of indescribable solemnity and fear. Sometimes there came a sensation as if a hand was drawn softly along my cheek and neck. Sometimes it was as if warm lips kissed me, and longer and longer and more lovingly as they reached my throat, but there the caress fixed itself. My heart beat faster, my breathing rose and fell rapidly and full drawn; a sobbing, that rose into a sense of strangulation, supervened, and turned into a dreadful convulsion, in which my senses left me and I became unconscious.

It was now three weeks since the commencement of this unaccountable state.

My sufferings had, during the last week, told upon my appearance. I had grown pale, my eyes were dilated and darkened underneath, and the languor which I had long felt began to display itself in my countenance.

My father asked me often whether I was ill; but, with an obstinacy which now seems to me unaccountable, I persisted in assuring him that I was quite well.

Carmilla

In a sense this was true. I had no pain, I could complain of no bodily derangement. My complaint seemed to be one of the imagination, or the nerves, and, horrible as my sufferings were, I kept them, with a morbid reserve, very nearly to myself.

It could not be that terrible complaint which the peasants called the oupire, for I had now been suffering for three weeks, and they were seldom ill for much more than three days, when death put an end to their miseries.

Carmilla complained of dreams and feverish sensations, but by no means of so alarming a kind as mine. I say that mine were extremely alarming. Had I been capable of comprehending my condition, I would have invoked aid and advice on my knees. The narcotic of an unsuspected influence was acting upon me, and my perceptions were benumbed.

I am going to tell you now of a dream that led immediately to an odd discovery.

One night, instead of the voice I was accustomed to hear in the dark, I heard one, sweet and tender, and at the same time terrible, which said,

"Your mother warns you to beware of the assassin." At the same time a light unexpectedly sprang up, and I saw Carmilla, standing, near the foot of my bed, in her white nightdress, bathed, from her chin to her feet, in one great stain of blood.

I wakened with a shriek, possessed with the one idea that Carmilla was being murdered. I remember springing from my bed, and my next recollection is that of standing on the lobby, crying for help.

Madame and Mademoiselle came scurrying out of their rooms in alarm; a lamp burned always on the lobby, and seeing me, they soon learned the cause of my terror.

I insisted on our knocking at Carmilla's door. Our knocking was unanswered.

It soon became a pounding and an uproar. We shrieked her name, but all was vain.

We all grew frightened, for the door was locked. We hurried

back, in panic, to my room. There we rang the bell long and furiously. If my father's room had been at that side of the house, we would have called him up at once to our aid. But, alas! he was quite out of hearing, and to reach him involved an excursion for which we none of us had courage.

Servants, however, soon came running up the stairs; I had got on my dressing gown and slippers meanwhile, and my companions were already similarly furnished. Recognizing the voices of the servants on the lobby, we sallied out together; and having renewed, as fruitlessly, our summons at Carmilla's door, I ordered the men to force the lock. They did so, and we stood, holding our lights aloft, in the doorway, and so stared into the room.

We called her by name; but there was still no reply. We looked round the room. Everything was undisturbed. It was exactly in the state in which I had left it on bidding her good night. But Carmilla was gone.

VIII.

Search

At sight of the room, perfectly undisturbed except for our violent entrance, we began to cool a little, and soon recovered our senses sufficiently to dismiss the men. It had struck Mademoiselle that possibly Carmilla had been wakened by the uproar at her door, and in her first panic had jumped from her bed, and hid herself in a press, or behind a curtain, from which she could not, of course, emerge until the majordomo and his myrmidons had withdrawn. We now recommenced our search, and began to call her name again.

It was all to no purpose. Our perplexity and agitation increased. We examined the windows, but they were secured. I implored of Carmilla, if she had concealed herself, to play this cruel trick no longer—to come out and to end our anxieties. It was all useless. I was by this time convinced that she was not in the room, nor in the dressing room, the door of which was still locked on this side. She could not have passed it. I was utterly puzzled. Had Carmilla discovered one of those secret passages which the old housekeeper said were known to exist in the schloss, although the tradition of their exact situation had been lost? A little time would, no doubt, explain all—utterly perplexed as, for the present, we were.

It was past four o'clock, and I preferred passing the remaining hours of darkness in Madame's room. Daylight brought no solution of the difficulty.

The whole household, with my father at its head, was in a state of agitation next morning. Every part of the chateau was searched. The grounds were explored. No trace of the missing lady could be discovered. The stream was about to be dragged; my father was in distraction; what a tale to have to tell the poor girl's mother on her return. I, too, was almost beside myself, though my grief was quite of a different kind.

The morning was passed in alarm and excitement. It was now one o'clock, and still no tidings. I ran up to Carmilla's room, and found her standing at her dressing table. I was astounded. I could not believe my eyes. She beckoned me to her with her pretty finger, in silence. Her face expressed extreme fear.

I ran to her in an ecstasy of joy; I kissed and embraced her again and again. I ran to the bell and rang it vehemently, to bring others to the spot who might at once relieve my father's anxiety.

"Dear Carmilla, what has become of you all this time? We have been in agonies of anxiety about you," I exclaimed. "Where have you been? How did you come back?"

"Last night has been a night of wonders," she said.

"For mercy's sake, explain all you can."

"It was past two last night," she said, "when I went to sleep as usual in my bed, with my doors locked, that of the dressing room, and that opening upon the gallery. My sleep was uninterrupted, and, so far as I know, dreamless; but I woke just now on the sofa in the dressing room there, and I found the door between the rooms open, and the other door forced. How could all this have happened without my being wakened? It must have been accompanied with a great deal of noise, and I am particularly easily wakened; and how could I have been carried out of my bed without my sleep having been interrupted, I whom the slightest stir startles?"

By this time, Madame, Mademoiselle, my father, and a number of the servants were in the room. Carmilla was, of course, overwhelmed with inquiries, congratulations, and welcomes. She had but one story to tell, and seemed the least able of all the party to suggest any way of accounting for what had happened.

My father took a turn up and down the room, thinking. I saw Carmilla's eye follow him for a moment with a sly, dark glance.

When my father had sent the servants away, Mademoiselle having gone in search of a little bottle of valerian and salvolatile, and there being no one now in the room with Carmilla, except my father, Madame, and myself, he came to her thoughtfully, took her hand very kindly, led her to the sofa, and sat down beside her.

Carmilla

"Will you forgive me, my dear, if I risk a conjecture, and ask a question?"

"Who can have a better right?" she said. "Ask what you please, and I will tell you everything. But my story is simply one of bewilderment and darkness. I know absolutely nothing. Put any question you please, but you know, of course, the limitations mamma has placed me under."

"Perfectly, my dear child. I need not approach the topics on which she desires our silence. Now, the marvel of last night consists in your having been removed from your bed and your room, without being wakened, and this removal having occurred apparently while the windows were still secured, and the two doors locked upon the inside. I will tell you my theory and ask you a question."

Carmilla was leaning on her hand dejectedly; Madame and I were listening breathlessly.

"Now, my question is this. Have you ever been suspected of walking in your sleep?"

"Never, since I was very young indeed."

"But you did walk in your sleep when you were young?"

"Yes; I know I did. I have been told so often by my old nurse."

My father smiled and nodded.

"Well, what has happened is this. You got up in your sleep, unlocked the door, not leaving the key, as usual, in the lock, but taking it out and locking it on the outside; you again took the key out, and carried it away with you to some one of the five-and-twenty rooms on this floor, or perhaps upstairs or downstairs. There are so many rooms and closets, so much heavy furniture, and such accumulations of lumber, that it would require a week to search this old house thoroughly. Do you see, now, what I mean?"

"I do, but not all," she answered.

"And how, papa, do you account for her finding herself on

the sofa in the dressing room, which we had searched so carefully?"

"She came there after you had searched it, still in her sleep, and at last awoke spontaneously, and was as much surprised to find herself where she was as any one else. I wish all mysteries were as easily and innocently explained as yours, Carmilla," he said, laughing. "And so we may congratulate ourselves on the certainty that the most natural explanation of the occurrence is one that involves no drugging, no tampering with locks, no burglars, or poisoners, or witches—nothing that need alarm Carmilla, or anyone else, for our safety."

Carmilla was looking charmingly. Nothing could be more beautiful than her tints. Her beauty was, I think, enhanced by that graceful languor that was peculiar to her. I think my father was silently contrasting her looks with mine, for he said:

"I wish my poor Laura was looking more like herself"; and he sighed.

So our alarms were happily ended, and Carmilla restored to her friends.

IX.

The Doctor

As Carmilla would not hear of an attendant sleeping in her room, my father arranged that a servant should sleep outside her door, so that she would not attempt to make another such excursion without being arrested at her own door.

That night passed quietly; and next morning early, the doctor, whom my father had sent for without telling me a word about it, arrived to see me.

Madame accompanied me to the library; and there the grave little doctor, with white hair and spectacles, whom I mentioned before, was waiting to receive me.

I told him my story, and as I proceeded he grew graver and graver.

We were standing, he and I, in the recess of one of the windows, facing one another. When my statement was over, he leaned with his shoulders against the wall, and with his eyes fixed on me earnestly, with an interest in which was a dash of horror.

After a minute's reflection, he asked Madame if he could see my father.

He was sent for accordingly, and as he entered, smiling, he said:

"I dare say, doctor, you are going to tell me that I am an old fool for having brought you here; I hope I am."

But his smile faded into shadow as the doctor, with a very grave face, beckoned him to him.

He and the doctor talked for some time in the same recess where I had just conferred with the physician. It seemed an earnest and argumentative conversation. The room is very large, and I and Madame stood together, burning with curiosity, at the farther end. Not a word could we hear, however, for they spoke in a very low tone, and the deep recess of the window quite concealed the doctor from view, and very nearly my father, whose foot, arm, and shoulder only could we see; and the voices were, I suppose, all the less audible for the sort of closet which the thick wall and window formed.

After a time my father's face looked into the room; it was pale, thoughtful, and, I fancied, agitated.

"Laura, dear, come here for a moment. Madame, we shan't trouble you, the doctor says, at present."

Accordingly I approached, for the first time a little alarmed; for, although I felt very weak, I did not feel ill; and strength, one always fancies, is a thing that may be picked up when we please.

My father held out his hand to me, as I drew near, but he was looking at the doctor, and he said:

"It certainly is very odd; I don't understand it quite. Laura, come here, dear; now attend to Doctor Spielsberg, and recollect yourself."

"You mentioned a sensation like that of two needles piercing the skin, somewhere about your neck, on the night when you experienced your first horrible dream. Is there still any soreness?"

"None at all," I answered.

"Can you indicate with your finger about the point at which you think this occurred?"

"Very little below my throat—here," I answered.

I wore a morning dress, which covered the place I pointed to.

"Now you can satisfy yourself," said the doctor. "You won't mind your papa's lowering your dress a very little. It is necessary, to detect a symptom of the complaint under which you have been suffering."

I acquiesced. It was only an inch or two below the edge of my collar.

"God bless me!—so it is," exclaimed my father, growing pale.

"You see it now with your own eyes," said the doctor, with a gloomy triumph.

"What is it?" I exclaimed, beginning to be frightened.

"Nothing, my dear young lady, but a small blue spot, about the size of the tip of your little finger; and now," he continued, turning to papa, "the question is what is best to be done?"

Is there any danger?"I urged, in great trepidation.

"I trust not, my dear," answered the doctor. "I don't see why you should not recover. I don't see why you should not begin immediately to get better. That is the point at which the sense of strangulation begins?"

"Yes," I answered.

"And—recollect as well as you can—the same point was a kind of center of that thrill which you described just now, like the current of a cold stream running against you?"

"It may have been; I think it was."

"Ay, you see?" he added, turning to my father. "Shall I say a word to Madame?"

"Certainly," said my father.

He called Madame to him, and said:

"I find my young friend here far from well. It won't be of any great consequence, I hope; but it will be necessary that some steps be taken, which I will explain by-and-by; but in the meantime, Madame, you will be so good as not to let Miss Laura be alone for one moment. That is the only direction I need give for the present. It is indispensable."

"We may rely upon your kindness, Madame, I know," added my father.

Madame satisfied him eagerly.

"And you, dear Laura, I know you will observe the doctor's direction."

"I shall have to ask your opinion upon another patient, whose symptoms slightly resemble those of my daughter, that have just been detailed to you — very much milder in degree, but I believe quite of the same sort. She is a young lady — our guest; but as you say you will be passing this way again this evening, you can't do better than take your supper here, and you can then see her. She does not come down till the afternoon."

"I thank you," said the doctor. "I shall be with you, then, at about seven this evening."

And then they repeated their directions to me and to Madame, and with this parting charge my father left us, and walked out with the doctor; and I saw them pacing together up and down between the road and the moat, on the grassy platform in front of the castle, evidently absorbed in earnest conversation.

The doctor did not return. I saw him mount his horse there, take his leave, and ride away eastward through the forest.

Nearly at the same time I saw the man arrive from Dranfield with the letters, and dismount and hand the bag to my father.

In the meantime, Madame and I were both busy, lost in conjecture as to the reasons of the singular and earnest direction which the doctor and my father had concurred in imposing. Madame, as she afterwards told me, was afraid the doctor apprehended a sudden seizure, and that, without prompt assistance, I might either lose my life in a fit, or at least be seriously hurt.

The interpretation did not strike me; and I fancied, perhaps luckily for my nerves, that the arrangement was prescribed simply to secure a companion, who would prevent my taking too much exercise, or eating unripe fruit, or doing any of the fifty foolish things to which young people are supposed to be prone.

About half an hour after my father came in — he had a letter in his hand — and said:

"This letter had been delayed; it is from General Spielsdorf. He might have been here yesterday, he may not come till tomorrow or he may be here today."

He put the open letter into my hand; but he did not look pleased, as he used when a guest, especially one so much loved as the General, was coming.

On the contrary, he looked as if he wished him at the bottom of the Red Sea. There was plainly something on his mind which he did not choose to divulge.

"Papa, darling, will you tell me this?" said I, suddenly laying my hand on his arm, and looking, I am sure, imploringly in his face.

"Perhaps," he answered, smoothing my hair caressingly over my eyes.

"Does the doctor think me very ill?"

"No, dear; he thinks, if right steps are taken, you will be quite well again, at least, on the high road to a complete recovery, in a day or two," he answered, a little dryly. "I wish our good friend, the General, had chosen any other time; that is, I wish you had been perfectly well to receive him."

"But do tell me, papa," I insisted, "what does he think is the matter with me?"

"Nothing; you must not plague me with questions," he answered, with more irritation than I ever remember him to have displayed before; and seeing that I looked wounded, I suppose, he kissed me, and added, "You shall know all about it in a day or two; that is, all that I know. In the meantime you are not to trouble your head about it."

He turned and left the room, but came back before I had done wondering and puzzling over the oddity of all this; it was merely to say that he was going to Karnstein, and had ordered the carriage to be ready at twelve, and that I and Madame should accompany him; he was going to see the priest who lived near those picturesque grounds, upon business, and as Carmilla had never seen them, she could follow, when she came down, with Mademoiselle, who would bring materials for what you call a picnic, which might be laid for us in the ruined castle.

At twelve o'clock, accordingly, I was ready, and not long after, my father, Madame and I set out upon our projected drive.

Passing the drawbridge we turn to the right, and follow the road over the steep Gothic bridge, westward, to reach the deserted village and ruined castle of Karnstein.

No sylvan drive can be fancied prettier. The ground breaks into gentle hills and hollows, all clothed with beautiful wood, totally destitute of the comparative formality which artificial planting and early culture and pruning impart.

The irregularities of the ground often lead the road out of its course, and cause it to wind beautifully round the sides of broken hollows and the steeper sides of the hills, among varieties of ground almost inexhaustible.

Turning one of these points, we suddenly encountered our old friend, the General, riding towards us, attended by a mounted servant. His portmanteaus were following in a hired wagon, such as we term a cart.

The General dismounted as we pulled up, and, after the usual greetings, was easily persuaded to accept the vacant seat in the carriage and send his horse on with his servant to the schloss.

X.
Bereaved

It was about ten months since we had last seen him: but that time had sufficed to make an alteration of years in his appearance. He had grown thinner; something of gloom and anxiety had taken the place of that cordial serenity which used to characterize his features. His dark blue eyes, always penetrating, now gleamed with a sterner light from under his shaggy grey eyebrows. It was not such a change as grief alone usually induces, and angrier passions seemed to have had their share in bringing it about.

We had not long resumed our drive, when the General began to talk, with his usual soldierly directness, of the bereavement, as he termed it, which he had sustained in the death of his beloved niece and ward; and he then broke out in a tone of intense bitterness and fury, inveighing against the "hellish arts" to which she had fallen a victim, and expressing, with more exasperation than piety, his wonder that Heaven should tolerate so monstrous an indulgence of the lusts and malignity of hell.

My father, who saw at once that something very extraordinary had befallen, asked him, if not too painful to him, to detail the circumstances which he thought justified the strong terms in which he expressed himself.

"I should tell you all with pleasure," said the General, "but you would not believe me."

"Why should I not?" he asked.

"Because," he answered testily, "you believe in nothing but what consists with your own prejudices and illusions. I remember when I was like you, but I have learned better."

"Try me," said my father; "I am not such a dogmatist as you suppose.

Besides which, I very well know that you generally require proof for what you believe, and am, therefore, very strongly predisposed to respect your conclusions."

"You are right in supposing that I have not been led lightly into a belief in the marvelous—for what I have experienced is marvelous—and I have been forced by extraordinary evidence to credit that which ran counter, diametrically, to all my theories. I have been made the dupe of a preternatural conspiracy."

Notwithstanding his professions of confidence in the General's penetration, I saw my father, at this point, glance at the General, with, as I thought, a marked suspicion of his sanity.

The General did not see it, luckily. He was looking gloomily and curiously into the glades and vistas of the woods that were opening before us.

"You are going to the Ruins of Karnstein?" he said. "Yes, it is a lucky coincidence; do you know I was going to ask you to bring me there to inspect them. I have a special object in exploring. There is a ruined chapel, ain't there, with a great many tombs of that extinct family?"

"So there are—highly interesting," said my father. "I hope you are thinking of claiming the title and estates?"

My father said this gaily, but the General did not recollect the laugh, or even the smile, which courtesy exacts for a friend's joke; on the contrary, he looked grave and even fierce, ruminating on a matter that stirred his anger and horror.

"Something very different," he said, gruffly. "I mean to unearth some of those fine people. I hope, by God's blessing, to accomplish a pious sacrilege here, which will relieve our earth of certain monsters, and enable honest people to sleep in their beds without being assailed by murderers. I have strange things to tell you, my dear friend, such as I myself would have scouted as incredible a few months since."

My father looked at him again, but this time not with a glance of suspicion—with an eye, rather, of keen intelligence and alarm.

"The house of Karnstein," he said, "has been long extinct: a hundred years at least. My dear wife was maternally descended from the Karnsteins. But the name and title have long ceased to exist. The castle is a ruin; the very village is deserted; it is fifty years since the smoke of a chimney was seen there; not a roof left."

"Quite true. I have heard a great deal about that since I last saw you; a great deal that will astonish you. But I had better relate everything in the order in which it occurred," said the General. "You saw my dear ward—my child, I may call her. No creature could have been more beautiful, and only three months ago none more blooming."

"Yes, poor thing! when I saw her last she certainly was quite lovely," said my father. "I was grieved and shocked more than I can tell you, my dear friend; I knew what a blow it was to you."

He took the General's hand, and they exchanged a kind pressure. Tears gathered in the old soldier's eyes. He did not seek to conceal them. He said:

"We have been very old friends; I knew you would feel for me, childless as I am. She had become an object of very near interest to me, and repaid my care by an affection that cheered my home and made my life happy. That is all gone. The years that remain to me on earth may not be very long; but by God's mercy I hope to accomplish a service to mankind before I die, and to subserve the vengeance of Heaven upon the fiends who have murdered my poor child in the spring of her hopes and beauty!"

"You said, just now, that you intended relating everything as it occurred," said my father. "Pray do; I assure you that it is not mere curiosity that prompts me."

By this time we had reached the point at which the Drunstall road, by which the General had come, diverges from the road which we were traveling to Karnstein.

"How far is it to the ruins?" inquired the General, looking anxiously forward.

"About half a league," answered my father. "Pray let us hear the story you were so good as to promise."

XI.

The Story

With all my heart," said the General, with an effort; and after a short pause in which to arrange his subject, he commenced one of the strangest narratives I ever heard.

"My dear child was looking forward with great pleasure to the visit you had been so good as to arrange for her to your charming daughter." Here he made me a gallant but melancholy bow. "In the meantime we had an invitation to my old friend the Count Carlsfeld, whose schloss is about six leagues to the other side of Karnstein. It was to attend the series of fetes which, you remember, were given by him in honor of his illustrious visitor, the Grand Duke Charles."

"Yes; and very splendid, I believe, they were," said my father.

"Princely! But then his hospitalities are quite regal. He has Aladdin's lamp. The night from which my sorrow dates was devoted to a magnificent masquerade. The grounds were thrown open, the trees hung with colored lamps. There was such a display of fireworks as Paris itself had never witnessed. And such music—music, you know, is my weakness—such ravishing music! The finest instrumental band, perhaps, in the world, and the finest singers who could be collected from all the great operas in Europe. As you wandered through these fantastically illuminated grounds, the moon-lighted chateau throwing a rosy light from its long rows of windows, you would suddenly hear these ravishing voices stealing from the silence of some grove, or rising from boats upon the lake. I felt myself, as I looked and listened, carried back into the romance and poetry of my early youth.

"When the fireworks were ended, and the ball beginning, we returned to the noble suite of rooms that were thrown open to the dancers. A masked ball, you know, is a beautiful sight; but so brilliant a spectacle of the kind I never saw before.

"It was a very aristocratic assembly. I was myself almost the only 'nobody' present.

"My dear child was looking quite beautiful. She wore no

mask. Her excitement and delight added an unspeakable charm to her features, always lovely. I remarked a young lady, dressed magnificently, but wearing a mask, who appeared to me to be observing my ward with extraordinary interest. I had seen her, earlier in the evening, in the great hall, and again, for a few minutes, walking near us, on the terrace under the castle windows, similarly employed. A lady, also masked, richly and gravely dressed, and with a stately air, like a person of rank, accompanied her as a chaperon.

Had the young lady not worn a mask, I could, of course, have been much more certain upon the question whether she was really watching my poor darling.

I am now well assured that she was.

"We were now in one of the salons. My poor dear child had been dancing, and was resting a little in one of the chairs near the door; I was standing near. The two ladies I have mentioned had approached and the younger took the chair next my ward; while her companion stood beside me, and for a little time addressed herself, in a low tone, to her charge.

"Availing herself of the privilege of her mask, she turned to me, and in the tone of an old friend, and calling me by my name, opened a conversation with me, which piqued my curiosity a good deal. She referred to many scenes where she had met me—at Court, and at distinguished houses. She alluded to little incidents which I had long ceased to think of, but which, I found, had only lain in abeyance in my memory, for they instantly started into life at her touch.

"I became more and more curious to ascertain who she was, every moment. She parried my attempts to discover very adroitly and pleasantly. The knowledge she showed of many passages in my life seemed to me all but unaccountable; and she appeared to take a not unnatural pleasure in foiling my curiosity, and in seeing me flounder in my eager perplexity, from one conjecture to another.

"In the meantime the young lady, whom her mother called by the odd name of Millarca, when she once or twice addressed her, had, with the same ease and grace, got into conversation with my ward.

"She introduced herself by saying that her mother was a very old acquaintance of mine. She spoke of the agreeable audacity which a mask rendered practicable; she talked like a friend; she admired her dress, and insinuated very prettily her admiration of her beauty. She amused her with laughing criticisms upon the people who crowded the ballroom, and laughed at my poor child's fun. She was very witty and lively when she pleased, and after a time they had grown very good friends, and the young stranger lowered her mask, displaying a remarkably beautiful face. I had never seen it before, neither had my dear child. But though it was new to us, the features were so engaging, as well as lovely, that it was impossible not to feel the attraction powerfully. My poor girl did so. I never saw anyone more taken with another at first sight, unless, indeed, it was the stranger herself, who seemed quite to have lost her heart to her.

"In the meantime, availing myself of the license of a masquerade, I put not a few questions to the elder lady.

"'You have puzzled me utterly,' I said, laughing. 'Is that not enough?

Won't you, now, consent to stand on equal terms, and do me the kindness to remove your mask?'

"'Can any request be more unreasonable?' she replied. 'Ask a lady to yield an advantage! Beside, how do you know you should recognize me? Years make changes.'

"'As you see,' I said, with a bow, and, I suppose, a rather melancholy little laugh.

"'As philosophers tell us,' she said; 'and how do you know that a sight of my face would help you?'

"'I should take chance for that,' I answered. 'It is vain trying to make yourself out an old woman; your figure betrays you.'

"'Years, nevertheless, have passed since I saw you, rather since you saw me, for that is what I am considering. Millarca, there, is my daughter; I cannot then be young, even in the opinion of people whom time has taught to be indulgent, and I may not like to be compared with what you remember me.

Carmilla

You have no mask to remove. You can offer me nothing in exchange.'

"'My petition is to your pity, to remove it.'

"'And mine to yours, to let it stay where it is,' she replied.

"'Well, then, at least you will tell me whether you are French or German; you speak both languages so perfectly.'

"'I don't think I shall tell you that, General; you intend a surprise, and are meditating the particular point of attack.'

"'At all events, you won't deny this,' I said, 'that being honored by your permission to converse, I ought to know how to address you. Shall I say Madame la Comtesse?'

"She laughed, and she would, no doubt, have met me with another evasion—if, indeed, I can treat any occurrence in an interview every circumstance of which was prearranged, as I now believe, with the profoundest cunning, as liable to be modified by accident.

"'As to that,' she began; but she was interrupted, almost as she opened her lips, by a gentleman, dressed in black, who looked particularly elegant and distinguished, with this drawback, that his face was the most deadly pale I ever saw, except in death. He was in no masquerade—in the plain evening dress of a gentleman; and he said, without a smile, but with a courtly and unusually low bow:—

"'Will Madame la Comtesse permit me to say a very few words which may interest her?'

"The lady turned quickly to him, and touched her lip in token of silence; she then said to me, 'Keep my place for me, General; I shall return when I have said a few words.'

"And with this injunction, playfully given, she walked a little aside with the gentleman in black, and talked for some minutes, apparently very earnestly. They then walked away slowly together in the crowd, and I lost them for some minutes.

"I spent the interval in cudgeling my brains for a conjecture as to the identity of the lady who seemed to remember me so kindly, and I was thinking of turning about and joining in the conversation between my pretty ward and the Countess's daughter, and trying whether, by the time she returned, I might not have a surprise in store for her, by having her name, title, chateau, and estates at my fingers' ends. But at this moment she returned, accompanied by the pale man in black, who said:

"'I shall return and inform Madame la Comtesse when her carriage is at the door.'

"He withdrew with a bow."

XII.

A Petition

"'Then we are to lose Madame la Comtesse, but I hope only for a few hours,' I said, with a low bow.

"'It may be that only, or it may be a few weeks. It was very unlucky his speaking to me just now as he did. Do you now know me?'

"I assured her I did not.

"'You shall know me,' she said, 'but not at present. We are older and better friends than, perhaps, you suspect. I cannot yet declare myself. I shall in three weeks pass your beautiful schloss, about which I have been making enquiries. I shall then look in upon you for an hour or two, and renew a friendship which I never think of without a thousand pleasant recollections. This moment a piece of news has reached me like a thunderbolt. I must set out now, and travel by a devious route, nearly a hundred miles, with all the dispatch I can possibly make. My perplexities multiply. I am only deterred by the compulsory reserve I practice as to my name from making a very singular request of you. My poor child has not quite recovered her strength. Her horse fell with her, at a hunt which she had ridden out to witness, her nerves have not yet recovered the shock, and our physician says that she must on no account exert herself for some time to come. We came here, in consequence, by very easy stages—hardly six leagues a day. I must now travel day and night, on a mission of life and death—a mission the critical and momentous nature of which I shall be able to explain to you when we meet, as I hope we shall, in a few weeks, without the necessity of any concealment.'

"She went on to make her petition, and it was in the tone of a person from whom such a request amounted to conferring, rather than seeking a favor.

"This was only in manner, and, as it seemed, quite unconsciously. Than the terms in which it was expressed, nothing could be more deprecatory. It was simply that I would consent to take charge of her daughter during her absence.

"This was, all things considered, a strange, not to say, an

audacious request. She in some sort disarmed me, by stating and admitting everything that could be urged against it, and throwing herself entirely upon my chivalry. At the same moment, by a fatality that seems to have predetermined all that happened, my poor child came to my side, and, in an undertone, besought me to invite her new friend, Millarca, to pay us a visit. She had just been sounding her, and thought, if her mamma would allow her, she would like it extremely.

"At another time I should have told her to wait a little, until, at least, we knew who they were. But I had not a moment to think in. The two ladies assailed me together, and I must confess the refined and beautiful face of the young lady, about which there was something extremely engaging, as well as the elegance and fire of high birth, determined me; and, quite overpowered, I submitted, and undertook, too easily, the care of the young lady, whom her mother called Millarca.

"The Countess beckoned to her daughter, who listened with grave attention while she told her, in general terms, how suddenly and peremptorily she had been summoned, and also of the arrangement she had made for her under my care, adding that I was one of her earliest and most valued friends.

"I made, of course, such speeches as the case seemed to call for, and found myself, on reflection, in a position which I did not half like.

"The gentleman in black returned, and very ceremoniously conducted the lady from the room.

"The demeanor of this gentleman was such as to impress me with the conviction that the Countess was a lady of very much more importance than her modest title alone might have led me to assume.

"Her last charge to me was that no attempt was to be made to learn more about her than I might have already guessed, until her return. Our distinguished host, whose guest she was, knew her reasons.

"'But here,' she said, 'neither I nor my daughter could safely remain for more than a day. I removed my mask imprudently for a moment, about an hour ago, and, too late, I fancied you saw me. So I resolved to seek an opportunity of talking a little to you. Had I found that you had seen me, I would have thrown myself on your high sense of honor to keep my secret some weeks. As it is, I am satisfied that you did not see me; but if you now suspect, or, on reflection, should suspect, who I am, I commit myself, in like manner, entirely to your honor. My daughter will observe the same secrecy, and I well know that you will, from time to time, remind her, lest she should thoughtlessly disclose it.'

"She whispered a few words to her daughter, kissed her hurriedly twice, and went away, accompanied by the pale gentleman in black, and disappeared in the crowd.

"'In the next room,' said Millarca, 'there is a window that looks upon the hall door. I should like to see the last of mamma, and to kiss my hand to her.'

"We assented, of course, and accompanied her to the window. We looked out, and saw a handsome old-fashioned carriage, with a troop of couriers and footmen. We saw the slim figure of the pale gentleman in black, as he held a thick velvet cloak, and placed it about her shoulders and threw the hood over her head. She nodded to him, and just touched his hand with hers. He bowed low repeatedly as the door closed, and the carriage began to move.

"'She is gone,' said Millarca, with a sigh.

"'She is gone,' I repeated to myself, for the first time—in the hurried moments that had elapsed since my consent—reflecting upon the folly of my act.

"'She did not look up,' said the young lady, plaintively.

"'The Countess had taken off her mask, perhaps, and did not care to show her face,' I said; 'and she could not know that you were in the window.'

"She sighed, and looked in my face. She was so beautiful that I relented. I was sorry I had for a moment repented of my hospitality, and I determined to make her amends for the unavowed churlishness of my reception.

"The young lady, replacing her mask, joined my ward in persuading me to return to the grounds, where the concert was soon to be renewed. We did so, and walked up and down the terrace that lies under the castle windows.

Millarca became very intimate with us, and amused us with lively descriptions and stories of most of the great people whom we saw upon the terrace. I liked her more and more every minute. Her gossip without being ill-natured, was extremely diverting to me, who had been so long out of the great world. I thought what life she would give to our sometimes lonely evenings at home.

"This ball was not over until the morning sun had almost reached the horizon. It pleased the Grand Duke to dance till then, so loyal people could not go away, or think of bed.

"We had just got through a crowded saloon, when my ward asked me what had become of Millarca. I thought she had been by her side, and she fancied she was by mine. The fact was, we had lost her.

"All my efforts to find her were vain. I feared that she had mistaken, in the confusion of a momentary separation from us, other people for her new friends, and had, possibly, pursued and lost them in the extensive grounds which were thrown open to us.

"Now, in its full force, I recognized a new folly in my having undertaken the charge of a young lady without so much as knowing her name; and fettered as I was by promises, of the reasons for imposing which I knew nothing, I could not even point my inquiries by saying that the missing young lady was the daughter of the Countess who had taken her departure a few hours before.

"Morning broke. It was clear daylight before I gave up my search. It was not till near two o'clock next day that we heard anything of my missing charge.

"At about that time a servant knocked at my niece's door, to say that he had been earnestly requested by a young lady, who appeared to be in great distress, to make out where she could find the General Baron Spielsdorf and the young lady his daughter, in whose charge she had been left by her mother.

"There could be no doubt, notwithstanding the slight

inaccuracy, that our young friend had turned up; and so she had. Would to heaven we had lost her!

"She told my poor child a story to account for her having failed to recover us for so long. Very late, she said, she had got to the housekeeper's bedroom in despair of finding us, and had then fallen into a deep sleep which, long as it was, had hardly sufficed to recruit her strength after the fatigues of the ball.

"That day Millarca came home with us. I was only too happy, after all, to have secured so charming a companion for my dear girl."

XIII.

The Woodman

"There soon, however, appeared some drawbacks. In the first place, Millarca complained of extreme languor — the weakness that remained after her late illness — and she never emerged from her room till the afternoon was pretty far advanced. In the next place, it was accidentally discovered, although she always locked her door on the inside, and never disturbed the key from its place till she admitted the maid to assist at her toilet, that she was undoubtedly sometimes absent from her room in the very early morning, and at various times later in the day, before she wished it to be understood that she was stirring. She was repeatedly seen from the windows of the schloss, in the first faint grey of the morning, walking through the trees, in an easterly direction, and looking like a person in a trance. This convinced me that she walked in her sleep. But this hypothesis did not solve the puzzle. How did she pass out from her room, leaving the door locked on the inside? How did she escape from the house without unbarring door or window?

"In the midst of my perplexities, an anxiety of a far more urgent kind presented itself.

"My dear child began to lose her looks and health, and that in a manner so mysterious, and even horrible, that I became thoroughly frightened.

"She was at first visited by appalling dreams; then, as she fancied, by a specter, sometimes resembling Millarca, sometimes in the shape of a beast, indistinctly seen, walking round the foot of her bed, from side to side.

"Lastly came sensations. One, not unpleasant, but very peculiar, she said, resembled the flow of an icy stream against her breast. At a later time, she felt something like a pair of large needles pierce her, a little below the throat, with a very sharp pain. A few nights after, followed a gradual and convulsive sense of strangulation; then came unconsciousness."

I could hear distinctly every word the kind old General was saying, because by this time we were driving upon the short grass that spreads on either side of the road as you approach the roofless village which had not shown the smoke of a chimney for more than half a century.

You may guess how strangely I felt as I heard my own symptoms so exactly described in those which had been experienced by the poor girl who, but for the catastrophe which followed, would have been at that moment a visitor at my father's chateau. You may suppose, also, how I felt as I heard him detail habits and mysterious peculiarities which were, in fact, those of our beautiful guest, Carmilla!

A vista opened in the forest; we were on a sudden under the chimneys and gables of the ruined village, and the towers and battlements of the dismantled castle, round which gigantic trees are grouped, overhung us from a slight eminence.

In a frightened dream I got down from the carriage, and in silence, for we had each abundant matter for thinking; we soon mounted the ascent, and were among the spacious chambers, winding stairs, and dark corridors of the castle.

"And this was once the palatial residence of the Karnsteins!" said the old General at length, as from a great window he looked out across the village, and saw the wide, undulating expanse of forest. "It was a bad family, and here its bloodstained annals were written," he continued. "It is hard that they should, after death, continue to plague the human race with their atrocious lusts. That is the chapel of the Karnsteins, down there."

He pointed down to the grey walls of the Gothic building partly visible through the foliage, a little way down the steep. "And I hear the axe of a woodman," he added, "busy among the trees that surround it; he possibly may give us the information of which I am in search, and point out the grave of Mircalla, Countess of Karnstein. These rustics preserve the local traditions of great families, whose stories die out among the rich and titled so soon as the families themselves become extinct."

"We have a portrait, at home, of Mircalla, the Countess Karnstein; should you like to see it?" asked my father.

"Time enough, dear friend," replied the General. "I believe that I have seen the original; and one motive which has led me to you earlier than I at first intended, was to explore the chapel which we are now approaching."

"What! see the Countess Mircalla," exclaimed my father; "why, she has been dead more than a century!"

"Not so dead as you fancy, I am told," answered the General.

"I confess, General, you puzzle me utterly," replied my father, looking at him, I fancied, for a moment with a return of the suspicion I detected before. But although there was anger and detestation, at times, in the old General's manner, there was nothing flighty.

"There remains to me," he said, as we passed under the heavy arch of the Gothic church — for its dimensions would have justified its being so styled — "but one object which can interest me during the few years that remain to me on earth, and that is to wreak on her the vengeance which, I thank God, may still be accomplished by a mortal arm."

"What vengeance can you mean?" asked my father, in increasing amazement.

"I mean, to decapitate the monster," he answered, with a fierce flush, and a stamp that echoed mournfully through the hollow ruin, and his clenched hand was at the same moment raised, as if it grasped the handle of an axe, while he shook it ferociously in the air.

"What?" exclaimed my father, more than ever bewildered.

"To strike her head off."

"Cut her head off!"

"Aye, with a hatchet, with a spade, or with anything that can cleave through her murderous throat. You shall hear," he answered, trembling with rage. And hurrying forward he said:

"That beam will answer for a seat; your dear child is fatigued; let her be seated, and I will, in a few sentences, close my dreadful story."

The squared block of wood, which lay on the grass-grown

pavement of the chapel, formed a bench on which I was very glad to seat myself, and in the meantime the General called to the woodman, who had been removing some boughs which leaned upon the old walls; and, axe in hand, the hardy old fellow stood before us.

He could not tell us anything of these monuments; but there was an old man, he said, a ranger of this forest, at present sojourning in the house of the priest, about two miles away, who could point out every monument of the old Karnstein family; and, for a trifle, he undertook to bring him back with him, if we would lend him one of our horses, in little more than half an hour.

"Have you been long employed about this forest?" asked my father of the old man.

"I have been a woodman here," he answered in his patois, "under the forester, all my days; so has my father before me, and so on, as many generations as I can count up. I could show you the very house in the village here, in which my ancestors lived."

"How came the village to be deserted?" asked the General.

"It was troubled by revenants, sir; several were tracked to their graves, there detected by the usual tests, and extinguished in the usual way, by decapitation, by the stake, and by burning; but not until many of the villagers were killed.

"But after all these proceedings according to law," he continued—"so many graves opened, and so many vampires deprived of their horrible animation—the village was not relieved. But a Moravian nobleman, who happened to be traveling this way, heard how matters were, and being skilled—as many people are in his country—in such affairs, he offered to deliver the village from its tormentor. He did so thus: There being a bright moon that night, he ascended, shortly after sunset, the towers of the chapel here, from whence he could distinctly see the churchyard beneath him; you can see it from that window. From this point he watched until he saw the vampire come out of his grave, and place near it the linen clothes in which he had been folded, and then glide away towards the village to plague its inhabitants.

"The stranger, having seen all this, came down from the steeple, took the linen wrappings of the vampire, and carried them up to the top of the tower, which he again mounted. When the vampire returned from his prowlings and missed his clothes, he cried furiously to the Moravian, whom he saw at the summit of the tower, and who, in reply, beckoned him to ascend and take them. Whereupon the vampire, accepting his invitation, began to climb the steeple, and so soon as he had reached the battlements, the Moravian, with a stroke of his sword, clove his skull in twain, hurling him down to the churchyard, whither, descending by the winding stairs, the stranger followed and cut his head off, and next day delivered it and the body to the villagers, who duly impaled and burnt them.

"This Moravian nobleman had authority from the then head of the family to remove the tomb of Mircalla, Countess Karnstein, which he did effectually, so that in a little while its site was quite forgotten."

"Can you point out where it stood?" asked the General, eagerly.

The forester shook his head, and smiled.

"Not a soul living could tell you that now," he said; "besides, they say her body was removed; but no one is sure of that either."

Having thus spoken, as time pressed, he dropped his axe and departed, leaving us to hear the remainder of the General's strange story.

XIV.

The Meeting

"My beloved child," he resumed, "was now growing rapidly worse. The physician who attended her had failed to produce the slightest impression on her disease, for such I then supposed it to be. He saw my alarm, and suggested a consultation. I called in an abler physician, from Gratz.

Several days elapsed before he arrived. He was a good and pious, as well as a learned man. Having seen my poor ward together, they withdrew to my library to confer and discuss. I, from the adjoining room, where I awaited their summons, heard these two gentlemen's voices raised in something sharper than a strictly philosophical discussion. I knocked at the door and entered. I found the old physician from Gratz maintaining his theory. His rival was combating it with undisguised ridicule, accompanied with bursts of laughter. This unseemly manifestation subsided and the altercation ended on my entrance.

"'Sir,' said my first physician,'my learned brother seems to think that you want a conjuror, and not a doctor.'

"'Pardon me,' said the old physician from Gratz, looking displeased, 'I shall state my own view of the case in my own way another time. I grieve, Monsieur le General, that by my skill and science I can be of no use.

Before I go I shall do myself the honor to suggest something to you.'

"He seemed thoughtful, and sat down at a table and began to write.

Profoundly disappointed, I made my bow, and as I turned to go, the other doctor pointed over his shoulder to his companion who was writing, and then, with a shrug, significantly touched his forehead.

"This consultation, then, left me precisely where I was. I walked out into the grounds, all but distracted. The doctor from Gratz, in ten or fifteen minutes, overtook me. He apologized for having followed me, but said that he could not conscientiously take his leave without a few words more. He told me that he could not be mistaken; no natural disease exhibited the same symptoms; and that death was already very near. There remained, however, a day, or possibly two, of life. If the fatal seizure were at once arrested, with great care and skill her strength might possibly return. But all hung now upon the confines of the irrevocable. One more assault might extinguish the last spark of vitality which is, every moment, ready to die.

"'And what is the nature of the seizure you speak of?' I entreated.

"'I have stated all fully in this note, which I place in your hands upon the distinct condition that you send for the nearest clergyman, and open my letter in his presence, and on no account read it till he is with you; you would despise it else, and it is a matter of life and death. Should the priest fail you, then, indeed, you may read it.'

"He asked me, before taking his leave finally, whether I would wish to see a man curiously learned upon the very subject, which, after I had read his letter, would probably interest me above all others, and he urged me earnestly to invite him to visit him there; and so took his leave.

"The ecclesiastic was absent, and I read the letter by myself. At another time, or in another case, it might have excited my ridicule. But into what quackeries will not people rush for a last chance, where all accustomed means have failed, and the life of a beloved object is at stake?

"Nothing, you will say, could be more absurd than the learned man's letter.

It was monstrous enough to have consigned him to a madhouse. He said that the patient was suffering from the visits of a vampire! The punctures which she described as having occurred near the throat, were, he insisted, the insertion of those two long, thin, and sharp teeth which, it is well known, are peculiar to vampires; and there could be no doubt, he added, as to the well-defined presence of the small livid mark which all concurred in describing as that induced by the demon's lips, and every symptom described by the sufferer was in exact conformity with those recorded in every case of a similar visitation.

Carmilla

"Being myself wholly skeptical as to the existence of any such portent as the vampire, the supernatural theory of the good doctor furnished, in my opinion, but another instance of learning and intelligence oddly associated with some one hallucination. I was so miserable, however, that, rather than try nothing, I acted upon the instructions of the letter.

"I concealed myself in the dark dressing room, that opened upon the poor patient's room, in which a candle was burning, and watched there till she was fast asleep. I stood at the door, peeping through the small crevice, my sword laid on the table beside me, as my directions prescribed, until, a little after one, I saw a large black object, very ill-defined, crawl, as it seemed to me, over the foot of the bed, and swiftly spread itself up to the poor girl's throat, where it swelled, in a moment, into a great, palpitating mass.

"For a few moments I had stood petrified. I now sprang forward, with my sword in my hand. The black creature suddenly contracted towards the foot of the bed, glided over it, and, standing on the floor about a yard below the foot of the bed, with a glare of skulking ferocity and horror fixed on me, I saw Millarca. Speculating I know not what, I struck at her instantly with my sword; but I saw her standing near the door, unscathed. Horrified, I pursued, and struck again. She was gone; and my sword flew to shivers against the door.

"I can't describe to you all that passed on that horrible night. The whole house was up and stirring. The specter Millarca was gone. But her victim was sinking fast, and before the morning dawned, she died."

The old General was agitated. We did not speak to him. My father walked to some little distance, and began reading the inscriptions on the tombstones; and thus occupied, he strolled into the door of a side chapel to prosecute his researches. The General leaned against the wall, dried his eyes, and sighed heavily. I was relieved on hearing the voices of Carmilla and Madame, who were at that moment approaching. The voices died away.

In this solitude, having just listened to so strange a story, connected, as it was, with the great and titled dead, whose monuments were moldering among the dust and ivy round us, and every incident of which bore so awfully upon my own mysterious case—in this haunted spot, darkened by the towering foliage that rose on every side, dense and high above its noiseless walls—a horror began to steal over me, and my heart sank as I thought that my friends were, after all, not about to enter and disturb this triste and ominous scene.

The old General's eyes were fixed on the ground, as he leaned with his hand upon the basement of a shattered monument.

Under a narrow, arched doorway, surmounted by one of those demoniacal grotesques in which the cynical and ghastly fancy of old Gothic carving delights, I saw very gladly the beautiful face and figure of Carmilla enter the shadowy chapel.

I was just about to rise and speak, and nodded smiling, in answer to her peculiarly engaging smile; when with a cry, the old man by my side caught up the woodman's hatchet, and started forward. On seeing him a brutalized change came over her features. It was an instantaneous and horrible transformation, as she made a crouching step backwards. Before I could utter a scream, he struck at her with all his force, but she dived under his blow, and unscathed, caught him in her tiny grasp by the wrist. He struggled for a moment to release his arm, but his hand opened, the axe fell to the ground, and the girl was gone.

He staggered against the wall. His grey hair stood upon his head, and a moisture shone over his face, as if he were at the point of death.

The frightful scene had passed in a moment. The first thing I recollect after, is Madame standing before me, and impatiently repeating again and again, the question, "Where is Mademoiselle Carmilla?"

I answered at length, "I don't know—I can't tell—she went there," and I pointed to the door through which Madame had just entered; "only a minute or two since."

"But I have been standing there, in the passage, ever since Mademoiselle Carmilla entered; and she did not return."

She then began to call "Carmilla," through every door and passage and from the windows, but no answer came.

"She called herself Carmilla?" asked the General, still agitated.

"Carmilla, yes," I answered.

"Aye," he said; "that is Millarca. That is the same person who long ago was called Mircalla, Countess Karnstein. Depart from this accursed ground, my poor child, as quickly as you can. Drive to the clergyman's house, and stay there till we come. Begone! May you never behold Carmilla more; you will not find her here."

XV.
Ordeal and Execution

As he spoke one of the strangest looking men I ever beheld entered the chapel at the door through which Carmilla had made her entrance and her exit. He was tall, narrow-chested, stooping, with high shoulders, and dressed in black. His face was brown and dried in with deep furrows; he wore an oddly-shaped hat with a broad leaf. His hair, long and grizzled, hung on his shoulders. He wore a pair of gold spectacles, and walked slowly, with an odd shambling gait, with his face sometimes turned up to the sky, and sometimes bowed down towards the ground, seemed to wear a perpetual smile; his long thin arms were swinging, and his lank hands, in old black gloves ever so much too wide for them, waving and gesticulating in utter abstraction.

"The very man!" exclaimed the General, advancing with manifest delight. "My dear Baron, how happy I am to see you, I had no hope of meeting you so soon." He signed to my father, who had by this time returned, and leading the fantastic old gentleman, whom he called the Baron to meet him. He introduced him formally, and they at once entered into earnest conversation. The stranger took a roll of paper from his pocket, and spread it on the worn surface of a tomb that stood by. He had a pencil case in his fingers, with which he traced imaginary lines from point to point on the paper, which from their often glancing from it, together, at certain points of the building, I concluded to be a plan of the chapel. He accompanied, what I may term, his lecture, with occasional readings from a dirty little book, whose yellow leaves were closely written over.

They sauntered together down the side aisle, opposite to the spot where I was standing, conversing as they went; then they began measuring distances by paces, and finally they all stood together, facing a piece of the sidewall, which they began to examine with great minuteness; pulling off the ivy that clung over it, and rapping the plaster with the ends of their sticks, scraping here, and knocking there. At length they ascertained the existence of a broad marble tablet, with letters carved in relief upon it.

With the assistance of the woodman, who soon returned, a

monumental inscription, and carved escutcheon, were disclosed. They proved to be those of the long lost monument of Mircalla, Countess Karnstein.

The old General, though not I fear given to the praying mood, raised his hands and eyes to heaven, in mute thanksgiving for some moments.

"Tomorrow," I heard him say; "the commissioner will be here, and the Inquisition will be held according to law."

Then turning to the old man with the gold spectacles, whom I have described, he shook him warmly by both hands and said:

"Baron, how can I thank you? How can we all thank you? You will have delivered this region from a plague that has scourged its inhabitants for more than a century. The horrible enemy, thank God, is at last tracked."

My father led the stranger aside, and the General followed. I know that he had led them out of hearing, that he might relate my case, and I saw them glance often quickly at me, as the discussion proceeded.

My father came to me, kissed me again and again, and leading me from the chapel, said:

"It is time to return, but before we go home, we must add to our party the good priest, who lives but a little way from this; and persuade him to accompany us to the schloss."

In this quest we were successful: and I was glad, being unspeakably fatigued when we reached home. But my satisfaction was changed to dismay, on discovering that there were no tidings of Carmilla. Of the scene that had occurred in the ruined chapel, no explanation was offered to me, and it was clear that it was a secret which my father for the present determined to keep from me.

The sinister absence of Carmilla made the remembrance of the scene more horrible to me. The arrangements for the night were singular. Two servants, and Madame were to sit up in my room that night; and the ecclesiastic with my father kept watch in the adjoining dressing room.

The priest had performed certain solemn rites that night, the purport of which I did not understand any more than I comprehended the reason of this extraordinary precaution taken for my safety during sleep.

I saw all clearly a few days later.

The disappearance of Carmilla was followed by the discontinuance of my nightly sufferings.

You have heard, no doubt, of the appalling superstition that prevails in Upper and Lower Styria, in Moravia, Silesia, in Turkish Serbia, in Poland, even in Russia; the superstition, so we must call it, of the Vampire.

If human testimony, taken with every care and solemnity, judicially, before commissions innumerable, each consisting of many members, all chosen for integrity and intelligence, and constituting reports more voluminous perhaps than exist upon any one other class of cases, is worth anything, it is difficult to deny, or even to doubt the existence of such a phenomenon as the Vampire.

For my part I have heard no theory by which to explain what I myself have witnessed and experienced, other than that supplied by the ancient and well-attested belief of the country.

The next day the formal proceedings took place in the Chapel of Karnstein.

The grave of the Countess Mircalla was opened; and the General and my father recognized each his perfidious and beautiful guest, in the face now disclosed to view. The features, though a hundred and fifty years had passed since her funeral, were tinted with the warmth of life. Her eyes were open; no cadaverous smell exhaled from the coffin. The two medical men, one officially present, the other on the part of the promoter of the inquiry, attested the marvelous fact that there was a faint but appreciable respiration, and a corresponding action of the heart. The limbs were perfectly flexible, the flesh elastic; and the leaden coffin floated with blood, in which to a depth of seven inches, the body lay immersed.

Here then, were all the admitted signs and proofs of vampirism. The body, therefore, in accordance with the ancient practice, was raised, and a sharp stake driven through the heart of the vampire, who uttered a piercing shriek at the moment, in all respects such as might escape from a living person in the last agony. Then the head was struck off, and a torrent of blood flowed from the severed neck. The body and head was next placed on a pile of wood, and reduced to ashes, which were thrown upon the river and borne away, and that territory has never since been plagued by the visits of a vampire.

My father has a copy of the report of the Imperial Commission, with the signatures of all who were present at these proceedings, attached in verification of the statement. It is from this official paper that I have summarized my account of this last shocking scene.

XVI.
Conclusion

I write all this you suppose with composure. But far from it; I cannot think of it without agitation. Nothing but your earnest desire so repeatedly expressed, could have induced me to sit down to a task that has unstrung my nerves for months to come, and reinduced a shadow of the unspeakable horror which years after my deliverance continued to make my days and nights dreadful, and solitude insupportably terrific.

Let me add a word or two about that quaint Baron Vordenburg, to whose curious lore we were indebted for the discovery of the Countess Mircalla's grave.

He had taken up his abode in Gratz, where, living upon a mere pittance, which was all that remained to him of the once princely estates of his family, in Upper Styria, he devoted himself to the minute and laborious investigation of the marvelously authenticated tradition of Vampirism. He had at his fingers' ends all the great and little works upon the subject.

"Magia Posthuma," "Phlegon de Mirabilibus," "Augustinus de cura pro Mortuis," "Philosophicae et Christianae Cogitationes de Vampiris," by John Christofer Herenberg; and a thousand others, among which I remember only a few of those which he lent to my father. He had a voluminous digest of all the judicial cases, from which he had extracted a system of principles that appear to govern—some always, and others occasionally only—the condition of the vampire. I may mention, in passing, that the deadly pallor attributed to that sort of revenants, is a mere melodramatic fiction. They present, in the grave, and when they show themselves in human society, the appearance of healthy life. When disclosed to light in their coffins, they exhibit all the symptoms that are enumerated as those which proved the vampire-life of the long-dead Countess Karnstein.

How they escape from their graves and return to them for certain hours every day, without displacing the clay or leaving any trace of disturbance in the state of the coffin or the cerements, has always been admitted to be utterly inexplicable. The amphibious existence of the vampire is sustained by daily renewed slumber in the grave. Its horrible lust for living blood supplies the vigor of its waking existence. The vampire is prone to be fascinated with an engrossing vehemence, resembling the passion of love, by particular persons. In pursuit of these it will exercise inexhaustible patience and stratagem, for access to a particular object may be obstructed in a hundred ways. It will never desist until it has satiated its passion, and drained the very life of its coveted victim. But it will, in these cases, husband and protract its murderous enjoyment with the refinement of an epicure, and heighten it by the gradual approaches of an artful courtship. In these cases it seems to yearn for something like sympathy and consent. In ordinary ones it goes direct to its object, overpowers with violence, and strangles and exhausts often at a single feast.

The vampire is, apparently, subject, in certain situations, to special conditions. In the particular instance of which I have given you a relation, Mircalla seemed to be limited to a name which, if not her real one, should at least reproduce, without the omission or addition of a single letter, those, as we say, anagrammatically, which compose it.

Carmilla did this; so did Millarca.

My father related to the Baron Vordenburg, who remained with us for two or three weeks after the expulsion of Carmilla, the story about the Moravian nobleman and the vampire at Karnstein churchyard, and then he asked the Baron how he had discovered the exact position of the long-concealed tomb of the Countess Mircalla? The Baron's grotesque features puckered up into a mysterious smile; he looked down, still smiling on his worn spectacle case and fumbled with it. Then looking up, he said:

"I have many journals, and other papers, written by that remarkable man; the most curious among them is one treating of the visit of which you speak, to Karnstein. The tradition, of course, discolors and distorts a little. He might have been termed a Moravian nobleman, for he had changed his abode to that territory, and was, beside, a noble. But he was, in truth, a native of Upper Styria. It is enough to say that in very early youth he had been a passionate and favored lover of the beautiful Mircalla, Countess Karnstein. Her early death plunged him into inconsolable grief. It is the nature of vampires to increase and multiply, but according to an ascertained and ghostly law.

"Assume, at starting, a territory perfectly free from that pest. How does it begin, and how does it multiply itself? I will tell you. A person, more or less wicked, puts an end to himself. A suicide, under certain circumstances, becomes a vampire. That specter visits living people in their slumbers; they die, and almost invariably, in the grave, develop into vampires. This happened in the case of the beautiful Mircalla, who was haunted by one of those demons. My ancestor, Vordenburg, whose title I still bear, soon discovered this, and in the course of the studies to which he devoted himself, learned a great deal more.

"Among other things, he concluded that suspicion of vampirism would probably fall, sooner or later, upon the dead Countess, who in life had been his idol. He conceived a horror, be she what she might, of her remains being profaned by the outrage of a posthumous execution. He has left a curious paper to prove that the vampire, on its expulsion from its amphibious existence, is projected into a far more horrible life; and he resolved to save his once beloved Mircalla from this.

"He adopted the stratagem of a journey here, a pretended removal of her remains, and a real obliteration of her monument. When age had stolen upon him, and from the vale of years, he looked back on the scenes he was leaving, he considered, in a different spirit, what he had done, and a horror took possession of him. He made the tracings and notes which have guided me to the very spot, and drew up a confession of the deception that he had practiced. If he had intended any further action in this matter, death prevented him; and the hand of a remote descendant has, too late for many, directed the pursuit to the lair of the beast."

We talked a little more, and among other things he said was this:

"One sign of the vampire is the power of the hand. The slender hand of Mircalla closed like a vice of steel on the General's wrist when he raised the hatchet to strike. But its power is not confined to its grasp; it leaves a numbness in the limb it seizes, which is slowly, if ever, recovered from."

Carmilla

The following Spring my father took me a tour through Italy. We remained away for more than a year. It was long before the terror of recent events subsided; and to this hour the image of Carmilla returns to memory with ambiguous alternations — sometimes the playful, languid, beautiful girl; sometimes the writhing fiend I saw in the ruined church; and often from a reverie I have started, fancying I heard the light step of Carmilla at the drawing room door.

In a Glass Darkly

By Joseph Sheridan Le Fanu

GREEN TEA.
PROLOGUE.
MARTIN HESSELIUS,
THE GERMAN PHYSICIAN.

    Though carefully educated in medicine and surgery, I have never practised either. The study of each continues, nevertheless, to interest me profoundly. Neither idleness nor caprice caused my secession from the honourable calling which I had just entered. The cause was a very trifling scratch inflicted by a dissecting knife. This trifle cost me the loss of two fingers, amputated promptly, and the more painful loss of my health, for I have never been quite well since, and have seldom been twelve months together in the same place.

    In my wanderings I became acquainted with Dr. Martin Hesselius, a wanderer like myself, like me a physician, and like me an enthusiast in his profession. Unlike me in this, that his wanderings were voluntary, and he a man, if not of fortune, as we estimate fortune in England, at least in what our forefathers used to term "easy circumstances." He was an old man when I first saw him; nearly five-and-thirty years my senior.

    In Dr. Martin Hesselius, I found my master. His knowledge was immense, his grasp of a case was an intuition. He was the very man to inspire a young enthusiast, like me, with awe and delight. My admiration has stood the test of time and survived the separation of death. I am sure it was well-founded.

    For nearly twenty years I acted as his medical secretary. His immense collection of papers he has left in my care, to be arranged, indexed and bound. His treatment of some of these cases is curious. He writes in two distinct characters. He describes what he saw and heard as an intelligent layman might, and when in this style of narrative he had seen the patient either through his own hall-door, to the light of day, or through the gates of darkness to the caverns of the dead, he returns upon the narrative, and in the terms of his art, and with all the force and originality of genius, proceeds to the work of analysis, diagnosis and illustration.

Here and there a case strikes me as of a kind to amuse or horrify a lay reader with an interest quite different from the peculiar one which it may possess for an expert. With slight modifications, chiefly of language, and of course a change of names, I copy the following. The narrator is Dr. Martin Hesselius. I find it among the voluminous notes of cases which he made during a tour in England about sixty-four years ago.

It is related in a series of letters to his friend Professor Van Loo of Leyden. The professor was not a physician, but a chemist, and a man who read history and metaphysics and medicine, and had, in his day, written a play.

The narrative is therefore, if somewhat less valuable as a medical record, necessarily written in a manner more likely to interest an unlearned reader.

These letters, from a memorandum attached, appear to have been returned on the death of the professor, in 1819, to Dr. Hesselius. They are written, some in English, some in French, but the greater part in German. I am a faithful, though I am conscious, by no means a graceful translator, and although here and there, I omit some passages, and shorten others and disguise names, I have interpolated nothing.

CHAPTER I.
DR. HESSELIUS RELATES HOW HE MET THE REV. MR. JENNINGS.

The Rev. Mr. Jennings is tall and thin. He is middle-aged, and dresses with a natty, old-fashioned, high-church precision. He is naturally a little stately, but not at all stiff. His features, without being handsome, are well formed, and their expression extremely kind, but also shy.

I met him one evening at Lady Mary Heyduke's. The modesty and benevolence of his countenance are extremely prepossessing. We were but a small party, and he joined agreeably enough in the conversation. He seems to enjoy listening very much more than contributing to the talk; but what he says is always to the purpose and well said. He is a great favourite of Lady Mary's, who it seems, consults him upon many things, and thinks him the most happy and blessed person on earth. Little knows she about him.

The Rev. Mr. Jennings is a bachelor, and has, they say, sixty thousand pounds in the funds. He is a charitable man. He is most anxious to be actively employed in his sacred profession, and yet though always tolerably well elsewhere, when he goes down to his vicarage in Warwickshire, to engage in the actual duties of his sacred calling his health soon fails him, and in a very strange way. So says Lady Mary.

There is no doubt that Mr. Jennings' health does break down in, generally a sudden and mysterious way, sometimes in the very act of officiating in his old and pretty church at Kenlis. It may be his heart, it may be his brain. But so it has happened three or four times, or oftener, that after proceeding a certain way in the service, he has on a sudden stopped short, and after a silence, apparently quite unable to resume, he has fallen into solitary, inaudible prayer, his hands and eyes uplifted, and then pale as death, and in the agitation of a strange shame and horror, descended trembling, and got into the vestry-room, leaving his congregation, without explanation, to themselves. This occurred when his curate was absent. When he goes down to Kenlis, now, he always takes care to provide a clergyman to share his duty, and to supply his place on the instant should he become thus suddenly incapacitated.

When Mr. Jennings breaks down quite, and beats a retreat from the vicarage, and returns to London, where, in a dark street off Piccadilly, he inhabits a very narrow house, Lady Mary says that he is always perfectly well. I have my own opinion about that. There are degrees of course. We shall see.

Mr. Jennings is a perfectly gentleman-like man. People, however, remark something odd. There is an impression a little ambiguous. One thing which certainly contributes to it, people I think don't remember; or, perhaps, distinctly remark. But I did, almost immediately. Mr. Jennings has a way of looking sidelong upon the carpet, as if his eye followed the movements of something there. This, of course, is not always. It occurs only now and then. But often enough to give a certain oddity, as I have said to his manner, and in this glance travelling along the floor there is something both shy and anxious.

A medical philosopher, as you are good enough to call me, elaborating theories by the aid of cases sought out by himself, and by him watched and scrutinised with more time at command, and consequently infinitely more minuteness than the ordinary practitioner can afford, falls insensibly into habits of observation, which accompany him everywhere, and are exercised, as some people would say, impertinently, upon every subject that presents itself with the least likelihood of rewarding inquiry.

There was a promise of this kind in the slight, timid, kindly, but reserved gentleman, whom I met for the first time at this agreeable little evening gathering. I observed, of course, more than I here set down; but I reserve all that borders on the technical for a strictly scientific paper.

I may remark, that when I here speak of medical science, I do so, as I hope some day to see it more generally understood, in a much more comprehensive sense than its generally material treatment would warrant. I believe the entire natural world is but the ultimate expression of that spiritual world from which, and in which alone, it has its life. I believe that the essential man is a spirit, that the spirit is an organised substance, but as different in point of material from what we ordinarily understand by matter, as light or electricity is; that the material body is, in the most literal sense, a vesture, and death consequently no interruption of the living man's existence, but simply his extrication from the natural body—a process which commences at the moment of what we term death, and the completion of which, at furthest a few days later, is the resurrection "in power."

The person who weighs the consequences of these positions

will probably see their practical bearing upon medical science. This is, however, by no means the proper place for displaying the proofs and discussing the consequences of this too generally unrecognised state of facts.

In pursuance of my habit, I was covertly observing Mr. Jennings, with all my caution—I think he perceived it—and I saw plainly that he was as cautiously observing me. Lady Mary happening to address me by my name, as Dr. Hesselius, I saw that he glanced at me more sharply, and then became thoughtful for a few minutes.

After this, as I conversed with a gentleman at the other end of the room, I saw him look at me more steadily, and with an interest which I thought I understood. I then saw him take an opportunity of chatting with Lady Mary, and was, as one always is, perfectly aware of being the subject of a distant inquiry and answer.

This tall clergyman approached me by-and-by: and in a little time we had got into conversation. When two people, who like reading, and know books and places, having travelled, wish to converse, it is very strange if they can't find topics. It was not accident that brought him near me, and led him into conversation. He knew German, and had read my Essays on Metaphysical Medicine which suggest more than they actually say.

This courteous man, gentle, shy, plainly a man of thought and reading, who moving and talking among us, was not altogether of us, and whom I already suspected of leading a life whose transactions and alarms were carefully concealed, with an impenetrable reserve from, not only the world, but his best beloved friends—was cautiously weighing in his own mind the idea of taking a certain step with regard to me.

I penetrated his thoughts without his being aware of it, and was careful to say nothing which could betray to his sensitive vigilance my suspicions respecting his position, or my surmises about his plans respecting myself.

We chatted upon indifferent subjects for a time; but at last he said:

"I was very much interested by some papers of yours, Dr. Hesselius, upon what you term Metaphysical Medicine—I read them in German, ten or twelve years ago—have they been translated?"

"No, I'm sure they have not—I should have heard. They would have asked my leave, I think."

"I asked the publishers here, a few months ago, to get the book for me in the original German; but they tell me it is out of print."

"So it is, and has been for some years; but it flatters me as an author to find that you have not forgotten my little book, although," I added, laughing, "ten or twelve years is a considerable time to have managed without it; but I suppose you have been turning the subject over again in your mind, or something has happened lately to revive your interest in it."

At this remark, accompanied by a glance of inquiry, a sudden embarrassment disturbed Mr. Jennings, analogous to that which makes a young lady blush and look foolish. He dropped his eyes, and folded his hands together uneasily, and looked oddly, and you would have said, guiltily for a moment.

I helped him out of his awkwardness in the best way, by appearing not to observe it, and going straight on, I said: "Those revivals of interest in a subject happen to me often; one book suggests another, and often sends me back a wild-goose chase over an interval of twenty years. But if you still care to possess a copy, I shall be only too happy to provide you; I have still got two or three by me—and if you allow me to present one I shall be very much honoured."

"You are very good indeed," he said, quite at his ease again, in a moment: "I almost despaired—I don't know how to thank you."

"Pray don't say a word; the thing is really so little worth that I am only ashamed of having offered it, and if you thank me any more I shall throw it into the fire in a fit of modesty."

Mr. Jennings laughed. He inquired where I was staying in London, and after a little more conversation on a variety of subjects, he took his departure.

CHAPTER II.
THE DOCTOR QUESTIONS LADY MARY, AND SHE ANSWERS.

"I like your vicar so much, Lady Mary," said I, so soon as he was gone. "He has read, travelled, and thought, and having also suffered, he ought to be an accomplished companion."

"So he is, and, better still, he is a really good man," said she. "His advice is invaluable about my schools, and all my little undertakings at Dawlbridge, and he's so painstaking, he takes so much trouble — you have no idea — wherever he thinks he can be of use: he's so good-natured and so sensible."

"It is pleasant to hear so good an account of his neighbourly virtues. I can only testify to his being an agreeable and gentle companion, and in addition to what you have told me, I think I can tell you two or three things about him," said I.

"Really!"

"Yes, to begin with, he's unmarried."

"Yes, that's right, — go on."

"He has been writing, that is he was, but for two or three years perhaps, he has not gone on with his work, and the book was upon some rather abstract subject — perhaps theology."

"Well, he was writing a book, as you say; I'm not quite sure what it was about, but only that it was nothing that I cared for, very likely you are right, and he certainly did stop — yes."

"And although he only drank a little coffee here to-night, he likes tea, at least, did like it, extravagantly."

"Yes, that's quite true."

"He drank green tea, a good deal, didn't he?" I pursued.

"Well, that's very odd! Green tea was a subject on which we used almost to quarrel."

"But he has quite given that up," said I.

"So he has."

626

"And, now, one more fact. His mother or his father, did you know them?"

"Yes, both; his father is only ten years dead, and their place is near Dawlbridge. We knew them very well," she answered.

"Well, either his mother or his father—I should rather think his father, saw a ghost," said I.

"Well, you really are a conjurer, Dr. Hesselius."

"Conjurer or no, haven't I said right?" I answered merrily.

"You certainly have, and it was his father: he was a silent, whimsical man, and he used to bore my father about his dreams, and at last he told him a story about a ghost he had seen and talked with, and a very odd story it was. I remember it particularly, because I was so afraid of him. This story was long before he died—when I was quite a child—and his ways were so silent and moping, and he used to drop in, sometimes, in the dusk, when I was alone in the drawing-room, and I used to fancy there were ghosts about him."

I smiled and nodded.

"And now having established my character as a conjurer I think I must say good-night," said I.

"But how did you find it out?"

"By the planets of course, as the gipsies do," I answered, and so, gaily, we said good-night.

Next morning I sent the little book he had been inquiring after, and a note to Mr. Jennings, and on returning late that evening, I found that he had called, at my lodgings, and left his card. He asked whether I was at home, and asked at what hour he would be most likely to find me.

Does he intend opening his case, and consulting me "professionally," as they say? I hope so. I have already conceived a theory about him. It is supported by Lady Mary's answers to my parting questions. I should like much to ascertain from his own lips. But what can I do consistently with good breeding to invite a confession? Nothing. I rather think he meditates one. At all events, my dear Van L., I shan't make myself difficult of access; I mean to return his visit to-morrow. It will be only civil in return for his politeness, to ask to see him.

Perhaps something may come of it. Whether much, little, or nothing, my dear Van L., you shall hear.

CHAPTER III.
DR. HESSELIUS PICKS UP SOMETHING IN LATIN BOOKS.

Well, I have called at Blank street.

On inquiring at the door, the servant told me that Mr. Jennings was engaged very particularly with a gentleman, a clergyman from Kenlis, his parish in the country. Intending to reserve my privilege and to call again, I merely intimated that I should try another time, and had turned to go, when the servant begged my pardon, and asked me, looking at me a little more attentively than well-bred persons of his order usually do, whether I was Dr. Hesselius; and, on learning that I was, he said, "Perhaps then, sir, you would allow me to mention it to Mr. Jennings, for I am sure he wishes to see you."

The servant returned in a moment, with a message from Mr. Jennings, asking me to go into his study, which was in effect his back drawing-room, promising to be with me in a very few minutes.

This was really a study—almost a library. The room was lofty, with two tall slender windows, and rich dark curtains. It was much larger than I had expected, and stored with books on every side, from the floor to the ceiling. The upper carpet—for to my tread it felt that there were two or three—was a Turkey carpet. My steps fell noiselessly. The book-cases standing out, placed the windows, particularly narrow ones, in deep recesses. The effect of the room was, although extremely comfortable, and even luxurious, decidedly gloomy, and aided by the silence, almost oppressive. Perhaps, however, I ought to have allowed something for association. My mind had connected peculiar ideas with Mr. Jennings. I stepped into this perfectly silent room, of a very silent house, with a peculiar foreboding; and its darkness, and solemn clothing of books, for except where two narrow looking-glasses were set in the wall, they were everywhere, helped this sombre feeling.

While awaiting Mr. Jennings' arrival, I amused myself by looking into some of the books with which his shelves were laden. Not among these, but immediately under them, with their backs upward, on the floor, I lighted upon a complete set of Swedenborg's Arcana Cælestia, in the original Latin, a very fine folio set, bound in the natty livery which theology affects, pure vellum, namely, gold letters, and carmine edges. There were paper markers in several of these volumes, I raised and placed them, one after the other, upon the table, and opening where these papers were placed, I read in the solemn Latin phraseology, a series of sentences indicated by a pencilled line at the margin. Of these I copy here a few, translating them into English.

"When man's interior sight is opened, which is that of his spirit, then there appear the things of another life, which cannot possibly be made visible to the bodily sight."...

"By the internal sight it has been granted me to see the things that are in the other life, more clearly than I see those that are in the world. From these considerations, it is evident that external vision exists from interior vision, and this from a vision still more interior, and so on."...

"There are with every man at least two evil spirits."...

"With wicked genii there is also a fluent speech, but harsh and grating. There is also among them a speech which is not fluent, wherein the dissent of the thoughts is perceived as something secretly creeping along within it."...

"The evil spirits associated with man are, indeed, from the hells, but when with man they are not then in hell, but are taken out thence. The place where they then are is in the midst between heaven and hell, and is called the world of spirits—when the evil spirits who are with man, are in that world, they are not in any infernal torment, but in every thought and affection of the man, and so, in all that the man himself enjoys. But when they are remitted into their hell, they return to their former state."...

"If evil spirits could perceive that they were associated with man, and yet that they were spirits separate from him, and if they could flow in into the things of his body, they would attempt by a thousand means to destroy him; for they hate man with a deadly hatred."...

"Knowing, therefore, that I was a man in the body, they were continually striving to destroy me, not as to the body only, but especially as to the soul; for to destroy any man or spirit is the very delight of the life of all who are in hell; but I have been continually protected by the Lord. Hence it appears how dangerous it is for man to be in a living consort with spirits, unless he be in the good of faith."...

In a Glass Darkly

"Nothing is more carefully guarded from the knowledge of associate spirits than their being thus conjoint with a man, for if they knew it they would speak to him, with the intention to destroy him."...

"The delight of hell is to do evil to man, and to hasten his eternal ruin."

A long note, written with a very sharp and fine pencil, in Mr. Jennings' neat hand, at the foot of the page, caught my eye. Expecting his criticism upon the text, I read a word or two, and stopped, for it was something quite different, and began with these words, Deus misereatur mei—"May God compassionate me." Thus warned of its private nature, I averted my eyes, and shut the book, replacing all the volumes as I had found them, except one which interested me, and in which, as men studious and solitary in their habits will do, I grew so absorbed as to take no cognisance of the outer world, nor to remember where I was.

I was reading some pages which refer to "representatives" and "correspondents," in the technical language of Swedenborg, and had arrived at a passage, the substance of which is, that evil spirits, when seen by other eyes than those of their infernal associates, present themselves, by "correspondence," in the shape of the beast (fera) which represents their particular lust and life, in aspect direful and atrocious. This is a long passage, and particularises a number of those bestial forms.

CHAPTER IV.
FOUR EYES WERE READING THE PASSAGE.

I was running the head of my pencil-case along the line as I read it, and something caused me to raise my eyes.

Directly before me was one of the mirrors I have mentioned, in which I saw reflected the tall shape of my friend Mr. Jennings leaning over my shoulder, and reading the page at which I was busy, and with a face so dark and wild that I should hardly have known him.

I turned and rose. He stood erect also, and with an effort laughed a little, saying:

"I came in and asked you how you did, but without succeeding in awaking you from your book; so I could not restrain my curiosity, and very impertinently, I'm afraid, peeped over your shoulder. This is not your first time of looking into those pages. You have looked into Swedenborg, no doubt, long ago?"

"Oh dear, yes! I owe Swedenborg a great deal; you will discover traces of him in the little book on Metaphysical Medicine, which you were so good as to remember."

Although my friend affected a gaiety of manner, there was a slight flush in his face, and I could perceive that he was inwardly much perturbed.

"I'm scarcely yet qualified, I know so little of Swedenborg. I've only had them a fortnight," he answered, "and I think they are rather likely to make a solitary man nervous—that is, judging from the very little I have read—I don't say that they have made me so," he laughed; "and I'm so very much obliged for the book. I hope you got my note?"

I made all proper acknowledgments and modest disclaimers.

"I never read a book that I go with, so entirely, as that of yours," he continued. "I saw at once there is more in it than is quite unfolded. Do you know Dr. Harley?" he asked, rather abruptly.

In passing, the editor remarks that the physician here named was one of the most eminent who had ever practised in England.

I did, having had letters to him, and had experienced from him great courtesy and considerable assistance during my visit to England.

"I think that man one of the very greatest fools I ever met in my life," said Mr. Jennings.

This was the first time I had ever heard him say a sharp thing of anybody, and such a term applied to so high a name a little startled me.

"Really! and in what way?" I asked.

"In his profession," he answered.

I smiled.

"I mean this," he said: "he seems to me, one half, blind—I mean one half of all he looks at is dark—preternaturally bright and vivid all the rest; and the worst of it is, it seems wilful. I can't get him—I mean he won't—I've had some experience of him as a physician, but I look on him as, in that sense, no better than a paralytic mind, an intellect half dead, I'll tell you—I know I shall some time—all about it," he said, with a little agitation. "You stay some months longer in England. If I should be out of town during your stay for a little time, would you allow me to trouble you with a letter?"

"I should be only too happy," I assured him.

"Very good of you. I am so utterly dissatisfied with Harley."

"A little leaning to the materialistic school," I said.

"A mere materialist," he corrected me; "you can't think how that sort of thing worries one who knows better. You won't tell any one—any of my friends you know—that I am hippish; now, for instance, no one knows—not even Lady Mary—that I have seen Dr. Harley, or any other doctor. So pray don't mention it; and, if I should have any threatening of an attack, you'll kindly let me write, or, should I be in town, have a little talk with you."

I was full of conjecture, and unconsciously I found I had fixed my eyes gravely on him, for he lowered his for a moment, and he said:

"I see you think I might as well tell you now, or else you are forming a conjecture; but you may as well give it up. If you were guessing all the rest of your life, you will never hit on it."

He shook his head smiling, and over that wintry sunshine a black cloud suddenly came down, and he drew his breath in, through his teeth as men do in pain.

"Sorry, of course, to learn that you apprehend occasion to consult any of us; but, command me when and how you like, and I need not assure you that your confidence is sacred."

He then talked of quite other things, and in a comparatively cheerful way and after a little time, I took my leave.

CHAPTER V.
DOCTOR HESSELIUS IS SUMMONED TO RICHMOND.

We parted cheerfully, but he was not cheerful, nor was I. There are certain expressions of that powerful organ of spirit—the human face—which, although I have seen them often, and possess a doctor's nerve, yet disturb me profoundly. One look of Mr. Jennings haunted me. It had seized my imagination with so dismal a power that I changed my plans for the evening, and went to the opera, feeling that I wanted a change of ideas.

I heard nothing of or from him for two or three days, when a note in his hand reached me. It was cheerful, and full of hope. He said that he had been for some little time so much better—quite well, in fact—that he was going to make a little experiment, and run down for a month or so to his parish, to try whether a little work might not quite set him up. There was in it a fervent religious expression of gratitude for his restoration, as he now almost hoped he might call it.

A day or two later I saw Lady Mary, who repeated what his note had announced, and told me that he was actually in Warwickshire, having resumed his clerical duties at Kenlis; and she added, "I begin to think that he is really perfectly well, and that there never was anything the matter, more than nerves and fancy; we are all nervous, but I fancy there is nothing like a little hard work for that kind of weakness, and he has made up his mind to try it. I should not be surprised if he did not come back for a year."

Notwithstanding all this confidence, only two days later I had this note, dated from his house off Piccadilly:

"Dear Sir.—I have returned disappointed. If I should feel at all able to see you, I shall write to ask you kindly to call. At present I am too low, and, in fact, simply unable to say all I wish to say. Pray don't mention my name to my friends. I can see no one. By-and-by, please God, you shall hear from me. I mean to take a run into Shropshire, where some of my people are. God bless you! May we, on my return, meet more happily than I can now write."

About a week after this I saw Lady Mary at her own house, the last person, she said, left in town, and just on the wing for Brighton, for the London season was quite over. She told me that she had heard from Mr. Jennings' niece, Martha, in Shropshire. There was nothing to be gathered from her letter, more than that he was low and nervous. In those words, of which healthy people think so lightly, what a world of suffering is sometimes hidden!

Nearly five weeks passed without any further news of Mr. Jennings. At the end of that time I received a note from him. He wrote:

"I have been in the country, and have had change of air, change of scene, change of faces, change of everything and in everything—but myself. I have made up my mind, so far as the most irresolute creature on earth can do it, to tell my case fully to you. If your engagements will permit, pray come to me to-day, to-morrow, or the next day; but, pray defer as little as possible. You know not how much I need help. I have a quiet house at Richmond, where I now am. Perhaps you can manage to come to dinner, or to luncheon, or even to tea. You shall have no trouble in finding me out. The servant at Blank street, who takes this note, will have a carriage at your door at any hour you please; and I am always to be found. You will say that I ought not to be alone. I have tried everything. Come and see."

I called up the servant, and decided on going out the same evening, which accordingly I did.

He would have been much better in a lodging-house, or hotel, I thought, as I drove up through a short double row of sombre elms to a very old-fashioned brick house, darkened by the foliage of these trees, which over-topped, and nearly surrounded it. It was a perverse choice, for nothing could be imagined more triste and silent. The house, I found, belonged to him. He had stayed for a day or two in town, and, finding it for some cause insupportable, had come out here, probably because being furnished and his own, he was relieved of the thought and delay of selection, by coming here.

The sun had already set, and the red reflected light of the western sky illuminated the scene with the peculiar effect with which we are all familiar. The hall seemed very dark, but, getting to the back drawing-room, whose windows command the west, I was again in the same dusky light.

I sat down, looking out upon the richly-wooded landscape that glowed in the grand and melancholy light which was every moment fading. The corners of the room were already dark; all was growing dim, and the gloom was insensibly toning my

In a Glass Darkly

mind, already prepared for what was sinister. I was waiting alone for his arrival, which soon took place. The door communicating with the front room opened, and the tall figure of Mr. Jennings, faintly seen in the ruddy twilight, came, with quiet stealthy steps, into the room.

We shook hands, and, taking a chair to the window, where there was still light enough to enable us to see each other's faces, he sat down beside me, and, placing his hand upon my arm, with scarcely a word of preface began his narrative.

CHAPTER VI.
HOW MR. JENNINGS MET HIS COMPANION.

The faint glow of the west, the pomp of the then lonely woods of Richmond, were before us, behind and about us the darkening room, and on the stony face or the sufferer—for the character of his face, though still gentle and sweet, was changed—rested that dim, odd glow which seems to descend and produce, where it touches, lights, sudden though faint, which are lost, almost without gradation, in darkness. The silence, too, was utter; not a distant wheel, or bark, or whistle from without; and within the depressing stillness of an invalid bachelor's house.

I guessed well the nature, though not even vaguely the particulars of the revelations I was about to receive, from that fixed face of suffering that so oddly flushed stood out, like a portrait of Schalken's, before its background of darkness.

"It began," he said, "on the 15th of October, three years and eleven weeks ago, and two days—I keep very accurate count, for every day is torment. If I leave anywhere a chasm in my narrative tell me.

"About four years ago I began a work, which had cost me very much thought and reading. It was upon the religious metaphysics of the ancients."

"I know," said I; "the actual religion of educated and thinking paganism, quite apart from symbolic worship? A wide and very interesting field."

"Yes; but not good for the mind—the Christian mind, I mean. Paganism is all bound together in essential unity, and, with evil sympathy, their religion involves their art, and both their manners, and the subject is a degrading fascination and the nemesis sure. God forgive me!

"I wrote a great deal; I wrote late at night. I was always thinking on the subject, walking about, wherever I was, everywhere. It thoroughly infected me. You are to remember that all the material ideas connected with it were more or less of the beautiful, the subject itself delightfully interesting, and I, then, without a care."

He sighed heavily.

"I believe that every one who sets about writing in earnest does his work, as a friend of mine phrased it, on something—tea, or coffee, or tobacco. I suppose there is a material waste that must be hourly supplied in such occupations, or that we should grow too abstracted, and the mind, as it were, pass out of the body, unless it were reminded often of the connection by actual sensation. At all events, I felt the want, and I supplied it. Tea was my companion—at first the ordinary black tea, made in the usual way, not too strong: but I drank a good deal, and increased its strength as I went on. I never experienced an uncomfortable symptom from it. I began to take a little green tea. I found the effect pleasanter, it cleared and intensified the power of thought so. I had come to take it frequently, but not stronger than one might take it for pleasure. I wrote a great deal out here, it was so quiet, and in this room. I used to sit up very late, and it became a habit with me to sip my tea—green tea—every now and then as my work proceeded. I had a little kettle on my table, that swung over a lamp, and made tea two or three times between eleven o'clock and two or three in the morning, my hours of going to bed. I used to go into town every day. I was not a monk, and, although I spent an hour or two in a library, hunting up authorities and looking out lights upon my theme, I was in no morbid state as far as I can judge. I met my friends pretty much as usual, and enjoyed their society, and, on the whole, existence had never been, I think, so pleasant before.

"I had met with a man who had some odd old books, German editions in mediæval Latin, and I was only too happy to be permitted access to them. This obliging person's books were in the City, a very out-of-the-way part of it. I had rather out-stayed my intended hour, and, on coming out, seeing no cab near, I was tempted to get into the omnibus which used to drive past this house. It was darker than this by the time the 'bus had reached an old house, you may have remarked, with four poplars at each side of the door, and there the last passenger but myself got out. We drove along rather faster. It was twilight now. I leaned back in my corner next the door ruminating pleasantly.

"The interior of the omnibus was nearly dark. I had observed in the corner opposite to me at the other side, and at the end next the horses, two small circular reflections, as it seemed to me of a reddish light. They were about two inches apart, and about the size of those small brass buttons that yachting men used to put upon their jackets. I began to speculate, as listless men will, upon this trifle, as it seemed.

From what centre did that faint but deep red light come, and from what—glass beads, buttons, toy decorations—was it reflected? We were lumbering along gently, having nearly a mile still to go. I had not solved the puzzle, and it became in another minute more odd, for these two luminous points, with a sudden jerk, descended nearer the floor, keeping still their relative distance and horizontal position, and then, as suddenly, they rose to the level of the seat on which I was sitting, and I saw them no more.

"My curiosity was now really excited, and, before I had time to think, I saw again these two dull lamps, again together near the floor; again they disappeared, and again in their old corner I saw them.

"So, keeping my eyes upon them, I edged quietly up my own side, towards the end at which I still saw these tiny discs of red.

"There was very little light in the 'bus. It was nearly dark. I leaned forward to aid my endeavour to discover what these little circles really were. They shifted their position a little as I did so. I began now to perceive an outline of something black, and I soon saw with tolerable distinctness the outline of a small black monkey, pushing its face forward in mimicry to meet mine; those were its eyes, and I now dimly saw its teeth grinning at me.

"I drew back, not knowing whether it might not meditate a spring. I fancied that one of the passengers had forgot this ugly pet, and wishing to ascertain something of its temper, though not caring to trust my fingers to it, I poked my umbrella softly towards it. It remained immovable—up to it—through it! For through it, and back and forward, it passed, without the slightest resistance.

"I can't, in the least, convey to you the kind of horror that I felt. When I had ascertained that the thing was an illusion, as I then supposed, there came a misgiving about myself and a terror that fascinated me in impotence to remove my gaze from the eyes of the brute for some moments. As I looked, it made a little skip back, quite into the corner, and I, in a panic, found myself at the door, having put my head out, drawing deep breaths of the outer air, and staring at the lights and trees we were passing, too glad to reassure myself of reality.

"I stopped the 'bus and got out. I perceived the man look oddly at me as I paid him. I daresay there was something unusual in my looks and manner, for I had never felt so strangely before."

CHAPTER VII.
THE JOURNEY: FIRST STAGE.

"When the omnibus drove on, and I was alone upon the road, I looked carefully round to ascertain whether the monkey had followed me. To my indescribable relief I saw it nowhere. I can't describe easily what a shock I had received, and my sense of genuine gratitude on finding myself, as I supposed, quite rid of it.

"I had got out a little before we reached this house, two or three hundred steps. A brick wall runs along the footpath, and inside the wall is a hedge of yew or some dark evergreen of that kind, and within that again the row of fine trees which you may have remarked as you came.

"This brick wall is about as high as my shoulder, and happening to raise my eyes I saw the monkey, with that stooping gait, on all fours, walking or creeping, close beside me on top of the wall. I stopped looking at it with a feeling of loathing and horror. As I stopped so did it. It sat up on the wall with its long hands on its knees looking at me. There was not light enough to see it much more than in outline, nor was it dark enough to bring the peculiar light of its eyes into strong relief. I still saw, however, that red foggy light plainly enough. It did not show its teeth, nor exhibit any sign of irritation, but seemed jaded and sulky, and was observing me steadily.

"I drew back into the middle of the road. It was an unconscious recoil, and there I stood, still looking at it, it did not move.

"With an instinctive determination to try something — anything, I turned about and walked briskly towards town with a skance look, all the time, watching the movements of the beast. It crept swiftly along the wall, at exactly my pace.

"Where the wall ends, near the turn of the road, it came down and with a wiry spring or two brought itself close to my feet, and continued to keep up with me, as I quickened my pace. It was at my left side, so close to my leg that I felt every moment as if I should tread upon it.

"The road was quite deserted and silent, and it was darker every moment. I stopped dismayed and bewildered, turning as I did so, the other way — I mean, towards this house, away from which I had been walking. When I stood still, the monkey drew back to a distance of, I suppose, about five or six yards, and remained stationary, watching me.

"I had been more agitated than I have said. I had read, of course, as every one has, something about 'spectral illusions,' as you physicians term the phenomena of such cases. I considered my situation, and looked my misfortune in the face.

"These affections, I had read, are sometimes transitory and sometimes obstinate. I had read of cases in which the appearance, at first harmless, had, step by step, degenerated into something direful and insupportable, and ended by wearing its victim out. Still as I stood there, but for my bestial companion, quite alone, I tried to comfort myself by repeating again and again the assurance, 'the thing is purely disease, a well-known physical affection, as distinctly as small-pox or neuralgia. Doctors are all agreed on that, philosophy demonstrates it. I must not be a fool. I've been sitting up too late, and I daresay my digestion is quite wrong, and with God's help, I shall be all right, and this is but a symptom of nervous dyspepsia.' Did I believe all this? Not one word of it, no more than any other miserable being ever did who is once seized and riveted in this satanic captivity. Against my convictions, I might say my knowledge, I was simply bullying myself into a false courage.

"I now walked homeward. I had only a few hundred yards to go. I had forced myself into a sort of resignation, but I had not got over the sickening shock and the flurry of the first certainty of my misfortune.

"I made up my mind to pass the night at home. The brute moved close beside me, and I fancied there was the sort of anxious drawing toward the house, which one sees in tired horses or dogs, sometimes as they come toward home.

"I was afraid to go into town, I was afraid of any one's seeing and recognising me. I was conscious of an irrepressible agitation in my manner. Also, I was afraid of any violent change in my habits, such as going to a place of amusement, or walking from home in order to fatigue myself. At the hall-door it waited till I mounted the steps, and when the door was opened entered with me.

"I drank no tea that night. I got cigars and some brandy-and-water. My idea was that I should act upon my material system, and by living for a while in sensation apart from thought, send myself forcibly, as it it were, into a new groove. I came up here to this drawing-room. I sat just here. The monkey then got upon a small table that then stood there. It looked dazed and languid. An irrepressible uneasiness as to its movements kept my eyes always upon it. Its eyes were half closed, but I could see them glow. It was looking steadily at me. In all situations, at all hours, it is awake and looking at me. That never changes.

"I shall not continue in detail my narrative of this particular night. I shall describe, rather, the phenomena of the first year, which never varied, essentially. I shall describe the monkey as it appeared in daylight. In the dark, as you shall presently hear, there are peculiarities. It is a small monkey, perfectly black. It had only one peculiarity—a character of malignity—unfathomable malignity. During the first year it looked sullen and sick. But this character of intense malice and vigilance was always underlying that surly languor. During all that time it acted as if on a plan of giving me as little trouble as was consistent with watching me. Its eyes were never off me, I have never lost sight of it, except in my sleep, light or dark, day or night, since it came here, excepting when it withdraws for some weeks at a time, unaccountably.

"In total dark it is visible as in daylight. I do not mean merely its eyes. It is all visible distinctly in a halo that resembles a glow of red embers, and which accompanies it in all its movements.

"When it leaves me for a time, it is always at night, in the dark, and in the same way. It grows at first uneasy, and then furious, and then advances towards me, grinning and shaking its paws clenched, and, at the same time, there comes the appearance of fire in the grate. I never have any fire. I can't sleep in the room where there is any, and it draws nearer and nearer to the chimney, quivering, it seems, with rage, and when its fury rises to the highest pitch, it springs into the grate, and up the chimney, and I see it no more.

"When first this happened I thought I was released. I was a new man. A day passed—a night—and no return, and a blessed week—a week—another week. I was always on my knees, Dr. Hesselius, always, thanking God and praying. A whole month passed of liberty, but on a sudden, it was with me again."

CHAPTER VIII.
THE SECOND STAGE.

"It was with me, and the malice which before was torpid under a sullen exterior, was now active. It was perfectly unchanged in every other respect. This new energy was apparent in its activity and its looks, and soon in other ways.

"For a time, you will understand, the change was shown only in an increased vivacity, and an air of menace, as if it was always brooding over some atrocious plan. Its eyes, as before, were never off me."

"Is it here now?" I asked.

"No," he replied, "it has been absent exactly a fortnight and a day—fifteen days. It has sometimes been away so long as nearly two months, once for three. Its absence always exceeds a fortnight, although it may be but by a single day. Fifteen days having past since I saw it last, it may return now at any moment."

"Is its return," I asked, "accompanied by any peculiar manifestation?"

"Nothing—no," he said. "It is simply with me again. On lifting my eyes from a book, or turning my head, I see it as usual, looking at me, and then it remains, as before, for its appointed time. I have never told so much and so minutely before to any one."

I perceived that he was agitated, and looking like death, and he repeatedly applied his handkerchief to his forehead; I suggested that he might be tired, and told him that I would call, with pleasure, in the morning, but he said:

"No, if you don't mind hearing it all now. I have got so far, and I should prefer making one effort of it. When I spoke to Dr. Harley, I had nothing like so much to tell. You are a philosophic physician. You give spirit its proper rank. If this thing is real—"

He paused, looking at me with agitated inquiry.

"We can discuss it by-and-by, and very fully. I will give you all I think," I answered, after an interval.

"Well—very well. If it is anything real, I say, it is prevailing, little by little, and drawing me more interiorly into hell. Optic nerves, he talked of. Ah! well — there are other nerves of communication. May God Almighty help me! You shall hear.

"Its power of action, I tell you, had increased. Its malice became, in a way aggressive. About two years ago, some questions that were pending between me and the bishop having been settled, I went down to my parish in Warwickshire, anxious to find occupation in my profession. I was not prepared for what happened, although I have since thought I might have apprehended something like it. The reason of my saying so, is this —"

He was beginning to speak with a great deal more effort and reluctance, and sighed often, and seemed at times nearly overcome. But at this time his manner was not agitated. It was more like that of a sinking patient, who has given himself up.

"Yes, but I will first tell you about Kenlis, my parish.

"It was with me when I left this place for Dawlbridge. It was my silent travelling companion, and it remained with me at the vicarage. When I entered on the discharge of my duties, another change took place. The thing exhibited an atrocious determination to thwart me. It was with me in the church — in the reading-desk — in the pulpit — within the communion rails. At last, it reached this extremity, that while I was reading to the congregation, it would spring upon the open book and squat there, so that I was unable to see the page. This happened more than once.

"I left Dawlbridge for a time. I placed myself in Dr. Harley's hands. I did everything he told me. He gave my case a great deal of thought. It interested him, I think. He seemed successful. For nearly three months I was perfectly free from a return. I began to think I was safe. With his full assent I returned to Dawlbridge.

"I travelled in a chaise. I was in good spirits. I was more — I was happy and grateful. I was returning, as I thought delivered from a dreadful hallucination, to the scene of duties which I longed to enter upon. It was a beautiful sunny evening, everything looked serene and cheerful, and I was delighted. I remember looking out of the window to see the spire of my church at Kenlis among the trees, at the point where one has the earliest view of it. It is exactly where the little stream that bounds the parish passes under the road by a culvert, and where it emerges at the road-side, a stone with an old inscription is placed. As we passed this point, I drew my head in and sat down, and in the corner of the chaise was the monkey.

"For a moment I felt faint, and then quite wild with despair and horror. I called to the driver, and got out, and sat down at the road-side, and prayed to God silently for mercy. A despairing resignation supervened. My companion was with me as I re-entered the vicarage. The same persecution followed. After a short struggle I submitted, and soon I left the place.

"I told you," he said, "that the beast has before this become in certain ways aggressive. I will explain a little. It seemed to be actuated by intense and increasing fury, whenever I said my prayers, or even meditated prayer. It amounted at last to a dreadful interruption. You will ask, how could a silent immaterial phantom effect that? It was thus, whenever I meditated praying; it was always before me, and nearer and nearer.

"It used to spring on a table, on the back of a chair, on the chimney-piece, and slowly to swing itself from side to side, looking at me all the time. There is in its motion an indefinable power to dissipate thought, and to contract one's attention to that monotony, till the ideas shrink, as it were, to a point, and at last to nothing—and unless I had started up, and shook off the catalepsy I have felt as if my mind were on the point of losing itself. There are other ways," he sighed heavily; "thus, for instance, while I pray with my eyes closed, it comes closer and closer, and I see it. I know it is not to be accounted for physically, but I do actually see it, though my lids are closed, and so it rocks my mind, as it were, and overpowers me, and I am obliged to rise from my knees. If you had ever yourself known this, you would be acquainted with desperation."

CHAPTER IX.
THE THIRD STAGE.

"I see, Dr. Hesselius, that you don't lose one word of my statement. I need not ask you to listen specially to what I am now going to tell you. They talk of the optic nerves, and of spectral illusions, as if the organ of sight was the only point assailable by the influences that have fastened upon me—I know better. For two years in my direful case that limitation prevailed. But as food is taken in softly at the lips, and then brought under the teeth, as the tip of the little finger caught in a mill crank will draw in the hand, and the arm, and the whole body, so the miserable mortal who has been once caught firmly by the end of the finest fibre of his nerve, is drawn in and in, by the enormous machinery of hell, until he is as I am. Yes, Doctor, as I am, for while I talk to you, and implore relief, I feel that my prayer is for the impossible, and my pleading with the inexorable."

I endeavoured to calm his visibly increasing agitation, and told him that he must not despair.

While we talked the night had overtaken us. The filmy moonlight was wide over the scene which the window commanded, and I said:

"Perhaps you would prefer having candles. This light, you know, is odd. I should wish you, as much as possible, under your usual conditions while I make my diagnosis, shall I call it—otherwise I don't care."

"All lights are the same to me," he said: "except when I read or write, I care not if night were perpetual. I am going to tell you what happened about a year ago. The thing began to speak to me."

"Speak! How do you mean—speak as a man does, do you mean?"

"Yes; speak in words and consecutive sentences, with perfect coherence and articulation; but there is a peculiarity. It is not like the tone of a human voice. It is not by my ears it reaches me—it comes like a singing through my head.

"This faculty, the power of speaking to me, will be my undoing. It won't let me pray, it interrupts me with dreadful blasphemies. I dare not go on, I could not. Oh! Doctor, can the skill, and thought, and prayers of man avail me nothing!"

"You must promise me, my dear sir, not to trouble yourself with unnecessarily exciting thoughts; confine yourself strictly to the narrative of facts; and recollect, above all, that even if the thing that infests you be as you seem to suppose, a reality with an actual independent life and will, yet it can have no power to hurt you, unless it be given from above: its access to your senses depends mainly upon your physical condition—this is, under God, your comfort and reliance: we are all alike environed. It is only that in your case, the 'paries,' the veil of the flesh, the screen, is a little out of repair, and sights and sounds are transmitted. We must enter on a new course, sir—be encouraged. I'll give to-night to the careful consideration of the whole case."

"You are very good, sir; you think it worth trying, you don't give me quite up; but, sir, you don't know, it is gaining such an influence over me: it orders me about, it is such a tyrant, and I'm growing so helpless. May God deliver me!"

"It orders you about—of course you mean by speech?"

"Yes, yes; it is always urging me to crimes, to injure others, or myself. You see, Doctor, the situation is urgent, it is indeed. When I was in Shropshire, a few weeks ago" (Mr. Jennings was speaking rapidly and trembling now, holding my arm with one hand, and looking in my face), "I went out one day with a party of friends for a walk: my persecutor, I tell you, was with me at the time. I lagged behind the rest: the country near the Dee, you know, is beautiful. Our path happened to lie near a coal mine, and at the verge of the wood is a perpendicular shaft, they say, a hundred and fifty feet deep. My niece had remained behind with me—she knows, of course, nothing of the nature of my sufferings. She knew, however, that I had been ill, and was low, and she remained to prevent my being quite alone. As we loitered slowly on together the brute that accompanied me was urging me to throw myself down the shaft. I tell you now—oh, sir, think of it!—the one consideration that saved me from that hideous death was the fear lest the shock of witnessing the occurrence should be too much for the poor girl. I asked her to go on and take her walk with her friends, saying that I could go no further. She made excuses, and the more I urged her the firmer she became. She looked doubtful and frightened. I suppose there was something in my looks or manner that alarmed her; but she would not go, and that literally saved me. You had no idea, sir, that a living man could be made so abject a slave of Satan," he said, with a ghastly groan and a shudder.

There was a pause here, and I said, "You were preserved nevertheless. It was the act of God. You are in his hands and in the power of no other being: be therefore confident for the future."

CHAPTER X.
HOME.

I made him have candles lighted, and saw the room looking cheery and inhabited before I left him. I told him that he must regard his illness strictly as one dependent on physical, though subtle physical, causes. I told him that he had evidence of God's care and love in the deliverance which he had just described, and that I had perceived with pain that he seemed to regard its peculiar features as indicating that he had been delivered over to spiritual reprobation. Than such a conclusion nothing could be, I insisted, less warranted; and not only so, but more contrary to facts, as disclosed in his mysterious deliverance from that murderous influence during his Shropshire excursion. First, his niece had been retained by his side without his intending to keep her near him; and, secondly, there had been infused into his mind an irresistible repugnance to execute the dreadful suggestion in her presence.

As I reasoned this point with him, Mr. Jennings wept. He seemed comforted. One promise I exacted, which was that should the monkey at any time return, I should be sent for immediately; and, repeating my assurance that I would give neither time nor thought to any other subject until I had thoroughly investigated his case, and that to-morrow he should hear the result, I took my leave.

Before getting into the carriage I told the servant that his master was far from well, and that he should make a point of frequently looking into his room.

My own arrangements I made with a view to being quite secure from interruption.

I merely called at my lodgings, and with a travelling-desk and carpet-bag, set off in a hackney-carriage for an inn about two miles out of town, called The Horns, a very quiet and comfortable house, with good thick walls. And there I resolved, without the possibility of intrusion or distraction, to devote some hours of the night, in my comfortable sitting-room, to Mr. Jennings' case, and so much of the morning as it might require.

(There occurs here a careful note of Dr. Hesselius' opinion upon the case and of the habits, dietary, and medicines which he prescribed. It is curious—some persons would say mystical. But on the whole I doubt whether it would sufficiently interest a reader of the kind I am likely to meet with, to warrant its being here reprinted. The whole letter was plainly written at the inn where he had hid himself for the occasion. The next letter is dated from his town lodgings.)

I left town for the inn where I slept last night at half-past nine, and did not arrive at my room in town until one o'clock this afternoon. I found a letter in Mr. Jennings' hand upon my table. It had not come by post, and, on inquiry, I learned that Mr. Jennings' servant had brought it, and on learning that I was not to return until to-day, and that no one could tell him my address, he seemed very uncomfortable, and said that his orders from his master were that he was not to return without an answer.

I opened the letter, and read:

"Dear Dr. Hesselius. It is here. You had not been an hour gone when it returned. It is speaking. It knows all that has happened. It knows everything—it knows you, and is frantic and atrocious. It reviles. I send you this. It knows every word I have written—I write. This I promised, and I therefore write, but I fear very confused, very incoherently. I am so interrupted, disturbed.

"Ever yours, sincerely yours,

"ROBERT LYNDER JENNINGS."

"When did this come?" I asked.

"About eleven last night: the man was here again, and has been here three times to-day. The last time is about an hour since."

Thus answered, and with the notes I had made upon his case in my pocket, I was in a few minutes driving towards Richmond, to see Mr. Jennings.

I by no means, as you perceive, despaired of Mr. Jennings' case. He had himself remembered and applied, though quite in a mistaken way, the principle which I lay down in my Metaphysical Medicine, and which governs all such cases. I was about to apply it in earnest. I was profoundly interested, and very anxious to see and examine him while the "enemy" was actually present.

I drove up to the sombre house, and ran up the steps, and knocked. The door, in a little time, was opened by a tall woman in black silk. She looked ill, and as if she had been crying. She curtseyed, and heard my question, but she did not answer. She turned her face away, extending her hand towards two men who were coming down-stairs; and thus having, as it were, tacitly made me over to them, she passed through a side-door hastily and shut it.

The man who was nearest the hall, I at once accosted, but being now close to him, I was shocked to see that both his hands were covered with blood.

I drew back a little, and the man passing down-stairs merely said in a low tone, "Here's the servant, sir."

The servant had stopped on the stairs, confounded and dumb at seeing me. He was rubbing his hands in a handkerchief, and it was steeped in blood.

"Jones, what is it, what has happened?" I asked, while a sickening suspicion overpowered me.

The man asked me to come up to the lobby. I was beside him in a moment, and frowning and pallid, with contracted eyes, he told me the horror which I already half guessed.

His master had made away with himself.

I went upstairs with him to the room—what I saw there I won't tell you. He had cut his throat with his razor. It was a frightful gash. The two men had laid him on the bed and composed his limbs. It had happened as the immense pool of blood on the floor declared, at some distance between the bed and the window. There was carpet round his bed, and a carpet under his dressing-table, but none on the rest of the floor, for the man said he did not like a carpet on his bedroom. In this sombre, and now terrible room, one of the great elms that darkened the house was slowly moving the shadow of one of its great boughs upon this dreadful floor.

I beckoned to the servant and we went down-stairs together. I turned off the hall into an old-fashioned panelled room, and there standing, I heard all the servant had to tell. It was not a great deal.

"I concluded, sir, from your words, and looks, sir, as you left last night, that you thought my master seriously ill. I thought it might be that you were afraid of a fit, or something. So I attended very close to your directions. He sat up late, till past three o'clock. He was not writing or reading. He was talking a great deal to himself, but that was nothing unusual. At about that hour I assisted him to undress, and left him in his slippers and dressing-gown. I went back softly in about half an hour. He was in his bed, quite undressed, and a pair of candles lighted on the table beside his bed. He was leaning on his elbow and looking out at the other side of the bed when I came in. I asked him if he wanted anything, and he said no.

"I don't know whether it was what you said to me, sir, or something a little unusual about him, but I was uneasy, uncommon uneasy about him last night.

"In another half hour, or it might be a little more, I went up again. I did not hear him talking as before. I opened the door a little. The candles were both out, which was not usual. I had a bedroom candle, and I let the light in, a little bit, looking softly round. I saw him sitting in that chair beside the dressing-table with his clothes on again. He turned round and looked at me. I thought it strange he should get up and dress, and put out the candles to sit in the dark, that way. But I only asked him again if I could do anything for him. He said, no, rather sharp, I thought. I asked if I might light the candles, and he said, 'Do as you like, Jones,' So I lighted them, and I lingered about the room, and he said, 'Tell me truth, Jones, why did you come again — you did not hear any one cursing?' 'No, sir,' I said, wondering what he could mean.

"'No,' said he, after me, 'of course, no;' and I said to him, 'Wouldn't it be well, sir, you went to bed? It's just five o'clock;' and he said nothing but, 'Very likely; good-night, Jones.' So I went, sir, but in less than hour I came again. The door was fast, and he heard me, and called as I thought from the bed to know what I wanted, and he desired me not to disturb him again. I lay down and slept for a little. It must have been between six and seven when I went up again. The door was still fast, and he made no answer, so I did not like to disturb him, and thinking he was asleep, I left him till nine. It was his custom to ring when he wished me to come, and I had no particular hour for calling him. I tapped very gently, and getting no answer, I stayed away a good while, supposing he was getting some rest then. It was not till eleven o'clock I grew really uncomfortable about him — for at the latest he was never, that I could remember, later than half-past ten. I got no answer. I knocked and called, and still no answer. So not being able to force the door, I called Thomas from the stables, and together we forced it, and found him in the shocking way you saw."

654

In a Glass Darkly

Jones had no more to tell. Poor Mr. Jennings was very gentle, and very kind. All his people were fond of him. I could see that the servant was very much moved.

So, dejected and agitated, I passed from that terrible house, and its dark canopy of elms, and I hope I shall never see it more. While I write to you I feel like a man who has but half waked from a frightful and monotonous dream. My memory rejects the picture with incredulity and horror. Yet I know it is true. It is the story of the process of a poison, a poison which excites the reciprocal action of spirit and nerve, and paralyses the tissue that separates those cognate functions of the senses, the external and the interior. Thus we find strange bed-fellows, and the mortal and immortal prematurely make acquaintance.

CONCLUSION.
A WORD FOR THOSE WHO SUFFER.

My dear Van L— —, you have suffered from an affection similar to that which I have just described. You twice complained of a return of it.

Who, under God, cured you? Your humble servant, Martin Hesselius. Let me rather adopt the more emphasised piety of a certain good old French surgeon of three hundred years ago: "I treated, and God cured you."

Come, my friend, you are not to be hippish. Let me tell you a fact.

I have met with, and treated, as my book shows, fifty-seven cases of this kind of vision, which I term indifferently "sublimated," "precocious," and "interior."

There is another class of affections which are truly termed — though commonly confounded with those which I describe — spectral illusions. These latter I look upon as being no less simply curable than a cold in the head or a trifling dyspepsia.

It is those which rank in the first category that test our promptitude of thought. Fifty-seven such cases have I encountered, neither more nor less. And in how many of these have I failed? In no one single instance.

There is no one affliction of mortality more easily and certainly reducible, with a little patience, and a rational confidence in the physician. With these simple conditions, I look upon the cure as absolutely certain.

You are to remember that I had not even commenced to treat Mr. Jennings' case. I have not any doubt that I should have cured him perfectly in eighteen months, or possibly it might have extended to two years. Some cases are very rapidly curable, others extremely tedious. Every intelligent physician who will give thought and diligence to the task, will effect a cure.

You know my tract on The Cardinal Functions of the Brain. I there, by the evidence of innumerable facts, prove, as I think, the high probability of a circulation arterial and venous in its mechanism, through the nerves. Of this system, thus considered, the brain is the heart. The fluid, which is propagated hence through one class of nerves, returns in an altered state through another, and the nature of that fluid is spiritual, though not immaterial, any more than, as I before remarked, light or electricity are so.

By various abuses, among which the habitual use of such agents as green tea is one, this fluid may be affected as to its quality, but it is more frequently disturbed as to equilibrium. This fluid being that which we have in common with spirits, a congestion found upon the masses of brain or nerve, connected with the interior sense, forms a surface unduly exposed, on which disembodied spirits may operate: communication is thus more or less effectually established. Between this brain circulation and the heart circulation there is an intimate sympathy. The seat, or rather the instrument of exterior vision, is the eye. The seat of interior vision is the nervous tissue and brain, immediately about and above the eyebrow. You remember how effectually I dissipated your pictures by the simple application of iced eau-de-cologne. Few cases, however, can be treated exactly alike with anything like rapid success. Cold acts powerfully as a repellant of the nervous fluid. Long enough continued it will even produce that permanent insensibility which we call numbness, and a little longer, muscular as well as sensational paralysis.

I have not, I repeat, the slightest doubt that I should have first dimmed and ultimately sealed that inner eye which Mr. Jennings had inadvertently opened. The same senses are opened in delirium tremens, and entirely shut up again when the over-action of the cerebral heart, and the prodigious nervous congestions that attend it, are terminated by a decided change in the state of the body. It is by acting steadily upon the body, by a simple process, that this result is produced — and inevitably produced — I have never yet failed.

Poor Mr. Jennings made away with himself. But that catastrophe was the result of a totally different malady, which, as it were, projected itself upon that disease which was established. His case was in the distinctive manner a complication, and the complaint under which he really succumbed, was hereditary suicidal mania. Poor Mr. Jennings I cannot call a patient of mine, for I had not even begun to treat his case, and he had not yet given me, I am convinced, his full and unreserved confidence. If the patient do not array himself on the side of the disease, his cure is certain.

THE FAMILIAR.
PROLOGUE.

Out of about two hundred and thirty cases, more or less nearly akin to that I have entitled "Green Tea," I select the following, which I call "The Familiar."

To this MS. Doctor Hesselius, has, after his wont, attached some sheets of letter-paper, on which are written, in his hand nearly as compact as print, his own remarks upon the case. He says—

"In point of conscience, no more unexceptionable narrator, than the venerable Irish Clergyman who has given me this paper, on Mr. Barton's case, could have been chosen. The statement is, however, medically imperfect. The report of an intelligent physician, who had marked its progress, and attended the patient, from its earlier stages to its close, would have supplied what is wanting to enable me to pronounce with confidence. I should have been acquainted with Mr. Barton's probable hereditary pre-dispositions; I should have known, possibly, by very early indications, something of a remoter origin of the disease than can now be ascertained.

"In a rough way, we may reduce all similar cases to three distinct classes. They are founded on the primary distinction between the subjective and the objective. Of those whose senses are alleged to be subject to supernatural impressions—some are simply visionaries, and propagate the illusions of which they complain, from diseased brain or nerves. Others are, unquestionably, infested by, as we term them, spiritual agencies, exterior to themselves. Others, again, owe their sufferings to a mixed condition. The interior sense, it is true, is opened; but it has been and continues open by the action of disease. This form of disease may, in one sense, be compared to the loss of the scarf-skin, and a consequent exposure of surfaces for whose excessive sensitiveness, nature has provided a muffling. The loss of this covering is attended by an habitual impassability, by influences against which we were intended to be guarded. But in the case of the brain, and the nerves immediately connected with its functions and its sensuous impressions, the cerebral circulation undergoes periodically that vibratory disturbance, which, I believe, I have satisfactorily examined and demonstrated, in my MS. Essay, A. 17. This vibratory disturbance differs, as I there prove, essentially from the congestive disturbance, the phenomena of which are examined in A. 19. It is, when excessive, invariably accompanied by illusions.

"Had I seen Mr. Barton, and examined him upon the points, in his case, which need elucidation, I should have without difficulty referred those phenomena to their proper disease. My diagnosis is now, necessarily, conjectural."

Thus writes Doctor Hesselius; and adds a great deal which is of interest only to a scientific physician.

The Narrative of the Rev. Thomas Herbert, which furnishes all that is known of the case, will be found in the chapters that follow.

CHAPTER I.
FOOT-STEPS.

I was a young man at the time, and intimately acquainted with some of the actors in this strange tale; the impression which its incidents made on me, therefore, were deep, and lasting. I shall now endeavour, with precision, to relate them all, combining, of course, in the narrative, whatever I have learned from various sources, tending, however imperfectly, to illuminate the darkness which involves its progress and termination.

Somewhere about the year 1794, the younger brother of a certain baronet, whom I shall call Sir James Barton, returned to Dublin. He had served in the navy with some distinction, having commanded one of His Majesty's frigates during the greater part of the American war. Captain Barton was apparently some two or three-and-forty years of age. He was an intelligent and agreeable companion when he pleased it, though generally reserved, and occasionally even moody.

In society, however, he deported himself as a man of the world, and a gentleman. He had not contracted any of the noisy brusqueness sometimes acquired at sea; on the contrary, his manners were remarkably easy, quiet, and even polished. He was in person about the middle size, and somewhat strongly formed—his countenance was marked with the lines of thought, and on the whole wore an expression of gravity and melancholy; being, however, as I have said, a man of perfect breeding, as well as of good family, and in affluent circumstances, he had, of course, ready access to the best society of Dublin, without the necessity of any other credentials.

In his personal habits Mr. Barton was unexpensive. He occupied lodgings in one of the then fashionable streets in the south side of the town—kept but one horse and one servant—and though a reputed free-thinker, yet lived an orderly and moral life—indulging neither in gaming, drinking, nor any other vicious pursuit—living very much to himself, without forming intimacies, or choosing any companions, and appearing to mix in gay society rather for the sake of its bustle and distraction, than for any opportunities it offered of interchanging thought or feeling with its votaries.

Barton was therefore pronounced a saving, prudent, unsocial sort of fellow, who bid fair to maintain his celibacy alike against stratagem and assault, and was likely to live to a good old age, die rich, and leave his money to an hospital.

It was now apparent, however, that the nature of Mr. Barton's plans had been totally misconceived. A young lady, whom I shall call Miss Montague, was at this time introduced into the gay world, by her aunt, the Dowager Lady L— —. Miss Montague was decidedly pretty and accomplished, and having some natural cleverness, and a great deal of gaiety, became for a while a reigning toast.

Her popularity, however, gained her, for a time, nothing more than that unsubstantial admiration which, however, pleasant as an incense to vanity, is by no means necessarily antecedent to matrimony — for, unhappily for the young lady in question, it was an understood thing, that beyond her personal attractions, she had no kind of earthly provision. Such being the state of affairs, it will readily be believed that no little surprise was consequent upon the appearance of Captain Barton as the avowed lover of the penniless Miss Montague.

His suit prospered, as might have been expected, and in a short time it was communicated by old Lady L— — to each of her hundred and fifty particular friends in succession, that Captain Barton had actually tendered proposals of marriage, with her approbation, to her niece, Miss Montague, who had, moreover, accepted the offer of his hand, conditionally upon the consent of her father, who was then upon his homeward voyage from India, and expected in two or three weeks at the furthest.

About this consent there could be no doubt — the delay, therefore, was one merely of form — they were looked upon as absolutely engaged, and Lady L— —, with a rigour of old-fashioned decorum with which her niece would, no doubt, gladly have dispensed, withdrew her thenceforward from all further participation in the gaieties of the town.

Captain Barton was a constant visitor, as well as a frequent guest at the house, and was permitted all the privileges of intimacy which a betrothed suitor is usually accorded. Such was the relation of parties, when the mysterious circumstances which darken this narrative first begun to unfold themselves.

Lady L— — resided in a handsome mansion at the north side of Dublin, and Captain Barton's lodgings, as we have already said, were situated at the south. The distance intervening was considerable, and it was Captain Barton's habit generally to walk home without an attendant, as often as he passed the evening with the old lady and her fair charge.

His shortest way in such nocturnal walks, lay, for a considerable space, through a line of street which had as yet merely been laid out, and little more than the foundations of the houses constructed.

One night, shortly after his engagement with Miss Montague had commenced, he happened to remain unusually late, in company with her and Lady L——. The conversation had turned upon the evidences of revelation, which he had disputed with the callous scepticism of a confirmed infidel. What were called "French principles," had in those days found their way a good deal into fashionable society, especially that portion of it which professed allegiance to Whiggism, and neither the old lady nor her charge were so perfectly free from the taint, as to look upon Mr. Barton's views as any serious objection to the proposed union.

The discussion had degenerated into one upon the supernatural and the marvellous, in which he had pursued precisely the same line of argument and ridicule. In all this, it is but truth to state, Captain Barton, was guilty of no affectation—the doctrines upon which he insisted, were, in reality, but, too truly the basis of his own fixed belief, if so it might be called; and perhaps not the least strange of the many strange circumstances connected with my narrative, was the fact, that the subject of the fearful influences I am about to describe, was himself, from the deliberate conviction of years, an utter disbeliever in what are usually termed preternatural agencies.

It was considerably past midnight when Mr. Barton took his leave, and set out upon his solitary walk homeward. He had now reached the lonely road, with its unfinished dwarf walls tracing the foundations of the projected row of houses on either side—the moon was shining mistily, and its imperfect light made the road he trod but additionally dreary—that utter silence which has in it something indefinably exciting, reigned there, and made the sound of his steps, which alone broke it, unnaturally loud and distinct.

He had proceeded thus some way, when he, on a sudden, heard other footfalls, pattering at a measured pace, and, as it seemed, about two score steps behind him.

The suspicion of being dogged is at all times unpleasant; it is, however, especially so in a spot so lonely; and this suspicion became so strong in the mind of Captain Barton, that he abruptly turned about to confront his pursuer, but, though there was quite sufficient moonlight to disclose any object upon the road he had traversed, no form of any kind was visible there.

The steps he had heard could not have been the reverberation of his own, for he stamped his foot upon the ground, and walked briskly up and down, in the vain attempt to awake an echo; though by no means a fanciful person, therefore he was at last fain to charge the sounds upon his imagination, and treat them as an illusion. Thus satisfying himself, he resumed his walk, and before he had proceeded a dozen paces, the mysterious footfall was again audible from behind, and this time, as if with the special design of showing that the sounds were not the responses of an echo—the steps sometimes slackened nearly to a halt, and sometimes hurried for six or eight strides to a run, and again abated to a walk.

Captain Barton, as before, turned suddenly round, and with the same result—no object was visible above the deserted level of the road. He walked back over the same ground, determined that, whatever might have been the cause of the sounds which had so disconcerted him, it should not escape his search—the endeavour, however, was unrewarded.

In spite of all his scepticism, he felt something like a superstitious fear stealing fast upon him, and with these unwonted and uncomfortable sensations, he once more turned and pursued his way. There was no repetition of these haunting sounds, until he had reached the point where he had last stopped to retrace his steps—here they were resumed—and with sudden starts of running, which threatened to bring the unseen pursuer up to the alarmed pedestrian.

Captain Barton arrested his course as formerly—the unaccountable nature of the occurrence filled him with vague and disagreeable sensations—and yielding to the excitement that was gaining upon him, he shouted sternly, "Who goes there?" The sound of one's own voice, thus exerted, in utter solitude, and followed by total silence, has in it something unpleasantly dismaying, and he felt a degree of nervousness which, perhaps, from no cause had he ever known before.

To the very end of this solitary street the steps pursued him—and it required a strong effort of stubborn pride on his part, to resist the impulse that prompted him every moment to run for safety at the top of his speed. It was not until he had reached his lodging, and sate by his own fire-side, that he felt sufficiently reassured to rearrange and reconsider in his own mind the occurrences which had so discomposed him. So little a matter, after all, is sufficient to upset the pride of scepticism and vindicate the old simple laws of nature within us.

CHAPTER II.
THE WATCHER.

Mr. Barton was next morning sitting at a late breakfast, reflecting upon the incidents of the previous night, with more of inquisitiveness than awe, so speedily do gloomy impressions upon the fancy disappear under the cheerful influence of day, when a letter just delivered by the postman was placed upon the table before him.

There was nothing remarkable in the address of this missive, except that it was written in a hand which he did not know — perhaps it was disguised — for the tall narrow characters were sloped backward; and with the self-inflicted suspense which we often see practised in such cases, he puzzled over the inscription for a full minute before he broke the seal. When he did so, he read the following words, written in the same hand:—

"Mr. Barton, late captain of the 'Dolphin,' is warned of DANGER. He will do wisely to avoid — — street—[here the locality of his last night's adventure was named]—if he walks there as usual he will meet with something unlucky—let him take warning, once for all, for he has reason to dread

"THE WATCHER."

Captain Barton read and re-read this strange effusion; in every light and in every direction he turned it over and over; he examined the paper on which it was written, and scrutinized the hand-writing once more. Defeated here, he turned to the seal; it was nothing but a patch of wax, upon which the accidental impression of a thumb was imperfectly visible.

There was not the slightest mark, or clue of any kind, to lead him to even a guess as to its possible origin. The writer's object seemed a friendly one, and yet he subscribed himself as one whom he had "reason to dread." Altogether the letter, its author, and its real purpose were to him an inexplicable puzzle, and one, moreover, unpleasantly suggestive, in his mind, of other associations connected with his last night's adventure.

In obedience to some feeling—perhaps of pride—Mr. Barton did not communicate, even to his intended bride, the occurrences which I have just detailed. Trifling as they might appear, they had in reality most disagreeably affected his imagination, and he cared not to disclose, even to the young lady in question, what she might possibly look upon as evidences of weakness. The letter might very well be but a hoax, and the mysterious footfall but a delusion or a trick. But although he affected to treat the whole affair as unworthy of a thought, it yet haunted him pertinaciously, tormenting him with perplexing doubts, and depressing him with undefined apprehensions. Certain it is, that for a considerable time afterwards he carefully avoided the street indicated in the letter as the scene of danger.

It was not until about a week after the receipt of the letter which I have transcribed, that anything further occurred to remind Captain Barton of its contents, or to counteract the gradual disappearance from his mind of the disagreeable impressions then received.

He was returning one night, after the interval I have stated, from the theatre, which was then situated in Crow-street, and having there seen Miss Montague and Lady L— — into their carriage, he loitered for some time with two or three acquaintances.

With these, however, he parted close to the college, and pursued his way alone. It was now fully one o'clock, and the streets were quite deserted. During the whole of his walk with the companions from whom he had just parted, he had been at times painfully aware of the sound of steps, as it seemed, dogging them on their way.

Once or twice he had looked back, in the uneasy anticipation that he was again about to experience the same mysterious annoyances which had so disconcerted him a week before, and earnestly hoping that he might see some form to account naturally for the sounds. But the street was deserted—no one was visible.

Proceeding now quite alone upon his homeward way, he grew really nervous and uncomfortable, as he became sensible, with increased distinctness, of the well-known and now absolutely dreaded sounds.

By the side of the dead wall which bounded the college park, the sounds followed, recommencing almost simultaneously with his own steps. The same unequal pace—sometimes slow, sometimes for a score yards or so, quickened almost to a run—was audible from behind him. Again and again he turned; quickly and stealthily he glanced over his shoulder—almost at every half-dozen steps; but no one was visible.

The irritation of this intangible and unseen pursuit became gradually all but intolerable; and when at last he reached his home, his nerves were strung to such a pitch of excitement that he could not rest, and did not attempt even to lie down until after the daylight had broken.

He was awakened by a knock at his chamber-door, and his servant entering, handed him several letters which had just been received by the penny post. One among them instantly arrested his attention — a single glance at the direction aroused him thoroughly. He at once recognized its character, and read as follows: —

"You may as well think, Captain Barton, to escape from your own shadow as from me; do what you may, I will see you as often as I please, and you shall see me, for I do not want to hide myself, as you fancy. Do not let it trouble your rest, Captain Barton; for, with a good conscience, what need you fear from the eye of

"THE WATCHER."

It is scarcely necessary to dwell upon the feelings that accompanied a perusal of this strange communication. Captain Barton was observed to be unusually absent and out of spirits for several days afterwards, but no one divined the cause.

Whatever he might think as to the phantom steps which followed him, there could be no possible illusion about the letters he had received; and, to say the least, their immediate sequence upon the mysterious sounds which had haunted him, was an odd coincidence.

The whole circumstance was, in his own mind, vaguely and instinctively connected with certain passages in his past life, which, of all others, he hated to remember.

It happened, however, that in addition to his own approaching nuptials, Captain Barton had just then — fortunately, perhaps, for himself — some business of an engrossing kind connected with the adjustment of a large and long-litigated claim upon certain properties.

The hurry and excitement of business had its natural effect in gradually dispelling the gloom which had for a time occasionally oppressed him, and in a little while his spirits had entirely recovered their accustomed tone.

In a Glass Darkly

During all this time, however, he was, now and then, dismayed by indistinct and half-heard repetitions of the same annoyance, and that in lonely places, in the day-time as well as after nightfall. These renewals of the strange impressions from which he had suffered so much, were, however, desultory and faint, insomuch that often he really could not, to his own satisfaction, distinguish between them and the mere suggestions of an excited imagination.

One evening he walked down to the House of Commons with a Member, an acquaintance of his and mine. This was one of the few occasions upon which I have been in company with Captain Barton. As we walked down together, I observed that he became absent and silent, and to a degree that seemed to argue the pressure of some urgent and absorbing anxiety.

I afterwards learned that during the whole of our walk, he had heard the well-known footsteps tracking him as we proceeded.

This, however, was the last time he suffered from this phase of the persecution, of which he was already the anxious victim. A new and a very different one was about to be presented.

CHAPTER III.
AN ADVERTISEMENT.

Of the new series of impressions which were afterwards gradually to work out his destiny, I that evening witnessed the first; and but for its relation to the train of events which followed, the incident would scarcely have been now remembered by me.

As we were walking in at the passage from College-Green, a man, of whom I remember only that he was short in stature, looked like a foreigner, and wore a kind of fur travelling-cap, walked very rapidly, and as if under fierce excitement, directly towards us, muttering to himself, fast and vehemently the while.

This odd-looking person walked straight toward Barton, who was foremost of the three, and halted, regarding him for a moment or two with a look of maniacal menace and fury; and then turning about as abruptly, he walked before us at the same agitated pace, and disappeared at a side passage. I do distinctly remember being a good deal shocked at the countenance and bearing of this man, which indeed irresistibly impressed me with an undefined sense of danger, such as I have never felt before or since from the presence of anything human; but these sensations were, on my part, far from amounting to anything so disconcerting as to flurry or excite me — I had seen only a singularly evil countenance, agitated, as it seemed, with the excitement of madness.

I was absolutely astonished, however, at the effect of this apparition upon Captain Barton. I knew him to be a man of proud courage and coolness in real danger — a circumstance which made his conduct upon this occasion the more conspicuously odd. He recoiled a step or two as the stranger advanced, and clutched my arm in silence, with what seemed to be a spasm of agony or terror! and then, as the figure disappeared, shoving me roughly back, he followed it for a few paces, stopped in great disorder, and sat down upon a form. I never beheld a countenance more ghastly and haggard.

"For God's sake, Barton, what is the matter?" said — —, our companion, really alarmed at his appearance. "You're not hurt, are you? — or unwell? What is it?"

"What did he say? — I did not hear it — what was it?" asked Barton, wholly disregarding the question.

"Nonsense," said — —, greatly surprised; "who cares what the fellow said. You are unwell, Barton—decidedly unwell; let me call a coach."

"Unwell! No—not unwell," he said, evidently making an effort to recover his self-possession; "but, to say the truth, I am fatigued—a little over-worked—and perhaps over anxious. You know I have been in chancery, and the winding up of a suit is always a nervous affair. I have felt uncomfortable all this evening; but I am better now. Come, come—shall we go on?"

"No, no. Take my advice, Barton, and go home; you really do need rest! you are looking quite ill. I really do insist on your allowing me to see you home," replied his friend.

I seconded — —'s advice, the more readily as it was obvious that Barton was not himself disinclined to be persuaded. He left us, declining our offered escort. I was not sufficiently intimate with — — to discuss the scene we had both just witnessed. I was, however, convinced from his manner in the few common-place comments and regrets we exchanged, that he was just as little satisfied as I with the extempore plea of illness with which he had accounted for the strange exhibition, and that we were both agreed in suspecting some lurking mystery in the matter.

I called next day at Barton's lodgings, to enquire for him, and learned from the servant that he had not left his room since his return the night before; but that he was not seriously indisposed, and hoped to be out in a few days. That evening he sent for Dr. R— —, then in large and fashionable practice in Dublin, and their interview was, it is said, an odd one.

He entered into a detail of his own symptoms in an abstracted and desultory way which seemed to argue a strange want of interest in his own cure, and, at all events, made it manifest that there was some topic engaging his mind of more engrossing importance than his present ailment. He complained of occasional palpitations and headache.

Doctor R— —, asked him among other questions, whether there was any irritating circumstance or anxiety then occupying his thoughts. This he denied quickly and almost peevishly; and the physician thereupon declared his opinion, that there was nothing amiss except some slight derangement of the digestion, for which he accordingly wrote a prescription, and was about to withdraw, when Mr. Barton, with the air of a man who recollects a topic which had nearly escaped him, recalled him.

"I beg your pardon, Doctor, but I really almost forgot; will you permit me to ask you two or three medical questions—rather odd ones, perhaps, but a wager depends upon their solution, you will, I hope, excuse my unreasonableness."

The physician readily undertook to satisfy the inquirer.

Barton seemed to have some difficulty about opening the proposed interrogatories, for he was silent for a minute, then walked to his book-case, and returned as he had gone; at last he sat down and said—

"You'll think them very childish questions, but I can't recover my wager without a decision; so I must put them. I want to know first about lock-jaw. If a man actually has had that complaint, and appears to have died of it—so much so, that a physician of average skill pronounces him actually dead—may he, after all, recover?"

The physician smiled, and shook his head.

"But—but a blunder may be made," resumed Barton. "Suppose an ignorant pretender to medical skill; may he be so deceived by any stage of the complaint, as to mistake what is only a part of the progress of the disease, for death itself?"

"No one who had ever seen death," answered he, "could mistake it in a case of lock-jaw."

Barton mused for a few minutes. "I am going to ask you a question, perhaps, still more childish; but first, tell me, are the regulations of foreign hospitals, such as that of, let us say, Naples, very lax and bungling. May not all kinds of blunders and slips occur in their entries of names, and soforth?"

Doctor R— — professed his incompetence to answer that query.

"Well, then, Doctor, here is the last of my questions. You will, probably, laugh at it; but it must out, nevertheless. Is there any disease, in all the range of human maladies, which would have the effect of perceptibly contracting the stature, and the whole frame—causing the man to shrink in all his proportions, and yet to preserve his exact resemblance to himself in every particular—with the one exception, his height and bulk; any disease, mark—no matter how rare—how little believed in, generally—which could possibly result in producing such an effect?"

The physician replied with a smile, and a very decided negative.

"Tell me, then," said Barton, abruptly, "if a man be in reasonable fear of assault from a lunatic who is at large, can he not procure a warrant for his arrest and detention?"

"Really that is more a lawyer's question than one in my way," replied Dr. R——: "but I believe, on applying to a magistrate, such a course would be directed."

The physician then took his leave; but, just as he reached the hall-door, remembered that he had left his cane up stairs, and returned. His reappearance was awkward, for a piece of paper, which he recognised as his own prescription, was slowly burning upon the fire, and Barton sitting close by with an expression of settled gloom and dismay.

Doctor R—— had too much tact to observe what presented itself; but he had seen quite enough to assure him that the mind, and not the body, of Captain Barton was in reality the seat of suffering.

A few days afterwards, the following advertisement appeared in the Dublin newspapers.

"If Sylvester Yelland, formerly a foremast-man on board his Majesty's frigate Dolphin, or his nearest of kin, will apply to Mr. Hubert Smith, attorney, at his office, Dame Street, he or they may hear of something greatly to his or their advantage. Admission may be had at any hour up to twelve o'clock at night, should parties desire to avoid observation; and the strictest secrecy, as to all communications intended to be confidential, shall be honourably observed."

The Dolphin, as I have mentioned, was the vessel which Captain Barton had commanded; and this circumstance, connected with the extraordinary exertions made by the circulation of hand-bills, &c., as well as by repeated advertisements, to secure for this strange notice the utmost possible publicity, suggested to Dr. R—— the idea that Captain Barton's extreme uneasiness was somehow connected with the individual to whom the advertisement was addressed, and he himself the author of it.

This, however, it is needless to add, was no more than a conjecture. No information whatsoever, as to the real purpose of the advertisement was divulged by the agent, nor yet any hint as to who his employer might be.

CHAPTER IV.
HE TALKS WITH A CLERGYMAN.

Mr. Barton, although he had latterly begun to earn for himself the character of an hypochondriac, was yet very far from deserving it. Though by no means lively, he had yet, naturally, what are termed "even spirits," and was not subject to undue depressions.

He soon, therefore, began to return to his former habits; and one of the earliest symptoms of this healthier tone of spirits was, his appearing at a grand dinner of the Freemasons, of which worthy fraternity he was himself a brother. Barton, who had been at first gloomy and abstracted, drank much more freely than was his wont—possibly with the purpose of dispelling his own secret anxieties—and under the influence of good wine, and pleasant company, became gradually (unlike himself) talkative, and even noisy.

It was under this unwonted excitement that he left his company at about half-past ten o'clock; and, as conviviality is a strong incentive to gallantry, it occurred to him to proceed forthwith to Lady L——'s and pass the remainder of the evening with her and his destined bride.

Accordingly, he was soon at —— street, and chatting gaily with the ladies. It is not to be supposed that Captain Barton had exceeded the limits which propriety prescribes to good fellowship—he had merely taken enough wine to raise his spirits, without, however, in the least degree unsteadying his mind, or affecting his manners.

With this undue elevation of spirits had supervened an entire oblivion or contempt of those undefined apprehensions which had for so long weighed upon his mind, and to a certain extent estranged him from society; but as the night wore away, and his artificial gaiety began to flag, these painful feelings gradually intruded themselves again, and he grew abstracted and anxious as heretofore.

He took his leave at length, with an unpleasant foreboding of some coming mischief, and with a mind haunted with a thousand mysterious apprehensions, such as, even while he acutely felt their pressure, he, nevertheless, inwardly strove, or affected to contemn.

It was this proud defiance of what he regarded as his own

weakness, which prompted him upon the present occasion to that course which brought about the adventure I am now about to relate.

Mr. Barton might have easily called a coach, but he was conscious that his strong inclination to do so proceeded from no cause other than what he desperately persisted in representing to himself to be his own superstitious tremors.

He might also have returned home by a route different from that against which he had been warned by his mysterious correspondent; but for the same reason he dismissed this idea also, and with a dogged and half desperate resolution to force matters to a crisis of some kind, if there were any reality in the causes of his former suffering, and if not, satisfactorily to bring their delusiveness to the proof, he determined to follow precisely the course which he had trodden upon the night so painfully memorable in his own mind as that on which his strange persecution commenced. Though, sooth to say, the pilot who for the first time steers his vessel under the muzzles of a hostile battery, never felt his resolution more severely tasked than did Captain Barton as he breathlessly pursued this solitary path—a path which, spite of every effort of scepticism and reason, he felt to be infested by some (as respected him) malignant being.

He pursued his way steadily and rapidly, scarcely breathing from intensity of suspense; he, however, was troubled by no renewal of the dreaded footsteps, and was beginning to feel a return of confidence, as more than three-fourths of the way being accomplished with impunity, he approached the long line of twinkling oil lamps which indicated the frequented streets.

This feeling of self-congratulation was, however, but momentary. The report of a musket at some hundred yards behind him, and the whistle of a bullet close to his head, disagreeably and startlingly dispelled it. His first impulse was to retrace his steps in pursuit of the assassin; but the road on either side was, as we have said, embarrassed by the foundations of a street, beyond which extended waste fields, full of rubbish and neglected lime and brick-kilns, and all now as utterly silent as though no sound had ever disturbed their dark and unsightly solitude. The futility of, single-handed, attempting, under such circumstances, a search for the murderer, was apparent, especially as no sound, either of retreating steps or any other kind, was audible to direct his pursuit.

With the tumultuous sensations of one whose life has just been exposed to a murderous attempt, and whose escape has been the narrowest possible, Captain Barton turned again; and without, however, quickening his pace actually to a run, hurriedly pursued his way.

He had turned, as I have said, after a pause of a few seconds, and had just commenced his rapid retreat, when on a sudden he met the well-remembered little man in the fur cap. The encounter was but momentary. The figure was walking at the same exaggerated pace, and with the same strange air of menace as before; and as it passed him, he thought he heard it say, in a furious whisper, "Still alive—still alive!"

The state of Mr. Barton's spirits began now to work a corresponding alteration in his health and looks, and to such a degree that it was impossible that the change should escape general remark.

For some reasons, known but to himself, he took no step whatsoever to bring the attempt upon his life, which he had so narrowly escaped, under the notice of the authorities; on the contrary, he kept it jealously to himself; and it was not for many weeks after the occurrence that he mentioned it, and then in strict confidence, to a gentleman, whom the torments of his mind at last compelled him to consult.

Spite of his blue devils, however, poor Barton, having no satisfactory reason to render to the public for any undue remissness in the attentions exacted by the relation subsisting between him and Miss Montague was obliged to exert himself, and present to the world a confident and cheerful bearing.

The true source of his sufferings, and every circumstance connected with them, he guarded with a reserve so jealous, that it seemed dictated by at least a suspicion that the origin of his strange persecution was known to himself, and that it was of a nature which, upon his own account, he could not or dared not disclose.

The mind thus turned in upon itself, and constantly occupied with a haunting anxiety which it dared not reveal or confide to any human breast, became daily more excited, and, of course, more vividly impressible, by a system of attack which operated through the nervous system; and in this state he was destined to sustain, with increasing frequency, the stealthy visitations of that apparition which from the first had seemed to possess so terrible a hold upon his imagination.

In a Glass Darkly

It was about this time that Captain Barton called upon the then celebrated preacher, Dr. — —, with whom he had a slight acquaintance, and an extraordinary conversation ensued.

The divine was seated in his chambers in college, surrounded with works upon his favourite pursuit, and deep in theology, when Barton was announced.

There was something at once embarrassed and excited in his manner, which, along with his wan and haggard countenance, impressed the student with the unpleasant consciousness that his visitor must have recently suffered terribly indeed, to account for an alteration so striking—almost shocking.

After the usual interchange of polite greeting, and a few common-place remarks, Captain Barton, who obviously perceived the surprise which his visit had excited, and which Doctor — — was unable wholly to conceal, interrupted a brief pause by remarking—

"This is a strange call, Doctor — —, perhaps scarcely warranted by an acquaintance so slight as mine with you. I should not under ordinary circumstances have ventured to disturb you; but my visit is neither an idle nor impertinent intrusion. I am sure you will not so account it, when I tell you how afflicted I am."

Doctor — — interrupted him with assurances such as good breeding suggested, and Barton resumed—

"I am come to task your patience by asking your advice. When I say your patience, I might, indeed, say more; I might have said your humanity—your compassion; for I have been and am a great sufferer."

"My dear sir," replied the churchman, "it will, indeed, afford me infinite gratification if I can give you comfort in any distress of mind; but—you know — —"

"I know what you would say," resumed Barton, quickly; "I am an unbeliever, and, therefore, incapable of deriving help from religion; but don't take that for granted. At least you must not assume that, however unsettled my convictions may be, I do not feel a deep—a very deep—interest in the subject. Circumstances have lately forced it upon my attention, in such a way as to compel me to review the whole question in a more candid and teachable spirit, I believe, than I ever studied it in before."

"Your difficulties, I take it for granted, refer to the evidences of revelation," suggested the clergyman.

"Why — no — not altogether; in fact I am ashamed to say I have not considered even my objections sufficiently to state them connectedly; but — but there is one subject on which I feel a peculiar interest."

He paused again, and Doctor — — pressed him to proceed.

"The fact is," said Barton, "whatever may be my uncertainty as to the authenticity of what we are taught to call revelation, of one fact I am deeply and horribly convinced, that there does exist beyond this a spiritual world — a system whose workings are generally in mercy hidden from us — a system which may be, and which is sometimes, partially and terribly revealed. I am sure — I know," continued Barton, with increasing excitement, "that there is a God — a dreadful God — and that retribution follows guilt, in ways the most mysterious and stupendous — by agencies the most inexplicable and terrific; — there is a spiritual system — great God, how I have been convinced! — a system malignant, and implacable, and omnipotent, under whose persecutions I am, and have been, suffering the torments of the damned! — yes, sir — yes — the fires and frenzy of hell!"

As Barton spoke, his agitation became so vehement that the Divine was shocked, and even alarmed. The wild and excited rapidity with which he spoke, and, above all, the indefinable horror, that stamped his features, afforded a contrast to his ordinary cool and unimpassioned self-possession striking and painful in the last degree.

CHAPTER V.
MR. BARTON STATES HIS CASE.

"My dear sir," said Doctor — —, after a brief pause, "I fear you have been very unhappy, indeed; but I venture to predict that the depression under which you labour will be found to originate in purely physical causes, and that with a change of air, and the aid of a few tonics, your spirits will return, and the tone of your mind be once more cheerful and tranquil as heretofore. There was, after all, more truth than we are quite willing to admit in the classic theories which assigned the undue predominance of any one affection of the mind, to the undue action or torpidity of one or other of our bodily organs. Believe me, that a little attention to diet, exercise, and the other essentials of health, under competent direction, will make you as much yourself as you can wish."

"Doctor — —" said Barton, with something like a shudder, "I cannot delude myself with such a hope. I have no hope to cling to but one, and that is, that by some other spiritual agency more potent than that which tortures me, it may be combated, and I delivered. If this may not be, I am lost—now and for ever lost."

"But, Mr. Barton, you must remember," urged his companion, "that others have suffered as you have done, and— —"

"No, no, no," interrupted he, with irritability—"no, sir, I am not a credulous—far from a superstitious man. I have been, perhaps, too much the reverse—too sceptical, too slow of belief; but unless I were one whom no amount of evidence could convince, unless I were to contemn the repeated, the perpetual evidence of my own senses, I am now—now at last constrained to believe—I have no escape from the conviction—the overwhelming certainty—that I am haunted and dogged, go where I may, by—by a DEMON!"

There was a preternatural energy of horror in Barton's face, as, with its damp and death-like lineaments turned towards his companion, he thus delivered himself.

"God help you, my poor friend," said Dr. — —, much shocked, "God help you; for, indeed, you are a sufferer, however your sufferings may have been caused."

"Ay, ay, God help me," echoed Barton, sternly; "but will he help me—will he help me?"

"Pray to him—pray in an humble and trusting spirit," said he.

"Pray, pray," echoed he again; "I can't pray—I could as easily move a mountain by an effort of my will. I have not belief enough to pray; there is something within me that will not pray. You prescribe impossibilities—literal impossibilities."

"You will not find it so, if you will but try," said Doctor ――.

"Try! I have tried, and the attempt only fills me with confusion; and, sometimes, terror; I have tried in vain, and more than in vain. The awful, unutterable idea of eternity and infinity oppresses and maddens my brain whenever my mind approaches the contemplation of the Creator; I recoil from the effort scared. I tell you, Doctor ――, if I am to be saved, it must be by other means. The idea of an eternal Creator is to me intolerable—my mind cannot support it."

"Say, then, my dear sir," urged he, "say how you would have me serve you—what you would learn of me—what I can do or say to relieve you?"

"Listen to me first," replied Captain Barton, with a subdued air, and an effort to suppress his excitement, "listen to me while I detail the circumstances of the persecution under which my life has become all but intolerable—a persecution which has made me fear death and the world beyond the grave as much as I have grown to hate existence."

Barton then proceeded to relate the circumstances which I have already detailed, and then continued:

"This has now become habitual—an accustomed thing. I do not mean the actual seeing him in the flesh—thank God, that at least is not permitted daily. Thank God, from the ineffable horrors of that visitation I have been mercifully allowed intervals of repose, though none of security; but from the consciousness that a malignant spirit is following and watching me wherever I go, I have never, for a single instant, a temporary respite. I am pursued with blasphemies, cries of despair and appalling hatred. I hear those dreadful sounds called after me as I turn the corners of the streets; they come in the night-time, while I sit in my chamber alone; they haunt me everywhere, charging me with hideous crimes, and—great God!—threatening me with coming vengeance and eternal misery. Hush! do you hear that?" he cried with a horrible smile of triumph; "there, there, will that convince you?"

The clergyman felt a chill of horror steal over him, while, during the wail of a sudden gust of wind, he heard, or fancied he heard, the half articulate sounds of rage and derision mingling in the sough.

"Well, what do you think of that?" at length Barton cried, drawing a long breath through his teeth.

"I heard the wind," said Doctor — —. "What should I think of it—what is there remarkable about it?"

"The prince of the powers of the air," muttered Barton, with a shudder.

"Tut, tut! my dear sir," said the student, with an effort to reassure himself; for though it was broad daylight, there was nevertheless something disagreeably contagious in the nervous excitement under which his visitor so miserably suffered. "You must not give way to those wild fancies; you must resist these impulses of the imagination."

"Ay, ay; 'resist the devil and he will flee from thee,'" said Barton, in the same tone; "but how resist him? ay, there it is—there is the rub. What—what am I to do? what can I do?"

"My dear sir, this is fancy," said the man of folios; "you are your own tormentor."

"No, no, sir—fancy has no part in it," answered Barton, somewhat sternly. "Fancy! was it that made you, as well as me, hear, but this moment, those accents of hell? Fancy, indeed! No, no."

"But you have seen this person frequently," said the ecclesiastic; "why have you not accosted or secured him? Is it not a little precipitate, to say no more, to assume, as you have done, the existence of preternatural agency, when, after all, everything may be easily accountable, if only proper means were taken to sift the matter."

"There are circumstances connected with this—this appearance," said Barton, "which it is needless to disclose, but which to me are proof of its horrible nature. I know that the being that follows me is not human—I say I know this; I could prove it to your own conviction." He paused for a minute, and then added, "And as to accosting it, I dare not, I could not;

when I see it I am powerless; I stand in the gaze of death, in the triumphant presence of infernal power and malignity. My strength, and faculties, and memory, all forsake me. O God, I fear, sir, you know not what you speak of. Mercy, mercy; heaven have pity on me!"

He leaned his elbow on the table, and passed his hand across his eyes, as if to exclude some image of horror, muttering the last words of the sentence he had just concluded, again and again.

"Doctor — —," he said, abruptly raising himself, and looking full upon the clergyman with an imploring eye, "I know you will do for me whatever may be done. You know now fully the circumstances and the nature of my affliction. I tell you I cannot help myself; I cannot hope to escape; I am utterly passive. I conjure you, then, to weigh my case well, and if anything may be done for me by vicarious supplication—by the intercession of the good—or by any aid or influence whatsoever, I implore of you, I adjure you in the name of the Most High, give me the benefit of that influence—deliver me from the body of this death. Strive for me, pity me; I know you will; you cannot refuse this; it is the purpose and object of my visit. Send me away with some hope, however little, some faint hope of ultimate deliverance, and I will nerve myself to endure, from hour to hour, the hideous dream into which my existence has been transformed."

Doctor — — assured him that all he could do was to pray earnestly for him, and that so much he would not fail to do. They parted with a hurried and melancholy valediction. Barton hastened to the carriage that awaited him at the door, drew down the blinds, and drove away, while Doctor — — returned to his chamber, to ruminate at leisure upon the strange interview which had just interrupted his studies.

CHAPTER VI.
SEEN AGAIN.

It was not to be expected that Captain Barton's changed and eccentric habits should long escape remark and discussion. Various were the theories suggested to account for it. Some attributed the alteration to the pressure of secret pecuniary embarrassments; others to a repugnance to fulfil an engagement into which he was presumed to have too precipitately entered; and others, again, to the supposed incipiency of mental disease, which latter, indeed, was the most plausible as well as the most generally, received, of the hypotheses circulated in the gossip of the day.

From the very commencement of this change, at first so gradual in its advances, Miss Montague had of course been aware of it. The intimacy involved in their peculiar relation, as well as the near interest which it inspired afforded, in her case, a like opportunity and motive for the successful exercise of that keen and penetrating observation peculiar to her sex.

His visits became, at length, so interrupted, and his manner, while they lasted, so abstracted, strange, and agitated, that Lady L— —, after hinting her anxiety and her suspicions more than once, at length distinctly stated her anxiety, and pressed for an explanation.

The explanation was given, and although its nature at first relieved the worst solicitudes of the old lady and her niece, yet the circumstances which attended it, and the really dreadful consequences which it obviously indicated, as regarded the spirits, and indeed the reason of the now wretched man, who made the strange declaration, were enough, upon little reflection, to fill their minds with perturbation and alarm.

General Montague, the young lady's father, at length arrived. He had himself slightly known Barton, some ten or twelve years previously, and being aware of his fortune and connexions, was disposed to regard him as an unexceptionable and indeed a most desirable match for his daughter. He laughed at the story of Barton's supernatural visitations, and lost no time in calling upon his intended son-in-law.

"My dear Barton," he continued, gaily, after a little conversation, "my sister tells me that you are a victim to blue devils, in quite a new and original shape."

Barton changed countenance, and sighed profoundly.

"Come, come; I protest this will never do," continued the General; "you are more like a man on his way to the gallows than to the altar. These devils have made quite a saint of you."

Barton made an effort to change the conversation.

"No, no, it won't do," said his visitor laughing; "I am resolved to say what I have to say upon this magnificent mock mystery of yours. You must not be angry, but really it is too bad to see you at your time of life, absolutely frightened into good behaviour, like a naughty child by a bugaboo, and as far as I can learn, a very contemptible one. Seriously, I have been a good deal annoyed at what they tell me; but at the same time thoroughly convinced that there is nothing in the matter that may not cleared up, with a little attention and management, within a week at furthest."

"Ah, General, you do not know—" he began.

"Yes, but I do know quite enough to warrant my confidence," interrupted the soldier, "don't I know that all your annoyance proceeds from the occasional appearance of a certain little man in a cap and great-coat, with a red vest and a bad face, who follows you about, and pops upon you at corners of lanes, and throws you into ague fits. Now, my dear fellow, I'll make it my business to catch this mischievous little mountebank, and either beat him to a jelly with my own hands, or have him whipped through the town, at the cart's-tail, before a month passes."

"If you knew what I knew," said Barton, with gloomy agitation, "you would speak very differently. Don't imagine that I am so weak as to assume, without proof the most overwhelming, the conclusion to which I have been forced—the proofs are here, locked up here." As he spoke he tapped upon his breast, and with an anxious sigh continued to walk up and down the room.

"Well, well, Barton," said his visitor, "I'll wager a rump and a dozen I collar the ghost, and convince even you before many days are over."

He was running on in the same strain when he was suddenly arrested, and not a little shocked, by observing Barton, who had approached the window, stagger slowly back, like one who had received a stunning blow; his arm extended toward the street—his face and his very lips white as ashes—while he muttered, "There—by heaven!—there—there!"

General Montague started mechanically to his feet, and from the window of the drawing-room, saw a figure corresponding as well as his hurry would permit him to discern, with the description of the person, whose appearance so persistently disturbed the repose of his friend.

The figure was just turning from the rails of the area upon which it had been leaning, and, without waiting to see more, the old gentleman snatched his cane and hat, and rushed down the stairs and into the street, in the furious hope of securing the person, and punishing the audacity of the mysterious stranger.

He looked round him, but in vain, for any trace of the person he had himself distinctly seen. He ran breathlessly to the nearest corner, expecting to see from thence the retiring figure, but no such form was visible. Back and forward, from crossing to crossing, he ran, at fault, and it was not until the curious gaze and laughing countenances of the passers-by reminded him of the absurdity of his pursuit, that he checked his hurried pace, lowered his walking cane from the menacing altitude which he had mechanically given it, adjusted his hat, and walked composedly back again, inwardly vexed and flurried. He found Barton pale and trembling in every joint; they both remained silent, though under emotions very different. At last Barton whispered, "You saw it?"

"It!—him—some one—you mean—to be sure I did," replied Montague, testily. "But where is the good or the harm of seeing him? The fellow runs like a lamp-lighter. I wanted to catch him, but he had stole away before I could reach the hall-door. However, it is no great matter; next time, I dare say, I'll do better; and egad, if I once come within reach of him, I'll introduce his shoulders to the weight of my cane."

Notwithstanding General Montague's undertakings and exhortations, however, Barton continued to suffer from the self-same unexplained cause; go how, when, or where he would, he was still constantly dogged or confronted by the being who had established over him so horrible an influence.

Nowhere and at no time was he secure against the odious appearance which haunted him with such diabolic perseverance.

His depression, misery, and excitement became more settled

and alarming every day, and the mental agonies that ceaselessly preyed upon him, began at last so sensibly to affect his health, that Lady L— — and General Montague succeeded, without, indeed, much difficulty, in persuading him to try a short tour on the Continent, in the hope that an entire change of scene would, at all events, have the effect of breaking through the influences of local association, which the more sceptical of his friends assumed to be by no means inoperative in suggesting and perpetuating what they conceived to be a mere form of nervous illusion.

General Montague indeed was persuaded that the figure which haunted his intended son-in-law was by no means the creation of his imagination, but, on the contrary, a substantial form of flesh and blood, animated by a resolution, perhaps with some murderous object in perspective, to watch and follow the unfortunate gentleman.

Even this hypothesis was not a very pleasant one; yet it was plain that if Barton could ever be convinced that there was nothing preternatural in the phenomenon which he had hitherto regarded in that light, the affair would lose all its terrors in his eyes, and wholly cease to exercise upon his health and spirits the baleful influence which it had hitherto done. He therefore reasoned, that if the annoyance were actually escaped by mere locomotion and change of scene, it obviously could not have originated in any supernatural agency.

CHAPTER VII.
FLIGHT.

Yielding to their persuasions, Barton left Dublin for England, accompanied by General Montague. They posted rapidly to London, and thence to Dover, whence they took the packet with a fair wind for Calais. The General's confidence in the result of the expedition on Barton's spirits had risen day by day, since their departure from the shores of Ireland; for to the inexpressible relief and delight of the latter, he had not since then, so much as even once fancied a repetition of those impressions which had, when at home, drawn him gradually down to the very depths of despair.

This exemption from what he had begun to regard as the inevitable condition of his existence, and the sense of security which began to pervade his mind, were inexpressibly delightful; and in the exultation of what he considered his deliverance, he indulged in a thousand happy anticipations for a future into which so lately he had hardly dared to look; and in short, both he and his companion secretly congratulated themselves upon the termination of that persecution which had been to its immediate victim a source of such unspeakable agony.

It was a beautiful day, and a crowd of idlers stood upon the jetty to receive the packet, and enjoy the bustle of the new arrivals. Montague walked a few paces in advance of his friend, and as he made his way through the crowd, a little man touched his arm, and said to him, in a broad provincial patois—

"Monsieur is walking too fast; he will lose his sick comrade in the throng, for, by my faith, the poor gentleman seems to be fainting."

Montague turned quickly, and observed that Barton did indeed look deadly pale. He hastened to his side.

"My dear fellow, are you ill?" he asked anxiously.

The question was unheeded and twice, repeated, ere Barton stammered—

"I saw him—by ——, I saw him!"

"Him!—the wretch—who—where now?—where is he?" cried Montague, looking around him.

"I saw him—but he is gone," repeated Barton, faintly.

"But where—where? For God's sake speak," urged Montague, vehemently.

"It is but this moment—here," said he.

"But what did he look like—what had he on—what did he wear—quick, quick," urged his excited companion, ready to dart among the crowd and collar the delinquent on the spot.

"He touched your arm—he spoke to you—he pointed to me. God be merciful to me, there is no escape," said Barton, in the low, subdued tones of despair.

Montague had already bustled away in all the flurry of mingled hope and rage; but though the singular personnel of the stranger who had accosted him was vividly impressed upon his recollection, he failed to discover among the crowd even the slightest resemblance to him.

After a fruitless search, in which he enlisted the services of several of the by-standers, who aided all the more zealously, as they believed he had been robbed, he at length, out of breath and baffled, gave over the attempt.

"Ah, my friend, it won't do," said Barton, with the faint voice and bewildered, ghastly look of one who had been stunned by some mortal shock; "there is no use in contending; whatever it is, the dreadful association between me and it, is now established—I shall never escape—never!"

"Nonsense, nonsense, my dear Barton; don't talk so," said Montague with something at once of irritation and dismay; "you must not, I say; we'll jockey the scoundrel yet; never mind, I say—never mind."

It was, however, but labour lost to endeavour henceforward to inspire Barton with one ray of hope; he became desponding.

This intangible, and, as it seemed, utterly inadequate influence was fast destroying his energies of intellect, character, and health. His first object was now to return to Ireland, there, as he believed, and now almost hoped, speedily to die.

To Ireland accordingly he came and one of the first faces he saw upon the shore, was again that of his implacable and dreaded attendant. Barton seemed at last to have lost not only all enjoyment and every hope in existence, but all independence of will besides. He now submitted himself passively to the management of the friends most nearly interested in his welfare.

With the apathy of entire despair, he implicitly assented to whatever measures they suggested and advised; and as a last resource, it was determined to remove him to a house of Lady L— —'s, in the neighbourhood of Clontarf, where, with the advice of his medical attendant, who persisted in his opinion that the whole train of consequences resulted merely from some nervous derangement, it was resolved that he was to confine himself, strictly to the house, and to make use only of those apartments which commanded a view of an enclosed yard, the gates of which were to be kept jealously locked.

Those precautions would certainly secure him against the casual appearance of any living form, that his excited imagination might possibly confound with the spectre which, as it was contended, his fancy recognised in every figure that bore even a distant or general resemblance to the peculiarities with which his fancy had at first invested it.

A month or six weeks' absolute seclusion under these conditions, it was hoped might, by interrupting the series of these terrible impressions, gradually dispel the predisposing apprehensions, and the associations which had confirmed the supposed disease, and rendered recovery hopeless.

Cheerful society and that of his friends was to be constantly supplied, and on the whole, very sanguine expectations were indulged in, that under the treatment thus detailed, the obstinate hypochondria of the patient might at length give way.

Accompanied, therefore, by Lady L— —, General Montague and his daughter—his own affianced bride—poor Barton—himself never daring to cherish a hope of his ultimate emancipation from the horrors under which his life was literally wasting away—took possession of the apartments, whose situation protected him against the intrusions, from which he shrank with such unutterable terror.

After a little time, a steady persistence in this system began to manifest its results, in a very marked though gradual improvement, alike in the health and spirits of the invalid. Not, indeed, that anything at all approaching complete recovery was yet discernible. On the contrary, to those who had not seen him since the commencement of his strange sufferings, such an alteration would have been apparent as might well have shocked them.

The improvement, however, such as it was, was welcomed with gratitude and delight, especially by the young lady, whom her attachment to him, as well as her now singularly painful position, consequent on his protracted illness, rendered an object scarcely one degree less to be commiserated than himself.

A week passed—a fortnight—a month—and yet there had been no recurrence of the hated visitation. The treatment had, so far forth, been followed by complete success. The chain of associations was broken. The constant pressure upon the overtasked spirits had been removed, and, under these comparatively favourable circumstances, the sense of social community with the world about him, and something of human interest, if not of enjoyment, began to reanimate him.

It was about this time that Lady L— — who, like most old ladies of the day, was deep in family receipts, and a great pretender to medical science, dispatched her own maid to the kitchen garden, with a list of herbs, which were there to be carefully culled, and brought back to her housekeeper for the purpose stated. The handmaiden, however, returned with her task scarce half completed, and a good deal flurried and alarmed. Her mode of accounting for her precipitate retreat and evident agitation was odd, and, to the old lady, startling.

CHAPTER VIII.
SOFTENED.

It appeared that she had repaired to the kitchen garden, pursuant to her mistress's directions, and had there begun to make the specified election among the rank and neglected herbs which crowded one corner of the enclosure, and while engaged in this pleasant labour, she carelessly sang a fragment of an old song, as she said, "to keep herself company." She was, however, interrupted by an ill-natured laugh; and, looking up, she saw through the old thorn hedge, which surrounded the garden, a singularly ill-looking little man, whose countenance wore the stamp of menace and malignity, standing close to her, at the other side of the hawthorn screen.

She described herself as utterly unable to move or speak, while he charged her with a message for Captain Barton; the substance of which she distinctly remembered to have been to the effect, that he, Captain Barton, must come abroad as usual, and show himself to his friends, out of doors, or else prepare for a visit in his own chamber.

On concluding this brief message, the stranger had, with a threatening air, got down into the outer ditch, and, seizing the hawthorn stems in his hands, seemed on the point of climbing through the fence—a feat which might have been accomplished without much difficulty.

Without, of course, awaiting this result, the girl—throwing down her treasures of thyme and rosemary—had turned and run, with the swiftness of terror, to the house. Lady L—— commanded her, on pain of instant dismissal, to observe an absolute silence respecting all that passed of the incident which related to Captain Barton; and, at the same time, directed instant search to be made by her men, in the garden and the fields adjacent. This measure, however, was as usual, unsuccessful, and, filled with undefinable misgivings, Lady L—— communicated the incident to her brother. The story, however, until long afterwards, went no further, and, of course, it was jealously guarded from Barton, who continued to amend, though slowly.

Barton now began to walk occasionally in the court-yard which I have mentioned, and which being enclosed by a high wall, commanded no view beyond its own extent. Here he, therefore, considered himself perfectly secure: and, but for a careless violation of orders by one of the grooms, he might have enjoyed, at least for some time longer, his much-prized immunity. Opening upon the public road, this yard was entered by a wooden gate, with a wicket in it, and was further defended by an iron gate upon the outside. Strict orders had been given to keep both carefully locked; but, spite of these, it had happened that one day, as Barton was slowly pacing this narrow enclosure, in his accustomed walk, and reaching the further extremity, was turning to retrace his steps, he saw the boarded wicket ajar, and the face of his tormentor immovably looking at him through the iron bars. For a few seconds he stood riveted to the earth — breathless and bloodless — in the fascination of that dreaded gaze, and then fell helplessly insensible, upon the pavement.

There he was found a few minutes afterwards, and conveyed to his room — the apartment which he was never afterwards to leave alive. Henceforward a marked and unaccountable change was observable in the tone of his mind. Captain Barton was now no longer the excited and despairing man he had been before; a strange alteration had passed upon him — an unearthly tranquillity reigned in his mind — it was the anticipated stillness of the grave.

"Montague, my friend, this struggle is nearly ended now," he said, tranquilly, but with a look of fixed and fearful awe. "I have, at last, some comfort from that world of spirits, from which my punishment has come. I now know that my sufferings will soon be over."

Montague pressed him to speak on.

"Yes," said he, in a softened voice, "my punishment is nearly ended. From sorrow, perhaps I shall never, in time or eternity, escape; but my agony is almost over. Comfort has been revealed to me, and what remains of my allotted struggle I will bear with submission — even with hope."

"I am glad to hear you speak so tranquilly, my dear Barton," said Montague; "peace and cheer of mind are all you need to make you what you were."

"No, no — I never can be that," said he mournfully. "I am no longer fit for life. I am soon to die. I am to see him but once again, and then all is ended."

"He said so, then?" suggested Montague.

"He? — No, no: good tidings could scarcely come through

him; and these were good and welcome; and they came so solemnly and sweetly—with unutterable love and melancholy, such as I could not—without saying more than is needful, or fitting, of other long-past scenes and persons—fully explain to you." As Barton said this he shed tears.

"Come, come," said Montague, mistaking the source of his emotions, "you must not give way. What is it, after all, but a pack of dreams and nonsense; or, at worst, the practices of a scheming rascal that enjoys his power of playing upon your nerves, and loves to exert it—a sneaking vagabond that owes you a grudge, and pays it off this way, not daring to try a more manly one."

"A grudge, indeed, he owes me—you say rightly," said Barton, with a sudden shudder; "a grudge as you call it. Oh, my God! when the justice of Heaven permits the Evil one to carry out a scheme of vengeance—when its execution is committed to the lost and terrible victim of sin, who owes his own ruin to the man, the very man, whom he is commissioned to pursue—then, indeed, the torments and terrors of hell are anticipated on earth. But heaven has dealt mercifully with me—hope has opened to me at last; and if death could come without the dreadful sight I am doomed to see, I would gladly close my eyes this moment upon the world. But though death is welcome, I shrink with an agony you cannot understand—an actual frenzy of terror—from the last encounter with that—that demon, who has drawn me thus to the verge of the chasm, and who is himself to plunge me down. I am to see him again—once more—but under circumstances unutterably more terrific than ever."

As Barton thus spoke, he trembled so violently that Montague was really alarmed at the extremity of his sudden agitation, and hastened to lead him back to the topic which had before seemed to exert so tranquillizing an effect upon his mind.

"It was not a dream," he said, after a time; "I was in a different state—I felt differently and strangely; and yet it was all as real, as clear, and vivid, as what I now see and hear—it was a reality."

"And what did you see and hear?" urged his companion.

"When I wakened from the swoon I fell into on seeing him," said Barton, continuing as if he had not heard the question, "it was slowly, very slowly—I was lying by the margin of a broad lake, with misty hills all round, and a soft, melancholy, rose-coloured light illuminated it all. It was unusually sad and lonely, and yet more beautiful than any earthly scene. My head was leaning on the lap of a girl, and she was singing a song, that told, I know not how — whether by words or harmonies — of all my life — all that is past, and all that is still to come; and with the song the old feelings that I thought had perished within me came back, and tears flowed from my eyes — partly for the song and its mysterious beauty, and partly for the unearthly sweetness of her voice; and yet I knew the voice — oh! how well; and I was spell-bound as I listened and looked at the solitary scene, without stirring, almost without breathing — and, alas! alas! without turning my eyes toward the face that I knew was near me, so sweetly powerful was the enchantment that held me. And so, slowly, the song and scene grew fainter, and fainter, to my senses, till all was dark and still again. And then I awoke to this world, as you saw, comforted, for I knew that I was forgiven much." Barton wept again long and bitterly.

From this time, as we have said, the prevailing tone of his mind was one of profound and tranquil melancholy. This, however, was not without its interruptions. He was thoroughly impressed with the conviction that he was to experience another and a final visitation, transcending in horror all he had before experienced. From this anticipated and unknown agony, he often shrank in such paroxysms of abject terror and distraction, as filled the whole household with dismay and superstitious panic. Even those among them who affected to discredit the theory of preternatural agency, were often in their secret souls visited during the silence of night with qualms and apprehensions, which they would not have readily confessed; and none of them attempted to dissuade Barton from the resolution on which he now systematically acted, of shutting himself up in his own apartment. The window-blinds of this room were kept jealously down; and his own man was seldom out of his presence, day or night, his bed being placed in the same chamber.

This man was an attached and respectable servant; and his duties, in addition to those ordinarily imposed upon valets, but which Barton's independent habits generally dispensed with, were to attend carefully to the simple precautions by means of which his master hoped to exclude the dreaded intrusion of the "Watcher." And, in addition to attending to those arrangements, which amounted merely to guarding against the possibility of his master's being, through any unscreened window or open door, exposed to the dreaded influence, the valet was never to suffer him to be alone — total solitude, even for a minute, had become to him now almost as intolerable as the idea of going abroad into the public ways — it was an instinctive anticipation of what was coming.

CHAPTER IX.
REQUIESCAT.

It is needless to say, that under these circumstances, no steps were taken toward the fulfilment of that engagement into which he had entered. There was quite disparity enough in point of years, and indeed of habits, between the young lady and Captain Barton, to have precluded anything like very vehement or romantic attachment on her part. Though grieved and anxious, therefore, she was very far from being heart-broken.

Miss Montague, however, devoted much of her time to the patient but fruitless attempt to cheer the unhappy invalid. She read for him, and conversed with him; but it was apparent that whatever exertions he made, the endeavour to escape from the one ever waking fear that preyed upon him, was utterly and miserably unavailing.

Young ladies are much given to the cultivation of pets; and among those who shared the favour of Miss Montague was a fine old owl, which the gardener, who caught him napping among the ivy of a ruined stable, had dutifully presented to that young lady.

The caprice which regulates such preferences was manifested in the extravagant favour with which this grim and ill-favoured bird was at once distinguished by his mistress; and, trifling as this whimsical circumstance may seem, I am forced to mention it, inasmuch as it is connected, oddly enough, with the concluding scene of the story.

Barton, so far from sharing in this liking for the new favourite, regarded it from the first with an antipathy as violent as it was utterly unaccountable. Its very vicinity was unsupportable to him. He seemed to hate and dread it with a vehemence absolutely laughable, and which to those who have never witnessed the exhibition of antipathies of this kind, would seem all but incredible.

With these few words of preliminary explanation, I shall proceed to state the particulars of the last scene in this strange series of incidents. It was almost two o'clock one winter's night, and Barton was, as usual at that hour, in his bed; the servant we have mentioned occupied a smaller bed in the same room, and a light was burning. The man was on a sudden aroused by his master, who said—

"I can't get it out of my head that that accursed bird has got out somehow, and is lurking in some corner of the room. I have been dreaming about him. Get up, Smith, and look about; search for him. Such hateful dreams!"

The servant rose, and examined the chamber, and while engaged in so doing, he heard the well-known sound, more like a long-drawn gasp than a hiss, with which these birds from their secret haunts affright the quiet of the night.

This ghostly indication of its proximity—for the sound proceeded from the passage upon which Barton's chamber-door opened—determined the search of the servant, who, opening the door, proceeded a step or two forward for the purpose of driving the bird away. He had however, hardly entered the lobby, when the door behind him slowly swung to under the impulse, as it seemed, of some gentle current of air; but as immediately over the door there was a kind of window, intended in the day time to aid in lighting the passage, and through which at present the rays of the candle were issuing, the valet could see quite enough for his purpose.

As he advanced he heard his master—who, lying in a well-curtained bed, had not, as it seemed, perceived his exit from the room—call him by name, and direct him to place the candle on the table by his bed. The servant, who was now some way in the long passage, and not liking to raise his voice for the purpose of replying, lest he should startle the sleeping inmates of the house, began to walk hurriedly and softly back again, when, to his amazement, he heard a voice in the interior of the chamber answering calmly, and actually saw, through the window which over-topped the door, that the light was slowly shifting, as if carried across the room in answer to his master's call. Palsied by a feeling akin to terror, yet not unmingled with curiosity, he stood breathless and listening at the threshold, unable to summon resolution to push open the door and enter. Then came a rustling of the curtains, and a sound like that of one who in a low voice hushes a child to rest, in the midst of which he heard Barton say, in a tone of stifled horror—"Oh, God—oh, my God!" and repeat the same exclamation several times. Then ensued a silence, which again was broken by the same strange soothing sound; and at last there burst forth, in one swelling peal, a yell of agony so appalling and hideous, that, under some impulse of ungovernable horror, the man rushed to the door, and with his whole strength strove to force it open. Whether it was that, in his agitation, he had himself but imperfectly turned the handle, or that the door was really secured upon the inside, he failed to effect an entrance; and as he tugged and pushed,

In a Glass Darkly

yell after yell rang louder and wilder through the chamber, accompanied all the while by the same hushed sounds. Actually freezing with terror, and scarce knowing what he did, the man turned and ran down the passage, wringing his hands in the extremity of horror and irresolution. At the stair-head he was encountered by General Montague, scared and eager, and just as they met the fearful sounds had ceased.

"What is it? Who—where is your master?" said Montague with the incoherence of extreme agitation. "Has anything—for God's sake is anything wrong?"

"Lord have mercy on us, it's all over," said the man staring wildly towards his master's chamber. "He's dead, sir, I'm sure he's dead."

Without waiting for inquiry or explanation, Montague, closely followed by the servant, hurried to the chamber-door, turned the handle, and pushed it open. As the door yielded to his pressure, the ill-omened bird of which the servant had been in search, uttering its spectral warning, started suddenly from the far side of the bed, and flying through the doorway close over their heads, and extinguishing, in his passage, the candle which Montague carried, crashed through the skylight that overlooked the lobby, and sailed away into the darkness of the outer space.

"There it is, God bless us," whispered the man, after a breathless pause.

"Curse that bird," muttered the General, startled by the suddenness of the apparition, and unable to conceal his discomposure.

"The candle is moved," said the man, after another breathless pause, pointing to the candle that still burned in the room; "see, they put it by the bed."

"Draw the curtains, fellow, and don't stand gaping there," whispered Montague, sternly.

The man hesitated.

"Hold this, then," said Montague, impatiently thrusting the candlestick into the servant's hand, and himself advancing to the bedside, he drew the curtains apart. The light of the candle, which was still burning at the bedside, fell upon a figure huddled together, and half upright, at the head of the bed. It seemed as though it had slunk back as far as the solid panelling would allow, and the hands were still clutched in the bed-clothes.

"Barton, Barton, Barton!" cried the General, with a strange mixture of awe and vehemence. He took the candle, and held it so that it shone full upon the face. The features were fixed, stern, and white; the jaw was fallen; and the sightless eyes, still open, gazed vacantly forward toward the front of the bed. "God Almighty! he's dead," muttered the General, as he looked upon this fearful spectacle. They both continued to gaze upon it in silence for a minute or more. "And cold, too," whispered Montague, withdrawing his hand from that of the dead man.

"And see, see—may I never have life, sir," added the man, after a another pause, with a shudder, "but there was something else on the bed with him. Look there—look there—see that, sir."

As the man thus spoke, he pointed to a deep indenture, as if caused by a heavy pressure, near the foot of the bed.

Montague was silent.

"Come, sir, come away, for God's sake," whispered the man, drawing close up to him, and holding fast by his arm, while he glanced fearfully round; "what good can be done here now—come away, for God's sake!"

At this moment they heard the steps of more than one approaching, and Montague, hastily desiring the servant to arrest their progress, endeavoured to loose the rigid gripe with which the fingers of the dead man were clutched in the bed-clothes, and drew, as well as he was able, the awful figure into a reclining posture; then closing the curtains carefully upon it, he hastened himself to meet those persons that were approaching.

It is needless to follow the personages so slightly connected with this narrative, into the events of their after life; it is enough to say, that no clue to the solution of these mysterious occurrences was ever after discovered; and so long an interval having now passed since the event which I have just described concluded this strange history, it is scarcely to be expected that time can throw any new lights upon its dark and inexplicable outline. Until the secrets of the earth shall be no longer hidden, therefore, these transactions must remain shrouded in their original obscurity.

The only occurrence in Captain Barton's former life to which reference was ever made, as having any possible connexion with the sufferings with which his existence closed, and which he himself seemed to regard as working out a retribution for some grievous sin of his past life, was a circumstance which not for several years after his death was brought to light. The nature of this disclosure was painful to his relatives, and discreditable to his memory.

It appeared that some six years before Captain Barton's final return to Dublin, he had formed, in the town of Plymouth, a guilty attachment, the object of which was the daughter of one of the ship's crew under his command. The father had visited the frailty of his unhappy child with extreme harshness, and even brutality, and it was said that she had died heart-broken. Presuming upon Barton's implication in her guilt, this man had conducted himself toward him with marked insolence, and Barton retaliated this, and what he resented with still more exasperated bitterness — his treatment of the unfortunate girl — by a systematic exercise of those terrible and arbitrary severities which the regulations of the navy placed at the command of those who are responsible for its discipline. The man had at length made his escape, while the vessel was in port at Naples, but died, as it was said, in an hospital in that town, of the wounds inflicted in one of his recent and sanguinary punishments.

Whether these circumstances in reality bear, or not, upon the occurrences of Barton's after life, it is, of course, impossible to say. It seems, however more than probable that they were at least, in his own mind, closely associated with them. But however the truth may be, as to the origin and motives of this mysterious persecution, there can be no doubt that, with respect to the agencies by which it was accomplished, absolute and impenetrable mystery is like to prevail until the day of doom.

POSTSCRIPT BY THE EDITOR.

The preceding narrative is given in the ipsissima verba of the good old clergyman, under whose hand it was delivered to Doctor Hesselius. Notwithstanding the occasional stiffness and redundancy of his sentences, I thought it better to reserve to myself the power of assuring the reader, that in handing to the printer, the M.S. of a statement so marvellous, the Editor has not altered one letter of the original text. — [Ed. Papers of Dr. Hesselius.]

MR. JUSTICE HARBOTTLE.
PROLOGUE.

On this case, Doctor Hesselius has inscribed nothing more than the words, "Harman's Report," and a simple reference to his own extraordinary Essay on "the Interior Sense, and the Conditions of the opening thereof."

The reference is to Vol. I. Section 317, Note Za. The note to which reference is thus made, simply says: "There are two accounts of the remarkable case of the Honourable Mr. Justice Harbottle, one furnished to me by Mrs. Trimmer of Tunbridge Wells (June, 1805); the other at a much later date, by Anthony Harman, Esq. I much prefer the former; in the first place, because it is minute and detailed, and written, it seems to me, with more caution and knowledge; and in the next, because the letters from Doctor Hedstone, which are embodied in it, furnish matter of the highest value to a right apprehension of the nature of the case. It was one of the best declared cases of an opening of the interior sense, which I have met with. It was affected, too, by the phenomenon, which occurs so frequently as to indicate a law of these eccentric conditions; that is to say, it exhibited, what I may term, the contagious character of this sort of intrusion of the spirit-world upon the proper domain of matter. So soon as the spirit-action has established itself in the case of one patient, its developed energy begins to radiate, more or less effectually, upon others. The interior vision of the child was opened; as was, also, that of its mother, Mrs. Pyneweck; and both the interior vision and hearing of the scullery-maid, were opened on the same occasion. After-appearances are the result of the law explained in Vol. II. Section 17 to 49. The common centre of association, simultaneously recalled, unites, or reunites, as the case may be, for a period measured, as we see, in Section 37. The maximum will extend to days, the minimum is little more than a second. We see the operation of this principle perfectly displayed, in certain cases of lunacy, of epilepsy, of catalepsy, and of mania, of a peculiar and painful character, though unattended by incapacity of business."

The memorandum of the case of Judge Harbottle, which was written by Mrs. Trimmer of Tunbridge Wells, which Doctor Hesselius thought the better of the two, I have been unable to discover among his papers. I found in his escritoire a note to the effect that he had lent the Report of Judge Harbottle's case, written by Mrs. Trimmer to Doctor F. Heyne. To that learned and able gentleman accordingly I wrote, and received from him, in his reply, which was full of alarms and regrets on account of the uncertain safety of that "valuable MS.," a line written long since by Doctor Hesselius, which completely exonerated him, inasmuch as it acknowledged the safe return of the papers. The Narrative of Mr. Harman, is, therefore, the only one available for this collection. The late Dr. Hesselius, in another passage of the note that I have cited, says, "As to the facts (non-medical) of the case, the narrative of Mr. Harman exactly tallies with that furnished by Mrs. Trimmer." The strictly scientific view of the case would scarcely interest the popular reader; and, possibly, for the purposes of this selection, I should, even had I both papers to choose between, have preferred that of Mr. Harman, which is given, in full, in the following pages.

CHAPTER I.
THE JUDGE'S HOUSE.

Thirty years ago, an elderly man, to whom I paid quarterly a small annuity charged on some property of mine, came on the quarter-day to receive it. He was a dry, sad, quiet man, who had known better days, and had always maintained an unexceptionable character. No better authority could be imagined for a ghost story.

He told me one, though with a manifest reluctance; he was drawn into the narration by his choosing to explain what I should not have remarked, that he had called two days earlier than that week after the strict day of payment, which he had usually allowed to elapse. His reason was a sudden determination to change his lodgings, and the consequent necessity of paying his rent a little before it was due.

He lodged in a dark street in Westminster, in a spacious old house, very warm, being wainscoted from top to bottom, and furnished with no undue abundance of windows, and those fitted with thick sashes and small panes.

This house was, as the bills upon the windows testified, offered to be sold or let. But no one seemed to care to look at it.

A thin matron, in rusty black silk, very taciturn, with large, steady, alarmed eyes, that seemed to look in your face, to read what you might have seen in the dark rooms and passages through which you had passed, was in charge of it, with a solitary 'maid-of-all-work' under her command. My poor friend had taken lodgings in this house, on account of their extraordinary cheapness. He had occupied them for nearly a year without the slightest disturbance, and was the only tenant, under rent, in the house. He had two rooms; a sitting-room, and a bedroom with a closet opening from it, in which he kept his books and papers locked up. He had gone to his bed, having also locked the outer door. Unable to sleep, he had lighted a candle, and after having read for a time, had laid the book beside him. He heard the old clock at the stair-head strike one; and very shortly after, to his alarm, he saw the closet-door, which he thought he had locked, open stealthily, and a slight dark man, particularly sinister, and somewhere about fifty, dressed in mourning of a very antique fashion, such a suit as we see in Hogarth, entered the room on tip-toe. He was followed by an elder man, stout, and blotched with scurvy, and whose features, fixed as a corpse's, were stamped with dreadful force

In a Glass Darkly

with a character of sensuality and villany.

This old man wore a flowered-silk dressing-gown and ruffles, and he remarked a gold ring on his finger, and on his head a cap of velvet, such as, in the days of perukes, gentlemen wore in undress.

This direful old man carried in his ringed and ruffled hand a coil of rope; and these two figures crossed the floor diagonally, passing the foot of his bed, from the closet-door at the farther end of the room, at the left, near the window, to the door opening upon the lobby, close to the bed's head, at his right.

He did not attempt to describe his sensations as these figures passed so near him. He merely said, that so far from sleeping in that room again, no consideration the world could offer would induce him so much as to enter it again alone, even in the daylight. He found both doors, that of the closet, and that of the room opening upon the lobby, in the morning fast locked, as he had left them before going to bed.

In answer to a question of mine, he said that neither appeared the least conscious of his presence. They did not seem to glide, but walked as living men do, but without any sound, and he felt a vibration on the floor as they crossed it. He so obviously suffered from speaking about the apparitions, that I asked him no more questions.

There were in his description, however, certain coincidences so very singular, as to induce me, by that very post, to write to a friend much my senior, then living in a remote part of England, for the information which I knew he could give me. He had himself more than once pointed out that old house to my attention, and told me, though very briefly, the strange story which I now asked him to give me in greater detail.

His answer satisfied me; and the following pages convey its substance.

Your letter (he wrote) tells me you desire some particulars about the closing years of the life of Mr. Justice Harbottle, one of the judges of the Court of Common Pleas. You refer, of course, to the extraordinary occurrences that made that period of his life long after a theme for 'winter tales' and metaphysical speculation. I happen to know perhaps more than any other man living of those mysterious particulars.

The old family mansion, when I revisited London, more than

thirty years ago, I examined for the last time. During the years that have passed since then, I hear that improvement, with its preliminary demolitions, has been doing wonders for the quarter of Westminster in which it stood. If I were quite certain that the house had been taken down, I should have no difficulty about naming the street in which it stood. As what I have to tell, however, is not likely to improve its letting value, and as I should not care to get into trouble, I prefer being silent on that particular point.

How old the house was, I can't tell. People said it was built by Roger Harbottle, a Turkey merchant, in the reign of King James I. I am not a good opinion upon such questions; but having been in it, though in its forlorn and deserted state. I can tell you in a general way what it was like. It was built of dark-red brick, and the door and windows were faced with stone that had turned yellow by time. It receded some feet from the line of the other houses in the street; and it had a florid and fanciful rail of iron about the broad steps that invited your ascent to the hall-door, in which were fixed, under a file of lamps, among scrolls and twisted leaves, two immense 'extinguishers,' like the conical caps of fairies, into which, in old times, the footmen used to thrust their flambeaux when their chairs or coaches had set down their great people, in the hall or at the steps, as the case might be. That hall is panelled up to the ceiling, and has a large fire-place. Two or three stately old rooms open from it at each side. The windows of these are tall, with many small panes. Passing through the arch at the back of the hall, you come upon the wide and heavy well-staircase. There is a back staircase also. The mansion is large, and has not as much light, by any means, in proportion to its extent, as modern houses enjoy. When I saw it, it had long been untenanted, and had the gloomy reputation beside of a haunted house. Cobwebs floated from the ceilings or spanned the corners of the cornices, and dust lay thick over everything. The windows were stained with the dust and rain of fifty years, and darkness had thus grown darker.

When I made it my first visit, it was in company with my father, when I was still a boy, in the year 1808. I was about twelve years old, and my imagination impressible, as it always is at that age. I looked about me with great awe. I was here in the very centre and scene of those occurrences which I had heard recounted at the fire-side at home, with so delightful a horror.

My father was an old bachelor of nearly sixty when he married. He had, when a child, seen Judge Harbottle on the bench in his robes and wig a dozen times at least before his death, which took place in 1748, and his appearance made a powerful and unpleasant impression, not only on his imagination, but upon his nerves.

The Judge was at that time a man of some sixty-seven years. He had a great mulberry-coloured face, a big, carbuncled nose, fierce eyes, and a grim and brutal mouth. My father, who was young at the time, thought it the most formidable face he had ever seen; for there were evidences of intellectual power in the formation and lines of the forehead. His voice was loud and harsh, and gave effect to the sarcasm which was his habitual weapon on the bench.

This old gentleman had the reputation of being about the wickedest man in England. Even on the bench he now and then showed his scorn of opinion. He had carried cases his own way, it was said, in spite of counsel, authorities, and even of juries, by a sort of cajolery, violence, and bamboozling, that somehow confused and overpowered resistance. He had never actually committed himself; he was too cunning to do that. He had the character of being, however, a dangerous and unscrupulous judge; but his character did not trouble him. The associates he chose for his hours of relaxation cared as little as he did about it.

CHAPTER II.
MR. PETERS.

One night during the session of 1746 this old Judge went down in his chair to wait in one of the rooms of the House of Lords for the result of a division in which he and his order were interested.

This over, he was about to return to his house close by, in his chair; but the night had become so soft and fine that he changed his mind, sent it home empty, and with two footmen, each with a flambeau, set out on foot in preference. Gout had made him rather a slow pedestrian. It took him some time to get through the two or three streets he had to pass before reaching his house.

In one of those narrow streets of tall houses, perfectly silent at that hour, he overtook, slowly as he was walking, a very singular-looking old gentleman.

He had a bottle-green coat on, with a cape to it, and large stone buttons, a broad-leafed low-crowned hat, from under which a big powdered wig escaped; he stooped very much, and supported his bending knees with the aid of a crutch-handled cane, and so shuffled and tottered along painfully.

"I ask your pardon, sir," said this old man in a very quavering voice, as the burly Judge came up with him, and he extended his hand feebly towards his arm.

Mr. Justice Harbottle saw that the man was by no means poorly dressed, and his manner that of a gentleman.

The Judge stopped short, and said, in his harsh peremptory tones, "Well, sir, how can I serve you?"

"Can you direct me to Judge Harbottle's house? I have some intelligence of the very last importance to communicate to him."

"Can you tell it before witnesses?" asked the Judge.

"By no means; it must reach his ear only," quavered the old man earnestly.

"If that be so, sir, you have only to accompany me a few steps farther to reach my house, and obtain a private audience; for I am Judge Harbottle."

In a Glass Darkly

With this invitation the infirm gentleman in the white wig complied very readily; and in another minute the stranger stood in what was then termed the front parlour of the Judge's house, tête-à-tête with that shrewd and dangerous functionary.

He had to sit down, being very much exhausted, and unable for a little time to speak; and then he had a fit of coughing, and after that a fit of gasping; and thus two or three minutes passed, during which the Judge dropped his roquelaure on an armchair, and threw his cocked-hat over that.

The venerable pedestrian in the white wig quickly recovered his voice. With closed doors they remained together for some time.

There were guests waiting in the drawing-rooms, and the sound of men's voices laughing, and then of a female voice singing to a harpsichord, were heard distinctly in the hall over the stairs; for old Judge Harbottle had arranged one of his dubious jollifications, such as might well make the hair of godly men's heads stand upright, for that night.

This old gentleman in the powdered white wig, that rested on his stooped shoulders, must have had something to say that interested the Judge very much; for he would not have parted on easy terms with the ten minutes and upwards which that conference filched from the sort of revelry in which he most delighted, and in which he was the roaring king, and in some sort the tyrant also, of his company.

The footman who showed the aged gentleman out observed that the Judge's mulberry-coloured face, pimples and all, were bleached to a dingy yellow, and there was the abstraction of agitated thought in his manner, as he bid the stranger goodnight. The servant saw that the conversation had been of serious import, and that the Judge was frightened.

Instead of stumping upstairs forthwith to his scandalous hilarities, his profane company, and his great china bowl of punch—the identical bowl from which a bygone Bishop of London, good easy man, had baptised this Judge's grandfather, now clinking round the rim with silver ladles, and hung with scrolls of lemon-peel—instead, I say, of stumping and clambering up the great staircase to the cavern of his Circean enchantment, he stood with his big nose flattened against the window-pane, watching the progress of the feeble old man, who clung stiffly to the iron rail as he got down, step by step, to the pavement.

The hall-door had hardly closed, when the old Judge was in the hall bawling hasty orders, with such stimulating expletives as old colonels under excitement sometimes indulge in now-a-days, with a stamp or two of his big foot, and a waving of his clenched fist in the air. He commanded the footman to overtake the old gentleman in the white wig, to offer him his protection on his way home, and in no case to show his face again without having ascertained where he lodged, and who he was, and all about him.

"By — —, sirrah! if you fail me in this, you doff my livery to-night!"

Forth bounced the stalwart footman, with his heavy cane under his arm, and skipped down the steps, and looked up and down the street after the singular figure, so easy to recognise.

What were his adventures I shall not tell you just now.

The old man, in the conference to which he had been admitted in that stately panelled room, had just told the Judge a very strange story. He might be himself a conspirator; he might possibly be crazed; or possibly his whole story was straight and true.

The aged gentleman in the bottle-green coat, on finding himself alone with Mr. Justice Harbottle, had become agitated. He said,

"There is, perhaps you are not aware, my lord, a prisoner in Shrewsbury jail, charged with having forged a bill of exchange for a hundred and twenty pounds, and his name is Lewis Pyneweck, a grocer of that town."

"Is there?" says the Judge, who knew well that there was.

"Yes, my lord," says the old man.

"Then you had better say nothing to affect this case. If you do, by — — I'll commit you; for I'm to try it," says the Judge, with his terrible look and tone.

"I am not going to do anything of the kind, my lord; of him or his case I know nothing, and care nothing. But a fact has come to my knowledge which it behoves you to well consider."

"And what may that fact be?" inquired the Judge; "I'm in haste, sir, and beg you will use dispatch."

"It has come to my knowledge, my lord, that a secret tribunal is in process of formation, the object of which is to take cognisance of the conduct of the judges; and first, of your conduct, my lord: it is a wicked conspiracy."

"Who are of it?" demands the Judge.

"I know not a single name as yet. I know but the fact, my lord; it is most certainly true."

"I'll have you before the Privy Council, sir," says the Judge.

"That is what I most desire; but not for a day or two, my lord."

"And why so?"

"I have not as yet a single name, as I told your lordship; but I expect to have a list of the most forward men in it, and some other papers connected with the plot, in two or three days."

"You said one or two just now."

"About that time, my lord."

"Is this a Jacobite plot?"

"In the main I think it is, my lord."

"Why, then, it is political. I have tried no State prisoners, nor am like to try any such. How, then, doth it concern me?"

"From what I can gather, my lord, there are those in it who desire private revenges upon certain judges."

"What do they call their cabal?"

"The High Court of Appeal, my lord."

"Who are you sir? What is your name?"

"Hugh Peters, my lord."

"That should be a Whig name?"

"It is, my lord."

"Where do you lodge, Mr. Peters?"

"In Thames-street, my lord, over against the sign of the Three Kings."

"Three Kings? Take care one be not too many for you, Mr. Peters! How come you, an honest Whig, as you say, to be privy to a Jacobite plot? Answer me that."

"My lord, a person in whom I take an interest has been seduced to take a part in it; and being frightened at the unexpected wickedness of their plans, he is resolved to become an informer for the Crown."

"He resolves like a wise man, sir. What does he say of the persons? Who are in the plot? Doth he know them?"

"Only two, my lord; but he will be introduced to the club in a few days, and he will then have a list, and more exact information of their plans, and above all of their oaths, and their hours and places of meeting, with which he wishes to be acquainted before they can have any suspicions of his intentions. And being so informed, to whom, think you, my lord, had he best go then?"

"To the king's attorney-general straight. But you say this concerns me, sir, in particular? How about this prisoner, Lewis Pyneweck? Is he one of them?"

"I can't tell, my lord; but for some reason, it is thought your lordship will be well advised if you try him not. For if you do, it is feared 'twill shorten your days."

"So far as I can learn, Mr. Peters, this business smells pretty strong of blood and treason. The king's attorney-general will know how to deal with it. When shall I see you again, sir?"

"If you give me leave, my lord, either before your lordship's court sits, or after it rises, to-morrow. I should like to come and tell your lordship what has passed."

"Do so, Mr. Peters, at nine o'clock to-morrow morning. And see you play me no trick, sir, in this matter; if you do, by — —, sir, I'll lay you by the heels!"

"You need fear no trick from me, my lord; had I not wished to serve you, and acquit my own conscience, I never would have come all this way to talk with your lordship."

"I'm willing to believe you, Mr. Peters; I'm willing to believe you, sir."

And upon this they parted.

"He has either painted his face, or he is consumedly sick," thought the old Judge.

The light had shone more effectually upon his features as he turned to leave the room with a low bow, and they looked, he fancied, unnaturally chalky.

"D— — him!" said the judge ungraciously, as he began to scale the stairs: "he has half-spoiled my supper."

But if he had, no one but the Judge himself perceived it, and the evidence was all, as any one might perceive, the other way.

CHAPTER III.
LEWIS PYNEWECK.

In the meantime, the footman dispatched in pursuit of Mr. Peters speedily overtook that feeble gentleman. The old man stopped when he heard the sound of pursuing steps, but any alarms that may have crossed his mind seemed to disappear on his recognising the livery. He very gratefully accepted the proferred assistance, and placed his tremulous arm within the servant's for support. They had not gone far, however, when the old man stopped suddenly, saying,

"Dear me! as I live, I have dropped it. You heard it fall. My eyes, I fear, won't serve me, and I'm unable to stoop low enough; but if you will look, you shall have half the find. It is a guinea; I carried it in my glove."

The street was silent and deserted. The footman had hardly descended to what he termed his "hunkers," and begun to search the pavement about the spot which the old man indicated, when Mr. Peters, who seemed very much exhausted, and breathed with difficulty, struck him a violent blow, from above, over the back of the head with a heavy instrument, and then another; and leaving him bleeding and senseless in the gutter, ran like a lamp-lighter down a lane to the right, and was gone.

When, an hour later, the watchman brought the man in livery home, still stupid and covered with blood, Judge Harbottle cursed his servant roundly, swore he was drunk, threatened him with an indictment for taking bribes to betray his master, and cheered him with a perspective of the broad street leading from the Old Bailey to Tyburn, the cart's tail, and the hangman's lash.

Notwithstanding this demonstration, the Judge was pleased. It was a disguised "affidavit man," or footpad, no doubt, who had been employed to frighten him. The trick had fallen through.

A "court of appeal," such as the false Hugh Peters had indicated, with assassination for its sanction, would be an uncomfortable institution for a "hanging judge" like the Honourable Justice Harbottle. That sarcastic and ferocious administrator of the criminal code of England, at that time a rather pharisaical, bloody, and heinous system of justice, had reasons of his own for choosing to try that very Lewis

In a Glass Darkly

Pyneweck, on whose behalf this audacious trick was devised. Try him he would. No man living should take that morsel out of his mouth.

Of Lewis Pyneweck of course, so far as the outer world could see, he knew nothing. He would try him after his fashion, without fear, favour, or affection.

But did he not remember a certain thin man, dressed in mourning, in whose house, in Shrewsbury, the Judge's lodgings used to be, until a scandal of his ill-treating his wife came suddenly to light? A grocer with a demure look, a soft step, and a lean face as dark as mahogany, with a nose sharp and long, standing ever so little awry, and a pair of dark steady brown eyes under thinly-traced black brows—a man whose thin lips wore always a faint unpleasant smile.

Had not that scoundrel an account to settle with the Judge? had he not been troublesome lately? and was not his name Lewis Pyneweck, some time grocer in Shrewsbury, and now prisoner in the jail of that town?

The reader may take it, if he pleases, as a sign that Judge Harbottle was a good Christian, that he suffered nothing ever from remorse. That was undoubtedly true. He had nevertheless done this grocer, forger, what you will, some five or six years before, a grievous wrong; but it was not that, but a possible scandal, and possible complications, that troubled the learned Judge now.

Did he not, as a lawyer, know, that to bring a man from his shop to the dock, the chances must be at least ninety-nine out of a hundred that he is guilty.

A weak man like his learned brother Withershins was not a judge to keep the high-roads safe, and make crime tremble. Old Judge Harbottle was the man to make the evil-disposed quiver, and to refresh the world with showers of wicked blood, and thus save the innocent, to the refrain of the ancient saw he loved to quote:

Foolish pity

Ruins a city.

In hanging that fellow he could not be wrong. The eye of a man accustomed to look upon the dock could not fail to read "villain" written sharp and clear in his plotting face. Of course he would try him, and no one else should.

A saucy-looking woman, still handsome, in a mob-cap gay with blue ribbons, in a saque of flowered silk, with lace and rings on, much too fine for the Judge's housekeeper, which nevertheless she was, peeped into his study next morning, and, seeing the Judge alone, stepped in.

"Here's another letter from him, come by the post this morning. Can't you do nothing for him?" she said wheedlingly, with her arm over his neck, and her delicate finger and thumb fiddling with the lobe of his purple ear.

"I'll try," said Judge Harbottle, not raising his eyes from the paper he was reading.

"I knew you'd do what I asked you," she said.

The Judge clapt his gouty claw over his heart, and made her an ironical bow.

"What," she asked, "will you do?"

"Hang him," said the Judge with a chuckle.

"You don't mean to; no, you don't, my little man," said she, surveying herself in a mirror on the wall.

"I'm d — — d but I think you're falling in love with your husband at last!" said Judge Harbottle.

"I'm blest but I think you're growing jealous of him," replied the lady with a laugh. "But no; he was always a bad one to me; I've done with him long ago."

"And he with you, by George! When he took your fortune and your spoons and your ear-rings, he had all he wanted of you. He drove you from his house; and when he discovered you had made yourself comfortable, and found a good situation, he'd have taken your guineas and your silver and your ear-rings over again, and then allowed you half-a-dozen years more to make a new harvest for his mill. You don't wish him good; if you say you do, you lie."

She laughed a wicked saucy laugh, and gave the terrible Rhadamanthus a playful tap on the chops.

"He wants me to send him money to fee a counsellor," she

said, while her eyes wandered over the pictures on the wall, and back again to the looking-glass; and certainly she did not look as if his jeopardy troubled her very much.

"Confound his impudence, the scoundrel!" thundered the old Judge, throwing himself back in his chair, as he used to do in furore on the bench, and the lines of his mouth looked brutal, and his eyes ready to leap from their sockets. "If you answer his letter from my house to please yourself, you'll write your next from somebody else's to please me. You understand, my pretty witch, I'll not be pestered. Come, no pouting; whimpering won't do. You don't care a brass farthing for the villain, body or soul. You came here but to make a row. You are one of Mother Carey's chickens; and where you come, the storm is up. Get you gone, baggage! get you gone!" he repeated with a stamp; for a knock at the hall-door made her instantaneous disappearance indispensable.

I need hardly say that the venerable Hugh Peters did not appear again. The Judge never mentioned him. But oddly enough, considering how he laughed to scorn the weak invention which he had blown into dust at the very first puff, his white-wigged visitor and the conference in the dark front parlour was often in his memory.

His shrewd eye told him that allowing for change of tints and such disguises as the playhouse affords every night, the features of this false old man, who had turned out too hard for his tall footman, were identical with those of Lewis Pyneweck.

Judge Harbottle made his registrar call upon the crown solicitor, and tell him that there was a man in town who bore a wonderful resemblance to a prisoner in Shrewsbury jail named Lewis Pyneweck, and to make inquiry through the post forthwith whether any one was personating Pyneweck in prison, and whether he had thus or otherwise made his escape.

The prisoner was safe, however, and no question as to his identity.

CHAPTER IV.
INTERRUPTION IN COURT.

In due time Judge Harbottle went circuit; and in due time the judges were in Shrewsbury. News travelled slowly in those days, and newspapers, like the wagons and stage-coaches, took matters easily. Mrs. Pyneweck, in the Judge's house, with a diminished household—the greater part of the Judge's servants having gone with him, for he had given up riding circuit, and travelled in his coach in state—kept house rather solitarily at home.

In spite of quarrels, in spite of mutual injuries—some of them, inflicted by herself, enormous—in spite of a married life of spited bickerings—a life in which there seemed no love or liking or forbearance, for years—now that Pyneweck stood in near danger of death, something like remorse came suddenly upon her. She knew that in Shrewsbury were transacting the scenes which were to determine his fate. She knew she did not love him; but she could not have supposed, even a fortnight before, that the hour of suspense could have affected her so powerfully.

She knew the day on which the trial was expected to take place. She could not get it out of her head for a minute; she felt faint as it drew towards evening.

Two or three days passed; and then she knew that the trial must be over by this time. There were floods between London and Shrewsbury, and news was long delayed. She wished the floods would last for ever. It was dreadful waiting to hear; dreadful to know that the event was over, and that she could not hear till self-willed rivers subsided; dreadful to know that they must subside and the news come at last.

She had some vague trust in the Judge's good-nature, and much in the resources of chance and accident. She had contrived to send the money he wanted. He would not be without legal advice and energetic and skilled support.

At last the news did come—a long arrear all in a gush: a letter from a female friend in Shrewsbury; a return of the sentences, sent up for the Judge; and most important, because most easily got at, being told with great aplomb and brevity, the long-deferred intelligence of the Shrewsbury Assizes in the Morning Advertiser. Like an impatient reader of a novel, who reads the last page first, she read with dizzy eyes the list of the

In a Glass Darkly

executions.

Two were respited, seven were hanged; and in that capital catalogue was this line:

"Lewis Pyneweck—forgery."

She had to read it half-a-dozen times over before she was sure she understood it. Here was the paragraph:

"Sentence, Death—7.

"Executed accordingly, on Friday the 13th instant, to wit:

"Thomas Primer, alias Duck—highway robbery.

"Flora Guy—stealing to the value of 11s. 6d.

"Arthur Pounden—burglary.

"Matilda Mummery—riot.

"Lewis Pyneweck—forgery, bill of exchange."

And when she reached this, she read it over and over, feeling very cold and sick. This buxom housekeeper was known in the house as Mrs. Carwell—Carwell being her maiden name, which she had resumed.

No one in the house except its master knew her history. Her introduction had been managed craftily. No one suspected that it had been concerted between her and the old reprobate in scarlet and ermine.

Flora Carwell ran up the stairs now, and snatched her little girl, hardly seven years of age, whom she met on the lobby, hurriedly up in her arms, and carried her into her bedroom, without well knowing what she was doing, and sat down, placing the child before her. She was not able to speak. She held the child before her, and looked in the little girl's wondering face, and burst into tears of horror.

She thought, the Judge could have saved him. I daresay he could. For a time she was furious with him; and hugged and kissed her bewildered little girl, who returned her gaze with large round eyes.

That little girl had lost her father, and knew nothing of the matter. She had been always told that her father was dead long ago.

A woman, coarse, uneducated, vain, and violent, does not reason, or even feel, very distinctly; but in these tears of consternation were mingling a self-upbraiding. She felt afraid of that little child.

But Mrs. Carwell was a person who lived not upon sentiment, but upon beef and pudding; she consoled herself with punch; she did not trouble herself long even with resentments; she was a gross and material person, and could not mourn over the irrevocable for more than a limited number of hours, even if she would.

Judge Harbottle was soon in London again. Except the gout, this savage old epicurean never knew a day's sickness. He laughed and coaxed and bullied away the young woman's faint upbraidings, and in a little time Lewis Pyneweck troubled her no more; and the Judge secretly chuckled over the perfectly fair removal of a bore, who might have grown little by little into something very like a tyrant.

It was the lot of the Judge whose adventures I am now recounting to try criminal cases at the Old Bailey shortly after his return. He had commenced his charge to the jury in a case of forgery, and was, after his wont, thundering dead against the prisoner, with many a hard aggravation and cynical gibe, when suddenly all died away in silence, and, instead of looking at the jury, the eloquent Judge was gaping at some person in the body of the court.

Among the persons of small importance who stand and listen at the sides was one tall enough to show with a little prominence; a slight mean figure, dressed in seedy black, lean and dark of visage. He had just handed a letter to the crier, before he caught the Judge's eye.

That Judge descried, to his amazement, the features of Lewis Pyneweck. He has the usual faint thin-lipped smile; and with his blue chin raised in air, and as it seemed quite unconscious of the distinguished notice he has attracted, he was stretching his low cravat with his crooked fingers, while he slowly turned his head from side to side — a process which enabled the Judge to see distinctly a stripe of swollen blue round his neck, which indicated, he thought, the grip of the rope.

This man, with a few others, had got a footing on a step,

from which he could better see the court. He now stepped down, and the Judge lost sight of him.

His lordship signed energetically with his hand in the direction in which this man had vanished. He turned to the tipstaff. His first effort to speak ended in a gasp. He cleared his throat, and told the astounded official to arrest that man who had interrupted the court.

"He's but this moment gone down there. Bring him in custody before me, within ten minutes' time, or I'll strip your gown from your shoulders and fine the sheriff!" he thundered, while his eyes flashed round the court in search of the functionary.

Attorneys, counsellors, idle spectators, gazed in the direction in which Mr. Justice Harbottle had shaken his gnarled old hand. They compared notes. Not one had seen any one making a disturbance. They asked one another if the Judge was losing his head.

Nothing came of the search. His lordship concluded his charge a great deal more tamely; and when the jury retired, he stared round the court with a wandering mind, and looked as if he would not have given sixpence to see the prisoner hanged.

CHAPTER V.
CALEB SEARCHER.

The Judge had received the letter; had he known from whom it came, he would no doubt have read it instantaneously. As it was he simply read the direction:

To the Honourable

The Lord Justice

Elijah Harbottle,

One of his Majesty's Justices of

the Honourable Court of Common Pleas.

It remained forgotten in his pocket till he reached home.

When he pulled out that and others from the capacious pocket of his coat, it had its turn, as he sat in his library in his thick silk dressing-gown; and then he found its contents to be a closely-written letter, in a clerk's hand, and an enclosure in 'secretary hand,' as I believe the angular scrivinary of law-writings in those days was termed, engrossed on a bit of parchment about the size of this page. The letter said:

"Mr. Justice Harbottle,—My Lord,

"I am ordered by the High Court of Appeal to acquaint your lordship, in order to your better preparing yourself for your trial, that a true bill hath been sent down, and the indictment lieth against your lordship for the murder of one Lewis Pyneweck of Shrewsbury, citizen, wrongfully executed for the forgery of a bill of exchange, on the—the day of — — last, by reason of the wilful perversion of the evidence, and the undue pressure put upon the jury, together with the illegal admission of evidence by your lordship, well knowing the same to be illegal, by all which the promoter of the prosecution of the said indictment, before the High Court of Appeal, hath lost his life.

"And the trial of the said indictment, I am farther ordered to acquaint your lordship is fixed for the 10th day of — — next ensuing, by the right honourable the Lord Chief-Justice Twofold, of the court aforesaid, to wit, the High Court of Appeal, on which day it will most certainly take place. And I am farther to acquaint your lordship, to prevent any surprise or miscarriage, that your case stands first for the said day, and that the said High Court of Appeal sits day and night, and never rises; and herewith, by order of the said court, I furnish your lordship with a copy (extract) of the record in this case, except of the indictment, whereof, notwithstanding, the substance and effect is supplied to your lordship in this Notice. And farther I am to inform you, that in case the jury then to try your lordship should find you guilty, the right honourable the Lord Chief-Justice will, in passing sentence of death upon you, fix the day of execution for the 10th day of – –, being one calendar month from the day of your trial."

It was signed by "CALEB SEARCHER,

"Officer of the Crown Solicitor in the

"Kingdom of Life and Death."

The Judge glanced through the parchment.

"'Sblood! Do they think a man like me is to be bamboozled by their buffoonery?"

The Judge's coarse features were wrung into one of his sneers; but he was pale. Possibly, after all, there was a conspiracy on foot. It was queer. Did they mean to pistol him in his carriage? or did they only aim at frightening him?

Judge Harbottle had more than enough of animal courage. He was not afraid of highwaymen, and he had fought more than his share of duels, being a foul-mouthed advocate while he held briefs at the bar. No one questioned his fighting qualities. But with respect to this particular case of Pyneweck, he lived in a house of glass. Was there not his pretty, dark-eyed, over-dressed housekeeper, Mrs. Flora Carwell? Very easy for people who knew Shrewsbury to identify Mrs. Pyneweck, if once put upon the scent; and had he not stormed and worked hard in that case? Had he not made it hard sailing for the prisoner? Did he not know very well what the bar thought of it? It would be the worst scandal that ever blasted judge.

So much there was intimidating in the matter, but nothing more. The Judge was a little bit gloomy for a day or two after, and more testy with every one than usual.

He locked up the papers; and about a week after he asked his housekeeper, one day, in the library:

"Had your husband never a brother?"

Mrs. Carwell squalled on this sudden introduction of the funereal topic, and cried exemplary "piggins full," as the Judge used pleasantly to say. But he was in no mood for trifling now, and he said sternly:

"Come, madam! this wearies me. Do it another time; and give me an answer to my question." So she did.

Pyneweck had no brother living. He once had one; but he died in Jamaica.

"How do you know he is dead?" asked the Judge.

"Because he told me so."

"Not the dead man?"

"Pyneweck told me so."

"Is that all?" sneered the Judge.

He pondered this matter; and time went on. The Judge was growing a little morose, and less enjoying. The subject struck nearer to his thoughts than he fancied it could have done. But so it is with most undivulged vexations, and there was no one to whom he could tell this one.

It was now the ninth; and Mr. Justice Harbottle was glad. He knew nothing would come of it. Still it bothered him; and to-morrow would see it well over.

[What of the paper, I have cited? No one saw it during his life; no one, after his death. He spoke of it to Dr. Hedstone; and what purported to be "a copy," in the old Judge's hand-writing, was found. The original was nowhere. Was it a copy of an illusion, incident to brain disease? Such is my belief.]

CHAPTER VI.
ARRESTED.

Judge Harbottle went this night to the play at Drury Lane. He was one of those old fellows who care nothing for late hours, and occasional knocking about in pursuit of pleasure. He had appointed with two cronies of Lincoln's Inn to come home in his coach with him to sup after the play.

They were not in his box, but were to meet him near the entrance, and to get into his carriage there; and Mr. Justice Harbottle, who hated waiting, was looking a little impatiently from the window.

The Judge yawned.

He told the footman to watch for Counsellor Thavies and Counsellor Beller, who were coming; and, with another yawn, he laid his cocked-hat on his knees, closed his eyes, leaned back in his corner, wrapped his mantle closer about him, and began to think of pretty Mrs. Abington.

And being a man who could sleep like a sailor, at a moment's notice, he was thinking of taking a nap. Those fellows had no business to keep a judge waiting.

He heard their voices now. Those rake-hell counsellors were laughing, and bantering, and sparring after their wont. The carriage swayed and jerked, as one got in, and then again as the other followed. The door clapped, and the coach was now jogging and rumbling over the pavement. The Judge was a little bit sulky. He did not care to sit up and open his eyes. Let them suppose he was asleep. He heard them laugh with more malice than good-humour, he thought, as they observed it. He would give them a d— —d hard knock or two when they got to his door, and till then he would counterfeit his nap.

The clocks were chiming twelve. Beller and Thavies were silent as tombstones. They were generally loquacious and merry rascals.

The Judge suddenly felt himself roughly seized and thrust from his corner into the middle of the seat, and opening his eyes, instantly he found himself between his two companions.

Before he could blurt out the oath that was at his lips, he saw that they were two strangers—evil-looking fellows, each with a pistol in his hand, and dressed like Bow Street officers.

The Judge clutched at the check-string. The coach pulled up. He stared about him. They were not among houses; but through the windows, under a broad moonlight, he saw a black moor stretching lifelessly from right to left, with rotting trees, pointing fantastic branches in the air, standing here and there in groups, as if they held up their arms and twigs like fingers, in horrible glee at the Judge's coming.

A footman came to the window. He knew his long face and sunken eyes. He knew it was Dingly Chuff, fifteen years ago a footman in his service, whom he had turned off at a moment's notice, in a burst of jealousy, and indicted for a missing spoon. The man had died in prison of the jail-fever.

The Judge drew back in utter amazement. His armed companions signed mutely; and they were again gliding over this unknown moor.

The bloated and gouty old man, in his horror, considered the question of resistance. But his athletic days were long over. This moor was a desert. There was no help to be had. He was in the hands of strange servants, even if his recognition turned out to be a delusion, and they were under the command of his captors. There was nothing for it but submission, for the present.

Suddenly the coach was brought nearly to a standstill, so that the prisoner saw an ominous sight from the window.

It was a gigantic gallows beside the road; it stood three-sided, and from each of its three broad beams at top depended in chains some eight or ten bodies, from several of which the cere-clothes had dropped away, leaving the skeletons swinging lightly by their chains. A tall ladder reached to the summit of the structure, and on the peat beneath lay bones.

On top of the dark transverse beam facing the road, from which, as from the other two completing the triangle of death, dangled a row of these unfortunates in chains, a hang-man, with a pipe in his mouth, much as we see him in the famous print of the 'Idle Apprentice,' though here his perch was ever so much higher, was reclining at his ease and listlessly shying bones, from a little heap at his elbow, at the skeletons that hung round, bringing down now a rib or two, now a hand, now half a leg. A long-sighted man could have discerned that he was a dark fellow, lean; and from continually looking down on the earth from the elevation over which, in another sense, he always hung, his nose, his lips, his chin were pendulous and loose, and drawn down into a monstrous grotesque.

This fellow took his pipe from his mouth on seeing the coach, stood up, and cut some solemn capers high on his beam, and shook a new rope in the air, crying with a voice high and distant as the caw of a raven hovering over a gibbet, "A rope for Judge Harbottle!"

The coach was now driving on at its old swift pace.

So high a gallows as that, the Judge had never, even in his most hilarious moments, dreamed of. He thought he must be raving. And the dead footman! He shook his ears and strained his eyelids; but if he was dreaming, he was unable to awake himself.

There was no good in threatening these scoundrels. A brutum fulmen might bring a real one on his head.

Any submission to get out of their hands; and then heaven and earth he would move to unearth and hunt them down.

Suddenly they drove round a corner of a vast white building, and under a porte-cochère.

CHAPTER VII.
CHIEF JUSTICE TWOFOLD.

The Judge found himself in a corridor lighted with dingy oil lamps, the walls of bare stone; it looked like a passage in a prison. His guards placed him in the hands of other people. Here and there he saw bony and gigantic soldiers passing to and fro, with muskets over their shoulders. They looked straight before them, grinding their teeth, in bleak fury, with no noise but the clank of their shoes. He saw these by glimpses, round corners, and at the ends of passages, but he did not actually pass them by.

And now, passing under a narrow doorway, he found himself in the dock, confronting a judge in his scarlet robes, in a large court-house. There was nothing to elevate this temple of Themis above its vulgar kind elsewhere. Dingy enough it looked, in spite of candles lighted in decent abundance. A case had just closed, and the last juror's back was seen escaping through the door in the wall of the jury-box. There were some dozen barristers, some fiddling with pen and ink, others buried in briefs, some beckoning, with the plumes of their pens, to their attorneys, of whom there were no lack; there were clerks to-ing and fro-ing, and the officers of the court, and the registrar, who was handing up a paper to the judge; and the tipstaff, who was presenting a note at the end of his wand to a king's counsel over the heads of the crowd between. If this was the High Court of Appeal, which never rose day or night, it might account for the pale and jaded aspect of everybody in it. An air of indescribable gloom hung upon the pallid features of all the people here; no one ever smiled; all looked more or less secretly suffering.

"The King against Elijah Harbottle!" shouted the officer.

"Is the appellant Lewis Pyneweck in court?" asked Chief-Justice Twofold, in a voice of thunder, that shook the woodwork of the Court, and boomed down the corridors.

Up stood Pyneweck from his place at the table.

"Arraign the prisoner!" roared the Chief; and Judge Harbottle felt the pannels of the dock round him, and the floor, and the rails quiver in the vibrations of that tremendous voice.

The prisoner, in limine, objected to this pretended court, as being a sham, and non-existent in point of law; and then, that, even if it were a court constituted by law, (the Judge was growing dazed), it had not and could not have any jurisdiction to try him for his conduct on the bench.

Whereupon the chief-justice laughed suddenly, and every one in court, turning round upon the prisoner, laughed also, till the laugh grew and roared all round like a deafening acclamation; he saw nothing but glittering eyes and teeth, a universal stare and grin; but though all the voices laughed, not a single face of all those that concentrated their gaze upon him looked like a laughing face. The mirth subsided as suddenly as it began.

The indictment was read. Judge Harbottle actually pleaded! He pleaded "Not guilty." A jury were sworn. The trial proceeded. Judge Harbottle was bewildered.

This could not be real. He must be either mad, or going mad, he thought.

One thing could not fail to strike even him. This Chief-Justice Twofold, who was knocking him about at every turn with sneer and gibe, and roaring him down with his tremendous voice, was a dilated effigy of himself; an image of Mr. Justice Harbottle, at least double his size, and with all his fierce colouring, and his ferocity of eye and visage, enhanced awfully.

Nothing the prisoner could argue, cite, or state was permitted to retard for a moment the march of the case towards its catastrophe.

The chief-justice seemed to feel his power over the jury, and to exult and riot in the display of it. He glared at them, he nodded to them; he seemed to have established an understanding with them. The lights were faint in that part of the court. The jurors were mere shadows, sitting in rows; the prisoner could see a dozen pair of white eyes shining, coldly, out of the darkness; and whenever the judge in his charge, which was contemptuously brief, nodded and grinned and gibed, the prisoner could see, in the obscurity, by the dip of all these rows of eyes together, that the jury nodded in acquiescence.

And now the charge was over, the huge chief-justice leaned back panting and gloating on the prisoner. Every one in the court turned about, and gazed with steadfast hatred on the man in the dock. From the jury-box where the twelve sworn brethren were whispering together, a sound in the general stillness like a prolonged "hiss-s-s!" was heard; and then, in answer to the challenge of the officer, "How say you, gentlemen of the jury, guilty or not guilty?" came in a melancholy voice the finding, "Guilty."

The place seemed to the eyes of the prisoner to grow gradually darker and darker, till he could discern nothing distinctly but the lumen of the eyes that were turned upon him from every bench and side and corner and gallery of the building. The prisoner doubtless thought that he had quite enough to say, and conclusive, why sentence of death should not be pronounced upon him; but the lord chief-justice puffed it contemptuously away, like so much smoke, and proceeded to pass sentence of death upon the prisoner, having named the 10th of the ensuing month for his execution.

Before he had recovered the stun of this ominous farce, in obedience to the mandate, 'Remove the prisoner,' he was led from the dock. The lamps seemed all to have gone out, and there were stoves and charcoal-fires here and there, that threw a faint crimson light on the walls of the corridors through which he passed. The stones that composed them looked now enormous, cracked and unhewn.

He came into a vaulted smithy, where two men, naked to the waist, with heads like bulls, round shoulders, and the arms of giants, were welding red-hot chains together with hammers that pelted like thunderbolts.

They looked on the prisoner with fierce red eyes, and rested on their hammers for a minute; and said the elder to his companion, "Take out Elijah Harbottle's gyves;" and with a pincers he plucked the end which lay dazzling in the fire from the furnace.

"One end locks," said he, taking the cool end of the iron in one hand, while with the grip of a vice he seized the leg of the Judge, and locked the ring round his ankle. "The other," he said with a grin, "is welded."

The iron band that was to form the ring for the other leg lay still red-hot upon the stone floor, with brilliant sparks sporting up and down its surface.

His companion in his gigantic hands seized the old Judge's other leg, and pressed his foot immovably to the stone floor; while his senior in a twinkling, with a masterly application of pincers and hammer, sped the glowing bar round his ankle so tight that the skin and sinews smoked and bubbled again, and old Judge Harbottle uttered a yell that seemed to chill the very stones, and make the iron chains quiver on the wall.

Chains, vaults, smiths, and smithy all vanished in a moment; but the pain continued. Mr. Justice Harbottle was suffering torture all round the ankle on which the infernal smiths had just been operating.

His friends Thavies and Beller were startled by the Judge's roar in the midst of their elegant trifling about a marriage à-la-mode case which was going on. The Judge was in panic as well as pain. The street-lamps and the light of his own hall-door restored him.

"I'm very bad," growled he between his set teeth; "my foot's blazing. Who was he that hurt my foot? 'Tis the gout—'tis the gout!" he said, awaking completely. "How many hours have we been coming from the playhouse? 'Sblood, what has happened on the way? I've slept half the night?"

There had been no hitch or delay, and they had driven home at a good pace.

The Judge, however, was in gout; he was feverish too; and the attack, though very short, was sharp; and when, in about a fortnight, it subsided, his ferocious joviality did not return. He could not get this dream, as he chose to call it, out of his head.

CHAPTER VIII.
SOMEBODY HAS GOT INTO THE HOUSE.

People remarked that the Judge was in the vapours. His doctor said he should go for a fortnight to Buxton.

Whenever the Judge fell into a brown study, he was always conning over the terms of the sentence pronounced upon him in his vision—"in one calendar month from the date of this day;" and then the usual form, "and you shall be hanged by the neck till you are dead," &c. "That will be the 10th—I'm not much in the way of being hanged. I know what stuff dreams are, and I laugh at them; but this is continually in my thoughts, as if it forecast misfortune of some sort. I wish the day my dream gave me were passed and over. I wish I were well purged of my gout. I wish I were as I used to be. 'Tis nothing but vapours, nothing but a maggot." The copy of the parchment and letter which had announced his trial with many a snort and sneer he would read over and over again, and the scenery and people of his dream would rise about him in places the most unlikely, and steal him in a moment from all that surrounded him into a world of shadows.

The Judge had lost his iron energy and banter. He was growing taciturn and morose. The Bar remarked the change, as well they might. His friends thought him ill. The doctor said he was troubled with hypochondria, and that his gout was still lurking in his system, and ordered him to that ancient haunt of crutches and chalk-stones, Buxton.

The Judge's spirits were very low; he was frightened about himself; and he described to his housekeeper, having sent for her to his study to drink a dish of tea, his strange dream in his drive home from Drury Lane playhouse. He was sinking into the state of nervous dejection in which men lose their faith in orthodox advice, and in despair consult quacks, astrologers, and nursery story-tellers. Could such a dream mean that he was to have a fit, and so die on the 10th? She did not think so. On the contrary, it was certain some good luck must happen on that day.

The Judge kindled; and for the first time for many days, he looked for a minute or two like himself, and he tapped her on the cheek with the hand that was not in flannel.

"Odsbud! odsheart! you dear rogue! I had forgot. There is young Tom—yellow Tom, my nephew, you know, lies sick at

Harrogate; why shouldn't he go that day as well as another, and if he does, I get an estate by it? Why, lookee, I asked Doctor Hedstone yesterday if I was like to take a fit any time, and he laughed, and swore I was the last man in town to go off that way."

The Judge sent most of his servants down to Buxton to make his lodgings and all things comfortable for him. He was to follow in a day or two.

It was now the 9th; and the next day well over, he might laugh at his visions and auguries.

On the evening of the 9th, Doctor Hedstone's footman knocked at the Judge's door. The doctor ran up the dusky stairs to the drawing-room. It was a March evening, near the hour of sunset, with an east wind whistling sharply through the chimney-stacks. A wood fire blazed cheerily on the hearth. And Judge Harbottle, in what was then called a brigadier-wig, with his red roquelaure on, helped the glowing effect of the darkened chamber, which looked red all over like a room on fire.

The Judge had his feet on a stool, and his huge grim purple face confronted the fire and seemed to pant and swell, as the blaze alternately spread upward and collapsed. He had fallen again among his blue devils, and was thinking of retiring from the Bench, and of fifty other gloomy things.

But the doctor, who was an energetic son of Æsculapius, would listen to no croaking, told the Judge he was full of gout, and in his present condition no judge even of his own case, but promised him leave to pronounce on all those melancholy questions, a fortnight later.

In the meantime the Judge must be very careful. He was over-charged with gout, and he must not provoke an attack, till the waters of Buxton should do that office for him, in their own salutary way.

The doctor did not think him perhaps quite so well as he pretended, for he told him he wanted rest, and would be better if he went forthwith to his bed.

Mr. Gerningham, his valet, assisted him, and gave him his drops; and the Judge told him to wait in his bedroom till he should go to sleep.

Three persons that night had specially odd stories to tell.

The housekeeper had got rid of the trouble of amusing her little girl at this anxious time by giving her leave to run about the sitting-rooms and look at the pictures and china, on the usual condition of touching nothing. It was not until the last gleam of sunset had for some time faded, and the twilight had so deepened that she could no longer discern the colours on the china figures on the chimney-piece or in the cabinets, that the child returned to the housekeeper's room to find her mother.

To her she related, after some prattle about the china, and the pictures, and the Judge's two grand wigs in the dressing-room off the library, an adventure of an extraordinary kind.

In the hall was placed, as was customary in those times, the sedan-chair which the master of the house occasionally used, covered with stamped leather, and studded with gilt nails, and with its red silk blinds down. In this case, the doors of this old-fashioned conveyance were locked, the windows up, and, as I said, the blinds down, but not so closely that the curious child could not peep underneath one of them, and see into the interior.

A parting beam from the setting sun, admitted through the window of a back room, shot obliquely through the open door, and lighting on the chair, shone with a dull transparency through the crimson blind.

To her surprise, the child saw in the shadow a thin man dressed in black seated in it; he had sharp dark features; his nose, she fancied, a little awry, and his brown eyes were looking straight before him; his hand was on his thigh, and he stirred no more than the waxen figure she had seen at Southwark fair.

A child is so often lectured for asking questions and on the propriety of silence, and the superior wisdom of its elders, that it accepts most things at last in good faith; and the little girl acquiesced respectfully in the occupation of the chair by this mahogany-faced person as being all right and proper.

It was not until she asked her mother who this man was, and observed her scared face as she questioned her more minutely upon the appearance of the stranger, that she began to understand that she had seen something unaccountable.

Mrs. Carwell took the key of the chair from its nail over the footman's shelf, and led the child by the hand up to the hall, having a lighted candle in her other hand. She stopped at a distance from the chair, and placed the candlestick in the child's hand.

"Peep in, Margery, again, and try if there's anything there," she whispered; "hold the candle near the blind so as to throw its light through the curtain."

The child peeped, this time with a very solemn face, and intimated at once that he was gone.

"Look again, and be sure," urged her mother.

The little girl was quite certain; and Mrs. Carwell, with her mob-cap of lace and cherry-coloured ribbons, and her dark brown hair, not yet powdered, over a very pale face, unlocked the door, looked in, and beheld emptiness.

"All a mistake, child, you see."

"There, ma'am! see there! He's gone round the corner," said the child.

"Where?" said Mrs. Carwell, stepping backward a step.

"Into that room."

"Tut, child! 'twas the shadow," cried Mrs. Carwell angrily, because she was frightened. "I moved the candle." But she clutched one of the poles of the chair, which leant against the wall in the corner, and pounded the floor furiously with one end of it, being afraid to pass the open door the child had pointed to.

The cook and two kitchen-maids came running upstairs, not knowing what to make of this unwonted alarm.

They all searched the room; but it was still and empty, and no sign of any one's having been there.

Some people may suppose that the direction given to her thoughts by this odd little incident will account for a very strange illusion which Mrs. Carwell herself experienced about two hours later.

CHAPTER IX.
THE JUDGE LEAVES HIS HOUSE.

Mrs. Flora Carwell was going up the great staircase with a posset for the Judge in a china bowl, on a little silver tray.

Across the top of the well-staircase there runs a massive oak rail; and, raising her eyes accidentally, she saw an extremely odd-looking stranger, slim and long, leaning carelessly over with a pipe between his finger and thumb. Nose, lips, and chin seemed all to droop downward into extraordinary length, as he leant his odd peering face over the banister. In his other hand he held a coil of rope, one end of which escaped from under his elbow and hung over the rail.

Mrs. Carwell, who had no suspicion at the moment, that he was not a real person, and fancied that he was some one employed in cording the Judge's luggage, called to know what he was doing there.

Instead of answering, he turned about, and walked across the lobby, at about the same leisurely pace at which she was ascending, and entered a room, into which she followed him. It was an uncarpeted and unfurnished chamber. An open trunk lay upon the floor empty, and beside it the coil of rope; but except herself there was no one in the room.

Mrs. Carwell was very much frightened, and now concluded that the child must have seen the same ghost that had just appeared to her. Perhaps, when she was able to think it over, it was a relief to believe so; for the face, figure, and dress described by the child were awfully like Pyneweck; and this certainly was not he.

Very much scared and very hysterical, Mrs. Carwell ran down to her room, afraid to look over her shoulder, and got some companions about her, and wept, and talked, and drank more than one cordial, and talked and wept again, and so on, until, in those early days, it was ten o'clock, and time to go to bed.

A scullery-maid remained up finishing some of her scouring and "scalding" for some time after the other servants — who, as I said, were few in number — that night had got to their beds. This was a low-browed, broad-faced, intrepid wench with black hair, who did not "vally a ghost not a button," and treated the housekeeper's hysterics with measureless scorn.

In a Glass Darkly

The old house was quiet, now. It was near twelve o'clock, no sounds were audible except the muffled wailing of the wintry winds, piping high among the roofs and chimneys, or rumbling at intervals, in under gusts, through the narrow channels of the street.

The spacious solitudes of the kitchen level were awfully dark, and this sceptical kitchen-wench was the only person now up and about, in the house. She hummed tunes to herself, for a time; and then stopped and listened; and then resumed her work again. At last, she was destined to be more terrified than even was the housekeeper.

There was a back-kitchen in this house, and from this she heard, as if coming from below its foundations, a sound like heavy strokes, that seemed to shake the earth beneath her feet. Sometimes a dozen in sequence, at regular intervals; sometimes fewer. She walked out softly into the passage, and was surprised to see a dusky glow issuing from this room, as if from a charcoal fire.

The room seemed thick with smoke.

Looking in, she very dimly beheld a monstrous figure, over a furnace, beating with a mighty hammer the rings and rivets of a chain.

The strokes, swift and heavy as they looked, sounded hollow and distant. The man stopped, and pointed to something on the floor, that, through the smoky haze, looked, she thought, like a dead body. She remarked no more; but the servants in the room close by, startled from their sleep by a hideous scream, found her in a swoon on the flags, close to the door, where she had just witnessed this ghastly vision.

Startled by the girl's incoherent asseverations that she had seen the Judge's corpse on the floor, two servants having first searched the lower part of the house, went rather frightened upstairs to inquire whether their master was well. They found him, not in his bed, but in his room. He had a table with candles burning at his bedside, and was getting on his clothes again; and he swore and cursed at them roundly in his old style, telling them that he had business, and that he would discharge on the spot any scoundrel who should dare to disturb him again.

So the invalid was left to his quietude.

In the morning it was rumoured here and there in the street that the Judge was dead. A servant was sent from the house three doors away, by Counsellor Traverse, to inquire at Judge Harbottle's hall-door.

The servant who opened it was pale and reserved, and would only say that the Judge was ill. He had had a dangerous accident; Doctor Hedstone had been with him at seven o'clock in the morning.

There were averted looks, short answers, pale and frowning faces, and all the usual signs that there was a secret that sat heavily upon their minds, and the time for disclosing which had not yet come. That time would arrive when the coroner had arrived, and the mortal scandal that had befallen the house could be no longer hidden. For that morning Mr. Justice Harbottle had been found hanging by the neck from the banister at the top of the great staircase, and quite dead.

There was not the smallest sign of any struggle or resistance. There had not been heard a cry or any other noise in the slightest degree indicative of violence. There was medical evidence to show that, in his atrabilious state, it was quite on the cards that he might have made away with himself. The jury found accordingly that it was a case of suicide. But to those who were acquainted with the strange story which Judge Harbottle had related to at least two persons, the fact that the catastrophe occurred on the morning of the 10th March seemed a startling coincidence.

A few days after, the pomp of a great funeral attended him to the grave; and so, in the language of Scripture, "the rich man died, and was buried."

END OF THE FIRST VOLUME.